Sun Wukong:
The Journey to the West

Sun Wukong:
The Journey to the West

By Jeff Pepper

IMAGIN8
PRESS

This book was previously published as *The Journey to the West* in 2023. It a compilation of the English language portions of all 31 books in the *Journey to the West* series written by Jeff Pepper and translated by Xiao Hui Wang, published by Imagin8 Press between 2017 and 2022. All 31 individual books are available in paperback and ebook formats, and can be purchased directly from the publisher on www.imagin8press.com and from all major online booksellers.

The authors and the publisher are not affiliated with Game Science, the publisher of the video game *Black Myth: Wukong*.

Published in the United States by Imagin8 Press LLC, Verona, Pennsylvania, US. For information, contact us via email at info@imagin8press.com, or visit www.imagin8press.com.

Our books may be purchased directly in quantity at a reduced price. Visit www.imagin8press.com for details.

Imagin8 Press, the Imagin8 logo and the sail image are all trademarks of Imagin8 Press LLC.

Written and designed by Jeff Pepper
Based on the original 16th century Chinese novel by Wu Cheng'en

ISBN: 978-1959043546
Version 3.3

Contents

Acknowledgements

We are deeply indebted to the late Anthony C. Yu for his incredible four-volume translation, *The Journey to the West* (University of Chicago Press, 1983, revised 2012).

We have also referred frequently to another unabridged translation, William J.F. Jenner's *The Journey to the West* (Collinson Fair, 1955; Silk Pagoda, 2005), as well as the original Chinese novel 西游记 by Wu Cheng'en (People's Literature Publishing House, Beijing, 1955). And we've gathered valuable background material from Jim R. McClanahan's *Journey to the West Research Blog* (www.journeytothewestresearch.com).

Thanks to Xiao Hui Wang, my longtime collaborator and translator, who made hundreds of helpful comments to improve the historical and cultural accuracy of these stories.

As always, many thanks to the team at Next Mars Media for their terrific illustrations, Jean Agapoff and Arnaud Ysmal for their careful proofreading, and Junyou Chen for his wonderful audiobook narration of the Chinese versions of the stories in this book.

Introduction

A long, long time ago, in a magical version of ancient China, an island called Aolai stood in the sea like a king in his palace. In the center of the island was Flower Fruit Mountain, and at the very top of the mountain was a large stone, as tall as six men. The stone was made pregnant by Heaven and earth, and one day the wind blew over the egg and it cracked open. A little stone monkey emerged. He opened his eyes, and two beams of light shot up to Heaven. The Jade Emperor on his throne saw the beams of light but he did not interfere.

The little stone monkey grew up to be Sun Wukong, the Handsome Monkey King. He had immense magical powers but little self control. And so, it wasn't long before he stormed the gates of Heaven, intent on taking the place of the Jade Emperor and declaring himself the Great Sage Equal to Heaven. All the gods and armies of Heaven could not defeat him. But finally he was outwitted by the Buddha himself and imprisoned under Five Finger Mountain.

Five hundred years later, the empire of Tang, in what is now eastern China, is ruled by Taizong. Emperor Taizong makes a serious mistake by accidentally ordering the execution of a dragon king for a crime he did not commit. The dead dragon files a complaint with the Lords of the Underworld, and soon the emperor is dragged down to hell to be judged and punished. He explains his mistake to the Lords of the Underworld. They agree to let him go, but leave it up to him to figure out how to return to the human world. He eventually escapes with the help of a deceased courtier, and he awakens in his coffin, a changed man.

Taizong decides to do something to free the souls who are trapped in the underworld, and also help his people. He selects a Buddhist monk and commands him to journey thousands of miles west to India, across vast stretches of unknown and dangerous country, to retrieve the Buddha's holy scriptures and bring them back to the Tang Empire.

The monk selected for the journey is a young man named Xuanzang. The emperor did not know that Xuanzang already met the Buddha in a previous lifetime. Centuries earlier the young monk was a student of the Buddha, but he fell asleep during one of the Buddha's lectures. As punishment the Buddha sentenced him to ten lifetimes of terrible suffering. In this, the tenth lifetime,

Xuanzang accepts the emperor's command that he undertake this perilous journey to the west.

And so, his journey begins. Almost immediately he runs into trouble with some local monsters and nearly loses his life. Then he stumbles upon the trapped Monkey King, converts him to Buddhism, and frees him from his prison under the mountain. Later he meets two other troublemakers, a pig-man named Zhu Bajie and a river monster named Sha Wujing. These two also have magical powers and are, to put it mildly, in great need of redemption. He converts them to Buddhism as well. Accompanied by these three powerful but unruly disciples, the monk spends the next fourteen years journeying to the Western Heaven. They cross hundreds of mountains and thousands of rivers, battling monsters, demons and a variety of devious humans. Eventually they arrive at the home of the Buddha, but the monk finds that his troubles are far from over.

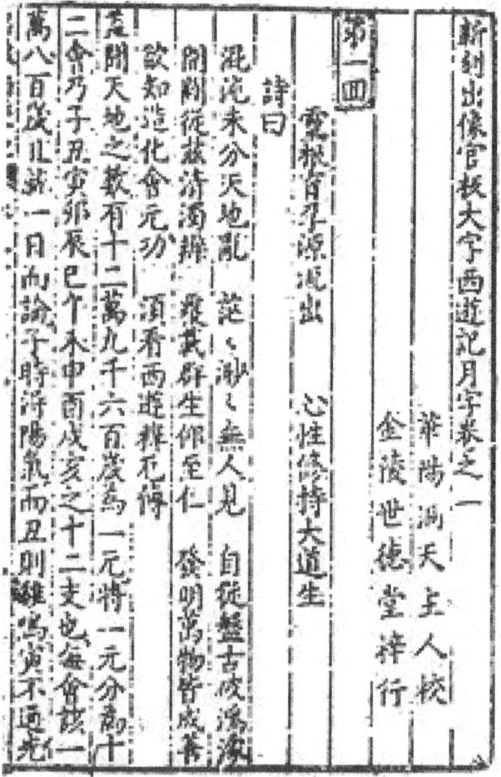

新刻出像官板大字西遊記月字卷之一

華陽洞天主人校

金陵世德堂梓行

第一回

靈根育孕源流出　心性修持大道生

詩曰

混沌未分天地亂　茫茫渺渺無人見

自從盤古破鴻濛　開闢從茲清濁辨

覆載群生仰至仁　發明萬物皆成善

欲知造化會元功　須看西遊釋厄傳

蓋聞天地之數，有十二萬九千六百歲為一元。將一元分為十二會，乃子丑寅卯辰巳午未申酉戌亥之十二支也。每會該一萬八百歲。且就一日而論，子時得陽氣，而丑則雞鳴，寅不通光

A woodblock print from the earliest known edition of Journey to the West.

This, in a nutshell, is the *Journey to the West*. This story was first told in detail in the 16th century A.D. in a two-thousand-page novel of the same name. The original author is believed to be a novelist and poet named Wu Cheng'en, but parts of the story already existed as written and oral folk tales well before he wrote his novel. The version of the story that we use was published anonymously in the year 1592.

Wu's novel is loosely based on an actual journey by the monk Xuanzang, who left China in the year 629. The real monk was not sent by the emperor; in fact, the real Taizong actually forbade him to go. But the young monk went anyway, in defiance of his emperor's command. He returned as a hero seventeen years later, leading twenty pack horses loaded down with Buddhist scriptures he brought from India.

Journey to the West is probably the most famous and best-loved novel in China and is considered one of the four great classical novels of Chinese literature. Its place in Chinese literature is roughly comparable to Homer's epic poem *The Odyssey* in Western literature. Wikipedia sums up the book's role perfectly, saying, "Enduringly popular, the tale is at once a comic adventure story, a humorous satire of Chinese bureaucracy, a spring of spiritual insight, and an extended allegory in which the group of pilgrims journeys towards enlightenment by the power and virtue of cooperation."

Journey to the West is a very, very long story. The original Chinese novel is over a half million Chinese characters long and uses a vocabulary of over four thousand different Chinese words. There are several English translations. The best one is by Dr. Joseph Yu, a scholarly work that runs over two thousand pages in four volumes.

However, what you are about to read is not a literal translation of the *Journey to the West*. Rather, it's a retelling of the story in easy-to-read English. Unlike the other full-text translations, this is a graded reader that uses a restricted vocabulary, simpler sentence structure, and fewer proper nouns. The chapters start off quite easy and gradually increase in complexity. The first chapter is written at a grade level of 2.6 (using the Flesh-Kincaid scale), while the final chapter is written at a grade level of 5.1.

All right, let's get to the story!

Chapter 1

My dear child, I know that the hour is late. You've been playing all day and you are tired, and now it is bedtime. But you say you want to hear a story before you sleep. So now I will tell you an old story about a monkey. He was very strong and very smart, but sometimes he was also very naughty. He needed to learn about love and helping others.

This monkey lived a thousand years ago in northern China. He had many names during his long life, but most people know him as Sun Wukong.

People tell many stories about Sun Wukong. If I told you all those stories, I would have to talk for many days! So tonight I will just tell you a little bit about his birth and how he became a great king.

In the beginning, when the Earth was young, the gods in Heaven made four continents: the Eastern Continent, the Western Continent, the Southern Continent, and the Northern Continent. The Eastern Continent had a country called Aolai, near a great ocean. In the middle of the ocean was a great mountain that stood in the sea like a king in his palace. It was called Flower Fruit Mountain. Around the mountain was a beautiful forest. In the forest were birds, animals, green grasses, beautiful flowers, and tall fruit trees. A hundred small rivers came out of the mountain and flowed into the ocean.

At the top of the mountain sat a very large stone. This stone was as tall as six tall men. Three large men could not encircle it. The stone was made at the same time as the Earth. For a million years it was fed by seeds of Heaven and Earth. Finally, after a million years, the rock became pregnant. The stone opened and a stone egg came out. The wind blew over it, the egg cracked open, and a small stone monkey walked out.

This monkey was small, but he was not a baby monkey. He was like an adult monkey. Every day the little stone monkey played and climbed and ran. All the animals were his friends.

One day the monkey opened his eyes. Two beams of light came out of his eyes and went straight to Heaven. In Heaven the great Jade Emperor saw the beams of light. The people in the palace saw this and were worried. But the Emperor did not worry because he knew that they came from the stone monkey. He smiled and said, "These beams come from a monkey who was born of Heaven and Earth. Don't worry."

The stone monkey lived happily in Flower Fruit Mountain. He played with all the animals who lived in the mountain. For many years he lived an easy life playing with his animal friends.

One day the weather was very hot. The stone monkey was playing in the cold river with his monkey friends. They used small stones to make houses under the water. When they were tired, they swam and washed in the river and rested on the shore.

One of the monkeys said, "We do not know where this river comes from. Today we have nothing to do. Let's go and find out!"

They walked along the river up the mountain, climbing rocks, calling to their friends, laughing and playing. After many hours they saw a great waterfall. They sat and watched the waterfall for a long time. In the daytime it looked like a rainbow. In the moonlight it glowed like fire. The nearby green trees drank its cold water.

All the monkeys shouted and clapped their hands. They said, "Marvelous water! Marvelous water! Who can go into the river and see behind the waterfall? He will be our king!"

The stone monkey heard, and he jumped up, shouting "I will go! I will go!" Dear monkey! He closed his eyes and jumped into the waterfall.

Behind the waterfall there was no water. There was just a large room with an iron bridge. He saw that the water flowed under the bridge to the top of the waterfall.

He looked around. He saw that he was in a beautiful cave. It looked like a cozy house, with stone beds, stone chairs, stone bottles, and stone cups. In the cave were many green trees. The stone monkey was very happy. He wanted to tell his friends. So he closed his eyes and jumped through the water and out of the cave.

The monkeys saw him. They asked, "What did you see?" The stone monkey said, "A beautiful place. No water. Just a large comfortable room with a bridge, and stone beds, stone chairs, stone cups, and stone bottles. We can live there. Let's call it the Water Curtain Cave. Come with me and see!"

"OK," said his friends happily, "you go in first." The stone monkey shouted, "Follow me!"

After all the monkeys were in the room, the stone monkey stood up. He said, "You all said that the monkey who finds this place will be your king. Now make me your king." So each monkey bowed to the stone monkey and said, "You are now my king."

From that day onward, the stone monkey was the king of all the monkeys. He took a new name, Handsome Monkey King. But we will just call him the Monkey King.

The Monkey King and his friends lived in the Water Curtain Cave for a very long time, three or four centuries. Every day they played on the mountain. Every night they slept in the cave. They were all very happy.

One day, while eating, the Monkey King became sad and cried a few tears. The other monkeys asked, "What's wrong?" The Monkey King said, "I am happy now, but I am worried about the days to come." The other monkeys laughed, "You should be happy. We have a wonderful life. We have food, we are safe, we are comfortable. Don't be sad!"

The Monkey King said, "Yes, we are happy today. But later we must still meet Yama, the King of the Underworld. If we are going to die later, how can we be happy today?" Then all the monkeys began to think about death, and they all began to cry.

Then one monkey jumped up and cried, "Great Monkey King, do you know, holy sages will never meet Yama because they live as long as Heaven and Earth."

The Monkey King said, "I did not know that. Where do the holy sages live?"

"They live in ancient caves, but I do not know where."

"No problem. Tomorrow I will go down the mountain and find holy sages. I will learn to be young forever and never meet the King of the Underworld."

All the monkeys clapped their hands and shouted, "Wonderful! Wonderful! Tomorrow we will find lots of fruit, and before you go, we will give you a great feast."

The next day the monkeys found many kinds of fruit and flowers. They put the fruit and flowers on the stone tables, they drank from the stone cups, and had a feast. They danced together and sang about how wonderful it was to be a mountain monkey. For a full day they ate, drank, sang and danced. They all gave gifts to the Monkey King. Afterwards, they slept.

In the morning the monkeys made a small boat for the Monkey King. The Monkey King got into the boat and used the wind to cross the ocean and go towards the Southern Continent. He sailed for many days. Finally he reached

the shore of the Southern Continent. He jumped off the boat. He saw some people fishing and preparing food. Dear Monkey King! He looked terrifying and the people ran away. But one man was too slow. So the Monkey King took the man's clothes and put them on himself. Now he looked like a man, but a little bit bigger and a little bit uglier.

The Monkey King walked a long way dressed like a man. Every day he looked for holy sages. But he only saw men who liked money and fame. The Monkey King thought, "Too bad! These men all seek money and fame. They all want more than what they have. But they never think about meeting Yama. They are all fools!"

The Monkey King looked and looked. He searched for eight or nine years. Finally, he came to the end of the Southern Continent at the Great Western Ocean. He thought, "There must be holy sages living on the other side of this ocean." So he made another small boat. He traveled for many days before arriving on the shore of the Western Continent.

Again he searched for holy sages. He met many frightening animals, but the Monkey King was not afraid.

One day he arrived at a tall and beautiful mountain with a forest of tall trees. He heard the sound of water from many rivers. "Such a beautiful place," he thought, "there must be holy sages living here!"

He walked into the forest. He heard a man singing about his happy and simple life. The man sang,

> "I chop wood, I sell the wood
> I buy a little rice, a little wine
> I sleep among the trees
> the ground is my bed
> I rest my head on a tree root
> I laugh easily, I do not worry
> I do not make plans
> My life is simple and happy!"

The Monkey King heard this song, and thought, "Here is a holy sage!" He ran to meet the man and said, "O Immortal One, O Immortal One."

The man jumped back and shouted, "I am just an old man. I have no money, no house, and little clothing. Why do you call me immortal?"

"I heard your song. Your words are the words of an Immortal. Please teach me."

The man laughed, "My friend, I tell you, I learned this song from my neighbor. He told me to sing this song if I was worried or sad. Just now I was worried, so I sang the song. I am no Immortal!"

The Monkey King said, "If your neighbor is an Immortal, why are you still here? You should be studying with him."

"I cannot. My father died and my mother is alone. I have no brothers or sisters to help her. Now she is very old, so I must stay and help her. I cannot study to become an Immortal."

"I understand," said the Monkey King, "You are a good man. Please tell me how to find this Immortal's house, so I can visit him."

"It is not far. He lives on the Mountain of Mind and Heart, in the Cave of the Crescent Moon and Three Stars. He has many students. It is seven or eight miles from here. Just walk down this road, you will see it."

"Thank you," said the Monkey King, "I will not forget you."

So the Monkey King walked down the road seven or eight miles and arrived at a cave. Above the cave mouth was a large stone. Written on the stone was *"Mountain of Mind and Heart, Cave of the Crescent Moon and Three Stars."* The Monkey King was very happy, and he thought, "The people in this region tell the truth. Here is the cave that I seek!" But he did not go into the cave. He climbed a tree and played while he waited.

After a short time, the cave door opened, and a handsome young man came out. "Who is making trouble here?" he asked. The Monkey King came down from the tree and said, "Immortal boy, I have come here to learn. I will not make trouble."

The youth laughed, "Do you seek the Way?"

"Yes."

"My Master just started teaching. But before he started teaching, he told me to go and open the door for a new student. You must be that student!"

The Monkey King smiled and said, "Yes, that is me."

"OK, please come with me."

And so, the Monkey King and the youth walked into the cave. After walking through many beautiful rooms, they met Master Subodhi. He was teaching a class of about thirty students.

The Monkey King bowed many times, saying, "Master, I am your new student. Please teach me!"

The Master said, "Where are you from? Tell me your name and country."

"Your student is from Water Curtain Cave in Flower Fruit Mountain, in the Aolai Country of the Eastern Continent."

"Leave now!" shouted Master Subodhi. "You are not telling the truth. Between Flower Fruit Mountain and here are two oceans and the entire Eastern Continent. How could you come here?"

The Monkey King bowed many times and replied, "Your student traveled ten years, across land and ocean, to meet this great teacher."

Master Subodhi relaxed and smiled, "I see. What is your surname?"

"I have no temper. If you shout at me, I am not angry. If you hit me, I do not fight. I only say kind words."

"Foolish monkey! I asked about your surname, not your temper[1]!"

"Oh, I am sorry! I have no surname, because I have no parents."

"You were born from a tree?"

"Not a tree, great Master. A rock. On Flower Fruit Mountain."

Master Subodhi was happy when he heard this. "Well, then your parents are Heaven and Earth. Show me how you walk."

The Monkey King got up. He was still dressed like a man but he walked like a monkey. Master Subodhi laughed, "You walk like a monkey and your face is not beautiful. You resemble a *husun*. So your surname shall be Sun."

"Thank you, Master! Now I know my surname. Now please tell me my personal name."

Master Subodhi said, "In my school we give each student one of twelve possible names. You are in the tenth position, called *wu*, which means 'understanding'. Because you seek to know truth, I will give you the name Wukong."

"Wonderful! Now I am called Sun Wukong. Thank you, Master!"

---

[1] This is a pun. In Chinese, the word for temper (性) and the word for surname (姓) are both pronounced xìng.

Chapter 2

From that day, Sun Wukong studied every day with the Master. He lived in the cave for seven years. One day in the seventh year, Master Subodhi said to Sun Wukong, "In my school there are 360 different paths. Each path leads to wisdom. Which one do you want to learn?"

"I will do as my Master tells me," replied Sun Wukong.

So Master Subodhi told Sun Wukong about each of the 360 different paths in his school. He talked for a long time. Every time Master Subodhi talked about a path, Sun Wukong asked, "If I study this path will I become an Immortal?" Every time, the Master replied "No." And every time, Sun Wukong said, "Then I will not learn that path."

Master Subodhi became angry, and shouted at Sun Wukong, "You are a very difficult monkey. I have told you about many different paths to wisdom, but you don't want any of them. You don't want to learn anything." He hit Sun Wukong three times on the head. Then he folded his arms behind his body and walked into his room and closed the door.

The other students heard this, and they were angry at Sun Wukong because he made the Master angry. But Sun Wukong was not angry or unhappy. He thought that the Master had told him a secret. Because the Master hit him three times on the head, he thought that meant "wait until the third watch" which starts at 11:00 PM. Because the Master put his arms behind his body, he thought that meant "Enter my room through the back door to receive my teaching."

So that night at the start of the third watch, Sun Wukong walked outside. He walked to the back door. It was open. He walked inside. The Master was sleeping in his bed. Sun Wukong sat down and waited for the Master to wake up.

When the Master woke up, he saw Sun Wukong and smiled, saying, "You are a very difficult monkey. Why are you here?"

"Master," said Sun Wukong, "yesterday you gave me a secret. You told me to wait until the third watch and then come through the back door to your room. Now I am here. Please teach me the secret of immortality."

So Master Subodhi spoke into Sun Wukong's ear a poem that contained the secret of immortality. Of course, I cannot tell you what was in the poem because it is a secret.

Sun Wukong heard the poem, and he said it to himself many times every day. He knew every word of the poem, and he did as the poem told him. He began to learn the secret of immortality.

But after three years, Master Subodhi said to Sun Wukong, "Be careful, my dear student. You have learned the secret of Heaven and Earth, but now you are in great danger. It is true that you will always be young. But five hundred years from now, Heaven will send you thunder. Use your wisdom to avoid the thunder, or you will die. Five hundred years after the thunder, Heaven will send you fire. Use your wisdom to avoid the fire, or you will die. And five hundred years after the fire, Heaven will send you a great wind. It will enter your head and go through your body. Use your wisdom to avoid the wind or you will die."

Sun Wukong was very afraid. His hair stood on end. "Please help me avoid these three things, Master. I will never forget you."

"Don't worry," said the Master. "Nothing in this world is difficult. Only the mind makes it difficult." Then Master Subodhi spoke a secret in Sun Wukong's ear. Sun Wukong listened, and soon he learned how to fly by doing a cloud somersault. He could fly 108,000 *li* by doing just one cloud somersault[1]. Now he could avoid the thunder, fire and wind sent by Heaven. He could be immortal.

He stayed with Master Subodhi for a few more years. Then one day the Master said to Sun Wukong, "Today you must leave. You are disturbing the other students."

"Where should I go?" said Sun Wukong sadly.

"Go to your home, wherever you came from." And so sadly, Sun Wukong turned and used the cloud somersault to go away.

He traveled very fast, and just an hour later he arrived back at his home in the cave in Flower Fruit Mountain. He heard the sound of monkeys. "My children, I have arrived," he said. Soon thousands of monkeys ran and greeted Sun Wukong. They asked, "Why did you go away? We were alone, waiting for your return. Recently a monster was here. He wanted our cave and he

---

[1] Sun Wukong's cloud somersault lets him travel 108,000 *li* at a time. The number 108 is considered sacred in Hinduism, Buddhism, and Jainism. There are many theories about the origin of this belief.

kidnapped many of our friends. We were very worried. But now we are happy because our Great King has returned."

Sun Wukong was very angry. "Tell me about this lawless monster. I will find him."

"He lives north of here. We do not know how far. He comes like a cloud and goes like the wind."

"Don't worry, I will find him." And Sun Wukong jumped up and used the cloud somersault to travel north until he came to a tall mountain. He saw some small demons and he knew this was the home of the monster. He said to the small demons, "I am the Monkey King of Flower Fruit Mountain. Your king, I don't care to know his name, is causing trouble for my friends. I want to speak with him." The small demons ran into the cave and told the monster, "There is an ugly monkey outside. He says he is a king. He wants to talk with you."

The monster just laughed. "I have often heard these monkeys talk about their king, who is far away studying with great Masters. But the king is never here. Now he has returned, eh?" The monster picked up his scimitar and walked out of the cave and said, "Where is this king of Flower Fruit Mountain?"

"Monster, you have big eyes but you cannot see this old monkey?"

"Old monkey, you are very small. Why do you talk to me like this?"

"You cannot see anything, foolish monster. You say I am small, but I can bring down the moon from Heaven if I want."

Then the monster shouted, and he began to fight with Sun Wukong. They fought for a long time, but the monster used his scimitar and Sun Wukong saw that he was losing. So he pulled a few hairs from his head, chewed them, then spat them out. The hairs became hundreds of small monkeys. The small monkeys helped Sun Wukong fight the monster. After some time, Sun Wukong and the small monkeys won the fight and killed the monster. Then Sun Wukong ate the hairs and the small monkeys returned to Sun Wukong's body.

But some hairs did not return to Sun Wukong's body. These were the kidnapped monkeys. Sun Wukong said to them, "Why are you here?"

They said, "After the Great King went to seek immortality, the monster came to Flower Fruit Mountain. For two years he came often and took some of us away. See? Here are some stone pots and stone bowls from our cave!"

"All of you, follow me home," said Sun Wukong.

"Great King," they said, "when we came here with the monster, we flew with him. We did not see the road, so we do not know how to return home."

"No problem," said Sun Wukong. "I know how to return you home. Close your eyes, all of you, and don't be afraid."

Dear Monkey King! He placed all the kidnapped monkeys on a cloud, and they rode the cloud back to Flower Fruit Mountain. "Open your eyes," said Sun Wukong, "You are home now!"

All the monkeys were very happy. They had a great banquet with wine and fruit. Sun Wukong told the monkeys about his time in the Western Continent and the Southern Continent. He said, "I learned many things from a great Master. Now I am an Immortal. And now our entire family has a new name."

"What is your new surname, Great King?"

"My surname is Sun."

All the monkeys were happy and said. "If the Great King is Old Sun, then we are all Young Sun. We are the Sun Family, in the Sun Nation, and we all live in the Sun Cave!" They all gave delicious fruits and good wine to Sun Wukong, they sang and danced all night, and they were all a big happy family.

Chapter 3

The monkeys learned how to fight, but one day Sun Wukong thought, "If people want to fight us, we also need good weapons. How can we get them?" Four old monkeys heard this. They came forward and said, "O Great King, two hundred miles east of Aolai, across the ocean, is another country. This country has a king with many weapons. If you buy weapons from that king, we will no longer be afraid."

"Good idea," said the Monkey King, "I will go there."

A few years earlier, the Monkey King had learned how to do a cloud somersault to travel very far in a short time. Now he did the cloud somersault and quickly crossed two hundred miles of ocean. He arrived in a large city and saw an armory with a great many weapons. He wanted the weapons, but he had no money so he could not buy them. But this was no problem for the Monkey King! He blew out a big wind. The wind made all the people go inside their homes, and all the stores closed their doors.

When all the people were in their homes, Sun Wukong was alone. He opened the armory doors. He saw many weapons, too many for him to take. No problem! He pulled out some hairs from his head, chewed them, and spat them out. The hairs changed into hundreds of small monkeys. Each monkey picked up some weapons. Then Sun Wukong made another big wind, and all the small monkeys and weapons flew on the wind back to Flower Fruit Mountain.

"My children," said Sun Wukong, "come and get your weapons!" Now all the monkeys had weapons and they were ready for war. Sun Wukong picked up a weapon for himself, but he did not like it. "This is too small for me," he said.

The four old monkeys came forward again and told him, "O Great King, below this mountain and under the ocean is the Dragon Palace. The great Dragon King lives there. Ask him to give you a good weapon."

Sun Wukong liked this idea, so he jumped into the water and swam down to the Dragon Palace to find the Dragon King. The Dragon King came out of his palace to meet him. "High Immortal," said the Dragon King, "welcome to my home. Please come in!"

The Dragon King and the Monkey King drank tea together. Afterwards, the Dragon King asked why Sun Wukong came to the Dragon Palace. "For many years I have studied the Way," said Sun Wukong, "and now I am immortal. I have taught my children how to fight and they all have good weapons. But I still do not have a weapon that I like. I have heard that my neighbor who lives under the ocean can help me."

The Dragon King sat and thought a bit. He was a little bit afraid of Sun Wukong, so he offered him several weapons. Some of the weapons were so big that ten men could not lift them. But Sun Wukong said, "all these weapons are too small. Do you have anything else? I can pay you."

Now the Dragon King was really afraid! "I'm sorry," he said, "those are the biggest weapons I have." The Monkey King became angry. But at that moment, the Dragon King's mother heard this conversation. She said to the Dragon King, "Dear son, here under the ocean there is a huge rod. For the last few days it has been glowing with a beautiful light. Let's just give it to the Monkey King. Maybe he will take it and go home!"

The Dragon King told Sun Wukong, "Here under the ocean we have a great rod. You can have it. However, it is too big and we cannot move it. Perhaps you can move it."

"Where is it?" said Sun Wukong. "Take me there."

So the Dragon King and Sun Wukong went together to see the great rod. It was twenty feet long and as wide as a big tree. Each end of the rod was wrapped in gold, and in the center was written, "Golden Hoop Rod." Sun Wukong said, "This rod is too long and too thick. Change!" Just as he said it, the rod became smaller and only as wide as a rice bowl. Sun Wukong picked it up. Now he liked it. He looked at the rod and said softly, "Still too big. Change!" Now the rod became very, very small. Sun Wukong picked it up and put it inside his ear.

"Thank you, my neighbor," he said to the Dragon King. "I like this rod! Now I just need one more thing. Do you have any good clothes for me?"

"Sorry," the Dragon King replied, "I don't have any clothes for you."

Sun Wukong looked at him and said coldly, "Do you want me to hit you with my golden rod?"

"Wait! Do not raise your hand," cried the Dragon King, "I will find some good clothes for you." The Dragon King called his three brothers, and together they found some good clothes for Sun Wukong, including a beautiful red gold hat and yellow gold armor. They gave these to Sun Wukong. He was happy. He took the clothes and went home. But the Dragon King and his brothers were all very angry, and they sent a letter to the Jade Emperor in Heaven.

When Sun Wukong returned home, he sat on his throne and put the golden rod on the ground. All the monkeys tried to pick it up but they could not move it. Sun Wukong laughed and told them the story of how he got the golden rod. The little monkeys laughed and danced, and they all ate food and drank wine until they fell asleep.

Now this is interesting! While Sun Wukong was asleep, he had a dream. In the dream, two men came up to him. They had a piece of paper with the words "Sun Wukong" on it. Not saying a word, the two men took Sun Wukong and dragged him down the road. As they were dragging him, Sun Wukong looked up and saw a sign above him with large letters, "Entering the Land of the Dead."

"What is this?" he cried, "The Land of the Dead is the home of Yama, the King of the Underworld. I am immortal. What am I doing here?" But the two men did not listen to him. Sun Wukong grew angry. He took his golden rod out of his ear and changed it to be as wide as a rice bowl, and he hit the two men hard with it. They let him go, and he ran into the City of the Underworld.

There he saw the ten Kings of the Underworld. The kings saw him but they did not know him, so they said, "Tell us your name!"

"I am Sun Wukong, the Monkey King from Flower Fruit Mountain," he replied, "You sent two men to drag me down the road. This has made me very angry. Tell me your names right now or I will hit you with my golden rod."

The kings were afraid, and they quickly told him their names. Sun Wukong said, "People call you great kings so you should be intelligent. However, I know that you sent those two men to take me. That was very stupid!"

"High Immortal," they replied, "please do not be angry. Perhaps our men took the wrong person. You know that many people have the same name."

"I don't believe you," said Sun Wukong, "Show me the Books of Life and Death. I want to see for myself if my name is there."

So the kings brought out the books called the Books of Life and Death. These books had the names of all living beings in them – men, monkeys, and animals. Sun Wukong looked in all the books but he could not find his own name. This was because he looked like a man but was not a man, but he was not a monkey either. He was special. Finally he saw a very small book with just one page. He opened it and read this: "Heaven-born stone monkey. Age: three hundred and forty two years. Dies of old age."

Sun Wukong said, "I don't know my age. But it's not a problem. I don't want my name to be in the Books of Life and Death. Bring me a brush and some ink." He used the brush and ink to cross out his own name. But he was not finished. He opened the ledger of monkey names and used the brush and ink to cross out the names of all the monkeys. "Now my name and my friends' names are not in the Books of Life and Death," he said, "and we will live forever." This made the ten Kings of the Underworld very angry, and they also sent a letter to the Jade Emperor in Heaven.

Just after that, Sun Wukong woke up and saw that it was all a dream. He told the four old monkeys about the dream, and how he had removed their names from the Books of Life and Death. When the four old monkeys learned that their names were not in the book, they were very happy because they knew they would live forever.

The Monkey King was happy, and so were the other monkeys and all his friends. In Heaven, though, the Jade Emperor was not happy. He had just received two letters. The first letter was from the Dragon King. It talked about Sun Wukong's visit to the Dragon Palace and what he did there. The second letter was from the Ten Kings of the Underworld. It talked about Sun Wukong's visit to the Underworld and what he did there.

After reading the two letters the Jade Emperor was very angry. He shouted, "Who is this lawless monkey? Where was he born? How did he learn so much, and how did he become so powerful?" Two of his ministers came forward and said, "O Emperor, this monkey is the little stone monkey born of Heaven and Earth that you saw three hundred years ago. At that time he was not strong. We do not know how he learned so much and became so powerful."

"Well, now he is too powerful and too dangerous. Go and arrest him," said the Jade Emperor.

One of the two ministers, the Gold Star of Venus, stepped forward and said, "O Jade Emperor, you know that all creatures can become immortal if they study. This monkey was born of Heaven and Earth, so of course he could also become immortal. Please do not arrest him. He should come and live in Heaven. Let's invite him here and give him a job."

Chapter 4

The Jade Emperor saw that this was good advice. So he told Gold Star to go meet with Sun Wukong and invite him to Heaven. Gold Star went down to Flower Fruit Mountain and said to Sun Wukong, "I am the Gold Star of Venus. The Jade Emperor wants you to come to Heaven and receive a job." Sun Wukong was happy to hear this, and he used his cloud somersault to go up to Heaven.

Sun Wukong traveled very fast and Gold Star could not stay with him, so he arrived at Heaven while Gold Star was still traveling. Nobody in Heaven knew him. When they saw him, they said, "You cannot come in." They stood in front of him, holding their weapons. Sun Wukong thought, "Gold Star did not tell me the truth. He invited me to Heaven. But these people do not want me here."

Just then, Gold Star arrived. "Don't worry, my friend," he said to Sun Wukong, "this is your first time here, of course the people in this place do not know you. That is why they will not let you come in! Now I am here and everything is ok. Later, when you live here and work here, who will stop you from coming and going?"

Then Gold Star said loudly to the people, "Move aside. This person was called by the Jade Emperor himself. Let him come in!" Everyone stepped aside, and Gold Star and Sun Wukong entered the palace. The palace was very beautiful. The palace had thirty-three layers, and inside were many valuable jewels. From far away they heard music. In the center of the palace the Jade Emperor was sitting on his throne.

Sun Wukong and Gold Star bowed in front of the Emperor. Gold Star said, "O Emperor, you asked me to bring the immortal monster to you."

"And who is this immortal?" asked the Emperor.

Before Gold Star could speak, Sun Wukong jumped up and said to the Emperor, "None other than this old monkey!"

The ministers all grew angry, but the Emperor said, "This immortal just recently became human. We will forgive him for saying these words."

Then the Emperor asked his ministers what jobs in Heaven were available for Sun Wukong. The ministers said that there were many jobs in Heaven, but almost all the jobs were already taken. There was only one job: taking care of the Emperor's horses in the stables. Sun Wukong liked horses, so he thought this would be a good job. Right away he went to the stables and started working.

He enjoyed the job, and the horses grew fat and happy. He worked for a couple of weeks. One day he was relaxing with his friends, eating and drinking. He lifted a cup of wine and asked them, "What rank is my job?"

"Your job does not have a rank," they replied.

"If it does not have a rank, it must be the highest job in Heaven!" said Sun Wukong.

"No," they laughed, "Your job has no rank because it is the lowest job in Heaven. You must make the horses fat and happy. Be careful, though, if the horses become thin or sick you will be in big trouble!"

"What?" he cried. "In Flower Fruit Mountain I am a great king. You say that here I am just a servant, feeding horses and working a low-rank job? This is not for me." He jumped up and took the golden rod out of his ear. Quickly it grew to the width of a rice bowl. He fought his way out of the stables and through the Gate of Heaven, then did a cloud somersault and returned to Flower Fruit Mountain.

The four old monkeys met him and said, "Great King, you have been in Heaven for ten years. We missed you! Did you enjoy your visit?"

"Ten years? It has only been two weeks," he replied.

"Great King, do you know, a year on Earth is only one day in Heaven. May we ask you what job you had during your time in Heaven?"

"Don't ask me that!" he said. "They gave me a very low-rank job, working in the stables. When I found out what rank job it was, I quit and returned here."

"We are happy that you have returned to us," they replied. "You can stay here in Flower Fruit Mountain and be our king." Then they said to the other monkeys, "Quick, bring wine for the King!"

Now, as they were all sitting and drinking wine, two demons arrived. They were very friendly and they brought gifts for the Monkey King, but they loved to cause trouble. The Monkey King gave them wine, and they all drank wine and talked together for a long time. When the demons heard that Sun Wukong had been to Heaven, they asked what job he had in Heaven. Sun Wukong told them about the stable job. "Oh no," said the demons, "that is not a good job for you. You are a great King, not a stable boy. You should be called 'Great

Sage Equal to Heaven.'" Sun Wukong loved this name so much, he told the monkeys to make a large flag saying, "The Great Sage Equal to Heaven."

But while Sun Wukong was chatting with the demons, there was trouble in Heaven. Two weeks earlier the Jade Emperor had been angry because of what the Monkey King had done on Earth. Now he was even more angry because the Monkey King had quit his job and left Heaven. He told one of his generals to find Sun Wukong, arrest him, and bring him back to Heaven. The general left Heaven and traveled quickly to Flower Fruit Mountain. He stood in front of the cave and called to Sun Wukong, "I have come to arrest you and bring you to Heaven. Come out quickly, or I must come in and kill you!"

Sun Wukong came out, but he did not want to go to Heaven. He was ready to fight. He wore his red gold hat and yellow gold armor, and in his hand he held the golden rod. His eyes glowed like fire, and his voice was like thunder. He said, "Who are you and why are you so stupid to come here like this? Tell me your name now."

"Lawless monkey," said the general, "you don't need to know my name. I have been sent by the Emperor to arrest you and take you back to Heaven. Put down your rod and come with me. If you say even half a 'no' you will be immediately killed."

"You stupid general," said Sun Wukong, "I could kill you right now, but I won't, because I want you to take my words back to the Emperor. Ask the Emperor why he gave me that low-rank job taking care of his horses. Do you see this flag? It says, 'Great Sage Equal to Heaven.' That is me! If the Emperor gives me this name, I will put down my rod and there will be no trouble. If he does not give me this name, I will fight my way to Heaven and cause so much trouble that the Emperor will not even be able to sit on his throne!"

The general just laughed. He said, "Lawless monkey, you want to be a Great Sage Equal to Heaven? Taste my axe first." Then the general and the Monkey King began to fight. They fought for a long time, the monkey using his golden rod and the general using his axe. Finally, Sun Wukong hit the general's head hard with his rod. The general ran away back to Heaven.

The Emperor sent a different general to Flower Fruit Mountain to fight the Monkey King. Again they fought, and again the Monkey King won the fight. The second general also ran away back to Heaven. He said to the Emperor, "Your servant is so sorry! He went down to Earth to bring the lawless monkey back to Heaven. But he could not do it!"

The Emperor wanted to send more generals to fight the Monkey King, but one of his ministers said, "Fighting this monkey is too difficult! Perhaps we should not fight him. Perhaps we should let him be the Great Sage Equal to Heaven. Give him the job that he wants, but do not give him any money, and do not give him anything to do. Maybe he will be happy and stop causing trouble!" The Emperor agreed and asked Gold Star to go down again to Flower Fruit Mountain to talk with Sun Wukong. This time Gold Star was not welcomed as a friend. This time everyone on Flower Fruit Mountain picked up weapons and began to fight him. "Wait," he shouted, "do not fight! I am here to talk with the Great Sage."

Sun Wukong saw him and said, "Please come in, my friend. Please forgive me for not meeting you when you first arrived."

Gold Star said, "Let me explain. When you first came to Heaven, the Emperor gave you a low-rank job because he did not know of your powers. Now we see that you are the Great Sage Equal to Heaven. So the Emperor wants you to return to Heaven. He will give you a new job that only you can perform."

Sun Wukong laughed, "Thank you, my friend. I am sorry that I caused you such problems in Heaven! Tell me, what is this new job?"

"Great Sage Equal to Heaven," Gold Star replied.

"Really? There is a job in Heaven called 'Great Sage Equal to Heaven'?"

"Yes. Trust me. If there is a problem, you can talk to me."

Sun Wukong heard this and was very pleased. So they traveled together back to Heaven and stood before the Jade Emperor on his throne. The Emperor said, "Let the Monkey King come forward." Sun Wukong came forward. "Let all men hear this. I now say to everyone that you are the Great Sage Equal to Heaven. This job is of the highest rank. Just don't cause any more trouble!" Sun Wukong was very happy and thanked the Emperor.

Then the Emperor gave Sun Wukong two bottles of wine, ten bunches of flowers, and a new house in Heaven next to the Garden of Immortal Peaches. This was a big mistake, because Sun Wukong loved to eat peaches! But that is a story for another time. Right now, everyone was happy. Sun Wukong sat down in his new house, and with his friends together he drank both bottles of wine.

Life was good. He was in Heaven, he was immortal, he had a good job, he had friends, and he had lots of wine to drink. What problems could he have?

Well, my child, you will learn that on the great wheel of life, things come and go. A person has many things for a while, and later those same things will go away. Suffering does not come from those things going away, it comes from holding too tightly to them. This is life. Maybe the Monkey King will learn this and get off the wheel of life. Maybe not. We don't know.

But for now, it's time for you to sleep.

Chapter 5

Sun Wukong was a very powerful monkey, so the Jade Emperor in Heaven did not want him to cause trouble. So he invited Sun Wukong to live in Heaven and be called "Great Sage Equal to Heaven." But Sun Wukong had no work to do. So he made friends, ate tasty meals, and traveled all around Heaven enjoying himself.

Now the Jade Emperor was worried that Sun Wukong would cause trouble because he had no work to do. So one day he called Sun Wukong to come see him. Sun Wukong arrived but did not bow to the Emperor. He just walked in and asked, "Great Emperor, what gift do you have for this old monkey?"

The Jade Emperor said, "I have no gift for you, but I have a job for you. You will take care of the Garden of Immortal Peaches. This is an important job. Be careful every day!"

Sun Wukong liked this, and right away he ran to the Garden of Immortal Peaches. He looked around. The garden looked beautiful and smelled wonderful. Everywhere he saw beautiful young trees with lovely flowers and fruits like large golden balls.

One of the garden workers, a local spirit, told Sun Wukong that the garden had 3600 peach trees. In the front, one third of the trees have small peaches that take 3000 years to ripen, and if a person eats them he will become immortal. In the middle, one third of the trees have sweet peaches that take 6000 years to ripen, and if a person eats them he will rise to Heaven and never grow old. And in the back, one third of the trees have beautiful purple peaches that take 9000 years to ripen, and if a person eats them, they will live to be as old as Heaven, the Earth, the sun and the moon.

Sun Wukong fell in love with the garden. He stopped traveling and stopped seeing his friends. Every day he was in the garden. One day he saw that some of the peaches were ripe. He really wanted to eat one, but he could not, because the workers were in the garden and he didn't want them to see him. So he asked the workers to leave the garden. Now he was all alone! He climbed up a tree and ate one of the peaches. It tasted very good. He ate another. He kept eating peaches until he was too full.

A few days later, the Queen Mother decided to give a feast. She wanted to have some immortal peaches in the feast. She asked seven of her immortal maidens – Red Gown, Blue Gown, White Gown, Black Gown, Purple Gown,

Yellow Gown and Green Gown – to gather some peaches for the feast. The maidens went to the garden, but the local spirit told them to wait. "This year is different from last year," he said, "this year we have a new boss, the Great Sage Equal to Heaven. I must tell him that you are here."

They asked, "Where is he?"

"In the garden. He is tired and sleeping."

"The Queen Mother told us to get peaches. We must not be late. We will go to see him now."

The maidens and the local spirit went into the garden, but they could not find Sun Wukong. He had eaten many peaches and was too full, so he made himself only two inches tall and fell asleep on a tree branch.

The maidens said, "The Queen Mother told us to get peaches. So we will get peaches, with or without the Great Sage."

They started to pick ripe peaches, but they could only find a few because Sun Wukong had eaten many of them. The Blue Gown maiden found a good ripe peach and she pulled it off the branch. The branch flew up and hit the Monkey

King. He fell to the ground. Waking up, he instantly grew to full size. He pulled his golden rod out of his ear and it grew to the thickness of a rice bowl. He shouted, "You monsters, where are you from, and why do you want to steal my peaches?"

The maidens were terrified, and said, "We are sorry, Great Sage! We are not monsters. We are just seven maidens, sent by the Queen Mother to get some immortal peaches for a great feast. We know that this is your garden, but we searched and could not find you. Please forgive us!"

Sun Wukong stopped being angry. He thought about the great feast and he smiled. "Thank you for inviting me to the feast!" he said.

The maidens didn't understand what he meant. They said, "We are sorry. We heard the names of the guests but did not hear your name, so we don't know if you are invited or not."

"No problem," he said. "Old Monkey will find out if he is invited. Stay here!" Then he used his magic so the maidens could not move. He did a cloud somersault and went to find the feast. As he was traveling, he met a handsome young man traveling the same direction as he was. He asked the man his name and where he was going.

"I am the Barefoot Immortal," said the handsome young man, "and I am going to the Feast of the Immortal Peaches."

"Oh," said Sun Wukong, "you are going the wrong way! This year the feast will be at the Palace of Light. The Emperor told me to tell everyone."

"I did not know that!" said the Barefoot Immortal. He turned around and went the other way, towards the Palace of Light. Then Sun Wukong changed himself to look like the Barefoot Immortal. He did another cloud somersault and arrived at the feast.

He was the first guest to arrive, but several workers were already there, preparing food. Looking around, he saw a hundred different kinds of tasty dishes. Then he smelled the aroma of wine. Sun Wukong was hungry and thirsty again, and he really wanted to taste the food and drink the wine! But he could not, because the other people would see him. What could he do? He used magic to make a cloud of insects. The insects flew and bit all the people, and they fell asleep.

Now Sun Wukong was all alone with the tasty food and the good-smelling wine. He ate until he was full, and he drank wine until he was very drunk.

Then he thought: "Bad monkey! Bad monkey! The guests will be here soon, and I will be in big trouble. I must leave now!"

But things became even worse for Sun Wukong. He was too drunk and could not find his way home. Instead of going home, he found himself in the house of Laozi, the great medicine man.

"Oh well," Sun Wukong thought, "I wanted to go home, but now I am here. I always wanted to meet this Laozi. This is a good time to meet him!"

But Laozi was not home. He was out, teaching a class. Sun Wukong walked through all the rooms of Laozi's house, looking for him. He did not find Laozi, but he found five bottles full of magic golden pills. Laozi was planning to give these pills to the guests at the feast, to give them immortality.

What did Sun Wukong do? Of course, he ate all the golden pills! But now he was really afraid, and he thought: "Bad! Bad! I have brought big trouble on myself. If the Jade Emperor hears about this, he will kill me!" So he ran out of Laozi's house and used the cloud somersault to return to his home in Flower Fruit Mountain.

The monkeys in Flower Fruit Mountain were very happy to see their King. They said, "Great King, you have been gone for over a hundred years. Where did you go and what were you doing?"

Sun Wukong was only in Heaven for a few months. But a day in Heaven is the same as a year on Earth.

He said, "I am happy to tell you that the Jade Emperor gave me a very good job. He gave me the job of 'Great Sage Equal to Heaven.' I took care of the Garden of Immortal Peaches. I ate one of the peaches. They tasted good so I ate a lot of them. Then I went to a great feast, even though I was not invited, and I ate a lot of food and drank a lot of wine. Then, drunk, I found myself in the house of the great Laozi, where I ate five bottles full of his golden pills. After I ate the pills, I was afraid that the Jade Emperor would hear about this, so I quickly came home."

The monkeys loved their king, so they prepared a feast for him and gave him a cup of home-made wine to drink. He tasted it, but immediately spat it out. "This taste very bad!" he said.

The monkeys said, "The Great King has been eating and drinking in Heaven. Of course the food and drink of Earth do not taste good to you!"

"No problem," he said, "I will get us some good wine!" Sun Wukong jumped up and used the cloud somersault to return to Heaven. He went to the feast and picked up four large bottles of the Emperor's best wine. He brought the bottles back to Flower Fruit Mountain, and he drank the wine with his friends.

Now, do you remember those seven immortal maidens? They were still in the same place! They could not move because of Sun Wukong's magic, so they stood under a tree in the garden of immortal peaches for a full day, until the magic ended and they could move again.

And now things started to get very bad for Sun Wukong. First, the immortal maidens told the Queen Mother that Sun Wukong ate many of the immortal peaches and used his magic to keep them in the garden. The Queen Mother went right to her son the Emperor and told him this story.

Before the Queen Mother was finished speaking, some workers from the Feast of the Immortal Peaches came and told the Emperor that someone had eaten all the food and drunk all the wine at the feast. Then the great Laozi himself came to the Emperor and told him that someone had entered his home and eaten all of his magic golden pills. And finally, the Barefoot Immortal came in and told the Emperor that someone had sent him to the wrong place for the Feast of the Immortal Peaches!

This was too much for the Emperor. He became very angry. He called many of the immortals together. He called the Stars of East and West, the Gods of North and South, the Immortals of the Five Mountains, the Dragon Gods of the Four Rivers, the Spirits of Heaven, and an army of a hundred thousand men. The Emperor told them all to go down to Flower Fruit Mountain and arrest Sun Wukong.

The army threw a large net around Flower Fruit Mountain to keep Sun Wukong inside. Then they all gathered outside the Water Curtain Cave and waited.

Chapter 6

Inside the cave, Sun Wukong was relaxing, drinking the Emperor's wine and chatting with his friends. Some frightened monkeys ran in and told him of the army outside the cave. But Sun Wukong was not worried. "You know the old saying: if you have wine today, drink it today, don't worry about troubles outside your door!"

But the troubles outside his door did not go away. The army of immortals broke down the door of his cave. One of them shouted, "You bad monkey! First, you ate the immortal peaches. Then you ate the food and drank the wine at the Feast of the Immortal Peaches. Then you ate Laozi's golden pills. And then you stole the Emperor's own wine for your pleasure."

"Ah, that is all true," smiled Sun Wukong. "But what are you going to do about it?"

"The Jade Emperor himself told us to come here and arrest you. Come with us, or we will kill all these monkeys and destroy your home."

Sun Wukong and the immortals shouted insults to each other for a while, then they began to fight. The fight went on for a very long time and I won't tell you all the details about it. It started when the sun came up in the east, and continued until the sun went down behind the western mountains. At nighttime, both sides rested and prepared to fight again the next day. The next day they fought again, but the huge army of immortals and soldiers could still not defeat Sun Wukong.

The Emperor did not know what to do. During the battle, a visitor came to see him. It was Guanyin, a Buddhist sage from the South Sea. She said, "Great Emperor, I know someone who can defeat this awful monkey. Your nephew, Erlang, is a great fighter. When he was young, he killed six monsters. These days he does not fight very much, but perhaps he will help you."

So the Emperor wrote a letter to Erlang, requesting his help. Erlang agreed to help, and he traveled to Flower Fruit Mountain with six of his brothers and a large army. The other soldiers opened a gap in the net to let the newcomers inside.

When they arrived at Water Curtain Cave, Erlang shouted to Sun Wukong, and they shouted insults to each other for a while. Then they began to fight. Sun Wukong had beaten other immortals, but this time Erlang was too much for him. Sun Wukong fought and fought, but he became tired and still could not win. So he changed into a small bird and flew away.

Erlang saw Sun Wukong change into a bird and fly away, so he quickly changed into a hawk and flew after him. Sun Wukong saw this, and he changed into a small fish and dove into the river. Erlang thought: "Where did he go?" He flew above the river, then he saw the small fish and dove into the water to catch it. Quickly, Sun Wukong changed into a water snake. The snake swam through the water and went into the tall grass. Erlang saw this, and he quickly changed into a crane and went into the tall grass to catch the snake.

Sun Wukong saw this and changed into a big bird, but he knew that he would be captured anyway. So he flew down a hill and changed into a small Buddhist temple. His mouth was the doorway. His eyes were the windows. But what about his tail? It stood straight up in the air and became a flagpole.

Erlang changed back into a man and walked towards the temple. "Very strange," he said, "I have seen many temples, but I have never seen one with a flagpole. It must be that bad monkey, Sun Wukong! If I go inside the temple, he will eat me. So I will stay outside and just smash the temple!"

But before he could smash the temple, it disappeared, and Sun Wukong stood several miles away. Erlang saw him, and they began to fight again, face to face. Erlang's six brothers also arrived to help him.

During the fight, Guanyin and Laozi were watching from up in Heaven. They both wanted to help Erlang. Laozi said, "I have a golden armlet made of steel. It has strong magic and cannot be harmed by fire or water. Let's try it!"

So Laozi threw down the armlet. It landed on Sun Wukong and wrapped itself around his head. Sun Wukong fell down, and right away the seven brothers wrapped him up with heavy ropes. They thrust a knife into his chest so he could not use his magic anymore. And then the guards from Heaven carried him up to Heaven so they could kill him there.

Chapter 7

But it was very difficult to kill Sun Wukong! He had studied the Way and was immortal. He also had eaten many immortal peaches and Laozi's golden pills, so his body could not be harmed. The guards used many weapons, but they could not hurt him. They tried fire but it had no effect. They threw lightning bolts but nothing happened. Nobody knew what to do.

Finally, Laozi stepped forward and said, "This monkey ate the immortal peaches, he drank the Emperor's wine, and he stole my golden pills. All this went into his stomach and gave him a diamond body. That is why it is so difficult to hurt him. But we can put him in a brazier and roast him slowly for forty-nine days. The fire will separate his body from the diamond, and he will die."

So the guards removed the knife from his chest, removed the ropes from his body, and threw him into the brazier. Laozi blew hard on the fire and made it very hot.

Forty-nine days later, Laozi opened the door of the brazier, thinking that Sun Wukong was dead. But he was not dead! Sun Wukong jumped out of the brazier, angry as a tiger. He hit everyone with his golden hoop rod, he smashed doors and buildings, he fought with everyone who came near to him. The immortals of Heaven were so frightened, they could only do one thing: they asked the great Buddha himself to come down and capture this dangerous monkey.

The Buddha himself arrived, with two of his students. They heard deafening shouts and the sound of breaking doors and buildings. He held up his hand and called for the fighters to stop. He said to Sun Wukong, "Come forward, monkey, and tell me your story. When were you born? How did you learn the Way? And why are you so very angry?"

So Sun Wukong told the Buddha the story of his life, from his birth as a small stone monkey on Flower Fruit Mountain until the present day. He said, "Now, the Earth is too small for me. I want to be Emperor in Heaven!"

The Buddha laughed. "Emperor in Heaven? You are just a monkey who learned a few things! You cannot be the Emperor. Look at the Jade Emperor. He started studying the Way when he was a small boy. He studied for 1,750 kalpas, where each kalpa is 129,600 years. Think of how many years he has studied. Compared to him, you are just a little animal who looks like a man.

Stop talking like this right now!"

Sun Wukong replied, "Even if the Jade Emperor has studied for a long time, he should not stay here forever. Nobody should be Emperor forever. Tell him to give the Emperor's throne to me, right now."

The Buddha smiled and said, "Let's make a bet. You stand here on my right hand. Use your cloud somersault to fly away. If you can leave my hand, you are the winner, and I will ask the Jade Emperor to give his throne to you. But, if you cannot get away, you will go back to Flower Fruit Mountain and stay there for a few more kalpas. Maybe you will learn something!"

Sun Wukong thought: "This man is a fool! Using one cloud somersault I can go a hundred thousand miles, but his hand is not even a foot wide. This will be easy!"

He said to the Buddha, "If I win this bet, you will really ask the Jade Emperor to give me his throne?"

The Buddha looked down at Sun Wukong and said, "Yes."

Sun Wukong jumped right up onto the Buddha's right hand, and he used the cloud somersault to fly away. The Buddha watched him fly and smiled. Sun Wukong flew for a long time, until he came to five tall pink mountains. He thought: "Good. I don't need to go any further. Now I will return to that foolish man, win the bet, and I will be the new Emperor. But first, I must leave something here."

He used his magic to make a brush and ink, and he wrote on one of the mountains, "The Great Sage was here." Also, he left a puddle of monkey urine at the base of the mountain. Bad monkey!

Sun Wukong turned around and used the cloud somersault to fly back to the Buddha. He said, "You lost the bet! I left your hand and flew very far. I arrived at a place with five pink mountains and wrote my name. Go there and see for yourself!"

"I don't need to go anywhere," said the Buddha. "Look here at my hand. And smell my hand too!" There on his fingers was written in tiny letters, "The Great Sage was here." And there was a smell of monkey urine. Sun Wukong saw that he had not left the Buddha's right hand.

He was very angry. He thought: "I don't believe it! I don't believe it! I will go there one more time!"

Sun Wukong started to fly again, but the Buddha quickly flipped his hand upside down. His five fingers became five mountains that surrounded Sun Wukong so he could not leave.

The immortals in Heaven were pleased by this, and they recited this poem:

> "He was born a monkey but learned to be human
> He learned the Way and lived like a king
> He wanted too much and caused trouble in Heaven
> He stole food, wine and medicine, he insulted the gods
> Who knows how long he will stay under the five mountains?"

The Buddha was getting ready to leave, but just then, the Jade Emperor arrived and said, "Thank you for defeating that frightening monkey. Please stay here for another day. We want to give you a wonderful feast!"

The Buddha stayed, and there was a great feast in Heaven. Many delicious foods were served, including a few immortal peaches. There was singing and dancing and reciting poetry. The guests asked the Buddha to give a name to the feast. He said, "My friends, if you want a name, let's call it 'The Great Feast for Peace in Heaven.'"

The Emperor, the Buddha, and all the guests stayed for a long time at The Great Feast for Peace in Heaven. Then a man came running up, saying: "The monkey is trying to get out!"

Everyone was frightened, but the Buddha said, "Don't worry." He took out a small sign with gold writing: "om mani padme hum[1]" and said, "Go put this sign on top of the mountain." The man did it, and right away the five mountains grew together tightly, so Sun Wukong could not leave.

The Buddha said, "Now the monkey cannot leave. But I do not want him to be hungry or thirsty." He called a local spirit and told him to give Sun Wukong iron balls if he was hungry, and hot melted copper if he was thirsty. He also told the local spirit to watch Sun Wukong until someone comes to take him away.

---

[1] A Buddhist mantra, literally "the jewel is in the lotus."

Chapter 8

The Buddha lived in Spirit Mountain in Heaven. One day he called all the holy men and women who lived in Spirit Mountain, and he said to them, "I have prepared a great bowl with a hundred kinds of beautiful flowers and a thousand kinds of tasty fruits. Please, sit and eat with me, and I will tell you about my plans."

So all the holy men and women sat around the Buddha and ate the delicious fruits in the bowl. They thanked the Buddha and gave him poems. When they were finished, they were silent and waited for the great Buddha to speak. When he began to speak, the people saw dragons flying in the sky overhead, and beautiful flowers fell like rain.

The Buddha said, "There are four continents, and I have seen the people who live there. The people in the East love Heaven and Earth, but they live a very simple life. The people in the North don't cause any trouble but they kill to live. The people in the West are easygoing and live a long time, but there are no wise people there. And the people in the South are the worst; they often do bad things; they fight with each other and kill their neighbors. I am not satisfied with this, so I have decided to do something to help these people."

"What will you do?" asked the holy men and women.

The Buddha replied, "I have made three rooms of holy books that will show the people how to do good, and why. The first speaks of Heaven. The second speaks of Earth. And the third helps people to leave the Underworld and reach Heaven. All together there are 15,144 books in these three rooms."

The Buddha continued, "I want to give these books to the people in the four continents. But I cannot do it myself, because those people are too stupid and they will not listen to me. We need an Easterner to do this. This man must journey to the West, get these holy books, and bring them back to the people. It will be a very difficult thing to do. He must climb a thousand mountains, cross ten thousand waters, and fight many monsters before arriving here."

The Buddha already knew who he wanted for this job. He wanted a young monk named Xuanzang, but he did not tell this to the others.

Why did the Buddha want Xuanzang? A long time ago, in an earlier lifetime, Xuanzang was a man named Gold Cicada, a student of the Buddha. Gold Cicada wasn't a good student. He did not study, he did not listen to the

Buddha, and did not listen carefully to what the Buddha told him. So the Buddha sent him down to the human world, and made him spend ten painful lifetimes as a human.

The story I will tell you tonight is about his tenth lifetime, which was the most difficult. In this life he was called Flowing River as a child, and later became known as Xuanzang.

Chapter 9

Xuanzang's father was named Guangrui. When Guangrui was a young man, before Xuanzang was born, he lived in the city of Chang'an. The emperor was a wise man named Taizong. The country was peaceful, and the people were well fed and happy.

One day Taizong said, "I will hold an imperial examination, to find the wisest people in the land, so they can become my ministers and help the people. Anyone in my land can come to Chang'an and take the examination."

Guangrui heard about the imperial examination, and he ran home to tell his mother. "The Emperor has invited people to take the examination," he said, "I want to take it. If I do well and become one of Taizong's ministers, it will bring honor to my parents, and it will help my wife and my children. Of course, I do not have a wife or children yet! But I want to take the examination. I think I will do very well."

His mother let him take the examination. So Guangrui journeyed to Chang'an. The examination was very difficult and took several days. But of all the people who took the examination, Guangrui was in first place. He was the "zhuangyuan" in this examination, which means "number one scholar." The people put him on a horse and led him through the city streets for three days.

As he was riding his horse through the streets, he passed the house of Prime Minister Yin, who had a beautiful daughter named Wenjiao. Wenjiao was not married, and she wanted to find a good husband. She made an embroidered ball, climbed up to the top of her house, and was ready to throw the ball, thinking that whoever caught the ball would be her husband. Just then she saw Guangrui on horseback. She thought he was very handsome and she also knew that he was the new zhuangyuan, so she carefully threw the ball and it hit Guangrui on the head. He looked up, saw Wenjiao, and smiled. Wenjiao's friends and family ran out and brought Guangrui into the house, and that same day they were married.

The next day, the Emperor Taizong asked his ministers, "What job should we give the new zhuangyuan?" One of his ministers replied, "Jiangzhou needs a county governor." Taizong immediately named Guangrui the governor of Jiangzhou and told him to leave right away. So Guangrui went home and told his wife. Then Guangrui, with his wife Wenjiao, his mother, and a servant, began the journey from Chang'an to Jiangzhou.

It was late spring. A soft wind blew through the trees, and a light rain fell on the flowers by the roadside.

After a few days on the road, they arrived in the town of Hongzhou. His mother said, "I do not feel well. Let's stay here for a few days so I can rest." Guangrui agreed, and they rested at an inn called the Inn of Ten Thousand Flowers.

Late that afternoon, Guangrui went outside to take a walk. He saw a man trying to sell a large fish. Guangrui purchased the fish and was planning to bring it back inside to cook it for dinner. But he looked at the fish and saw that it was rapidly blinking its eyes at him. Guangrui said to the man, "I have heard that when a fish blinks its eyes like that, it is a special creature, not just a fish! I cannot eat this fish. Where did you catch it?"

"I caught it in the Hong River," said the man. So Guangrui bought the fish, then he took it back to the Hong River and threw it into the water. The fish looked at him for a long time, blinked his eyes, then went under the water. Remember this, because Guangrui will meet the fish again later!

Three days passed, but Guangrui's mother was still not feeling well. Guangrui said to her, "The Emperor told me that I must go to Jiangzhou quickly. I cannot wait any longer. Please stay here until you feel better. I will give you some money. Wait for me, I will return and bring you to Jiangzhou."

So Guangrui, Wenjiao and the servant left the inn and continued towards Jiangzhou. They soon arrived at the Hong River. Two boatmen, Liu Hong and Li Biao, offered to take them across the river.

Now, I told you that Wenjiao was very beautiful. People say that her face was like the moon, her eyes were like the water of autumn, and she was so beautiful that birds would fall from the sky and fish would sink to the bottom of the sea. One of the boatmen, Liu Hong, fell in love with her beauty, and wanted her to be his wife. So the two boatmen took the boat to a place where nobody could see them. That night they killed the servant, then they beat Guangrui and threw him into the water.

Wenjiao tried to jump into the water to help her husband. But Liu Hong grabbed her and said, "Your husband is already dead. You will die too, or you can become my wife." Wenjiao knew that she was pregnant, and she wanted to protect her child. If she died, her child would die too. So she agreed to be Liu Hong's wife. Liu Hong took the boat to the other side of the river, and with Wenjiao he went to Jiangzhou. When they arrived at Jiangzhou, he put on Guangrui's clothes and told the people that he was Guangrui. Now he had Guangrui's job and he had Wenjiao as his wife.

Now let's return to the Hong River. Guangrui was dead, and his body sank to the bottom of the river. A river spirit saw it and rushed to the palace of the Dragon King, saying, "O Great King, a scholar has been killed and his body thrown into the river. It is now at the bottom of the river."

"Bring it here," said the Dragon King. The river spirit brought the body in, and the Dragon King looked at it. He said, "I know this man! He helped me just a few days ago. I was a fish, and this man bought me and returned me to the water. He was kind to me, so of course I must be kind to him." He told the river spirit to go to the Underworld and get Guangrui's soul. Then the Dragon King put Guangrui's soul back into his body. Guangrui sat up and opened his eyes.

"Scholar," said the Dragon King, "what is your name? Where did you come from? And why are you dead?"

"My name is Guangrui. I was traveling from Chang'an to Jiangzhou with my wife and servant. When I tried to cross the Hong River, the boatman decided he wanted my wife for himself, so he killed me and threw my body in the river. I am a young man with much to live for. Please return me to life, O Great King!"

"My friend," said the Dragon King, "you do not know it, but you helped me. I was a fish, and you bought me and returned me to the river. Now I will help you."

The Dragon King put a magic pearl in Guangrui's mouth, to keep his body and soul together. "For now, you can wait here in my palace. I will try to return you to life later."

Now let's return to Wenjiao, who had no choice but to be the wife of the bandit Liu Hong. She really wanted to kill him but she could not. She was also looking forward to the birth of her child and was afraid that Liu Hong would kill the child.

One day Liu Hong was out of town, and Wenjiao was thinking about her dead husband. Suddenly she felt a sharp pain in her belly, and she gave birth to a baby boy. Later, she fell asleep with the baby in her hands and she dreamed.

In her dream she heard a voice saying, "Listen carefully, dear Wenjiao! I am the Star Spirit of the South. One day your child will be a famous man, a servant of the Buddha himself, but right now he is in danger. You must protect him! Don't worry about your dear husband, he is alive and waiting for you in the palace of the Dragon King. You will all be together again in the future. Remember my words. Now wake up! Wake up!"

Wenjiao woke up and remembered the words from the dream. But just then, Liu Hong returned to the house. He saw the baby boy and wanted to kill the baby right away. But Wenjiao said, "It is late today, my husband. Let's wait till tomorrow, then we will go together and throw the baby in the river." Liu Hong agreed.

But the next morning, Liu Hong had to go away again. Wenjiao knew that she did not have much time. She wanted to write a letter but did not have a brush and ink, so she bit her finger and wrote the letter with blood. The letter explained the child's story and asked that someone take care of him. She wrapped up the letter and tied it to the baby. Then she bit off a small toe from the child's left foot, so she would know him if she met him later.

Wenjiao ran with the baby down to the river. She saw a wooden plank floating on the water. She put the baby on the plank and tied him to it, with the letter. She stood and watched as he floated down the river and out of sight.

The baby floated down the river for several hours, until he arrived at Gold Mountain Temple. The abbot of the temple heard the baby crying, ran down to the river, and picked him up. He read the letter written in blood. He took the baby into the temple and gave him the name Flowing River.

Flowing River lived at the temple. He studied with the abbot but he never knew anything about his parents or his birth, because the abbot did not tell him. When Flowing River turned eighteen, the abbot had his head shaved and gave him the name Xuanzang.

One day Xuanzang was discussing the Buddha's teachings with another young monk. This young monk was angry because Xuanzang had outwitted him, and he shouted, "What are you? You don't even know your own name, or the names of your parents. Why are you even here with us?"

 Xuanzang went to the abbot and cried. So the abbot said, "Follow me, Xuanzang," and the two of them went into the abbot's room. The abbot reached into a secret place and pulled out the letter written in blood, and gave it to Xuanzang.

Xuanzang read the letter, and said to the abbot, "For eighteen years I have lived here, not knowing my name or my family. Now I understand who I am.

Dear abbot, please allow me to go and seek my mother and avenge my father's death!"

The abbot replied, "Of course you may go. Put on the clothing of an ordinary monk, and go the governor's home where your mother lives."

Xuanzang dressed as a lowly monk and went to the governor's home. Liu Hong was again away on business, because Heaven wanted mother and son to meet. Also, the previous night Wenjiao had dreamed of seeing her son again. So when Xuanzang arrived at her house, she opened the door right away and asked, "Who are you?"

"I am a humble monk from Gold Mountain Temple," said Xuanzang.

Wenjiao looked him over. She invited him to come inside, and gave him vegetables and rice to eat. Again she asked, "Who are you? Why did you leave your family?"

"I did not leave my family," he said. "My father was killed, and my mother was forced to marry the man who killed him. My anger is as deep as the ocean, and I want to avenge my father and mother."

And who are your father and mother?" asked Wenjiao.

"My father's name is Guangrui. My mother's name is Wenjiao. I was called Flowing River, but on my eighteenth birthday the abbot gave me the name Xuanzang." Then he showed Wenjiao the letter written in blood. Then Wenjiao knew that this monk was her son, and Xuanzang knew that this woman was his mother.

But before he could say anything, Wenjiao cried, "You must leave at once!"

"Why?" asked Xuanzang. "I have lived for eighteen years not knowing my parents. Now I meet my mother, and she tells me to leave at once. Why?"

"You must leave as if you are on fire," she replied. "The bandit Liu Hong will return soon, and if he sees you he will kill you immediately. But I have an idea. Go back to your temple and wait for me."

Xuanzang did as he was told. The next day, Wenjiao would not get out of bed and would not eat. She told the servants that she was feeling very sick. Liu Hong came into her room. She said to him, "When I was young, I wanted to donate a hundred pairs of shoes to temple monks. I never did it. But last night I had a dream that a monk was angry with me and told me I had to donate the shoes. Now I am sick because of this."

Liu Hong said, "Such a small problem! Don't worry about it." Then he ordered that a hundred families must each bring him a pair of shoes. Five days later, he had a hundred pairs of shoes. "Now we have the shoes," he said to Wenjiao, "where do you want to take them?"

Wenjiao said, "I have heard that Gold Mountain Temple is a good place. I will go there. You stay here, you are busy and I don't need your help. Just give me two servants."

Wenjiao arrived at the temple, and the servants prepared a great feast for the monks of the temple. Then she gave the shoes to the abbot, who gave them to the monks. Later, the monks left the room, and she was alone with the abbot. Xuanzang came in. Wenjiao looked at his feet, and she saw that he only had four toes on his left foot. Together they wept with joy, and they thanked the abbot for his help.

Then Wenjiao said to her son, "There are two things you must do.

"First, go to Hongzhou and find the Inn of Ten Thousand Flowers. There you will find your grandmother. She was traveling with your father and me, but she became ill and could not travel, so she stayed at the inn. It has been many years, I hope she is still there! You must find her."

Wenjiao continued, "Second, you must avenge your father's death. Go to the Emperor Taizong's palace and find Chief Minister Yin. He is my father. Take this letter that I have written to him. The letter asks the Emperor to send his men and horses to arrest and kill the bandit Liu Hong. Only then can your father's death be avenged. Now, go quickly. I must return home before Liu Hong thinks something is wrong."

Early the next morning, Xuanzang left the monastery and traveled to Hongzhou. He soon found the Inn of Ten Thousand Flowers. He said to the innkeeper, "Many years ago a small group of travelers arrived here. The woman was not feeling well, and she stayed while the rest of the group continued. Do you remember that woman, and do you know where she is now?"

The innkeeper said, "Yes, I remember the woman. She stayed at my inn for a long time, crying every day because she thought her family had forgotten about her. She cried so much that she became blind. She had no money so she could no longer remain here. So after a few years, she left. She now lives in a shack outside the city. Every day she goes begging for food in the street. I do not know why her family did not return for her."

Xuanzang went out and found the shack where his grandmother lived. She was sitting in front of the shack with a begging bowl in her hand. He greeted her respectfully, saying, "Grandmother, how are you?" She said, "You sound like my son Guangrui!"

"I am Guangrui's son, my name is Xuanzang. I am sorry to say that many years ago your son was killed by a bandit who wanted his wife Wenjiao. That is why Guangrui did not return for you. Wenjiao wanted to return for you, but she could not, because the bandit made her live with him in Jiangzhou. She told me to find you, and that the last time she saw you was at the Inn of Ten Thousand Flowers. The innkeeper there told me that I could find you here."

The grandmother began to cry and said, "Oh, this is terrible news and wonderful news. Terrible that my son was killed, but wonderful that you are here, my child!"

Then Xuanzang closed his eyes and said softly, "Dear Heaven, please listen to the words of this worthless young man, who is eighteen years old and has not yet avenged the death of his father. Here you see his grandmother, who is blind from years of crying over her missing son. Please give her sight back to her!"

Then he licked his grandmother's eyes, one at a time, with his tongue. And just like that, she could see again.

Xuanzang said, "I must leave now, to avenge my father's death. Please wait for me." He helped her to leave the shack and return to the Inn of Ten Thousand Flowers. He gave the innkeeper money to take care of her. Then he went to the Emperor's palace and found the house of Chief Minister Yin. He came to the door. A servant answered. "I am here to see the Chief Minister," said Xuanzang.

The servant told Yin that a monk was at the door to see him. "I do not know any monks," said Yin.

But just then, Yin's wife said, "Last night I had a dream that our daughter Wenjiao returned to us. And now, this monk is at our door. Let him in, and let's hear what he has to say!"

So Yin told the servant to let Xuanzang enter the house. When Xuanzang saw Yin and his wife, he fell down, crying, and handed Wenjiao's letter to them. Yin read the letter. "What does the letter say?" asked his wife.

Yin said, "It is from our daughter Wenjiao. This monk is her son. Our daughter's husband Guangrui was killed by a bandit, and Wenjiao has been forced to be the bandit's wife for eighteen years. She asks for our help. Of course, we will do so immediately!"

Yin went to see the Emperor Taizong and showed him the letter. Taizong became very angry. He ordered Yin to ride out with sixty thousand soldiers to capture the bandit Liu Hong. They marched by day and rested by night, and in several days they reached Jiangzhou. They arrived at the home of Liu Hong, who was asleep in his bed. The soldiers broke down the door of his home and captured Liu Hong without a fight.

The next day, Chief Minister Yin took a seat in the governor's home where Liu Hong had lived. Wenjiao came into the room to meet her father. She fell down, weeping, and said, "Oh father, I want to die. My husband was killed by that bandit. How could I remain alive and be the wife of this terrible man?"

Yin said to her, "My child, you did not do anything wrong. You did what you had to do to protect your child. There is nothing wrong with this, only great honor! You and your son should be happy today. I have captured the terrible bandit. Now we will finish this and avenge your dead husband."

They went outside. Liu Hong was there with the other bandit, Li Biao, who had also been captured by the soldiers. Li Biao was killed immediately. Liu Hong was taken to the river, to the exact place where he had killed Guangrui so many years before. Then they took out Liu Hong's heart from his body, and they offered it to the soul of Guangrui. Yin, Wenjiao and Xuanzang all stood on the riverbank and cried loudly.

Far below, deep under the water, their cries were heard by the Dragon King in his palace, and he saw the offering of Liu Hong's heart. The Dragon King told his servants to bring Guangrui to him. The King said to Guangrui, "Rejoice, my old friend! Your wife, your son and your mother's father are all standing on the riverbank, making offerings to you. Now it is time for me to return you to your family."

The Dragon King told a river spirit to bring Guangrui to the surface of the river. Guangrui drifted to the riverbank where his family was standing. Wenjiao saw him and cried even more loudly, thinking he was dead. But then Guangrui woke up. He took a deep breath, stretched, and climbed up onto the riverbank and sat down. Everyone stared at him, speechless. Guangrui blinked his eyes, looked at them and just said, "Why are you all here?"

Wenjiao stopped crying, and happily said to Guangrui, "My dear husband, eighteen years ago you were killed at this place by two bandits, and one of them forced me to be his wife. Later, your child was born, and I helped him get away from the bandit. Your child drifted down the river to Gold Mountain Temple, where the abbot took care of him. Now your son is a grown man. He went to see my father, Chief Minster Yin, and Yin brought an army of men to capture and kill the bandit Liu Hong. The bandit is dead. But how can you still be alive after all this time?"

"Well, for a long time I was not alive but I was not dead! When I was killed, my body fell to the bottom of the river. The Dragon King found me. Do you remember when we were at the Inn of Ten Thousand Flowers, and I bought the big fish and returned it to the river? Well, that big fish was actually the Dragon King! He was grateful to me, so he kept my body and soul in his palace until now. Then he heard your cries, and now he has returned me to you!" Then they cried together with happiness, and Wenjiao recalled that the Star Spirit of the South had told her about this in a dream, on the day of Xuanzang's birth.

Later, Guangrui and Xuanzang returned to the Inn of Ten Thousand Flowers, and Guangrui saw his mother for first time in eighteen years. Then they all returned to the Emperor's Palace, where the Emperor gave a great feast that he called the Festival of Reunion. The Emperor offered Xuanzang a high position. Xuanzang thanked him but said that he wanted to resume his studies of Buddhism. And so he returned to Gold Mountain Temple.

Chapter 10

Now I will tell you about three powerful and famous people: an emperor who lived in a palace in Chang'an, the emperor's wise prime minister, and a dragon king who lived under the river.

People say that a great river always starts as a tiny stream. And so, tonight's story begins with two ordinary people: a woodsman and a fisherman. These two were not scholars, but they were intelligent men and they loved to talk. They were also very good friends. Every day the fisherman sold the fish that he had caught, and the woodsman sold the wood that he had cut. At the end of the day they met at a tavern to eat dinner, drink wine and talk.

One evening, after they were done eating and drinking, they walked side by side on a small path alongside the Jing River to return home. They were both a little drunk, and each held a bottle of wine in his hand.

"My friend," said the woodsman, "I think that people who want to be famous will lose their lives because of fame, and people who want to be rich will be unhappy because of their money. Our lives are much better, because we are not famous and we have no money. We live in the beautiful mountains near the river. What more could we want?"

"You are correct," said the fisherman, "we both have happy lives, and we both live in beautiful places. But my river is much better than your mountains. Every day I sail in my little boat. My friends are the sun and wind, the birds in the sky, and the fish in the river. Every day I see my wife and son. My mind is clear, I have no worries, and I sleep very well at night."

"No, my friend," said the woodsman, "you are wrong. My forest is much better than your river. Every day in spring I walk through the woods, listening happily to the song of the birds. Summer comes, and the fragrance of flowers is all around me. Then autumn arrives, and then the cold of winter. I have no king and no master. I am happy in all four seasons!"

The woodsman and the fisherman walked home this way, talking about their lives, their jobs and their families. Each one said that his life was better than the other's. Finally, they came to a place where one road went east and the other went west, and it was time for the two friends to say goodbye. "Be careful, my old friend," said the fisherman. "When you climb your mountain tomorrow, be careful and watch for tigers. If a tiger were to eat you, I would miss you!"

The woodsman became angry at this, and shouted, "You fool! Good friends would die for each other. But now you say that I might be eaten by a tiger? Well, maybe you will fall into the river and die! Nobody knows what will happen tomorrow."

The fisherman was not angry. He replied, "Ah, but I do know what will happen tomorrow."

"How can you know that?" cried the woodsman.

The fisherman said, "I will tell you a secret. In the city of Chang'an, on a small street near the west gate, there is a man who can see the future. Every day I go and find him. I give him a fish, and he tells me where to find more fish the next day. I have listened to him a hundred times, and he is never wrong. Just today, he told me where to catch fish tomorrow in the Jing River. I will do as he says. Tomorrow I will sell many fish, and I will buy you a bottle of fine wine!"

After that, the woodsman and the fisherman each went to their homes. But that is not the end of our story, because you know the old saying, "words said on the road are heard in the grass." A river spirit was nearby. He heard the fisherman say that he had caught many fish for a hundred days in a row. The river spirit was very frightened. He rushed to the palace of the Dragon King of the Jing River, shouting "Disaster! Disaster!"

"What kind of disaster?" asked the Dragon King.

The river spirit replied, "Just now I was in the river near a small path. I heard two men talking. One of them, a fisherman, said that every day he goes to see a man in Chang'an who can see the future. This man tells the fisherman where to fish the next day. And he is never wrong! You must do something. If you don't, the fisherman will catch all the fish in the river and we will all die!"

The Dragon King became very angry. He picked up his sword and started to rush out of his palace to kill the man. But before he could leave, one of his ministers said, "Your Majesty, please wait, don't do this! You are the King of Eight Rivers and you can change the weather. If you go to Chang'an in anger, you will bring great thunder and heavy rains to the city. The people will be frightened, and Heaven will be angry with you. Instead, go slowly and quietly and learn more about this man. You can change into any man or animal. So, change into a man and go see him. Then you can decide what to do."

The Dragon King thought this was a good idea. So he walked up out of the water onto the riverbank, then he changed into a tall and handsome scholar wearing a white robe. He walked into Chang'an.

Near the west gate he saw a man standing in front of his house, surrounded by a noisy crowd. The man was telling people what would happen in their future.

The Dragon King pushed the people aside and walked right past the fortune teller and into the house. The fortune teller followed him into the house. He told a boy to serve tea, then he sat down and looked at the Dragon King.

"What do you want to know?" asked the fortune teller.

"Please tell me tomorrow's weather."

"Tomorrow at the hour of the Dragon[1], clouds will come. At the hour of the Snake, thunder will come. At the hour of the Horse rain will start to fall, and at the hour of the Sheep it will finish. Altogether, there will be three feet and three inches of rain."

"I'll tell you what," laughed the Dragon King, "if you are right, I will come back and give you fifty pieces of gold. But if you are wrong even a little bit, I will smash your house and chase you out of Chang'an."

"Of course, that is no problem," said the fortune teller. "Goodbye for now. Please come again tomorrow after the rain."

The Dragon King returned to his palace, and he sat on his throne and told his ministers and friends the story of the stupid man he had met in Chang'an. The Dragon King did not think that anyone could know the future. But just then, a messenger from the Jade Emperor arrived. He said, "The Jade Emperor commands the King of the Eight Rivers to bring rain to Chang'an tomorrow," and then the messenger told the Dragon King to bring the same amount of rain at the same time that the fortune teller had said.

"Oh no!" cried the Dragon King. "I should not have made this bet with the fortune teller. Now I will lose! I don't care about the gold, but I really don't like to lose a bet!"

"Don't worry," said his ministers. "This is not a problem. Make the rain tomorrow as the Jade Emperor commands. But make it rain just a little bit less, perhaps a half inch less. Then the fortune teller will be wrong, and you can smash his house and chase him out of Chang'an."

---

[1] In traditional Chinese timekeeping, the hour of the dragon is 7 to 9 am, the snake is 9 to 11 am, the horse is 11 am to 1 pm, and the goat is 1 to 3 pm.

The Dragon King made the rain, but he made it rain a half inch less than what the Jade Emperor had commanded. When the rain was finished, he went to the fortune teller's house and began smashing the door, the chairs and tables, the sign, and the entire house. The fortune teller just sat watching him and did nothing.

"You cannot see the future!" shouted the Dragon King. "You just take money from the people and tell them meaningless stories. You must leave Chang'an at once!"

The fortune teller just smiled and looked up at the sky. Then he said quietly, "I am not afraid of you. You are not a scholar at all, you are the Dragon King. And you have failed to send the rain as the Jade Emperor commanded. Now you will be brought to Prime Minister Wei, and then you will be killed. Prepare to die, Dragon King!"

Now the Dragon King was not angry, he was afraid. He knew the fortune teller was correct and that he would soon be killed. So he left the fortune teller's house with tears in his eyes, changed into a dragon, and flew slowly to Emperor Taizong's palace[1]. Then he changed back into a man and waited in the palace garden for the Emperor to come. He waited a long time, until the middle of the night.

Emperor Taizong was asleep in his bed. In his dream he entered the garden and saw the Dragon King waiting for him. The Dragon King cried, "O Emperor, please help me!"

"Why should I help you?" replied the Emperor.

"I am the Dragon King of the Jing River. The Jade Emperor commanded me to send rain to the city of Chang'an, but I sent less rain than The Jade Emperor commanded."

The Emperor already knew that the Dragon King had done this, and he had already commanded Prime Minister Wei to execute the Dragon King. But the Emperor said, "Don't worry, I will speak with my Prime Minister about this matter. You will not be hurt, believe me!"

Right after that, the Emperor woke up and remembered the dream. He went to his throne room and saw all his ministers and generals, but he did not see Prime Minister Wei. So he commanded Wei to come to the throne room.

---

[1] There are two emperors in this story: the Jade Emperor in Heaven who ordered the rain, and Emperor Taizong, a mortal.

Wei arrived. The Emperor did not say anything about the Dragon King. He said to Wei, "Let's play a game of chess." They began to play. But after an hour, Wei's head fell on the table and he fell asleep. The Emperor said nothing. He just let Wei sleep and waited for him to wake up.

An hour later, Wei woke up. He bowed low to the Emperor and said, "Your Majesty, your servant is so sorry that he fell asleep in front of you. Please kill me now!" But the Emperor told him not to worry, and they started to play another game of chess.

Just then, two ministers ran into the throne room, holding a huge dragon's head, and shouting, "Your Majesty, we have seen many things, but we have never seen this! Look at this dragon's head, it just fell from the sky!"

The Emperor looked at Wei. "What is this?" he asked.

"This is the head of the dragon that your useless servant just executed, as you commanded. Just now we were playing chess, and I fell asleep. While I was sleeping, I flew into the sky, above the clouds. There I saw the Dragon King waiting to be executed. I told him, 'You have broken Heaven's law, now you must die.' And then I killed him."

When the Emperor heard this, he was both happy and unhappy. He was happy to know he had such a good prime minister as Wei. But he was unhappy because he had told the Dragon King that he would help him. He left the throne room and went to bed. While in bed, he kept thinking about the Dragon King crying and asking him for help.

For a long time he could not fall sleep. Around midnight he did sleep, but in his dream the Dragon King came to him, holding his own head, dripping blood, and crying, "Taizong, Taizong, give me back my head! Give me back my life!" The Dragon King grabbed the Emperor and would not let go.

In the dream, the Emperor tried to get away from the Dragon King, but he could not. He became very tired and thought he was going to die. But then he heard beautiful music, and looking to the South he saw colorful clouds. A beautiful woman was standing in the clouds. It was Guanyin, the Buddhist teacher.

Guanyin had come to Chang'an to find someone to journey to the West and bring back the Buddha's teachings. Guanyin had been sleeping in a nearby temple when she heard the cries of the Dragon King and the Emperor. She made the Dragon King let go of the Emperor, and then she took the Dragon King down to the underworld.

Right after that, the Emperor woke up. He was terrified, and shouted, "Ghost! Ghost!" Everyone in the palace woke up, and they stayed awake for the entire night. The next day the Emperor did not talk to anyone and did not leave his bed. He stayed in bed for six days, not eating or drinking. On the seventh day the Queen Mother called a doctor to come and examine him.

The doctor examined the Emperor. Afterwards, he said to the Queen Mother, "The Emperor is very ill. I do not know why. He talks about seeing ghosts. His heart is sometimes quick and sometimes slow. I am afraid that he will die within a week." This frightened the Queen Mother and the ministers.

Later that day, the Emperor commanded several of his minsters and generals to come and see him. He said to them, "Since I was nineteen years old, I have been your Emperor. I have fought many wars and traveled to every place on earth - East, South, West and North. I have seen many things and fought many monsters, but I've never seen a ghost. Now I hear them screaming all day and all night. During the day it's not so bad, but at night it is so loud that I cannot sleep at all."

"Don't worry about those ghosts!" said one of the generals. "Tonight, two of us will stand outside your room. We won't let any ghosts inside your bedroom. You will be able to sleep tonight."

And so that evening the two generals, wearing bright golden armor and carrying swords, stood outside the Emperor's bedroom door. They stood there all night but did not see any ghosts. The Emperor did not hear any ghosts, and he had no trouble sleeping.

The two generals returned the next night, and the night after that. They did not see any ghosts, and the Emperor slept well. But the Emperor did not want his generals to work all night every night. So he commanded an artist to make paintings of the two generals, and the paintings of the generals were put outside his room.

For a few nights no ghosts came to the door. But then the Emperor began to hear ghosts again. He was very unhappy and would not eat or drink anything. He knew that he was going to die soon. So he bathed and put on clean clothing, and lay down on his bed, waiting to die.

Wei came to him and said, "Don't worry, Your Majesty. I can give you a long life."

"My friend," said the Emperor, "it is too late for that. My heart is sick, and soon I will die."

Wei said, "A long time ago, a man named Cui Jue was a minister here in the palace. He was a good friend of mine. When he died, he went to the underworld and became a judge. I still meet with him frequently in my dreams. I think he can help you." And then Wei gave the Emperor a letter. "When you arrive in the underworld, look for Cui Jue. Give him this letter. After he reads it, I think he will help you return to the world of the living!"

Taizong heard these words, smiled at Wei, and took the letter in his hand. Then he closed his eyes and died.

My child, do not be afraid of death! Listen:

> A hundred years pass like water
> A lifetime is but a single dream
> The face that was the color of peaches
> Is now edged with snow
> If you quietly do good deeds
> Heaven will give you a long and happy life

Chapter 11

Taizong's soul drifted upwards, out of the palace. He did not know where he was or what he was doing. He saw clouds. He thought that some men on horses arrived and wanted to take him riding with them. But a little while later he could not see the men and horses, and he was alone again. He began to walk. It was cold and dark, the wind was blowing, and he could not see anything.

Taizong walked for a long time. Finally, he heard a voice in the darkness. It said, "Your Majesty, come over here! Come over here! Taizong looked and saw a tall man standing in front of him. The man was wearing a white robe. He had long white hair under a black hat, and his long white beard was blowing in the wind. In one hand he held a Book of Life and Death.

"Who are you, and why have you come to meet me?" asked Taizong.

The man said, "Two weeks ago the Dragon King of the Jing River came here. He told the Kings of the Underworld that you promised to save him, but then you had him killed. The Kings of the Underworld wanted to talk with you. So they sent ghosts to the human world to bring you here. That is why you became ill and died. I heard that you were coming to the underworld, so I came here to meet you."

"What is your name," asked Taizong again, "and what is your rank?"

"When your lowly subject was alive, he served as a minister in your palace. My name is Cui Jue."

Taizong said, "I am very happy to see you! My prime minister Wei gave me this letter to give to you." And he handed the letter to Cui Jue. Cui Jue opened the letter and read it. It said,

> "Your beloved brother Wei sends this letter to the Great Judge of the Underworld, my brother Mr. Cui. I remember our friendship, and your voice and handsome face are always with me. Several years have passed since we last talked together in my dreams. I have only given you a few vegetables and fruits during the festivals, and I hope you have enjoyed them. I am glad that you have not forgotten me, and I am also glad that you are now a judge in the underworld. The worlds of men and the underworld are far apart, so we cannot meet. I write you now because of the sudden death of my Emperor Taizong. I ask you to not forget our

friendship, and allow the Emperor to return to life."

"I know the story of the Dragon King, and I think you did the correct thing," said Cui Jue. "I am happy to help you return to the world of the living, if I can. But first, you must come with me and meet with the Kings of the Underworld."

Just then, two servant boys arrived. They wore blue robes and carried flags, and they shouted, "The Kings of the Underworld want to meet with you." Taizong and Cui Jue walked behind the boys. Soon they arrived at the gate of the Palace of the Kings of the Underworld. The palace had a tall green tower that reached to the sky. Taizong saw red lightning in the sky, and monsters all around. Outside the gate, two servants stood holding large burning torches.

Taizong and Cui Jue walked inside the gate and waited. Soon, the Ten Kings of the Underworld came out, bowed to Taizong, and waited for him. Taizong bowed to them, but he did not move. One of them said to Taizong, "You are an Emperor in the world of men, we are only ghosts here in the underworld. Why do you not lead the way?"

"I am very sorry," said Taizong, "I do not know the ways of the underworld." They all stood for a while, not moving. Finally, Taizong decided to start walking, so they all walked together into another room and sat down.

One of the Kings looked at Taizong and said, "The Dragon King says that you promised to save him, then you had him killed. Why?"

Taizong replied, "Yes, I did promise him that he would be safe. But before that, I had already told my prime minister Wei to execute him. I tried to save the dragon by inviting Wei to play a game of chess with me. But Wei was clever, he fell asleep and executed the dragon in his dream. I did not know about this, so I don't see how I caused the dragon's death."

The King of the Underworld said, "We understand. Even before the Dragon King was born, it was written in the Book of Life and Death that he would die by the hand of a human judge. And of course, the Dragon King did not obey the Emperor's command to send the rain. So we have already sent the him to the Wheel of Rebirth. We apologize for bringing you here."

But the Kings of the Underworld did not let Taizong leave yet. They said to Cui Jue, "Bring out the Books of Life and Death, we want to see how long Taizong should live."

Cui Jue went into another room to look in the Book of Life and Death, and he saw that Taizong would die in the thirteenth year of his reign. Quickly, Cui Jue used his brush and ink to add two strokes to the character ten (十), making it a thirty (卅). Then he brought the book to the Kings of the Underworld.

"How many years have you been the Emperor?" they asked.

"Thirteen years," replied Taizong.

"Don't worry, then, you have twenty more years of life. Now we are finished, and you may return to the human world. Again, we are sorry for bringing you here."

Taizong bowed and thanked the Kings. "Is there anything I can give you when I return to the human world?" he asked.

"Well, we would love to have some pumpkins!" said the Kings.

"That's not a problem at all," said Taizong, "I would be happy to send you some pumpkins."

Then the Kings ordered Cui Jue and another man, General Zhu, to take Taizong back to the human world. As they left, Taizong saw that they were taking a different road than the road that they had taken when they entered. "Aren't we going the wrong way?" he asked Cui Jue.

"No. It is easy to enter the underworld when you die, but you can only leave through the Wheel of Rebirth. Now we are going to the Wheel. But it is a long walk, and I will show you a little bit of hell as we walk!"

Now my dear child, I must tell you some of the things that Taizong saw in the underworld. Please don't be afraid!

Taizong, Cui Jue and General Zhu walked for several miles, then they saw a very tall mountain. Black clouds surrounded it. "This is the Mountain of Darkness," said Cui Jue. "There are no animals here, only hungry ghosts and monsters." Taizong looked around. He saw no grass on the ground, no trees on the sides of the mountain, no water in the rivers, no birds in the sky. He saw only black clouds and heard only the cold wind and the shouts of demons and ghosts. He was very afraid, but Cui Jue helped him to pass the mountain.

But after they passed the mountain, Taizong saw something that frightened him even more. It was a place with many buildings, each with many rooms, and in each room, souls were crying loudly.

"Who are all these people?" asked Taizong.

"These are the Eighteen Levels of Hell," said Cui Jue. "Many different kinds of people are here. You will see people who had the mouth of a Buddha but the heart of a snake. You will see people who say one thing but do something else. You will see people who took money from others through deception. You will see people who turned against their king and country. And of course, you will see people who killed other living creatures. Those people must stay here for a thousand years, bound tightly with ropes. If they move, red-hair demons and black-hair demons strike them with long swords. It is terrible to see!"

By this time, Taizong was so afraid that he could hardly walk. But Cui Jue helped him, and they walked down the road. Soon they came to three bridges. The first was a golden bridge, which Taizong and Cui Jue walked across. The second was a silver bridge, where many good people walked across, led by flags.

"What is that third bridge?" asked Taizong.

"That is the Bridge of Punishment," said Cui Jue. "When you return to the world of the living, please tell others about this bridge. It is many miles long but only as wide as three fingers, and there are no railings. A hundred feet below is a river as cold as ice, full of demons and monsters. Ghosts with bare feet and dirty hair try to cross this bridge. If they fall, demons and monsters rise up from the river, grab them and pull them under the water."

Taizong was even more afraid than before. Next, they came to a city full of headless ghosts. "Give us back our lives!" they all shouted. "Give us back our lives!" Some of them tried to grab Taizong.

"Help me, Judge Cui!" cried Taizong. "Who are these people?"

"These are the forgotten ghosts of soldiers who died fighting for nothing. Nobody has given them a home or cared for them. They cannot enter the Wheel of Rebirth because they have no money. So they stay here, cold and hungry. Perhaps you can help them."

"How can I help them?" asked Taizong. "I also have no money here in the underworld!"

"There is a man living in the human world, a Mr. Xiang, who has put a large amount of gold and silver here in the underworld. You can borrow money from him and give it to me. I will give it to the hungry ghosts so they can enter the Wheel of Rebirth. If I do this, they will let us pass and we can finish our journey. Later, when you return to the human world, you can repay Mr.

Xiang."

So Taizong borrowed the money and gave it to Cui Jue, and Cui Jue gave the money to the hungry ghosts, saying, "Here is the great emperor Taizong. I am taking him back to the human world. Use this gold and silver to buy entry to the Wheel of Rebirth. Now let him pass!" The hungry ghosts took the money and let them pass.

They kept walking, and after a long time they arrived at a very large wheel. Taizong looked and saw people, animals, birds, ghosts and monsters. Each of them walked under the wheel and came out on the other side, walking on one of six different roads.

"What is this?" asked Taizong.

"You must remember this and tell people in the human world about it. This is the Wheel of Rebirth. When people die, they come here and their souls go under this wheel. When they come out on the other side, each soul takes one of six paths. Five of them are: the Path of Immortals, the Path of Honor, the Path of Happiness, the Path of Man, and the Path of Wealth. Otherwise, they fall down to the Path of Demons. This decides what their next life will be. But you will not go under the Wheel of Rebirth today. You will go directly to the Gate of Rebirth on the Path of Honor."

After they walked around the Wheel and through the Path of Honor's Gate of Rebirth, Cui Jue said, "Now I must leave you. General Zhu will take you the rest of the way back to the human world. When you return to the human world, you must hold a Great Mass of Land and Water ceremony to help these hungry ghosts be reborn. Do not forget! If you want peace in your country, there must not be any hungry ghosts in the underworld. Teach all your people to be good. This will make your family happy and your country safe."

Taizong walked through the Gate of Rebirth with General Zhu. On the other side of the gate two beautiful horses waited for them. They rode swiftly until they arrived at the banks of a wide river. After being in the underworld for so long, Taizong thought the river was the most beautiful thing he had ever seen. He just sat on his horse, looking at the river. Zhu tried to push him, but Taizong just kept looking at the river.

Finally, Zhu shouted, "What are you waiting for? Get moving!" and he pushed Taizong off his horse and into the river. Now Taizong was in the water but he was also in the land of the living, inside his coffin. He pounded on the coffin door, shouting, "Help me! I am underwater!" Some of the ministers thought it must be a ghost, but Prime Minister Wei quickly opened the coffin. Taizong stepped out, dripping wet, onto the palace floor.

"I was just riding my horse along the river, when that terrible man Zhu pushed me off the horse and into the river!" he said.

His ministers looked at him. "Your Majesty, you have nothing to fear. There is no river here, no horse, and no Zhu!" His doctor gave him a little medicine and a little soup, and Taizong went to bed and slept all night.

Early in the morning, Taizong got out of bed and called all his ministers and generals to the throne room. He told them the story of his time in the underworld. "I am so happy to be back in the human world," he said. "Now there are many things I must do!"

First, Taizong held a Great Mass of Land and Water for the souls of the hungry ghosts, to let them enter the Wheel of Rebirth and be born again. Then he sent one of his ministers to repay Mr. Xiang for the gold that Taizong had borrowed from him in the underworld. And finally, he sent pumpkins down to the Ten Kings of the underworld, but the story of how he did that is too long for me to tell you tonight!

Taizong remained as the Tang Emperor for another twenty years, and he never forgot about his time in the underworld. He remembered all the things he saw there, and he tried to help all of his people to lead good lives.

Chapter 12

While the emperor Taizong was in the Underworld, he met a group of hungry ghosts. He promised to help the ghosts so that they could enter the Wheel of Rebirth and be born again. To do this, he held a Great Mass of Land and Water for the souls of the hungry ghosts.

Taizong invited all the Buddhist monks in Chang'an to come to the palace, and he asked them to select one person to lead the Great Mass. The ministers discussed this matter, then they came to Taizong and said, "Your Highness, we have selected a monk to lead the Great Mass. You should already know him!

> In a previous life, he was a student of the Buddha
> He did not listen to the Buddha, so he had to suffer
> His father, a zhuangyuan, was killed by a bandit
> His mother was the beautiful daughter of a prime minister
> The young monk was born but was in great danger
> His mother put him in a river, he floated on the water
> Finally he arrived at Gold Mountain Temple
> He lived there for eighteen years
> Then he learned the story of his birth
> He asked his maternal grandfather to avenge his father
> The grandfather's army killed the bandit
> Then Your Majesty offered the young monk a job
> But the monk chose to live a life of study
> In a previous life his name was Golden Cicada
> When he was young he was called River Flow
> Now you know his name as Xuanzang."

Emperor Taizong remembered Xuanzang, and asked him to lead the Great Mass. It lasted for 49 days, and 1,200 Buddhist monks were there.

During the Great Mass, the Buddhist teacher Guanyin was staying at a small temple in Chang'an. She was searching for someone to journey to the West to get Buddhist scriptures and bring them to China. When she heard that Emperor Taizong had selected Xuanzang to lead the Great Mass, she decided that she would also select this young monk to journey to the West.

So Guanyin changed into an ugly old monk. She went out into the street and called out, "I have an embroidered cassock and a priest's staff for sale. Just seven thousand pieces of gold!" Just then, the Prime Minister arrived, riding on his horse. He liked the cassock and staff, and he recognized Guanyin as a great Buddhist teacher. So he brought Guanyin to meet Emperor Taizong.

Taizong looked at the cassock and staff, and asked Guanyin, "These two items are very expensive. Why do you want so much money for them?"

Guanyin replied, "You cannot find another cassock like this anywhere in this world. It is made of silk from ice silkworms. It is woven by immortal women and girls. It shines with the light of Heaven, and lights up the whole human world. But not everyone can wear it. If you are a good person, you can wear this cassock; nobody can hurt you and you will not suffer in the underworld. But if you are not a good person, forget it, you will not even see this cassock!"

"And the staff?" asked Taizong.

"Ah, the staff! It has nine rings made of iron and copper. It has gone through the gates of Heaven and has broken down the gates of Hell. It cannot be touched by the dirt of this world. If you hold it, you will not grow old. It will lead your holy monk to the tops of mountains!"

"Wonderful!" cried Taizong. "I will buy these and give them to Xuanzang."

"If this young monk is a good man, then I will not take your money. Please give the cassock and staff to him." And before Taizong could say anything to her, Guanyin handed the cassock and staff to Taizong, left the palace and returned to her temple in Chang'an.

Taizong summoned Xuanzang to the palace and gave him the cassock and staff. "Are you ready to travel to the West?" asked Taizong. Xuanzang bowed low and replied, "Although this useless monk has no talent, he is willing to do the work of a cow and a horse. I will bring back the wisdom of the Buddha, so that our empire will be strong and last forever!"

Taizong raised up Xuanzang to a standing position, and said to him, "If you are ready to go on this journey and are not frightened, then I will become your brother." Then Taizong bowed towards Xuanzang four times, calling him "younger brother" and "holy monk".

Xuanzang said, "Your Majesty, this worthless monk cannot take such honor from you! However, I will go to the West and bring back the Buddha's wisdom. If I cannot finish this journey, I will die and I will fall into the underworld, never to return."

Then Xuanzang went to the temple and said to the monks, "My brothers, wait for me. Watch the tree near the temple gate. If its branches point to the East, you will know that I am coming back soon. If after seven years the branches don't point to the East, then you will know that I will not return."

The next morning, the Emperor's ministers wrote a paper that gave Xuanzang permission to go anywhere in the Tang empire. Taizong gave the paper to Xuanzang. He also gave him a beautiful horse, a golden begging bowl, and two servants to help him during the journey.

They walked together to the city gate. Taizong picked up two cups of wine, and handed one to Xuanzang. He

asked Xuanzang, "As a child you were called Flowing River, and your name now is Xuanzang. But do you have a nickname?"

Xuanzang replied, "This worthless monk has left his family. He has no nickname."

 "The teacher Guanyin said yesterday that there are three rooms full of books that you will be searching for. Please take that as a nickname, and call yourself Sanzang. Now drink with me!"

"I am very sorry, Your Majesty," said Xuanzang, who was now called Sanzang, "but monks cannot drink wine. I have never had wine in my entire life!"

Taizong replied, "My brother, today is not like other days, and this journey is special. Please drink this one cup of wine, with our good wishes." Sanzang had to agree, so he picked up the cup. But before he could drink it, the Emperor picked up a handful of dirt and dropped a little of it in the cup of wine. Sanzang did not understand. He just stared at the cup with the dirt in it, then he looked at Taizong.

"Dear brother," said Taizong, "how long will you be gone?"

"I hope to return in three years."

"The years will be long, the mountains will be high, and the road will be long. Remember to love this dirt from your home more than ten thousand pieces of foreign gold!"

Then Sanzang understood. He thanked the Emperor again, and drank the wine. Then he mounted his horse and rode out the gate, accompanied by his two servants. Taizong returned to the palace.

Chapter 13

Sanzang and the servants rode westward for several days. They arrived at a temple, where the monks sat down with Sanzang to discuss Buddhism. They talked into the night, and the monks gave the travelers a vegetarian meal and a place to sleep. The next day they left, and traveled for several more days until they arrived at the city of Gongzhou and rested there for one night.

Several days after that, they arrived at the district of Hezhou, at the western border of the Tang Empire. They rested at a temple there. In the morning Sanzang arose when the cock crowed around the time of the fourth watch. It was still dark, but the moon was bright in the sky and there was frost on the ground.

They walked by the light of the moon for a few miles. The road was in very bad condition, and the travelers had to leave the road and walk through some bushes. Suddenly they all fell into a deep pit. They heard voices shouting, "Seize them! Seize them!" Fifty ogres seized Sanzang and his servants and pulled them up out of the pit.

Sanzang looked up and saw a terrifying monster sitting on a high throne. He was huge. His eyes were like lightning and his voice was like thunder. His teeth were too large for his mouth, and looked like long knives. The Monster King shouted, "Tie them up and prepare to cook them for dinner!"

Just then, an ogre ran up to the Monster King and said, "The Bear Mountain Lord and the Steer Hermit have arrived!" Two very large men, the Bear Mountain Lord and the Steer Hermit, walked into the camp. The Monster King smiled and said, "Hello, how are you two gentlemen today?"

"I'm fine, there's nothing I have to do," said the Bear Mountain Lord.

"I'm just getting by," added the Steer Hermit.

Just then, one of Sanzang's servants began to cry loudly, because his ropes were so tight. The Bear Mountain Lord looked at him. "These three look tasty," he said to the Monster King, "but let's not eat all of them at once. We'll eat two of them now, and save one for breakfast." The Monster King agreed, and they killed and ate both of the servants. Sanzang almost died from fear.

The three monsters ate, drank wine, and talked all night. When it was early morning, the Bear Mountain Lord and Steer Hermit thanked the Monster King for the good dinner, and they left. The Monster King was feeling tired and went to bed. The red sun climbed into the sky. Sanzang was alone but he could not move, because he was still tied tightly with ropes.

Suddenly an old man arrived, holding a staff in his hand. He walked up to Sanzang and waved his staff. The ropes all snapped and fell off. Sanzang fell on the ground and said, "I thank you for helping this poor monk!"

"Get up," replied the old man. "Have you lost anything?"

"I have lost both of my servants. Last night we fell into a pit and were captured by the Monster King and his two friends the Bear Mountain Lord and the Steer Hermit, and a lot of ogres. They ate my servants for dinner! And I don't know where my horse or baggage are."

"Isn't that your horse over there?" asked the old man, pointing with his staff.

Sanzang looked, and recognized his horse and his baggage. He walked over to the horse and started putting his baggage on his horse. He said to the old man, "Tell me, what is this place, and who were those creatures?"

"You are in the land of spirits," replied the old man. "That Monster King was really a tiger spirit. The Bear Mountain Lord was a bear spirit, and the Steer Hermit was a bull spirit. The ogres are all spirits of the mountains, trees, and animals. Because of your pure nature, they could not eat you. Now follow me and I will lead you out of here."

Together they walked back to the road. Sanzang turned to thank the old man. Just then a gentle breeze came, and the old man rose up, riding a white crane with a red head. As they flew away, a slip of paper fell to the ground. Sanzang picked it up and read, "I am the Bright Star of Venus, come to help you. Others will also help you. Remember, if you have trouble, it won't be coming from Heaven!"

Sanzang bowed to the sky and thanked the Bright Star of Venus for helping him. Then he mounted his tired horse, and together they rode slowly westward. They saw some animals in the forest, but no other people. They were alone, cold, tired and hungry.

They rode all day. Late in the afternoon, he saw two huge tigers on the road ahead of him. He looked behind him and saw two huge snakes. On his left were more animals and on his right were monsters. Sanzang knew he could not fight all these creatures. Then his horse lay down on the ground, too tired to stand. Sanzang knew he was going to die right then and there. But suddenly all the creatures ran away. Sanzang saw a big man walking towards him on the road. He had a steel trident in his hand, and a bow and arrows hung at his waist.

"Great King, help me!" cried Sanzang, kneeling in the road.

"Don't be afraid," replied the big man. "I live in these mountains. My name is Boqin. I was looking for something to eat. I hope I did not frighten you!"

"This poor monk was sent by His Majesty the Tang Emperor, to seek Buddhist scriptures in the West. I was surrounded by tigers and other animals, and I thought I was going to be killed. But the animals saw you and ran away. Thank you!"

"Yes, the animals know me, and so they are afraid of me. If you were sent by the Tang Emperor then you are of this place, for this is still part of the Tang empire. You and I are both of the same nation. Come with me. You can rest your horse at my house, and you can continue your journey in the morning."

They walked together down the road. Suddenly they heard the sound of the wind. "Don't move," said Boqin, "a mountain cat is nearby. I will take him home and we can have a good meal tonight!" Boqin walked forward, holding his trident in his hands. A great tiger roared and jumped towards him. Boqin raised his trident and roared back at the tiger. Sanzang lay down on the ground, his hands over his head, terrified.

Boqin and the tiger fought for over two hours. Finally, the tiger became tired and Boqin killed it. Boqin grabbed the dead tiger by the ear and began dragging it along the road. Sanzang said, "You are truly a god of the mountain!"

They arrived at a small mountain village. The village had white buildings, narrow roads, and several stone bridges over small rivers. There were many large trees, and a light breeze blew through the streets. Yellow autumn leaves were falling to the ground. White clouds drifted over the distant mountains.

They entered Boqin's house. Boqin threw down the tiger on the floor and shouted, "Little ones, where are you?" From the back of the house came an old woman, a middle-aged woman, and four ugly servants. Boqin introduced them to Sanzang, saying, "This is my mother, this is my wife, and these are my four servants."

Then Boqin said to his mother, "Mother, this monk has been sent by the Emperor Taizong to journey to the West and bring Buddhist scriptures to the

Tang empire. Just now your son met him in the mountains. Since we are both of the Tang empire, I invited him to stay tonight and rest in our home."

"You are welcome in our home!" said the old woman. "You have arrived at a very good time. Tomorrow it will be one year since my late husband's death. Would you please recite some words from the holy books for us?"

Sanzang agreed. He drank tea with Boqin and his wife and mother. Soon the servants brought out steaming plates of cooked tiger meat.

"Oh dear," said Sanzang. "I am so sorry, but I cannot eat your wonderful food. I have been a monk since I was born and I have never eaten meat."

Boqin thought about this for a while. "Well, for many years this family has lived by eating meat. We don't have any vegetables in the house. And even our cooking pots and dishes have been used for many years for meat. I must beg your pardon, but I don't see how we can give you a vegetarian meal."

"That is no problem," replied Sanzang. "I can easily go several days without eating anything at all, and for me, that is better than eating meat. Please, enjoy your dinner!"

"Oh, stop this!" cried Boqin's mother. "You are our guest. Of course, we would not let you stay here without giving you something that you can eat. I will prepare a vegetarian dish for you." Then she went into the kitchen with Boqin's wife. They heated up a cooking pan until all the grease burned off. Then they washed it again and again, then they put it on the stove and added water, leaves, vegetables, and rice, to make a vegetarian soup.

"Please eat this," she said to Sanzang, "it is the cleanest food that we have ever prepared."

Sanzang ate the vegetarian soup. Boqin went into another room and ate a very large plate of tiger meat, snake meat, and deer meat.

After dinner, Sanzang and Boqin took a walk outside. They sat in the garden and talked for a while. As they sat, several deer walked by them. "These deer are not afraid of you!" said Sanzang.

"In your city of Chang'an, people store up wealth in case of future hard times. In farms, the families store up grain for the same reason. Here, we keep these animals."

That night, the soul of Boqin's father came in a dream to Boqin, and also came to his mother and his wife. In each dream, he said the same thing: "For the past year I have suffered in the underworld because of things that I did in the land of the living. Yama, the King of the Underworld, would not allow me to leave. But the holy monk's prayers have changed all that. Now Yama will send me to the rich land of China, where I will be born again into a wealthy family. You all must thank the holy monk and take care of him!"

In the morning, the family went to Sanzang and thanked him again and again for helping their dead relative. They offered him money, but Sanzang only said to Boqin, "I cannot take your money. But would you please accompany me on the next part of my journey?"

So that same day, Boqin and Sanzang and several servants set out on the road, traveling westward over the beautiful mountains. After several hours of walking, they came to a particularly large mountain. They climbed halfway up. Then Boqin stopped and said, "Holy monk, please go on yourself. I cannot go any further. This is the Mountain of the Two Frontiers. The eastern side is in the great Tang empire, but the western side belongs to the Tartars. I cannot cross the border. You must go by yourself."

Chapter 14

Sanzang was very unhappy, and he begged Boqin to change his mind. Just then, a thunderous voice came from under the mountain, shouting, "My master has come! My master has come!" Boqin and Sanzang were both terrified. But the servants just laughed and said, "It must be the old monkey in the stone box underneath the mountain who is shouting."

Boqin nodded his head and said, "Yes, you are right, it must be him."

"Who is this old monkey?" asked Sanzang.

"It is a very old story," said Boqin. "This mountain is called the Mountain of Two Frontiers because the Tang Emperor conquered this region. But long before that, it was called Five Finger Mountain. It is said that centuries ago this mountain fell from Heaven, with a monkey inside it. This monkey was not afraid of heat or cold, and was immortal. He was imprisoned by the spirits of the earth, who fed him iron balls when he was hungry, and liquid copper when he was thirsty. We don't need to be afraid. Let's go down the mountain and take a look."

Sanzang agreed, and they walked back down the mountain. They soon found a stone box, and inside the box was a monkey. The monkey, of course, was Sun Wukong. He had been in the stone box for five hundred years, and now he was filthy and covered from head to foot with dirt and grass.

Sun Wukong pushed his head out of the box, waved his arms wildly, and cried, "Master, why have you taken so long to arrive? Welcome! Welcome! Get me out of here, and I will protect you on your way to the West!"

Sanzang did not move, but Boqin walked right up to the monkey and pulled away some of the grass and dirt that was on his face. He asked Sun Wukong, "Now I can see you. What do you have to say?"

"I have nothing to say to you," said Sun Wukong coldly. "But ask my Master to come here. I have a question for him."

Sanzang came over. "What is your question?" he asked.

"Did the great Emperor in the East send you to go seek holy books in the West?"

"Yes."

"I am Sun Wukong, the Great Sage Equal to Heaven. Five hundred years ago, I caused a lot of trouble in Heaven and earth, so the Buddha himself put me in this box. Recently I met the Buddhist teacher Guanyin, who was looking for a holy monk to journey to the West. I asked her to help me. She told me to obey the teachings of the Buddha and to protect the holy monk. She said if I did that, nothing bad would happen to me. So I have been waiting for you to come. Let me protect you in your travels, and let me be your disciple!"

Sanzang said, "I would be happy to have you as my disciple. But how can I let you out of this stone box?"

Sun Wukong said, "On top of this mountain is a tag with words written by the Buddha. Go there and pick up the tag. Then I can come out."

Sanzang and Boqin climbed to the top of the tall mountain. Standing on the top, they could see for hundreds of miles in all directions. Ten thousand shafts of golden light arose from a huge stone. On top of the stone was a small tag with the golden letters, "om mani padme hum."

Sanzang knelt down in front of the stone. Closing his eyes, he spoke to the Buddha, saying, "You told your disciple to seek the holy scriptures. If you want this monkey to help me and be my disciple, then let me lift up the tag. But if he is only a cold-blooded monster who wants to hurt me, then do not let me lift up the tag." Then he reached out and pulled on the tag. It came up easily.

Immediately a breeze came and blew the tag out of his hand. He heard a voice saying, "I am the guardian of the Great Sage. Today his time inside the stone box is finished, and my job is done. Now I will return this tag to the Buddha."

Sanzang and Boqin walked down the mountain and returned to the stone box. They said to Sun Wukong, "The tag has been lifted. You can come out now."

Sun Wukong said happily, "Thank you Master! Now please walk away from here, so I can come out. Don't be afraid!"

Sanzang and Boqin walked until they were five miles away. But the monkey shouted, "Keep going, keep going!" They kept walking until they were completely off the mountain. They heard a thunderous sound, like the mountain itself was breaking in half. Suddenly the monkey was standing in front of Sanzang, completely naked.

He knelt down and cried, "Master, I'm out!" and bowed four times to Sanzang. Then he turned to Boqin and said, "I thank Elder Brother for helping my master to come here. Also, thank you for removing the dirt and grass from my face." Then he began preparing Sanzang's baggage.

Boqin said goodbye to Sanzang and Sun Wukong, and returned home. Sanzang mounted his horse, and Sun Wukong picked up the baggage. They started walking westward.

As they passed the Mountain of Two Frontiers, they saw another tiger standing in the road. Again, Sanzang became afraid, but Sun Wukong said, "Don't worry, Master. This tiger wants to give me some clothes!"

Sun Wukong took a tiny needle from his ear, and it quickly grew into a long iron rod, as thick as a rice bowl. He said to Sanzang, "Master, this is my Golden Hoop Rod. I have not used this for five hundred years. I think it needs some exercise!" Then he walked up to the tiger, swung the Golden Hoop Rod at its head, and instantly killed the tiger.

Then he took some hairs from his head and blew on them. The hairs changed into a long knife. Sun Wukong used the knife to remove the skin from the tiger. "Too big," he said to himself. So he used the knife to cut the skin into two pieces. He wrapped one piece around his waist, and he put the other piece in the luggage.

"Let's go, Master," he said. "When we get to a house, I can make this into good clothing."

Sanzang was still frightened from seeing Sun Wukong kill the tiger so quickly and easily. "What is that rod?" he asked.

"Master, this is the Golden Hoop Rod. There is nothing else like it in the world. I got it a long time ago, when I was still causing trouble in Heaven and earth. I don't cause any more trouble, but this rod is still with me. You just saw that it's very useful!"

The day was getting late. As the sun set, clouds began to fill the sky. Birds sang on a thousand mountains, flying into the forests for the night. The animals began to return to their homes, the moon rose in the sky, and ten thousand stars shone down on Sanzang and his new disciple.

"Master," said Sun Wukong, "it is late. Let's walk quickly. There must be a house in those trees up ahead. Let's stay there tonight."

There was indeed a house in the trees. They arrived at the front door, and Sanzang knocked on the door. An old man opened the door. He took one look at Sun Wukong, a large dirty monkey with a tiger skin wrapped around his waist. "Ghost! Ghost!" he cried, very frightened.

"Don't be afraid, my old friend," said Sanzang. "He is not a ghost. He is my disciple."

The man looked at Sun Wukong again, then he looked at Sanzang and said, "Who are you, and why do you bring this monster to my house?"

"I am just a poor monk from Tang, traveling westward to seek holy scriptures. It is getting late, so we came to your beautiful home and ask to stay the night. We will not cause you any trouble, and we will leave early tomorrow morning."

"Well," said the old man, "you may be a Tang man, but this monster beside you is certainly no sugar man.[1]"

 "Old man," said Sun Wukong, "have you no eyes in your head? Of course I am no sugar man. I am the disciple of this holy monk. I am also the Great Sage Equal to Heaven. We have met before. Don't you recognize me?"

"No, I don't recognize you," replied the old man.

"Yes, you do. When you were young, many times you passed near my home. I lived in a stone box on the Mountain of Two Frontiers. Do you recognize me now?"

The old man looked carefully at Sun Wukong. "Yes, I know you now. I saw you when I was a child, but you had dirt and grass on your face. And I remember my grandfather told me an old, old story about this mountain falling from the sky. He said there was a magical monkey inside it, in a stone box. But that was centuries ago. I don't understand how you can still be alive now. But it doesn't matter. Let's eat!"

The old man's family prepared a delicious vegetarian meal. After they finished eating, Sun Wukong said, "Old man, I have not had a bath for five hundred years. Please heat up some water so my master and I can wash ourselves." Then master and disciple had hot baths, and then Sun Wukong borrowed a needle and made the tiger skin into clothing that he could wear comfortably. Then the old man led them to their beds.

The next morning after breakfast, Sanzang and Sun Wukong left the old man's house and walked westward. The weather was cold, and the clouds in the sky looked like snow.

---

[1] This is a pun. 唐 (Tang, as in Tang Empire) and 糖 (sugar) are both pronounced *táng*.

As they were walking down the road, six men suddenly jumped in front of them. All the men were holding long knives. "Stop, monk!" one of them cried. "Give us your horse and your baggage, and we will let you go. If you fight us, you will die."

Sanzang was so frightened that he fell to the ground. But Sun Wukong just laughed and said to him, "Master, don't worry. These six gentlemen are here to give us some clothing and some money for our journey."

"Didn't you hear them? They want to kill us!" cried Sanzang.

"Don't worry, Master. Let Old Monkey take care of this." Turning to the six men, he said, "Gentlemen, I am sorry to say that I do not recognize you. Please tell me your names."

"You don't know us, you stupid monkey? We are famous!" said one of the men. "I am Eye That Sees Happiness. Over there are Ear that Hears Anger, and Nose that Smells Love, and Tongue that Tastes Thought, the Mind that Knows Desire, and the Body that Hurts and Suffers.[1]"

Sanzang understood immediately that these were not ordinary men, but they were really the six different senses of the body that made it difficult for men to become enlightened. He told this to Sun Wukong.

Sun Wukong just said, "Master, I just see six ugly bandits." Then he said to the bandits, "Show me what you have taken from others, so that we can take what we need. If you do that, you will live to see tomorrow."

Each of the six men heard Sun Wukong's words, but each one reacted differently. They were happy, angry, loving, thoughtful, desiring, and sad. But they all attacked Sun Wukong with their knives and tried to kill him. They hit him seventy or eighty times on the head with their knives. Sun Wukong just stood there and did nothing.

"This monkey has a head like a stone!" said one of the bandits.

"My friends," replied Sun Wukong. "you all must be getting tired. Time for me to take out my needle for some exercise!"

"What, are you an acupuncturist?" asked one of the bandits. Sun Wukong took a needle out of his ear, and it quickly grew into a large rod. "Now let me try this rod on you!" he shouted. The six bandits saw the rod and tried to run away, but Sun Wukong ran after them and killed them all. Then he looked at

---

[1] These six are not ordinary bandits of course, they are obstacles to enlightenment.

Sanzang, smiled, and said, "OK my master, we can go now. The bandits are all dead."

Sanzang was very upset. "Why did you do that?" he asked. "Those men were bandits, but you did not have to kill them. You should have just made them go away. How can you be a Buddhist monk if you kill others so easily? A monk is careful not to hurt any creature!"

"Master," said Sun Wukong, "if I hadn't killed them, they would have killed you."

"I am a monk. I would rather die than kill another person. If I died, only one person dies. But you have made six people die. That is much worse."

"When I was the Monkey King on Flower Fruit Mountain, I don't know how many people I killed. That is how I became Great Sage Equal to Heaven."

"And that is why you had to stay under the mountain for five hundred years! You caused great trouble in Heaven and earth. But now that you are a monk, you cannot do these things anymore!"

Sun Wukong's heart became filled with fire, and he shouted, "So, you think I can't be a monk? Then I will leave and never come back." And he jumped into the air and flew to the East.

Sanzang could do nothing about this, so he sadly started walking westward, alone, with just his horse. He walked for just a few miles when he saw an old woman standing in the road. She was holding a silk shirt and an embroidered cap.

"Where do you come from?" asked the woman.

Sanzang bowed and said, "Your child was sent by the Tang Emperor to journey to the West, to find the teachings of Buddha and bring them back to the East."

"The Buddha in the West lives in the Great Thunderclap Temple in India. It is a hundred and eight thousand miles away. How can you hope to get there all by yourself?"

Sanzang said unhappily, "Ah, I had a disciple to help me, but he was a troublemaker. He is gone now."

"I can help you with that. Please take this silk shirt and cap. And let me teach you a magic spell, called the Words to Calm the Mind. Remember every word of this spell, and don't tell it to anyone. When you see your disciple again, give him the shirt and cap. If he gives you trouble, just speak the spell silently to yourself. Your disciple will certainly obey you!"

After saying this, the old woman rose into the air, and flew away towards the East. Sanzang realized that the woman was Guanyin, helping him again. He picked up a little bit of dirt and tossed it towards the East, then he bowed and spoke some words of thanks. He walked westward. As he walked, he practiced the Words to Calm the Mind.

What about Sun Wukong? He had used the cloud somersault to fly far away and visit an old friend, the Dragon King of the Eastern Ocean. The Dragon King came out of his palace to welcome Sun Wukong. He said, "Hello, my old friend. I am glad to see you are not under the mountain anymore! Have you returned to your cave on Flower Fruit Mountain to become Monkey King again? Or are you again causing trouble in Heaven?"

"I wanted to return home," replied Sun Wukong, "but I met Guanyin, the great Buddhist teacher. She convinced me to become a Buddhist, and to help a Tang monk find some holy books."

"Good! But why are you here in the East, instead of journeying to the West?"

Sun Wukong laughed and said, "Ah, that Tang monk knows nothing of this world! We met a few bandits on the road, they gave us a little bit of trouble, so of course I killed them all. You would think the monk would be happy. But no, he scolded me and told me I made a mistake. Old Monkey would not stay and listen to that, so I left him there. I was going back home to Flower Fruit Mountain, but I decided to visit you and have some tea."

The Dragon King said nothing, and the two of them sat quietly drinking their tea. After a while, the Dragon King said, "There once was a holy man named Huang, and a young man named Zhang. One day the two of them were sitting on a bridge. One of Huang's shoes fell into the river below. Zhang immediately went and picked up the shoe out of the river and gave it to Huang. Huang said nothing, but again dropped his shoe into the river. Again Zhang brought it back and gave it to Huang. A third time, Huang dropped his shoe into the river. And a third time, Zhang gave it back to him. All this time, Zhang was not angry. He just did it. So Huang made Zhang his student, and a few years later Zhang became enlightened."

The Dragon King continued, "My friend, if you do not go back to help the Tang monk and obey his instructions, you will just be a fake immortal and you will never become enlightened. Don't allow temporary comfort to rule your actions!"

Sun Wukong sat silently for a long time. Then he jumped up and said, "Not another word! I will return to the Tang monk!" And he used the cloud somersault to return to Sanzang.

He found the monk sitting on the side of the road. He said, "Master, why are you just sitting there?"

Sanzang said, "You left me here all alone. It's easy for you to go thousands of miles in a moment, but I am just a poor monk. I can only walk. I was afraid to go forward or backward, so I just stayed here waiting for you."

Sun Wukong did not reply to this, but he said, "Master, are you hungry?"

"Yes, I have some fruit in the luggage."

Sun Wukong opened the luggage to get the fruit. He saw the beautiful silk shirt and embroidered cap in the bag. "Did you bring these from the East?" he asked.

"Oh, those old things. Yes, I wore them when I was young. You can wear them if you like."

When Sanzang saw the shirt and hat on Sun Wukong, he spoke the magic spell. Sun Wukong grabbed his head with his hands and cried, "Oh, it hurts. It hurts!" He fell to the ground, holding his head. "Master, did you put a magic spell on me?"

"Now will you obey me?" asked Sanzang.

"Yes, I will!" replied Sun Wukong, but in his heart, he was not willing. As soon as Sanzang stopped saying the spell, Sun Wukong took the tiny Golden Hoop Rod out of his ear, made it into a large weapon, and swung it at Sanzang's head. Sanzang quickly moved away and said the spell three more times. Sun Wukong dropped the rod and again fell to the ground, holding his head.

"You bad monkey!" shouted Sanzang. "While you were gone and I was all alone, Guanyin came. She wanted you to be my disciple and help me journey to the West, but she knew that you would not listen to me. So she gave me this shirt and the cap, and she taught me this spell. Now will you listen?"

Sun Wukong had no choice. He knelt down and said, "Master, I have no choice. I will obey you and follow you to the West. And I will not think about leaving you again. But you must not think of this spell as a game to play with me!"

"Agreed," said Sanzang. "Now let's get going." He stood up and brushed the dirt off his clothes.

Sun Wukong picked up the baggage, and they headed again on their journey to the West.

Chapter 15

It was winter. The sky was cold, snow was falling, and a strong wind was blowing from the west. Tangseng was riding his horse. Sun Wukong's horse carried their baggage, and Sun Wukong walked beside it.

Tangseng heard the sound of running water. He said, "I have heard that the name of this place is Eagle Grief Creek. I think I can hear the sound of the water now."

Soon they arrived at the creek. As the horses began to drink, there was a loud sound. A small dragon came out of the water. Tangseng was so frightened that he fell to the ground. The dragon opened its great mouth and ate Tangseng's horse in one big bite, then it turned and dove back into the water.

Sun Wukong picked up Tangseng and set him down on higher ground. "Master," he said, "you wait here. I will get our baggage."

"The water is deep and wide. How can you find our baggage?" asked Tangseng.

"Don't worry," replied Sun Wukong, "it is not a problem. You just wait here."

Sun Wukong jumped up into the air, shaded his eyes with his hand, and looked in all four directions. He saw the baggage. He jumped into the water and pulled the baggage up onto the bank.

"Ah, what will we do now?" cried Tangseng. "If my horse was eaten, I will have to walk. How can I pass through these mountains? How can I walk ten thousand miles to the West, to do the job that the great Buddha asked me to do?"

"Ah, stop crying," said Sun Wukong. "You sound like a baby. Just wait here and let Old Monkey find that dragon. I will ask it to give us back our horse."

As Sun Wukong was saying this, a voice called out, "Sun Wukong, please don't be angry. And Tangseng, please don't be afraid. We will help you. I am the Golden Headed Guardian. I bring you the six Gods of Darkness and the six Gods of Light. Each of us will help you, one at a time."

"OK, good," said Sun Wukong. "You take care of my Master. I will go and find that stupid dragon and bring back our horse." He stood up tall, holding his golden hoop rod in his hand. He called loudly, "Lawless snake, return my horse! Return my horse now!"

The dragon was resting at the bottom of the creek. He had just eaten a horse and he did not want to do anything except rest. But when he heard the monkey shouting at him, he came up out of the water and said, "Who comes here and scolds me with his big mouth?"

"Don't ask questions. Just return my horse!" replied Sun Wukong, and they began to fight. They fought for a long time. Sun Wukong used his rod to hit the dragon on the head and body; the dragon tried to bite the monkey and hurt him with his tail and claws. Neither one could win the fight, so after a while the dragon became very tired, so he just dove down into the creek.

Sun Wukong returned to the monk, saying that he could not win the fight against the dragon. Tangseng smiled and said, "You once told me that you could kill any tiger and any dragon. Why can't you kill this one?"

This made the Monkey King very angry. He jumped up and shouted, "Not one more word from you! I will show this stupid dragon who is the master!" Then he used magic to make the water very dirty. The dragon had to come up out of the water. He shouted, "What monster are you? Where do you come from? And why are you causing me all this trouble?"

"Never mind who I am and where I come from," replied Sun Wukong. "Just give me back my horse and you can live."

"Stupid monkey, I ate your horse," shouted the dragon. "It's in my belly. How can I return it to you now?"

"If you don't return my horse, I will take your life!" replied Sun Wukong, and they started to fight again. But like before, neither one could win. So the dragon changed into a water snake and went into the tall grass. This made Sun Wukong so angry that smoke came out of his ears!

He knew that he needed help to find the dragon. So he spoke some magic words, and immediately the local spirit and the local mountain god were standing before him. Sun Wukong was still angry. "Stand there. Don't move," he said, "I will hit each of you with my rod five times, just to make myself feel better."

"Please don't be angry," said the local spirit, "Let us tell you about this creek and this dragon. The creek is called Eagle Grief Creek because its water is so clean that birds see themselves in the water. They dive into the water to fight those other birds, and needless to say, they die.

"Now, let me tell you about this dragon. He is the son of the Great King of the Western Ocean. A long time ago he was young and careless, and one day he accidentally set fire to the palace. Many valuable things were destroyed by the fire. His father was angry, and he was going to let his son be killed by the Jade Emperor himself. But then the great monk Guanyin arrived. She said that she needed a creature to wait in this river for the Tang Monk who would come one day and need help. The dragon's job was to wait until the monk arrived, and then carry the monk on his journey to the Western Heaven. That was his job. I don't know why he ate the monk's horse instead!"

"But he did not help us at all!" said Sun Wukong. "He ate our horse, he fought with me, and then he changed into a water snake and ran away. Now I need to find him and get my horse back."

The local spirit said, "I think you should ask Guanyin to help you. If she asks the dragon to come out, he certainly will!"

"That's a good idea," replied Sun Wukong. He went back to Tangseng to tell him that he was going to see Guanyin. But Tangseng was afraid to be alone without Sun Wukong. So Sun Wukong stayed with Tangseng, and the Golden Headed Guardian went to Potalaka Mountain to find Guanyin. Guanyin listened to his story, then she agreed to come and help.

Soon Guanyin arrived. She waited in the clouds and asked the Golden Headed Guardian to bring Sun Wukong to her. But when Sun Wukong arrived, he did not even bow to Guanyin. He said, "You call yourself a teacher and a bodhisattva. But you used tricks to harm me and my Master!"

Guanyin just laughed, saying, "Oh, you stupid red-butt! I worked very hard to find a monk who would save your life and free you from the mountain where you lived for five hundred years. And now you find fault with me?"

"Yes, you saved me," replied Sun Wukong. "But you made me serve this Tang monk. Then you gave the monk a magic headband, which is now on my head, and now whenever he wants to hurt me, he says some magic words, the headband becomes tight, and it really hurts!"

"Oh my dear monkey," replied Guanyin, "you don't listen to me, and you don't listen to the monk. The magic headband is just a way to keep you out of trouble! Without it, you would cause Heaven to be angry with you again." Then she turned to the Golden Headed Guardian and said, "Go to the edge of the creek and say, 'Come out, third son of the Dragon King Auron. Guanyin from the South Sea is here.'"

The Golden Headed Guardian went to the edge of the creek and said the words. Right away, the dragon jumped out of the water, saying, "Thank you for saving my life, Guanyin. I have been waiting for the monk, but he has not arrived yet."

Guanyin pointed to Sun Wukong and said to the dragon, "And isn't this the disciple of the monk that you are waiting for?"

"Him? Who is he? I just met him yesterday. I was hungry, so I ate his horse. He never said anything about a monk. I even asked him his name and where he came from, but he did not tell me."

Guanyin just looked off into the distance and said, "Yes, he is a very difficult monkey." Then she walked up to the dragon and stood in front of him. She blew softly on him. "Change!" she said. The dragon changed into a horse that looked just like the one that he ate the day before.

Guanyin said to the dragon horse, "Now, remember the job I gave you. You will serve the monk and carry him to the Western Heaven. But you will do it as a horse, not a dragon. When you are finished, you will not be a horse or a dragon, you will become like a perfect golden fruit." Then she prepared to leave. But Tangseng stopped her, saying, "Please don't go. I cannot travel to the Western Heaven with this monkey. We will not survive!"

"Please don't worry," replied Guanyin. "If you run into trouble, ask Heaven for help, and Heaven will help you. Ask Earth for help, and Earth will also help you. Ask me for help, and I will also help you. Now, I have one more thing to give you. Come closer." Then she placed three green leaves on the back of Tangseng's head and said, "Change!" The three leaves became three magic hairs. "If you ever are in extreme danger, use these hairs, they will save you." Then she rose into the air and returned to Potalaka Mountain.

Tangseng mounted the dragon horse, and together with Sun Wukong they continued their journey. It was late in the day, the sun was low in the western sky, and the sky grew dark. They were alone on the road and the weather was getting cold. Ahead, Tangseng saw a village with many small buildings. A sign across the entrance said, "Lishe Shrine."

Tangseng and Sun Wukong left the horses outside and walked into the shrine. An old man met them, and invited them inside for tea.

"Thank you for letting us in," said Tangseng. "Please tell me, why is this place called Lishe Shrine?"

"There is a village behind the shrine," replied the man. "Li is the name of the village. In every season, families from the village bring food to the shrine, so that their fields will give them much food to eat."

"In my country, we do not do these things. You know the saying, 'Just three miles from your home, the people do things differently.'"

"Ah. And where do you come from?"

"This poor monk was sent from Chang'an by the Tang Emperor to seek Buddhist scriptures in the Western Heaven. We were walking on the road, it was getting late, and we saw your fine shrine, so we ask to stay here tonight. We will leave early tomorrow morning." And then Tangseng told the old man the story of their meeting with the dragon in Eagle Grief Creek.

When Tangseng was finished telling his story, the old man asked a youth to prepare a vegetarian dinner for the two travelers. Afterwards, they all went to bed for the night.

In the morning, the old man gave Tangseng a beautiful harness for his horse. As Tangseng was thanking him, the old man and the shrine both disappeared in a cloud of smoke. From the sky, a voice said, "Holy monk, I am the local spirit of Potalaka Mountain. The great Guanyin asked me to give you this harness and last night's lodging. Now you must continue your westward journey. Remember to always work hard!"

Tangseng was so frightened that he fell down on the ground. He bowed again and again to the sky. Sun Wukong just stood and laughed at him, saying, "Master, get up! He is a long time gone; he cannot hear you anymore!"

"Stop that meaningless talk," muttered Tangseng. "Now let's get going." He mounted his horse again, and they resumed their journey.

They traveled for another two months with no trouble. The season changed from winter to early spring. One day, when the trees were beginning to turn green and new grass was appearing on the ground, they saw buildings in the distance. As they came closer, they saw that it was a beautiful temple. It had many buildings and several tall towers. It was surrounded by tall trees. They saw many monks quietly sitting on the ground with their eyes closed.

Chapter 16

As they approached the gate, a monk came out. The monk wore a hat, a cassock with a silk sash, and shoes made of straw. In his hand he held a wooden fish[1], telling him to always work hard to achieve enlightenment. Tangseng put both of his hands together at his chest. The monk did the same, but then he saw Sun Wukong and was afraid. Tangseng told him not to be afraid of his disciple.

The monk invited the visitors inside to have tea with him. Tangseng told him that they were traveling to the Western Heaven to seek Buddhist scriptures for the Tang Emperor. He also said quietly to the monk, "Be careful, do not anything bad about the monkey. He is easily angered!"

Together they entered the great hall. Tangseng bowed to the golden Buddha. One of the young monks struck a large bell several times. But when he finished, Sun Wukong continued to strike the bell loudly, again and again. All the monks in the temple came to the great hall, asking, "Who is the fool who is striking the bell?"

Sun Wukong jumped up and shouted, "It is your Grandpa Sun, striking the bell to amuse himself!"

When the monks saw the large ugly monkey, they were frightened and fell onto the ground. Sun Wukong laughed at them. Finally they got up off the floor, and sat down in the back of the room while Tangseng, Sun Wukong and the monk had tea and a vegetarian meal.

After dinner, a very old man arrived. He was so old that two young boys had to help him walk. His face was full of wrinkles so he looked like an old witch. He could not see very well, and several teeth were missing from his mouth. The monk said, "The old abbot is here!"

Tangseng bowed to him, saying, "Your disciple bows to you." The old abbot returned the bow, and they all sat down.

The old abbot said, "Just now I heard from the young ones that two holy fathers from the Tang Court have arrived from the East. I came here to greet you."

"We are just two poor monks traveling through your country. Please excuse

---

[1] A wooden fish is used as a sort of drum, played during recitation of Daoist scriptures.

us for entering your temple," replied Tangseng.

"May I ask the holy Tang monk how far he has traveled?"

"After leaving Chang'an I traveled five thousand miles. Then I picked up my disciple, and since then we have traveled another five thousand miles."

"So, you have traveled ten thousand miles. This foolish old monk has never even gone outside this temple. He is like a frog sitting in a well, looking up at the sky![1]"

"May I ask, what is the age of the great abbot?"

"Foolishly I have spent two hundred and seventy years." Then looking at the Monkey King, he asked, "And you, disciple, how old are you?"

"I cannot say," replied Sun Wukong. He did not want to tell the old abbot that he was thousands of years old. But the old abbot simply nodded, drank his tea and said nothing.

A young man brought tea in a beautiful teacup. Tangseng told the old abbot that the teacup was very beautiful. "Oh, it is nothing," the old abbot replied. "But you come from a great city. Did you bring any beautiful things from Chang'an?"

"I'm sorry, there is nothing valuable in Chang'an," replied Tangseng. "And if there was, we could not bring it on our long journey." Of course, Tangseng did not want to talk about valuable things in front of these strangers.

The Monkey King looked up when he heard this. "Master, we have a beautiful cassock, perhaps you could show that to the great abbot?"

When the other monks heard this, they laughed. One monk said, "Cassocks are very common. Most monks own twenty or thirty of them. And our great abbot has lived for a long time and owns seven hundred cassocks! Do you want to see them?" And with that, some of the young monks brought out a great many cassocks. They took out the cassocks for Tangseng and Sun Wukong to see. The cassocks were made of fine silk, embroidered with gold and silver thread. They were beautiful, but Sun Wukong only said, "OK, OK, now put these away. We have a cassock that is more beautiful than any of these!"

Tangseng was horrified by this. Turning to Sun Wukong he whispered,

---

[1] A famous Chinese proverb about a conceited frog who, from his narrow viewpoint in the bottom of a well, thinks he has seen the whole world.

"Don't say these things! We are strangers here, far from home. You should not show valuable goods to someone who is dishonest. Once he sees it, he will want it. And if he wants it, he will try to take it!"

"Relax," replied Sun Wukong, "Old Monkey will take care of everything!" Then he took out Tangseng's cassock and showed it to the old abbot and all the other monks in the room. When he held up the cassock, a bright red light filled the room, and sweet-smelling air filled the great hall.

The old abbot walked up to the cassock, knelt down, and began to cry.

"Why are you crying?" asked Tangseng.

"It is late in the day, and my old eyes cannot see this cassock," he replied. "Would you let me take it back to my room so that I may have a better look at it? I will return it to you tomorrow morning."

Tangseng did not like this, and he glared at Sun Wukong. But then he said to the abbot, "Of course you may have it until the morning. But please be very careful with it!"

After that, the abbot gave instructions for the young monks to give Tangseng and Sun Wukong beds in the great hall, and everyone else went to their rooms for the night. Everyone went to sleep, but the old abbot did not sleep. He sat in his room in front of the cassock, crying loudly. Several monks came into his room. One of them asked, "Why are you crying?"

"It is too late!" replied the abbot.

"What do you mean?"

"I can only look at this cassock for one night. Look at me! I am two hundred and seventy years old. I have hundreds of cassocks, but I really want to keep this one."

"That's no problem. Put it on for tonight and be happy. Tomorrow we will ask our guests to stay one more day, and you can wear the cassock tomorrow. If you want, we can ask them to stay ten more days, and you can wear it for ten days. If you want to wear it for a year, we will ask them to stay here for a year."

"But then they will go, right?"

Another monk spoke, "This is also not a problem. We will just kill them while they sleep!" At this, the abbot clapped his hands with joy and said, "Yes, this idea is very good!"

But a third monk spoke, "No, that will not work. We can kill the monk. But the monkey is big, strong, and dangerous. I don't think we can kill him. And we do not want to make him angry!"

"Do you have any good ideas?" asked the abbot.

"We have two hundred monks here at the monastery. Let's call every monk and ask them to bring wood. We will set the wood all around the great hall. We will lock the doors. Then we will light the wood. The great hall will burn, the visitors will die in the fire, but it will look like the fire started by itself. And you can keep the cassock for yourself."

The old abbot loved this idea, and he told the monks to start bringing the wood.

Now, Tangseng was sleeping, but the Monkey King was not sleeping. He was resting but his eyes were open. He heard sounds outside the room. "That is strange," he thought. "It is night, a time for rest. Why are people carrying things around outside the room?" So he changed into an insect and flew outside the room to see what was going on. He saw monks putting a lot of firewood outside the room.

"My master was right," he thought. "They want to kill us and steal the cassock. I could just use my golden hoop rod to kill them all, but then my master would be angry at me again. I must do something else."

So he did a cloud somersault, and right away he was in Heaven. He went to see his friend Guangmu Tianwang[1], a powerful spirit who lived in Heaven. "Hello, my old friend!" said Guangmu, "How are you? I heard you became a disciple of a monk who is traveling to the West. How's it going?"

"No time to discuss that!" snapped Sun Wukong. "Some bad people are trying to kill my master with fire. I need to borrow your Fire Repelling Cover, right now. I will return it to you as soon as I can."

"That is foolish. It's easy to put out a fire. Just use water."

"I can't do that. I need to let the fire burn. Hurry up, just give me the Fire Repelling Cover!"

Guangmu said nothing to Sun Wukong, he just gave him the Fire Repelling Cover. Sun Wukong took it back to the monastery, and used it to cover

---

[1] Guǎngmù is a major Buddhist deity, the guardian of the West, called Virupaksa in Sanskrit.

Tangseng, the white horse, and their baggage. Then he went outside to sit on the roof and watch.

One of the monks lit the fire. It began to spread rapidly, burning all the wood. Sun Wukong blew out a long breath, and it turned into a strong wind that made the fire even larger. Black smoke and red flames rose up to the sky. The stars vanished. The bright red flames rose two miles into the sky and could be seen from a thousand miles away. Tangseng and the horse were safe underneath the Fire Repelling Cover, but the rest of the great hall was in flames.

While the great hall was burning, twenty miles away a monster was sleeping in his cave. The cave was called Black Wind Cave, and it was in Black Wind Mountain. The monster was awakened by light, and he thought it was morning. He looked at it for a time, and he could see that the light was coming from a distant fire.

"It must be the monastery on fire," he thought. He and the old abbot were friends, so he decided to go and help the abbot. He flew on a cloud and arrived at the monastery. He looked around. First, he saw that the abbot's room was not on fire. Then he saw a big ugly monkey sitting on the roof, making a wind that fed the fire. He understood that the monkey was making the fire bigger. He went into the abbot's room to see if the abbot was ok, and then he saw the beautiful cassock. He forgot about helping the abbot. He grabbed the cassock, ran out of the room, and flew back to Black Wind Mountain.

Sun Wukong was watching the fire and helping it to grow, so he did not see the monster take the cassock. He waited until the fifth watch[1], when the fire had burned out. Then he picked up the Fire Repelling Cover and returned it to his friend Guangmu. Then he went back to Tangseng and woke him up. Tangseng stood up, looked around, and asked, "Where is the great hall? What happened?"

"There was a fire last night. Old Monkey protected you from it!"

"If you could protect me, why didn't you just put out the fire?"

"Because I wanted you to see the truth. The old abbot fell in love with the cassock. He and the other monks started the fire because they wanted to kill us and keep the cassock."

---

[1] Fifth watch, the night's fifth 2-hour period, is from 3 to 5 am.

"Is that right? I don't think so. I think you started the fire yourself, because the monks made you angry."

"Do you really think Old Monkey would do something like that? No, I didn't start the fire. The monks started it. Of course, it's true that I did not help them put the fire out. In fact, I must tell you, I helped the fire a little bit."

"My God! When a fire starts, you should put it out! Why didn't you do that?"

"You know the old saying, 'If a man does not hurt the tiger, the tiger will not hurt the man.' They started the fire. I just helped it a little bit. Now, let's get your cassock and get out of this place."

Sun Wukong walked over to the monks. The monks saw Tangseng and the big ugly monkey walking out of the place where the great hall had burned to the ground, and they were terrified. They put their hands over their heads and fell to the ground, crying, "Are you men or ghosts?"

"Stop that!" cried Sun Wukong. "I am just Old Monkey. Give me the cassock and we will be going."

The monks all ran to the room of the old abbot, shouting, "Great father, the Tang monk and the monkey must be gods. They were not burned by the fire. Give them the cassock, right now!" The abbot looked for the cassock, but of course it was not there. The old abbot was overwhelmed with grief. He saw that the cassock was gone, and so was most of the monastery. The old man fell down, his head hit heavily against the ground, and he died.

Sun Wukong looked everywhere for the cassock. He searched every one of the monks. He searched their rooms. He searched the old abbot's body and his room. He looked in every place in the monastery. But he could not find the cassock. He sat and thought for a while. Then he asked, "Tell me, is there a spirit or monster living nearby?"

"Yes," replied a monk, "about twenty miles southeast is Black Wind Mountain. In the mountain is Black Wind Cave. And living in the cave is the Great Black King. He and our abbot were friends, they met often to discuss the Dao."

"That's it, Master!" said Sun Wukong to Tangseng. "Last night's big fire could have been seen for two hundred miles. The monster saw the light, came here, grabbed the cassock, and flew back to his cave. Don't worry, Old Monkey will take care of this!"

Sun Wukong turned to look at the monks. He said slowly, "I know that you will take good care of my master and his horse. Be cheerful and pleasant. Give good food to both of them. If you don't, you will meet my rod." And he took his rod in his hand and smashed it into a wall. The wall collapsed to the ground, and so did seven or eight more walls that were behind it. Tangseng said, "As you can see, my disciple has a short temper. You really do not want to make him angry!" The monks were terrified, and they said they would take very good care of Tangseng and his horse.

Chapter 17

Sun Wukong flew to Black Wind Mountain. He sat on his cloud for a while, looking at the beautiful mountain. There were no people, but there were many trees, streams, birds and animals. Sun Wukong was looking at the beautiful mountain, but then he heard voices. Looking down, he saw three monsters sitting on the ground, talking. On the left was a monster who looked like a Daoist priest. In the middle was a black monster who looked a little bit like a bear. And on the right was a monster wearing the white robes of a scholar.

The black monster laughed and said, "Tomorrow is my birthday. Will you two come visit me?"

"Of course," said the white robed scholar. "We come every year. Why would we not come this year?"

"I have something special to show you. Last night I picked up a new treasure, a cassock that is good enough for the Buddha himself to wear. So I will give a feast and call it 'The Feast of the Buddha Robe.'"

Sun Wukong heard these words, and he became very angry. He jumped down to the ground and shouted, "You thieving monsters! You took my cassock! Give it back to me right now, and don't try to run away." Then he swung his rod at all three of the monsters. The black monster flew away on the wind. The Daoist priest escaped into the clouds. But the rod struck the white-robed scholar on the head, and he fell dead. When he died, he turned into a dead white snake.

Sun Wukong followed the black monster until he arrived at a great door. Above the door was a sign: "Black Wind Mountain, Black Wind Cave." He struck the door with his rod, shouting, "Open the door! Open the door!" A little demon came out, and Sun Wukong told the demon that he had come to see the monster.

The little demon ran back inside and said to the monster, "Great King, there is a monk outside, with a hairy face and a voice like thunder. He says the cassock belongs to him, and he wants it back."

The monster stood up. He put on a black silk robe, heavy armor, and black shoes. He picked up a sword and went outside to meet Sun Wukong.

Sun Wukong said, "My cassock was in the monastery, in the room of the old abbot. There was a fire. The monastery burned, but the cassock was taken. I know you took it, because I heard you talk about the Feast of the Buddha Robe you are planning for tomorrow. Give me the cassock right now. If you say even half a 'no' I will smash you, your cave and everything in it."

The monster just looked at the monkey. "And who are you? What can you do?"

"Well, that's a long story," said Sun Wukong, and he began to tell the monster his whole life story: his birth as a stone monkey, his early years on Flower Fruit Mountain, his first teacher Master Subodhi, his time in Heaven, his meetings with Laozi, Guanyin, the Jade Emperor and the Buddha himself, the five hundred years he lived under a mountain, and his meeting with Tangseng. Then he told the monster all the things he could do with his golden hoop rod.

The monster sat quietly and listened to this story, which lasted a long time. When the story was finally over, the monster laughed and said, "I've heard of you! You are the stupid monkey who caused big trouble in Heaven!"

"Don't you call me a stupid monkey!" shouted Sun Wukong, and he struck the monster with his rod. The two began to fight in front of the cave. One was a disciple of the monk, the other was a monster. One used a rod, the other used a sword. One used the "white tiger climbing the mountain," the other used "yellow dragon on the ground."

They fought for half a day. Finally the monster said, "Sun, we are both tired. Can we just take a rest and eat some lunch?"

"You useless devil," replied Sun Wukong. "How can you be tired after only half a day of fighting? Look at me. I lived under a mountain for five hundred years with no water to drink. And now you want to eat lunch? Stop talking and just give me the cassock, then you can go eat."

The monster said nothing, he ran away back to his cave and shut the door. Sun Wukong could not enter the cave, so he returned to the monastery.

"Wukong, you have returned!" said Tangseng. "Do you have my cassock?"

"No, but I met the monster who took it. He lives in Black Wind Mountain. I heard him telling two friends that he took the cassock. I killed one of them who looked like a scholar but was really a white snake who had become a spirit. The other one looked like a Daoist monk, he got away. I fought with the monster for half a day, but he ran away into his cave and closed the door. Now I must go back and get the cassock." Then Sun Wukong looked at the monks. "I hope you have given good food to my master, and good hay to my horse."

"Oh yes," they cried.

"Yes," agreed Tangseng. "You have only been gone for half a day, but they have already given me tea three times and served me a tasty vegetarian meal."

"That's good," replied Sun Wukong. "Don't worry about a thing. I will get the cassock."

Sun Wukong flew back to Black Wind Mountain. About halfway there, he saw a small demon on the road carrying a small package. Sun Wukong came down to the road, killed the demon with his rod, and took the package. He opened it. Inside the package were two pills, and a letter that read,

> Dear great abbot, greetings from your friend the Black Bear. Thank you for all the gifts you have given me. I am sorry I could not help you last night when your monastery was burned. I hope you are not hurt. I now have a very nice Buddhist robe, and I want to invite you to a Festival of the Buddha Robe, with fine wine and good food. I hope you can come. It is two days from now.

The Monkey King sat on the ground and laughed, saying, "Oh, now I see! The old abbot was friends with the black monster. That's how he lived to be two hundred and seventy years old, the monster must have given him some magic to give him longer life. I will change my appearance, so I look like the abbot and enter the monster's cave!"

And so Sun Wukong changed his appearance. Now he looked just like the old abbot. He walked up to the cave and banged on the door, saying, "Open the door!"

The monster said to his little demon, "How did the abbot get here so quickly? I think the Monkey King sent him here to get the cassock. Put it away so the abbot does not see it!" Then the monster put on a fine jacket made of dark green silk and put on black leather shoes. Then he went to the front door and let Sun Wukong into the cave.

"My old friend," he said, "we have not seen each other for several days. Please sit down and have some tea!" Then he continued, "I just sent you an invitation to come in two days, for a Festival of the Buddha Robe. Why are you here so early?"

"I was coming anyway, just to say hello. Then I ran into your messenger on the road, learned about the Festival, and decided to come early so I could see the cassock."

"But you have already seen it, in your monastery. Why do you want to see it again?"

Just as Sun Wukong was about to answer, another little demon ran into the cave, saying, "Disaster, O Great King! Your servant who carried the invitation was killed on the road by the Monkey King. We think that the Monkey King read the invitation, and changed his appearance so he looks like the old abbot!"

The black monster jumped up and took his sword in his hand. Sun Wukong changed back to his original appearance and took his rod in his hand. The two began to fight, much harder than before. They started fighting in the cave, but then they continued their fight outside the cave. Then they kept fighting at the top of Black Wind Mountain. Finally they rose up to the clouds and fought there. All day they battled, until the sun grew red in the west.

"I am tired," said the monster, "can we just continue this tomorrow?"

But Sun Wukong just kept hitting the monster with his rod. Finally the monster changed into the wind, and blew back into his cave. He shut the door.

Sun Wukong had no choice. He turned around and flew back to the monastery to discuss the matter with Tangseng. Tangseng asked him, "Who is the better fighter, you or the monster?"

"We are evenly matched," said Sun Wukong. "I don't know if I can win against him."

Then Tangseng and Sun Wukong read the letter together. "Aha!" said Sun Wukong, "now I understand. That monster is really a bear spirit. He originally was an animal, a bear, but after much work and study he became a spirit. I also was born an animal, a monkey, and through hard work and study I became the Great Sage Equal to Heaven."

"That is why you are evenly matched," said Tangseng.

They had a vegetarian meal prepared by the monks, then they went to sleep. In the morning, Sun Wukong decided to go see Guanyin, because she had said that she would help them if they ever needed her help. Using his cloud somersault, he flew rapidly to Potalaka Mountain in the South Sea, where Guanyin lived. He arrived, walked to the garden where Guanyin was sitting, and bowed low to her.

"Why are you here?" she asked, "You were supposed to be helping the Tang monk."

"We were traveling west, and arrived at a temple where the local people bow to you and offer you food. But you let a bear monster live nearby. He has taken the master's cassock and will not return it."

"I know about that, you ignorant monkey. I also know that you created this problem yourself. You showed the cassock to the monks, to make them want it. And you created the wind to make the fire bigger, so that it destroyed my temple. And after all that, you want my help?"

In that moment, the monkey understood that Guanyin could see things from the past, and also things in the future. He understood that she had great wisdom. He bowed and said, "I am sorry, great teacher. Everything you say is true. But I must return the cassock to my master. If I don't, he will make the headband tight on my head, giving me great pain. The pain is too great. Please help me get the cassock so we can continue on our journey west."

Guanyin agreed, and the two of them flew from Potalaka to Black Wind Mountain. But as they were coming close to the mountain, they looked down and saw the white-robed Daoist monk. He was carrying a tray, and on the tray were two pills. Sun Wukong didn't say a word, he just dropped down on the monk and hit him on the head with the rod. The monk fell down and died.

"Why did you do that?" asked Guanyin. "He didn't do anything to you."

"You don't know him, but I do. He is a friend of the black bear monster. They were talking together yesterday. I think he was going to the big festival at Black Wind Mountain."

They looked at the dead monk, and as they watched, he changed into a dead wolf. Sun Wukong laughed and said, "Great teacher, I have a good idea!" He quickly told Guanyin. She agreed.

Instantly she changed her appearance so that she looked just like the white-robed Daoist monk. Sun Wukong cried out, "Marvelous! Is the great teacher the Daoist monk, or is the Daoist monk the great teacher?"

Guanyin smiled and replied, "Monkey, I tell you, both the teacher and the monk exist in a single thought. They are both nothing." Sun Wukong looked at her thoughtfully but did not say anything.

Then Sun Wukong also changed his appearance, so he looked like a pill, but slightly larger than the pills on the tray. Guanyin saw that the two pills were different size. She put one of the original pills inside her clothes. Then she put the large pill and the other small pill on the tray, and she walked up to the doorway of the cave. She knocked on the door.

One of the little demons saw Guanyin, who looked like the white robed monk. The demon told the black bear monster that the monk had arrived.

The monster went and opened the door. "My old friend," he said, "I am so happy that you came to see me!"

"This humble Daoist monk has a small gift for you," said Guanyin. She picked up the large pill and gave it to the black bear monster, saying, "May you live for a thousand years!"

"Thank you!" the monster replied, "and you, please take the other pill for yourself." Guanyin picked up the pill and waited. The monster moved the large pill to his mouth. Suddenly the pill jumped into his mouth. Inside the monster, Sun Wukong returned to his original appearance. He hit the monster from the inside a few times, then flew out through the monster's nose. The monster fell to the ground. Guanyin changed back to her own appearance and grabbed the cassock. Then she put a magic headband on the monster, just like the one on Sun Wukong's head.

The monster stood up and started to pick up his sword. But Guanyin recited some magic words. The headband became very tight on the monster's head, and he fell down, crying in pain. Sun Wukong saw what Guanyin had done, and began to laugh loudly.

"Now, will you do as I say?" said Guanyin to the monster.

"Yes, I will. Please don't kill me!"

While the monster was on the ground, Sun Wukong moved to strike him with his rod. But Guanyin said, "Don't hurt him, I have a job for him."

"He is just a monster. What use could he be?" asked Sun Wukong.

"He is not just a monster. He can help me. I need someone to guard the back side of Potalaka Mountain. He is just right for the job." And then Guanyin touched the monster's head and told him that his new job was to serve her. The monster nodded his head but said nothing.

Turning to Sun Wukong, she said, "Now we are finished here. You must return to serve the Tang monk. And please, please don't cause any more trouble."

Sun Wukong bowed deeply to Guanyin, and left to return the cassock to his master. Guanyin returned to Potalaka Mountain, leading the bear monster. As she flew, bright colors surrounded her, and there was beautiful music in the air.

Now do you understand, my child? The things that you see depend on the thoughts in your mind. Sun Wukong likes to fight, so when he looked at the bear monster, he saw only a monster. But when Guanyin looked at the same monster, she saw someone who could become good.

Chapter 18

After Sun Wukong finished fighting with the bear monster, he returned the cassock to the monastery and gave it to Tangseng. The monks in the monastery were happy, and they gave a great vegetarian feast to the two travelers.

In the morning, Sun Wukong and Tangseng thanked the monks and they continued walking westward. They walked for six or seven days. One day they arrived at a small village. It was late in the afternoon. The sun was low and red in the sky. "I would like to rest here," said Tangseng.

 "Wait a bit," replied Sun Wukong. "I need to take a look around, to see if this is a good or bad place." He used his golden fire eyes to look at the village. He saw many small houses surrounded by tall trees. The air was full of smoke from cooking fires. Cattle were walking home on every path. Fat pigs and chickens were sleeping near the houses. A drunken old man sang a song as he walked slowly towards his home.

"Everything looks ok to me," said Sun Wukong. "This village has good families living in it. We can stay here tonight."

They entered the village. Right away they saw a young man. He wore a blue shirt and a white hat. In his hand was a straw umbrella and he had a bundle of straw on his back. Sun Wukong walked up to him, grabbed his arm tightly, and asked, "Where are you going? What is this place?"

The young man was frightened of the monkey and tried to get away, but Sun Wukong was too strong. The young man cried, "Go ask your questions to somebody else and leave me alone!" He tried to hit Sun Wukong, but the monkey just held him tightly and did not move.

Finally, the young man stopped fighting. He said, "All right. You are in the kingdom of Wusizang. We call this Old Gao Village, because most of the families here are named Gao. Now let me go!"

"So I suppose your name is Gao," said Sun Wukong. "I will let you go if you tell me where you are going and what you are doing."

"My name is Gao Cai. The head of our family is my father's older brother, we call him Old Man Gao. He has a twenty-year-old daughter named Green Orchid. Three years ago, a monster took her to be his wife. Old Man Gao was very unhappy because he did not want a monster for a son-in-law. He tried to stop this, but the monster refused. The monster kept the girl locked up for six months so she could not see her family. The old man gave me some money and told me to find a Master of the Law who could get rid of the monster. I could not find a good exorcist. I only found some worthless monks and helpless Daoists. So the old man gave me a little more money and told me to try one more time. I am still trying to find a good exorcist, but you are making me late!"

"Well," said Sun Wukong, "today is your lucky day. Your problem and my abilities fit together perfectly! As the saying goes, 'Not only do you have a good doctor, but now your eyes are good too!' We are holy monks from the east. We are traveling west to get holy books to bring back to the Tang Emperor. We have already fought several monsters, and we won each time. So yes, we can help you. Lead us to the door of your house."

The young man picked up his umbrella and his bundle of straw, and the three of them walked to his house. "Please wait here," he said when they reached the door. The young man went inside and told Old Man Gao about the two monks. He said, "These men say that they are holy monks from the east. One of them says he is a brother to the Tang Emperor himself. I think they can help us."

Old Man Gao came to the front door. "Welcome!" he said, and bowed to Tangseng. Tangseng bowed back to Gao. Sun Wukong did not bow, he just stood there. "Why don't you say hello to me?" he demanded. The old man looked with fear at the ugly monkey. Then he turned to Gao Cai and said, "Young man, what have you done? We already have one monster in our house. Now we have two!"

"Old Gao," said Sun Wukong, "you have lived for many years but you are still a fool. You think that a good-looking person is a good person! I am Old Monkey. I may be ugly but I can capture this monster and get your daughter back. Is that good enough for you?"

The old man was still frightened but he liked Sun Wukong's words, so he said, "Please come in." When they were all inside the house, Tangseng told him the story of their journey to the west to seek Buddhist books to bring back to the Tang Emperor. He also asked if they could stay a night at the old man's house.

"You just want to stay for one night?" asked Gao, "Then how can you catch my monster?"

"We are asking to stay here for one night," said Sun Wukong, "but we thought we could catch a few monsters too, just for fun. Tell me, how many monsters do you have in your house?"

"Just one, but he has brought much trouble to us."

"Tell us."

"From ancient times this village has never had problems with ghosts, spirits or monsters. We were all happy here. I have three daughters. I have already agreed to give the two older ones to men in the village. But I hoped that my youngest daughter, named Green Orchid, would marry a man who would stay with our family and have children to take our name. Three years ago, a young man came to our village. He was good looking and strong, and he liked Green Orchid. He said his name was Zhu Ganglie. Because he had no family, I thought he would be a good son. He joined our family and he worked very hard. He started early in the day and worked until late in the evening."

"That sounds good. What happened?"

"His appearance began to change. His ears began to grow large. His nose became long and hairy. Hair grew from behind his ears. I tell you, he really started looking like a big pig. And so hungry! In a single meal he might eat as much rice as twenty men. For breakfast he ate a hundred buns. It's a good thing he is a vegetarian, because if he ate meat, we could not afford to feed him at all!"

"Well, maybe he is hungry because he works so hard," said Tangseng.

"The food is not really a big problem. The big problem is my daughter. I have not seen her for six months. I don't know if she is dead or alive. Now I am sure that Zhu is a monster. We must get rid of him!"

"That is not difficult, old man!" said Sun Wukong. "Tonight I will catch him. I will get him to agree to a divorce, and your daughter will return to you.

How's that?"

The old man was very happy to hear this. He had a vegetarian meal prepared for the visitors. After dinner, he asked, "What weapons do you need and what attendants?"

"I don't need your weapons," replied Sun Wukong, "I have this!" And he pulled a needle out of ear, waved it around, and it changed into his magic golden hoop rod. "And I don't need any attendants. However, I would like some good elderly people to come and stay with my master, to keep him company while I catch the monster for you."

The old man agreed. Soon several elderly men and women arrived at the house to sit with Tangseng and talk with him. Sun Wukong said to him, "Master, you should feel safe with these people. I am going to fight the monster!" Then turning to Old Man Gao, he said, "Old man, where is the house where the monster lives?"

Gao walked to a building in back of the house. They stood in front of the front door. "Quickly, old man, get the key to the door!" said Sun Wukong.

"If I had a key to this door, I would not need you," snapped Gao.

Sun Wukong said, "Old man, you are quite old but you still can't recognize a joke. I was just teasing you a little." Then he used his golden hoop rod to smash the door with one blow. They looked inside. It was pitch black. "Old Gao, call your daughter."

The old man was frightened, but he called out, "My Daughter! My dear Green Orchid!" The girl replied faintly, "Papa! I'm over here!" They looked at her. Her lovely face and hair were dirty, and she had lost a lot of weight. She ran to her father and cried.

Sun Wukong said, "Stop that crying! Where is the monster?"

"I don't know," she replied. "He leaves early in the morning and he returns late in the evening. I don't know where he goes. But he is careful to not let Papa see him, because he knows Papa is trying to get rid of him."

"OK. No more talk. Go with your father. Old Monkey will wait here." So the father and daughter left. Sun Wukong changed his form so he looked just like the girl. Then he sat down and waited.

He didn't have to wait long. Soon there was a tremendous wind, causing dirt and stones to fly through the air. Trees fell to the ground. Animals lost their way in the forest. Rivers and seas were churned up. Rocks and mountains were broken. In the north, parts of the Great Wall itself fell down.

When the wind subsided, a great monster appeared. It was Zhu Ganglie. His black face was covered with short hair. He had a long nose and huge ears. He wore a blue-green shirt. On his head he wore a spotted handkerchief.

Sun Wukong didn't say anything when Zhu entered the room. He just lay on the bed and pretended to be sick. Zhu walked over to the bed, grabbed the monkey who looked like a girl, and demanded a kiss. But Sun Wukong grabbed the monster's nose tightly, causing him to fall to the floor with a crash.

"My dear, it seems you are a little annoyed with me today," said Zhu. "Is it because I came home late?"

"I am not annoyed. But what makes you think you can just come in here and demand a kiss? Can't you see that I am not feeling well? You know that if I was feeling better, I would get up from the bed and open the door for you. Now take off your clothes and go to sleep."

Zhu took off his clothes, but just before he got into bed, Sun Wukong got out of bed and went to the chamber pot. "Dear wife, where have you gone?" asked Zhu.

"I have to use the chamber pot. When I am finished I will come to bed." Then he said, "Oh, I have such bad luck!"

"Why do you say you have bad luck? It's true that I eat a lot of your family's food. But I work very hard every day. I work in the fields and also inside the house. You wear fine clothes, you have gold and silver, you have lots of rice and vegetables year-round. But still, you cry and say you have bad luck. Why?"

"Today I was scolded by my father. He says that you are very ugly and you don't know how to behave. You come and go with great wind and clouds. Nobody knows where you go. You have ruined our family's reputation."

"It's true that I am not handsome. But your family knew that when I first arrived here. My family is named Zhu, we come from Fuling Mountain. Of course your family knew what I looked like. I entered your family with your father's consent and I have worked very hard. Why do they bring this up today?"

Sun Wukong sat on the chamber pot, and he thought to himself, "This monster certainly tells the truth! He does not seem like a bad man." Then he said to Zhu, "My parents are trying to get a Master of the Law to make you go away."

"That does not worry me at all!" said Zhu. "You just go to sleep. Don't worry about them at all. I can change into as many different forms as there are stars in the Heavenly Ladle[1]. And I have a nine-pronged rake that I can use as a weapon."

"They said they were hoping to get someone named Sun. They say he is the Great Sage Equal to Heaven who caused trouble in the Palace of Heaven five hundred years ago. They were going to ask Sun to come and catch you."

Zhu became very alarmed when he heard this. "If this is true, I must leave. We cannot live together anymore! That Sun has real power. I cannot fight him."

Zhu put on his clothes quickly and walked to the door. Sun Wukong shook his body again and changed back into his original monkey form. He grabbed Zhu by the shirt and shouted, "Monster, where do you think you're going? Look at me and see who I am!" Zhu looked and saw the big hairy face of Sun Wukong. Instantly he tore his shirt and got free of Sun's grip. He changed into the wind. Sun struck at the wind with his golden hoop rod. Zhu changed from a wind into beams of sunlight and flew back to his family home in Fuling Mountain.

Sun Wukong shouted, "Where are you running to? If you fly to Heaven, I will chase you to the Heavenly Palace. If you go down to earth, I will chase you to the Underworld. You cannot get away from me!"

---

[1] Tiāngāng is the Heavenly Ladle, a constellation with 36 stars corresponding to the Big Dipper.

Chapter 19

Zhu, in his form as a beam of sunlight, flew away to Fuling Mountain, with Sun Wukong close behind him. Zhu arrived at the mountain, ran into his cave, and came out holding his rake. He was ready to fight.

"Lawless monster!" shouted Sun Wukong, "How do you know my name? Tell me now, and I might let you live!"

"Come up here, you ugly old monkey," replied Zhu. "Sit down and I will tell you my story." Sun Wukong calmed down a bit. He sat down and listened to Zhu's story.

> "Ever since I was young, I have not been very smart
> I just wanted to relax and play every day
> I hated work and I never wanted to study
> One day I met an immortal being
> He who spoke to me of cold and heat[1]
> He told me that one day my life would end
> And it will be too late to change
> I listened to him and asked him to be my teacher
> For many years I worked day and night to learn the ways of Heaven
> Finally I became enlightened and I flew up to Heaven
> There I met the Jade Emperor himself
> He gave a great banquet in my honor
> The Jade Emperor named me Marshal of Heaven
> And gave me all his ships and 80,000 warriors
> I was so happy!
> Later that day, I came to the Queen Mother's Peach Festival
> But I drank too much alcohol and became drunk
> While drunk, I met the beautiful Goddess of the Moon
> Without thinking, I asked her to come to bed with me
> She said no
> I asked her again and she said no
> Five times I asked her, and five times she said no
> I became angry and roared like thunder
> The gods caught me and brought me back to the Jade Emperor

---

[1] This is not a reference to the weather, but to the inner alchemy of transformation as taught in Daoism.

He was ready to have me killed
But the Gold Star of Venus arrived
He bowed to the Jade Emperor
He asked him not to have me killed
But I was beaten five thousand times
Then I was sent out of Heaven and down here to earth
When I arrived on earth, my soul became lost
I ended up in the belly of a sow
Now I must live the rest of my life as a lowly pig!"

Sun Wukong sat and listened to Zhu's story. When it was finished, he said, "I also was in Heaven, at the Queen Mother's Peach Festival. I also got very drunk. And I also was sent out of Heaven. So I understand your problems! Now I know that you are actually the Marshal of Heaven."

"Yes, and you are the terrible monkey who caused so much trouble in Heaven! Do you know how many people suffered because of you? Now taste my rake, you monster!"

They began to fight, shouting insults at each other. The pig used his rake, the monkey used his golden hoop rod. They fought all night, until the second watch came and the sun rose in the east. Zhu was tired and could not fight any more. He ran away back into his cave, and locked the door. Sun Wukong did not try to break down the door. Instead, he flew back to see Tangseng.

Now, Tangseng had spent all night talking with the elderly men and women from the village. He looked up when Sun Wukong arrived.

"Master, I have returned!" said Sun Wukong.

"Wukong, you were gone all night. Where is the monster?"

"He is no monster. He is the Marshal of Heaven. He took the wrong path of rebirth, that is why he looks like a pig. But he still has a spiritual nature. I fought him with my rod in the rear building, but he changed into a beam of light and flew to Fuling Mountain. I followed him and we fought again. Then he ran away into his cave. I thought about breaking down the cave door, but first I had to come back here and see if you were ok."

After he finished speaking, Old Man Gao came forward, saying, "O great monk, I must say this. You chased the monster away, but what if he comes back? Please arrest the monster, so we will not have any more worries. I will be very happy, and I will give you half of everything that I own!"

"Well, old man, you are asking a lot from me, aren't you?" laughed Sun Wukong. "I was chatting with your monster. He said that yes, he did eat a lot of food, but he also did a lot of work for you. And yes, he is not good-looking, but you knew that when he first arrived in your house. And he has not hurt your daughter at all. It seems that you should be grateful for all that Mr. Zhu has done for you." And before Old Gao could reply, Sun Wukong flew away again to Fuling Mountain.

When Sun Wukong was speaking with Old Man Gao, he praised Zhu. But now he smashed down the cave door and shouted at Zhu, "Come out and fight me, you fat coolie!"

Zhu was still tired from his earlier fight with the monkey, and he was resting in his cave. But when he heard himself called a "fat coolie" he jumped up, grabbed his rake, and ran to the front of the cave. "You stupid monkey! Don't you know the law? You cannot just smash down someone's door like that. You are a criminal, and you can be put to death!"

"Oh, and what about you? You took a young girl away from her family. You didn't give the family any tea and wine. You didn't even use a matchmaker. In my eyes, you are the criminal, not me."

"This is not the time for talk. It's time for me to give you a taste of my rake!"

"Ha! That old thing? Don't you use that for growing vegetables in your farm?"

"Don't say that! This is the greatest weapon in Heaven and earth. The Jade Emperor himself gave it to me. It is made of the finest steel. All the warriors of Heaven fear it, and the Ten Kings of the Underworld bow before it. You may be a stone monkey, but my rake will break your head!"

Sun Wukong just smiled. He put down his golden hoop rod and stood in front of Zhu. He said, "OK, let's see if that's true. Go ahead, hit me hard on the head."

Zhu brought the rake down on the monkey's head as hard as he could. It hit his head and bounced back. Sun's head was not hurt even a little bit. Zhu was so scared that his legs became weak and he dropped the rake. "Such a head," he muttered.

"You don't know, do you?" said Sun Wukong. "Five hundred years ago, when I made trouble in Heaven, the great sage Laozi put me in a brazier and cooked me for three weeks. The fire made me stronger. Now I have eyes of golden fire, a bronze head, and iron arms. Go ahead, hit me a few more times and see for yourself!"

"Monkey," said Zhu, "I remember you from long ago. You lived on Flower Fruit Mountain, in the country of Aolai. You caused a lot of trouble in Heaven. Then nobody saw you for many years. Now you are here. Did my wife's father bring you here?"

"No, he did not call me. For many years I was on the wrong path, but now I am on the right path. I am traveling with a holy monk, the brother of the Tang Emperor, we are going to the west to seek holy books from the Buddha. We saw Gao Village and asked if we could stay for one night. It was Old Man Gao who asked us to help his daughter. She was unhappy because of you, you fat coolie!"

Sun Wukong thought that saying "fat coolie" would make Zhu angry again. But Zhu threw down his rake and said, "Where is this holy monk? Can you introduce me to him?"

"Why?" said Sun Wukong, puzzled.

"One of my teachers was the holy monk Guanyin. She told me to study, eat a vegetarian diet, and wait here for a holy monk who was traveling to the west. When I met him, I was to go with him to get the fruits of truth. You are the holy monk's disciple, why didn't you say anything about him earlier? Why did you shout at me, insult me, hit me, and smash down my door?"

Tell me the truth, you fat coolie. If you really want to meet the holy monk, you must face Heaven and say that you are telling the truth!"

Right away, the pig knelt down and bowed so rapidly that it looked like he was pounding rice with his head. "Holy Buddha!" he cried, "if I am not speaking the truth, kill me now!"

Sun Wukong thought, "Well, I suppose he is telling the truth after all!" To Zhu he said, "All right. Burn everything in this cave, and then let's go."

Zhu picked up firewood, brought it into the cave, and started a fire. Everything in the cave burned. Then Sun Wukong said, "Now give me your rake." He blew on the rake and it turned into a piece of rope, then he used the rope to tie Zhu's hands together. Zhu did not argue or fight. Together they flew back to Gao Village.

They arrived in Gao Village. Sun said to Zhu, "Look, there is my master." Zhu fell to the ground in front of Tangseng and kowtowed, saying, "Master, your disciple is sorry for not coming to meet you. If I knew you were here, I would have come at once."

"Wukong," said Tangseng, "what's going on here? Tell me what happened." But Sun Wukong just hit Zhu on the back of the head with his golden hoop rod. He told Zhu, "Say something!" So Zhu told Tangseng his story of his troubles in Heaven, his meeting with Guanyin, his return to earth, and his fight with Sun Wukong.

Tangseng was very pleased to hear this story. He turned to Old Man Gao. "Dear sir," he said, "may I borrow your incense table?" Old Gao brought the table. Tangseng washed his hands, then lit the incense. He bowed to the south and thanked Guanyin for her help. All the elders came and put more incense on the table. Tangseng asked Sun Wukong to remove the rope from Zhu's hands.

"Now," said Tangseng to Zhu, "you are my disciple. I must give you a new name."

"Master," replied Zhu, "my teacher Guanyin already gave me a name, it is Zhu Wuneng.[1]"

"That is a good name! Your elder brother is called Wukong and you are called Wuneng."

"Master, when I became a student of the holy monk Guanyin, she told me I was not allowed to eat any of the five stinking foods or the three forbidden meats[2]. Since then, I have only eaten vegetarian food. Now that I am your disciple, will you release me from this?"

"No, no, no," replied Tangseng. "But since you have not eaten the five stinking foods or the three forbidden meats, I will give you another name: Bajie, meaning 'Eight Prohibitions.'"

"Thank you, Master," said Zhu Bajie. "And now, may I please ask my humble wife to come out and meet you and Elder Brother?"

"Younger Brother," laughed Sun Wukong, "you are now a Buddhist monk. It's true that some Daoist monks have wives. But have you ever heard of a

---

[1] Zhu's new name Zhū Wùnéng, meaning "Pig Awaken to Power."
[2] There are five forbidden vegetables: onions, garlic, chives, green onions and leeks. There are also three forbidden meats: wild goose, dog, and snake. Together they are the Eight Prohibitions (bā jiè). This might also refer to the Eightfold Path of Buddhism.

married Buddhist monk? Forget about your wife. Just sit down and enjoy your vegetarian meal. Soon we will leave for the west!"

So they all had a good vegetarian meal. Old Man Gao brought out some wine. Tangseng did not drink any. He told Sun Wukong and Zhu Bajie that they could drink a little bit, as long as they did not get drunk and cause trouble.

After the dinner, Old Man Gao brought out a tray with two hundred gold and silver coins. He offered them to the visitors, saying that they were for travel expenses. Tangseng said they could not take the money. But Sun Wukong grabbed a handful of coins and gave them to the young man Gao Cai to thank him for his help.

Then Old Man Gao brought out three beautiful silk cassocks. Tangseng said they could not take the cassocks. But Zhu asked if he could take one, because the cassock he was wearing had been torn by Sun Wukong in the fight. Tangseng agreed to this.

In the morning, they resumed their journey to the west. Zhu Bajie was in the rear, carrying baggage tied to a long pole. Tangseng was in the middle, riding his white horse. And Sun Wukong led the way, with the golden hoop rod across his back.

They traveled for about a month, leaving the western edge of the Kingdom of Wusizang. One day they saw a tall mountain far away. "What mountain is this?" asked Tangseng.

Zhu said, "This is Pagoda Mountain. A Chan Master[1] lives there. I have met him. He once invited me to stay with him, but I did not do it." They came closer to the mountain. They heard the sounds of thousands of birds singing and flying together. They saw a thousand flowers and a green stream flowing down the mountainside. Looking up, they saw a great tree. In the tree branches was a large nest made of wood and straw. And inside the nest was a man.

"Look!" said Zhu. "That is the Chan Master."

As they watched, the Chan Master jumped down from the nest to greet them. Tangseng got off his horse and bowed to him. The Chan Master said, "Please get up. Welcome to my home at Pagoda Mountain!" Then, looking at Zhu, he said, "I know you! You are Zhu Ganglie of Fuling Mountain!" And looking at Sun Wukong he said, "And who are you?"

Sun Wukong laughed and said, "So, you recognize that old pig, but you don't recognize me?"

"I have not had the pleasure of meeting you," the Chan Master replied.

"This is my eldest disciple, Sun Wukong," said Tangseng. "Please tell me, how far is it to the temple at Thunder Mountain?"

"Oh, very far away! The road is long and filled with dangers. One day you will arrive at Thunder Mountain. I think I can help you a little. I have a special prayer here[2]. It is the door to becoming Buddha. If you ever meet trouble, just say the words in this prayer, and no troubles will come to you."

"Please give us this prayer, o great monk!" cried Tangseng. And so, the Chan Master spoke the prayer. It was 54 sentences and 270 characters. Tangseng

---

[1] Chán is a Chinese school of Mahayana Buddhism, better known in the West as Zen.
[2] This is the heart sutra, the most commonly recited scripture in East Asian Buddhism. It is said to have been written in India, then translated to Chinese and brought to China by the real monk Tangseng in the 7th Century.

heard the prayer once, and remembered it perfectly.

After the Chan Master finished saying the prayer, he prepared to return to his nest in the tree. But Tangseng asked him, "Please tell us about the road to Thunder Mountain!"

The Chan Master laughed and said,

> "Listen to my words
> This road is not difficult to walk
> You will see a thousand mountains
> And many deep rivers
> When you come to the edge of a high cliff
> Put your feet sideways
> Be careful in the Black Pine Forest
> Spirits will try to stop you
> You will meet many monsters and animals of the forest
> An old pig carries a long pole
> You will meet a water spirit
> You have already met an angry old stone monkey
> He knows the way to the West!"

Then the Chan Master changed into a beam of light and returned to his nest in the tree. Sun Wukong became angry and tried to hit the nest with his golden hoop rod, but his rod turned into many colored flowers.

"Don't try to hit the Chan Master!" said Tangseng. "Why did you do that?"

"Don't you understand?" replied Sun Wukong. "He insulted your disciple Zhu. He called me an angry old stone monkey." Sun Wukong was also unhappy that the Chan Master said that he knew the way to the west, but he did not say anything about that.

"Don't worry about that," said Zhu. "Let's see if his words are true. Let's see if we come to a high cliff or the Black Tree Forest, and if we meet a water spirit. Then we will know."

Chapter 20

And so, the three travelers began walking west again. They walked for many days and weeks and months. Fall became winter, winter became spring, and summer arrived. Every day Tangseng said the Chan Master's prayer, and it opened the doorway to his understanding. Spiritual light filled his body and his mind.

Zhu Wuneng was always hungry. If they received food at a village, Sun Wukong and Tangseng would generally eat two bowls of rice, but sometimes Zhu would eat ten bowls of rice. Zhu complained when there was no food, and he also complained that he missed his family. Finally Tangseng said to him, "Wuneng, it sounds like your heart misses your family. If this is true, then maybe this is not the right path for you. Maybe you should leave us and return home."

When he heard these words, Zhu fell to his knees and said, "Master, please do not send me home. The holy monk Guanyin herself told me I should go with you, and you have been very good to me. Please let me stay!" And so, Tangseng allowed Zhu to stay.

After a few weeks, they came to a high cliff, just as the Chan Master had said. Tangseng sat sideways on his horse, just as the Chan Master had said. He looked down from the cliff. The cliff was ten thousand feet deep, and it was so deep that it appeared to go all the way down to the underworld.

The three walked slowly and carefully on the edge of the cliff, staying close to the mountain. Suddenly there was a great wind. Tangseng and Zhu were afraid, but Sun Wukong stood facing the wind, unafraid.

"Elder Brother," said Zhu, "be careful, this wind is too strong!"

"Why are you afraid?" asked Sun Wukong. "This wind is nothing. What would you do if you met a monster spirit face to face?"

"Nothing would happen to us if we just waited for a while," Zhu replied.

"Stop talking. I have magic that allows me to seize wind. I will just seize this wind and smell it." Sun Wukong waited until the head of the wind had passed him, then he seized the tail of the wind. He held it to his nose and smelled it. "Yes, this is not a good wind. It smells like a tiger, or maybe a monster."

Suddenly a huge tiger appeared in the path, just in front of them. It stood up on its rear legs and roared at them. Tangseng was frightened, and fell to the ground. Zhu threw down the luggage that he was carrying, he grabbed his rake, and he attacked the tiger, shouting "You monster, where are you going?"

But the tiger raised his left front paw and cut his own skin from his neck down to his belly. He stepped out of his own skin and stood in front of the three. He was still a tiger, but now he was covered with red blood and looked even more frightening than before. The tiger shouted, "Wait right there! I am no ordinary tiger. I am the leader of the Great King Yellow Wind's army. The Great King told me to watch this mountain, seize any travelers that I see, and bring them to him to eat for dinner. You three look like you would taste very good."

"Don't you recognize us?" shouted Zhu. "We are disciples of Tangseng, brother to the great Tang Emperor. We are traveling to the Western Heaven to find Buddhist scriptures and bring them back to the east. Move aside and let us pass, and you will live. If not, my rake will be your last teacher!"

Zhu began to fight with the tiger monster. The monster had claws but no other weapons, so he quickly ran away to a cave where he picked up a pair of golden swords and continued to fight.

Sun Wukong picked up Tangseng off his horse and put him on the ground, saying, "Don't worry, Master. You rest here, I will help Zhu fight the monster." Then the pig and the monkey chased the tiger monster down the mountainside. The tiger monster wrapped up a large rock with his own skin, then he turned into a wind. He blew past Zhu and Sun Wukong.

As the tiger monster passed, he looked down and saw Tangseng sitting on the ground. He quickly picked up Tangseng and carried him on the wind back to the cave of Great King Yellow Wind. When he arrived at the cave, he said to one of his soldiers, "Quick, go tell the King that I have captured a very tasty looking monk. I await word from the King!" Soon the soldier returned and allowed the tiger monster to enter the cave.

The tiger monster entered the cave, with his two golden swords on his belt and with Tangseng in his arms. He said, "Great King! Your servant thanks you for allowing him to watch the cliff. Today I found this monk. He says that he is the brother of the great Tang Emperor, and that he is traveling to the west. He looks very tasty. So I bring him to you!"

The king replied, "I have heard that a monk is traveling to the west in search of Buddhist scriptures. But people say that he is with a disciple named Sun Wukong who is extremely dangerous. How did you capture this monk?"

"The monk has two disciples, a monkey and a pig. The pig attacked me with a rake and the monkey attacked me with a rod. But I was able to get away, capture this monk, and bring him to you."

"Let's not eat him yet," said the king.

"Great King, a good horse always eats food when he can."

"My good soldier, think about this. The monk's two disciples may come looking for him. Let's tie up the monk and leave him outside in the garden for a few days. If the disciples don't come, we can relax and eat the monk for dinner."

"You are very wise, my king," said the tiger monster. Then he told some of the soldiers to tie up Tangseng and leave him in the garden.

Meanwhile, Zhu and Sun Wukong arrived at the place where the tiger skin was wrapped around a rock. Sun Wukong thought that the skin was the tiger. He struck the tiger skin with his Golden Hoop Rod, but the rod just bounced back and hurt his hands. Then Zhu struck the tiger skin with his rake, but the rake also bounced back. "Oh," said Sun Wukong, "we are just hitting a rock. The tiger monster has escaped!"

Zhu was very unhappy and he started to cry. "Don't cry," said Sun Wukong. "When you start to cry, you have already lost the fight. The Master and the monster are both in the mountains, we just have to look for them."

So the pig and the monkey began to search for their master. They looked up and down, left and right, for a long time. After several hours they arrived at a cave. Above the door was a sign with six characters: "Yellow Wind Cave, Yellow Wind Mountain." He held his golden hoop rod in his hand and shouted, "Monster! Give my master back to me right now, or I will smash your cave!"

Inside the cave, the king heard this. He said to the tiger monster, "What have you done? I just asked you to watch the mountain and bring back some animals for me to eat. Why did you have to bring back a Tang monk? Now we have a lot of trouble!"

"Don't worry," replied the tiger monster. "Give me fifty soldiers. I will go out there and show him who's boss, and then I'll give him to you. Tonight at dinner you can put him on your rice, right next to the Tang monk."

So the king gave fifty soldiers to the tiger monster, and together they went out to fight Sun Wukong. The monster shouted at Sun Wukong, "You ugly monkey, where did you come from, and why are you making such a big noise here?"

"Don't ask me questions, you beast," replied Sun Wukong. "Just give me my master and you will live to see tomorrow."

"Yes, I took your master. He will look good on my king's dinner plate tonight. And you will look good next to him. This is good, it is like 'buy one, get one free.'"

Sun Wukong became very angry when he heard this. The two of them began to fight. Sun Wukong used his Golden Hoop Rod to rain blows down on the monster's head. After five or six rounds, the monster became tired and ran away. But he did not go back to the king's cave because he was also afraid of the king. So he ran down the mountainside. Sun Wukong ran after him. Zhu saw them and also ran after the monster. Zhu caught the monster first and hit him hard with his rake, killing him instantly.

"Thanks!" said Sun Wukong. "You stay here and watch our luggage." Then Sun Wukong grabbed the dead monster and began to drag him back to the king's cave.

Chapter 21

Now, the king was sitting in his cave, waiting for the tiger monster to return. But he did not return. Later, a soldier ran into the cave and told the king that Sun Wukong had killed the tiger monster. This made the king very angry. "I will fight this monkey myself," he said. He put on his golden armor, golden helmet, and leather shoes, and picked up his steel trident. Then he went out of the cave, followed by his soldiers.

"I am looking for the old monkey Sun. Where are you?" he cried.

Sun Wukong stood outside the cave. He had the Golden Hoop Rod in his hand, and one foot on the dead monster. He replied, "Your grandpa Sun is here. Now give me back my master."

The king looked down at Sun Wukong, who was really only about four feet tall and very thin. "I was looking for a great fighter," he said, "but all I see is a small sickly ghost."

"You are very foolish, old man," said Sun Wukong. "You think I am small? Just hit me on the head and I will grow to be ten feet tall." So the king used his trident to hit Sun Wukong on the head. This did not bother Sun Wukong at all, but he quickly grew to be ten feet tall. The two of them began to fight outside the cave. They fought for a long time, but neither one could win.

Sun Wukong pulled some hairs from his head and blew on them. Each hair became another Sun Wukong, and now there were a hundred monkeys, all fighting the king. But the king made a great wind that blew away all the hundred monkeys. The wind also put dirt into Sun Wukong's eyes, so he could not see.

Now, I must tell you, Sun Wukong did not know what to do. He did not want Tangseng to be dinner for the king, but he also did not know how to win the fight against the king. He could not see well, but he found Zhu and talked with him. They decided to walk down the mountain and find a place to stay for the night.

When they arrived at the bottom of the mountain, they found a small house in a village. Inside the house was an old man. The old man gave some eye medicine to Sun Wukong. Sun and Zhu slept in the old man's house that night. In the morning the house was gone, they were lying in the grass, and Sun Wukong's eyes were better again. Then knew that the old man was really a spirit sent by Guanyin to help them.

"Little Brother," said Sun Wukong, "you wait here and keep an eye on our baggage. I will go back to the cave and try to learn if our master is okay." Then he changed into a small insect and flew under the door and into the king's cave. In the back of the cave was another door. He flew under that door also, and he found himself in a garden under the sky. In the middle of the garden was Tangseng, tied up and crying.

Sun Wukong landed on the monk's head and said, "Master! I am on your head. Calm down and do not worry. We killed the tiger monster, but now we have to capture the king. Then you can leave this place!"

Sun Wukong flew back into the cave, and he heard the king talking with his soldiers. The king said, "I am not worried about that monkey or that pig. My wind is too strong for them. There is only one person who can overcome that wind, and that is the great monk Lingji!"

This made Sun Wukong very happy, because now he knew how to win the fight against the king. But he did not know anything about the monk called Lingji. He flew out of the cave to tell Zhu what he had learned. Just then, a man walked by. Sun Wukong put his rod back into his ear, and walked up to the man. "Tell me, sir, do you know anything about a monk named Lingji?"

The man just pointed south with his hand and said, "Follow that path for three thousand miles. You will find him." Sun Wukong turned his head to look at the path. When he looked back, the man was gone.

Zhu stayed to watch the baggage, while Sun Wukong used his cloud somersault to travel the three thousand miles to the home of the monk Lingli. He told Lingji that his master was in danger because of the king of Yellow Wind Mountain. Lingji was unhappy to hear this, and said, "I know that king. I captured him a long time ago. I let him live, but only if he would not eat any humans, only animals. I see that he has not listened to me!" And so, the monkey and the monk traveled back to Yellow Wind Mountain.

They arrived at the cave of the king. Sun Wukong smashed the cave door with his golden hoop rod. The king angrily came out from the cave, steel trident in hand. They fought for a short time. Then the king threw his trident at Sun Wukong. Sun Wukong moved to the side and the trident hit the cave wall. The king opened his mouth to say the words that would create the wind, but just then, Lingji threw down his walking stick. It changed into the Eight Clawed Golden Dragon. Two of the dragon's claws grabbed the king's head and threw it against the cave wall. The king fell down, and changed into a mink with yellow fur.

Sun Wukong ran up to the mink and was ready to kill it with his golden hoop rod. But Lingji stopped him, saying, "Do not hurt him. This creature was once an animal, a mink, who learned the way of the Buddha. But he took a little bit of the Buddha's holy oil. He became afraid and tried to run away. The Buddha told me not to kill him, but to capture him and put him here, at this mountain. Now it looks like he has not learned anything. So I must bring him back to the Buddha, so that the Buddha can decide what to do with him."

Sun Wukong thanked Lingji. The monk and the mink flew away to the Western Heaven, to meet with the Buddha.

Then Sun Wukong and Zhu returned to the cave. They entered, found their master, and told him everything that had happened. Tangseng was very happy of course! They found some tea and rice in the cave and had lunch together. Then the monkey, the pig and the holy monk collected their horse and baggage, and continued their journey to the West.

Chapter 22

After the monkey and the pig stopped the king from eating Tangseng for dinner, the three continued to walk westward, towards Thunder Mountain. They walked for a month and met no trouble. Summer became autumn, and the air became cooler.

One day they arrived at a very wide river. Sun Wukong shaded his eyes and looked across the river. "Master," he said, "we have a problem. This river is eight hundred miles wide. I can cross it easily of course; I just have to use my cloud somersault. But for you, it is a thousand times more difficult."

Tangseng was unhappy when he heard these words. He got down from his horse. Then he looked down at the ground, and saw three words written in stone: 'Flowing Sand River'.

Just as he read these words, the water came up quickly, like a tall mountain. A giant monster jumped out. The monster's hair was red like fire, his eyes were black, and his face was a greenish black. Around his neck were nine skulls. In his hand he held a large staff.

The monster ran up onto the riverbank and tried to grab Tangseng. But the Monkey King was faster than the monster, he grabbed Tangseng and carried him away to higher ground. Zhu Bajie hit the monster with his nine-pronged rake. Zhu and the monster fought for a long time. The pig used his rake, the monster used his staff. They fought for twenty rounds but neither one could win.

As they fought, Sun Wukong watched from high ground. At first he was just amused by the fight. But as the fight continued, he became angry and wanted to fight too. He took out his Golden Hoop Rod, and said to Tangseng, "Master, please wait here. Don't be afraid. Let Old Monkey play with this monster a little!"

Zhu and the monster did not even see Sun Wukong coming, because they were fighting so hard. So Sun Wukong was able to come up behind the monster and whack him on the head with his rod. The monster was surprised. He stopped fighting, then he jumped into the Flowing Sand River and disappeared.

"Elder Brother, why did you do that?" cried Zhu Bajie. "The monster was getting tired. In another four or five rounds I would have won the fight! Now the monster has run away. What will we do now?"

Sun Wukong just laughed and said, "Brother, I must tell you. It's been a long time since I used my rod to fight and win against the King of Yellow Wind Mountain. I have not used it in a month. I just wanted to play a little! But it looks like the monster does not know how to play, and so he just ran away."

The two of them returned to Tangseng, laughing and talking. When they arrived at the place where Tangseng was waiting, they told him about the fight at the riverbank.

Tangseng said, "This monster has probably lived here a long time. So he knows this river. He knows where to wait for us. We cannot cross the river while he is waiting there."

"Yes," replied Sun Wukong. "When we catch the monster, we should not kill him. We should make him take you across the river."

"Good idea," said Zhu. "You should go into the river and catch the monster."

"Well, I could fight him on the land or in the sky, but I am just not comfortable fighting in the water. Of course I could change into a fish, but I could not use my rod so I might not win the fight."

"No problem," Zhu replied, "I am comfortable in water. Remember, I was Marshal of the Heavenly Reeds when I lived in Heaven a long time ago. But I worry that the monster may have a lot of friends and relatives down there. They might help him in a fight."

Sun Wukong said, "OK. You go down there and begin fighting the monster. Then run back to the riverbank. When the monster follows you, I will fight him here on the land."

While they were talking, the monster was resting at the bottom of the river. He saw Zhu coming towards him. He shouted, "Be careful, monk. If you come closer, I might hit you with my staff!"

Zhu replied, "What kind of monster are you, and why do you try to stop us?"

"I am no monster. I have a name."

"If you are no monster, why do you want to kill people?"

"Wait there, monk, while I tell you my story. Ever since I was a child, I have had a strong spirit. Many times I traveled across the earth and into Heaven. For many years I searched for a true teacher of the Way. Finally, I found a teacher of the Great Path of Golden Light. I studied with him until I found the

Hall of Light[1] within myself. I saw the face of Heaven, and I met the Jade Emperor himself. He made me the Curtain-Raising Captain. I wore golden armor and I was guardian of the throne.

"One day the Queen Mother gave a Peach Festival. I held a priceless jade cup in my hand. But I had been drinking, and I dropped and broke it. The Jade Emperor was very angry and prepared to kill me. But the Barefoot Immortal begged him to stop. So the Jade Emperor did not kill me, but he sent me to live in this river. Now I must eat people to live. The woodsman sees me and his life is ended. The fisherman sees me and he dies. I have eaten many men. And now I will eat you too. But I tell you, you don't look very tasty."

Zhu listened to this story, and he became very angry. He shouted, "So, you don't think I will taste good? All right, then taste my rake instead!" And so, they began to fight a second time, but this fight was under the water. For two hours they fought, but neither one could win.

While they fought, Sun Wukong waited on the riverbank, holding his Golden Hoop Rod and pacing back and forth. He really wanted Zhu to bring the monster out of the water and onto the land. Finally he could not wait any longer. He ran down into the water and tried to hit the monster with his rod. The monster saw him coming, turned, and dove down to the bottom of the river again.

"You stupid ape!" cried Zhu, "If you had waited, I would have brought him up to high ground. You could have stepped between him and the river, and we would have won the fight!"

"Stop shouting at me," laughed Sun Wukong. "Let's go back to Master and discuss this."

They returned to Tangseng and told him about the fight with the monster. "What should we do now?" asked Tangseng.

"Master, you just relax," said Sun Wukong. "It's getting late. I will go and beg some vegetarian food. We can eat and rest tonight, and find a solution to the problem tomorrow." Sun Wukong jumped in the air and disappeared. He returned a short time later with some delicious food.

"Wukong," said Tangseng, "why don't we just go to the family who gave you the food, and ask them for help in crossing the river?"

---

[1] The Hall of Light, guāngmíng diàn, refers to the third eye, a point of focus in meditation.

"You can't do that. That family is seven thousand miles away."

"Stop telling such stories," said Zhu. "How could you go seven thousand miles, get food, and come back so quickly?"

Sun Wukong replied, "You don't know about my cloud somersault. Doing it just one time, I can travel one hundred and eight thousand miles. So traveling a few thousand miles to get food was easy for me."

"If that is easy for you, why don't you just pick up Tangseng and me, and carry us across the river?" asked Zhu.

"Well, why don't you carry him?" replied Sun Wukong.

"I cannot carry him. When I fly in the clouds, the Master would be as heavy as Tai Mountain."

"It is the same for me. But even if I could do it, it would not be a good idea. You know the saying, 'A thing easily gotten is soon forgotten'. Our Master must make this journey himself. Our job is just to guard his body and his life, but we cannot save him from the woes of this journey, and by ourselves we cannot bring back the holy books from the Western Heaven. The Master must do it."

Zhu did not say any more about it, so the three of them sat down and ate the vegetarian food.

The next morning, Sun Wukong said to Zhu, "Ok, let's try again. You go back into the water and bring the monster up onto the riverbank. This time I will try to wait for you!" So Zhu walked into the water again, holding his rake high in his hands. Again he met the monster, who shouted "You again? Watch out for my staff!"

"That old thing?" replied Zhu. "Why should I be worried?"

The monster held it in his hands and said, "This staff is quite famous. It was not made by men. It was cut from a huge tree by Wu Gang[1] himself. It is gold at the center, and it is wrapped by pearls. I can make it large or small by just wishing it. The Jade Emperor himself gave it to me, to guard his throne. You and your little rake cannot stand against it."

"That's what you say now," replied Zhu. "But when I hit you with this rake,

---

[1] In Chinese legend, Wú Gāng lived on the moon, where he tried repeatedly to cut down a great cassia tree, only to see it grow back again. The expression "Wu Gang chopping the tree" is used to describe any endless toil.

your blood will run out from nine holes in your body. If you don't die right away, you will die later from loss of blood!"

And so, for a third time they fought. This time Zhu tried to pull the monster onto the riverbank, but the monster understood what Zhu was trying to do and he refused to come out. Instead, the monster tried to pull Zhu down under the water.

Finally, Zhu came out of the river and stood on the riverbank. He said to Sun Wukong, "That monster is too smart, we cannot make him come up onto the riverbank."

"Yes, that's true. I think we need help. It's time for me to go to the South Sea and talk to Guanyin. This westward journey was her idea. And she has helped us many times before. Maybe she will help us again." He used the cloud somersault to travel to Potalaka Mountain in the South Sea. He arrived at Guanyin's temple. One of the local spirits met him there, and took him to see Guanyin.

"What brings you here?" she asked. "You are supposed to be with the Tang monk."

"Great Guanyin, my master took on another disciple at Gao Village. He is a pig named Zhu Bajie, and he has the religious name Zhu Wuneng. The three of us left Yellow Wind Mountain and traveled for a month. We arrived at a great river called Flowing Sands River. It is eight hundred miles wide, and we cannot cross it. Even worse, there is a monster who lives in the river. Zhu fought with him three times, but he fights very well and we cannot defeat him. We ask for your help!"

"Ah, you foolish monkey. Did you think to mention that you are a disciple of the Tang monk?"

"We just wanted to catch the monster and make him help us cross the river. I am not good in the water, so Zhu did all the fighting. Zhu had some conversation with the monster, but I don't know if he mentioned the Tang monk or not."

"That is no monster. That is the Curtain-Raising Captain, sent to the river by the Jade Emperor himself. I told him to wait for a monk who was traveling to the Western Heaven to find the Buddha's holy books and bring them back to China. If you had mentioned that you were traveling with the Tang monk, he would have gladly helped you to cross the river."

"Well, I don't know anything about that. The monster is very afraid of us now. He is at the bottom of the river and he won't come out. How can we bring him out?"

Guanyin called her disciple Moksa and handed him a small red gourd. "Go to the Flowing Sands River and call out, 'Wujing!'. He will come out right away. Bring him to the Tang monk. Then take the nine skulls from Wujing's neck and arrange them in the same positions as the Nine Palaces[1]. Put this gourd in the center. The nine skulls and the gourd will change into a boat that will carry you across Flowing Sands River."

Moksa and Sun Wukong returned to Flowing Sands River. Moksa stood on a cloud above the water and shouted, "Wujing! Wujing! The holy monk has been here for a long time. Why have you not submitted to him yet?"

Now, the monster was still at the bottom of the river. He was very afraid of Sun Wukong. But when he heard his name, he knew that it was Moksa calling him. He lost his fear and came right out of the river to meet Moksa. He smiled and said, "Please forgive me for not greeting you earlier! Where is Guanyin?"

"She did not come. But she told me to tell you to become the disciple of the Tang monk right away. We will take the nine skulls from your neck, and this gourd, to make a boat. Then we will use the boat to take the Tang monk to the other side of this river."

"Where is this holy monk?"

Moksa looked at the riverbank and saw Zhu Bajie. "Isn't that him?"

The monster, whose name was Wujing, laughed. "That lawless pig is no holy monk. He has been fighting with me for two days!"

Moksa looked again and pointed to Sun Wukong. "Well, what about him?"

Wujing said, "That is the pig's helper. He is worse than the pig. I am not going anywhere near those two!"

"All right. Those two must be disciples of the Tang monk. Come with me and we will find the monk."

So Wujing came out of the water and onto the riverbank. They walked onto higher ground and saw Tangseng. Wujing bowed to Tangseng and said, "Master, this poor disciple has eyes but he cannot see. I beg you to forgive me

---

[1] The "positions of the Nine Palaces" refers to an 3x3 grid arrangement.

and accept me as your disciple."

Zhu walked up to them. "You worthless monster! Now you bow before our Master, but you fought with me for two days. What do you have to say about that?"

Sun Wukong laughed and said, "Brother, don't shout at him. We forgot to tell him that we were traveling to the west with the Tang monk, and of course we did not tell him our names. So the monster did not know who we were."

Tangseng agreed to take Wujing as his newest and youngest disciple. He gave him the name 'Sha Monk', and told him to build the boat right away. Sha Monk took the nine skulls from his neck and arranged them like the Nine Palaces. Then he put the gourd in the middle, and they changed into a boat.

Tangseng got on the boat and stood in the center. Zhu Bajie was on his left and Sha Monk was on his right. Sun Wukong stood in the front of the boat, holding the dragon horse. Moksa stayed behind the boat, riding on a cloud. In this way they traveled across the river as fast as an arrow. The wind was calm and the water was peaceful, but the boat traveled quickly.

Soon they reached the other side. Moksa picked up the gourd and flew back on a cloud to the South Sea. The boat changed back to nine skulls, then the nine skulls changed into smoke and disappeared. Tangseng mounted his horse, and they all walked westwards again.

Chapter 23

They walked for many days, always walking away from the morning sun and towards the evening sun. In this way they traveled for two months. It was now late autumn. The trees on the mountainside were turning red, and birds were flying south in the sky above.

One day, in late afternoon, Tangseng asked, "Where should we sleep tonight?"

Sun Wukong replied, "Master, your words are not quite correct. We left our homes long ago. We dine on the wind, we rest beside the river, we sleep under the moon, and we rest upon the cold ground. Any place can be our home. Why ask where we will sleep tonight?"

But Zhu Bajie was tired and hungry, and not feeling good. He said, "Elder Brother, I listen to your words, and I think you do not care about the comfort of others. You always want to keep going west. But think about me! I have been carrying our baggage every day, and I am tired. I wanted to be the Master's disciple, but every day I am just a coolie, carrying your baggage. Let's just look for a nice house where we can have some tea and rice, and sleep in beds."

Sun Wukong laughed and said, "Pig, I only care about one thing: the safety of the Master, and helping him get to the Western Heaven and back again. You and Sha worry about the baggage, I will worry about the Master. And if you ever don't do your job, you will taste my rod!"

"Don't talk about hitting me with your rod," replied Zhu. "I am carrying heavy bags, but you only carry your rod. And look at that horse, he only carries the Master. Why can't he carry some baggage too?"

"That is no horse. That is the son of Aurun, the Dragon King of the Western Ocean. A long time ago he started a fire in his father's palace. His father was angry and wanted to kill him. But Guanyin stopped him, and sent him to wait in Eagle Grief Stream for the arrival of the Tang monk. When Tangseng arrived, he changed from a dragon to a horse, and now he is carrying the Master to the Western Heaven. He is like you, he is on the path to the Buddha, and you should not bother him."

But then, just for fun, Sun Wukong took his rod and smacked the horse on the rump. The horse ran away, up a mountainside, with Tangseng holding on tight. After a while the horse stopped running. Tangseng looked down and saw several buildings in the forest.

The other three arrived, and they all looked down at the buildings. "Look," said Tangseng, "there is a large house. Perhaps we can stay there tonight."

Sun Wukong looked at the village. Then he looked up in the sky and saw strange clouds over the village. Right away he knew that was a place where spirits lived, but he did not say anything about it to Tangseng or the others.

They walked down the mountain and arrived at the gate to the house. The gate was very beautiful, and Sha Monk said, "This must be the home of some wealthy people."

Sun Wukong started to walk inside, but Tangseng stopped him, saying, "No. We are monks, we should not just walk into someone's home. We should wait until we are invited." So the four of them sat down and waited. They waited for a really long time. Finally, Sun Wukong could not wait anymore. He stood up and walked through the gate.

Inside, he saw three great halls. He walked into the middle hall, and saw a table and six chairs. He was looking at this when he heard a woman's voice behind him, saying, "Who are you, to enter someone's home without permission?"

Sun Wukong was surprised and could only say, "This poor monk comes from the Tang land in the East. He is traveling west to seek the Buddha's scriptures. There are four of us. It was late afternoon when we found your noble home. We ask you to please give us a place to sleep tonight."

The woman smiled and said, "And where are your three friends? Please invite them to come in." Sun Wukong called to the others. Sha Monk tied up the horse outside, then they all entered the hall. Zhu Bajie carried the baggage.

The woman was beautiful. Even though she was middle-aged, she looked like a young woman. Zhu looked at her with hunger in his eyes.

The woman invited the four travelers to sit down. A servant girl came in and gave them tea in white jade cups. The smell of fine tea filled the air. The woman told the servant girl to prepare some vegetarian food for the travelers.

"Dear lady," said Tangseng, "what is your noble surname?"

She replied, "My maiden surname is Jia[1]. My husband's family surname is

---

[1] The name Jiǎ means "unreal." The name Mò means "non-existing." The three

Mo. His parents died and my husband inherited their fortune. He inherited ten thousand pieces of gold and silver and a tremendous amount of good land. We had no sons, only three daughters. Then two years ago my husband died. Now it is just the four of us. We have no relatives, and nobody to inherit our fortune. We have been living here by ourselves. But now we are very happy to see that the four of you have arrived. We would like very much to invite you to marry us. I don't know what you think about this!"

Tangseng heard these words, but he was so surprised that he did not know what to say. So he just sat and said nothing at all.

Lady Jia continued, "Please think about this. We have hundreds of sheep, pigs and horses, we have enough food to last for eight years, we have more gold and silver than you could ever use, and we have comfortable silk sheets.

"I am now forty-five years old. My eldest daughter Zhenzhen is twenty years old. My second daughter, Aiai, is eighteen. And my youngest daughter, Lianlian, is sixteen. It is true that I am not much to look at, but my daughters are each quite lovely. Each one is well trained in everything that a wife needs to know, to take care of a home and please her husband. If you four are willing to forget about your journey, you can become masters of this house. Isn't gold and silk better than straw and dirt? Isn't it better to sleep in a warm bed than the cold ground?"

Sitting in his chair, Tangseng was like a child struck by lightning. His eyes rolled upwards, and he almost fell over. But Zhu Bajie, hearing of this wealth and seeing this beauty, became so full of desire that he could not sit. He jumped up and said to Tangseng, "Master! Didn't you hear what this woman is saying?"

Tangseng looked at him and shouted angrily, "You animal! How can you forget who you are? We are people who have left our homes. How can we be moved by wealth and beauty?"

"Ah, I am so sorry that I upset you," said Lady Jia. "Tell me, what is so good about leaving home?"

Tangseng snapped back, "Well, tell me what is so good about staying at home?"

"Let me tell you," she said, smiling. "When spring comes, we wear beautiful

---

daughters are named Zhēn Zhēn, Ài Ài and Lián Lián. Taken together, Zhēn Ài Lián means "truly worthy of love and sympathy."

new silk. In the summer, we change to wearing light silk clothes. In the autumn we drink rice wine. And in the cold of winter, our rooms are warm and our faces glow with wine. We have the delicious fruits of all four seasons. And the comfortable silk sheets of our beds will make you forget about the hard life of a monk."

Tangseng replied, "Lady, I believe that my life is much better than yours. Yes, it is true that those who stay at home have riches and comfort, and children by their side. That is a good life. But the life of a monk is also a good life. I have no worries. My body has equal amounts of yin and yang. When my life is finished, I will face the end of my life with an enlightened mind and return to my home in Heaven. You only care about your beautiful body, but that will soon become old and ugly!"

When Lady Jia heard this, she became angry, and said, "How dare you say these things to me! I wanted to give you a comfortable home and a good life, but you use words to hurt me instead. If you want to remain a monk, that is all right. But what about your disciples? Do any of them want to marry us and stay here?"

Tangseng thought about this for a minute, then he turned to Sun Wukong and said, "Wukong, do you want to stay here?"

"No, Master," he replied, "I know nothing of these things. Perhaps Younger Brother Zhu would like to stay."

Zhu Bajie said, "Elder Brother, don't play with me like this!" Then they all looked at Sha Monk.

Sha Monk said, "Master, I waited for you for many years. And now I have been with you just two months, please don't send me away now. I will travel with you to the Western Heaven, or die trying!"

After all the disciples had spoken, Lady Jia turned and walked out of the room, leaving Tangseng and the disciples alone. They sat there for a while, but nobody came out to offer them tea.

"See what you have done!" said Zhu. "You hurt that nice woman. Now she has gone away, the door is shut, and nobody will come out again. We will not get any more food, and we have no place to sleep tonight."

"Younger Brother, why don't you stay here and get married?" asked Sun Wukong. "You can marry one of the girls. Her family will become our family. There will be a great wedding feast. We can all eat as much as we want, and we can all stay here for a few days. Then we will leave, but you can stay, and you will be comfortable for the rest of your life."

Zhu replied, "Thank you, Elder Brother, but I have already given up that life. Why would I give up one wife only to take another wife? But I must tell you, I am hungry and I want a good meal tonight. Also, think about our horse. He has not eaten all day. If we don't feed him, he will not be able to carry Master tomorrow." And with that, Zhu walked out of the hall and went outside.

Sun Wukong waited a few minutes, then he also went outside. He was thinking about Zhu's words. So he changed into a flying insect so he could watch Zhu without Zhu seeing him.

Zhu walked over to the horse and set him free, then he shouted in its ear. The horse was frightened and ran away towards the back of the house. Lady Jia was standing there. Zhu followed the horse and approached her.

"Young monk," she said, "where are you going?"

"Hello!" he said. "I am just taking a walk in this beautiful evening, and I am also grazing my horse."

"Your Master is being foolish, I think. Why does he not want to stay here and marry?"

"Mama, we are all afraid of the Tang Emperor. He commanded us to go to the Western Heaven. Also, I would like to stay here, but I worry that your daughters will find me too ugly to marry."

"We have no man here, so having an ugly man is certainly better than having no man at all. But I agree, my daughters might be unhappy with the idea of marrying a pig."

"Please tell your daughters to not think like that. Yes, I may be a little bit ugly, but I can work very hard. Using my rake, I can quickly prepare land for farming. If there is no rain, I can make rain. If there is no wind, I can make wind. If you want your house to be taller, I can make it taller. I can do all the work that you need."

"That sounds wonderful. I want you to stay. But first you must ask your Master."

"I will not do that. He is not my father. I decide whether to stay, not him!"

"All right. Then let me talk with my daughters." Lady Jia went inside the house.

Now, Sun Wukong was still an insect, sitting in a nearby tree. He heard every word of this conversation. He flew back to Tangseng, changed back into his original form, and told Tangseng everything that Zhu and Lady Jia had discussed. Tangseng listened to this story, but he was not sure if it was true or not.

Later, Zhu returned. Tangseng asked him, "Did you graze the horse?"

"No," replied Zhu, "there is no good grass here for the horse."

Sun Wukong looked at him and said, "Yes, this is no place to graze a horse. But it is a very good place to lead a horse[1]."

When Zhu heard this, he knew that Sun Wukong knew what was going on. He just looked down at the ground and didn't say anything. But just then, they all heard the sound of the door opening. Two servants came out carrying red lanterns. Following them was Lady Jia and her three daughters. The daughters all bowed to the travelers.

Lady Jia was as beautiful as before, but her three daughters were more beautiful than any girls that the travelers had ever seen before. They were all dressed in golden robes. They had beautiful jade and pearls in their long black hair. They were so beautiful that they looked like fairies coming down from Heaven. Tangseng could not look at them, so he just looked down at the ground. Sun Wukong looked but could not speak. Sha Monk turned away. Only Zhu looked at them. His eyes were wide, and he was so filled with desire that he had trouble standing. He said softly, "Mama, we are very happy to meet such beautiful immortals. Now please ask these dear daughters to leave."

The girls went out, but they left the two red lanterns behind. Lady Jia said, "Well, have you decided who will marry who?"

Sha Monk said, "We have discussed this matter, and we have decided that Zhu Bajie will enter your esteemed family."

Zhu held up both of his hands and said, "No, I cannot do this." But Sun Wukong scolded him, saying, "There is nothing more to discuss! I heard you talking at the back door with Lady Jia. You called her 'Mama'. We should have the wedding ceremony today. Now come here and bow to the Master.

---

[1] Dài mǎ zǒu zǒu means "to lead a horse." The original novel uses qiān, an archaic word for "lead," and when Sun Wukong says "qiān mǎ zǒu zǒu" he is using an old Chinese idiom for "to arrange a marriage."

Then you can get married and have the comfortable life that you want."

"No!" shouted Zhu again. "I will not do this!"

"Of course you will do this. You have already called Lady Jia 'Mama'. So we all know that you want to do this. Now no more talk. Let's get started with the wedding ceremony. The sooner you get married, the sooner we all can have some good food and wine."

Then Sun Wukong grabbed Zhu's arm and pulled him towards Lady Jia. "Mother, take him inside," he said to her. Lady Jia walked into the house, and Zhu walked after her. She said to a servant, "Bring out some tables and chairs for our guests, and prepare a vegetarian meal for them. I will take our new master inside."

Zhu and Jia walked through the house, and they passed many rooms. Zhu looked left and right with wide eyes. "Mother," he said, "please walk more slowly. I just arrived here and do not know this house. It is so large!"

"Yes," she replied, "these rooms have all of our gold, silver, food, fine clothing, and other things. Keep walking, we are getting close to the kitchen."

Then she added, "You know, we are doing this marriage so quickly that we have forgotten some important things. Right now, you should bow eight times towards the sky."

"Of course," said Zhu. "You are right. Please sit down. I will bow to you, and that show my gratitude to Heaven and Earth, and to you." This pleased Lady Jia, so she sat down and waited while Zhu bowed to her.

When he was finished, Zhu asked, "Please tell me, which of your daughters do you plan to give me?"

"Well," she replied, "that is a hard problem. I wanted to give you my eldest daughter, but that might make my second daughter unhappy. If I give you my second daughter, that might make my youngest daughter unhappy. But if I give you my youngest daughter, that might make my eldest unhappy. So I cannot make up my mind."

"I have a solution to this problem. Just give me all three daughters. That way, there will be no difficulties in your family."

"What? You want all three of my daughters?"

"This is not strange at all. Nowadays everyone has three or four girlfriends. Marrying all three of your daughters would not be a problem for me at all. I would certainly make them all quite happy!"

"Forget it, pig. I will not give you all three. But I have a different idea. Here is a handkerchief. Put it over your eyes so you cannot see. I will ask all three of my daughters to walk past you. Grab one, and she will be your wife."

Zhu put on the handkerchief so that it was in front of his eyes. Then Lady Jia called out, "Zhenzhen, Aiai, Lianlian! Come here, and find out which one of you will marry this man."

Zhu stood in the center of the room with the handkerchief over his eyes. He heard the three young women enter the room, and he smelled the scent of beautiful flowers. Eagerly he stretched out his arms, but he could not grab anything. He heard a sound on the left, but when he reached there, he only grabbed the air. He heard a sound on the right, but when he reached there, he only hit the wall with his hand. Left, right, left, right. Again and again he heard the sounds of the young women moving past him, and he kept trying to grab them, but he could not. Finally, he was so tired that he simply sat down on the ground, with nothing in his hands.

"Mama," he said, "your daughters are too quick for me. I could not catch even one of them. What should I do?"

Lady Jia replied, "My son, take off the handkerchief. You say that my daughters are too quick, but that is not why you could not grab them. They all care only for their sisters. None of them wants to be your wife if it means that the others could not. That is why they all run away from you."

"Mama, if none of them wants me, how about you? Would you be my wife?"

"Dear son, thank you, but I am much too old for you. Here's what we will do. Each of my daughters has made a beautiful silk shirt for you. Put each of them on. Whichever shirt fits you best, that is the daughter you can marry."

"Fine, fine," said Zhu. "Bring all three shirts. I will try them on. But I'm telling you, if all three of them fit me, then I want all three daughters."

"You really are a very hungry pig," said Lady Jia. "Let's see what happens."

Zhu took off his own shirt, and picked up the first silk shirt. He put it on. It fit him very well. But then suddenly the shirt changed to heavy rope, wrapped tightly around Zhu's body. It became tighter and tighter. Zhu was in terrible pain. He fell to the ground, and when he hit the ground, all four of the women disappeared.

While this was going on, the other three travelers – Tangseng, Sun Wukong

and Sha Monk – were sleeping in comfortable beds in another room. But as soon as Zhu fell to the ground, all three travelers woke up. They saw that they had been sleeping outside on the cold ground. And the great house had disappeared.

Tangseng was frightened and called out for Sun Wukong. Sha Monk also was afraid, and he cried, "Elder Brother, help us! We have met some ghosts!"

But Sun Wukong just smiled. He was the only one who understood what had happened. He said, "I think that this pine forest is very comfortable. And I also think that our friend Zhu Bajie is learning an important lesson right now."

"What do you mean?" asked Sha Monk.

Sun Wukong said, "Those four women were really holy monks, just like Guanyin. They wanted to test us, to learn if we were more interested in the life of spirit than the life of this world. Zhu wanted the life of this world, and now he must learn a painful lesson."

Tangseng closed his eyes and bowed to the place where the buildings had been. Then he looked up and saw a piece of paper on a nearby tree. He picked it off the tree and read it:

> The lady of the mountain had no desire
> But Guanyin asked her to leave her home
> Her daughters also were guests in this house
> All of them looked so beautiful!
> The holy monk only wished to find Buddha
> But the pig wanted the things of this world
> Now he must learn with a quiet heart
> If he does not, life will be hard for him!

Tangseng read these words aloud to the others. Then they heard someone shouting from the forest, "Master, help me! These ropes are too tight, they are killing me!"

"Wukong," said Tangseng, "do you hear something?"

"It's nothing, just Zhu Wuneng playing again," he replied. "Don't worry about him, let's go now."

But Tangseng said, "No, we should not do that. Your younger brother Zhu is stupid and causes trouble. But his heart is good, and we need his strong back to carry our luggage. Lady Jia gave us this test to help us, not to stop us. So let's help Zhu. I don't think he will do this again!"

The three of them walked into the forest. They found Zhu tied tightly to a tree, screaming in pain. Sun Wukong just laughed and said to him, "Younger Brother, it's getting late, but you have not finished your marriage ceremony yet. You have not thanked your parents, and you have not told Master about your marriage. What are you doing? Where is your mama? Where is your wife? Stop playing around here!"

Zhu Bajie stopped screaming and just cried quietly. Sha Monk walked up to him and cut the ropes, freeing him. Zhu fell to the ground and kowtowed again and again to the sky.

Sun Wukong stood over him and laughed again. He said to Zhu, "Younger Brother, didn't you recognize those women as holy monks?"

"How could I?" Zhu replied. "My eyes were open but I could not see anything."

Sun Wukong handed him the slip of paper that was on the tree. Zhu read it and cried some more. Sha Monk smiled and said, "Zhu is the lucky one here. He almost had four holy monks for his wives!"

"Brother," said Zhu, "please don't ever talk about this again. I will never do anything like this for the rest of my life. I will carry Master's baggage to the Western Heaven, even if it kills me."

"You are finally speaking the words that you should have spoken several days ago," said Tangseng. "Now let's not talk about this anymore. Let's go."

And the holy monk, the three disciples and the dragon horse, all began walking westward again.

Chapter 24

The monk Tangseng was riding his horse westward along the great Silk Road, with his three disciples – the powerful but difficult monkey Sun Wukong, the hungry pig Zhu Bajie, and the kind-hearted Sha Wujing.

One day they arrived at a tall mountain. "Let's be careful," said Tangseng, "there may be monsters on this mountain."

But Sun Wukong just replied, "What do you have to be afraid of, Master? You have three powerful disciples to protect you. Don't worry!"

The mountain was beautiful, with countless birds, monkeys and animals living in the trees and grasses near the bottom. The top of the mountain reached to the sky, and was white with snow. "This mountain is so beautiful!" said Tangseng, "Perhaps we are close to Thunderclap Mountain!"

But Sun Wukong just laughed and said, "Sorry, Master, but we are still one hundred and eight thousand miles away."

"How long will it take us to get there?" asked Zhu Bajie.

"I could go to Thunderclap Mountain and come back fifty times in a single day. You and Sha Wujing could get there in ten days. But for the Master, don't even ask me!"

"How long?" asked Tangseng.

"Start walking as a child, keep walking until you are old, then die and be born again, and keep walking. Do that a thousand lifetimes and you still might find it difficult to get to Thunderclap Mountain. But there is another way. If you learn how to see the Buddha in everything, and when every one of your thoughts returns to the place where it began, then you will arrive."

Tangseng and the other disciples walked silently for a time. Finally Sha Wujing said, "Well, it is still a beautiful mountain. I think it must be the home of a good man, or maybe even an immortal."

Sha Wujing was correct. The name of the mountain was Long Life Mountain. On the side of the mountain was a Daoist monastery called Five Villages monastery. And the master of the monastery was an immortal called Master Zhenyuanzi, the Lord Equal to Earth. Forty-eight of the Master's disciples also lived at the monastery.

There was something very special about this monastery. In a garden in the middle of the monastery was a large ginseng tree. This tree flowered just once every three thousand years. Then three thousand years later it produced fruit, and three thousand years after that, the fruit became ripe. Although the tree was very large, it only produced thirty ripe fruits after nine thousand years. The fruits were strange. Each fruit looked like a newborn baby, with a head, two arms and two legs. But the fruit had powerful magic: if a person ate one of these fruits they would live for forty-seven thousand years.

On the day that Tangseng and his disciples arrived at Long Life Mountain, Master Zhenyuanzi was not home. One of the Immortals in Heaven had invited him to hear a lecture on the Dao, and so he went to Heaven, taking forty-six disciples with him. He told the two youngest disciples, Clear Breeze and Bright Moon, to stay at the monastery. They were both quite young. Clear Breeze was one thousand three hundred twenty years old, and Bright Moon was only one thousand two hundred years old.

Master Zhenyuanzi said to the two disciples, "I must go and listen to this lecture. You two take care of the monastery while I am gone. An old friend of mine will arrive soon. He is a holy monk from the land of the Tang Emperor. Treat him well. You may give him two of the fruits from the ginseng tree. But just two, no more."

The Master turned to go, then he stopped and said, "Oh, one more thing. This monk will have some disciples with him. Be careful, because I have heard that these disciples can be troublemakers. Don't tell them about the fruits or the tree, they may cause trouble if they hear about these things!" And then he flew up to Heaven with the other disciples to hear the lecture.

The next day, Tangseng and his three disciples arrived at the monastery. The monastery was in middle of a forest, with a bamboo path leading to the front gate. Tangseng dismounted from his horse and they walked through the front gate. They came to a second gate. On the ground just outside the second gate was a large stone, with these words carved into it:

> Living long, ever young
> This immortal Daoist home
> Is the same age as Heaven itself

Sun Wukong said, "Such big words! When I was causing trouble in Heaven five hundred years ago, I was in many fine homes, even the home of Laozi, and I never saw words like this."

"Don't listen to him," said Zhu Bajie. "Let's go inside and meet this old Daoist."

As they walked through the second gate, Bright Moon and Clear Breeze arrived to greet them, saying, "Old Master, please forgive us for arriving late to meet you! Please come in." There were five large rooms. Tangseng and the disciples followed them into the main room in the center. On the back wall, two large characters, "Heaven" and "Earth" were embroidered in five colors.

Tangseng looked at the characters for a while, then he turned and said to the two young men, "Your monastery is truly a beautiful place! But why do you only write Heaven and Earth on the wall? Don't you worship the Three Pure Ones[1], the Gods of the Four Quarters, or the many Lords of Heaven?"

One of the young men replied, "The Three Pure Ones and the Four Gods are his old friends, and the Lords of Heaven are his junior colleagues. We use the word Heaven to flatter them."

"And where is your teacher now?"

"Our teacher has been invited to hear a lecture on the Dao in a palace in Heaven. He's not home."

Sun Wukong laughed and shouted, "Just listen to this stupid kid! Who invited his master to Heaven? What kind of lecture is he going to hear?"

Tangseng was worried that Sun Wukong would become angry and cause trouble, so he said, "Wukong, stop this right now. Go outside and graze the horse. Sha, take care of the luggage. Zhu, get some grain from our bags. We can fix some dinner for ourselves, pay these young men a little bit for the firewood that we use, and we will leave. We won't bother them anymore."

After this, the two young men served tea to Tangseng. Then the young men went into another room to talk. Clear Breeze said, "I don't like these people, but we must obey our master. We must give two ginseng fruits to the Tang monk." So they went to the garden and Clear Breeze climbed the tree. He gently hit one of the ginseng fruits with a golden rod. The fruit fell. Before it reached the ground, Bright Moon caught it in a silk handkerchief. Clear

---

[1] According to the Dao De Jing, "The Dao produced One; One produced Two; Two produced Three; and the Three produced the Ten Thousand Things." The Three Pure Ones are manifestations of those Three. They are also called the Jade Pure One (Lord of Primordial Beginnings), the Supreme Pure One (Lord of Numinous Treasure), and the Grand Pure One (Lord of the Way and Its Virtue) manifested as the sage Laozi.

Breeze hit another fruit and Bright Moon caught it in the handkerchief.

The two young men returned to Tangseng and showed him the two fruits, saying, "Master, we have very little to offer you except these fruits that we grow here in the monastery. Please enjoy them!"

Tangseng looked down at the fruits, which looked just like newborn babies. His eyes grew big, his mouth opened, and he backed away three feet. "This is terrible! Do you have so little food that you must eat little babies? How can you give these to me?"

The two young men thought to themselves, "This foolish monk has eyes but he cannot see." Bright Moon said aloud, "Master, don't worry, these are not babies. They are ginseng fruit. They will give you health and long life. It is all right for you to eat them!"

"No, I cannot! Their parents brought these babies into the world. How can you offer them to me as if they were fruits?"

"But they grew on a tree!"

"Of course they did not grow on a tree. It's clear to see that they are babies!"

The two young men did not discuss it anymore. They just took the fruits and went back to their own room. They knew that the fruits had to be eaten quickly. If not, they would become hard and inedible. So they each ate one of them.

Now, Zhu Bajie was in the kitchen, preparing dinner. He heard everything. He did not see the ginseng fruits, but he heard the two young men talking and eating the fruits, and he became very hungry. He ran outside and grabbed Sun Wukong and said, "There is treasure in this temple!"

"What kind of treasure?"

"It's something you have never seen before!"

"Younger brother, I have traveled all over the world and throughout all of Heaven. I have seen everything!"

"Elder Brother, have you ever seen a ginseng fruit?"

"No, I have never seen one. But I have heard that it will give you long life if you eat one."

"They have ginseng fruits right here in this monastery. They offered two of the fruits to our Master, but he could not see what they were. He only thought they were newborn babies! So the two young men took the fruits back to their room and ate them both. Ah, I am so hungry, I really, really want one right now! Can you help?" And then he told Sun Wukong about the small golden rod.

Sun Wukong walked quietly into the young men's' room, found the golden rod, and picked it up. Then he entered the garden, where he found a huge tree. The tree was a thousand feet tall, and the trunk was sixty feet around. He looked up and saw a ginseng fruit on the tree. It looked just like a baby. Sun Wukong climbed up the tree and tapped the fruit with the small golden rod. The fruit dropped to the ground. He jumped down to pick up the fruit, but he could not find it.

"Where is the fruit?" he asked. "Someone must have taken it!" He spoke a magic spell to summon the local spirit of the garden. The local spirit appeared and bowed to Sun Wukong, saying, "Great sage, what can I do for you?"

"Why did you take my fruit? Tell me now, or I will strike you with my rod!"

"Oh great sage, I did not take it. I must tell you about this fruit. If it touches gold, it will fall. If it touches wood, it will harden. If it touches water, it will melt. If it touches fire, it will dry out. And if touches earth, it will disappear. So, if you want the fruit, you must tap it with a golden mallet, then you must catch it with a silk handkerchief before it touches the ground."

Sun Wukong climbed the tree again and found three more fruits. He tapped them with the gold mallet, and they fell. He caught them in the front of his silk shirt, and ran back into the kitchen. "Call Sha Wujing," he said to Zhu Bajie, "we can each eat one of them."

Zhu called Sha, who came in and saw the ginseng fruits. "I have never eaten one of these before," he said. "But when I was the Curtain Raising Captain, I was in the palace during the Festival of the Immortal Peaches. I saw immortals give this gift to the Queen Mother as a birthday gift. Elder Brother, will you let me try one?"

"Of course!" said Sun Wukong, and he gave one to Zhu and one to Sha. Sun Wukong and Sha ate theirs slowly. But Zhu opened his mouth and swallowed it. He looked at Sun Wukong and asked, "So, how did you like it?"

"You just ate one!" said Sun Wukong. "You tell me."

"I ate it too fast, and I could not taste it. And now I am even more hungry. Please, give me another one!"

"You hungry pig, you don't know when to stop. This is not like eating rice or noodles. There are only thirty of these fruits in nine thousand years."

That was the end of the discussion, but Zhu was still hungry. He was talking to himself about wanting to eat more of the ginseng fruits when Clear Breeze and Bright Moon came back into the kitchen to prepare tea for Tangseng. They heard him talking to himself. Clear Breeze said, "Bright Moon, did you hear that pig talking about wanting to eat more ginseng fruit? I think this is what our Master told us. These disciples are troublemakers. Maybe they stole our treasure!"

They ran into the garden and looked up at the great tree. They carefully counted all the ginseng fruits in the tree. There were just twenty-two. Bright Moon said, "There were originally thirty fruits. Last week Master gave two to all of his disciples, and yesterday he told us to give two to the Tang Monk. So, there should be twenty-six. That foolish monk and his troublemaking disciples must have taken four of our fruits!"

They returned to Tangseng and began shouting at him, calling him a thief and other terrible things. "What are you talking about?" asked Tangseng. "What are these fruits you are talking about?"

"You know these fruits," said Bright Moon. "They look like little babies."

"Ah, Buddha! In my whole life I would not eat one of those terrible things!"

"That may be true. But your disciples are troublemaking thieves. They probably took the fruits."

"That may be," replied Tangseng, "but no need to get angry. Let's ask them." He raised his voice. "Disciples, come here, all of you."

Chapter 25

"Ah no," cried Zhu. "We are in big trouble now." So the three disciples went to see Tangseng. "Master," said Zhu, "why did you call us? The rice is not ready to eat yet."

"I did not call you to ask about the rice," said Tangseng. "These two young men say that several babies, I mean ginseng fruits, have been taken from the great tree. They think that you did it. Now tell me the truth. Did you take the fruits?"

Sun Wukong said, "I only took the fruits because Zhu wanted them." Then Zhu looked at him and said, "What? You took the fruits. And you told me you only took three fruits, but these young men say four were taken. Did you keep one for yourself and not tell us?"

Clear Breeze and Bright Moon started shouting at Tangseng and the three disciples, calling them thieves. Sun Wukong listened to them shouting, and he became more and more angry. He said to himself, "OK, I can solve this problem. I will make sure nobody has any more fruits to eat." He pulled a hair from his head, blew on it, and said, "Change!" The hair changed into a monkey that looked just like Sun Wukong. This second Sun Wukong stood quietly and listened to the shouting, while the first Sun Wukong flew into the garden. He brought out his golden hoop rod, and hit the tree as hard as he could. The tree fell to the ground with a huge sound. Broken branches and leaves were scattered everywhere. All the fruits fell off the tree, hit the ground, and disappeared.

He returned to the room where the two young men were still shouting. He took the second Sun Wukong back into his body so quickly that nobody saw the change.

After a while, Clear Breeze said to Bright Moon, "You know, we have been shouting at these monks for a long time now, and they have not said anything. Do you think that perhaps they did not take the fruits? Maybe we counted wrong. Let's go back to the tree and count the fruits again."

So they returned to the garden. But they did not see a great tree. They saw a mountain of broken branches, roots, and leaves. Both were very frightened. Bright Moon began to shake and he could not speak. Clear Breeze fell to the ground and shouted, "Disaster! Disaster! The magic tree of our monastery is broken! What will we tell our Master when he returns?"

Bright Moon said, "Stop shouting and quiet down, my friend. I think the monkey did this. But he is very powerful. If he becomes angry, we cannot win a fight against him, much less against all four of them. But I have another idea. Let's go back and give them their dinner of rice and vegetables. While they are eating, we will leave the room and lock the door from the outside. Then we will just wait for our Master to return. He will know what to do!"

They returned and said to Tangseng, "Master, we are sorry for using such bad language and shouting at you. We have counted the fruits again, and now we see that all the fruits are still on the tree. We are really, really sorry. Now, we would like to give you your dinner."

Of course, Sun Wukong and the other disciples knew that this was just a story. But Tangseng did not know. He said, "All right, then please just bring us some rice and vegetables. We will eat, and then we will leave right away."

The young men brought out rice, vegetables, and hot tea for the visitors. Tangseng and his disciples picked up their bowls and began to eat. The young men left the room, then they quickly closed the great door and locked it from the outside. Clear Breeze shouted at them through the locked door, "You terrible thieves! You took our fruit without asking. And then you killed our great tree. Who are you, to do such things? Do you really think that you can do such things and then journey to the Western Heaven to see the face of Buddha? Never! You will have to ride the Wheel of Rebirth and try again in another lifetime!"

When he heard this, Tangseng put down his food and began to cry. "Don't cry," said Sun Wukong, "Old Monkey will get us out of here." Of course, Tangseng was not just crying because he was locked in the room. He was crying because he knew that Clear Breeze was telling the truth. How could he and his disciples see the face of Buddha after everything they had just done?

Sun Wukong was not worried about this. He just wanted to get out of the room. He took out his golden hoop rod, pointed it at the door, said some magic words, and the door opened. "Master, get on your horse. Zhu and Sha, pick up the baggage. Start walking down the road. I will find you later. First, I must make sure the young men sleep for a long time."

Tangseng's eyes grew big. He said, "Don't you dare hurt them, or you will be a killer as well as a thief."

"Don't worry," replied Sun Wukong, "I won't hurt them." He went to the room where the young men were sleeping. A long time ago, he had played a game of guess-fingers[1] with one of the Heavenly kings, and he had won a few sleep-causing insects. He still had a few of them in his bag. He took out two of the insects. They flew straight towards the two young men, and bit them. The two young men fell into a deep sleep and could not be awakened. Then Sun Wukong left the monastery and together with Tangseng, Zhu and Sha they walked westward.

They walked all through the night. At dawn, Tangseng said, "Monkey, you have almost killed me! I am so tired." So they walked off the road, into the woods a little bit. Tangseng lay down on the ground with his head on a tree root and fell asleep. Zhu and Sha also slept. But Sun Wukong was not tired. He wanted to play, so he climbed some trees and jumped from branch to branch.

Now, during all this, the great immortal, Master Zhenyuanzi, was in one of the Heavenly palaces with his disciples, listening to a lecture on the Dao.

---

[1] Cāiquán is "guess fist" or "guess fingers," a game similar to rock-paper-scissors.

When the lecture was finished, he returned to the monastery with the forty-six disciples. He saw that the gates were open. He thought that Bright Moon and Clear Breeze had opened the gate to welcome him home. But he could not find them anywhere. "Well," he thought, "maybe they just forgot to close the gates last night before they went to bed." He went into their room and found them deeply asleep. He could not wake them up. So he asked one of his other disciples to get a cup of water. The Master recited a magic spell, then spat some water into the faces of Bright Moon and Clear Breeze. This broke the sleep spell, and the two young men woke up.

Bright Moon and Clear Breeze opened their eyes. They saw the face of their Master. Right away they knelt down, cried, and kowtowed again and again, saying, "Master, your old friend the Tang Monk is a terrible thief! He arrived just as you said he would, with three disciples. We obeyed your command and gave him two ginseng fruits. But the old man was a fool, he could not see the fruits clearly, he thought they were babies! He refused to eat them. So we had to eat the fruits ourselves. But then one of his disciples, a monkey, took four fruits and ate them. And then, oh, I really don't know how to say this, he struck down the great tree!" And he began to cry and kowtow again.

Master Zhenyuanzi was not angry. He just said, "Don't cry. Don't cry. That monkey has great power, he is an immortal himself, and a long time ago he caused much trouble in Heaven. Just tell me: if you see these four again, will you recognize them?"

"Certainly!" they both said.

"Then come with me." Then he told his other disciples to prepare some ropes and a whip.

Master Zhenyuanzi, Clear Breeze and Bright Moon flew quickly a thousand miles to the west. Zhenyuanzi looked down but he could not see Tangseng. He looked to the west and could not see him. Then he looked east, and nine hundred miles away he saw Tangseng and the other disciples. They all flew back, and looked down from the clouds. "Master," said one of the young men, "that's the Tang Monk sitting beneath that tree, drinking tea."

"I see him," said Master Zhenyuanzi. "You go back to the monastery now. I will catch these thieves myself." Then he came down to earth and changed into an old man, a poor Daoist monk. He wore an old robe, old straw sandals on his feet, and in his hand he held a yak's tail.

He walked up to Tangseng and said, "Elder, this poor monk greets you!"

Tangseng stood up quickly and replied, "Pardon me for not greeting you first."

"May I ask, where did the elder come from, and why was he sitting on the ground?"

"I am a monk sent by the great Tang Emperor to India to find the Buddha's books and bring them back to the East."

"Ah, I see. Tell me, when you came from the East, did you pass through my poor mountain home? I live in the Five Villages monastery. Perhaps you saw it."

Sun Wukong was standing nearby. Before Tangseng could answer, he said, "No, no, we came by a different road."

The great Immortal pointed a finger at Sun Wukong and said, "Lying monkey, what story are you telling me now? You struck down my ginseng tree, then you ran away into the night! Don't lie to me. Just bring me another tree right away."

Without saying a word, Sun Wukong took out his golden hoop rod and tried to strike the Immortal's head. Zhenyuanzi easily stepped aside to avoid the blow, then he flew up to the clouds. Sun Wukong followed him, and they began to fight in the sky. Zhenyuanzi had no weapon, just the little yak's tail. Sun Wukong struck at him again and again, but he could not hit Zhenyuanzi. After a while, Zhenyuanzi opened the sleeve of his robe and scooped up all four of them plus the horse.

"Well, now we are all together in a bag!" said Zhu.

"This isn't a bag, you fool, this is the sleeve of his gown," replied Sun Wukong.

Zhu tried to use his rake to make a hole in the sleeve, but no matter how hard he tried, he could not make any holes.

Zhenyuanzi flew back to the monastery. He reached into his sleeve and picked up Tangseng first, and had him tied to one of the large pillars in the main room. Then he picked up the other three disciples, one at a time, and had each of them tied to one of the other pillars. Finally he took out the horse and put it outside, and he told one of his disciples to give it some hay.

Then he turned to his disciples and said, "Disciples, these travelers are monks who have left their homes. We should not kill them. However, we must punish them for striking down our ginseng tree. So we will whip them."

One of the disciples asked, "Master, which one should we whip first?"

"Tangseng is the eldest one, he is the leader. We will start with him."

This worried Sun Wukong, because he knew that Tangseng could not take a whipping like this. So he said to Zhenyuanzi, "Sir, you are wrong. I took the fruits, I ate the fruits, and I struck down your tree. So if you want to whip someone, whip me."

Zhenyuanzi said, "All right, monkey." Then he turned to the disciple who was holding the whip and said, "Give him one lash for each fruit that was on the tree. Thirty lashes." Just as the disciple started to whip him, Sun Wukong looked behind himself and saw that the whip was going to hit his legs. So he changed his legs to be as hard as steel.

When the whipping was finished. Zhenyuanzi said, "Now give the old monk a whipping, because he does not know how to control his disciples."

Quickly, Sun Wukong said, "Sir, you are wrong again. When the fruits were taken, my master was talking with your two disciples. He knew nothing about the fruits. Perhaps he should have controlled us better, it's true. But he had nothing to do with this. Whip us instead. And start with me."

Zhenyuanzi thought to himself, "This ape is a thief, but he is telling the truth here." So he told his disciple to lash Sun Wukong again. But of course, Sun Wukong's legs were still as hard as steel and he was not hurt at all.

By now it was evening, and everyone was tired. So Zhenyuanzi said, "Let's stop for now. Put the whip in water, and tomorrow we will lash them again."

Tangseng began to cry again, saying, "Monkey, you did this, but I have to be punished because of it! I have not been whipped, but my body hurts from being tied up all day. What are you going to do now?"

"Stop crying," replied Sun Wukong. "Soon you can all get out." Then he made his body small. He easily escaped from the ropes that were holding him. He stood up, returned to his own size, and untied the ropes of the others. They all walked out of the monastery. Sun Wukong said to Sha, "Go over there and bring back four small willow trees."

Sha used his great strength to pull up four small willow trees, and gave them to Sun Wukong. Sun Wukong brought the willow trees into the monastery. He tied each willow tree to a pillar. Then he bit his finger and spat a little bit of blood onto each tree, saying, "Change!" Each of the four willow trees changed into one of the travelers. They looked just like the travelers, they could see and hear, and they could even answer simple questions. Then the travelers got onto the main road again and began to walk west. They walked all night, and only stopped to rest when the morning came.

In the morning, Zhenyuanzi woke up, ate his breakfast, and walked into the main hall. "Pick up the whip. Today we will whip the old monk." The disciple said to Tangseng, "I am going to flog you." "Go ahead," replied the tree that looked like Tangseng. The disciple gave him thirty lashes with the whip. Then he said to Zhu, "I am going to flog you." "Go ahead," replied the tree that looked like Zhu. And the disciple gave him thirty lashes. Then he said to Sha, "I am going to flog you." "Go ahead," replied the tree that looked like Sha. And the disciple gave him thirty lashes.

Finally, he started to whip Sun Wukong again. As soon as he started, the real Sun Wukong began to feel terrible pain. "Something is wrong," he said. "I used my magic to make these four bodies, but I did not think that they would whip me again. This really hurts! I need to stop the magic now."

He stopped the magic, and the four bodies changed into willow trees again. Master Zhenyuanzi saw this and said, "This Monkey King has powerful magic! But now I will catch him and bring him back again." Zhenyuanzi flew west, only a hundred miles this time, and he easily found Tangseng and the disciples.

Sun Wukong saw that Zhenyuanzi had returned. He said to Tangseng, "Master, let's forget about that little word 'kindness' for a while, ok?" Tangseng was too frightened to say anything. So Sun Wukong picked up his golden hoop rod, Zhu Bajie picked up his rake, and Sha Wujing picked up his staff. The three of them began to fight with Zhenyuanzi. But they could not win. Zhenyuanzi easily blocked their blows with his little yak tail. After only a half hour of fighting, Zhenyuanzi scooped them up in his sleeve and brought them back to the monastery.

He had them tied up, but this time he told his disciples to wrap up each man in cloth. Their entire bodies were covered except for their faces. Zhu said, "Sir, thank you for leaving my face uncovered. But if I have to wait for a long time, I would be more comfortable if you also made another hole lower down."

The disciples brought out a huge frying pan, filled it with oil, and put it on a big fire. Sun Wukong thought this would be no problem for him, but he was worried about his friends. He also was worried that the frying pan might have some powerful magic. What could he do? He looked and saw a large stone lion near the gate. So he used his magic to quickly fly up to the clouds, and put the stone lion in his own place. It was done so quickly that nobody saw it.

The oil was now very hot. "Pick up the monkey and put him in the frying pan," said Zhenyuanzi. Four disciples tried to pick him up, but he was too heavy. It took twenty disciples to pick him up and put him in the frying pan. The frying pan broke, all the oil burned in the fire, and all that was left was a stone lion.

Zhenyuanzi was very, very angry. "All right," he said, "let the monkey go. We will put the Tang monk in the frying pan instead." This worried Sun Wukong because he knew that Tangseng would die quickly in the frying pan. So he came down from the clouds, stood in front of Zhenyuanzi, and said, "Don't do that. Put me in the pan instead."

Chapter 26

"I really don't want to put anyone in the frying pan," said Zhenyuanzi. "I just want my ginseng tree returned to me."

"Oh, is that all you want? You should have told me that a long time ago. It's no problem. Just untie my master and my friends, and I will return your ginseng tree to you." Zhenyuanzi thought about this. He did not trust the monkey, but he knew that Tangseng could not travel quickly. So he told his disciples to untie Tangseng, Zhu and Sha.

Zhu said to Tangseng, "This is a trick, but the trick is on us. Old Monkey knows that the tree is dead, and nobody can bring it back to life. He tells Zhenyuanzi that he is going to find medicine for the tree. But he will just leave and we will never see him again. Do you think he cares about us?"

"He would not leave us," said Tangseng. "Let's ask him what he is planning." Raising his voice, he called, "Wukong, what game are you playing? Where are you going?"

Sun Wukong replied, "Old Monkey is speaking the truth, and only the truth. You know the old saying, 'the cure comes from the sea'? I must go to the Great Eastern Ocean, visit the Immortals who live there, and find out how to bring the ginseng tree back to life."

"That's a big job. How long will it take you?"

"No longer than three days."

"All right, I will give you three days. After that, I will recite the spell to tighten the headband around your head, and you will have a terrible headache!"

"I hear you! I hear you!" replied Sun Wukong. Then he said to Zhenyuanzi, "I am leaving now. You must take good care of my Master. Make sure he gets three good meals every day, and drinks tea six times. If his clothes become dirty, wash them. If anything happens to my Master, I will make trouble for you when I return!"

"Go, go," said Zhenyuanzi. "I will see to it that your Master is well fed."

Sun Wukong used his cloud somersault to travel quickly to the Great Eastern Ocean, many thousands of miles away. He arrived at Penglai, the home of three of his friends, all of them immortal Stars. He saw the Star of Blessing and the Star of Wealth playing a game of chess, while the Star of Long Life looked on. Sun Wukong called out, "Brothers, I bow to you!" The three Stars stopped their game and greeted him.

"Great sage," they said, "why did you come here? We heard that you stopped studying Daoism to follow the Buddha, and you are now traveling with a Tang monk to the Western Heaven. The journey must be difficult. How did you find the time to visit us?"

Sun Wukong said, "I must tell you, we have a little problem." Then he told them the story of how he arrived at the monastery, took the ginseng fruits and ate them, and then struck down the great tree. Then he told the story of how Master Zhenyuanzi returned and captured them – twice – and how he got away both times.

"And so," he concluded, "I told Master Zhenyuanzi that I would find a way to let his tree live again. I must do this, or he will put my Master in hot oil! If you know any way to restore this tree, please tell me."

"Ah, you have a problem," said the Star of Blessing. "Master Zhenyuanzi is the grandfather of the Earth Immortals, You cannot win against him in a fight and you cannot escape from him. If you had just killed an animal or a bird, I could give you some medicine to restore it to life. But the great ginseng tree is the root of all divine trees. I don't know how to help you!"

Sun Wukong said nothing to this. So the Star of Blessing continued, "However, you might find a solution in another place."

"That may be, but remember, I only have three days. After that, my Master will recite a magic spell and my head will hurt!"

"Don't worry about that," said the Star of Long Life. "Master Zhenyuanzi knows us. We will go and tell him that you are searching for a way to heal his tree. Zhenyuanzi will ask your master to give you another few days." And so, the three Stars traveled to the monastery, talked with Zhenyuanzi, and got Tangseng to agree to give Sun Wukong a few more days.

My child, I will not tell you about everything that Sun Wukong did for the next few days, or all the Immortals that he talked with. But nobody could help him bring the ginseng tree back to life. After several days of searching, he decided to go to Potalaka Mountain and talk with Guanyin, the great Buddhist teacher. He arrived at Potalaka Mountain. Immediately, a large bear stood in front of him, saying, "Sun Wukong, you old monkey, where do you think you are going?"

Sun Wukong saw that it was the monster of Black Wind Mountain, who now served Guanyin as guardian of her mountain. He said, "Oh, it's just you! Don't shout at me, you old bear. You should thank me and call me 'Great Father.' If not for me, you would be dead back on Black Wind Mountain. But instead, you serve the great Guanyin, you listen to her lectures on Buddhism, and you have a comfortable life. What do you say now?"

The bear monster just replied, "Let's forget the past. The great Guanyin asked me to meet you. Come with me." They walked together to a bamboo grove, where Guanyin was seated. The bear left. Sun Wukong bowed to her and waited for her to speak.

"Tell me, monkey, where is the Tang monk?"

"He is at Long Life Mountain."

"There is a monastery there, the home of the great Immortal Master Zhenyuanzi. Did you meet him?"

Sun Wukong hit his head on the ground several times and said, "Yes. Your foolish disciple made him angry by hurting his tree. Well, to tell the truth, I killed his tree. The Master was not home, he left two young disciples to meet us. Zhu Wuneng learned about the fruits, and he wanted to try one. So I took some fruits for him, Sha and myself. The young disciples found out and started shouting at us. I became angry, and, well, I struck down the ginseng tree. Now Master Zhenyuanzi is holding my master and wants to put him in hot oil. He will not let him go until I restore the tree to health. Please help us!"

"Of course I can help you," she said. "This is no problem. Many years ago, Laozi put a small willow tree in his brazier, and left it there until it was completely blackened and dried. Then he gave it back to me. I put the willow tree in my vase. After one day and one night, the willow tree was alive again and had green leaves. If I can do this for Laozi's willow tree, I can do it for that ginseng tree."

Guanyin stood up, picked up the vase, and left. Sun Wukong followed her, smiling.

A short time later, at the monastery, Master Zhenyuanzi looked up and saw Guanyin and Sun Wukong in the clouds, flying towards them. "Quick," he shouted, "The great teacher Guanyin has arrived. Come and meet her!" The three Stars, Tangseng, Zhu, Sha, and all of Zhenyuanzi's disciples all came out to meet Guanyin.

When Guanyin arrived, Master Zhenyuanzi said to her, "Great immortal, welcome to our monastery. But tell me, why should our small and unimportant affairs be of interest to this great teacher?"

"The Tang monk is my disciple," she replied. "And the monkey is his disciple. So this is of interest to me. Now I am ready to bring your precious tree back to life." She led the way into the garden. Master Zhenyuanzi followed her, then the three Stars, Tangseng and his three disciples, and all the other disciples. They all arrived at the garden. They all saw the great tree, lying on its side, with broken branches everywhere.

"Wukong, give me your hand," said Guanyin. He gave her his left hand. Guanyin took a small willow twig, dipped it in the vase, then used it as a brush to draw a magic spell on Sun Wukong's hand. "Now put your hand on tree, near the bottom, and wait." Wukong walked over to the tree and put his hand on one of the broken roots.

Soon, a spring of sweet water began to come up from the ground. Guanyin said, "This is magic water. It should not be touched by fire, water, wood, metal or earth. It must be scooped up by something made of jade. Now push the tree so it is standing upright again, scoop up the magic water with the jade, and pour it on the tree."

One of the disciples said, "We have jade cups for drinking tea, and jade wine glasses. Will that be all right?"

"Cups, glasses, it does not matter. As long as they are jade and can hold water. Now go get them!"

Sun Wukong pushed the tree until it was standing upright. The monastery's disciples ran into the kitchen and came back with thirty jade teacups and fifty jade wine glasses. They all scooped up water in the teacups and wine glasses, and poured it on the base of the tree. Guanyin stood and recited a magic spell. Soon, the tree turned green, with many leaves and new branches. Everyone looked up, and counted twenty-three ginseng fruits.

"Why are there twenty-three and not twenty-two?" asked Clear Breeze.

Sun Wukong said, "Old Monkey tried to take four fruits the other day, but one of them fell into the ground and disappeared. It looks like that one is back on the tree, along with twenty-two other fruits. Zhu, you said I kept that fruit for myself, but as you can see, I did not!"

Master Zhenyuanzi was very happy. He asked for the gold mallet, and had ten fruits knocked down. Then he invited everyone to the main hall for a Festival of Ginseng Fruits. Guanyin sat in the place of highest honor. The three Stars were on her left, Tangseng was on the right. The host, Master Zhenyuanzi, sat across from her. Guanyin stood and recited this poem,

> At the cave in Long Life Mountain
> Ginseng fruits ripen every nine thousand years
> The tree was struck down, the roots came out
> But sweet water brings it back to life
> Three Stars meet their old friends
> Four monks find new friends
> Now they have learned to eat the ginseng fruits
> They will live long and never grow old.

Tangseng looked at the ginseng fruit for a long time. Then he slowly opened his mouth and took a small bite. He smiled. "It's very good. I like it!" he said.

Everyone had a wonderful feast, and then, tired, they all slept through the night. The four travelers were ready to leave the next day, but Master Zhenyuanzi had become good friends with Sun Wukong, and they both said they wanted to spend a few days together. Finally, after five more days of feasting, talking and resting, the four travelers said goodbye to their new friends, and continued their journey to the West.

Chapter 27

The travelers walked westward along the great Silk Road for several months. They were cold, they were tired, they were hungry, and they were all becoming a little grumpy.

One day they arrived at a very tall mountain covered with forest. They all looked up at the mountain. The top was so high that it was in the clouds. In the forest they could see many animals. Sun Wukong saw that Tangseng was afraid of the animals, so he shouted loudly and the animals all ran away.

They kept walking. Later that same day, they arrived at the top of the mountain. Tangseng said to Sun Wukong, "I am tired and hungry. Go and beg some vegetarian food for us."

Sun Wukong looked at him and said, "Master, you are not very smart. We are on top of a mountain, far from any village. There is no inn and there are no people. How can I get food?"

"You difficult monkey!" replied Tangseng. "Don't you remember when you were under the mountain for five hundred years? Who helped you get out of there? I did! Now you are my disciple, and your life belongs to me. But you will not even go and get some food for us. You don't help us at all!"

"I do help you! I work hard for you every day."

"Then go and get us some food. I am very tired and very hungry. And the air on this mountain is not good. I am starting to feel a little sick. Go now!"

"Master, please don't get upset. Just get off your horse, sit down, and rest for a while. I will find someone to give us some good food." Sun Wukong jumped up to the clouds. Shading his diamond eyes with his hand, he looked in all four directions. He saw many trees and many animals, but no people and no houses. But far away, to the south, he saw a little bit of red color on the ground.

He returned to Tangseng and said, "Master, there are no people near here. But to the south I see some red. I think there are some ripe peaches there. I will go and get them." He did a cloud somersault and flew off to pick up some peaches.

My child, you know the old saying, 'A tall mountain will always have monsters.' I have told you many stories, and often there is a monster in the mountains. Well, this story is no different! There really was a monster living on this mountain. The monster was flying through the clouds when she saw Sun Wukong flying off to the south. Then she looked down and saw Tangseng sitting on the ground. She was very happy to see him! She said to herself, "I have heard stories of a Tang monk from the east who was going to the Western Heaven. I have heard that anyone who eats his flesh will gain long life. And now I see him, sitting all alone on my mountain!"

But when she came closer, she saw two powerful warriors standing near Tangseng and protecting him. Of course, these were two of Tangseng's disciples, the pig-man Zhu Bajie and the big man Sha Wujing. She was a little bit afraid of these two, so she changed into a beautiful young woman. Her face was like the moon, and her eyes were as bright as stars. She was barefoot and wore a silk robe. In her hand she held a small blue pot.

Tangseng was resting on the ground when he saw the young woman. He called out, "Zhu, Sha, I thought Sun Wukong said that there were no people in this region. But I see a person walking towards us."

Zhu Bajie was the senior disciple while Sun Wukong was away. He said to Tangseng, "Master, you sit here with Sha. Let this old pig take a look."

Zhu walked up to her and said, "My lady, where are you going? What are you holding in your hands?"

"Elder, in this pot I have some very tasty rice. I want to give it to you and the other monks."

Zhu was happy to hear this, because he is always hungry. So he ran back to Tangseng, shouting, "Master, we don't have to be hungry anymore. Don't wait for Sun Wukong's peaches. He will be gone for a long time, if he comes back at all. Also, if you eat too many peaches you will get sick. This beautiful woman has some tasty rice for us."

So Tangseng and Zhu went to see the woman. Of course, she was really a monster, but Tangseng and Zhu were very hungry so they did not see this. They only saw a woman. "Lady," said Tangseng, "where do you live? What is your family? And why have you come here to give rice to hungry monks?"

"Master," she said, "you are on White Tiger Mountain. I live nearby with my parents and my husband. My parents have no son, and I am their only daughter. They wanted me to marry, but they also wanted someone to take care of them when they got old. So they found a husband for me, and asked him to come and live in our house."

"Lady," said Tangseng, "if your words are true, then your husband should be the one walking around and feeding monks. You should not go out by yourself."

The woman smiled and replied, "You are right, Master. But today my husband is working on the northern side of the mountain, with several of his workers. I made this lunch for them. Nobody is at home except me and my parents, but they are old. So I must bring the food myself. But now that I have met you, I want to give some of this rice to you and the other monks."

"Ah, thank you, but I cannot eat this food. If I ate your husband's rice, what would he say? He would scold you. This poor monk cannot become that kind of person!"

The young woman tried again to give the rice to Tangseng, but again he said no. Zhu was getting very hungry, and he said to himself, "There are many monks in the world, but none are as wishy-washy as my Master! Here is rice, ready to eat. But Master will not eat it. He wants to wait for that troublesome monkey to return. Then we will have one more mouth to feed, and we will have to divide the rice in four."

Just then, Sun Wukong returned. He flew through the sky, carrying a bag of peaches in one hand and his golden hoop rod in the other. He looked down and saw the young woman. Right away he knew that she was a monster. He got ready to strike her with his rod. But Tangseng stopped him, saying, "Monkey, why do you want to hit this beautiful young woman? She only wants to help us!"

"Master," he said, "in the past you could see clearly, but today you have eyes but you cannot see. A long time ago, when I was a king in Flower Fruit Mountain, I did the same thing that this monster is doing now. If I was hungry and wanted to eat human flesh, I would change into a beautiful woman, or an old man, or a drunk. If someone was foolish and did not see my true nature, I would invite him to come back to my cave. Then I would cook and eat them!"

Tangseng did not believe these words. He did not believe that the beautiful woman was really a monster. So Sun Wukong said, "Master, I understand. I think you have desire for this woman. If that is true, it is no problem. We three disciples can build a little house for the two of you, and you can be together, nobody will see you. You don't even need to be married first! Then when you are finished, we can continue our westward journey."

Tangseng's face turned red, his mouth opened, but he could not say anything. He just stood and looked at Sun Wukong. Sun Wukong used his golden hoop rod to strike the monster on the head. But the monster used the magic called 'releasing the corpse.' Her spirit flew into the sky so quickly that nobody could see her, and she left her body behind. It lay on the ground, dead.

Tangseng said, "Monkey, you killed that person without knowing anything about them."

"Master, come and look, see what is in that pot." He opened the pot and they all looked inside. There was no rice in the pot. There were just a lot of large worms.

Tangseng was surprised, and he thought that perhaps Sun Wukong was right. But Zhu caused trouble again. He said to Tangseng, "Master, this woman was just trying to help us. But the monkey was angry, as always. He wanted to hit someone with his rod, as always. So he killed the woman. Then he changed her tasty rice to a bunch of worms. Why? So you would not use the 'tight headband spell' on him!"

Tangseng believed Zhu's words. Right away he used the 'tight headband spell' and the magic headband on Sun Wukong's head became tight. His head started to hurt. "My head! My head!" he cried.

"Monkey, you must be kind to everyone. Do not hurt any living creature! You killed this beautiful woman, so you cannot stay with us. Go back to your home. I don't want you as a disciple. Leave us!"

"Master, if I am not here to protect you, you will not reach the Western Heaven!"

"My life is in the hands of Heaven. If I must be food for a monster, it's ok with me. Now go."

"But I cannot leave you. You saved my life, and I must use my life to protect you. I cannot let you be in danger." When Tangseng heard these words, he changed his mind. He told Sun Wukong that he could stay.

The monster was sitting up in the clouds, listening to Tangseng and Sun Wukong. She was angry. She knew that if the monk ate even a little bit of the rice, she could take him back to her cave and eat him. But Sun Wukong stopped her. "That monkey is stronger and smarter than I thought," she said to herself. "I must go back and try again."

So she changed again. This time she changed into an eighty-year-old woman. She walked slowly through the forest and came to the place where Tangseng and his disciples were. Tangseng, Zhu Bajie and Sha Wujing all looked at her and saw an old woman. But Sun Wukong knew that she was really the same monster. So he did not say anything. He just used his rod again and struck the old woman on the head. The monster used the 'releasing the corpse' magic again. Her spirit flew into the air, and the body of the old woman lay on the ground, dead.

Tangseng saw this. He was so angry, he could not say anything to Sun Wukong. He just fell off his horse and lay on the ground. While he lay on the ground, he spoke the tight headband spell twenty times. The magic headband around Sun Wukong's head became so tight that his head looked like a gourd. He was in great pain. "Stop it, Master!" he cried. "Just say what you must say to me."

"What can I say? I have tried to teach you, but you do not listen. You only want to hurt people. Today you have already killed two people. I cannot have you as a disciple anymore. You must leave."

"Master, a long time ago I lived on Flower Fruit Mountain. I was the king of forty-seven thousand little monkeys and the demons of seventy-two caves. But then I met you and I became your disciple. I wear this headband on my head. If you want me to leave, I will leave. But please, speak the loose headband spell so that I can take the headband off my head and go home again."

"Monkey, I learned the tight headband spell from the great monk Guanyin. She did not teach me a loose headband spell. I cannot take the headband off your head."

"Then you must keep me as a disciple."

"All right," Tangseng agreed. "But you must not hurt anyone again."

Sun Wukong helped Tangseng get up on his horse, and they prepared to travel west again. Up in the sky, the monster watched them. She said to herself, "I really want to eat that monk's flesh. I must do something soon, because if they travel a few miles more, they will leave my mountain and I will not be able to do anything to them." So she changed into an old man with a long white beard. He walked slowly, reciting Buddhist prayers to himself.

Tangseng saw the old man, and again, he could not see that the creature was really a monster. "Ah, look," he said, "this old man can hardly walk, but still he prays to the Buddha." Turning to the old man, he said, "Hello, Elder!"

The old man replied, "Holy monk, this old man has lived here for many years. All my life I have tried to do good. I give food to monks and I read the Buddha's holy books. But today has been a very bad day. My daughter left to take rice to her husband, but we have not seen her. Then my wife went to look for her, and I have not seen my wife either. I fear that they both have been eaten by tigers."

Sun Wukong just laughed and said, "You are not an old man. I can see you are a monster." And he prepared to strike the old man on the head with his rod. But then he stopped. He said to himself, "This is a problem. If I hit the old man, my Master will recite the tight headband spell. But if I don't hit the old man, he will eat my Master. What should I do?"

Quickly, he called the local spirits of the mountain, and told them to watch the monster and catch its spirit if it left the old man's body. Then he used his rod to strike the old man on the head. The monster's spirit could not leave the body, so it stayed inside the old man's body, and died.

Tangseng, Zhu and Sha all saw this. Zhu said, "That monkey is really having a bad day. It's not even lunchtime and already he has killed three people!"

"Master," said Sun Wukong, "this was not a person. This was a monster. Come and look!" He led them over to look at the body, but there was no body, just a pile of white bones. "See? I killed it, and now you can see its true form."

But Zhu said, "Don't believe him, Master. He is just telling you a story. He changed the old man's body into a pile of bones. He really killed three people today."

Tangseng listened to Zhu's words, and looked at the bones. Then he said to

Sun Wukong, "Monkey, you must go. The actions of a good man are like grass in the spring, there are more every day. But your actions are not like this at all. You have killed three people today, and we are in the mountains. What if we arrive at a city? Will you kill hundreds of people? No, you cannot be my disciple. Go now."

Sun Wukong said, "Master, your words hurt me. You listen to that foolish Zhu, but you have forgotten all the good things I did for you. Many times I saved you from monsters and demons. I gave you Zhu and Sha as junior disciples. But I see that you forgot all that. So if you want me to go, I will go."

Sun Wukong tried to bow to his master, but Tangseng turned away. So Sun Wukong took three hairs from his head, blew on them and said, "Change!" They changed and they all looked just like Sun Wukong. The four monkeys surrounded Tangseng on all four sides, so he could not turn away. All four monkeys bowed low to Tangseng. Then Sun Wukong took the three hairs back into his body, jumped into the air, and flew away to Flower Fruit Mountain.

Chapter 28

Tangseng mounted his horse and started walking west again. Zhu walked in front of him and Sha walked behind him. They entered a large and dark forest. Tangseng was afraid of the forest. He also was hungry. Since Sun Wukong was gone, he asked Zhu to find some vegetarian food. Zhu told him to wait and rest, then he picked up the begging bowl and walked west. He walked for several hours but he saw no villages, no houses, no people, and no food. He became tired and just wanted to sleep.

"If I return to Master with no food, he will be angry at me," he said to himself. "I should just rest here for a little while, to pass the time. Then I will return later." He lay down to rest, but soon he fell into a deep sleep.

Tangseng was getting more and more hungry. "Where is that pig?" he asked Sha Wujing. "Master," said Sha, "that pig is always hungry, and always thinking only about himself. He is not thinking about you at all. He is probably eating all the food himself. When he is full, he will come back. Probably."

Sha Wujing picked up his staff and went into the forest to look for Zhu. Now Tangseng was alone in the forest. He waited for a short time. Then he got on his horse and started riding west, then he rode south, then he rode east. Soon he did not know where he was or which direction he was going. He kept riding. Soon he came to a beautiful golden pagoda. There were no trees near it, so the golden sunlight came down from the sky and made the pagoda shine brightly.

Tangseng dismounted from the white horse and tied it to a nearby tree. Then he walked into the pagoda. When he stepped inside, he saw a big old monster sleeping in a chair. The monster had a red face, a purple beard, and long white teeth. He wore an old yellow robe, and he was not wearing shoes. Tangseng turned and ran out the door. But the monster heard him. He woke up and shouted, "Little ones! Who is outside our door?"

A little demon replied, "Great King, it is a monk. His body has a lot of tasty meat. I think he will make a good dinner for you."

"Bring him here!" shouted the monster. The little demons brought Tangseng back into the pagoda. Tangseng was very frightened. The monster said,

"Where did you come from? Where are you going? Tell me quickly!"

Tangseng said that he was sent by the Tang Emperor to the Western Heaven, to find the Buddha's books and bring them back to the east.

The monster laughed and said, "I am happy that you are here. I want to eat you!" And he told the little demons to tie up Tangseng.

"Be careful, sir. I have two great and powerful warriors with me," said Tangseng.

"That is even better. You plus your two disciples equals three. And if I add your horse, that equals four! We can have a good meal." Then he told the little demons to close the door to the pagoda and wait for Tangseng's two disciples to arrive.

While this was happening, Sha Wujing searched the forest and finally he found Zhu Bajie. Zhu was still sleeping. Sha woke him, then they returned to the place where they had left Tangseng. Of course, Tangseng was not there. They started searching for him. After searching for an hour, they found the golden pagoda. "Wonderful!" said Zhu. "This place is beautiful. I think our master must be inside, eating lots of good vegetarian food. Let's get some for ourselves."

"I don't like the look of this place," replied Sha. "I think it the cave of a monster."

But Zhu did not listen to him. He walked right up to the door of the pagoda and shouted, "Open the door! Open the door!"

"Great King," said one of the little demons, "a monk has arrived. He has large ears and a long mouth. And there is another very large monk with him. What should we do?"

"Our dinner has arrived! Invite them to come in!" said the monster. When Zhu and Sha came in, the monster said, "Where are you from, and why do you make so much noise outside my door? Please enter and eat some tasty buns filled with human flesh."

Zhu started to come inside. But quickly Sha said to him, "Elder brother, did you forget? You don't eat human flesh anymore!" Zhu felt as if he was waking up from a dream. He brought out his rake, and tried to strike the

Yellow Robed Monster. The two of them rose up into the sky to fight. Sha joined the fight. They fought for a long time. Zhu used his nine-pronged rake, Sha used his staff, and the Yellow Robed Monster used his scimitar. They fought until the sky was filled with cloud and mist. Rocks broke, mountains fell down, but they continued to fight.

Chapter 29

While they fought in the sky, Tangseng was sitting tied up inside the pagoda. He could now see that it was a cave. He started to cry. He heard a sound nearby. He looked up, and saw a woman standing in front of him. She was about thirty years old. She said, "Elder, where did you come from? And why are you tied up?"

"Don't ask me any questions," replied Tangseng tiredly. "If you are hungry, just go ahead and eat me."

"I don't eat people! I come from Precious Image Kingdom, three hundred miles west of here. I am the third daughter of the king. Thirteen years ago, the Yellow Robed Monster came to my city, grabbed me, and brought me back here to be his wife. I could not stop him. I have not been able to send a letter to my parents, so they don't know where I am. They probably think I am dead."

"This poor monk is traveling to the Western Heaven to find the Buddha's books and bring them back to the east. I came to this place, and now I think I will be the monster's dinner."

"Dear elder, don't worry. I can ask my husband to let you go. But you must do something for me. Please deliver a letter to my parents when you arrive at their city. Will you do that?"

"Of course," said Tangseng. So the woman untied him. She wrote a letter and gave it to him. Then Tangseng went out the back door of the pagoda and into the forest. He waited there to see if Zhu and Sha would win the fight against the monster.

The woman walked out the front door. She looked up and saw her husband in the sky, fighting Zhu and Sha. She called to him, "Dear husband, I just had a dream."

The monster stopped fighting and came down to the ground. "Tell me," he said.

"I didn't tell you earlier, but when I was a child, I made a secret vow. My vow was that if I found a good husband, I would thank Heaven by giving food to hungry monks. Just now in my dream, a golden deity came to me and said that I must do what was in my vow. I woke up and came to tell you about the dream. But as I walked through the house, I saw a monk tied up. Can you let him go? Letting him go would be the same as me feeding him. Will you do that for me?"

"Of course, my dear. Go ahead and let the monk leave." Then the monster called up to Zhu and Sha, "You two, in the sky. Come down here. I will not fight you anymore. You can leave. Go with the monk, and don't come back here again. If I am hungry, I can always find other humans to eat."

Zhu and Sha were very tired from fighting with the monster, so they were happy that the fight had ended without them being killed. They thanked the monster. They quickly found Tangseng in the forest. Then the three of them started walking westward.

Now, my child, you might think this is the end of the story. But there is more to tell. The three travelers walked west for almost three hundred miles. Then, coming down from the mountains, they saw a beautiful city. It was Precious Image Kingdom. The city was large, with many palaces, temples and farmlands. The travelers were happy to see the city. They arrived at an inn, tied up their horse, and sat down to rest.

Later, after they rested, the Tang monk went to the palace of the king. "This poor monk would like to see the king," he said. "I have an important letter for him." He was taken to the throne room to see the king.

"Your Majesty, this humble monk comes from the Tang Kingdom and is traveling to the Western Heaven. I must tell you that your daughter, the third princess, was taken many years ago by the Yellow Robed Monster. I met her, and she asked me to give you this letter." He gave this letter to the king:

"Your poor daughter kowtows a hundred times to you, my father the King, and to you, my mother the Queen. Thirteen years ago, on the fifteenth day of the eighth month, you gave a great banquet on a summer evening. During the banquet, an evil wind brought the Yellow Robed Monster to our home. He carried me away to his mountain, and made me his wife. I could not fight him. I have been with him for thirteen years, and have given him two monster sons. Recently your poor daughter met this holy Tang monk who was also taken by the monster. I gave him this letter. I beg you to quickly send your generals and your army to capture this monster and bring your daughter back home. Your daughter kowtows again and again."

The king and queen cried when they heard the letter. Afterwards, the king said, "Elder, we have no generals and no army. We have some guards, but no real soldiers. We are a peaceful kingdom here in the mountains. We cannot fight this monster. But you are a powerful monk. Can you help us?"

"This poor monk knows a little bit about Buddhism, but truly, he knows nothing of fighting monsters."

"If you cannot fight, how can you possibly hope to travel to the Western Heaven and back again?"

"Your Majesty, I do have two disciples who protect me. They are called Zhu Bajie and Sha Wujing. They are a little bit ugly. Actually, they are very ugly. That is why I did not bring them into your fine palace. They are waiting outside."

"Well, now that you have told us about them, we are ready to meet them. Bring them in!"

Zhu and Sha came into the throne room. "You," said the king to Zhu. "Your master says that you are a great warrior. Show us your power."

Zhu made a magic sign with his finger, and recited a spell. Then he shouted, "Grow!" He became ten times bigger than he was before. Everyone in the throne room was frightened, but the king was very happy. He poured a cup of wine for Zhu, looked up at him, and said, "Elder, this wine is for you. Please capture the monster and bring back our little girl. Then we will have a great banquet. We will thank you, and give you a thousand pieces of gold." Zhu returned to his normal size and drank the wine. The king also gave a cup of wine to Tangseng and Sha Wujing, but of course Tangseng did not drink. Then they all had a vegetarian dinner and went to sleep.

The next day, Zhu and Sha flew on clouds to the cave of the Yellow Robed Monster. Zhu hit the front door as hard as he could, and made a hole in it. One of the little demons ran to the monster and said, "Master, the monk with huge ears and a long nose has returned, and broken our front door!"

The monster was quite angry about the breaking of his front door. He went outside and said, "Monks, I have already let you and your master leave without harm. Why have you returned to my home? And why have you broken my beautiful front door?"

"Yes, you let us go. But we just heard that you captured the king's third daughter and made her your wife. You have kept her for thirteen years. Now the king has asked us to bring her home. Give her to us right now. If you don't, I might have to raise my hand."

The monster laughed at this. He drew his scimitar and tried to kill Zhu. The fight began. Zhu used his rake, shouting, "You harmed the nation and must die!" Sha used his staff, shouting, "You took a princess and brought shame to her country!" And the monster used his scimitar, shouting, "It's none of your business, get out of here!"

They fought for a long time. Zhu and Sha were becoming very tired. Finally, Zhu said, "Younger brother, you fight the monster. I have to go into the woods for a few minutes." Zhu ran into the trees and went to sleep. Sha could not fight the monster alone, and soon the monster captured Sha and tied him up.

Chapter 30

Now, this monster was very smart. He knew that there was a reason why the two disciples returned to his home to fight him. Their master must have sent them. But for what reason? Then he understood. His wife must have met with the Tang monk and told him her story. He became very angry at his wife, and went to look for her.

"Wife," he said to her, "what have you done? I brought you here and gave you silk and gold. You have my love. Anything you want, I give you. But now you tell the Tang monk stories about me, and make him send his disciples to fight me? Why do you do these things to me?"

"I did nothing!" she cried.

"Oh? Let's see what this one has to say!" And he dragged Sha Wujing into the room. "Now tell us, did the princess give a letter to your master?"

Sha thought to himself, "I cannot cause the princess to be harmed." So he said to the monster, "Sir, there was no letter. When my master was tied up in your house, he saw your beautiful wife. Later, we visited the king of Precious Image Kingdom and my master told him about the woman he had seen. The king knew it was his daughter. So the king commanded us to come back and get her, to bring her home. Your wife did nothing to harm you. If you must kill someone, kill me."

The monster felt really bad, and he said to his wife, "I am sorry I shouted at you. Please forgive me!" He tied up Sha again. Then he sat down and had dinner with his wife. They both drank a lot of wine. Finally, the monster said, "My dear, I must go and say hello to my wife's father. I have not met him before. I think it is time."

The princess was worried about this. "Please don't do this. You are my husband but you are also a monster. You will frighten my father if he sees you."

"You are right!" he replied. So he changed his appearance. Now he looked like a tall handsome middle-aged man. He had an attractive face, long black hair, and he wore a white silk robe and black shoes. Then he quickly flew three hundred miles to the palace of the king. He stood outside the gate, knocked on the door, and said, "The husband of the king's third daughter is here to see the king."

He was brought in to see the king. The king was sitting with Tangseng, talking. "I don't know you," said the king. "Who are you, where do you live, and when did you marry our daughter?"

"Let me tell you my story. Thirteen years ago, I was walking with my friends in the forest. I saw a large tiger with a young girl in his mouth. I hit the tiger with an arrow and brought the girl back to my home. My friends brought the tiger back to my home. The girl did not say she was a princess, so I thought she was a girl from the village. We got married. I wanted to kill the tiger to eat it at the wedding, but she told me that the tiger was our go-between and we should let it go. So I let it go. Later I learned that the tiger had become a powerful tiger spirit, killing and eating monks and taking their form. Now I see the tiger right here!" And he pointed his finger straight at Tangseng.

The king did not know if Tangseng a monk or a tiger. So he said to the monster, "If this monk is really a tiger, show me his true form."

"All right. Give me a cup of clean water." A servant brought the water. The monster spat some water on Tangseng and spoke a magic spell that made Tangseng appear to be a tiger. The king's guards all rushed forward to kill the tiger. If they killed the tiger, Tangseng would have also been killed. But Tangseng had the secret protection of the Gods of Light and the Gods of Darkness, so he was not harmed. After a while, the king told them to stop trying to kill the tiger, and they put him in a cage.

The king believed that the monster had shown him Tangseng's true form, and he was grateful. But he was also very tired so he went to bed. Before he went to bed, he ordered food and drink to be brought to the monster by eighteen beautiful serving girls. The monster ate and drank a great deal, and he became drunk. He jumped up, grabbed the nearest serving girl, bit off her head and ate it. The other seventeen girls ran away, but they didn't scream because the king was sleeping. So the monster sat down, drank more wine and ate the rest of the dead serving girl.

People ran out of the palace, and the story quickly passed from one person to another. Soon the story reached the inn where Tangseng's white horse was tied up. Now, remember that the white horse was really the son of the King of the Western Ocean. Guanyin had ordered him to carry the Tang Monk to the west. The horse knew that he was the only one who could help Tangseng. He changed back into his dragon form, and he ran into the throne room to fight the monster.

The dragon and the monster fought, but the dragon was not strong enough. The monster threw a sword at the dragon, hitting it on the leg. The dragon ran out on three legs. He ran back to the inn, where he changed back into a horse and fell down, asleep.

Now, let's go back to Zhu, who was sleeping in the woods. He had been sleeping for a long time. He did not know that Tangseng was trapped in a cage and Sha Wujing was tied up in the monster's house. He decided to go look for Sha. So he went back to the inn. He did not see Sha, but he saw the white horse on the ground with a hurt leg. "What's going on?" he asked the horse. And the horse told Zhu the whole story of what happened in the palace.

"Well, that's that," said Zhu. "It's all finished. You should return home to the Western Ocean. I think I will go back to my home in Old Gao Village and see if my wife is still there."

The horse began to cry. "Elder, please don't give up. I know you want to save our master. There is only one person who can help him. You must go to Flower Fruit Mountain and ask Sun Wukong to come and help."

"He will not come. He is still angry with me. He might hit me with his rod and kill me."

"He won't hit you. Go and tell him that our master is thinking about him. When he comes here and sees what happened to our master, he will get angry at the monster, and he will take care of everything!"

"All right, I will try. But if the monkey does not come back, then I will not come back either."

So Zhu flew on a cloud to Flower Fruit Mountain. Looking down, he saw Sun Wukong sitting on a big rock. All around him were thousands of monkeys, shouting, "Long live grandfather Great Sage!" Zhu was afraid of Sun Wukong, so he did not walk right up to him. Instead, he sat down in the middle of all the monkeys, with his head down. But Sun Wukong saw him, and said, "Bring that big one to the front!" All the little monkeys pushed Zhu to the front. Zhu kept his head down. "Who are you?" asked Sun Wukong.

"What, you don't recognize me? You and I have been brothers for several years." And he lifted up his head.

"Ah. My friend Zhu Bajie! Why have you come here? Is your master angry at you too?"

"No, he is not angry. But he is thinking about you."

"Well, let's not worry about him right now. Come, look at my beautiful home!" And Sun Wukong began to walk around the mountain, showing Zhu all the lovely things in Flower Fruit Mountain. Some little monkeys brought fruits for the two brothers to eat.

After a while, Zhu said, "Elder brother, this is a beautiful place. But our master is waiting for us."

"Why should I leave? This place is my home. Leave if you wish, but I will not come with you."

Zhu became angry and started to shout at Sun Wukong. Of course, the Monkey King did not like this. He said, "You fat coolie, why do you scold me?" Then he told his little monkeys to capture Zhu and bring him into Water Curtain Cave. Sun Wukong picked up a whip and prepared to lash Zhu.

Chapter 31

"Elder brother," cried Zhu, "for the sake of our master, for the sake of the great Buddha, please forgive me!"

When Sun Wukong heard the name Buddha, he put down the whip and said, "Brother, I won't whip you right now. But you must tell me the truth. Where is our master, and what is happening with him?"

So Zhu told Sun Wukong the long story. You know the story, of course: Tangseng, Zhu and Sha arrived at the forest; Zhu went to beg for food, got tired and took a nap; Sha went to look for Zhu; Tangseng was alone and went for a walk; Tangseng found the golden pagoda and the monster; the monster caught Tangseng and wanted to eat him; Zhu and Sha found the pagoda and fought the monster; Tangseng met the princess; the princess asked the monster to let Tangseng go; Tangseng took the princess's letter to the king; the monster changed into a handsome man and visited the king; the monster changed Tangseng into a tiger; the monster got drunk, ate a serving girl and hurt the white horse; and finally the white horse asked Zhu to ask Sun Wukong for help.

Then, Zhu added something new to the story. He said, "Elder Brother, I told the monster about you. I said that you are a great warrior, and that you would come and kill him. But the monster just laughed and said, 'Let him come. I will kill him quickly and easily. I will eat his heart. The monkey's body is small and thin, but I will cut it up, put it in the pan of oil, and eat it for dinner.'"

Well, my child, you know what happened next! Sun Wukong was so angry, he started jumping up and down and waving his rod. Then he said, "I will go right now. I will capture that monster and kill him!"

"Good idea," said Zhu. "You should go and kill that monster. I will wait here for you. The fruit here is very tasty."

"No. You come with me. I want you to watch this." Then Sun Wukong grabbed Zhu's arm, and together they flew across the ocean to White Tiger Mountain. Sun Wukong looked down and saw the golden pagoda. He said to Zhu, "You wait here in the clouds. I will go down to the pagoda. I know the monster is not home, but I need to pick up something there." Then he jumped

down to the ground and picked up the monster's two small children. He also
went into the house, found Sha, and told him to come outside. Then he told
Zhu and Sha to take the two boys to the king's palace and tell the monster that
they had arrived.

So Zhu and Sha went to the king's palace. First, they left the boys in the
woods. Then Zhu pounded on the palace door and shouted "Hey, monster!
We are two disciples of the Tang monk. We have returned, and we have your
two children!" The monster heard this and ran outside. He saw Zhu and Sha
but he did not see the children. He did not want to fight Zhu and Sha, because
he was still feeling sick from drinking wine and eating the serving girl. So he
quickly jumped into the sky and flew back to his cave to see if his boys were
there.

While this was happening, Sun Wukong was talking with the princess. He
told her that her husband was coming back and would be very angry. He told
the princess to go into the forest. Then he changed his appearance so that he
looked like the princess. Then he waited.

Soon the monster returned. He saw a woman who looked like his wife. She
was crying. "Wife, why are you crying?" he asked.

"Oh my dear husband," said Sun Wukong, "this morning that ugly pig
returned. He took the other monk, and he took our two children!"

"Don't worry, my dear. I will go and bring back our two boys. And I will kill
those monks too."

"I don't think so," said Sun Wukong. He changed his appearance again, back
to his true form. "Now, do you know me?"

The monster was surprised to see his beautiful wife turn into an ugly monkey.
But he looked more seriously at Sun Wukong. "Actually, I think I do know
you."

"Of course you don't know me. I am the eldest disciple of the Tang monk.
My name is Sun Wukong, the Lord of Heaven, and I am over five hundred
years old. I like to kill monsters. For that reason, my master was unhappy
with me, and he told me to leave. But you know the old saying, 'between
father and son, no anger remains overnight.' I heard that you planned to harm
my master, so I returned. Now, I don't need to kill you. Just put your head
down right here. I will hit you once with my rod, and we will call it finished."

Well of course, the monster did not put his head down. He knew Sun Wukong was very powerful. So he called all the other monsters who lived within a hundred miles of his cave, and told them to help him defeat Sun Wukong. Soon Sun Wukong saw monsters in all directions, all wanting to kill him. This made him very happy! He changed his appearance so that he had six arms and three heads, and he used three rods to fight the monsters.

The fight went on for a long time. Finally, Sun Wukong had killed all the monsters except Yellow Robed Monster. To finish the fight, he used the 'stealing peaches under the leaves' method, and smashed his rod down on the monster's head. But the monster did not die. He just disappeared. Sun Wukong was standing alone.

He looked down but did not see any blood. Then he jumped up to a cloud and looked in all four directions, but he could not see the monster. Then he said to himself, "That monster said that he knew me. How could that be? Maybe I met him in Heaven five hundred years ago. Maybe he is a spirit from Heaven."

He used his cloud somersault to fly up to the South Gate of Heaven, and he walked into the Hall of Light. One of the Heavenly masters asked him, "Great sage, why are you here?"

"I was helping the Tang monk go to the Western Heaven. We arrived at the Precious Image Kingdom and had some trouble with a monster. But then I could not find him. I don't think he is a monster from earth. I think he is from here. Have you lost any monsters, spirits or deities?"

The Heavenly masters checked to make sure all the Heavenly beings were really in Heaven. They checked all the mountains gods, the river gods, the sky gods, the sun gods and the moon gods, but everyone was there. Then they checked the twenty-eight gods of the constellations. But they could only find twenty-seven of them. Kui the Wolf was missing. Every god needed to check in every three days. But Kui had missed the last four check ins, including yesterday. Four times three is twelve, and twelve plus one is thirteen.

The Heavenly masters went to the palace and told the Jade Emperor that Kui was missing for thirteen days. A day in Heaven is equal to a year on earth, so Kui had been on earth for thirteen years. When the Jade Emperor heard this, he called out to Kui. Kui was under a waterfall on earth. When he heard the Emperor calling him, he came to the palace right away. He walked past Sun

Wukong, who tried to hit him, but the other gods grabbed his arm first. Kui
did not look at Sun Wukong. He continued into the palace and bowed to the
Emperor.

"Kui," said the Emperor. "There is so much beauty here in Heaven. Why did
you go down to earth?"

"Your Majesty," Kui replied, "please forgive me. In your great Incense Hall
there was a jade girl in charge of the incense. We fell in love. But we could
not be together in Heaven. So she went down to earth and took the form of a
girl, born as the third daughter of a king. I also went down to earth and took
the form of the Yellow Robed Monster on White Tiger Mountain. I found the
princess, we married, and we have lived happily together for the last thirteen
years."

The Jade Emperor told him that he could not have his job as a constellation
anymore. His new job was to be a lowly fire tender in the house of Laozi. Kui
bowed low and left the palace.

Sun Wukong also bowed to the Emperor, turned and left. The Jade Emperor smiled and said to the Heavenly masters, "Let us be happy that he left quickly and did not cause any trouble in Heaven."

Sun Wukong returned to earth. He met Zhu and Sha, and together the three of them returned to the king's palace. They met with the king, the queen, and the princess. Sun Wukong told the story of his visit to Heaven. He said to the king and queen, "Now you know that your daughter is really an incense girl in the Incense Hall in Heaven. And your daughter has two boys. Now, let's go get our master."

They all went to find the tiger, who was still in his cage. Everyone saw a tiger, but Sun Wukong saw that it really was Tangseng. "Master," he laughed, "usually you are a good monk. Why do you now look like a tiger?" Then he got some water and spat a little bit in the tiger's face. Instantly the tiger changed back to Tangseng.

Tangseng was so happy to see Sun Wukong! He said, "Disciple, you have saved my life again. I hope that we reach the West soon. Then we will return to the East, and I will report your good works to the Tang Emperor."

"Don't mention it," replied Sun Wukong. "Just don't say that spell to me again, and I will be happy enough."

Then the king called for a great vegetarian feast, and there was much eating, drinking, singing, and telling of stories. And the next day, the four travelers and their horse headed westward again.

Chapter 32

The four travelers – the monkey Sun Wukong, the monk Tangseng, the pig-man Zhu Bajie, and the strong but quiet man Sha Wujing – continued walking along the Silk Road in Western China. They were walking west towards India. Winter had turned to spring, and the trees and grasses turned green.

One day the travelers arrived at a tall mountain. The mountain was so tall that they could not see the sun during the day, or the moon and stars at night. They followed the road as it turned left and right and left again. The road became a mountain path. They walked up the mountain.

A woodcutter was standing in a green meadow above them. The woodcutter wore an old blue hat on his head, and a black monks' robe. In his hands he held an axe. When the woodcutter saw Tangseng and his disciples, he said, "You who are going to the West, please stop. I have something to tell you. There are monsters and demons in this mountain. They wait for travelers coming from the East, and they eat them!"

Tangseng heard these words and was very frightened. But Sun Wukong just laughed. He said to the woodcutter, "Elder brother, we were sent by the Tang Emperor to bring back the Buddha's books from India. That man on the white horse is my master. He is a bit timid, so he asked me to talk with you, to learn more about these monsters. Tell me about them. Then I will tell the mountain gods and local spirits to help me capture these monsters."

"You are mad," replied the woodcutter. "Why do you think the mountain gods and local spirits will help you? How will you capture the monsters, and what will you do with them?"

"I am the Monkey King, the Great Sage Equal to Heaven. Of course the mountain gods and local spirits will help me. If the demons are from Heaven, I will send them to the Jade Emperor. If the demons are from Earth, I will send them to the Palace of Earth. If they are dragons, I will send them to the Lords of Oceans. If they are ghosts, I will send them to King Yama. Every kind of demon has its own home, and Old Monkey knows all of them. I will tell them and they will do as I say!"

The woodcutter laughed at these words. "Then you are a fool. I will tell you about these demons. This is Level Top Mountain. In the mountain is the Lotus Flower Cave. In the cave are two very large and powerful monsters. They have a picture on the wall of the Tang monk, and they are waiting for you to arrive. They will cook you and eat you!"

"How will they eat us? Starting with the head or with the feet?"

"Why do you ask?"

"If they eat my head first, I will not feel any pain. But if they start eating me at my feet first, it will take a long time and it will be very painful. I would not like that at all."

"Don't worry, monkey, these monsters will eat you in a single bite. It will be very quick! And be careful, because these monsters have five treasures that have great magical power. It does not matter if you are powerful, it will still be very difficult for you to protect the Tang monk. You must become a little bit mad to pass this place!"

"Ah, that's very good. I am already a little bit mad. Thank you!" Sun Wukong turned and walked back to Tangseng and the others. He was very happy. "No problem, master, the old man says there are a couple of small monsters here. Don't worry. Let's go, let's go."

Just then, the woodcutter disappeared. "That's not good," said Zhu Bajie. "We have just met a ghost in the middle of the day." Sun Wukong looked in all four directions but did not see the woodcutter. Then he looked up in the sky and saw the Sky Sentinel sitting on a cloud. He flew up and shouted, "If you had something to say, why did you change into a woodcutter? You could have just told us." The Sky Sentinel was frightened and said he was sorry, and Sun Wukong chased him away. Then he returned to the ground and started walking back to the others.

As Sun Wukong returned, he said to himself, "What should I do? If I tell Master the truth about these monsters, he will be very afraid and he might fall off his horse and hurt himself. But if I don't tell him, he might do something foolish and the monsters will kill him." He thought for a while. Then he decided to trick Zhu Bajie into going to find out more about the monsters.

Sun Wukong made some water flow from his eyes, so it looked like he was crying. Zhu saw this and became very afraid. He said, "That's it. Our journey is over. Sha, you should return to your river and become a monster again. I will return to my village and see if my wife is still there. We can sell the horse. And we can use the money to buy a coffin for our master for his old age."

"Why are you talking like this, you stupid coolie?" asked Tangseng.

"Didn't you see Sun Wukong crying? He is a great warrior. If he is crying, he must be very afraid. And if he is afraid, what can we do?"

Tangseng said, "Stop talking like this. Wukong, why are you unhappy? And why are you showing us those tears which are not tears?"

"Master, I just spoke with the Sky Sentinel. He told me that the monsters in this mountain are extremely dangerous. I am strong, but I don't know if I can win a fight against all of them."

"Ah, that is true. As the book says, 'the few cannot win against the many[1].' But remember, you are not alone. You have Zhu Bajie and Sha Wujing here to help you. I will let you use them to help you."

This was exactly what Sun Wukong wanted to hear from his master! He said to Zhu, "You must do two things. First, you must take care of our master. Second, you must go into the mountain and look for monsters."

Zhu replied, "I don't understand, elder brother. To take care of our master I must stay here. To look for monsters I must go out. I cannot do both!"

"Then just do one of them."

"I don't know which one to do. Tell me more about the two jobs."

"Ok. To take care of our master, you must do everything he asks. If he wants to go for a walk, go with him. If he is hungry, go and beg vegetarian food for him. If he needs to go into the woods to use the bathroom, help him do that."

"That sounds very dangerous. If I go and beg food for him, I might meet people on the road. They won't know that I am with the Tang monk. They will only see a big fat pig that is ready to be eaten. They will kill and eat me!"

"Then go into the mountain and look for monsters. Find out how many there are, and where they live."

"Ah, that is easy," said Zhu. He picked up his rake and walked off to look for monsters. As he left, Sun Wukong laughed and said to Tangseng, "You and I both know that Zhu will not look for monsters. He will walk for a little while, then he will find a nice place to rest on the ground and go to sleep. Then he will come back and tell us some stupid story. You just wait. I will follow him and see what he does."

---

[1] This is a quote from the *Mencius*, a book written by the Confucian philosopher of the same name during the Warring States period, 4th century B.C.

Sun Wukong said softly, "Change!" and his body changed into a small insect. He flew towards Zhu and landed on his ear. Sure enough, Zhu found some comfortable grass, rested on it, and went to sleep. A few hours later he got up and began to walk back towards the others. He stopped walking when he saw three large flat rocks. He stood in front of the rocks. He told the three rocks a long story about finding a cave where mountain spirits lived, and looking inside the cave. When he was finished, he continued saying the story to himself as he walked towards Tangseng and the others.

But Sun Wukong flew ahead of Zhu and arrived before him. He changed back to his monkey form and said to Tangseng, "Zhu is coming. He spent the day sleeping. But then he made up a story about finding a mountain spirit cave. I heard the story. Now you just wait and you will hear it for yourself."

Soon Zhu returned. He stood in front of Tangseng, Sun Wukong and Sha Monk, and told the same story that he had told to the three flat rocks. "Idiot!" cried Sun Wukong, and hit Zhu with his rod. "I heard you tell this same story to the three flat rocks. You did not find a cave, you just found a nice place to sleep. Why don't you tell us the truth?"

Zhu grabbed Tangseng's robe and said, "Please, great master, protect me from this monkey!"

Tangseng said, "Wukong, don't hit Zhu anymore. But Zhu, you must go back into the mountains again. This time, do your job!" And so Zhu went back into the mountains. He was terribly afraid but he did his job. We will talk more about him later.

Now, you remember that this mountain was called Level Top Mountain, and there was a large cave called Lotus Flower Cave. Two monsters lived there. The older one was called Great King Golden Horn and the younger one was called Great King Silver Horn. Golden Horn said to Silver Horn, "Do you know what I heard today? The Tang Emperor has sent his younger brother, the Tang monk, to find holy books in the West. He will be on the Silk Road, passing through our mountain and close to our cave. He is a very powerful holy man. His body has strong magic. If we eat him, we will live for a very, very long time. Go find him and bring him back here, so we can eat him for dinner."

So Silver Horn went out with thirty little demons to look for Tangseng. They did not find Tangseng, but they soon found Zhu walking along a mountain path. Zhu saw the monster and the little demons. He was afraid, but he used his rake to fight them.

Silver Horn laughed. "I think you became a monk when you were older. You must have been a farmer in your younger years. You have a farmer's rake!"

Zhu replied, "My child, you don't know this rake! When I use it in a fight, it brings cold wind and bright fire, it hides the sun and the moon. It catches monsters and it kills demons. It brings down Mount Tai[1]. Tigers and dragons run away when they see it. You may be powerful, but when you meet this rake, I will see your blood!"

The monster had a weapon also, it was the sword of seven stars. He raised the sword and ran towards Zhu, and the two of them fought for a long time. Zhu was beginning to win the fight, but then the thirty little demons came to help the monster. Zhu could not fight them all. He fell to the ground, the demons grabbed his arms and legs, and they carried him back to Lotus Flower Cave.

---

[1] Mount Tai (Tài Shān) is a large mountain in Shandong. It appears on the Chinese 5 RMB bank note. It is mentioned in many stories and idioms, for example, "Though death befalls all men alike, it may be weightier than Mount Tai or lighter than a feather."

Chapter 33

Silver Horn shouted, "Elder brother, look what we have! We caught the Tang monk!"

The older monster, Great King Golden Horn, looked at Zhu. He said, "Younger brother, this is not the Tang monk. This one is just a large pig. He is useless."

"Yes, I am useless!" said Zhu. "You should let me go."

"No," said the younger monster. "He was traveling with the Tang monk. We should keep him. Put him in the pool of water in the back of the cave. Keep him in the water for a few days, then remove his skin, then put him in the sun and let him dry. Later, we can eat him for lunch, with some wine."

"All right," said Golden Horn. So he told his little demons to tie up Zhu and throw him into the water.

Meanwhile, Tangseng was becoming worried because Zhu had not returned. He said, "This region is dangerous. It has very few people, it's not like a village or town. Where will we meet him?"

"Don't worry, Master," replied Sun Wukong. "Just make your horse walk a little faster, and we will catch up to him."

Tangseng got on his horse and started walking quickly down the mountain path. He did not know it, but Golden Horn was watching him from a few miles away. "Here comes the Tang monk!" he said to his little demons, and he pointed his finger at the monk. Immediately Tangseng's body trembled, but he did not know why. Silver Horn looked in the same direction, pointed at Tangseng, and said, "Is that him?" Tangseng trembled again.

"Why am I trembling like this?" he asked the others.

"I think you are not feeling well," said Sha Wujing, "That's why you are feeling cold and shaking."

"I think you are just afraid," said Sun Wukong. "Let me show you something to make you feel better." He took out his golden hoop rod and began exercising with it. He moved the rod up and down, then left and right, then in a circle. He pushed it forward and pulled it backward. He was very graceful and strong.

Sun Wukong did this exercise because he wanted to make Tangseng less afraid. But when Silver Horn saw Sun Wukong's exercises with the golden hoop rod he became very, very afraid. "Look at that monkey and his rod," he said to the little demons. "He is too powerful. He can fight and win against ten thousand of us. And we only have a few hundred soldiers. We cannot fight against this monkey!"

One of the little demons replied, "If we cannot fight the monkey, should we just release the pig?"

"No, said Silver Horn, "we have to use a different method. All of you, go back to the cave. I will capture the Tang monk by myself."

The little demons all returned to Lotus Flower Cave. The monster changed into an old Daoist monk. Now he had white hair, a blue silk gown, and yellow shoes. His leg was covered with blood, and he lay behind a large rock near the mountain path. He cried, "Save me! Save me!"

Tangseng arrived on his horse with Sun Wukong and Sha Wujing. He heard the monk crying. He said, "Who is here?"

The monk crawled out from behind the big rock, onto the mountain path. He kowtowed again and again. Tangseng got off his horse and grabbed the monk's arm, saying, "Please, grandfather, get up!" Then Tangseng saw the blood on the monk's leg. He asked, "What happened to you? Why is your leg hurt?"

"Last night I was walking home with my disciple, when we met a large tiger on the mountain path. The tiger grabbed my disciple and dragged him away. I ran away as fast as I could, but I fell on some rocks and hurt my leg. Thank you, Master, for helping me today!"

Tangseng said, "Of course we will help you. Wukong, put this man on your back and carry him. We will take him back to his temple."

Sun Wukong picked up the monk and began to carry him on his back. But he said quietly, "I know you are not a monk. You are a monster. The Tang monk thinks your words are true, but I have lived for a long time and I don't believe you at all. I think you want to kill my master and eat him. But if you do, you should give me half!"

"I am no monster!" said the monster. "I am a poor Daoist monk who met a tiger on the road today."

Sun Wukong replied, "My master is a kind man, but sometimes he is also foolish. He believes what he sees with his eyes. He does not see what is inside you. But I see inside you and I know what you are. You are no monk."

The monkey carried the monk for several miles, but then he started to walk more slowly. Soon Tangseng and Sha Wujing were far ahead of them. When Sun Wukong could not see Tangseng and Sha, he decided to kill the monk. But the monk knew what Sun Wukong was planning. Before Sun Wukong could kill him, he flew up into the sky and made a magic sign with his hand. Mount Meru[1] lifted up into the air and came down on Sun Wukong's head. Sun Wukong moved his head to the right side, and the mountain came down on his left shoulder. He laughed and said, "What kind of magic is this? I feel a bit lopsided." The monster made another magic sign, and Mount Emei[2] lifted up into the air and came down on Sun Wukong's right shoulder. "Thanks," said Sun Wukong. "I feel much better now." And carrying two huge mountains on his shoulders, he began to run towards Tangseng and Sha Monk.

The monster saw this and said to himself, "This monkey is very strong. But I am stronger!" Then the monster made another magic sign, and Mount Tai, the largest mountain in China, lifted up and came down on Sun Wukong's head. This was too much for Sun Wukong. He fell to the ground. Blood came out of his ears, eyes, nose and mouth.

The monster left Sun Wukong trapped under the three mountains, and caught up to Tangseng and Sha Monk. Sha Wujing tried to fight, but the monster was too strong. The monster picked up Tangseng, Sha, the horse and the luggage, and carried all of them back to Lotus Flower Cave.

But when he arrived at the cave, his older brother was not happy. "Where is Sun Wukong?" he asked. "If we eat the monk and the other two disciples, that monkey will be very angry. He will come here, and he will make life very difficult for us."

"Don't worry, elder brother. The monkey is trapped under three very large mountains. One of them is Mount Tai. He cannot move."

"Ok, that's good. But let's be safe. Capture him and bring him here." Then the older monster told two of his demons to go and capture Sun Wukong. "Take two of my treasures," he said. "Take the gourd of purple gold and the jade

---

[1] Mt. Meru, also known as Mt. Sumeru, is known in Buddhism as the central axis of the universe, reaching up into Heaven.
[2] Mt. Emei is one of the four sacred Buddhist mountains. It is believed that Buddha arrived from India and his teachings spread from this mountain throughout China.

vase. Go and find Sun Wukong. When you find him, call his name. When he answers, open the gourd. The monkey will be sucked inside the gourd. Close the gourd and bring him back here."

Sun Wukong was trapped under the three mountains. He was badly hurt, and he was unhappy because he could not help the Tang monk and his friends. He cried loudly. His cries were heard by the mountain god, the local spirit, and the Golden Headed Guardian. The Golden Headed Guardian said to the other two, "Ah, this is very bad. Do you know who is trapped under your mountains? It is Sun Wukong, the Great Sage Equal to Heaven. He caused great trouble in Heaven five hundred years ago. Now he is a disciple of the Tang monk. You have allowed a monster to trap him under three mountains. When he escapes, he will be very angry, and he will probably kill both of you."

"We did not know!" cried the mountain god and the local spirit. "We just did our job. We heard someone say the magic words for moving mountains, so we moved them. That's all. We didn't know the mountains would land on the Great Sage Equal to Heaven."

Now the mountain god and the local spirit were both very afraid. They walked up to the three mountains and shouted, "Great Sage! The mountain god, the local spirit, and the Golden Headed Guardian have come to help you. We ask you to let us move the mountains away, so you can come out. We are very sorry. Please pardon us!"

Sun Wukong replied, "Just move the mountains. I won't hurt you." The mountain god and the local spirit said magic words, and the three mountains lifted up and moved back to where they belonged. Sun Wukong jumped up. He lifted his face to the sky, and said in a loud voice, "O Heaven! All my life, ever since I was born on Flower Fruit Mountain, I searched for a teacher to help me learn the secret of long life. I can kill tigers, I can fight dragons, I can cause trouble in Heaven, and I was named Great Sage Equal to Heaven. But I have never seen anything like this before. I cannot move three mountains like this monster did. This monster talks to the mountain god and the local spirit as if they were coolies! O Heaven, if you gave birth to Old Monkey, why did you give birth to these monsters also[1]?"

---

[1] This is a parody of the dying words of General Zhou Yu at the end of the Battle of Red Cliff in the classic novel *Romance of the Three Kingdoms*. His adversary was the strategist Zhuge Liang. As he died, Zhou cried out, "O Heaven, you let Zhou Yu be born, why did you let Zhuge Liang be born also?"

Sun Wukong waited but did not hear an answer from Heaven. But far away, he saw two lights. He asked the mountain god what the lights were. The god replied, "They are treasures of the two monsters, Golden Horn and Silver Horn."

"Good!" said Sun Wukong. "I think I will visit them in their cave. Tell me, what kind of people do they like to visit with?"

"They enjoy sitting and drinking tea with Daoist monks," the god replied. The mountain god and the local spirit left. Sun Wukong changed into an old Daoist monk. Now he wore an old robe and held a wooden fish in his hand. He sat down at the side of the mountain path and waited.

Soon the two demons who were sent to capture Sun Wukong arrived. They saw the old Daoist monk. Their master liked to visit with Daoist monks, so the two demons stopped, bowed, and greeted him.

"Hello, my two young friends," said the monkey who looked like a monk. "I am an immortal from Penglai Mountain. I have come here to help people become immortals. Would you like to become immortal?"

When the two demons heard this, they became very excited. "Of course!" they both said.

"Good. Tell me who you are and what you are doing today."

One of the demons replied, "Our master is Great King Golden Horn. He has powerful magic. His younger brother Great King Silver Horn lifted three huge mountains and dropped them on the old monkey Sun Wukong. Now the monkey is trapped under the mountains. Our master sent us to put the monkey into this gourd."

"How will you do that?"

"I will call him by his name. When he replies, I will open the gourd. He will be sucked into the gourd. I will then close the gourd and he will be trapped inside. In one and three quarters hours, he will turn into liquid."

"Very nice!" said the monk. "I have something just like it." Sun Wukong pulled a hair from his head, said, "Change!" and the hair turned into a gourd just like the one that the two demons had. He said to the demons, "Do you like it?"

"Well, it's very nice, but it doesn't have any magic. Our gourd has powerful magic. We can put a thousand people inside it."

"That's interesting. But my gourd is even more powerful than yours. I can store Heaven itself inside it! Sometimes Heaven makes me angry. When that happens, I store Heaven inside the gourd for a while, then I let it go again."

One of the demons laughed and said, "That is very powerful magic indeed! If what you say is true, we would like to trade gourds with you. But first, you must show us your gourd's magic."

"All right," said the monk, "but when we trade, you must also give me the jade vase." The demons agreed, because they wanted to become immortal. "Wait here for a minute," he said. Then he quickly flew up to Heaven and went to the palace of the Jade Emperor. "O Emperor, I am traveling with the Tang monk to acquire holy books in the West. Our path is blocked by some powerful monsters. I need their magic gourd. To do that, I must show them that I can capture Heaven in my own gourd. So, I need to borrow Heaven for about a half hour. Do this for me. If you don't, I will start a war in Heaven!"

The Jade Emperor became angry and was about to say no. But Third Prince Nezha said to him, "Your Majesty, I know this monkey is very difficult and has caused trouble in Heaven. But he is a disciple of the Tang monk, and we Nezhad must help the monk. I have an idea. We can cover Heaven with a large black banner. People on earth won't be able to see the sun, the moon, or the stars. They will think that the monkey has indeed stored Heaven in his gourd."

The Jade Emperor nodded his head and turned to Sun Wukong. "All right. We will do this, not to help you but to help the Tang monk."

Sun Wukong flew back down to earth and changed back into a Daoist monk. He said to the two demons, "All right. Here we go. Watch this." Then he threw the gourd up in the air. Prince Nezha saw this and covered Heaven with a black banner. The sun, moon and stars all disappeared. The sky turned black, and darkness covered the earth.

The demons were terrified. "Stop it, stop it!" they cried. The monk said some magic words. Nezha heard him. He rolled up the black banner, and the sun appeared in the sky again. The two demons were shaking. They gave their gourd and the jade vase to the monk. The monk gave his gourd to the demons and he walked away quickly. The two demons tried to use the gourd but of course it did not have any magic because it was just an ordinary gourd. Sun Wukong was on a cloud in the sky watching this and laughing. Then he changed the gourd back into a hair and put the hair back on his head. Now the demons had nothing – no gourd, no vase, and no Sun Wukong.

Chapter 34

They returned to the cave and told Great King Golden Horn and Great King Silver Horn what happened. The two monsters were angry at the Daoist monk, but they did not know that the monk was really Sun Wukong. Golden Horn said to his younger brother, "We need a different method to capture this monkey. Let's use our other three treasures. I have the sword of seven stars, and I have the palm leaf fan. The other treasure is the yellow gold rope. Our mother has that treasure. Let's ask her to come visit us at our cave and bring the rope with her. We can use the three treasures to capture the monkey."

The monsters called two more little demons. They told the demons to go to the home of their mother to invite her to the cave. But Sun Wukong had turned into a small insect and heard every word that they said. He followed the two little demons for two or three miles. Then he flew ahead of them and changed into a little demon wearing a tiger skin. He ran up to the two demons and said, "Hey you! Wait for me!"

"Who are you?" asked one of the little demons. "We have never seen you before."

"I also work for the Great King Golden Horn and Great King Silver Horn. They want their mother to visit them right away. They thought that the two of you would walk too slowly. So they sent me to make sure you moved quickly. Now start running!" The two demons believed him. So the three of them ran down the mountain path. As soon as they got close to the mother's house, Sun Wukong changed back to his original form, took out his Golden Hoop Rod, and hit them both on the head, killing them. Then he changed himself to look like one of the demons, and he used one of his hairs to look like the other demon. Then the two of them walked up to the mother's house.

The demon knocked on the door. When the mother came to the door, he bowed low to her. He said, "I come from Lotus Flower Cave. Your two sons told me to come here. They invite you to come to their cave to eat the flesh of the Tang monk. They also ask you to bring the yellow-gold rope, because they need it to catch the monkey, Sun Wukong."

The mother was happy to hear this. She came out and got into her sedan chair. The two Sun Wukong demons picked up the sedan chair and carried her along the mountain path for a few miles. Then when they were far away from the house, Sun Wukong hit the mother on the head with his Golden Hoop Rod.

The mother died instantly. After she died, her body changed into its true form, a nine-tailed fox. Sun Wukong picked up the yellow-gold rope and put it in his sleeve. Now he had three of the five treasures.

He changed his form so that now he looked like the mother. He pulled another hair from his head and changed it into the other little demon. Then the two little demons carried the mother on the sedan chair, but of course all three of them were really Sun Wukong!

Soon they arrived at the cave. The old woman got out of the sedan chair and walked slowly into the cave. She sat down, facing south. Great King Golden Horn and Great King Silver Horn kowtowed to her, saying, "Mother, your children bow to you."

"My sons, please rise," said the mother.

Now, remember that Zhu Bajie was also in the cave, along with Sha Wujing and Tangseng. Zhu was tied up and sitting in a pool of water. When the mother turned around, Zhu saw that she had a monkey's tail. Zhu laughed loudly. "It's Sun Wukong!" he said to Sha Wujing.

"Be quiet," said Sha. "Let's see what Old Monkey will do."

The old mother said, "My dear sons, why did you ask me to come here today?"

Golden Horn replied, "Dear mother, we asked you to come and eat the flesh of the Tang monk with us. We will cook him and eat him for dinner."

"Well, I am not really hungry for monk. But I really would like to taste some pork. Let's eat that large pig over there. We can start with his ears, I hear they are very tasty."

When Zhu heard this, he cried out, "So, you came here to taste my ears, eh? I should tell these monsters who you really are!"

Both monsters heard this. They looked at Zhu, then they looked at each other, then they looked at their mother. They both jumped up. But just then, a little demon ran into the cave, saying, "Disaster, disaster! Sun Wukong has killed your mother, and changed his form so that he looks just like her. There he is!" Silver Horn immediately picked up his sword of seven stars and prepared to fight with Sun Wukong. But Golden Horn held up his hand to stop him. "You cannot win this fight, younger brother. He is very powerful. Let him go. And let the others go also."

Silver Horn said, "What? Are you afraid of them? I am not afraid. Let's do this: I will fight this monkey for three rounds. If I win, we will eat the Tang monk for dinner, and eat the others tomorrow. If I lose, we will let them all go. All right?" Golden Horn agreed, and Silver Horn went to put on his armor and prepare for the fight. Sun Wukong changed back to his true form and waited for him, smiling.

"Old monkey!" Silver Horn shouted at Sun Wukong. "Give us our mother and our treasures. I will let you and the others go. You can go to the west with no more trouble from us." Of course, he knew that Sun Wukong would not like these words.

Sun Wukong just laughed at him. "You foolish monster, Old Monkey will not let you go so easily. Give me my master, my friends, the white horse, and our luggage. Also, give us some travel money. If I hear even half a 'no' from you, it will be the end of your life. You should just hang yourself with the yellow-gold rope and save me the trouble of killing you."

Silver Horn and Sun Wukong both jumped up into the clouds and began to fight. It was the biggest fight of Sun Wukong's life. It was like two tigers fighting on the mountain, two dragons fighting over the ocean. They used a thousand different methods of fighting. One used the golden hoop rod, the other used the sword of seven stars. They fought all day and all night. They fought for thirty rounds, but neither one was the winner.

Finally, Sun Wukong took out the yellow-gold rope and threw it around Silver Horn. But Silver Horn knew the loose-rope spell. He said the words, and the rope fell off him. Then Silver Horn grabbed the rope and threw it around Sun Wukong. Sun Wukong tried to use the loose-rope spell, but Silver Horn was faster, he used the tight-rope spell. The rope became tight around Sun Wukong. The monkey could not move. The monster pulled the gourd and the vase out from Sun Wukong's sleeve. Then he took the monkey back to the cave.

When they returned to the cave, Silver Horn told some little demons to tie Sun Wukong to a pillar. Then he went into another room to drink wine and talk with his older brother. As soon as the monster was gone, Sun Wukong shook his head. His golden hoop rod fell out of his ear and into his hand. He blew on it, and the rod changed into a diamond knife. He used the knife to cut the yellow-gold rope. Then he pulled another hair from his head, blew on it, and it changed into another monkey just like himself. He tied up the second monkey with the yellow-gold rope. Then he changed himself so he looked like a little demon.

Zhu Bajie was still in the pool of water. He saw all this. He shouted loudly to the monsters, "Bad news, bad news! The monkey that is tied up is not the real monkey. The real monkey has escaped!"

"What is he yelling about?" asked Golden Horn, holding his cup of red wine.

"That fat pig is just trying to cause trouble," said the little demon who was Sun Wukong. "He wants the monkey to try to escape, but the monkey will not do it. That's why the pig is shouting. But we must be careful. The monkey might be able to escape. Let's use a bigger rope to hold him to the pillar."

"You're right," said the monster. He took off his heavy belt and gave it to the little demon. "Use this."

The little demon tied the belt around the form of the monkey. Then he quickly blew on one of his hairs and made a second yellow-gold rope, tied it around the monkey, and put the real yellow-gold rope in his sleeve. Golden Horn had been drinking a lot of wine, so he did not see this.

The real Sun Wukong, still using the form of a little demon, ran out of the cave. He changed back into his monkey form and shouted, "Hey, you in there! I am Sun Grimpil[1], the brother of Pilgrim Sun. I am here to make some trouble for you!"

Silver Horn came to the door and said, "I have your brother. He is tied up in my cave. I think you want to fight with me, but I will not fight you. I will call your name. Are you afraid to answer me?"

"Call my name a thousand times, I am not afraid to answer," Sun Wukong replied. But he was afraid. He knew that if he said his real name, he would be trapped inside the magic gourd. But he did not know what would happen if he used "Sun Grimpil" instead of his real name.

The monster shouted, "Sun Grimpil!" Sun Wukong replied, "I am Sun Grimpil!" Instantly he was pulled into the gourd. The monster closed the gourd, and Sun Wukong was trapped inside. He tried to get out but he could not move. This was a magic gourd. Anyone trapped in it would be turned to liquid in one and three quarters hours. Sun Wukong's body was as hard as diamond, so he was not turned into liquid. But he was still trapped inside.

The two monsters were very happy because they had caught Sun Grimpil. "Let's wait a couple of hours," said one of them, "then we will shake the

---

[1] Sun Wukong is sometimes called sūn xíng zhě, Pilgrim Sun. Here he says his name backwards, giving us zhě xíng sūn, Sun Grimpil.

gourd. If we feel liquid moving around inside, we know the monkey is dead."

Sun Wukong was thinking. He needed to make the monsters think that he was dead and turned to liquid. What could he do? He could make a lot of urine, but that would smell bad and make his clothes dirty. He decided to use spit. So he began spitting again and again, filling up half of the gourd with saliva. Then he cried out, "Ah, no! My legs have turned to liquid. My arms have turned to liquid. My belly has turned to liquid. I fear my head will be liquid soon!" And then he changed into a tiny insect and landed on the mouth of the gourd.

Chapter 35

Golden Horn opened the gourd. Instantly, Sun Wukong flew out of the gourd, leaving behind a pool of saliva. Then he changed from an insect to a little demon. He stood and watched as the two monsters laughed and drank wine, thinking that they had killed Sun Grimpil. When they were not looking, Sun Wukong put the magic gourd in his sleeve, and put a second, non-magic gourd in its place. As the monsters continued to laugh and drink, Sun Wukong walked out of the cave.

Sun Wukong rested for a while outside the cave. Then he went back and banged on the door. "Open this door. It is me, Pilgrim Sun!"

"What is this?" said Golden Horn to his younger brother. "We already have Sun Grimpil in our gourd. Pilgrim Sun must be his brother. How many Suns are there?"

Silver Horn replied, "Don't worry, we have room in the gourd for a thousand people. We can just put this Pilgrim Sun inside, next to his brother. They will both turn to liquid." Then he walked out of the cave to meet Sun Wukong. He carried a gourd, but of course it was not the magic gourd, it was the gourd that Sun Wukong had made. He said to the monkey, "Who are you, and why are you causing trouble here?"

"I am Sun Wukong, the Great Sage Equal to Heaven. I was born on Flower Fruit Mountain five hundred years ago. I caused trouble in Heaven, and was trapped under a mountain for a long time. I found a teacher and now we are traveling to the West to find Buddhist scripture. Now we have a little bit of trouble with some monsters on this mountain. We do not want to fight you. Let us continue our journey. We will leave you and not cause any trouble."

"Yes, we should not fight. I will call your name. Answer me, and then you can leave."

"All right. But then I will call your name, and you must answer me."

"That's fine," said the monster. Then he shouted, "Pilgrim Sun!"

"Yes, I am Pilgrim Sun," replied Sun Wukong. The monster opened his gourd, but of course nothing happened. The monster looked at the gourd, then he looked at Sun Wukong. Then Sun Wukong said, "Now I will call you. Great King Silver Horn!" he cried.

"Yes, I am Great King Silver Horn!" replied the monster. Instantly he was sucked into the gourd that was in Sun Wukong's sleeve. Sun Wukong laughed and shook the gourd. He could feel the liquid inside, and he knew that Silver Horn was dead. He walked to the door of the cave, holding the gourd and shaking it. "Great King Golden Horn!" he shouted into the cave. "I have your younger brother. He has turned to liquid. Soon I will have you too!"

When Golden Horn heard that his brother was dead, he began to cry. Zhu Bajie heard this, and he said, "Monster, don't cry. Old Pig will tell you something. Pilgrim Sun and Sun Grimpil and Sun Wukong are all the same person. He stole your treasures, and he killed your brother. Now stop crying and prepare a nice vegetarian dinner for us. We will eat dinner and then we will leave you alone."

"Cook that pig!" shouted Golden Horn. "I will eat him first. Then when my belly is full, I will fight this Sun Wukong." Then he said, "No, wait, don't cook the pig yet. I have to fight this monkey first." Then he turned to one of the little demons and said, "Tell me quickly. How many treasures do we have in the cave right now?"

"Three treasures."

"Which three?"

"The sword of seven stars, the palm leaf fan, and the jade vase."

"I don't need the vase right now. Bring me the sword and the fan." The demon brought the two treasures to Golden Horn. He put the fan in his sleeve and he held the sword in his hand. Then he walked out of the cave, right past Sun Wukong. He walked into a clearing. He called every demon in the region. Three hundred demons came, all carrying weapons. Golden Horn turned and faced Sun Wukong, with the three hundred demons behind him. How did he look, you ask?

> The monster wore a long red cape, it looked like fire
> Behind him, the demons held up a long red banner
> His eyes were open wide, lightning flashed from them
> In his hand was the sword of seven stars
> He moved quickly like a cloud in the sky
> His voice was like thunder, shaking the mountains
> He was a great warrior, ready to fight Heaven itself
> Leading many demons, he was ready to fight Old Monkey

"You ugly ape!" he shouted. "You killed my younger brother and my dear mother. Now you must die."

"Monster, you are the one asking to die. Are you saying that the life of a monster is worth more than the lives of my Master and my friends? Do you think I would be ok with you eating them for dinner? Give them to me now. Also, give me some money for our journey. Then I might let you live."

Golden Horn did not answer. He just tried to hit Sun Wukong's head with this sword. The fight began. They fought until day turned into night. The sky grew dark. Dragons hid in their caves and tigers hid in the forest. One using his sword and the other using his rod, the two great ones fought for many hours.

Golden Horn was becoming tired, so he called his three hundred demons. The demons fought Sun Wukong on all four sides. Sun Wukong used his rod, but there were just too many demons. Quickly he pulled a hundred hairs from his left arm, shouted "Change!" and each one became another copy of Sun Wukong. The long hairs became big monkeys with golden hoop rods. The medium hairs became medium size monkeys with powerful fists. The short hairs became small monkeys who grabbed the demons by the legs.

The demons began to lose the fight. They ran away, shouting, "We can't fight all these monkeys!" Now Golden Horn was alone fighting all the monkeys. He pulled the palm leaf fan from his sleeve and waved it towards Sun Wukong and the army of monkeys. Fire came up from the ground all around him. It was a magic fire, very hot, with no smoke. All the animals ran away from it, all the birds flew away in fear. The fire was so hot that rivers became dry and the earth turned red.

The fire was so hot that it burned the hairs on Sun Wukong's arms. When the hairs burned, all the monkeys burned also. Now Sun Wukong and Golden Horn stood alone in the clearing. Sun Wukong jumped up and flew back to the cave. But when he arrived there, he saw a hundred more little demons standing outside the cave. Sun Wukong was angry now, he used his golden hoop rod to kill every one of the little demons.

Inside the cave, he saw a red light. "Oh, no!" he said, "the cave is on fire too!" But it was not on fire. He was just seeing the light from the jade vase. Quickly he put the vase in his sleeve. Just then, Golden Horn ran into the cave and tried again to kill Sun Wukong with his seven-star sword. The two of them fought inside the cave. But this time the monkey was too powerful for the monster. Golden Horn ran away.

Sun Wukong turned and saw Tangseng and his friends tied up in the cave. He untied them. "Disciple, you have been working very hard!" said Tangseng.

"Yes, my legs are tired," he replied. "I have been walking more than a mail carrier, no rest for me at all. But everything is good. One monster is trapped inside the gourd and turned to liquid. The other monster has run away. And most of the little demons are dead. It's been a very long day. Let's have some dinner!" They looked around the cave and found some rice, noodles and vegetables. They cooked a nice vegetarian dinner, then they sat down and ate it with a little bit of wine. Tangseng, of course, did not drink any wine, he only drank water. When they were finished, they found some beds in the back of the cave and went to sleep.

Now you may think that is the end of the story, but it is not. Golden Horn was still angry. So he flew away to Crush Dragon Mountain and met several hundred female demons. He told them that Sun Wukong killed his brother and his mother. When the female demons heard this, they were very angry and wanted revenge.

Then his maternal uncle arrived, his name was Great King Fox Number Seven. The uncle had heard about the death of his sister. So he came with two hundred more little demons. Together they now had a large army of demons, and they all wanted revenge on Sun Wukong.

The two monsters and the hundreds of little demons arrived at the cave in the morning. Sun Wukong, Zhu Bajie and Sha Wujing were waiting for them. But Sun Wukong changed into the form of a little demon. He called out, "Great King Golden Horn! Great King Golden Horn!" Golden Horn thought the demon needed his help, so he replied. As soon as he did, Sun Wukong opened his magic gourd and sucked the monster inside. But just before the monster went inside the gourd, Sun Wukong grabbed the monster's sword of seven stars.

There was some more fighting, but it was over quickly. Great King Fox Number Seven was killed, and turned into a nine-tailed fox just like his sister. All the little demons ran away.

Now, finally, all the fighting was over. Sun Wukong said to Tangseng, "Master, the mountain is safe now. The monsters have been killed. The demons have run away. And we have all five of the treasures." Tangseng was happy to hear this. They had a good breakfast, then they all began walking west again.

As they walked, an old blind man came up to them. He grabbed Tangseng's horse and said, "Give me back my treasures!"

"Ah, not more monsters!" said Zhu Bajie. But Sun Wukong looked carefully at the blind man and recognized that he was the great Daoist saint Laozi. He bowed deeply to Laozi.

Laozi said, "My child, you have five treasures. They are mine. I use the gourd to store magic elixir. I use the jade vase to store my water. I use the sword of seven stars to fight demons. I use the fan to tend my fire. And the yellow-gold rope is the belt of my gown. Also, I must tell you that the two monsters that you killed are really two Daoist youths. One tends my golden brazier and the other tends my silver brazier. Guanyin asked me to give the youths to her for a short time. She wanted to see if you really want to continue your journey to the west."

Sun Wukong thought to himself, "This Guanyin said she would help us. But it looks like she is more interested in causing trouble for us!" But he did not say this to Laozi. He just said, "Sir, I am happy to return your five treasures to you."

Laozi took the five treasures from Sun Wukong. He opened the gourd, turned it upside down, and liquid flowed from the gourd onto the ground. As they all watched, the liquid changed into two young men. They stood up, one standing on Laozi's right side, the other on his left side. A beam of golden light came down from Heaven. Laozi and the two youths flew up the golden light and disappeared into Heaven.

Tangseng, Sun Wukong, Zhu Bajie and Sha Wujing watched them fly up into the sky. Then, with the morning sun at their backs, they began walking west again.

Chapter 36

Sha Wujing was leading the horse and Zhu Bajie was carrying the luggage. Sun Wukong was in front, carrying his iron rod across his shoulders and looking in all four directions for trouble.

"Disciples," said Tangseng, "why is it so difficult to reach the Western Heaven? We have seen springtime come and go four or five times. Each time spring has turned to summer, then fall, then winter, then spring again. But still, we travel on this road. When will we reach the end?"

Sun Wukong replied, "Don't worry, Master, the road is long. We have just begun. Look at it like this: we are still in our house. All of Heaven and Earth is just one room in our home. The blue sky is our roof, the sun and moon are our windows, and the mountains are the pillars that hold up our home. We have not left our house yet. But don't worry, just follow me!"

They came to a tall mountain. Sun Wukong walked quickly up the mountain path, and the others followed close behind him. They heard wolves, and Tangseng became afraid. Sun Wukong saw this and laughed. "Don't be afraid, Master, and keep going. We will reach the end when we have done everything that Heaven asks of us."

They walked until evening. They could see thousands of stars in the sky, and the moon rose in the east. Tangseng wanted to find a place to rest for the night. He saw several large buildings. "Disciples, I see a place. Perhaps it is a temple."

"Wait," said Sun Wukong. "Let me take a look first." He jumped into the air and flew towards the building. He saw that it was indeed a Buddhist monastery. All around the monastery was a high red stone wall, with a large golden gate. He looked inside the wall and saw many monks. Some of the monks were teaching classes. Some were playing music, cooking food, burning incense, or just walking around. He returned and said, "Master, this looks all right to me. We can stay here tonight."

They walked towards the golden gate. Above the gate was a sign, covered by dirt. Sun Wukong cleaned the sign, and read it: "Precious Grove Monastery."

"Wait here," said Tangseng to Sun Wukong. "You are an ugly monkey. If you frighten the monks, we will have no place to stay tonight." He got off his horse, folded his hands in front of him, and walked slowly through the gate.

There was a large golden lion statue on his left side, and another one on his right side. He walked through a second gate and saw a statue of the bodhisattva Guanyin. She was giving food to fish and other creatures of the ocean. He thought, "Ah, look at these creatures all praying to Buddha. Why can't people do this?"

As he was thinking about this, a worker came through the third gate and met him, saying, "Where does the Master come from?"

Tangseng replied, "This poor monk comes from the Tang kingdom. He was sent by the Tang Emperor to journey to the west and find Buddhist books to bring back to the Tang Emperor. We were traveling nearby and saw your beautiful monastery. The hour is getting late, so we ask you to give us a place to rest for the night. We will leave in the morning."

The worker replied, "I cannot say if you can or cannot stay here tonight. I am just a poor worker. I will go and ask my master." The worker ran into the monastery and said to the old master, "Sir, there is a monk outside."

The old master looked outside. He saw Tangseng wearing torn and dirty clothing and old sandals on his feet. The old master became angry, and said to the worker, "That is no monk, that is just a beggar. I don't want him bringing dirt into our beautiful clean monastery. Tell him to go away!"

Tangseng heard this. He did not wait for the worker. He walked right into the monastery and said to the old master, "How sad, how sad. It is as people say, 'A man away from home is cheap!' This poor monk left home long ago to become a monk. I don't know what I did to cause you to say these things to me. If I told my monkey disciple what you told me, he would use his iron rod to teach you a lesson that you will never forget."

The monk was sitting at his desk. He looked up at Tangseng and said, "Who are you and where did you come from?"

"This poor monk was sent by the Tang emperor to the Western Heaven, to find and bring back the Buddha's books. I was passing through your beautiful neighborhood. The hour was getting late, so I thought to stop here and rest. I will leave early tomorrow morning. Please let me stay tonight."

The old master looked at Tangseng, and said, "Are you Tangseng?"

"Yes."

"I have heard of you. Well, you cannot stay here. There is a nice inn about five miles west of here. They sell food there, and they also have beds. Now go away."

Tangseng was getting a little bit angry. He folded his hands again and said, "Dear sir, the ancients said that a monk may come to any abbot or monastery, and take three percent of the food in that place. Why do you tell me to go away?"

The old master replied, "I will not let beggars come in here! A long time ago, some poor monks like you arrived here. They sat in front of the gate and asked for food. I let them in and gave them vegetarian food. I even gave each of them new clothes, and I invited them to stay for a few days. Do you know, they stayed here for eight years and caused a lot of trouble!"

Now Tangseng was really angry. He did not reply to the old master, he just walked out. He told his disciples that the old master would not let them stay. Sun Wukong said, "You know what the ancients say, 'when people come together for the Buddha, they are all one family.' This old master is not a true Buddhist. You wait here. I will see what's going on."

Sun Wukong walked through the first gate and second gate, right up to the monastery door. The worker saw him and was terrified. He ran back into the monastery and said to the old master, "Holy father, there is another monk outside. He is not like the first one. He has big yellow eyes, pointed ears, a hairy face, and a nose like a thunder god. And he is holding in his hands a huge iron rod. I think he wants to beat someone with it!"

The old monk got up and walked outside to see who was there. He took one look at Sun Wukong, turned, and ran back inside. He quickly closed the monastery door.

This was no problem for Sun Wukong. He just used his iron rod to smash the door. Then he shouted, "Hurry up! I want to take a nap. I need one thousand rooms right now!"

The old master was shaking in his shoes. He shouted through the door to Sun Wukong, "Elder brother, I am sorry but we only have three hundred rooms in our monastery. We have no rooms for you. Please go somewhere else."

Sun Wukong smashed his iron rod down onto the floor. Stones flew up to the sky. He said to the old master, "It is time for you to leave. All of you. Now."

"But sir, there are five hundred monks here. We have lived here since we were young men. There is no other place for us to go."

"All right. Then come out and I will beat you with my iron rod."

The old master and the worker did not know which person Sun Wukong wanted to beat. They started arguing about who should go out and get the beating. While they were arguing, Sun Wukong looked around. He saw a large stone lion. He raised his iron rod and smashed it down on the lion, turning it into a pile of stones. This made the old master even more afraid. "All right, all right!" he cried, "You can stay here tonight."

"Good. Call all the monks. Tell them all to come here and welcome the Tang monk." The old master told the worker to do this. Sun Wukong called to Tangseng and the others, telling them to come inside.

Soon, five hundred monks were standing in the main hall. They all kowtowed to Tangseng. Zhu Bajie thought this was very funny. He said to Tangseng, "Master, when you went into the monastery, you came out crying. But when Old Monkey went inside, he came back with five hundred monks kowtowing to him. Why is that?"

"You fool," replied Tangseng. "The ancients say, 'Even ghosts are afraid of nasty people.'" The he turned to the kowtowing monks and said, "My friends, please rise." He said to the old master, "Thank you for welcoming us to your home. Truly, we are all brothers following the Buddha."

The old master replied, "Please forgive us for not recognizing you as the great Tangseng. We are all very happy to meet you. Tell me, do you want meat or vegetables for dinner?" Tangseng told him that they all were monks and lived only on vegetarian food. So the old master told his monks to go to the kitchen and prepare dinner for the visitors.

They all enjoyed a nice vegetarian dinner, then they went to their beds to rest for the night. All five hundred monks followed them. Tangseng looked at them and said, "Please, go back to your own rooms! We don't need any more of your help tonight."

After the monks left, Tangseng walked outside and looked up to the sky. There was a large bright moon in the sky. He said to the others,

> "Look at the bright moon in the sky
> Her light covers all the world
> It fills great temples and small homes
> Ten thousand miles are made bright
> She is a wheel of ice in the green sky
> A ball of snow over the blue sea
> An old traveler sleeps in the inn

An old man sleeps in his mountain home
The moon enters and turns black hair to gray
And gray hair to white
She lights each window like white snow
And comes to see us here tonight."

He said, "My friends, you are all tired from the day's journey. Go to sleep. I will stay here and meditate on the teachings of the Buddha."

Sun Wukong asked him, "Master, you have studied the Buddha's words since you were a young boy. Why do you need to study them again now?"

"Since we left Chang'an, we have been traveling day and night. I fear that I will forget what I learned when I was a youth." Sun Wukong nodded, and he went to sleep. Tangseng stayed outside for a long time, under the bright moon.

Chapter 37

Finally, around the time of the third watch, Tangseng went to bed. He was tired and quickly fell asleep. He began to dream. In his dream he heard the sound of a strange and powerful wind. He listened to the wind. It seemed to be calling him. "Master!" said the wind. Tangseng saw a man standing there, soaking wet as if he was in a heavy rain. The man said again, "Master!"

In his dream Tangseng asked, "Who are you? Are you a ghost here to cause trouble? I am a good man. I am a monk. I am traveling to the Western Heaven with three disciples. They are all great warriors. They can kill you instantly if you cause trouble. Now go away while you still can, and don't come here to the doors of this monastery."

"I am not a ghost," said the man. "Look at me!" Tangseng looked carefully at the man. On his head was a rising-to-Heaven hat. He wore a red robe with flying dragons, tied with a green belt. On his feet were boots embroidered with white clouds. His face was strong like the king of Mount Tai. Tangseng could see that this was a great king.

Tangseng bowed deeply and said, "Your majesty, did you have trouble in your kingdom? Did evil ministers try to take your throne away from you? Is that why you are here at this monastery in the middle of the night?"

The man replied, "No, I had no trouble with evil ministers. My kingdom is about forty miles west of here. It is called the Black Rooster Kingdom. About five years ago there was a terrible drought. The people had no water. They could not grow any food, and many people died from hunger."

Tangseng said, "Your majesty, the ancients say, 'when the kingdom is upright, then Heaven will smile.' If there is no food, the king must open up the storehouses and give food to your people. But instead, you are here, all alone, telling your story to this poor monk. What did you do that caused Heaven to become angry with you?"

"I did just as you say. We opened the storehouses and gave away all the food. We had no money, so we stopped paying the ministers. I also went hungry, to share the pain of our people. Night and day we all prayed to the gods. We did this for three years, but still there was no rain. Our people were dying. Then one day a Daoist monk came to our kingdom. He called the wind, and the wind brought rain. He turned rock into gold. Once again, our people had food to eat and water to drink. I was so happy, I made him my brother."

"If this Daoist monk could make rain anytime he wanted, then your kingdom should be wealthy and happy. Why are you here tonight?"

"Yes, our kingdom was wealthy and happy. But one day in the springtime, I was walking in the garden with the Daoist monk. We came to an eight-sided well. Suddenly the monk pushed me into the well. Then he covered the well with a large flat stone. He covered the well with dirt, and he planted a tree on top of it! And so, I have been dead for three years."

Tangseng listened to this, then he said, "Your Majesty, you say you have been dead for three years. Didn't your ministers miss you and search for you?"

"As soon as the Daoist monk pushed me into the well, he changed his form and looked just like me. Then everything belonged to him: my kingdom, my army, my four hundred ministers and my many wives. Truly this man is a demon!"

"My friend, I think you are too timid. Yes, the Daoist certainly had powerful magic. But after your death you could have brought the matter to Yama, the King of the Underworld."

"I could not do that. This demon is good friends with Yama's ministers. The Ten Kings of the Underworld are his brothers. He even goes drinking with the dragon king of the ocean. There is no place I can go for help."

"If you cannot get help in the world of darkness, why do you come to me in the world of light?"

"Ah great Tang monk, I have heard of you! You are a great man. You are protected by the Six Gods of Darkness, the Six Gods of Light, and many other gods. Just now, one of the Gods of Darkness brought me here on the strange wind. He told me that you have a disciple, the Monkey King, who is powerful. So I ask you to please come to my kingdom, seize the demon monk, and return me to our throne!"

"Well, if you ask my monkey disciple to fight demons and catch monsters, that will make him very happy. But I'm afraid this will be a very difficult job."

"Why?"

"You say that this demon looks exactly like you. That means that everyone in your kingdom thinks that the demon really is you. If my monkey disciple does something to harm the demon, the people of your kingdom will think that he harmed the true king. He would be in serious trouble."

"That may be true. But my son, the prince, is still in the palace. He does not know that I have been killed and the demon is now sitting on the throne instead of me. But the demon will not let my son speak with his mother. He is afraid that if the two of them talk together, they will learn the truth."

"How can I meet the prince? I am just a lowly traveling monk."

"My son is leaving the palace tomorrow. He plans to go hunting. He will bring three thousand men and horses. Perhaps you can meet him while he is on this hunting trip."

"Why would he believe me?" asked Tangseng. "For years he has believed that you are alive. He thinks that he talks with you every day."

"Use this." The king showed a white jade statue to Tangseng. "After the demon pushed me into the well, he took everything in the palace, everything in the whole kingdom. But he could not find this jade statue because it was in my robe when he pushed me into the well. Show this to my son."

"All right, I will do it. Please wait here."

"No, I cannot. I have one more job to do tonight. I must go to the queen and talk to her in a dream." The ghost king left the room. Tangseng tried to follow him, but he fell and hit his head on the floor. As soon as that happened, he woke from his dream.

"Disciples, disciples, come quickly!" he called. "I had a dream. I must tell you about it!"

Sun Wukong came into the room. He said, "Master, your mind is too busy. Yesterday you were worried about meeting monsters on this mountain. Then you were worried about how far it is to the Western Heaven. Then you thought about your home in Chang'an. Because of this mind is too busy, and you dream. Look at me. I have a quiet mind, and I have no dreams at all."

"No, this was not a dream of home or a dream of fear. I met a ghost king." Then Tangseng told his three disciples about the dream. Then he looked around the room, and he saw the white jade statue lying on the floor. He picked it up and showed it to the three disciples. "This is the statue that the king gave me in my dream!"

Sun Wukong laughed and said, "It looks like this ghost king wants to let me have some fun. If there's a demon on the throne, my iron rod will take care of him!" Then the monkey pulled a hair from his head and blew on it. Instantly it changed into a small red wooden box. Sun Wukong put the jade statue in the box. "Master, go sit in the main hall. Hold the box in your hands. Wait for me. I will bring the prince to you. When he arrives, open the box a little bit. I will make myself just two inches high and jump into the box. Do not stand up or even look at him. This will make him angry, and he will have you arrested."

"What?" cried Tangseng. "Then what will happen?"

"Don't worry, I will be there to protect you. Tell him that you are a monk traveling to the Western Heaven, which of course is true. Tell him that there is a treasure inside this box. The treasure knows everything about the past five hundred years, the present five hundred years, and the future five hundred years. Then I will come out and tell the prince everything that you heard in your dream. The prince will believe me. Then I can go to the palace and kill the demon."

Tangseng thought this was a good plan. The next morning, Sun Wukong jumped into the air and flew forty miles to the city. He saw that it was covered in a dark fog. "Truly, if a true king sits on the throne, the city will be full of light. But now a demon sits on the throne, so of course the city is covered in dark fog."

As he looked at the city, the eastern gates opened and three thousand men and horses came out. They soon reached the rice fields about twenty miles from the monastery. In front was a tall handsome young man, holding a sword of blue steel. Sun Wukong recognized that this was the prince. "Let me have a little fun with him," he thought to himself.

Sun Wukong changed into a small white rabbit. He ran right in front of the prince's horse. The prince shouted with delight and shot the rabbit with an arrow. He did not see Sun Wukong grab the arrow before it hit his body, so the rabbit was not hurt. The rabbit ran away towards the monastery. The prince followed. When the rabbit arrived at the monastery, it ran inside and changed back to Sun Wukong's monkey form. "Master, the prince is here!" shouted Sun Wukong.

The prince arrived, jumped down from his horse, and entered the main hall of the monastery. Three thousand men on horses arrived shortly afterwards, and many of them also crowded into the hall. At the other end of the hall, the five hundred monks entered and kowtowed to the prince. The prince looked around. He saw the beautiful paintings in the main hall. Then he saw a monk sitting in the middle of the hall. The monk did not get up or bow to the prince.

The prince was very angry. "Seize him!" he cried. The prince's men tried to grab Tangseng. But Sun Wukong, hiding inside the box, made a magic spell that protected Tangseng like a wall of stone, so the men could not touch him. The prince said, "Who are you, monk, to use magic against me?"

Tangseng replied, "Sir, I am just a poor monk from the Tang empire. I am traveling to the Western Heaven to find the Buddha's books and bring them back to my emperor. But I know you. You have not honored your father."

"What?" cried the prince. "Of course I honor my father. I see him every day, and I do as he tells me."

"Great prince, look inside this red box. You will find a treasure. This treasure can see five hundred years in the past, five hundred years in the present, and five hundred years in the future. And this treasure knows that you have not honored your father." Then Tangseng opened the box. Sun Wukong jumped out, and grew from two inches tall to his usual height.

The prince said to him, "This old monk says that you have knowledge of the past, present and future. Tell me the truth: have I or have I not honored my father?"

Sun Wukong replied, "Your highness, you are the son of the king of Black Rooster Kingdom. You may remember that there was no rain in your kingdom for several years. The people had no water and no food. Then a Daoist monk arrived. He brought rain, and the people could eat again. The monk and your father became brothers."

"Yes, I know this. What of it?"

"I will tell you, but it is a secret. No one else can hear this." So the prince told his three thousand men to leave the main hall. And Tangseng told the five hundred monks to leave. Now it was just the three of them in the main hall.

Sun Wukong continued, "Your Highness, the Daoist monk is really a demon. Three years ago he killed your father. He then took the form of your father, and became king of your land. He could not be in two bodies at the same time, so he told you that the Daoist monk had returned to the mountains where he came from. But this is not true. The man who sits on the throne is not your father. It is the demon!"

"That cannot be true," said the prince. "If our king was a demon, things would be very bad for us. But for the last few years our kingdom has been happy. We have plenty of rain, we have plenty of food, and there is no war. You are wrong. The Daoist monk is gone, my father is on the throne, and all is well in our kingdom."

Sun Wukong turned to Tangseng and said, "See, he does not believe me. Show him the treasure." Tangseng held the jade statue out for the prince to see.

"Thief! Thief!" cried the prince. "You have stolen this statue, and now you try to give it back to me while you lie about my father. I will have you arrested and killed for this!"

Tangseng became very afraid. He turned to Sun Wukong and said, "Monkey, look at the trouble you have caused. Do something!"

Sun Wukong said, "Your Highness, my name is Sun Wukong. I am the elder disciple of this monk Tangseng. We were traveling west yesterday. It became late so we stopped at this monastery to spend the night. During the night, my master met your father in a dream. Your father told my master that the Daoist monk had killed him and thrown him into a well. Then the Daoist monk changed his form to look like your father. He seized the throne and has been the king for three years. The demon is afraid that your mother knows the difference between him and your real father. For that reason, he will not let you see your mother. He is afraid that the two of you will discuss this and learn the truth."

The prince did not know what to think. He stood there, just thinking about Sun Wukong's words.

Sun Wukong said, "Your Highness, I know this is a lot to think about. But it is all true. You can find the truth for yourself. Leave your three thousand men here. Go back quietly to the palace. Go in through the servant's gate in the back, and find your mother. Talk with her!"

Chapter 38

The prince did as Sun Wukong told him. He told his three thousand men to wait at the monastery. Then he rode his horse quickly back to the palace, entered through the servant's gate, and soon found his mother. The Queen was sitting in the garden, crying. She remembered an important dream from the previous night, but she could only remember the first half of the dream. When she saw her son arrive, she ran to him. "Ah my son, I am so happy to see you! It has been many years." She saw that he was unhappy, and said, "Why are you unhappy? Your life is good. And sometime in the future, your father will return to Heaven and you will sit on the throne. How can you be unhappy?"

"Mother, I must ask you a question. Who sits on the throne?"

"My son, are you mad? It is your father of course."

"Mother, I must ask you another more difficult question. Is your husband different than he was a few years ago?"

"No, he is the same as he was before."

"Mother, when you are in bed with him, is everything the same as before?"

The queen looked down at the ground. She said quietly, "Well, three years ago he was loving and warm. But for the past three years he has been as cold as ice. I have tried to invite him to give his love to me, but he just says that he is old and cannot do it anymore."

The prince jumped up and mounted his horse. He said, "Mother, I must go. Earlier today I was out hunting and I met a traveling monk and his disciple. They told me that the man sitting on the throne is not my father, but a demon. I did not believe them, but I believe them now!"

"My son, how can you believe the words of these people? You just met them today!"

"They gave me this." He handed her the white jade statue.

The queen saw it and began to cry. She just remembered the rest of her dream. She said, "My son, last night I saw your father in a dream. He was covered with water. He told me he was dead, that the Daoist monk had thrown him down a well. He said that there is a traveling monk who can help us. My son, you must go to that monk and get his help right away!"

The prince rode his horse back to the monastery. He got off the horse and walked into the main hall. He saw Sun Wukong and Tangseng. He told them everything that had happened. Sun Wukong said, "Ah, if the demon king is cold in bed, he is probably a cold-blooded creature of some sort. Don't worry, I will take care of this demon. I'll do it tomorrow. For now, go back to the palace and wait for me."

"I cannot go back right now. I left the palace with three thousand men to go hunting. How can I return with no meat?"

Sun Wukong flew into the sky and called for the local spirit and the mountain god. He told them that he needed them to put several hundred animals by the side of the road. The local spirit and mountain god did as they were told. Sun Wukong returned to the monastery and told the prince, "Your highness, you can go back. You will find plenty of animals by the side of the road. You can pick them up and bring them to the palace."

The prince kowtowed to Sun Wukong. Then he walked out of the monastery and told the soldiers that the hunt was finished and it was time to return to the palace. As they traveled on the road, they saw the animals lying on the ground and picked them all up. Then they returned to the palace.

That night, Sun Wukong was resting in his bed. Suddenly he jumped up and ran over to wake up Tangseng. "Master, wake up!"

"What is it," asked Tangseng.

"We have a problem. Of course, we can go back to the palace and try to seize the demon king, or even kill him. But if we say that the demon killed the true king, nobody will believe us. We have to go back to the well and find the body of the true king."

"Good idea. Go get Zhu Bajie to help you."

Sun Wukong walked over to Zhu's bed. "Wake up! Wake up!" he shouted in Zhu's ear.

"Let me sleep," said Zhu, "we have to travel tomorrow."

"You must help me tonight. I have to fight the demon king tomorrow. He is very powerful. I must find his treasure and steal it, to take away his power. I need you to help me steal the treasure."

Zhu was not happy about this. He said, "All right, but I want to keep the treasure. When we are traveling I will probably get very hungry. I can sell the treasure and get some food." Sun Wukong agreed to this. So Zhu got out of bed and followed Sun Wukong. They used Sun Wukong's cloud somersault to fly back to the city. Then they walked to the palace and jumped over the high stone wall. They were in the garden. They arrived at the well where the king had died. It had a large tree growing on top of it.

Zhu used his rake to push over the tree. Then he used his snout to push away dirt, until he came to a large flat stone that covered the well. Sun Wukong helped Zhu push the flat stone to the side. They looked into the well. They saw light coming from the bottom of the well. "Look!" said Zhu, "I see treasure at the bottom of the well! But how can we get to the bottom? We have no ropes."

"No problem," said Sun Wukong. "Give me your clothes." Then Sun Wukong changed his iron rod into a very long wooden pole, long enough to reach the bottom of the well. He tied Zhu's clothes around the end of the pole, tied Zhu to his clothes, and lowered Zhu down into the well.

Down, down, down went Zhu. His foot touched the water. "Stop!" he cried. But Sun Wukong pushed down on the pole, and Zhu fell into the water.

"I think the treasure is at the bottom of the water," said Sun Wukong. "Swim down and see if you can find it." Zhu swam down. He opened his eyes and looked around. He saw a sign saying, "Water Crystal Palace." Zhu thought this was strange. How could there be a palace at the bottom of a well? He did not know that the Well Dragon King lived here.

The Well Dragon King heard Zhu arrive. He came out of his crystal palace to meet Zhu. He said, "Hello my friend. We do not get many visitors here. Are you the Marshal of Heaven?"

Zhu replied, "Yes, I was the Marshal of Heaven. I am now a disciple of Tangseng, who is journeying to the Western Heaven in search of Buddha's books. My elder brother is Sun Wukong. He is above us right now, waiting for me to return. He asked me to get a treasure and bring it back to him. Do you have it?"

"I have no treasures. I am not like the other dragon kings who live in the ocean or in large rivers. They have a lot of treasure. But I live in this well. It is very small, and I rarely see the sun or the moon. I certainly don't have any treasure for you."

"You have nothing?"

"Well, I do have one thing. Come with me." The dragon king swam into another room, and Zhu followed. They came to the body of a dead king. The dead king was still wearing a rising-to-Heaven hat on his head. He wore a red robe with flying dragons, tied with a green belt. On his feet were boots

embroidered with white clouds. "Here is your treasure," said the dragon king.

 "Treasure? Before I met the Tang monk, I used to eat people. I call this food!"

"Please do not think of this as food. This is the body of the king of Black Rooster Kingdom. He arrived here several years ago. I have used my small magic to keep his body from decaying. You may bring this body back to Sun Wukong. Perhaps the monkey can bring him back to life."

Zhu picked up the body of the dead king and swam back to the wooden pole. He called up to Sun Wukong, "I have your treasure. Pull me up!" Sun

Wukong pulled the wooden pole up, bringing out Zhu and the body. All three of them fell onto the ground.

"All right, now carry the body back to Master," said Sun Wukong. Zhu was not happy to be carrying a dead body, but Sun Wukong took out his iron rod and waved it at Zhu. Then Zhu picked up the dead body and they walked out of the garden. Sun Wukong grabbed Zhu, and using his cloud somersault they flew back to the monastery.

When they arrived at the monastery, they walked into the main hall where Tangseng waited for them. Zhu dropped the body on the floor and said, "Here is Old Monkey's grandfather." Sun Wukong laughed and said, "That's not my grandfather, you idiot. That is the king of Black Rooster Kingdom."

Tangseng said, "Yes, and he has been dead for several years. Wukong, can you bring him back to life?"

Sun Wukong replied, "I don't think so. When someone dies, they go to the Underworld for some time, to pay for all the bad things they did during life. If they were a good person this could take a few weeks. Or it can take a few years. Then they return to life in a new body. But this man has been dead for several years. How can I bring him back?"

"Think. You must find a way."

Sun Wukong thought for a couple of minutes. Then he said, "OK, I have an idea. I will go to the Underworld to talk with the Ten Kings of the Underworld. I will find out which king has the soul of this dead man. Then I will bring the soul back and put it into this dead body."

Zhu heard this. He said, "Ah monkey, you need a better plan than that! You told me that you could bring this man back to life without needing to go to the Underworld." This was not true, of course. But Tangseng believed it. He began to say the tight headband spell. The headband on Sun Wukong's head began to tighten, and Sun Wukong began to get a terrible pain in his head.

Chapter 39

"Stop, Master, stop! All right, I have a better idea. I will use my cloud somersault to go up to the thirty-third Heaven, to the home of the great Laozi. He has magic pills that can bring a person back to life. I will get one of these pills and give it to the dead king."

Tangseng agreed to this. So Sun Wukong used his cloud somersault and flew up to the South Heaven Gate. He went through the gate, then he flew up to the thirty-third Heaven and arrived at the home of Laozi. He entered. He saw Laozi with two or three young men, making magic pills. Laozi looked up and saw Sun Wukong. He said to the young men, "Be careful, here is the troublesome monkey who stole our magic pills. And later, he gave me a hard time when I asked for my five treasures back. Why have you returned to my home, monkey?"

"Sir, if you remember correctly, I did not give you any trouble when you asked for your five treasures. I gave them to you. Then my master and I continued on our journey west. We came to Black Rooster Kingdom. We learned that the king had been killed by a demon. The demon took the form of the king and now sits on the king's throne. Two nights ago, the ghost of the dead king came to visit my master in a dream. He asked my master for help. Now we want to bring the king back to life so he can take back the throne."

"And what do you want from me?"

"I need a thousand of your magic pills."

"What, do you think you can eat these pills like rice?"

"All right," laughed Sun Wukong. "Then just give me a hundred pills."

"I don't have any pills for you."

"All right, how about ten pills?"

"I told you, I don't have any."

"All right, then I will just go somewhere else to get them." Sun Wukong turned to go. But Laozi started to worry that Sun Wukong might return later and steal his magic pills.

"You troublemaking monkey," he said, "I will give you one pill. Now take it and never come back." Sun Wukong took the pill, and flew back down to the monastery. He walked over to the body of the dead king. He used both of his hands to pull open the king's mouth. Then he put the magic pill in the king's mouth, and then he poured in a cup of cold water into his mouth. Sun Wukong, Tangseng, Zhu and Sha all waited to see what would happen. They waited for almost a half hour. Then the king's belly started making loud sounds.

They continued to wait, but the king did not start breathing. "You have to help him," said Tangseng. Sun Wukong opened the king's mouth again, and blew hard into it. Sun Wukong's breath traveled throughout the king's body and awakened it. The king took a deep breath and sat up.

"Thank you!" said the king to Tangseng. "I remember visiting you in your dream. I asked you for help, but I never expected to wake up in the land of the living again!" Tangseng helped the king to stand up. Then they all went into the main hall. The monks gave them breakfast. Then the monks removed the king's old and dirty clothing and gave him some clean monk's clothing to wear. Sun Wukong told the monks to clean the king's old clothing and bring it to the palace later in the day.

After breakfast, they left the monastery and walked towards the palace. The king was dressed in monk's clothing and was carrying some luggage, looking just like a servant or worker.

They walked forty miles and arrived at the palace. Sun Wukong walked up to the palace gate. He said to a guard, "We are monks sent by the Tang Emperor to journey to the west. We would like to visit with your king." The guard told this to the demon king. The demon king told the guard to bring the visitors into the throne room.

The four travelers and the true king entered the throne room. The true king looked around at the throne room and began to cry quietly. Sun Wukong said into his ear, "Please don't cry, Your Majesty. We don't want the demon king to know who you are. Soon my iron rod will do its work, and the demon king will be killed. Don't worry!"

When they got near the throne, four of them stopped walking. But Sun Wukong kept walking until he stood right in front of the demon king. He did not kowtow and he did not bow.

The demon king was angry that this visitor did not bow to him. "Where do you come from?" he asked.

"I am from the great Tang nation, traveling to the west to find Buddha's books and bring them back. We arrived here and wish to greet you."

The king was angry. He said, "So, you are from the East? I don't care about you or your kingdom. When you are in my throne room, you must bow to me. Guards, seize all of them!" The guards all ran forward to seize Sun Wukong, but he just pointed his finger at them, said some magic words, and the guards all froze.

The demon king saw this. He jumped up and wanted to fight Sun Wukong. But the prince put his hand on the demon king's arm. The prince was afraid that the demon king would hurt Tangseng. He did not know that Sun Wukong had strong magic and an iron rod. The prince said to the king, "Father, please let go of your anger. I have heard of this Tang monk who was sent by his emperor to seek the Buddha's books in the west. You are strong, but the Tang Empire is very large and very strong. If you harm this Tang monk, the Tang emperor will send a large army. We will not be able to fight them, and the Tang Emperor will punish our kingdom."

The king turned to Sun Wukong again, and said, "When did you leave the land of the east? Why did the Tang Emperor send you to the west?"

Sun Wukong told the demon king everything about their journey. He told him about his own birth on Flower Fruit Mountain, how the Buddha put him under a mountain for five hundred years, and how he met Tangseng and became his disciple. Then he told the demon king the life stories of Tangseng, Zhu Bajie and Sha Wujing. Finally he pointed to the true king and said, "And yesterday as we passed the Precious Grove Monastery, we picked up this worker."

The demon king looked carefully at the true king. "I don't like him. You say he is a monk? Let me see his papers."

"Your Highness," replied Sun Wukong, "this man cannot hear, and he cannot speak. Several years ago he lived in your kingdom. No rain came for three years. The people were hungry. They prayed to Heaven, but no help came. Then a Daoist monk arrived and brought rain. But the monk took this man's life by throwing him into a well. I brought him back to life. Now I say this to you and everyone else in this room: you are a demon, and this man is the true king of Black Rooster Kingdom!"

The demon king ran over to one of his frozen guards. He grabbed the guard's sword. Then he flew up into the air. Sun Wukong followed him, shouting, "Demon, where do you think you are going. Old Monkey is coming for you!"

The demon replied, "Monkey, go away. Why are you interested in the matters of this kingdom? This is not your problem."

Sun Wukong laughed. "You lawless demon, do you think you should be king here? This kingdom is not yours. Now prepare to meet my rod!"

They began to fight. The demon could not hope to win against Sun Wukong. He flew away, back down to the palace, and changed his appearance so he looked exactly like Tangseng. Sun Wukong returned to the palace and prepared to kill the demon with his rod.

"Don't hit me, Sun Wukong. It's me, your master Tangseng!" said the demon. Sun Wukong turned to hit the other man.

"Don't hit me, Sun Wukong. It's me, your master Tangseng!" said Tangseng.

Sun Wukong said to Zhu and Sha, "Which one of these is our master and which is the demon?" But Zhu and Sha did not know, because they did not see the demon come back and take the form of Tangseng.

Sun Wukong did not know what to do. He looked at one Tangseng, then the other. They looked exactly the same. "What should I do?" he said to Zhu.

"You are very stupid, my elder brother. This is easy," replied Zhu. "Put one Tangseng on the left side of the room with Sha. Put the other Tangseng on the right side of the room with me. Tell them both to recite the secret scripture that was given to Tangseng by the bodhisattva Guanyin. Only our master knows this scripture."

"All right." Sun Wukong put the two Tangsengs on different sides of the throne room, and told them both to recite the secret scripture. One of them was standing next to Sha, he started saying the scripture quietly. The other one was standing next to Zhu, he started mumbling. Zhu pointed to him and said, "Elder brother, this one is mumbling. He is the demon!"

The demon flew up into the air again. Sun Wukong followed. He was about to kill the demon with one blow from his iron rod. But just then, a loud voice came from a colored cloud in the northeast. The voice said, "Sun Wukong, don't do it!" Sun Wukong looked at the cloud, and saw the bodhisattva Wenshu[1]. He bowed to Wenshu.

Wenshu said, "I am here to put away this demon for you. Look!" Wenshu held a mirror in his hand. Sun Wukong used the mirror to look at the demon.

---

[1] Wenshu, also known as Manjusri, is a boddhisadva who represents the transcendent wisdom which cuts down ignorance and duality.

He saw the demon's true form: big red eyes, big head, a green body covered with green hair, four large feet, two large ears, and a long tail. He was a lion!

Sun Wukong said, "Bodhisattva, I know this green-haired lion. This is the lion who is your servant. How did he escape and come here to cause trouble in this kingdom?"

Wenshu replied, "He did not escape. I sent him here. A long time ago the king of Black Rooster Kingdom was a good man. The Buddha sent me here to lead him to the Western Heaven. I took the form of a poor monk and asked him for food. He did not like that, so he told his guards to tie me up with rope and throw me into the deep water that surrounds the palace. I was under the water for three days, then the Six Gods of Darkness saw me and helped me to escape. The Buddha sent this lion to punish the king by throwing him into a well and leaving him there for three years. Now you have come, and his punishment is finished."

"That's a nice story," said Sun Wukong, "and I am happy that you punished the king. But how many people were harmed by this? How many died?"

"Nobody has been harmed and nobody has died. The demon king has brought good weather and plentiful food to the kingdom."

"And what of the king's wives? Didn't the demon sleep with them for three years, breaking the law of Heaven?"

"No. He may look like a powerful lion, but he is a gelding. No laws were broken with the king's wives."

Zhu laughed at this and said, "So, he has a red nose but he does not drink, eh?"

"All right," said Sun Wukong. "Take him away." The bodhisattva Wenshu recited a spell, and the demon changed into his original lion form. Wenshu and the lion flew up to Heaven.

Sun Wukong returned to the throne room. All the ministers kowtowed to the true king and to Tangseng and to the disciples. Four monks arrived from the monastery, bringing the true king's clean clothes. The king took off his monk's clothing. He put on his red robe with flying dragons and tied it with his green belt. Then he put on his boots and his hat. The king looked at the throne for a minute, but he did not sit on it. He said to Tangseng and the disciples, "My friends, I have been dead for three years. I do not feel like a king anymore. One of you should sit on the throne instead of me."

Sun Wukong said, "Your Majesty, why would I want to be a king? A king has too many things to worry about. I like the simple life of a disciple." Tangseng of course said no, and so did Zhu and Sha. So finally, the king walked to the throne, sat on it, and said, "All right. I am the king again."

Tangseng smiled and said, "I think you will be a very good king."

The king asked them to stay overnight in the palace, and that evening he held a great feast. In the morning the Tang monk and his disciples all said goodbye to the king, the queen, and the prince. They walked out of the palace and continued on their journey to the west.

Chapter 40

Tangseng and his three disciples left Black Rooster Kingdom and continued on their journey. Their minds were on the teachings of Buddha and their goal was Thunderclap Mountain, far away in India. Winter was coming, the air was cool, and they could hear the wind blowing softly through the green bamboo trees.

Two weeks after leaving Black Rooster Kingdom, they arrived at a tall mountain. Tangseng said, "Be careful, I am afraid a dangerous creature or monster lives here." The path led them up the mountain. They heard animals in the forest but could not see them.

They continued on the path, climbing the mountain. Suddenly they saw a dark red cloud rising up from the mountain ahead of them. As they watched, the cloud became a bright red fireball. Sun Wukong pulled Tangseng down from his horse, saying, "Be careful, Master, a monster is coming!" The three disciples surrounded their master, holding their weapons. The monkey king Sun Wukong held his golden hoop rod, the pig-man Zhu Wuneng held his rake, and the quiet but powerful Sha Wujing held his staff. They waited for the monster to approach.

There was indeed a monster inside the red fireball. His name was Red Boy[1] and he lived in the mountain. Several years earlier he had heard people talking of the Tang monk who was traveling west to India. He heard that anyone who tasted the flesh of the Tang monk would achieve immortality. So when Red Boy saw the monk arrive, he knew that he wanted to kill and eat the monk.

The monster thought, "The monk looks very tasty, but those three disciples look dangerous. I do not want to fight all of them." Using his powerful magic, he changed his appearance so he looked like a small boy around seven years old. He tied himself up with rope and hung himself upside down from a tree. Then he started shouting, "Help me! Help me!"

Sun Wukong, the elder disciple, saw the red cloud disappear. "It's ok to continue," he said to the others. "I think there was a monster in the red cloud,

---

[1] Red Boy is the son of Princess Iron Fan and the Bull Demon King. The story of his battle with Sun Wukong is told in chapters 40 – 43. After his defeat, Red Boy became a devoted disciple of Guanyin and was given the new name Shancai (or Sudhana), "Boy Skilled in Wealth."

but I don't see him anymore. He was probably just passing by."

Zhu laughed and said, "Elder brother, I did not know that monsters would just pass by!"

"Of course. Perhaps a demon king is having a festival, and he wants to invite all the local monsters to come. So of course he would send out invitations. Those monsters would not care about harming people like us, they would just be passing by on their way to the festival."

Zhu laughed again but did not reply. They continued on the path. Soon they heard the boy crying for help. Sun Wukong knew that his master would want to stop and help. He said, "Master, we are in a dangerous place. We should not stop. Mind your own business."

Tangseng wanted to stop, but he agreed to keep moving. But the shouting continued. Finally Tangseng said, "Listen to that boy crying. If it was a demon or a monster, there would be no echo. I know that I heard an echo. Let's stop and help him."

"Please, master," said Sun Wukong, "put away your kindness until we have passed over this mountain. You know that any creature can become an evil spirit. They call you. If you answer, the spirit takes your soul!"

They continued walking, and they came to a place where they could see the little boy hanging upside down in a tree. Tangseng became angry. He shouted at Sun Wukong, "You trouble-making ape. You were just trying to frighten me! Look at that poor boy. He needs our help!" Sun Wukong did not reply, because he was afraid that Tangseng would recite the Tight Headband Spell and cause him great pain.

Tangseng said to the boy, "Where do you come from, boy? Why are you hanging from this tree?"

The demon began to cry. He said, "Oh Master, please help me. My family lives in a village just west of this mountain. My grandfather's name was Red. He was very wealthy, so people called him Red Millions. When he died, the fortune passed to my father. My father was a good man but he was a poor businessman. He lost most of the money, so people called him Red Thousands. He owed money to some bad people. The bad people came, they burned our house and killed my father. As they carried my mother away, she begged them not to kill me, so they tied me up and hung me from this tree. Please save my life so I can return home. I will do anything you ask, to repay your kindness."

Tangseng could not see that this boy was really a demon. He told Zhu to cut the ropes. But Sun Wukong shouted, "You monster! I recognize you. Don't think that you can fool me. If your story is true, then you have no home and no family. But you say that we should return you to your family. Your story does not add up."

The monster was frightened by this, because he realized that Sun Wukong could see his true form and could also see through his lies. But he said to Tangseng, "Master, it is true that my parents are gone. But I have other relatives. My mother's family lives south of this mountain, and I have several relatives in different villages. Please save my life. I will tell them of your kindness and they will be happy to repay you."

Zhu pushed Sun Wukong aside, saying, "Elder brother, can't you see this is just a child? We should help him." Zhu cut the ropes and freed the little monster. Tangseng told Sun Wukong to carry him.

When Sun Wukong picked up the little monster, he found that the boy weighed just a few catties[1]. He said to the monster, "You don't fool me for a minute. I know who you are. But tell me, little monster, why do you weigh so little?"

"I didn't get enough milk when I was a baby," the monster replied.

Sun Wukong laughed and said, "All right, I'll carry you. But tell me if you need to piss."

They walked silently for a while, then Sun Wukong began to talk quietly to himself, saying, "It's difficult enough to climb this mountain, but Master also wants me to carry this monster on my back. Why? I'm sure that the monster will cause trouble for us. I should just kill him now."

The monster heard Sun Wukong's thoughts. He took four deep breaths and blew onto the monkey's back. Immediately Sun Wukong felt as if he were carrying a thousand catties. Then the monster used his magic to leave his body and rise into the air.

Sun Wukong felt the heavy weight on his back. He became angry. He grabbed the monster and threw him down hard on the ground, killing him. But of course he only killed the body that the monster had created. The spirit of the monster was still alive.

---

[1] During the Ming Dynasty when this was written, a cattie was 590 grams, about 1.3 pounds.

Then, the monster created a huge storm. The sky turned black as night. The wind pulled trees out of the ground. It moved huge rocks. Streams became rivers, and rivers became oceans. The three disciples hid on the ground and covered their heads. When Red Boy saw that, he came down, grabbed Tangseng, and flew away.

When the wind stopped, the three disciples stood up and looked around. Their luggage was on the ground. Tangseng's white horse was still there, but the monk was gone. "Where is Master?" asked Sha Wujing. Nobody knew. The three disciples just stood there, not knowing what to do.

Sun Wukong finally said, "Brothers, we must work together. We must pick up the luggage, climb this mountain, and save our Master."

They climbed for seventy miles, crossing rivers and deep valleys. They did not see any animals or birds at all. Sun Wukong became worried. He jumped into the air, shouting, "Change!" He now had three heads and six arms. Using three Golden Hoop Rods, he began to smash trees and rocks all around. Zhu said to Sha, "My brother, this is bad. Sun Wukong has lost his mind."

Soon, a large group of deities arrived. They were dressed in old dirty clothes and they looked hungry. One of them said to Sun Wukong, "Great sage, the mountain gods and the local spirits are here to see you!"

Sun Wukong looked at them and said, "Why are there so many of you?"

"Great sage," he replied, "this is Six Hundred Mile Mountain. So this side of the mountain is three hundred miles from bottom to top. Every ten miles there is one local spirit and one mountain god. So all together, we are thirty local spirits and thirty mountain gods. We heard yesterday that you were coming, but we needed time to gather together. Please forgive us for being late."

"All right, I forgive you," replied Sun Wukong. "Tell me, how many monsters are on this mountain?"

"Ah, there is just one. And he has caused us great trouble. We have burned all of our incense and paper money, and used up all our food."

"And where does this monster live?"

"He lives in the Cave of Fire. He has very powerful magic. Often, he will grab one of us and make us into his servants. And his little demons come to us, demanding protection money."

"But you are immortals! You don't have any money."

"True, we have no money. So we cannot give money to the little demons. Instead, we give them deer meat and other gifts[1]. But sometimes they don't like our gifts. Then they smash our temples and take our good clothing. We cannot live in peace. We ask the Great Sage to get rid of this monster for us, and save the creatures who live on this mountain!"

"And what is the name of this monster?"

"He is the son of the Bull Demon King. His powers are great indeed. He studied for three hundred years until he learned how to make the true fire of Samadhi[2]. His father told him to come here and guard this mountain. His title is Great King Holy Child, but behind his back we all call him by his childhood name, Red Boy."

Sun Wukong was pleased to hear this. He thanked the local spirits and mountain gods and told them to go home. Then he returned to Zhu and Sha and said, "Good news, my brothers. This monster is relative of old Monkey!"

Zhu laughed and said, "Elder Brother, that cannot be true. You grew up on Flower Fruit Mountain on the island of Aolai. That is ten thousand miles and two oceans away from here!"

"This monster is called Red Boy, and his father is Bull Demon King. Five hundred years ago when I was causing trouble in Heaven, I traveled all around the world to find the great heroes of this world. I found six of them, and we formed a kind of family or alliance. The Bull Demon King was the most powerful of the six. He is my brother, and so I am an old uncle to this Red Boy. How could he harm his old uncle? Let's go and see him."

Sha laughed and said, "Elder brother, you know what the ancients say: 'three years away from my door, you are my relative no more.' You have not seen the Bull Demon King for more than five hundred years. You have not shared a cup of wine or given gifts at festival time. Why would Red Boy think of you as his uncle?"

"Well, the ancients also say, 'if the leaf can flow to the ocean, where would people not meet as they come and go?' Yes, it's been a long time. Maybe he won't give us a great feast. But at the very least, he should return Master to us."

---

[1] The mountain gods and local spirits had to give meat and other goods to the little demons. They had to use all their resources to give these gifts, leaving no food or clothes for themselves.
[2] Samadhi, a state of intense concentration achieved through meditation.

They traveled night and day, covering a hundred miles. Finally they came to a pine forest with a cold stream running through it. On the other side of the stream was a cliff. At the base of the cliff was a large cave with a heavy stone door. Sun Wukong told Sha to stay and watch the horse and the luggage, while he and Zhu headed to the cave to search for Tangseng.

Chapter 41

When they arrived at the Cave of Fire, they saw dozens of small demons standing in front of the stone door. The demons were all holding swords. Sun Wukong shouted to them, "Quick, go and tell your master to give us the Tang monk. If you say even half a 'no' we will smash your cave and everyone in it. Now go!"

Inside the cave, Red Boy was sitting in his chair. Several other small demons were washing Tangseng, preparing him to be cooked and eaten. The soldier demons ran inside and told Red Boy that two ugly monks were standing outside wanting the Tang monk. "What do they look like?" asked Red Boy.

"One of them has a hairy face and a nose like a thunder god. The other one is also hairy, with long ears and a very long nose. They are both quite ugly."

"Ah, that must be Sun Wukong and Zhu Bajie," said Red Boy. He pointed to several small demons, saying, "You and you and you, get the carts and push them out the door. And you, get me my spear." One small demon gave Red Boy an eighteen-foot-long fire-tipped spear. The others pushed five small wooden carts out the door.

Zhu saw this and said, "What's this? They are afraid of us, so they have decided to move out of their cave and go somewhere else?"

"No," replied Sun Wukong, "Look at where they put the carts." Zhu looked, and he saw that the five carts were placed in a pentagram shape, corresponding to the five phases of metal, wood, water, fire and earth[1]. One small demon stood guard next to each cart.

Red Boy came out of the cave. What did he look like, you ask?

> His face white as snow,
> His lips red as blood,
> His hair black as night,
> His eyebrows like two moons carved by knives,
> The big man lifts up his spear.
> He walks out covered in bright light,
> He roars like thunder,

---

[1] These are the wǔxíng, the five phases or essential processes. Wood feeds fire, fire makes earth (ash), earth yields metal (mining), metal collects water (condensation), and water nourishes wood.

His eyes glow like lightning,
Call him Red Boy, the name of lasting fame.

"Who dares to make noise outside my cave?" he roared.

Sun Wukong smiled. "It's your old uncle! Why do you look like this? This morning you were just a small boy hanging from a tree. Do you remember, I carried you on my back? Now you want to repay my kindness with this? Stop playing around and give me my master. If you don't do that, I might have to talk with your father, and you wouldn't want that, would you?"

"What are you talking about, you ugly ape? You are no uncle of mine."

"Oh yes, I am your uncle. I am Sun Wukong, the Great Sage Equal to Heaven. Five hundred years ago I caused great trouble in Heaven. At that time I traveled all around the world, looking for the great heroes of the earth. I met your father, Bull Monster King, and we became good friends. There were five others: the Dragon Monster King, the Eagle Monster King, the Lion Monster King, a female monkey king who called herself the Fair Wind Great Sage, and the Giant Ape Monster King. We seven became a family. This was long before you were born."

Red Boy did not reply. He didn't care that Sun Wukong was his uncle, but he remembered that Sun Wukong had tried to kill him earlier that morning. He tried to stab the monkey with his fire-tipped spear. Sun Wukong easily stepped aside, and tried to smash the monster with his rod. They fought for a long time. Each one wanted the Tang monk but for different reasons. Sun Wukong wanted to protect the monk, but Red Boy wanted to eat the monk.

Zhu watched the battle for a while. Then he stepped forward and brought his rake down hard on Red Boy's head. Red Boy staggered, then he ran away as fast as he could. Zhu and Sun Wukong followed him. Red Boy ran to one of the carts. Then he punched himself in the nose! Zhu laughed and said, "Look at him, punching himself like that. I think he wants to make himself bleed, so he can go to a judge and sue us!"

Just then, Red Boy recited a magic spell. Fire and black smoke poured out of his mouth. The area around the cave became as hot as a brazier. Zhu said, "We'd better get out of here. I don't want to be cooked. That monster will want to eat me for dinner."

Sun Wukong jumped into the fire, using his magic to protect himself. He tried to find Red Boy, but there was too much smoke and he could not see anything. Red Boy and the little demons ran back into the cave and locked the

stone door behind them.

Sun Wukong returned to the other side of the stream, where Zhu and Sha were waiting for him. He shouted at Zhu, "You idiot, why didn't you help me? I had to go into the fire all by myself, while you ran away to safety. I guess I will have to do all the fighting myself. Tell me, how is the monster's fighting ability compared to mine?"

"Not as good," said Zhu. Then the two of them started talking about different methods of fighting the monster and his Samadhi fire. They could not find a good way to fight Red Boy. After a few minutes, Sha Wujing started laughing.

"What are you laughing about?" asked Sun Wukong.

"You two are not thinking clearly," he replied. "Of course, you are a better fighter than he is. But you cannot win because of the fire and smoke. But you have forgotten one important thing. Tell me, what overcomes fire?"

"You are right!" said Sun Wukong. "Water overcomes fire. I just need to find enough water to put out the monster's fire. Then it will be easy to win the fight against him, and we can rescue Master. You two stay here. I will go to the Great Eastern Ocean to talk with my old friend Auron, the Dragon King of Four Oceans. He will bring us water."

Old Monkey used his cloud somersault to travel quickly to the Great Eastern Ocean. Then he used his magic to open up a dry path through the water. A water spirit saw him and told Auron that the monkey king had arrived. A few minutes later, the Dragon King met Sun Wukong. He invited Sun Wukong to sit down with him and have some tea.

"No time for that, my old friend," said Sun Wukong. "I must talk with you about something that will cause you some trouble. I am traveling with my master. We are going to the Western Heaven to find the Buddha's books and bring them back to the Tang Empire. We met a monster named Red Boy. The monster captured my master. I am stronger than the monster and I am a better fighter. But the monster uses black smoke and hot fire. We cannot fight against this. So I came to ask you for some water. I ask you to bring heavy rain to put out the monster's fire. Then we can rescue the Tang monk."

"I am sorry my friend," replied the Dragon King. "I cannot help you."

"But you are Auron, the great Dragon King of the Four Oceans. You make all the rain in the world. If I can't ask you, who can I ask?"

"It's true that I bring rain, but I cannot just make it rain anytime that I want. That is up to the Jade Emperor. He decides how many feet and inches of rain should fall, and the day and hour that it should come. He writes it down, and the document is sent to the North Star. Then I call the Thunder God, the Lightning Mother, the Wind Uncle, and the Cloud Boy, and together we make it rain."

"I don't need thunder, lightning, wind or clouds. Just a lot of rain."

"All right, then I can help you. But I will need help from my brothers." Then the Dragon King beat his great drum and hit his great bell. Soon three more dragons arrived: the Dragon King of the Southern Ocean, the Dragon King of the Western Ocean, and the Dragon King of the Northern Ocean. Sun Wukong told them about the problem, and they all agreed to help. We have a poem for this:

> The Dragon Kings of the four seas are happy to help
> When the Great Sage Equal to Heaven asks for it
> The great Tang monk meets trouble

These four bring water to put out the great red fire

Sun Wukong and the four dragon kings traveled quickly back to the Cave of Fire. He said to them, "This is the cave of the demon. Please stay here and do not let anyone see you. I will go and fight with Red Boy. If I win, I will not need your help. If I lose, I will be dead and I will not need your help. But if he starts his fire and I ask you for help, please send the rain." The four dragon kings agreed.

Then the monkey ran up to the cave door and shouted, "Open the door!"

The stone door opened and Red Boy came out. Right behind him were five little demons, each one pushing a small cart. He said, "Why did you return? You must be a very stupid monkey. I have an idea for you: just forget about your master. We will eat him for dinner, and you can be on your way without him."

This made Sun Wukong very angry, and he tried to hit Red Boy with his rod. They began to fight again. They fought for a long time. Both of them fought well and neither could win. Finally Red Boy tried to hit Sun Wukong with his spear, then he quickly turned and punched himself twice, hard, on the nose. Fire and smoke poured out of his nose and mouth. More fire came from the five carts that surrounded him.

"Quick, Dragon Kings, send the rain now!" shouted Sun Wukong. It started to rain. At first the rain was light, like a morning mist. Then it rained harder, like a springtime shower. Then it rained even harder, like a summer thunderstorm. Harder and harder fell the rain. Water poured down the mountainsides like jade waterfalls. Rivers overflowed their banks, birds hid in the trees, and animals ran to high ground.

But the rain did not put out Red Boy's fire. This was because the rain was just ordinary rain. It was not sent by the Jade Emperor, and so it could not put out the Samadhi fire that Red Boy had made. The rain just made the fire bigger and hotter, like adding oil. Sun Wukong tried to walk into the fire to find Red Boy. The monster spat out a big cloud of black smoke at him. It was too much for Sun Wukong. He flew away with his body on fire. He dove into the cold mountain stream to put out the fire. But the cold water was too much for him, and he fainted.

The four Dragon Kings saw this, and they were terrified. They shouted at Zhu Bajie and Sha Wujing to come and help the Monkey King. The two disciples ran to the stream bank and looked in the water. They saw Sun Wukong floating on top of the water, face down, not moving. Sha jumped into the stream, picked him up, and carried him to the riverbank. His body was as cold as the stream water.

Sha thought he was dead, but Zhu said, "Don't worry, this old monkey has lived for a long time. I think he has seventy-two lives. Let's wake him up." They sat him up, and Zhu began to massage him. After a few minutes the massage released his breath, and Sun Wukong opened his eyes. He blinked a few times, then he looked around. He saw Sha and Zhu, but he did not see the dragons.

"Brothers of the ocean, where are you?" he asked.

The four dragon kings replied, "Your little dragons are here. We wait on you."

"I am sorry to have caused you all this trouble. But we did not win the fight. Please go home, I will thank you another day." The four dragon kings rose up into the air and flew away in four different directions.

Sun Wukong was feeling very tired, and his body hurt all over. He did not know what to do. Sha Wujing said, "Brothers, I remember that the Bodhisattva Guanyin told us that Heaven would help us if we ever needed it. Well, now we need it. I wonder where we should go for help."

"This monster is very powerful," said Sun Wukong. "We must get help from someone who is more powerful than me. I think we must ask Guanyin herself for help. But I am feeling unwell and I don't think I can travel to the South Sea to meet her. Zhu, can you go instead of me?" Zhu agreed, and he flew south towards the South Sea to find Guanyin.

Inside the cave, Red Boy was resting with his little demons. "I wonder what those troublemakers are doing now?" he said to himself. He walked outside the cave and looked up in the sky. He saw Zhu Bajie flying south. He thought to himself, "That can only mean one thing: the pig-man is going to ask Guanyin for help. But I know a faster way to go." He flew out of the cave and took a shorter way to the South Sea. Then he came down to the ground, changed his appearance so that he looked like Guanyin, and waited for Zhu.

Zhu was flying south towards the South Sea. He looked down and saw Guanyin. Zhu could not tell the difference between true and not true, so he thought it was really Guanyin. He bowed low and said, "Bodhisattva, your disciple Zhu Wujing kowtows to you."

The monster said, "Why are you here, and not protecting your master?"

"We were traveling west. We met a powerful monster named Red Boy. The monster knows how to fight with hot fire and black smoke. Our elder disciple Sun Wukong fought with the monster but could not win. He was badly burned and he cannot move. He asked me to come and ask you to save our master."

"I don't think that Red Boy would hurt you or your master. Perhaps you said something to make him angry."

"I did not. But my elder brother tried to kill him, and I think that made the monster a little bit angry."

"I will be happy to help you, come with me," said the monster. Then he quickly pulled out a large leather bag, put it over Zhu, and pulled the rope tight so that Zhu could not escape. He carried Zhu back to his cave. He said, "I will keep you here for four or five days, then I will steam you and give you to my little demons to eat for dinner. I think you will taste very good with some red wine."

Across the stream, Sun Wukong and Sha were waiting for Zhu to return with Guanyin. They waited a long time. As they were waiting, a bad-smelling wind blew past them. "This is a bad wind," said Sun Wukong. "I think that something bad has happened to Zhu." Even though he was in great pain, he ran up to the door of the cave and shouted, "It's Old Monkey again. Open the door!" A crowd of little demons came out of the cave. Sun Wukong was hurting too much to fight. So he changed into a small piece of cloth.

The demons saw the cloth and brought it back into the cave to show to Red Boy. "The monkey ran away," they said, "and he dropped this on the ground."

"It's not important," said Red Boy, "but maybe we can use it to mend some old clothing." They threw the cloth into a corner of the cave. Sun Wukong changed into a little insect. He flew around the cave. Soon he found Zhu tied up in the leather bag, talking to himself about all the terrible things he was planning to do to the monster and the little demons. Sun Wukong laughed to himself. But then he heard Red Boy say, "It's time to prepare the Tang monk for dinner. You six," and he pointed to six of the little demons, "go to my father the Bull Demon King. Invite him to come here for dinner. Tell him that if he eats the flesh of this monk, his life will be a thousand times longer."

Chapter 42

The six little demons left the cave and started running southwest towards the home of the Bull Demon King. Sun Wukong said to himself, "So, they are going to visit my brother, the Bull Demon King. Our friendship was strong, but that was a long time ago. Now I am on the path of the Buddha, while he is still a demon. I still remember what he looks like. I will change my appearance to look like him, then we will see if I can fool Red Boy!"

He flew to a place about ten miles southwest from the cave. He changed his appearance so he looked like the Bull Demon King. Then he pulled some hairs from his head, said, "Change!" and they turned into little sword-carrying demons. He pulled more hairs and turned them into dogs. Now it looked like the Bull Demon King was on a hunting party.

The six demons arrived and saw the Bull Demon King. They kowtowed and one of them said, "Father, we have been sent by your son, the Great King Holy Child. He invites you to come to his home and join him in eating the flesh of the Tang monk. Your life will be increased a thousandfold."

Sun Wukong replied, "Please get up, children. I would be happy to go with you. Come with me back to my house so that I can put on better clothes for the dinner."

"Father, we beg you to please come with us without returning home. It is a long way to the cave, and we are afraid that our master will be unhappy with us if we return too late!"

"You are very good children!" said Sun Wukong. "All right, let's go." They returned to the Cave of Fire. Sun Wukong entered the cave and sat down at the seat of honor.

Red Boy said to him, "Father King, your child bows to you." Then he kowtowed four times.

Sun Wukong smiled and replied, "Thank you, but my child does not need to bow. Tell me, why did you invite me here?"

"Father, your child has no talent, but he did manage to capture a traveling monk. This monk has been studying the teachings of Buddha for ten lifetimes. Anyone who eats his flesh will achieve immortality. Your foolish son does not dare to eat this monk all by himself. So I invite you to join me, so you may have long life."

Sun Wukong asked, "My child, is this monk the master of the Monkey King, the Great Sage Equal to Heaven?"

"Yes, he is."

"My child, do not provoke him! You can provoke others, but not him. He has great power. Once when he was creating trouble in the Heavenly Palace, the Jade Emperor sent a hundred thousand soldiers to capture him, but they could not do it. And now you want to provoke him by eating his master? Don't do it! Let the monk go. If you don't, the monkey will use his golden hoop rod and smash you and your cave. Then you will die, and who will then take care of me when I am old?"

"Father, you talk of the great powers of this monkey, but what about the powers of your own son? I have already fought with this monkey, and his powers are no greater than mine. He was so frightened that he asked the four Dragon Kings for help. That did not work, of course. The monkey was nearly killed, and he has run away. Now we can relax and enjoy our dinner, so you may have long life without growing old."

"My boy, you do not know this monkey. He can change his appearance into anything. He can become very small, like an insect. He can become something very ordinary, like a piece of cloth. He can even change to look like a different person, like me! How would you recognize him?"

"Father, I have nearly killed him already. He would not dare to come back here."

"Well, my boy, it sounds like you are a great warrior, perhaps greater than the monkey. But unfortunately, I cannot eat meat today. I am feeling old these days, so I have decided to become a vegetarian."

"Ah, that is interesting news. Are you a vegetarian every day?"

"No, only four days every month. Today is the last of those four days. Let's wait and eat the Tang monk tomorrow."

Red Boy heard this, and he thought to himself, "Something is strange. My father has lived for a thousand years by eating the flesh of people. Now he suddenly decides to become a vegetarian?" He walked out and said to one of his little demons, "Tell me, where did you find the Great King?"

"We were traveling to his home, and we met him on the way. He was hunting."

"Ah! I think that is not my father. It looks like him, but his words do not sound like his words. Be careful, all of you! I will go back and talk with him. If his words are not right, I will shout, and you all must attack him."

Red Boy returned to his father and said, "Your foolish son asked you to come here for two reasons. First of course, to invite you to eat the flesh of the Tang monk. But also, I have a question for you. Last week I was traveling in the Ninth Heaven and I ran into Master Zhang, the Daoist priest. He said that he would tell me about my future. To do that, he needs to know the hour, date, month and year of my birth. I do not know this, so I am hoping you can tell me so that I can tell Master Zhang."

Sun Wukong was surprised by this, thinking to himself, "Ah, this is a very clever monster indeed!" He smiled and said to Red Boy, "My boy, I'm afraid that at my age I have forgotten many things. I do not remember when you were born. I will ask your mother when I return home tomorrow."

Immediately Red Boy knew that this was not his father, because his father was always telling him about the auspicious date and time of his birth. He shouted for the little demons to attack Sun Wukong. Sun Wukong changed into a beam of light and left the cave.

Red Boy did not try to chase after him. He was feeling a little bit uncomfortable because he had just told his little demons to attack someone who looked like his father. He waved his hand and said to the little demons, "All right, all right, just let him go. Wash the Tang monk and prepare him for cooking."

Sun Wukong crossed the stream and met up with Sha. He was laughing and said, "Brother, I have won a round against the monster. Our brother Zhu was captured and is inside the cave, trapped in a leather bag. I wanted to enter the cave, so I changed my appearance to look like the monster's father. The monster did not know it was me, so he kowtowed to me four times. That was a real pleasure!"

Sha replied, "Elder brother, I am afraid that your desire for small victories will stop us from rescuing our master."

Sun Wukong replied, "Don't worry, my friend. This small victory makes me forget about my pain! Now I will go to the South Sea to ask Guanyin to help us. You take care of the luggage and keep an eye on the horse while I'm gone." Then he used his cloud somersault to fly to Potalaka Mountain in the South Sea. He flew swiftly, arriving after only a half hour. He entered Guanyin's home and kowtowed to her.

Guanyin said, "Wukong, why are you here? You should be leading your master to the Western Heaven."

The Monkey King replied, "Please let me tell you what happened. We were traveling west and came to a tall mountain. There we met a very clever monster called Red Boy. He grabbed my master and took him back to the Cave of Fire. Zhu Wuneng and I fought against him, but he used powerful magic to send Samadhi fire and black smoke at us. We could not win the fight. I asked the Dragon King of the Four Oceans for help. He came with three other Dragon Kings. The four of them brought a lot of rain, but the rain did not put out the monster's fire. Your disciple was badly burned and almost died."

"If he has Samadhi fire, why did you go to the Dragon Kings? You should have asked me for help."

"I could not come because of my burns. I sent Zhu Wuneng to ask you for help."

"He did not come here."

"Indeed, he did not. The monster took your form and tricked Zhu. He captured Zhu in a leather bag and brought him back to the Cave of Fire. Now the monster has the Tang monk and Zhu in his cave. He plans to cook and eat both of them."

"How dare that monster take my form!" she said angrily. She grabbed a white porcelain vase and threw it into the ocean. A few seconds later the vase came back. It was riding on the back of a giant black tortoise. The tortoise walked out of the water and nodded its head twenty-four times to Guanyin, to show that he was bowing to her twenty-four times. The vase slid off the turtle's back and onto the ground. Then the turtle returned to the ocean.

"Wukong, go pick up that vase and give it to me," she said. Sun Wukong tried to pick it up but he could not lift it. He felt like an insect trying to move a large rock. He knelt before Guanyin and said, "I am sorry, but your disciple cannot pick up this vase."

"Monkey, if you cannot even pick up a small vase, how can you possibly fight against powerful monsters?"

"I do not know. Maybe my burns have made me weak today."

"Normally this vase is empty and weighs almost nothing. But when I threw it in the ocean, it traveled around the world, through all the oceans and rivers of the world, and picked up an oceanful of water. You may be strong, but even you cannot pick up an ocean." Then she reached down and picked up the vase, as easily as picking up a bunch of spring flowers.

"Wukong, the water in my vase is not like the rain brought by the Dragon Kings. This water can put out the Samadhi fire. I want you to take it, but I fear that you will steal it. You must leave something with me so I know you will return the vase when you are finished."

"Bodhisattva, I have nothing to give you. My clothing is old and worthless. My rod is valuable but I need it to fight against the monster. I would gladly give you my headband, but I cannot take it off my head, and anyway I think you will not allow me to be without it."

"All right, you clever monkey. I will go with you myself. Let's go. You go first."

"Your disciple dares not go first. We will be traveling in strong winds. My clothing might blow upwards, and I would not want to offend you by letting you see my body."

Guanyin laughed. She told Sun Wukong to jump into a large lotus flower that was floating on the water. Then she blew on the flower, and it traveled quickly across the water. Guanyin called one of her disciples, Moksha, and told him to go up to Heaven and borrow the Swords of Constellations. Moksha went, and returned a short time later with the swords. Guanyin threw all the swords into the air. When they came down, they formed a large lotus flower with a thousand petals. Guanyin sat on the lotus flower. Then she and Sun Wukong flew together to meet Sha, who was waiting across the stream from the Cave of Fire.

Guanyin recited a prayer, and immediately all the mountain gods and local spirits gathered in front of her. She said, "Go, all of you. Find every animal, every bird, and every insect within three hundred miles of here. Carry them far away, where they will be safe." She waited while they did this.

Then Guanyin turned the vase upside down. A torrent of water came from the vase. The water poured out like a waterfall. It flowed over the entire mountain, covering everything and turning the area into a vast ocean that looked exactly like the South Sea. Then she shouted, "Wukong, give me your hand." He held out his hand. She used a willow branch to write the word "delusion" on his hand. "Now go and fight the monster. But do not win the fight. You must lose. Make him chase you back here. I will be waiting."

Sun Wukong ran up to the stone door of the cave. "Open the door!" he shouted. Red Boy was inside the cave, but he ignored the shouting. Sun Wukong hit the door with his rod, smashing it. Red Boy came running out of the cave. Sun Wukong said to him, "You are a terrible son. You chased your own father away. What punishment should you receive?"

This made Red Boy very, very angry. They began to fight. Sun Wukong did not try to win the fight, though. He kept moving backwards, drawing Red Boy away from the cave and towards Guanyin. Red Boy shouted, "Why are you fighting so badly? The last time we fought, you did much better."

Sun Wukong shouted, "I am afraid of your fire. Come and get me!" Then he opened his fist and showed the word "delusion" to the monster. Now the monster's mind was clouded. He could only think of one thing: chasing and fighting Sun Wukong. The monkey ran away as fast as an arrow, with the monster close behind.

They arrived at the place where Guanyin was waiting. Sun Wukong said, "You have chased me all the way to the South Sea, the home of the Bodhisattva Guanyin. Why are you still chasing me?" Then he ran behind Guanyin and disappeared. Red Boy thrust his spear at Guanyin, but she immediately changed into a beam of light and also disappeared.

Now Red Boy was standing alone. He shouted, "Stupid monkey, you could not win a fight with me, so you have run away. And your lady friend has also run away. But she left behind this nice lotus flower. I think I will sit on it and relax for a while." And he sat down cross-legged in the middle of the lotus flower.

This was the moment that Guanyin was waiting for. She pointed her willow stick downward and cried, "Withdraw!" The lotus flower disappeared, and now Red Boy was sitting on the points of the Swords of Constellations. Guanyin said to Moksha, "strike the swords with your hammer!" Moksha began to hit the handles of the swords with his hammer. Each time he hit a sword handle, it went deep into Red Boy's body. Blood began to come out of dozens of holes in his body.

"Stop now," said Guanyin to Moksha. Then she recited another spell. The swords turned into large hooks, sharp as the teeth of wolves. Now Red Boy could not pull himself free. He said to Guanyin, "Bodhisattva, this foolish monster has eyes but he could not see. Now I see your great power. Please let me live. I will never hurt another creature again. I will follow you and your teachings."

Guanyin said to him, "You wish to follow me?"

"If you let me live, I am willing to enter the gate of your teachings." Guanyin took a golden razor from her sleeve, and she shaved off all of Red Boy's hair except for three little tufts of hair. Then she pointed with her finger and cried, "Withdraw!" The swords fell to the ground, and all of Red Boy's injuries disappeared.

As soon as Red Boy saw that his injuries were gone, he stood up and said, "You tricked me! Those were not real swords, and I did not have any real injuries. I will not follow you. Prepare to meet my spear!"

Sun Wukong was about to hit the monster with his rod, but Guanyin told him to wait. Then she took a golden headband from her sleeve. She said, "This treasure once belonged to the Buddha himself. He gave me three golden headbands. One is on the head of the Monkey King. The other is on the head of the guardian of my mountain home. And now I know what to do with the third one." She threw the headband in the air and cried, "Change!" It changed into five bands. One landed on the monster's head, two landed on his arms, and two on his legs. All five wrapped themselves around him. Then Guanyin recited the Tight Headband Spell, and all five bands became rooted in his flesh and became very small and tight. Red Boy fell to the ground and cried in pain. She cried again, "Close!" His two hands pressed together, as if he was in prayer. He could not move at all. He bowed his head in defeat.

Guanyin said to Sun Wukong, "I think this boy needs a lesson. I will have him walk all the way to Potalaka Mountain. He must kowtow with each step. Maybe that will teach him something. Now, you must return to the Cave of Fire to rescue your master and your younger brother." Sun Wukong bowed low to her, turned and left.

While this was happening, Sha Monk was waiting with the luggage and the horse. He had been waiting a long time. Finally he picked up the luggage and began walking with the horse towards the south. He met Sun Wukong on the road. Sun Wukong told him everything that had happened, then said, "Let's go rescue Master and Zhu."

They returned to the Cave of Fire, ran through the doorway, and killed all the little demons that were there. They found Zhu still hanging in a leather bag. They cut open the bag to free him. Zhu fell out of the bag onto the ground. He jumped up and shouted, "Where is that evil monster? I want to give him a taste of my rake!"

"The monster has gone to Potalaka Mountain to study with Guanyin," replied Sun Wukong. "But I think it will take him a long time to get there."

Then the three disciples searched for Tangseng. They looked all around the cave but could not find him. Then they went to the back of the cave and found a large room. Tangseng was tied up in the center of the room. He had no clothes on, and he was crying. They freed him also.

Tangseng thanked them and said, "Disciples, you have worked hard! What happened to the monster?" Sun Wukong told him the story. At the end of the story he described how Guanyin came, defeated the monster, and turned him into one of her disciples. Tangseng knelt down and bowed to the south.

"No need to thank her," said Sun Wukong, "We gave her a new disciple!"

Guanyin's new disciple Red Boy made his way, slowly, to Potalaka Mountain. It was a journey of many miles. After every step he stopped, knelt to the ground, and kowtowed to the south. During this long journey he learned how to let go of his anger. Later he became one of Guanyin's most devoted disciples, taking the Buddhist name Shancai[1] which means "Child of Wealth." He traveled the world searching for enlightenment, meeting fifty-three teachers. One of his teachers was the Buddha himself, who gave Shancai a vision of all the Heavenly worlds. Shancai became famous in Buddhist, Taoist and folk tales.

As for Tangseng and his three disciples, their problems were finished for the day. They looked around the cave, found some rice and vegetables, and made a simple dinner. That night they slept in the Cave of Fire.

---

[1] Shancai is also known by his Hindu name Sudhana. His story is told in the *Avatamsaka Sutra*, as well as the 18th century Chinese book *Precious Scroll of Shancai and Longnü.*

Chapter 43

The next day, Tangseng and his three disciples began walking westward again. After a month of traveling, they arrived at a place where they heard the sound of water. Tangseng was worried. He asked Sun Wukong, "Where is that sound of water coming from?"

Sun Wukong smiled and said, "Master, you worry too much! You have forgotten the Heart Sutra that the Chan master taught you."

"Which part have I forgotten?" asked Tangseng.

"You have forgotten the words, 'no eye, no ear, no nose, no tongue, no body, no mind.' We who have left our families must give up these six things. This is called the 'killing of the six bandits.' You say that you seek the Buddha, but you are still carrying all six bandits with you. How can you get to the Western Heaven and see the Buddha?"

Tangseng was silent for a long time, thinking about this.

They continued walking, and soon they came to a very wide river. The water was as black as ink. Animals would not drink it and birds would not fly over it.

"Disciples," said Tangseng, "why is the water so black?"

Sha said, "Maybe someone is washing the ink from their brushes."

"It does not matter," replied Sun Wukong. "This river is ten miles wide. We must find a way to get our master to the other side. Zhu, can you carry him?"

"No, I can't," replied Zhu. "I can fly by myself, but if I try to carry our master, I can't even get three feet off the ground. You know what the ancients say, 'A man is heavier than a mountain.'"

As they were discussing this, a man came down the river in a small boat. They saw it was a small canoe that could only carry two people plus the boatman.

Zhu said to Sun Wukong and Sha, "I will go across with our master. You two can just fly across the river." Sun Wukong agreed. Zhu and Tangseng got into the boat and the boatman started to take them across the river.

They did not know that the boatman was really a monster who lived in the river. Soon after they started to cross the river, the monster called up a great storm. High winds, heavy rain and mountainous waves hit the little boat, and it soon disappeared underneath the black water.

Sun Wukong and Sha looked but could not see the others. Sha said, "I have spent a lot of time in rivers. Do you remember that I was once a monster in Flowing Sands River? Let me go and look for them." And without waiting for a reply, he grabbed his staff and jumped into the black water. He held up his staff and the water parted in front of him.

Looking ahead, Sha saw a beautiful pavilion. On the door was written, "Home of the Black River God." He walked up to the gate. He heard someone inside the pavilion saying, "Ah, this is good! This monk has studied the Way for ten lifetimes. If I can eat his flesh I will live forever and never grow old!" Then the voice said, "Little ones, bring me two iron cages. We will steam these two. And I will invite my uncle to visit and share in the feast."

This made Sha very angry. He began to smash the door with his staff. "Disaster!" cried the little demons. "There is a big man with a dark face outside, hitting our door." The monster stood up and called for the little demons to bring him his iron armor and gold helmet. He put these on. Then he picked up his weapon, a riding crop, and went to the door.

The monster shouted, "Who is banging on my door?"

Sha shouted back, "You monster, you have taken my master and my brother! Give them back to me and I will let you live."

"Yes, I have your master and the pig too. I will steam them and eat their flesh. Now come here and fight me. If you can last three rounds, you can take them and go. If not, I will steam and eat you too."

They began to fight at the bottom of the river, Sha using his staff and the monster using his riding crop. They fought for thirty rounds but neither could win. Finally, Sha turned and ran away. The monster shouted, "I will not chase you. I have other things to do." And of course he did not give the two prisoners to Sha.

Sha returned to the riverbank and told Sun Wukong everything that happened.

Sun Wukong asked, "What kind of monster is he?"

"I'm not sure. Maybe an iguana of some kind."

Just then, a man came out of the river and walked towards them. Sun Wukong picked up his golden hoop rod and prepared to fight, but the man kowtowed and said, "Great Sage, the water god of Black River bows to you!"

Sun Wukong said, "Are you that monster, come back to cause more trouble?"

"No, I am truly the god of this river. Let me tell you my story. Last year in the fifth month, a monster arrived from the Western Ocean. He fought me. He was much stronger than I was, so I could not fight him. He took my home and began to live in my river. I went to the Dragon King of the Western Ocean to make a complaint against the monster, but I learned that the Dragon King is actually the monster's uncle. The Dragon King told me that I must let the monster live in my home. I am a lowly god and cannot go to the Jade Emperor. So there is nothing I can do. I ask you, Great Sage, please help me!"

"I understand," said Sun Wukong. "All right. You stay here with my brother. I will go and find the Dragon King." The monkey held up his fingers to make a magic sign. The waters parted and he walked into the river.

He saw a black fish carrying a golden box. He hit the fish on the head, killing it. Looking inside the box, he found a letter. It said,

> Mr. Ao, your foolish nephew touches his head to the ground a hundred times. You have been very kind to me. Now I have just captured two monks from the east. They are very good to eat. Your birthday is coming soon, so I invite you to come to my home. Together we will eat the flesh of these monks. I hope you will come.

Sun Wukong put the letter in his sleeve. Then he continued to the palace of Aoshun, the Dragon King of the Western Ocean. When he arrived, the Dragon King said, "Great King, please come in and have some tea with me."

"I will not have tea with you. You have committed a great crime."

"What crime are you talking about?"

Sun Wukong took the letter from his sleeve and showed it to the Dragon King. The Dragon King read the letter. His mouth opened but he could not speak. Then he fell to his knees and said, "Great Sage, please forgive me. This young dragon is the ninth child of my sister. Her husband was the Dragon King of Jing River. He made a terrible mistake, sending the wrong amount of wind and rain, and the Tang Emperor had him killed in a dream. With her husband dead, my sister had no place to go. She came here with her children. Two years ago she became ill and died. Her son needed a place to live, so I told him to go to the Black River. I did not know he would do such terrible things."

"How many sons did your sister have?"

"Nine sons. They are all different kinds of dragons. Eight of them are good and live in different rivers and mountains. Only this one has become bad."

"I was planning to make a complaint against you with the Jade Emperor. But it looks like the iguana is at fault, not you. Quick, send someone to arrest him and rescue my master."

Aoshun called his son Prince Moang and told him to gather five hundred fish soldiers to arrest the iguana and rescue Tangseng and Zhu. Then he asked Sun Wukong to stay for some food and wine. But Sun Wukong said he needed to go with Moang to rescue his master.

Sun Wukong, Moang, and the fish army went to the Black River. Sun Wukong left them to return to the riverbank, where he met with Sha and told him everything that had happened. They sat down on the riverbank to wait.

The iguana monster was sitting in the pavilion under the Black River when heard a voice shouting, "Prince Moang is here to see you." Then a little demon came to him and said there was a large army of fish waiting outside. The monster did not understand what was happening. But he was worried. So he called for his armor, his helmet, and his riding crop. He put on the armor and walked out the door.

When he got outside, the iguana monster saw his cousin Moang waiting for him. He also saw five hundred fish soldiers. Some were big, some were small. They held silver swords, long lances and short knives. Some held fluttering banners. The monster shouted, "Cousin, this morning I sent a letter to Uncle, inviting him to dinner. It looks like he cannot come. But why are you here, and why have you brought so many soldiers with you?"

"Tell me," replied Prince Moang, "why did you invite your uncle to dinner?"

"Uncle Aoshun has been very good to me, and I have not seen him in a long time. Yesterday I captured a monk who has been studying the Way for ten lifetimes. His flesh will be very good to eat. I wanted Uncle to join me in eating the monk's flesh for dinner."

"You fool!" shouted Moang. "Don't you know who you have captured? This monk has three disciples. You have met two of them. But the third is the Great Sage Equal to Heaven. He caused great trouble in the palace of Heaven five hundred years ago. He took your letter to Uncle. Now if you want to live, you must return the monk and the pig, and beg the Great Sage to spare your life!"

Now the iguana monster was angry. He said, "Cousin, you may be afraid of this Great Sage but I am not. Tell him to come here and fight me. If he can last three rounds, I will let him and the others go. If not, I will steam and eat him too."

"You truly are a fool. I won't ask the Great Sage to fight you. I will fight you myself!" The two of them began to fight, and Prince Moang's soldiers began to fight with the monster's little demons. What a battle! The river was full of fighting fish and monsters.

Finally, Moang hit the monster hard on the head with his club. The monster fell to the ground. Moang kicked him and knocked the riding crop from his hand. The soldiers tied him up and carried him out of the river to face Sun Wukong.

Sun Wukong stood on the riverbank and looked down at the iguana monster. "You have been a very bad dragon. Your uncle sent you here to study the Way and become wise. But you pushed the river god out of his house. You used magic to trick me, my brothers, and my master. I should kill you right now. But instead I will ask you to let my master and my younger brother go free."

The iguana monster fell to his knees. He said, "Great Sage, I knew nothing about you until just now. Thank you for letting me live. Your master is in my pavilion, still tied up. Let me go. I will return to the pavilion and bring them back to you."

"Don't do it!" said Moang. "He will swim away and you will never see him again."

Sha said, "I will go. I know where they are." Sha and the river god jumped into the water and swam quickly to the pavilion. They found Tangseng and Zhu both tied up. They untied the two prisoners and brought them quickly back to the riverbank.

Zhu saw the iguana monster and ran over to him, his rake held high in his hands. Just before he smashed the rake down on the monster's head, Sun Wukong said, "Brother, let him go. Think of the feelings of Aoshun and his son." Zhu stopped and put away his rake.

Moang said to Sun Wukong, "Great Sage, I must bring this iguana back to see my father. I am sure my father will punish him in some way. I am sorry for all the trouble he caused you!" Then Moang and his soldiers returned to the Great Western Ocean.

Tangseng said, "Disciples, we are still on the eastern shore of this river. How can we cross?"

The river god of Black River said, "Great Sage, thank you for letting me return to my home. Now please let me open a path for you to the other side of the river."

Tangseng got up on his horse. Zhu led the horse while Sha picked up the luggage. The river god used his magic to open a path to the western side of the river. They walked up onto high ground and continued on their journey to the west.

Chapter 44

Tangseng and his three disciples continued on their journey to the west. They traveled all winter, through cold wind and deep snow. They were no longer in China. After several years of traveling on the Silk Road they had arrived in the wild country beyond the country's western borders.

The days passed, and the cold winter turned to early spring. Snow and ice melted, the rivers flowed rapidly, the air was filled with the songs of birds, and the trees turned green again. The poem says,

> The god of the new year arrives
> The god of the woods goes for a walk
> Warm breezes carry the smell of flowers
> Clouds part before the sun
> The rains bring new life
> All things show the beauty of spring

The travelers were walking west when suddenly they heard a sound as loud as ten thousand voices.

"What was that sound?" asked Tangseng, the Tang monk.

"It sounded like the earth was breaking apart," said Zhu Bajie, the pig-man and middle disciple.

"It sounded like thunder," said Sha Wujing, the big quiet man and youngest disciple.

"None of you are correct," laughed Sun Wukong, the Monkey King and eldest disciple. "Wait here, I will take a look." He jumped into the air and used his cloud somersault to fly quickly ahead. He looked down and saw a large city covered in fog. Looking carefully, he saw that the fog was not caused by evil magic. Outside the city gate he saw several hundred Buddhist monks trying to pull a heavy wooden cart up a hill. The cart was full of rocks and was too heavy for them. They all cried loudly for the Buddha to help them. This was the sound that the travelers had heard. Sun Wukong decided to take a closer look.

He came down to the ground and walked up to the monks. They were thin and dressed in old rags. This was surprising, since monks usually wear nicer clothing. Sun Wukong thought, "Perhaps they are trying to build or repair a local monastery and they cannot find local workers, so they must do the work themselves."

Then he saw two young Daoist priests come out of the city gate. They were dressed in beautiful clothes. They were well fed and their faces were as bright and handsome as two full moons. When the monks saw the two Daoist priests, they put their heads down and tried even harder to pull the cart up the hill. They looked very frightened. "Ah, that's it," Sun Wukong thought. "The monks are afraid of the Daoist priests. I have heard of a city where Daoism is revered and Buddhism is not. This must be the place. I must tell Master of this, but first I need to understand what is happening here."

He shook his body and changed his appearance. Now he looked like a traveling Daoist priest, in old clothes. He carried a wooden fish which he hit with a stick, and he sang a Daoist song. He walked up to the two well-dressed Daoist priests and said, "Masters, this old Daoist greets you."

"Where do you come from?" asked one of the Daoist priests.

"This poor disciple has wandered to the ends of the oceans and across the borders of Heaven. Just this morning I arrived at your beautiful city. Can you please tell me which streets have people who are friends of the Dao, and which streets I should avoid?"

"Why do you ask that?"

"I wish to beg for some vegetarian food, and I do not want trouble."

"And why do you wish to beg for this food?"

"That is a strange question! We who have left our families must always beg for food. We have no money and cannot buy it for ourselves."

The Daoist laughed at this, and said, "My friend, you come from far away and you do not know our city. This is the Slow Cart Kingdom. All the ministers and all of the people in the city are friends of the Dao. They are happy to give us food. Even our king is fond of the Dao."

"Are you saying that your king is a Daoist?"

"No, but he is a friend of the Dao. Many years ago, the weather was very bad here. There was no rain. The crops died, the land turned brown, and the people had nothing to eat. The king and the people all prayed but still the rain did not come. Then one day, when it looked like we all would die of hunger, three Immortals arrived."

"Who were these Immortals?"

"The first is called Tiger Strength Immortal, the second is called Deer Strength Immortal, and the third is called Goat Strength Immortal. They have deep knowledge of the Dao, and their magic is powerful. They can command the sun, the wind and the rain as easily as you turn over your hand. Soon after they arrived, they brought rain. The land turned green and the people had plenty to eat."

Sun Wukong said, "Your king is indeed a lucky man. As the ancients say, 'Magic moves ministers.' Do you think that I could meet these three immortals?"

"That would be no problem at all. We will introduce you to them. But first, we have some work to do. Do you see these useless monks? They are Buddhists. During our time of hunger, the Buddhists prayed to their god for rain, but nothing happened. Then the Daoist immortals came and easily brought rain. This made our king angry at the Buddhists. He said that they were useless. He smashed their temples and told them they could not leave the city. He made them work. Our job is to keep an eye on the monks to make sure they don't relax when they should be working."

Sun Wukong nodded his head, thinking about this but saying nothing. Then he had an idea. He said, "My friends, maybe you can help me. I have a relative, an uncle, who lives in this region. He is a Buddhist monk. I have not seen him in many years. I think he might be living here in your city. Can I see if he is one of these workers?"

"Of course. Go down and take a look at the monks. There should be five hundred of them. You can help us by counting them to make sure all five hundred are there. While you are there, you can look for your uncle. Come back later and we will introduce you to the three Immortals."

Sun Wukong thanked them, then he walked down to where the monks were working. As he walked, he hit his wooden fish and sang a Daoist song. The monks saw him coming. They all stopped work and kowtowed to him. One of them said, "Oh great master, do not be angry. All five hundred of us have been working very hard!"

He replied, "Please get up, don't be afraid. I am not here to look at your work. I am looking for my uncle." The monks surrounded him, all hoping that Sun Wukong would claim him as his uncle. He asked, "My friends, why are you working like slaves? You should be in the monastery, chanting the holy words of the Buddha. Why do you work for these Daoist priests?"

One of them told the same story that the Daoist had told about the hunger, the arrival of the three Immortals, and the king's anger at the Buddhists. He said, "Now the king will not allow us to be monks anymore. We can only be slaves of the Daoist priests!"

"Why don't you just run away?"

"That would not help us. The king has had portraits painted of each of us, and these are hung up in all four corners of the kingdom. If we run away, we will be recognized and captured."

"Well then, you might as well just give up and wait to die."

"Indeed, many of us have already died. Originally there were two thousand of us. Fifteen hundred have died from overwork. But for us, the last five hundred, we cannot die. Many of have tried to kill ourselves, but we always fail. So we work all day, every day. In the evening we eat a little soup with rice. At night we sleep outdoors on the ground. And every night, the Six Gods of Darkness and the Six Gods of Light come to us in our dreams. They tell us to stay strong and wait for the arrival of the Tang Monk and his disciple, the Great Sage Equal to Heaven. They tell us that when the Great Sage comes, he will help those who suffer. He will destroy the Daoist priests and bring back the love of the Buddha!"

Sun Wukong was surprised to hear this. He decided this was not a good time to tell the monks that he was, indeed, the Great Sage Equal to Heaven. He turned and walked back to the two well dressed Daoist priests. One of them said, "Little brother, did you find your uncle?"

"Yes, I did. All five hundred of them are my uncles."

"How can that be?"

"I come from a very large family. One hundred are neighbors on my right. One hundred are neighbors on my left. One hundred are on my father's side and one hundred are on my mother's side. And one hundred are my blood brothers. All are my relatives and friends. Let them all go. Now."

The Daoist said, "Of course we will not do that. If we let them go, who will do the work in this city?"

"That is not my problem. Let them go!" shouted Sun Wukong. They refused. He asked them three more times. Each time they refused, and each time he became angrier. Finally, he took out his golden hoop rod and smashed the two Daoist priests on their heads, killing them instantly.

When the monks saw this, they came running up to Sun Wukong, crying "Disaster! Disaster! Now the king will be very angry and we will be the ones to suffer for it. Why did you do this?"

"Stop shouting, all of you. I am no traveling Daoist monk. I am Sun Wukong, the Great Sage Equal to Heaven. I am traveling with the Tang monk. I have come to save your lives."

One of the monks cried, "No, you cannot be the Great Sage. In our dreams, we met an old man who calls himself Gold Star of Venus. He says that the Great Sage has a round head, a hairy face, golden eyes and a pointed mouth. He carries a golden hoop rod that he used to smash the gates of Heaven. They also say he is quite rude."

Sun Wukong was pleased to hear the gods were talking about him, but he was also a little bit annoyed because the gods had been telling these monks too much about him. He said, "OK, I am not the Great Sage. I am just his disciple. There is the Great Sage!" And he pointed to a place behind the monks. As they turned to look, he changed into his true form and shouted, "Here I am!"

They looked back and saw him, then they all went down on their knees, saying, "Oh Father, we are sorry we did not recognize you. We beg you to avenge us. Enter the city and kill those demons!"

Sun Wukong used his magic to pick up the heavy cart and smash it on the ground. He shouted, "Go away! I will see this foolish king tomorrow, and I will kill those Daoist priests."

"But Father, we are afraid. What will we do when you are gone? What if the Daoist priests come back?"

Sun Wukong pulled a bunch of hairs from his head. He chewed them until he had five hundred little pieces of hair. He gave one piece to each monk. He told them to put the little hair under the fingernail of their fourth finger. "If anyone gives you trouble, close your fist tightly and say, 'Great Sage Equal to Heaven.' I will come and protect you."

This was difficult for the monks to believe. One of the monks held up his fist and whispered, "Great Sage Equal to Heaven." Immediately a thunder spirit appeared in front of him, holding an iron rod. The thunder spirit was so big and powerful that nobody would dare attack the monk. Encouraged by this, several other monks also said, "Great Sage Equal to Heaven." Each time, a thunder spirit appeared in front of them.

"When you want the thunder spirit to go away, just say the word, 'Stop' and it will disappear." The monks, feeling more confident now, all shouted "Stop!" and the thunder spirits all disappeared.

While all this was happening, Tangseng and the other two disciples were waiting on the road. They grew tired of waiting, so they started to walk towards the city. Soon they saw Sun Wukong standing with a crowd of monks around him. He asked Sun Wukong to explain what was happening. Sun Wukong told him the full story. Tangseng was horrified, and asked the Monkey King what they should do.

One of the monks spoke up, saying to Tangseng, "Great father, do not be afraid. Great Sage Sun has great magical powers, he will protect you from danger. There is still one monastery in the city that the king has not destroyed. Please come to our monastery and rest there. Tomorrow the Great Sage will know what to do."

The four travelers and the crowd of monks all walked to the monastery. When they entered, they saw a large golden Buddha. Tangseng prostrated himself before the Buddha. Then an old monk came out to meet them. He looked at Sun Wukong and prostrated himself on the ground, saying, "Father, you have arrived! You are the Great Sage Equal to Heaven, the one who we see in our dreams!"

"Please get up," laughed Sun Wukong. "Tomorrow we will take care of your problem." The monks all went to prepare a simple vegetarian meal for the travelers. Then the travelers went to their beds for the night's sleep.

But Sun Wukong could not sleep. He was thinking of the events of the day, and what he would do tomorrow. Around the time of the second watch, he heard the sound of music. He got up, put on his clothes, and jumped into the air on his cloud. Looking down, he saw the Daoist temple which was called the Temple of the Three Pure Ones. In the courtyard outside the temple, in the bright light of torches, he saw the three Daoist Immortals wearing beautiful robes. There were also seven or eight hundred Daoist monks. They were singing, beating drums, burning incense, and sending prayers up to Heaven. There was a lot of food on tables. He thought to himself, "I'd like to go there and have some fun. First, though, I'll get Zhu and Sha to help me."

He returned to the Buddhist monastery to wake up Zhu and Sha. He said, "Come with me to the Temple of the Three Pure Ones. The Daoist priests are having some sort of ceremony there. There are tables full of fruits, buns as big as barrels, and cakes that must weight fifty catties each. Let's enjoy ourselves!"

The three of them left the monastery and flew to the Daoist temple. They looked down and saw the Daoist priests and all the delicious food. "We should not go down there," said Sha, "there are too many people."

"Let me use a little magic," replied Sun Wukong. He blew out a strong wind. The wind became a storm. It blew out all the lamps and torches, and knocked over the tables and chairs. Tiger Strength Immortal said, "Disciples, the weather has turned bad. Let's go indoors and go to bed. We will finish our prayers tomorrow."

 After the Daoist priests left, the three disciples arrived at the courtyard. Zhu immediately grabbed one of the buns. Sun Wukong smacked his hand and said, "Don't do that. Let's sit down and eat with proper manners."

"Are you kidding me?" replied Zhu. "Here you are, stealing food from a temple, and you're talking to me about manners?"

Sun Wukong looked up and saw three statues near the wall. "Who are those?"

he asked.

"Don't you know anything?" replied Zhu. "Those are the Three Pure Ones. On the left is the Jade Pure One. In the middle is the Supreme Pure One. And on the right is Laozi himself, the Grand Pure One." Zhu used his long nose to push over the statue of Laozi. Then he changed his appearance so he looked just like the statue of Laozi. Sha laughed and changed into the Supreme Pure One, and Sun Wukong changed into the Jade Pure One. "OK," said Zhu, "let's eat!"

"Not yet," replied Sun Wukong. "We need to hide these three statues. Just outside this room I saw a little door on the right. It smells really bad, so I think it is the Room of Five Grain Transformation[1]. Put the statues in there." Of course, when Sun Wukong said this, he meant that it was the bathroom. Zhu carried the three statues into the bathroom and threw them into the toilet. They landed in the dirty water. Then he returned to the courtyard, laughing. The three of them, looking like the Three Pure Ones, sat down at the table. They drank all the wine and they ate every last mouthful of food.

One of the young Daoist monks was trying to sleep, but he remembered that he had left a handbell in the courtyard. He got up in the dark and walked to the courtyard to get the bell. He heard the sound of breathing and became very frightened. He tried to run out of the courtyard but he slipped on a banana. Zhu saw this and laughed loudly. This made the young Daoist even more frightened. He ran to the residence of the three Daoist Immortals and cried, "Masters, come quickly! I heard the sound of breathing in the courtyard, then I heard someone laughing!"

Tiger Strength Immortal shouted, "Bring some light. Let's see who is there." Then all three Daoist immortals and hundreds of Daoist monks grab bed lamps and torches and ran to the courtyard.

---

[1] This is the toilet.

Chapter 45

Sun Wukong heard the crowd coming. He said, "Watch me!" to Zhu and Sha. Then he became silent and sat unmoving, like a statue. Zhu and Sha saw what he did. They also sat unmoving. Now they looked just like the Three Pure Ones.

Tiger Strength Immortal arrived in the courtyard with the others. He held a torch and looked closely at the three statues, but they looked exactly like the statues of the Three Pure Ones. Then he said, "There are no thieves here, just these three statues. But who ate all the food?"

Goat Strength Immortal replied, "I think that the Three Pure Ones have come down to earth, visited our temple, and eaten our food. We are very fortunate! Let's ask them to give us some golden elixir. We can give it to our king."

The three immortals and all the Daoist disciples began to sing and dance and recite the holy Daoist scriptures. Then Tiger Strength Immortal prostrated himself on the ground, held out his arms, and asked the Three Pure Ones to give them golden elixir for the king.

Sun Wukong said to them, "You young immortals, please stop asking us for golden elixir. We have just returned from the Festival of the Immortal Peaches. Right now, we do not have the elixir that you want. Come back tomorrow and we will give them to you."

The Daoist monks saw the Jade Pure One open his mouth and speak. They were terrified and fell to the ground. Deer Strength Immortal came forward and also prostrated himself on the ground, saying,

Oh Pure Ones Three
Your disciples pray to you
With our heads in the dust
Your disciples sing to you
With torches by night and incense by day
We came here and set the king free
Now we ask you to give him long life
Please hear our prayers
And give us some golden elixir!

Sun Wukong said, "All right, young immortals, enough of this. We hear your prayers and will give you the golden elixir that you ask for. Give us something to hold the gifts." Right away, the three Immortals ran to find three large buckets. Soon they returned, carrying the empty buckets. "Good," said Sun Wukong. "Now go away, and close all the doors and shutters. The mysteries of Heaven must not be seen by the eyes of men. We will call you when the elixir is ready." The three Immortals and all the Daoist monks left the courtyard. They closed all the doors and shutters, so nobody could see into the courtyard.

Sun Wukong stood up, walked over to one of the buckets, lifted his tiger skin, and pissed into the bucket until it was full. Zhu saw this, laughed, and said, "Elder brother, we have been friends for a long time, but this is the most fun I have ever had with you!" and he filled up the second bucket with urine. Sha pissed into the third bucket and filled it up.

Then Sun Wukong called out, "Little ones, come and get your golden elixir!" The Daoist priests came back into the courtyard. They kowtowed to the Three Pure Ones. Then they picked up the three buckets and poured the liquid into a large barrel, mixing the contents together. "Disciples," called Tiger Strength Immortal, "bring me a cup." One of them brought him a large cup. He dipped the cup into the barrel, filled it with the warm liquid, and drank all of it at once. The others watch him. He blinked his eyes a couple of times.

"Elder brother," said Deer Strength Immortal, "how does it taste?"

"I have to say, it does not taste good," said Tiger Strength Immortal. "The taste is very strong and bitter."

Goat Strength Immortal tasted the liquid. "I think it tastes like pig urine," he said.

Sun Wukong could not stop himself from laughing. He stood up and said, "Oh Daoist priests, you are such fools! Let me tell you our true names. We are not Pure Ones. We are disciples of the Tang monk, traveling west by command of the Tang Emperor. We came to your city looking for a place to rest a bit. Tonight we found this good food, and ate and drank all of it. We wanted a way to pay you for the good food and drink, so here it is. We hope you enjoy your golden elixir!"

The Daoist priests were furious. They picked up anything they could find – rakes, sticks, torches, rocks – and attacked the three Tang disciples. Quickly, the three Buddhist disciples flew into the air and returned to the Buddhist monastery. When they arrived, they went quietly back to bed, trying not to wake up their master. Their bellies were full and they slept until late the next morning.

In the morning, Tangseng got out of bed and said to them, "Disciples, get up. I need to go and see the king. He needs to sign our travel rescript[1]."

The three disciples also got up, put on their clothes, and waited for Tangseng. They said, "Master, please be careful. This king is a friend to the Daoist priests, and has no love for Buddhists. We fear that if he sees that we are Buddhists, he will refuse to sign our travel rescript. Please let us come with you to see the king." Tangseng agreed, and they left the monastery to walk to the palace of the king.

They arrived at the palace and told one of the ministers that they were monks traveling from the east, traveling to India, and wished to greet the king and have their travel rescript signed. The minister told the king, and the four travelers were invited to come into the throne room.

The king looked at the four Buddhists. He said to his minister, "If these monks are looking to die, why do they want to do it here?"

The minister replied, "Your Majesty, they come from the Tang Empire. It is in China, ten thousand miles east of here. The road from Tang to here is very dangerous, with many monsters and wild animals. Yet these four are still alive. They must have very powerful magic. Please, sign their rescript and allow them to continue on their journey."

Tangseng and the three disciples came forward and presented the rescript to the king. The king took it, read it, and was about to sign it. But just then, the three Daoist Immortals arrived. They walked into the throne room without being invited. The king bowed to them. They stood tall and did not return the bow. The king said to them, "Oh great Immortals, we were not expecting to see you today. Why have you come?"

One of them replied, "We have something to tell you. But first, tell us, where do these four monks come from?"

"They say that they came from the Tang Empire, ten thousand miles to the east, in China," the king replied. "They are traveling west to India. They asked us to sign their travel rescript, and we agreed, wanting to keep a good

------

[1] Tōngguān wénshū is a travel rescript, similar to an imperial passport that needs to be stamped by each kingdom to guarantee legal passage, in this case along the quest to India. It contains an introductory letter from the Tang emperor and the stamps of all the kingdoms already visited.

relationship with the Tang Empire."

The three Immortals laughed. Tiger Strength Immortal said, "I must tell you what happened yesterday. As soon as these monks arrived at our city, they killed two of our disciples outside the eastern gate. Then they released five hundred Buddhist monks and smashed their cart. Then last night they came to our temple. They took the form of the Three Pure Ones and ate all of the food that we had set out for the Pure Ones. We thought they really were the Three Pure Ones, so we asked them to give us some golden elixir. We wanted to give the golden elixir to you, to give you long life. But they gave us their urine instead of golden elixir. We learned of this after we drank some of the awful stuff. We tried to grab them but they escaped. We did not think they would dare to remain in our city, but here they are!"

The king heard this. He was about to give the order to kill the four travelers. But quickly Sun Wukong said, "Your Majesty, please, let your anger cool and let this poor monk speak."

"What?" said the king, "Are you saying that these holy Immortals are not telling the truth?"

Sun Wukong had seen that the king was a bit muddle-headed and not very smart. So he decided to try to trick the king. "Your Majesty, they say that we killed two disciples. But there are no witnesses. Even if this is true, that crime should only result in two of us being killed, not four. Then they say that we smashed a cart. Again, there are no witnesses. And even if this is true, it is not a serious crime, and I do not think even one of us should be killed. And finally, they say that we caused trouble in their temple. Clearly this is a trap they set for us."

"How can you say that it was a trap?"

"Your Majesty, we are travelers from the east. We just arrived. We do not know your city; we do not know one street from another. How could we even know the location of their temple, and at night no less? If last night we really gave them urine instead of golden elixir, why would they wait until this morning to tell you? Many people look alike. Perhaps someone else gave them the urine, not us. This matter is not clear at all. We ask you to set up a committee to look into this matter carefully before you make any decisions."

Now the king was very confused. He did not know what to do or what to say. But as he was standing there, a minister came in and said, "Your Majesty, many village elders are waiting to see you." The king returned to his throne and told the minister to bring them in.

The elders came in. They all kowtowed to the king, and one of them said, "Your Majesty, there has been no rain this spring. Our farms are turning brown and we are afraid that soon there will be no food. We ask the three Immortals to pray for rain, so that your people will have food."

The king said to Tangseng, "Now do you understand why we love the Dao and have no use for Buddhists? In years past, the Buddhist monks prayed for rain but there was no rain. Then the three Daoist Immortals arrived, they prayed for rain and the rain came. The Immortals saved our city, while the Buddhists did nothing. Now you come here and cause trouble for these Immortals. I should have you killed, but I have a better idea. We will have a rainmaking competition. If you bring rain, I will sign your travel rescript and you can continue on your journey to the west. If you fail, you will all lose your heads!"

The king and his ministers climbed to the top of a great tower to watch the competition. The four travelers and the three Immortals also climbed to the top of the tower. Tiger Strength Immortal walked forward to the edge of the tower. On all sides flags were flying in the wind with the names of the twenty-eight constellations on them. There was a large table. On the table was a brazier with incense burning in it.

Sun Wukong said, "Wait a minute! If we both try to bring rain, and the rain comes, nobody will know who brought the rain. We need a way to know the winner of the competition."

Tiger Strength Immortal smiled and said, "No problem, little monkey. I will bang on this table five times. The first time the wind will come. The second time the clouds will come. The third time the lightning and thunder will come. The fourth time the rains will come. And the fifth time the rain will stop and the clouds will go away."

"Wonderful!" said Sun Wukong. "I have never seen this before. Please, begin!"

The Daoist banged loudly on the table. The wind began to rise. "Oh no," said Zhu, "we are in trouble now!"

"Be quiet, brother," said Sun Wukong. "Let me work." He pulled out one of his hairs, blew on it, and it changed into the image of the monkey. That monkey stood still. The spirit of Sun Wukong flew up into the air. He shouted, "Who is in charge of the wind around here?"

The Old Woman of the Wind appeared, holding a large bag that she used to make the wind. "I make the wind," she said. "Who are you?"

"I am the Great Sage Equal to Heaven, and a disciple of the Tang monk. We are traveling west to India, and stopped at Slow Cart Kingdom. Now I am having a competition with one of the Daoist priests. He is trying to bring the wind. I want you to stop the wind. If you don't do it right away, I will hit you twenty times with my rod!"

Immediately the Old Woman of the Wind stopped the wind. On the tower, everyone saw that the wind had stopped. The Daoist burned some incense and banged on the table again, and clouds began to form. In the sky Sun Wukong shouted again, "Who brings the clouds?" Cloud-Pushing Boy and Fog-Spreading Boy came up to him. He told them the same story, and gave them the same orders. Immediately they stopped the clouds from forming, and the sun came out.

On the tower, Zhu laughed loudly and said, "This old Daoist has fooled the king and the people. He has no magic power at all. Look, there's no wind, and not a single cloud in the sky!"

The Daoist was becoming a little bit frightened, but he continued to try making his magic. He said more prayers, burned more incense, and banged the table a third time. In the sky, Lord Deng[1] came down from the South Heaven Gate, along with the Prince of Thunder and the Mother of Lightning. Lord Deng said, "We have been called by the Jade Emperor himself to assist with the rainmaking."

Sun Wukong replied, "That's fine, but please wait a moment. You can still do as the Jade Emperor commands, but you can help me at the same time." Lord Deng agreed, and he stopped the thunder and lightning.

Now the Daoist was becoming desperate. He burned all the rest of the incense, said some prayers, and banged the table a fourth time. In the sky, the Dragon Kings of the Four Oceans all appeared. But they were all old friends of Sun Wukong. He greeted them and told them the same story. They agreed to wait and did not bring any rain.

Lord Deng said, "Great Sage, we have all done as you asked. Now we will

---

[1] Dèng Tiānjūn, or Lord Deng, is a Daoist deity also known as the Statutory Commander of Scorching Fire. He has a red-haired bird head, wings, and eagle claws. He holds a drill in his left hand and a mallet in his right.

wait for your order."

Sun Wukong replied, "Thank you. I will point my rod upwards five times. Each time I point my rod, that will tell you to make the wind blow, then bring the clouds, then bring the thunder and lightning, then bring the rain, and then stop the rain." All the weather spirits agreed to follow his commands. Then he flew down to the tower and returned to his body. He said to the Daoist, "Sir, you have tried to bring the wind, clouds, thunder, lightning and rain, but you have failed. Now let me try."

The Daoist walked slowly away from the table, saying to the king, "I am sorry, Your Majesty, the dragon kings are not at home today."

Sun Wukong heard this. He said, "Your Majesty, the dragon kings are indeed home today. But your Daoist friend does not have enough magic to bring the rain. Let the Buddhists monk try!"

"Please go ahead," said the king.

Sun Wukong said quietly to Tangseng, "OK, now it's time for you to bring the rain."

Tangseng replied, "But I don't know anything about bringing rain!"

"Don't worry. You know how to recite scriptures. Just go there and say some Buddhist prayers. I will take care of everything."

Tangseng recited the Heart Sutra. When he finished, Sun Wukong took his rod out of his ear, pointed it to the sky, and raised it one time. The Old Woman of the Wind saw this. She opened her bag and the wind started to rise. It grew stronger and stronger. All over the city, clouds of dust rose up and filled the air. But the tower was higher than the dust clouds.

Sun Wukong raised his rod a second time The Cloud-Pushing Boy and the Fog-Spreading Boy saw this. They brought a thick blanket of clouds. The cloud blanket was so deep and dark that daytime turned to nighttime in the city. He raised his rod a third time. The Prince of Thunder brought thunder that was so loud that it awakened sleeping animals for a hundred miles. The Mother of Lightning brought lightning that was so bright that it lit up the sky like a dragon breathing fire across the sky. The people in the city were frightened. They burned incense and paper money.

Now the Monkey King raised his rod a fourth time, and the four Dragon Kings brought rain. It rained so hard, it was as if the entire Yangtze River came down onto the city. All the streets were flooded. The king said, "Please, stop this rain. We have enough! I am afraid that it will destroy the crops in the farmers' fields!" Sun Wukong raised his rod a fifth time. The rain stopped. The thunder and lightning stopped. The wind stopped. The clouds drifted away and the sun returned to the sky.

The king was very pleased by this. He was getting ready to sign the travelers' rescript and send them on their way. But the Daoist priests were angry. They said, "Your Majesty, this rain was not brought by those Buddhist monks. It came from our strength, not theirs."

"How can you say that?" replied the king. "You just said that the Dragon Kings were not home. But the Buddhist monk showed us that the Dragon Kings were here, and they brought the rain."

Tiger Strength Immortal said, "You must remember, I said prayers and I burned incense first. The Dragon Kings and the other weather spirits must have been busy somewhere else at the time. They came as soon as they could. It was my prayer that brought them, not this foolish Buddhist monk."

The king again became confused. He did not know what to think. Sun Wukong laughed and said, "Your Majesty, this old Daoist is telling you stories again. But it should be easy for you to know if he is telling the truth or not. He says that he commanded the four Dragon Kings to bring the rain. So tell him to command those dragons to show themselves!"

"I have sat on the throne for twenty-three years," the king replied, "but I have never seen a living dragon!" And he ordered the Daoist to bring the dragons. The Daoist called the dragons, but they simply ignored him. No dragons appeared in the sky. Then the king turned to Sun Wukong and said, "Can you do this?"

"Of course!" said Sun Wukong. He turned his face to the sky and called, "Auron, Dragon King of the Western Ocean! I ask you and your three brothers to please show yourselves!"

All four Dragon Kings appeared in the sky above the city. They danced over the city, their bodies shining like mirrors in the sky. Sun Wukong waited for a while, then he shouted to them, "Thank you, dragon kings and weather spirits. You can all return home now. The king will say a special mass for you on another day." The dragons returned to their oceans, the weather spirits disappeared, and the sky was clear again.

Chapter 46

Later that day, the king signed Tangseng's travel rescript. He was getting ready to hand it over to Tangseng, but just then the three Daoist Immortals came in again.

"What do you want now?" asked the king.

"Your Majesty, we have lived in your kingdom for twenty years. We have brought rain; we have protected you and your people. Now this traveling monk arrives and shows you a little magic, and you are ready to return to Buddhism and forget about us? How can you treat us like this? We ask for one more competition to see whose magic is stronger."

This king's mind was quite weak. It was difficult for him to make decisions, and he always agreed with the last person who spoke to him. So he put away the travel rescript and asked, "What sort of competition do you have in mind?"

"We call it the Competition of Cloud Ladders. We need one hundred tables. Build two towers of fifty tables each, one on top of the other. I will climb to the top of one tower without using my hands or a ladder, only by using a cloud. The Buddhist will climb the other tower the same way. Then we will both mediate silently. Whoever meditates the longest will win the competition."

The king liked this idea. He told his workers to gather a hundred tables and build two towers in the courtyard. Then he told one of his ministers to explain the competition to the four travelers.

Sun Wukong was not happy about this. He said, "I am very good at smashing things. But I am not good at meditating. I cannot sit still for any long period of time. I'm afraid I will lose this contest."

"I can meditate!" said Tangseng.

"Wonderful!" replied Sun Wukong. "How long can you sit still?"

"Oh, for at least two or three years."

"We will not need that much time."

Soon all the travelers and Daoist priests gathered in the courtyard next to the two towers. Tiger Strength Immortal jumped into the air. Clouds formed at his feet, and he rose up in the air. When he got to the top of the tower, he stepped off the clouds onto the topmost table. He sat down and began to meditate.

Sun Wukong changed into a five-colored cloud. The cloud rested on the ground next to Tangseng. The monk stepped on the cloud, and it carried him up to the top of the other tower. Tangseng stepped off the cloud, sat down, and also started to meditate.

Now, Deer Strength Immortal decided to help his brother a little bit. He pulled a hair from his head and blew on it. It floated up to the top of Tangseng's tower. It landed on Tangseng's head and changed into an insect. The insect started to bite Tangseng's head. Tangseng really wanted to scratch his head, but he knew that if he moved his hand, he would lose the competition.

Sun Wukong saw that his master was having trouble. He turned into a cricket and flew up to the top of Tangseng's tower. He saw the insect on Tangseng's head. He pushed the insect off. Then he used his little legs to scratch Tangseng's head, stopping the itching.

Sun Wukong knew that there was no way an insect could have flown up to the top of the tower. It had to be the work of one of the Daoist priests. So he flew over to the other tower, just above the meditating Daoist. He changed into a seven-inch-long centipede. The centipede dropped down onto the face of the Daoist and gave him a huge bite on the upper lip. The Daoist jumped up and fell off the tower. His friends caught him when he reached the ground. They carried him away, and the king declared Tangseng the winner of the competition.

But before the king could let the travelers go, Deer Strength Immortal spoke to him, saying, "Your Majesty, my elder brother sometimes has difficulty when the weather is cold and windy. That's why he could not win the meditation competition. Please allow us to have a second competition. We call it the Competition of Hidden Things. This poor Daoist has the ability to see what is hidden behind boards. Let's see if the traveling monk can do the same."

The king was confused again, and so he agreed to another competition. He asked the queen to put something of great value into a red lacquered chest, then the chest was brought into the courtyard. He said, "Let both sides guess what treasure is in the chest."

Tangseng said to Sun Wukong, "Disciple, I do not know how to see inside this chest!"

"No worries, Master," replied Sun Wukong. "I will take a look and tell you what's inside." He changed into a cricket and found a small crack in the bottom of the chest. He entered the chest and saw that the treasure was a beautiful palace robe. He bit his lip and spat a drop of blood on the robe, using his magic to change the robe into an old worn-out cassock. Then just for fun, he changed into a cat and pissed on it. Then he changed back into a cricket, left the chest, and flew up to Tangseng's ear. He said quietly, "It's an old worn-out monk's cassock."

"Well?" asked the king. "What's in the chest?"

"It is a beautiful palace robe," said Deer Strength Immortal.

"No, no, no," replied Tangseng. "It's an old worn-out cassock."

"How dare you!" shouted the king. "Do you think we have no treasure in our kingdom?"

Tangseng was very frightened. He replied, "Your Majesty, your humble monk begs you to wait and see if my words are true or not!" Then he waited nervously as the chest was opened. Inside was an old worn-out cassock that smelled like cat urine.

Now the king and queen were both angry. The queen was angry because her beautiful palace robe had turned to rags, and the king was angry because such an old dirty thing was found in his palace. He said, "We will have one more contest. This time, I will hide the thing myself." He had two servants carry the chest into the garden. There he found a very large peach, as big as two fists, and he placed it in the chest. They returned to the courtyard.

Again Sun Wukong changed into a cricket and entered the chest. He was very happy to find the peach. He ate the entire fruit, leaving only the pit. Then he left the chest, flew up to Tangseng's ear, and told him that there was a peach pit inside.

Again the king asked what was in the chest. The Daoist said, "Inside the chest is a large peach."

Tangseng said, "No, Your Majesty, there is only a peach pit in the chest."

They opened the chest and of course there was only a peach pit. The king shook his head, saying, "I put that peach in the chest myself. Truly, this Buddhist monk has very powerful magic."

"Yes," said Tiger Strength Immortal, "he has some magic. But these are just small tricks. We want to have one final competition with them. We want you to cut off our heads."

"But that will mean certain death!" cried the king.

"Not for us. But perhaps for these monks," replied the Immortal.

Sun Wukong heard this and laughed. "It is my lucky day!" he said. "It looks like business has come to my door!" Turning to the king, he said, "Please, Your Majesty, since we won each of the last three competitions, please allow us to change the rules for this final competition. I wish to enter this competition alone. I will allow my head to be cut off. For the Daoist priests, each of them will also lose their heads. Will you allow this?"

The king agreed. Sun Wukong was tied up with ropes and his head was put on a wooden block. Three thousand soldiers stood guard. The executioner lifted his ax and brought it down on the monkey's neck. His head came off and rolled on the ground. The executioner kicked the head and it rolled away. As the head was rolling away, it shouted, "Grow!" and a new head grew from Sun Wukong's neck.

Now the king was very frightened. He told Tangseng and the three disciples to leave his city and never return. But Sun Wukong said, "We will be happy to go, but the competition is not finished. The three Daoist priests must also lose their heads."

The three Daoist Immortals were tied up. Three executioners brought down three axes at the same time, and three heads rolled along the ground. All three of the Daoist priests' bodies called for their heads to return, but Sun Wukong blew on three hairs, changing them into three dogs. The dogs grabbed the three heads and ran away with them. The Daoist priests could not bring their heads back. After a minute, blood flowed out from their necks and they died. Their bodies changed. One was a headless yellow tiger, one was a headless white deer, and one was a headless gray goat.

The king saw that the three Immortals were dead. He knelt down and cried without stopping. Sun Wukong listened to this for a while, then he shouted at the king, "How could you be so foolish? These were not Daoist Immortals, they were demons! Can't you see that? They were just waiting for your power to weaken, then they would kill you and take over your kingdom. You are very lucky that we came here and saved your life and saved your kingdom. But you don't see that. No problem, just give us our travel rescript and we will be on our way."

The king's prime minister said, "Your highness, the monkey is correct. These were demons, not Daoist priests."

The king said, "In that case, we thank the Tang monk and his disciples. Please rest tonight at the Buddhist monastery. Tomorrow we will have a great vegetarian feast for you, and you can continue on your journey to the west."

The next day, the king gave a great feast for the four travelers. He declared that the Buddhist monks could safely return to the city. The five hundred monks returned. They gave their little monkey hairs back to Sun Wukong, and they thanked him for saving their lives.

Sun Wukong stood up and said to the king and the people, "I must confess. I released these five hundred monks. I smashed the cart. And I killed the two Daoist priests outside the gate. I did those things to save your city from the three demons. From now on, please remember the way of the Buddha. Do not believe false words from others. Also, remember to revere the Buddhist monks, revere the Daoist priests also, and revere the talented and wise. Do these things and your kingdom will be safe."

The king agreed. He thanked the four travelers again and handed the travel rescript to Tangseng. Then the Tang monk and the three disciples left the city and continued their journey to the west.

Chapter 47

The four travelers drank when they were thirsty, they ate when they were hungry, they rested when they were tired. Spring became summer, summer became fall. One day in early fall as the cool wind blew through the trees, Tangseng spoke to his disciples. He said, "It is getting late. Where can we find a place to sleep tonight?"

Sun Wukong replied, "Master, long ago we left our families. We do not have comfortable beds, we do not have wives to keep us warm at night, we do not have children to make us happy. We live under the sun, the moon and the stars. If there is a road, we travel. If the road ends, we stop."

"Easy for you to say!" said the pig-man Zhu Bajie. "All day I carry your heavy baggage. I am tired, I am hungry, my feet hurt, and I want to stop right now!"

"The moon is bright tonight. Let's walk a little further," said Sun Wukong. The others did not argue with him, they just walked behind him.

The road ended at a large river. They could not see the far side. Sun Wukong used his cloud somersault to jump up into the air. He used his diamond eyes, but he could not see the river's far side. "This river is very wide," he said. "I can see a thousand miles in daytime and five hundred miles at night, but I cannot see the far side of this river. I don't know how we can get to the far side."

Tangseng did not say a word, but he started to cry quietly.

"Don't cry, Master," said Sha. "I see a man over there, standing near the water. Maybe he can help us." Sun Wukong walked over to take a look. When he got close, he saw that it was not a man, it was a tall stone pillar. Three large words were on the stone: "Heaven Reaching River." Below that were smaller words:

> Eight hundred miles wide,
> Very few have ever crossed it

The four travelers read the words but said nothing. Sun Wukong, Zhu and Sha could fly across the river with no trouble, but Tangseng had no magical powers and could not fly. How could they all cross the river?

Then they heard the sound of music coming from a mile or so up the river.

"That music does not sound like Daoist music," said Tangseng. "It might be Buddhist. I will go and talk with them. I will beg some vegetarian food and a place for us to sleep. You wait here. You are all quite ugly and I don't want to frighten these people."

Tangseng rode his white horse along the riverbank. He arrived at a large temple. Candles burned in every window, and more candles burned inside. He took off his hat and waited just outside the front door. After a few minutes, an old man came out.

Tangseng bowed and said, "Grandfather, this poor monk salutes you."

The man said, "You are too late. If you had arrived earlier, you would have gotten some rice, some cloth, and a few pennies. Now you will get nothing. Go away." He turned to go back inside the temple.

Tangseng said quickly, "Grandfather, please wait a minute. We have been sent by the Tang Emperor to journey to the Western Heaven. We seek the Buddha's holy books to bring back to the Tang Empire. It is getting late in the day, and we just seek a place to stay tonight. We will leave in the morning."

"Monk, a man who has left his family should not lie. The Tang Empire is fifty-four thousand miles to the east. Traveling alone, you could not get here."

"That is true. I have three disciples with me. They are very good at fighting monsters, demons and tigers. But they are a bit ugly. I didn't bring them here because I didn't want to frighten you."

"You cannot frighten me tonight," said the old man. "Bring them in." Tangseng did not understand this, but he called the three disciples. Sun Wukong, Zhu and Sha ran into the temple laughing and shouting. They brought the horse and the luggage with them. The old man fell to the ground, shouting, "Monsters are here! Monsters are here!"

"Don't be afraid, Grandfather," said Tangseng, "they won't hurt you." Then he turned to the three disciples and shouted at them, "Why are you so rude? I have told you every day to act like Buddhist monks, but you act like wild animals instead!"

The old man heard this. He looked at Sun Wukong, Zhu and Sha and saw that they did not reply at all. Then he understood that the three really were the monk's disciples, not monsters. He called his servants to bring food for the four travelers. The servants were very frightened. They brought the food, then they ran out of the room as fast as they could.

The old man introduced himself as Chen Cheng. He and the four travelers sat down to eat dinner. Then a door opened and another old man entered the room. He used a cane to walk. He said to them, "What kind of demons are you? Why do you come to our home in the middle of the night and frighten all of our servants?"

Chen Cheng said to the travelers, "My friends, this is my elder brother, Chen Qing." He turned to his brother and said, "Elder Brother, please don't worry. This monk has come from the Tang Empire. He is traveling to the west with his three disciples." The second man nodded his head. He called for servants to bring out some low tables. Tangseng was given the seat of honor in the middle of the room. On one side, three tables were given to Sun Wukong, Zhu and Sha. On the other side two tables were given to the two old men. Servants brought out fruit, vegetables, rice, noodles, and buns. One of the servants took the horse outside and gave him some grass to eat.

After the food was put down, Tangseng lifted his chopsticks and started to recite the Fast Breaking Sutra. But before he finished, Zhu picked up a large bowl of rice and poured all of it into his mouth. A servant ran over and filled the bowl again. Tangseng continued to recite the sutra, and Zhu ate another bowl of rice. And another. And another. He finished six bowls of rice before Tangseng finished reciting the sutra.

After dinner, Tangseng asked, "Honored grandfather, please tell me, what was this feast that you were having when we arrived? I did not recognize the music." Cheng replied, "It is a preparatory mass for the dead."

Zhu laughed so hard that rice came out of his mouth. "Grandfather, we know when someone is lying. There is no such thing as a preparatory mass for the dead. Sometimes there is a mass for the dead, but that is after they die. We don't see any dead people here!"

Cheng replied, "Tell me, travelers. When you arrived at the river, what did you see?"

"We saw a stone pillar with words on it," said Sun Wukong. "We could not walk any further because of the river. So we turned and came to your temple."

"If you had walked a mile in the other direction, you would have come to the temple of the Great King of Bright Power."

"We did not see that. Tell us, who is this Great King of Bright Power?"

"This Great King sends blessings to all people far and near. He sends sweet rains every month, and auspicious clouds from year to year." Then he started to cry.

"That does not sound bad," said Sun Wukong. "Why are you crying?"

"There is a cost for these blessings. The Great King loves to eat young boys and girls, plus cows and pigs and chickens of course. Every year he selects a family. The family must give him one boy and one girl. The Great King eats them."

"And so, this year your family must give young children to the Great King?" asked Sun Wukong.

"Yes, this year it is my family. I am an old man. For many years I never had a child. I gave all my money to the village to repair their roads and bridges. In all, I gave them thirty catties of gold. Thirty catties is equal to one cart-load. So when my daughter was finally born eight years ago, I called her One Load of Gold."

"And what about the young boy?"

Chen Qing spoke up. He said, "The two of us are brothers. Since my brother does not have a son, the Great King wants to eat my son. His name is Guanbao. Together, my brother and I have lived for one hundred and twenty years. We have only these two children. And soon they will be dead because of the Great King!" He began to cry. "We cannot say no to the Great King, but it is hard for us to give up our precious children."

Tangseng also started to cry, saying, "Ah, Heaven is so cruel to a childless man!"

But Sun Wukong just said, "Old man, how wealthy are you?"

Qing replied, "Quite wealthy. My brother and I together have a very large farm. We have many horses, hogs, sheep, chickens and geese. We also have gold and silver. Why do you ask?"

"If you have so much money, why not just buy a boy and a girl? I hear that you can buy both for a hundred and fifty taels of silver."

"That would not work. The Great King comes to visit us often. We do not see him, but we can feel the cold wind when he comes through. He knows every person in the village. He knows my son, and he knows my brother's daughter. We could not buy a boy and a girl with the same age and appearance."

Sun Wukong nodded his head. "I understand. I have an idea. Please bring out your son." The old man called out, and Guanbao came into the room. He was a happy young boy, dancing and laughing. Sun Wukong shook himself, and instantly he looked exactly like Guanbao. Now there were two happy young boys in the room. Both of them were dancing and laughing.

The old man's mouth fell open. He could not believe what he was seeing. Sun Wukong shook himself and changed back to his true form. He said, "Do you think I could be the sacrifice?"

"If you look like that, yes of course!" said Qing. "If you can save my son, I will give a thousand taels of silver to the Tang Monk to thank him and help him on his journey to the west."

"Why won't you thank me?" asked Sun Wukong.

"The Great King will eat you. You will be dead. How can I thank you if you are dead?"

"Leave that up to me."

Qing was very happy. But his brother Cheng cried. Sun Wukong understood why. "Grandfather, don't cry. I know that you do not want your daughter eaten by this Great King. We can stop that. Please give a lot of rice, vegetables and noodles for my pig friend. Let him eat as much as he wants. Then I will ask him to change into the form of your daughter. We will save your two children, and we will gain merit in Heaven!"

Zhu heard this. "Oh no, Elder Brother, don't get me involved in this. You can do whatever you want, but I do not want to be dinner for the Great King!"

"Younger Brother, why do you say that? When we arrived at this house, the two brothers gave us food and drink. Now we must pay. What's wrong with that?"

"I do not want to pay with my life!" cried Zhu.

Tangseng said, "Wuneng, your elder brother speaks the truth. The ancient ones say, 'the saving of a life is better than building a seven storied pagoda.' You can repay these monks for feeding you, and you can gain merit in Heaven. You and Sun Wukong should do this. It will be fun."

"Fun?" cried Zhu. "This is not fun. And I don't know how to change into a little girl. A horse, yes. A mountain, yes. But a little girl? No."

"Grandfather," said Sun Wukong to Cheng, "please bring out your daughter." Cheng called out, and One Load of Gold came into the room. Sun Wukong said to Zhu, "Okay, my friend. It's time. Change!"

Zhu was not happy, but he spoke some magic words and shook his head several times. His head changed to look like One Load of Gold, but his body did not change, it was still the body of a fat pig-man.

"Change more!" laughed Sun Wukong.

"I cannot!" cried Zhu.

"Okay, I will help you," said Sun Wukong. He blew a magic breath towards Zhu. Instantly Zhu's body changed to look just like One Load of Gold.

Then Sun Wukong said to the Chen brothers, "Please take your children inside so there will be no confusion about who is who. Tell them to be very quiet and not come out until this is finished." Then he changed into the form of Guanbao. He said to the Chen brothers, "How will you deliver us to the Great King?"

Cheng said, "I will show you." He called for four servants to bring out two large red lacquered trays. He told Sun Wukong and Zhu to sit on the trays. He told the servants to pick up the trays and put them on two tables. Then he told them to carry the tables to the temple of Great King Bright Power.

As they were being carried to the temple, Sun Wukong said to Zhu, "Stay on the tray. Don't move, don't talk. Wait until the Great King grabs me. Then run out of the temple as fast as you can."

Zhu replied, "But what if he grabs me first?"

Cheng was walking beside them. He said, "A few years ago, some people from the village hid behind the temple to watch the Great King. He ate the boy first, and then the girl. So I think it will happen like that again. Probably."

Just then, a group of villagers met them on the road, carrying torches and banging on gongs. "Bring the boy to the temple! Bring the girl to the temple!" they shouted. The four servants carried the tables into the Great King's temple.

Chapter 48

When they arrived at the Great King's temple, they saw a large stone. On the stone in gold letters were the words "Great King Bright Power." On the temple floor were offerings of dead hogs and sheep. The villagers placed the boy and girl on top of the offerings. They lit many candles and burned incense. Then they all sang,

> "Great Father King, we come to you today
> We do this every year on the same day
> Chen Cheng gives you his daughter, One Load of Gold
> Chen Qing gives you his son, Chen Guanbao
> We also bring you hogs and sheep for your enjoyment
> Please bring us rain and wind to make the land green
> And bring us a rich harvest of the five grains."

Then they burned paper money and paper horses and returned to their homes.

Sun Wukong and Zhu waited for a few minutes. Then Zhu said, "Let's go home now, ok?"

Sun Wukong said, "You fool, stop talking like that. If we leave early, the Great King will do terrible things to the village. We agreed to help the village, and so we must help them until the end. We must wait for the Great King to come and eat us."

Just then, they heard a very loud wind outside. "Oh dear," said Zhu. The temple door opened, and there stood the Great King of Bright Power. He was very large and very tall. He wore a gold helmet, a red robe, and he had a gold sword at his belt and large brown boots. His eyes were like bright stars, his teeth were like steel swords. Gray mist surrounded him. When he walked into the temple, a cold wind followed him.

He saw the two young children. In a voice like thunder, he shouted, "Which family gives the sacrifice this year?"

Sun Wukong laughed and said, "Good question! This year the Chen brothers give you the sacrifices."

The Great King was a little bit confused by this. He thought, "This is strange. Usually the children are frightened out of their minds and cannot answer any questions. How can this boy speak so easily? I must be careful here!" He said, "And what are your names, little ones?"

"I am called Chen Guanbao," said Sun Wukong, "The girl is called One Load of Gold."

"This sacrifice is an annual custom. You have been offered to me. So I will eat you."

"Go ahead!"

The Great King's confusion turned to anger. "Don't talk to me like that! In past years I always ate the little boy first. But this year I will change the custom. I will eat the little girl first."

"Oh, no!" cried Zhu, "please don't change the custom! Follow the old ways!"

The Great King reached out his hand to grab Zhu. Zhu jumped down onto the floor, changed back into his true form, and brought his rake down hard on the Great King's head. The Great King staggered. Two small fish scales fell to the floor. Sun Wukong also jumped down to the floor and changed back to his true form. He tried to hit the Great King with his rod. The Great King had thought he was coming to a feast, so he only had the gold sword on his belt. That sword was not strong enough to fight Sun Wukong and Zhu.

The Great King flew up to the sky as fast as he could. Sun Wukong and Zhu chased him. Standing on the edge of a cloud he shouted, "You two, where did you come from? How dare you come here, steal my dinner, and give me a bad name?"

Sun Wukong shouted back, "We are disciples of the Tang Monk. He was sent by his Emperor to journey to the Western Heaven to obtain holy scriptures. Last night we stayed with the Chen family. They told us about the demon who calls himself the Great King and eats young children. We decided to save lives and arrest you. Now you must tell us everything. How many children have you killed and eaten? If you tell us everything, we might let you live."

The demon heard these words and was afraid. He turned into a gust of wind that blew across the Heaven Reaching River. "He probably lives in the river," said Sun Wukong. "Let's wait until tomorrow. We can catch him and ask him to take Master across the river." Then the two disciples picked up the hogs, sheep, tables and trays. They carried all of it back to the Chen house and dropped all of it in the courtyard. They told Tangseng and the Chen brothers everything that happened at the Great King's temple.

Meanwhile, the demon changed back to his true form and went to his palace at the bottom of Heaven Reaching River. He sat in his chair for a long time, not saying a word. His friends and relatives were worried about him. One of them said, "Great King, usually you are happy when you return from the sacrifice. This year you are very quiet. What happened?"

"I had some very bad luck," he replied. "There were two disciples of a holy monk who is traveling to the Western Heaven to get the Buddha's books. One of them changed into a little boy, the other changed into a little girl. They nearly killed me!"

He continued, "I have heard of this Tang monk. They say that he has studied the Way for ten lifetimes. They say that to eat even a little bit of his flesh will give a person long life. That sounds like a good idea. But ah, these disciples! They are very dangerous. I would like to eat the Tang monk, but I dare not go near those disciples."

A large fish-mother bowed to him and said, "Great King, it is not difficult to catch the Tang monk. I can help you. But if I help you, how will you help me?"

The demon replied, "If you can show me how to capture the Tang monk, I will become your bond brother[1]. We will sit down together and eat his flesh."

"Thank you! Great King, I know that you can bring the wind and rain, and you can stir up the rivers and oceans. But can you bring ice and snow?"

"Of course, that is easy for me."

"Well then, you can capture the Tank monk. Tonight, you must bring cold weather and heavy snow. The Heaven Reaching River will turn to ice. Then, you must change us into human form. We will walk across the river from east to west. We will carry umbrellas and we will push carts. The Tang monk will see us. He will think we are traders, and that it is safe to cross the river. Wait until the monk and his disciples are halfway across the river, then melt the ice under their feet. They will fall into the river. You will have them. Easy!"

"Wonderful!" shouted the demon. He flew up to the clouds and began to bring cold weather and heavy snow. The river quickly turned to ice.

Inside the Chan home, the four travelers were asleep. The weather turned cold and they woke up shivering. "I am so cold," shivered Zhu.

"Idiot," replied Sun Wukong, "you need to grow up. We have left the family. We should not be bothered by heat or cold. How can you be afraid of the cold?" But when they walked outside the Chan house, they saw that the trees were covered with ice. Snow was falling from the sky like threads of silk and chips of jade. Wind blew the snow into huge snowdrifts. Far away they could see the river covered with ice.

Old man Cheng came into the room with some servants to light a fire. Tangseng asked him, "Grandfather, tell me, do you have four seasons here – spring, summer, fall and winter?"

"Of course," he replied, "we live under the same sun as everyone else."

"Then tell me, why do we have ice-cold weather and heavy snow in early fall?"

"Perhaps our kingdom is colder than yours. We often have a little snow in

---

[1] In Chinese, literally "dear brother." This is similar to the Western idea of "bond brother" or "blood brother," when unrelated people choose to form a bond as close as that of two brothers. Earlier, Tangseng became the bond brother of the king Taizong.

early fall. But don't worry, we have plenty of food and firewood. You will be quite comfortable staying here."

"Grandfather, many years ago I left my home to begin this journey. The Tang Emperor himself drank a cup of wine with me and became my bond brother. He asked me how long my journey would last. I told him three years. But it has already been eight or nine years and I have not even come close to the Western Heaven yet. Now we must wait because of this cold weather. I do not know if we will be able to cross the Heaven Reaching River."

Cheng laughed. "Please, holy father, just relax and enjoy the beautiful weather!"

The next day, the weather was even colder. There was a fire burning in Cheng's house but the travelers could see their breath like white clouds in the air. They put on heavy coats but they were still cold. "I have never seen cold weather like this," said Zhu. "I think the river must be covered with thick ice by now."

Tangseng looked at him for a minute. Then he said to Cheng, "Grandfather, thank you for taking care of us these past few days. Now the river is covered with thick ice. It is time for us to walk across the river to continue our journey to the west."

"Please wait," replied Cheng. "In a few days the ice will melt. Then I can use my boat to take you across the river."

"Thank you but we cannot wait. If you can, please give us three more horses, one for each of my disciples. The four of us will ride our horses across the river."

Cheng was not happy about this, but he agreed. His servants brought out three horses. The four travelers got on their horses and looked at the ice-covered river. "What are those people?" asked Tangseng, pointing to a group of people walking across the river.

"I think they are traders. Many traders go to the Western Kingdom of Women on the far side of the river. Things that sell for a penny on this side of the river sell for a hundred pennies on the other side. And things sold for a penny on the other side sell for a hundred pennies here. So of course, there is much profit to be made. The traders love profit, so they will cross the river even if it is dangerous."

Tangseng thought about this. "Truly, men are slaves to fame and profit. Many would give up their lives for fame and profit. But here I am, giving up my life for my Emperor. Perhaps I am also looking for fame. Perhaps I am no different from those traders." He turned to Sun Wukong. "Elder disciple, get the horses ready. We will leave now."

"Wait!" shouted Zhu. He ran out onto the ice a hundred feet. He lifted his nine-pronged rake and brought it down hard onto the ice. The rake bounced off the ice. Zhu's hands were hurt, but the ice was not broken. "Okay," he shouted, "it's safe to walk on the ice."

The four travelers began to slowly ride their horses on the ice. Immediately Tangseng's horse slipped and almost fell down. Zhu told them to wait. Then he ran back to Cheng's house and got a large bundle of straw. He ran back to Tangseng and the others. They wrapped the horses' hooves with straw. This stopped the horses from slipping on the ice.

They rode for three or four miles. Zhu said to Tangseng, "Master, please take my rake. Hold it sideways as we ride."

"Why? I don't need your rake," replied Tangseng.

"Master, you don't know this, but ice sometimes has holes. If your horse steps in a hole, you and the horse will both fall through the ice and you will drown in the cold water. This rake will stop you from falling through the ice. The horse will drown, of course, but you will not die."

So Tangseng held the rake crosswise. Sun Wukong saw this and held his rod crosswise. Sha Monk held his staff the same way. Zhu did not have his rake, but he held the luggage pole crosswise as he rode.

Night came but the four travelers dared not stop. They continued to ride under the light of the moon and the stars. They ate a little bit of cold food. They rode all night and into the next day.

While the four travelers were riding their horses on top of the ice, the demon waited in his palace below the ice. He heard the sound of horses' hoofs on the ice. He used his magic power to melt the ice underneath the travelers. The ice broke. Sun Wukong jumped into the air, but the other three travelers and all four horses fell into the water. Zhu and Sha and the white horse swam to the surface and climbed onto the ice. "Where is Master?" shouted Sun Wukong.

Under the water, the demon grabbed Tangseng and carried him down to his palace under the water. "Fish Mother, come quickly!" he shouted. "Your idea was very good. We have the Tang monk. Let's cook him and eat him!"

"Great King, thank you," replied the fish mother, "but please wait a bit. The monk's disciples are probably very angry right now. You should watch out for them, because you will need to fight them if they arrive. Let's save the Tang monk and eat him in a day or two, when the trouble is finished. We will have singing and dancing, and a great feast!"

The three disciples rose into the air and flew back to the village while the horse ran as fast as the wind. They all arrived at the Chan house. "Where is your master?" asked Chan Cheng.

Zhu replied, "His family name is now 'Sink' and his given name is 'To The Bottom.'"

"How sad!" cried Cheng. "We told him that we could take him in a boat, but he could not wait. Now he is dead."

"I don't think our master is dead yet," said Sun Wukong. "That demon, the Great King of Bright Power, did this. Grandfather, please give us some dry clothes, wash these wet clothes, dry our travel rescript, and feed our white horse. We need to go back and deal with this demon. We will save our master, and we will also kill this evil demon. Your village will be able to live in peace!"

The Chen brothers were happy to hear this. They gave the three disciples a good hot meal and dry clothing. After they finished eating, the three disciples picked up their weapons and went back to the river to search for their master and capture the demon.

Chapter 49

They arrived at the place where Tangseng fell into the water. Sun Wukong did not want to go into the water. He said to Zhu and Sha, "You two are much better in the water than I am. If this demon were in a mountain cave, it would be no problem, but I can't do business well in the water. I need to make a water-repelling sign with my hand. That means that I only have one hand to use my Golden Hoop Rod."

Sha said that he could carry Sun Wukong until they got to the demon's home. But Zhu said that he was stronger and he wanted to carry Sun Wukong on his back. "All right," said Sun Wukong. But he had a feeling that Zhu planned to play a trick on him.

Sha used magic to open a path to the bottom of the river. The three brothers jumped down towards the bottom. Sun Wukong thought that Zhu was getting ready to play a trick on him. So he pulled a hair from his head and made a copy of himself. He put the copy on Zhu's back, and he changed his form into a louse and crawled into Zhu's ear.

A few minutes later, Zhu stumbled and fell, sending the copy of Sun Wukong flying to the ground in front of him. The copy changed back into a hair and floated away in the water. "Now you did it," said Sha. "Elder Brother has floated away. How can we fight the demon without him?"

"Don't worry," said Zhu, "we don't need that monkey. The two of us can fight the demon with no problem."

"No, I won't go any further. Elder Brother is very strong and very fast, and a very good fighter. We need him. I will not go without him."

Sun Wukong could not keep quiet anymore. He shouted in Zhu's ear, "I AM RIGHT HERE!" Zhu was so frightened, he fell to his knees and kowtowed in every direction.

"Elder Brother, I am so sorry!" he cried. "Where are you? I want to say I am sorry but I don't know where you are!"

"I am a louse right here in your ear. Now I will change back to my true form. Don't play any more tricks!"

They traveled for another hundred miles or so. They arrived at a large building. A sign on the building read, "Sea Turtle House." Sun Wukong told

Zhu and Sha to hide. He walked through the gate. He changed his form so he was a small fish. He looked around. He saw the demon sitting in a big chair. All around him were his friends and relatives. They were talking about the best way to eat Tangseng. Should they steam him, roast him, bake him, or stir-fry him with vegetables?

Sun Wukong was happy to learn that his master was still alive. But where was he? Sun Wukong swam up to another small fish and asked, "Friend, I hear the Great King talking about how to cook the Tang monk that he captured yesterday. I would like to taste that monk. Where is he?"

The small fish replied, "He is in a stone box at the rear of the palace. The Great King is waiting to see if the monk's disciples come to save him. If they don't come by tomorrow, we will all eat a little bit of the monk."

Sun Wukong chatted with her a bit more, then he swam off to find the stone box. He found it in the rear of the palace. He swam closer and heard Tangseng crying inside, saying

> I have had many river troubles in this life!
> When I was born my mother put me in the river.
> I had great problems at Black River
> And now I may die in this icy cold river
> I don't know if my disciples will save me
> Or if this will be the end of my life.

Sun Wukong just laughed and said, "Master, why are you saying these things? Earth is the mother of everything, but everything comes from water. Without earth there is no life, but without water there is no growth."

Tangseng cried, "Oh disciple, please save me!"

"Try to relax. I will take care of this demon, then you can leave this place."

Sun Wukong left the palace and met Zhu and Sha. He said, "Our master is still alive. He is imprisoned in a stone box. The demon is planning to eat him tomorrow. You two must start a fight with the demon. Try to defeat him. But if you cannot defeat him, try to get him to come out of the river. Then I can defeat him!" Then he made a water-repelling sign with his hand and went up to wait on the riverbank.

Zhu ran up to the gate, shouting, "Evil demon! Send my master out!" The little fish-demons heard this and reported to the Great King that a large pig was at the front gate.

The Great King said, "That must be one of the monk's disciples. Quick, get my armor!" He put on his golden helmet and armor. In one hand he held a large bronze mallet. In the other hand he held a thin green pond weed. He walked out of the gate to meet Zhu. His voice was like summer thunder. "You ugly pig, where do you come from, and why are you here?"

Zhu shouted back, "Don't ask questions! You call yourself Great King of Bright Power but you are really just an evil demon. Do you remember, you tried to eat me yesterday! Don't you recognize me? I am One Load of Gold from the Chen family."

The demon replied, "Monk, I did nothing wrong. I did not eat you. But you hit my hand and injured me. And you have committed a crime. You took the form of another person. After all that you dare to come back to cause trouble again?"

"It is you who caused trouble again! You sent cold wind, ice and snow. And you melted the ice to capture my master. Now give him to me. If you give me even half a 'no' you will taste my rake!"

The demon raised his bronze mallet and brought it down on Zhu's head. Zhu blocked it with his rake. Sha saw that the fight was starting, so he ran over and began to hit the demon with his staff.

The demon said, "You two are not real monks. Pig, you must have been a farmer, that is why you are using a rake as a weapon." The demon turned to Sha and said, "And you must have been a baker, that is why you are using a rolling pin as a weapon. You are not monks and you are not very good fighters!"

All three were now very angry. They fought at the bottom of the river for over two hours. Zhu winked at Sha, and the two of them pretended to be defeated. They ran away towards the surface of the river. The demon followed them.

Sun Wukong was sitting on the eastern shore of the river, watching the water carefully. Suddenly huge waves appeared. Zhu and Sha came bursting out of the river, with Zhu shouting, "He's coming! He's coming!" Then the Great King burst out of the river, chasing them.

Sun Wukong shouted, "Watch my rod!" and smashed it down on the demon. The demon blocked the rod. The four of them fought for a short time. Then the demon turned and dove back into the water. He returned to his palace and told his friends and relatives what happened.

The fish-mother said, "Great King, what did this third disciple look like?"

The demon replied, "He looks like a monkey. He has a hairy face, a broken nose, and diamond eyes. To tell the truth, he is generally quite ugly."

She said, "Great King, I know who this monkey is. A long time ago I lived in the Great Eastern Ocean. I heard the old Dragon King talking about him. He is the Handsome Monkey King, the Great Sage Equal to Heaven. Five hundred years ago he caused great trouble in Heaven, but now he is a Buddhist, a disciple of the Tang Monk. He changed his name to Sun Wukong. He has great powers. Please do not try to fight with him!"

"Ok, thanks!" said the demon. He turned to his little demons and said, "Little ones, go and shut the gates. Behind the gates build a wall of rocks and mud. Don't let those disciples in. After a day or two they will get tired of waiting and they will go away. Then we can eat the Tang monk and live in peace again."

Zhu and Sha arrived. Zhu smashed the gate with his rake, but they could not get through the wall of rocks and mud. They returned to the river's eastern shore to discuss the matter with Sun Wukong.

After a long discussion, Sun Wukong told them, "I don't see any way to get inside that palace to rescue our master. You two go back and watch the demon's palace. Make sure he does not try to move our master to another location. I will go to Potalaka Mountain to talk with Guanyin. I want to learn the demon's name, where he came from, and how I can save our master."

Sun Wukong used his cloud somersault to fly quickly to the South Sea and then to Potalaka Mountain. When he arrived, he was met by several of Guanyin's disciples. One of them was Child Sudhana. "Hello, my friend!" said Sun Wukong. "I remember when you were called Red Boy and caused so much trouble for me and my brothers."

Sudhana replied, "Great Sage Sun, thank you for your kindness. The Bodhisattva was kind and took me in, and I am happy to serve her."

One of the disciples told Sun Wukong to wait. "The Bodhisattva is not here right now. She is in the bamboo grove. She told us that you were coming. She said that you must wait for her to return."

Sun Wukong tried to wait, but he could not. After a short time he ran into the bamboo grove. He saw Guanyin. She was sitting on the ground under a large tree with her legs crossed. She was barefoot and wore simple clothing. He called to her, "Bodhisattva, your disciple Sun Wukong begs to speak with you!"

Guanyin did not move or look at him. "Wait outside," she said.

"Bodhisattva, my master is in terrible danger. I came to ask you about the demon at the bottom of the Heaven Reaching River. He has captured my master."

"Leave the bamboo grove and wait for me," she said again. Sun Wukong had no choice. He left the bamboo grove and waited for her. After a while, she came out of the bamboo grove. She was still barefoot and wearing simple clothes. In her hand was a purple bamboo basket. "Wukong, I will go with you to rescue the Tang monk."

Sun Wukong and Guanyin flew together to the Heaven Reaching River. They came down on the eastern riverbank. Sun Wukong called Zhu and Sha, and they came out of the river. Seeing Guanyin, they kowtowed to her.

Guanyin removed her sash and tied it to the basket. Then she rose into the air and flew over the river. She lowered the basket into the river. She said, "The dead leave, the living stay. The dead leave, the living stay." After a few minutes she pulled the basket out of the river. There was a small goldfish in the basket.

"Wukong," she cried, "go into the water and get your master."

"But we have not captured the demon yet," he replied.

"The demon is here in the basket. I will tell you his story. Once he was a goldfish living in a pond near my home. Every day he came to the surface of the pond to listen to my lectures. He learned the Way from my lectures, and he developed great magical powers. Nine years ago, I came out of my house but he was not in the pond. I realized that a high tide had carried him out of my pond and into this river. He became an evil demon here. That bronze mallet is really a lotus bud that he made into a weapon."

The three disciples bowed to her. Sun Wukong asked if she would wait for a little while so the villagers could come out and see her. She agreed. Zhu and Sha ran into the village, shouting, "Come all of you, see the Bodhisattva Guanyin!" Every person in the village, young and old, came out. They all knelt down and kowtowed to Guanyin. One of them painted a picture of Guanyin holding the basket. That is why even today you will see pictures of Guanyin holding a bamboo basket.

Zhu and Sha jumped into the river and went quickly to Sea Turtle House. All the little demons were dead. They found the stone box with Tangseng inside. They opened the box. They pulled him out and brought him out of the river and back to the riverbank. Chen Cheng and Chen Qing were waiting to meet him. Cheng said, "Father, you should have listened to us!"

Tangseng smiled and said, "No need to discuss that anymore. Your problems are finished. No more sacrifices to the Great King, no more children eaten by the demon. Now, can you please find a boat for us, so we may cross this river and continue on our journey?"

Before the Chen brothers could say anything, a loud voice came from the river. "I will take you across the river!" Everyone was very frightened. Then a large creature crawled out of the river onto the riverbank. It was a huge old turtle.

Sun Wukong lifted his rod, saying, "Don't come any closer! I will kill you with my rod!"

The turtle spoke slowly, in a low voice, "I am grateful to all of you. The Sea Turtle House used to be my home. I lived there with my relatives. Then nine years ago an evil demon arrived. He killed many of my relatives. He turned the rest into servants. I could not fight him so I had to leave my home. Now you have come. You saved your master, but you also saved my home and this village. Please let me do this small thing for you!"

Sun Wukong put away his rod, but he said, "Are you really telling us the truth?"

The turtle replied, "If I am not telling the truth, may Heaven change my body into blood!"

Sun Wukong nodded. "All right, then. Come here." The old turtle swam to the riverbank and climbed up on the shore. Sun Wukong led the white horse onto the turtle's back. Tangseng stood on the left side. Sha stood on the right. Zhu stood in the back. Sun Wukong stood in front. He did not completely trust the turtle, so he wrapped his tiger-skin sash around the turtle's neck so it was like the rein of a horse. He held the sash in one hand and his golden hoop rod in the other. "Turtle, be very careful. One wrong move and I will hit your head with my rod!"

"I dare not! I dare not!" said the turtle. He began to swim rapidly across the river. The four travelers and the white horse rode on his back. In one day he crossed the entire eight hundred miles of the river. They arrived on the western riverbank.

"Thank you," said Tangseng. "I have nothing to give you now. But when we return from the Western Heaven, I will have a gift for you."

"I need no gift," said the turtle. "But you can do something for me. I have studied the Way for thirteen hundred years. I have lived a long time, but I have not learned how to lose my original form. When you meet the Buddha, please ask him how I can lose my original form and be reborn in human form."

"I promise to ask," replied Tangseng.

The turtle turned and disappeared in the water. Sun Wukong helped Tangseng to mount his horse. Zhu picked up the luggage. They found the main road and began walking again towards the West. Truly,

> The holy monk seeks the Buddha's books
> Through many years and many difficulties
> His mind is strong, not afraid of death
> He crossed Heaven's River on a turtle's back.

Chapter 50

Autumn turned to early winter. Snow began to fall, the weather turned cold. The road became narrow. It climbed upwards towards the top of a mountain. Tangseng's white horse had trouble walking. Finally, the horse could not carry the Tang monk anymore. Tangseng said to his disciples, "We have arrived at a very tall mountain. I don't think we can continue. What should we do?"

Sun Wukong said, "Let's keep going. Master, please get down off your horse. We must walk." And so they slowly climbed until they reached the top of the mountain. They looked around in all four directions. Ahead of them, to the west, they saw a tall tower. Next to the tower were some small buildings.

"Disciples," said Tangseng, "look! Ahead of us is something. Perhaps it is a monastery, or maybe a small village. I'm hungry. Let's go there and beg some food."

Sun Wukong looked at the village with his diamond eyes. "Please don't go there," he said. "I can see that there is something wrong with that place. There is evil in the air. This is not a good place."

"What's wrong with it?" asked the monk. "There is a tower and some houses. It looks ok to me."

Sun Wukong laughed quietly. "Oh Master, you look but you cannot see. Already we have met many demons on our journey. They can use magic to make any kind of towers and buildings that they wish. You know what the ancients say, 'A dragon can have nine different kinds of offspring.' Demons can make these things. When a traveler comes too close, the demon eats them!"

"All right. We will not go there. But I am quite hungry. Can you go somewhere else and beg some food for us?"

"I will do that, Master. But it is not safe here. Let me protect you." Sun Wukong used his golden hoop rod to draw a large circle on the ground. He told Tangseng and the other two disciples to step inside the circle. He led the white horse inside the circle. Then he picked up the luggage and put it inside the circle too.

"Master, please stay inside this circle. It is as strong as a stone wall. Nothing can come inside this circle. Not tigers, not wolves, not monsters, not demons. As long as you stay here you will be safe. If you step outside the circle, I am afraid that something will kill you and eat you." He paused. "And they will probably eat Zhu and Sha and the white horse too!"

Tangseng agreed to this. He, Zhu and Sha sat down in the circle. "Please don't leave the circle!" said Sun Wukong again. Then he used his cloud somersault to fly into the air. He flew a thousand miles in just a few minutes. Looking down, he saw a village. In the village was a large house surrounded by tall trees. He came down to the ground, walked up to the front gate, and hit the wooden gate with his rod.

A few minutes later an old man opened the gate. He wore an old robe, straw sandals, and an old wool hat. A small dog ran out the gate and barked at Sun Wukong. The man looked at him and said, "What do you want?"

Sun Wukong held his begging bowl in front of him. "Old father, this poor traveler comes from the land of the Great Tang. I am traveling to the Western Heaven with my master and two other disciples. We were passing through your region. My master is hungry. I am here to beg for some vegetarian food for us. Can you give us a little rice?"

The man replied, "Young man, you have taken the wrong road. The road to the Western Heaven is a thousand miles north of here."

Sun Wukong laughed. "Yes, old father, you are right. And right now, my master is sitting on that road, waiting for me to bring him some food."

"Walking from there to here has taken you at least a week. It will take you another week to get back to him. He will be dead long before you return."

"No, I left him just a short time ago, about the same time it takes you to drink a cup of tea."

The man shouted, "Ghost! Ghost!" He hit Sun Wukong several times on the head with his staff. Sun Wukong just stood without moving as the staff bounced off his head. The man turned and ran inside. He shut the gate and bolted it from inside.

Sun Wukong shouted at him, "Old man, please remember how many times you hit me. Each one will cost you a bowl of rice!" He waited but the old man did not open the gate. So Sun Wukong used his magic to become invisible. He jumped over the gate and walked into the kitchen. He saw a large pot full of delicious rice. He filled his begging bowl with rice. Then he walked outside and used his cloud somersault to go back to Tangseng and the other two disciples.

Now, while Sun Wukong was away, Tangseng and the other two disciples waited inside the circle. Tangseng was getting very hungry. He said to the others, "Where is that monkey? He has been gone for a long time."

Zhu replied, "Who knows? He is probably just playing somewhere. He wants to keep us in this prison, just for fun."

"What do you mean, keep us in prison?"

"Think about it, Master. Do you really think that a circle on the ground would keep out a tiger, or a wolf, or a demon? Of course not. That monkey put us in this circle to play a trick on us. We should just start walking. When the monkey returns, he can easily find us on the road."

Tangseng foolishly agreed with Zhu. They walked out of the circle. They walked down the narrow road until they arrived at the tower. It had a high white wall, with corners that looked like the number eight. There was a large gate with carvings of lovebirds. The gate was painted in five colors. They did not see any people.

"Master," said Zhu, "I don't see anyone. The people must all be inside, keeping warm by a fire. I will go inside and look around."

He walked into the tower. He walked through three large rooms. He came to a large hall with a ceiling two stories high. Near the ceiling were open windows with yellow silk curtains that fluttered in the wind. There was no furniture. The whole building was as quiet as death. "Where are the people?" he thought. "They probably trying to stay warm and are sleeping in their beds."

Zhu continued up to the second floor. He walked into a large room. There was a large bed in the middle of the room. On the bed was large a white skeleton. The skeleton's skull was as big as a jar. The legs were four or five feet long.

He said to the skeleton, "I wonder who you were. Perhaps you were a great general. Now all we see are your bones. You have no family to keep you company, you have no soldiers to burn incense for you. Once you were a great man, now you are just a skeleton!"

Behind the bed was a silk curtain. Zhu saw a light coming from behind the curtains. He walked behind the curtain. He saw that the light was coming from an open window. There was a low table. On the table were three beautiful, embroidered silk vests. Without thinking, Zhu picked up the three vests. He walked outside to talk with Tangseng.

"Master," he said, "look what I found." Then he told Tangseng about the rooms, the skeleton, the curtain, and the vests. "There were no people in the house, so I took these vests. Please put on one of them, it will keep you warm."

"No, no, no!" shouted Tangseng. "If you take things, you are a thief. It does not matter if anyone saw you or not. Men might not know, but Heaven knows. As Xuandi[1] said, 'the gods have eyes like lightning.' Quickly, put them back!"

Of course, Zhu did not listen. He put on the vest. Then he gave a vest to Sha, who also put it on. Tangseng watched but said nothing. After a few seconds, though, the vests became extremely tight. Zhu and Sha could not move their arms. They could barely breathe. Tangseng tried to take the vests off them, but he could not.

Then the situation became much worse. A monster spirit lived in a nearby cave and he used the tower to trap foolish travelers. As soon as Zhu and Sha put on the vests, the tower disappeared. The monster told his little demons to grab the three travelers, along with the horse and luggage. The little demons took the three of them to the monster's cave.

The little demons pushed Tangseng to his knees in front of the monster. "Who are you and where did you come from?" he growled. "And why did you take things that belonged to me?"

Tangseng began to cry and said, "This poor monk was sent by the Tang Emperor to journey to the Western Heaven and bring back the Buddha's holy books. We were traveling over a high mountain. I became hungry, so I told my elder disciple to go and beg some food. He told us to wait for him, but foolishly we started walking again. Then my other two disciples saw your

---

[1] Xuandi, the eighth emperor of the Han Dynasty, ruled for 26 years and was known as a wise ruler who brought peace and prosperity to his kingdom.

vests and took them because they were cold. I told them to put the vests back but they did not listen to me. Please be merciful and let us go, so we can continue our journey to the west. I will always be grateful to you."

The monster just laughed. "Did you really think I would let you go? I have heard of you, Tang monk. I have heard that if someone eats just a little of your flesh their white hair will turn black, their missing teeth will grow back, and they will become young again. We will soon find out!" Then he told his little demons to tie up all three travelers and sharpen their weapons to prepare for meeting the fourth traveler, Sun Wukong.

Of course, Zhu and Sha were not the only thieves. Sun Wukong also was a thief. He had taken a begging bowl full of rice from the old man. Holding the rice bowl in one hand, he used his cloud somersault to return to the place where he had left the other travelers. He saw the circle on the ground, but it was empty. The travelers were not there.

Sun Wukong started running westward on the road. After running for five or six miles, he heard a sound and stopped. Looking around, he saw an old man and a young servant. "Grandfather," said Sun Wukong, "this poor monk salutes you. I am traveling to the west with my master and two other disciples. My master was hungry so I went to find him some food. When I returned, they were gone. Have you seen them?"

The old man replied, "Did one of the travelers have a long snout and large ears? Was another one tall and a bit ugly? And was there a short fat man with pale skin?"

"Yes, yes, yes!" cried Sun Wukong. "The man with pale skin is my master. The other two are my younger brothers. Where are they?"

"Forget about them and run for your life!" said the old man. "I saw them taking a road that leads to the cave of a powerful demon. This mountain is Golden Mountain. It has a cave called Golden Cave. And living in the cave is Great Buffalo King. If you meet him, you will probably get yourself killed."

Sun Wukong thanked the old man and bowed to him. He was about to give the old man the rice that he had in his begging bowl. But then the old man and the servant changed to their true forms. They both kowtowed to Sun Wukong. "We are the mountain god and the local spirit for this region. We will hold your bowl and rice for the moment. Please use all of your powers to fight the Great Buffalo King."

Sun Wukong was not happy about this. "You stupid ghosts, you should have come sooner and told me about the danger before this monster captured my master. Now matters have become more difficult. I should beat you with my rod. But for now, just hold my rice. I will be right back."

He handed the rice bowl to the mountain god and ran to the mouth of the cave. He shouted, "Little demons, tell your master that the Great Sage Equal to Heaven has arrived! Tell him to send out my master, or he will pay with his life!"

The little demons told the Great Buffalo King that an ugly monkey was at the mouth of the cave. "Oh good, it must be Sun Wukong," said the monster. "Little ones, bring me my lance!" The little demons brought him a twelve-foot steel lance.

The monster came out of the cave. He looked like a giant buffalo-man. One large horn came out of his head. He had dark skin, a wide mouth with yellow teeth, and a long tongue that sometimes licked his big nose. In his large strong hands he held the steel lance. "Where is this foolish monkey?" he called.

Sun Wukong walked right up to him and replied, "Here is your grandpa Sun. Give me my master quickly. If you say even half a 'no' you will die so quickly that you won't have time to say where your grave should be."

"Your master is a thief. I will not give him to you. He deserves to be killed and eaten."

"How can you call my master a thief? He is a holy monk. He would never steal anything!"

"Oh yes, he certainly is a thief. There are witnesses. He is a criminal, and soon he will be my dinner."

The two of them shouted at each other for a while, then they stopped talking and started fighting. The monkey king used his golden hoop rod, the monster used his steel lance. They fought for thirty rounds, but neither one could win. The monster was impressed with Sun Wukong's fighting ability, saying, "Marvelous ape! Marvelous ape! Now I see how you caused such trouble in Heaven!" Sun Wukong was impressed with the monster's fighting ability, saying, "Marvelous spirit! Marvelous spirit! This monster knows how to use his lance!" And so, they fought for another twenty rounds.

Finally, the monster shouted, "Attack!" All his little demons ran forward to attack Sun Wukong. "Oh, wonderful!" cried Sun Wukong. He threw his golden hoop rod into the air and shouted, "Change!" Instantly the rod changed to a thousand small rods. The small rods came down like rain onto the heads of the little demons. The little demons were terrified. They covered their heads and ran back to the cave.

The monster laughed and shouted, "Now watch my trick!" He took a white hoop from his sleeve and threw it into the air, shouting "Hit!" All the iron rods changed back to a single rod again. That single rod was sucked up by the hoop. It disappeared.

Sun Wukong had no weapon. Quickly he used his cloud somersault to fly away, barely escaping with his life.

Chapter 51

Sun Wukong flew to a safe place on the other side of the mountain. He sat down and cried. He lost his golden hoop rod, his greatest treasure. Now his hands were empty. He had no weapon. His master and his two younger brothers were trapped in the monster's cave. He did not know what to do.

Then he thought of something. "That monster knows me!" he thought. "While we were fighting, he said 'Now I see how you caused such trouble in Heaven!' I did not tell him that. So he must know me from long ago when I caused trouble in Heaven. He must be a spirit or a star that wanted to live on earth because of a longing for this world. I wonder who he is and where he came from. I must go to Heaven to find out."

He used his cloud somersault and soon arrived at the South Heaven Gate. A guard bowed to him and asked, "Where is the Great Sage going?"

"I must see the Jade Emperor," replied Sun Wukong.

Four minsters of Heaven arrived, bowed to Sun Wukong, and invited him to join them for tea. "Have you finished your journey to the west with the Tang monk?" asked one of the ministers.

"No," replied Old Monkey. "We are less than halfway to the Western Heaven. Our trip is taking a long time because of all the demons and monsters we have met on the road. Yesterday we arrived at Golden Mountain. A very dangerous monster lives there. He has captured the Tang monk. I fought with him. He had great powers, and he was able to take my golden hoop rod. I think he might be a spirit from the Heavenly worlds who has come down to earth because of longing for the world. I need to know who he is, where he came from, and how I can fight him. I must speak with the Jade Emperor and ask him why he cannot keep the people in his house under control!"

The minister laughed and said, "I see that you are still causing trouble in Heaven. OK, I will tell the Jade Emperor you wish to see him."

A short time later, the minister returned and led Sun Wukong to the throne room of the Jade Emperor. Sun Wukong bowed and said, "Your majesty, thank you for seeing me. For several years I have been traveling with the Tang monk towards the Western Heaven to bring back the Buddha's books. It has been a very slow journey because of all the monsters, demons and wild animals we have met. Now a buffalo monster has captured the Tang monk in the Golden Cave on Golden Mountain. I don't know if my master will be steamed, fried, or boiled. This monster has great powers. Also, this monster knows me but I do not recognize him. I think this monster is really an evil star from Heaven who has left the Heavens because of longing for the world. Your majesty, only you can help my master. Please help me to learn his name, and send soldiers to arrest him. Old Monkey asks you with great fear and trembling."

One of the ministers was standing nearby. He laughed and said, "Wukong, usually you cause trouble in Heaven. Why do you act with such fear today?"

Sun Wukong replied, "Right now I am a monkey with no rod to play with."

The Jade Emperor said Lord Kehan[1], "Kehan, this monkey has asked us for help. This is my decree. Go with Wukong and learn the name of this evil star. Search all the Heavens, talk with all the stars and planets. See if anyone has left these places out of longing for the world. Report to me when you are done."

Lord Kehan and Sun Wukong left the palace and began their search. They spoke with all the ministers. Then they spoke with all the immortals. Then they spoke with all the stars and planets. Then they spoke with the thunder gods and lightning gods. Then they searched the thirty-three Heavens. Finally they searched the twenty-eight houses of the moon. All were in their correct places.

Sun Wukong said to Lord Kehan, "Thank you, Lord Kehan. Old Monkey does not need to return to the palace and disturb the Jade Emperor again. Please go and report to the Emperor. I will wait here."

Lord Kehan reported to the Jade Emperor, "Your majesty, we have traveled to all four corners of your Heavenly kingdom. Every star, planet and god is in their correct place. None have left out of longing for the world."

The Jade Emperor replied, "This is my decree. Let Wukong select a few warriors from Heaven to help him capture the demon in the world below."

---

[1] Lord Kehan was one of the nine monarchs in the Shenxiao School of Daoism during the Southern Song dynasty (1127-1279 A.D.).

Lord Kehan returned to Sun Wukong and told him of the Emperor's decree.

Sun Wukong was silent for a few minutes. He thought to himself, "There are many warriors in Heaven but most of them are not as strong as I am. Why should I get help from them? But on the other hand, I cannot defy a decree from the Jade Emperor!"

Lord Kehan understood why Sun Wukong was silent. He said, "Wukong, you must not defy the Emperor's decree! Please select a few warriors from Heaven to help you."

Sun Wukong thought about it, then he said, "All right. I want the god-king Li and his son Prince Nata. They are both great warriors. I want them to lead an army of Heaven's soldiers. Also, I want two thunder gods. They will watch the fight from a high cloud and throw thunderbolts at the monster, killing him."

Lord Kehan called to the god-king Li, Prince Nata, the two thunder gods, and the army of Heavenly soldiers. They all met up with Sun Wukong. Together they went out the South Heaven Gate and returned to Golden Mountain. When they arrived at Golden Cave, Li said to Sun Wukong, "Please let my son begin the fight. He is the greatest warrior in all of Heaven."

Sun Wukong and Prince Nata stood outside the cave door. Sun Wukong shouted, "Evil demon, open this door and let my master go!" The little demons ran to tell their master. The demon came out, holding his steel lance. He saw an ugly monkey. Next to the monkey he saw a handsome young boy wearing silver armor.

The monster laughed. "Aha, it's the little boy Nata, third son of Li. What are you doing here?"

Prince Nata replied, "I am here because of the trouble you have caused! The Jade Emperor himself has decreed that I come and arrest you. Let the Tang monk go and come with me."

The monster tried to stab Prince Nata. Nata met the lance with his silver sword. They began to fight. Sun Wukong flew up into the sky and called to the thunder gods, "Quick! Throw your thunderbolts at the monster!"

Nata said some magic words. Instantly he had three heads and six arms. Each arm held a sword. The monster also changed into a monster with three heads and six arms. Each arm held a lance. The prince threw his six swords into the air and shouted, "Change!" The six swords became six thousand swords, all of them flying towards the monster. The monster took out his white hoop and shouted, "Hit!" Instantly all six thousand swords were sucked into the hoop and disappeared. Nata stood there with nothing in his hands. The monster laughed and walked back inside the cave.

One thunder god said to the other, "It's a good thing we did not throw our thunderbolts at that monster! If the monster's hand sucked our thunderbolts into his white hoop, what would we do? We need our thunderbolts to make thunderstorms."

Li, Nata and Sun Wukong discussed the matter. Sun Wukong said, "We must find a weapon that cannot be sucked into that white hoop."

Li said, "Only water and fire can resist being sucked away, because their power has no limits."

"Of course, you are right!" replied Sun Wukong. He jumped into the air and used his cloud somersault to go up to Heaven and through the South Heavenly Gate. This time he did not go to see the Jade Emperor. He went to see Mars, the star of fire. Mars came out to meet him and said, "Why are you here again? You were here yesterday. I told you that nobody from my house has gone to earth. Why did you come back?"

"We need your help."

"How can I help you? The great Prince Nata has defeated the demons of ninety-six caves. If he cannot defeat this monster, how can I?"

"The monster has a magic hoop that can suck up any weapon. It has already sucked my golden hoop rod and Prince Nata's sword. We don't know what it is. But fire can destroy anything. Please come with us. Start a fire that will burn up the demon. You must save my master!"

Mars agreed. He returned with Sun Wukong to the Golden Cave. This time, Li himself stood in front of the cave and shouted at the monster to come out. The monster came out and saw Li. "So, you are unhappy because I took your little boy's sword? Too bad!" He laughed.

The god-king Li replied, "No, I am here to arrest you. Give me the Tang monk!" Of course the monster did not give Tangseng to him. They began to fight. Sun Wukong flew up to the clouds and told Mars, "Get ready to use your fire on the monster!"

Li fought with the monster. Then he saw the monster take out the white hoop. Li did not wait. He flew away. "Quick, use your fire!" shouted Sun Wukong to Mars. Mars threw a huge fireball at the monster. Inside the fireball were five fire dragons, five fire horses, and five fire birds. The monster raised his white hoop. The fireball was sucked into the hoop. It disappeared. All the dragons, horses and birds disappeared. The monster turned and walked back into his cave.

Sadly, Mars sat down on the ground. "I have lost my fire," he said. "What can I do now?"

"Just wait," said Sun Wukong. "We all know that water can defeat fire." He flew up to the Northern Heaven Gate to ask the Star of Water to help. "Please bring water. Flood the cave. Drown the monster!"

"Of course I can do that," replied the Star of Water, "but that will also drown your master."

"Don't worry about that, I can bring him back from death."

"All right," the Star of Water replied. He took a chalice from his robe and held it up. "This chalice looks small. But it can hold the entire Yellow River."

Sun Wukong laughed. "I think half a chalice will be quite enough! Come with me to the Golden Cave. As soon as the monster opens the cave door, pour the water into the cave. Don't wait for the fight to start."

Sun Wukong went up to the cave door and called to the monster to come out. The monster opened the door. The Star of Water opened his chalice. Half the water from the Yellow River poured out of the chalice. Quickly the monster lifted his white hoop and sucked up all the water. Then the water came out of the other side of the hoop. It rushed out of the cave and onto the mountain. Sun Wukong and the Star of Water had to leap into the air to avoid the rushing water. The water became a flood, covering the land for miles around. It covered roads, villages and farms. "This is bad," said Sun Wukong. "The monster is not troubled by this at all, but look at all the trouble we have caused."

He became really angry. He ran back to the cave door and pounded on it with his fists. "Come out, you evil monster. I don't need my rod. I will fight you with my fists!"

"Your fists are as small as walnuts," said the monster. "But if you want to fight with your fists, we will fight." He threw away his lance and began to fight bare-handed with Sun Wukong. They fought for a long time, each one using his fists and feet to hit the other. God-king Li, Prince Nata, Mars, the Star of Water and the two thunder gods all watched from nearby and shouted at them. Hundreds of little demons also shouted and beat their drums. Sun Wukong pulled fifty hairs from his head and shouted "Change." The hairs changed to fifty little monkeys. They all attacked the monster, biting and scratching and kicking him.

The monster became a little frightened. He took out his white hoop. When Sun Wukong and the others saw this, they flew away. All fifty little monkeys were sucked into the hoop. The fight was over. The monster walked back into the cave, laughing.

Sun Wukong went back to talk with the others. He said, "What do you think of the monster's fighting ability?"

Li replied, "He is not as good as you, Wukong. But he has the white hoop. He cannot lose a fight. If you cannot beat him in a fight, you must steal his treasure! You are quite good at stealing things. I know that you stole Laozi's elixir from his house in Heaven many centuries ago. Now you must steal the hoop."

"Good idea!" said Sun Wukong. He changed into a tiny insect and crawled inside the cave. He saw hundreds of little demons, all dancing and singing. The Great Buffalo King was sitting in a large chair, drinking wine and eating. Sun Wukong flew around the cave looking for the hoop. He did not see it. But in the back of the cave he saw the five fire horses, five fire dragons and five fire birds. Next to them was the golden hoop rod. Sun Wukong changed back to his true form and grabbed the rod. He turned and fought his way out of the cave.

Chapter 52

Sun Wukong returned to the place where the gods were waiting for him. They asked him what happened. He replied, "I changed into a tiny insect and entered the cave. I saw the monster eating and drinking and talking with his little demons. Then I heard the sound of horses coming from the back of the cave. I went back there and found my golden hoop rod. Then I used the rod to fight my way out of the cave."

"We are glad you have your treasure," said the gods, "but what about our treasures?"

"Don't worry, I will get them back for you," said Sun Wukong. Just then he heard a crowd of people coming down the road towards him. In front of the crowd was the Great Buffalo King himself. Behind him were hundreds of little demons. "Stupid demon, where are you going," shouted Sun Wukong.

"You little thief!" shouted the monster. "You took my treasures. How dare you!"

"You are the thief! You stole my treasures with your white hoop. You also stole the treasures of my friends. Don't run away. Have a taste of Old Monkey's rod!"

They began to fight again. Three hours later they were still fighting. Neither one could win. The day was nearly finished. "Wukong," said the monster, "let's stop this for now. We can continue our fight tomorrow morning."

"Shut up, you lawless monster!" said Sun Wukong. "I don't care if it's getting late. I want to find out who is a better fighter." But the monster turned and ran back into his cave. His little demons followed him. Then he closed the cave door and locked it tight.

The god-king Li said to Sun Wukong, "Well, that's all for today. Let's rest for the night and start fighting again tomorrow."

"Forget it," said Sun Wukong. "Now is the best time for me to go back inside the cave. The monster is tired. He will not be looking for me. And of course, you know that night is the best time to be a thief! Now is the best time for me to go into the cave and look around. Maybe I can grab some of your treasures."

The monkey king changed into a small insect again. He crawled into the cave.
He saw the monster sleeping in his bed. The monster's white hoop was
wrapped around his upper arm like an armlet. "Ah, that monster is careful!"
Sun Wukong thought. Then he changed into a flea. He crawled under the
blanket and bit the monster on the arm. The monster jumped up but he kept
the hoop on his arm. "Well, that won't work," thought Sun Wukong.

So he flew into another room in the cave. He saw that it was brightly lit.
Inside the room were the weapons that the monster had taken from the gods.
Then he saw a little pile of about fifty monkey hairs on a table. "Oh, good!"
he thought. He changed back to his true form. He picked up the hairs, blew on
them, and whispered, "Change!" All fifty hairs changed into fifty small
monkeys. Some monkeys picked up weapons. Other monkeys went into the
back of the cave and picked up the five fire horses, the five fire dragons, and
the five fire birds. To distract the little demons Sun Wukong started a fire.
The little demons were terrified of the fire and tried to put it out. While they
were doing that, Sun Wukong and the fifty little monkeys ran out of the cave
with the treasures.

The Great Buffalo King woke up. He jumped out of bed. He ran around the
cave, using his white hoop to capture the fire. Every time he held out the
hoop, fire was sucked into it and disappeared. Finally, all the fire was gone.
"That thieving monkey did this!" he shouted. "I will find him and kill him!"

The next morning, Sun Wukong and the gods returned to the cave. "Lawless
demon," he shouted, "Come and fight with Old Monkey!"

"Monkey, you are an arsonist and a thief!" replied the monster. "Why do you
think you can win a fight with me?"

"Oh, you lawless monster," said Sun Wukong. "Let me tell you my story.

    I have been a great fighter since my birth
    When I was young I studied with a great sage
    I learned how to use the power of Heaven
    The cloud somersault, the golden hoop rod
    All of earth and Heaven was mine
    I fought tigers on the mountain
    I fought dragons in the ocean

On Flower Fruit Mountain I had a throne
In Water Curtain Cave I had a home
But wanting more I flew to Heaven
Foolishly I stole from the world above
I became the Great Sage Equal to Heaven
The Handsome Monkey King
One day there was a peach festival
I was not invited but I came anyway
I ate all the food, I drank all the wine
The Jade Emperor saw my evil deeds
He sent an army but I defeated them
Finally the great Laozi caught me
He put me in a brazier for forty nine days
I came out as strong as steel,
As hard as diamond,
As strong as a tiger!
The gods themselves were afraid of me
Then the Buddha himself tricked me
He trapped me for five hundred years
No food but fire, no drink but hot iron
Until the Tang monk released me
and the Bodhisattva Guanyin taught me
Now I go west with the Tang monk
Release the monk, you lawless demon
Release the monk, bow to the Buddha!"

The monster listened, then he said, "So, you are the thief who stole treasures from Heaven! Your life is finished. Prepare to die!" They began to fight. All the gods and warriors of Heaven fought against the monster. But this fight ended the same way that the other fights did. The monster just held his white hoop, said the word "Hit," and all of the weapons were sucked into the hoop and disappeared. Sun Wukong and the gods were empty-handed again.

The gods were very unhappy, but Sun Wukong smiled and said, "Please don't be unhappy. You know what the ancients say, 'victory and defeat are both common for a soldier.' I will find out who this monster is. I have already gone to Heaven and asked the Jade Emperor. I have searched all through Heaven but I have not found out who the monster is. Now I must look somewhere else."

"Where will you go?" asked the god-king Li.

"I will go all the way to the western Heaven and I will ask the Buddha himself. He knows everything. He can help us."

"If you want to go, then go quickly," said Li.

Sun Wukong used his cloud somersault, and in a few minutes he arrived at the western Heaven. He saw a beautiful little village at the foot of a very tall mountain. Flowers were everywhere, birds were singing, and a soft wind blew through the trees. He could hear the sound of bells and flowing waters. Holy men and women were teaching their students under great old trees, while others walked slowly on the paths. This was truly a place filled with the Buddha's spirit.

Sun Wukong just stood, looking at the beautiful place. Then he heard someone speaking to him. He turned around and saw the Bodhisattva Bhikkuni. He said to her, "I have an important matter that I must discuss with the Buddha himself."

Bhikkuni replied, "If you want to see the Buddha, you must go to Thunderclap Monastery at the top of this mountain. Follow me." They flew to the gate of Thunderclap Monastery at the top of the mountain. It was guarded by eight Diamond Guardians. Bhikkuni said to them, "Sun Wukong needs to see the great Buddha." The Diamond Guardians moved aside to let them enter.

The Buddha was sitting under a tree with his legs crossed. He wore a yellow robe and sandals. He looked at Sun Wukong and said, "Wukong, I heard that the Tang monk released you from the prison where I put you five hundred years ago. I also heard that you have changed, and you are now helping the Tang monk travel here to Thunderclap Monastery. But why are you here alone?"

Sun Wukong touched his head to the ground. He said, "Let me tell the Buddha my story. Your disciple now follows your path. I am helping the Tang monk to come to this place. It is a very difficult journey. We have been traveling for several years. We have met many demons, monsters and wild animals. Recently we arrived at Golden Mountain where we met the Great Buffalo King. He is an evil demon. He captured my master. He has a powerful weapon, a white hoop. It can make any weapon disappear. He has defeated me and also the greatest warriors of Heaven. The demon is holding my master and plans to eat him soon.

"I believe that this demon has left Heaven out of longing for the world. But I do not know who he is or how to defeat him. I have traveled to Heaven to ask the Jade Emperor himself, but he could not help me. Now I ask you to tell me the true name of this demon, where he comes from, and how I can defeat him."

The Buddha sat for a minute. He used his wisdom eye to look into the distance. Soon he understood the whole matter. He said to Sun Wukong, "Now I know the name of this demon. But I will not tell you, because you have the tongue of a monkey and you will talk too much. If you tell the demon that I helped you, he will just start an argument here in Thunderclap Monastery. That would cause me a lot of trouble. That is why I will not tell you. However, I will help you in a different way."

Sun Wukong, kowtowed again and replied, "Please tell me, O great one!"

"I will give eighteen grains of golden cinnabar[1] sand to my eighteen arhats. They will go with you back to the cave. Find the demon. Tell him that you want to fight him again. When he comes out, my arhats[2] will release the cinnabar sand. It will trap him. He will not be able to move his hands or feet."

"Wonderful, wonderful!" said Sun Wukong, clapping his hands.

Sun Wukong flew into the air, joined by sixteen arhats. "Where are the other two arhats?" he asked. Soon the last two arhats, Dragon Fighter and Tiger Fighter, joined them. Then all eighteen arhats and Sun Wukong flew back to Golden Cave. They were met by the god-king Li, his son Nata, and the other gods and warriors.

"Where were you?" asked Li.

"It's a long story, no time to explain," said one of the arhats. "Wukong, go and meet this demon. We will wait in the clouds."

---

[1] Cinnabar, mercury sulphide, is a naturally occurring bright red ore that can be distilled to produce pure mercury. Daoists believed that through alchemy it could bring immortality.
[2] An arhat is one who has gained insight into the true nature of existence and has achieved nirvana.

Sun Wukong walked up to the cave, banged his fist on the door, and shouted, "Come out, come out, you fat old monster. Try your hand against Old Monkey again!"

The demon just sat in his cave. He shook his head and said, "That monkey is here again? Every time he fights me, he loses. He has no weapons. His friends have no weapons. Why does he keep coming back?" Slowly he stood up, walked to the door, and opened it. "All right, you stupid monkey. I am here. What do you want this time?"

"If you don't want to see me again, just say you are sorry and give me back my Master and my younger brothers."

"We have just finished washing your master and your brothers. Soon we will cook and eat them. After we eat them, will you finally go away and stop bothering me?"

Sun Wukong attacked the demon. The demon used his lance to fight back. Sun Wukong moved left and right to avoid the lance. The demon moved forward, attacking again and again. Soon he was outside of the cave. Sun Wukong shouted to the arhats, "Now!"

The arhats stood on a cloud and poured sand down on the demon. The sand fell like a white fog. It covered everything. The demon looked down and saw that his feet and legs were buried in the sand. He tried to pull one leg out of the sand but he could not move it. He grabbed his white hoop, threw it in the air, and shouted, "Hit!" All eighteen magic grains of cinnabar sand were sucked into the hoop and disappeared. All the sand disappeared. The demon turned and walked back into his cave.

Sun Wukong flew up to the cloud and shouted, "Why did you stop sending the sand?"

"We lost our golden cinnabar!" replied one of the arhats. "That white hoop sucked them right out of our hands. Now what do we do?"

Dragon Fighter and Tiger Fighter said, "We have one more idea. Before we left Thunderclap Monastery, the Buddha told us to wait. He gave special instructions to the two of us. He said that if the demon won the fight, we should tell you to go and see Laozi. He will know what to do."

Sun Wukong laughed and said, "So, even the great Buddha is playing games with me. If he knew that Laozi could help us, why did he let us lose this fight? Well, no matter. I will go see Laozi and finally settle this matter." He used his cloud somersault to fly up to the South Heaven Gate. He was in a hurry. He did not stop to talk with any of the guards, but went through the gate and right up to Laozi's house in the thirty third Heaven.

Two young men were guarding the house. Sun Wukong walked right past them. They tried to grab him but he ignored them. He saw Laozi. Bowing, he said, "Sir, I haven't seen you for a while!"

"You lawless ape, why are you here? You should be helping your master travel to the west."

"We ran into a bit of a problem," replied Sun Wukong. Then he started looking around Laozi's house. In the back of the house was a corral. It was empty. A boy was sleeping nearby. Sun Wukong said to Laozi, "Sir, I believe your buffalo has escaped."

"What?" shouted Laozi. This caused the boy to wake up. He bowed to Laozi and said, "Great father, I don't know how the buffalo escaped."

"I know," replied Laozi. "We were making the Elixir of Seven Returns to the Fire. You are a thief. You stole a little bit for yourself and drank it. That is why you have been sleeping for the past seven days. During that time, the buffalo has been in the world of men, causing a lot of trouble."

"It's worse than that," said Sun Wukong. "This buffalo demon has a white hoop. He is living on earth, causing trouble and eating people."

"Oh, no," said Laozi. "That white hoop is my diamond snare. It is stronger than any weapon I have except for my leaf fan."

Laozi picked up his leaf fan, and together with Sun Wukong he flew down to Golden Cave. They were met by the eighteen arhats, the two thunder gods, the Star of Water, the Star of Fire, the god-king Li and his son Nata. They explained everything.

"Wukong," said Laozi, "please go to the cave and get my buffalo to come out."

So again, Sun Wukong went to the cave door and shouted at the demon to come out. As soon as the demon opened the door, Sun Wukong ran right up to him and slapped him on the face! Furious, the demon chased after the monkey.

As soon as the demon was outside the cave, he heard a voice saying, "Is that my little buffalo? Why is he here, and not at home where he should be?"

The Great Buffalo King looked up and saw Laozi. Laozi waved his fan and all the strength left the demon. The demon threw his white hoop at Laozi. Laozi caught it easily and waved his fan again. Now the demon changed; he was not the Great Buffalo King, he was just an ordinary green buffalo. Laozi waved the white hoop. It changed into a brass ring that went through the buffalo's nose. Laozi took off his belt and tied it to the brass ring. Then he climbed onto the back of the buffalo. They rode away together back to Laozi's home in the thirty third Heaven.

Sun Wukong and the other gods and warriors went back into the cave. They killed the rest of the little demons and grabbed the weapons. The god-king Li and his son Nata returned to Heaven. The Star of Water returned to the river. The Star of Fire returned to the sky. The thunder gods returned to the clouds. The eighteen arhats returned to Thunderclap Monastery.

Sun Wukong found Tangseng, Zhu and Sha. He untied them. They found the horse and the luggage nearby. Together, they left the cave and began walking westward again.

But just as they started walking, they heard a voice. It said, "O holy monk! Before you continue on your journey, please eat a little food."

Tangseng heard the voice and was frightened, thinking that it might be another monster or demon. But it was just the mountain god and the local spirit of Golden Mountain. They said to the travelers, "This is the rice that the Great Sage begged several days ago. He was trying to help you. He told you to stay in the circle but you did not listen to him. That was the reason for your recent troubles."

Sun Wukong said, "They are right. Zhu, you stupid coolie, it was your foolish words that brought this trouble to Master and the rest of us. I had to go and see the Buddha himself to save you."

Tangseng said, "Elder disciple, you are right. From now on I will always listen to you!"

Tangseng and the three disciples ate the rice and thanked the mountain god and local spirit. When they were finished, Tangseng mounted his horse and they began walking. The poem says,

> Their minds clear and free of worries
> The travelers dined on wind
> And rested by the waters
> As they journeyed to the west.

Chapter 53

Tangseng and his three disciples left Golden Mountain and continued their journey to the west. They traveled for several months. The snows of winter arrived, and melted in the spring rain. The cold ground became soft and wet under their feet. The mountains and valleys turned from brown to green. Birds sang in the trees.

One day in early spring the travelers arrived at a river. They could see across to the other side but it was too wide and deep for Tangseng's horse to cross. There were some small houses on the other side of the river. Sun Wukong said, "That is a small village. There must be a ferry to take people across the river."

They looked for a ferry but did not see one. Zhu dropped the luggage and shouted, "Hey ferryman! Hey ferryman! Come here now!" A few minutes later a small boat emerged from under some willow trees and began slowly crossing the river. The boat was small but the travelers could see that it was large enough for them, their horse, and their luggage.

The ferry arrived at the riverbank. The person on the boat called, "Well, if you want to cross the river, get moving." Tangseng urged his horse to move forward. He looked carefully at the person in the boat. He was surprised to see that it was an old woman wearing an old coat and hat. Her hands were strong and her skin was brown and weathered.

Sun Wukong walked to the boat and said, "You are running this boat?"

"Yes," said the woman.

"Where is the ferryman?"

The woman smiled but did not answer. She waited for the four travelers and the horse to walk onto the boat. Then she pushed the boat away from the bank and rowed across the river to the other side. She tied a rope from the boat to a pillar and waited for the travelers to get off the boat. Tangseng told Sha Wujing to give her a few pennies. The woman took the money and walked away. They could hear her laughing as she walked.

Tangseng felt very thirsty. He looked at the water. It appeared to be clear and clean. "Zhu," he said, "get the begging bowl and fill it with water. I am thirsty." Zhu put the bowl in the river and filled it with water. He gave the bowl to Tangseng, who drank about a cupful of it. Then Zhu poured the rest of the water into his own mouth.

They continued walking west. In less than a half hour, though, both Tangseng and Zhu began feeling terrible pain in their stomachs. "The pain is awful!" they both cried. Their bellies began to swell. Tangseng put his hand on his belly. He felt something moving under his skin.

Soon they came to another small village. "Wait here," said Sun Wukong. "I will find someone to give you some medicine."

He walked over to an old woman who was sitting in front of her house. He said to her, "Grandmother, this poor monk has come from the land of Tang in the east. My master is traveling to the Western Heaven to find the Buddha's holy books. A little while ago he drank some water from a river. Now he is feeling quite ill. Is there someone here who can help us?"

The woman laughed and said, "So, you people drank water from the river? Come inside my house, all of you, I will tell you something." The four travelers followed her into her house. Sun Wukong helped Tangseng to walk, while Sha helped Zhu.

Sun Wukong said to her, "Grandmother, please give my master some warm water to drink." But the old woman ran outside and called to her friends to come and look. Soon several middle-aged women came into the house. They pointed at the travelers and laughed loudly.

This made Sun Wukong angry. He grabbed the old woman and said, "Give us some hot water right now, or I will smash you with my rod."

But the woman just said, "Hot water will not help you. let me go and I'll tell you."

Sun Wukong let her go. She said, "You are in the Country of Women, in the Kingdom of Western Liang. There are no men here, only women and girls. You foolishly drank water from the Mother and Child River. When a young woman turns twenty years old and wants to become pregnant, she drinks from that river. Your master drank from that river, and so did that ugly pig. They both are pregnant now. Hot water will not change the situation!"

"Oh no!" cried Zhu. "We are men. How can a baby come out of us?"

"Don't worry," laughed Sun Wukong. "The ancients say, 'When a fruit is ripe, it will fall by itself.' Maybe the baby will come out of a hole in your armpit."

"I'm going to die, I'm going to die," cried Zhu, shaking his body.

Sha said to him, "Second elder brother, don't shake so much. You might hurt the baby."

Sun Wukong said to the woman, "Do you have any drugs that we can use to end this pregnancy?"

The woman replied, "Drugs cannot help you. But if you go south a few miles you will come to Male Undoing Mountain[1]. In the mountain is a cave. In the cave is a well. If you drink from that well you can end the pregnancy."

"That sounds good," said Sun Wukong.

"Ah, but it's not easy. Last year a Daoist came to the cave. He stopped giving the magic water away for free. You must give him money, meat, wine and fruit. Then he will give you a tiny cup of water. But you are poor monks. You have no money, so you cannot get any water from him."

---

[1] The Male Undoing Mountain is jiě yáng shān. Jiě means to untie or undo, yáng is the male principle in Daoism, and shān is mountain.

"Grandmother," said Sun Wukong, "how far is it to the Male Undoing Mountain?"

"About three thousand miles," she replied.

"Excellent!" he said. He told Sha Wujing to take care of Tangseng and Zhu. The woman gave him a large bowl and asked him to fill it with magic water. Sun Wukong took the bowl. He jumped into the air and used his cloud somersault to fly south to the Male Undoing Mountain.

A little while later he arrived at a tall mountain. Near the bottom of the mountain he saw a building. It was quite beautiful. In front of the building, a small stream ran under a wooden bridge. He walked up to the gate. An old Daoist sat on the ground outside the gate. Sun Wukong put down the bowl and bowed to the Daoist.

The Daoist nodded his head and said, "Where did you come from? Why have you come to my little cave?"

Sun Wukong replied, "This poor monk is traveling with a holy monk from the Tang Empire. We are journeying to the western Heaven. My master was thirsty and foolishly drank water from the Mother and Child River. Now his belly is swollen and he is in great pain. I was told that in this cave there is water that can help him. I ask you to give us some of that water."

The Daoist replied, "My master is the True Immortal. This is his cave and this is his water. If you want some of his water you must bring gifts. I see you are a poor monk and you have no gifts. Please go away now. We have nothing for you."

"Please tell your master that Sun Wukong, the Great Sage Equal to Heaven, is here. Perhaps he will give me some water. Perhaps he will give me the whole cave."

The Daoist went inside the cave and said to his master, "Sir, there is a Buddhist monk outside. He says he is Sun Wukong, the Great Sage Equal to Heaven. He would like to have some of our water."

The Immortal became very angry when he heard this. He jumped up and ran outside the cave. He shouted, "Are you really Sun Wukong, or are you another man using his name?"

Sun Wukong looked at the Immortal. He had a red beard, red hair, and sharp white teeth. He wore a red robe with golden threads. On his head was a cap of many colors. In his right hand was a sharp golden hook. Sun Wukong said to the Immortal, "Of course I am Sun Wukong. The ancients say, 'A good man does not change his surname when he stands, nor his given name when he sits.'"

"Do you recognize me?"

"Sir, I have been traveling for several years, but I have never seen your handsome face."

"Is your master the Tang monk?"

"Yes."

"In your journey to the west, did you happen to meet a Great King Holy Child?"

"Yes, that is the nickname of the demon called Red Boy. Why does the True Immortal ask?"

"I am his uncle. The Bull Demon King is my older brother. Some time ago he wrote me a letter and said that Sun Wukong, the eldest disciple of the Tang monk, brought terrible harm to his son, the Great King Holy Child. I did not know where to look for you. But now here you are, standing in front of my cave, asking for water!"

Sun Wukong smiled, trying to calm down the Immortal. "Sir, you are wrong. Your older brother was my friend, my bond brother. His son was not harmed at all. He became a disciple of the Bodhisattva Guanyin. His name is now Sudhana."

"Stop flapping your tongue, you old monkey! Do you think that Red Boy is better off a slave to Guanyin than when he was a king? Of course not. I will have my revenge!" He struck at Sun Wukong with his hook.

Sun Wukong blocked the hook and said, "Sir, please stop this warlike talk. Just give me some water and I will leave."

"You idiot! You cannot fight against me. If you can live for fifteen minutes, I will give you water. If not, I will cut you up and use you as meat for my dinner!"

And so, the two of them began to fight in front of the cave. The poem says,

> The holy monk drank from the stream
> And so the Great Sage must seek magic water
> Who knew it was guarded by a True Immortal?
> They speak with angry words, they fight to the death

One comes seeking water for his master
The other seeks revenge for his brother's son
Quick as a scorpion is the hook
Trying to grab the monkey's leg
Strong as a dragon is the Golden Hoop Rod
Trying to stab the Immortal's chest
All day they fight, both trying to win
Again the hook hooks, again the rod strikes
But neither one can win the fight.

The True Immortal became tired. He ran into the back of the cave and disappeared. Sun Wukong did not follow him. He ran a short distance into the cave with the bowl. He filled the bowl with water from the well. Just then, the True Immortal came out from the back of the cave, swinging his hook.

Sun Wukong held the bowl in one hand and his Golden Hoop Rod in the other. This made it difficult for him to fight. The True Immortal hooked his hook around Sun Wukong's leg, making him fall and drop the bowl. Sun Wukong could not fight and also get water, so he turned and flew out of the cave, saying, "I need help."

He returned to the old woman's house and told Tangseng and Zhu everything that happened in the cave. "Now I need Sha to come with me. I will fight with the True Immortal while Sha gets the water."

Tangseng said, "But while you are gone, who will take care of us?"

"Don't worry," said the old woman, "I will take care of you. You are lucky to have come to my house."

"Why are we lucky?" asked Sun Wukong.

"Remember, there are no men in this village. I am old and not interested in love anymore. But there are younger women in some of the other houses. If you came to their houses, they would want to make love to you. If you refused, they would kill you and cut you into small pieces."

"That doesn't sound so bad," said Zhu. "Except for the killing part."

"Save your strength, Zhu," said Sun Wukong. "You will need it when it's time for your baby to come out."

Sun Wukong and Sha left the house, carrying a bucket and two ropes. They flew to the Male Undoing Mountain. Sun Wukong said to Sha, "take this bucket and ropes. Hide outside the cave. I will start a fight with the True

Immortal. When the fighting starts you go into the cave and get the water from the well. Then leave quickly."

Sun Wukong walked up to the cave and shouted, "Open the door! Open the door!"

The True Immortal came out and replied, "This is my cave, this is my water. Even a king must beg me for a little water. You have nothing to give me and I don't see you begging. So get out of here."

Sun Wukong rushed at the True Immortal with his Golden Hoop Rod, and the two began to fight again. While they were fighting, Sha entered the cave, found the well, and filled the bucket. The old Daoist saw him. He said, "Who are you to steal our water?"

Sha hit him with his staff, breaking the Daoist's shoulder and arm. The Daoist fell to the ground. Sha said, "I will not kill you, old man. Just stay out of my way." He picked up the bucket and ran out of the cave. He shouted to Sun Wukong, "Elder Brother, I have the water. You don't need to kill the True Immortal!"

Sun Wukong stopped fighting. He said to the True Immortal, "I could kill you easily. But it is better to let someone live than to kill him, so I will let you go. But from now on, you must give water free to anyone who asks for it."

"Never!" cried the True Immortal, and he rushed at Sun Wukong. The monkey grabbed the immortal's hook. He broke it into two pieces. Then he broke those two pieces into four pieces. He threw the pieces on the ground, shouting, "Now do you agree to give water freely?" The immortal said nothing, he just looked at his broken weapon and nodded his head. Sun Wukong used his cloud somersault to fly quickly back to the village.

Sun Wukong and Sha entered the house. They saw that Tangseng and Zhu were almost ready to give birth. The old woman said, "Quick, give me the water!" she dipped a cup into the bucket, filling the cup with water. "Drink this slowly," she said to Tangseng, "it will dissolve the baby in your belly."

Zhu grabbed the bucket and said, "I don't need a cup!"

"WAIT!" she shouted at him. "If you drink the whole bucket of water, everything inside your body will dissolve and you will die in great pain." Zhu drank just half of the bucket of water.

Soon their pain became less. They both felt a strong urge to go to the bathroom. The old woman gave chamber pots to both of them. They went outside and spent some time filling the chamber pots. Their pain stopped and their bellies returned to normal size. Some of the women prepared some soup for them to eat.

"Holy father, may we have the rest of the water?" asked the old woman.

"Zhu, do you need any more water?" asked Tangseng.

"No, I feel fine," Zhu replied. So Tangseng gave the rest of the water to the old woman. The women prepared a vegetarian meal for the four travelers. They all had a good dinner, then they rested for the night. The next morning, they left the village and continued on their way.

Chapter 54

After walking about forty miles the travelers arrived at a city. Tangseng said to the disciples, "Remember that we are still in the Country of Women. All of you must act like monks and not wild animals. Be respectful and keep your desires under control."

They entered the city. Soon they were in the marketplace. They saw hundreds of women and girls buying and selling many different things. There were stores selling food, medicine and clothing. There were wine shops and tea shops and small restaurants. Many people were in the street. When the people saw the travelers several of them clapped their hands and shouted, "Look, human seeds are coming! Human seeds are coming!" The travelers could not move forward because the street was full of shouting people.

"Quick," shouted Sun Wukong, "frighten them away!" Zhu flapped his ears and lips. Sha waved his arms. Sun Wukong jumped up and down. The women became frightened. They backed away from the disciples but they continued to look at the handsome Tang monk. Slowly the travelers crossed the marketplace, followed by hundreds of women and girls.

They reached the end of the marketplace. A woman stood in the middle of the road. She said to them, "Visitors are not allowed in this city without permission. You must go to the Men's Post House[1] and wait there. I will announce you to the queen. If she decides to help you, she will sign your rescript and you may continue on your journey."

The woman pointed to a nearby building. It had a sign saying, "Men's Post House." They entered and sat down. A housekeeper served them tea. After about an hour the official came and asked, "Where do the visitors come from?"

Sun Wukong told her, "We are poor monks traveling from the land of Tang. We are going to the Western Heaven to seek holy books. There are four of us plus the horse. We beg you to sign our rescript and allow us to continue on our journey."

The official told the housekeeper to prepare food for the travelers. Then she hurried to the palace. She told the guard at the gate that she needed to see the

---

[1] In ancient China, post houses were established along main roads for changing horses. They also served as hotels for officials and traveling businessmen.

queen immediately. A few minutes later she was standing in front of the queen.

"Why does the official of the Men's Post House wish to see me?" asked the queen.

The official told the queen about the travelers who were waiting in the Men's Post House. The queen smiled and said, "Last night I had a dream. Beautiful colors came from golden screens, and rays of sunlight came from mirrors of jade. Now I think that the Heavens have sent a gift to us. This Tang monk will be my husband. We will have children, they will have children of their own, and our country will continue for thousands of years."

The official replied, "Your Majesty, this is a good idea. But I have seen the disciples of the Tang Monk. They do not look like men. They are like wild animals or spirits."

"That will not be a problem," replied the queen. "We will sign the travel rescript for the three disciples. We will give them food and money and let them go westward. The Tang monk will stay here and be my husband."

Tangseng and the three disciples were waiting in the Men's Post House. They ate vegetarian food and drank tea. "What do you think will happen?" asked Tangseng.

"Oh, they are probably going to ask you to marry the queen," replied Sun Wukong.

"If they do that, what should we do?"

"Master, just say yes to them. Old Monkey will take care of the matter."

Just then the official returned to the Men's Post House. She bowed low to Tangseng. Tangseng said, "Dear lady, I am a poor monk who has left his family. Why do you bow to me?"

The official replied, "Father, we wish you ten thousand happinesses."

"I am just a poor monk. Where does my happiness come from?"

"Father, this is the Country of Women. We have not had any men here for many, many years. We are lucky that you have arrived. My queen has decided to use all the silver and gold of this kingdom to make you an offer of marriage. You will have the seat of honor facing south[1], and you will be the

---

[1] The south-facing seat is the place of honor in a Chinese home.

man set apart from others[1]. The queen will remain as the ruler of this land but you will be her husband. We will give your disciples money and food so that they can continue to the Western Heaven. When they return, we will give them more money and food to help them return to the land of Tang."

Tangseng said nothing. The official continued, "This is a wonderful opportunity for you, father. My queen would like your answer quickly."

When Tangseng still said nothing, Zhu stepped forward and said, "You don't understand. My master is a holy monk. He has studied the way of the Buddha for ten lifetimes. He has no interest in wealth or power or marriage. You should just sign his rescript and let him go. I will stay and be the queen's husband."

The official looked at Zhu. She closed her eyes for a moment and then opened them again. "Sir, it's true that you are a male. However, you are extremely ugly. Our queen would not want to marry you."

"I think you are being much too inflexible," said Zhu. "I would be a very good husband."

"Oh, stop this," said Sun Wukong to Zhu. He said to the official, "We will let our master stay here and marry the queen. The three of us will continue to the Western Heaven. When we return, we will visit the queen and her husband to ask for money and food to finish our journey back to our home.

The official bowed and thanked Sun Wukong. Zhu said, "And we would like a great feast tonight, with lots of food and drink!"

"Of course," replied the official, and she left the Men's Post House.

As soon as she was gone, Tangseng grabbed Sun Wukong and shouted at him, "You devil monkey! Your tricks are killing me! how can you tell them that I will marry the queen? I would not dare to do such a thing."

"Relax, Master," said Sun Wukong, "I understand how you feel. But we must use our tricks against their tricks."

"What do you mean?"

"Think about it. What would happen if you said no to marrying the queen? Do you think they would just sign our rescript and let us leave? Of course not. They would try to force you to marry her. You would say no again. Then

---

[1] "The man set apart from others" refers to the king, who is believed to suffer from loneliness because of his great power.

there would be a big fight. I would have to use my rod. You know that my rod is for fighting demons, not ordinary women. I would have to kill hundreds of them. Do you really want me to do that? Do you want the blood of so many people on your hands?"

Tangseng nodded his head. He said, "I understand. You are wise. But what can we do? If the queen asks me to come into her palace, she will want me to do what husbands do. How can I agree to that? How can I give up my yang and leave the path of the Buddha?"

"Don't say no to her. let her send her chariot to pick you up and bring you to the palace. Ask her to sign the rescript. Have a nice dinner with her but do not go into the bedroom with her. After dinner, tell her that you wish to use the chariot to say goodbye to your disciples. Of course she will give you the chariot. Ride the chariot outside the city and meet us. Then you can get on the white horse and we will leave this place."

"Won't they just follow us?"

"Old Monkey will take care of that. I will use my magic to make them unable to move for a full day and night. That will give us time to get away. After a day and a night they will be able to move again, but we will be gone. Nobody will be hurt."

Tangseng felt like he had awakened from a terrible dream. He thanked Sun Wukong for his wisdom.

While this was happening, the official ran into the palace and said to the queen, "Your Majesty, your dream will soon come true. You will soon have the happiness of marriage! I talked with the travelers and told them that you wanted to marry the Tang monk. The monk was hesitant, but his senior disciple agreed to the marriage. He only asks that you sign their travel rescript so they can continue on their journey."

"Did the Tang monk say anything at all?"

"No. I think he did not know whether he wanted to get married. The first disciple did all the talking. Oh, and the second disciple wanted a banquet with lots of drinking."

The queen told her servants to prepare a great banquet for the travelers. Then she told the servants to bring her chariot and horses. She rode the chariot out of the palace gate and to the Men's Post House. A hundred officials from the palace followed the chariot. Tangseng and the three disciples walked out of the Men's Post House to meet her. She looked at each of them. "Which one of you is the man who I will marry?" The official pointed to Tangseng.

She was filled with desire for the handsome monk. She smiled at him and said, "Royal brother, aren't you coming to ride the phoenix with me?" Tangseng's face turned red.

Sun Wukong laughed and said, "Don't worry, master, I think she just wants you to ride on the chariot with her." Tangseng nodded his head and relaxed a little bit. Zhu stared at the beautiful queen and drool fell from his mouth.

The queen dismounted from the chariot. She walked up to Tangseng and said softly in his ear, "Dear brother, come with me now. Climb onto the phoenix chariot and ride with me to the palace. We will become husband and wife!"

Tangseng did not move. Sun Wukong pushed him a little bit. He whispered in Tangseng's other ear, "Go ahead, Master. Don't worry." Tangseng gave the queen a little smile and mounted the phoenix chariot. The chariot turned around and went back into the palace, followed by the officials. Zhu ran after the chariot, shouting, "Wait! We have to drink the wedding wine!"

The queen leaned close to Tangseng. She said softly in his ear, "Who is that ugly pig-man following us?"

"That is my second disciple, Zhu Wuneng. He is always hungry and thirsty. Just give him some food and wine, then we can continue with our business."

"Dear," she said, smiling at him, "do you eat meat or are you a vegetarian?"

"This poor monk is a vegetarian, but my disciples do like wine. My second disciple likes wine very much."

They arrived at the palace. White birds flew in the sky above them. They heard music coming from the towers. Dozens of servants waited and watched as they rode past.

They entered the main hall of the palace. There were tables for the guests. The queen and Tangseng sat at the head table, with the queen on the right and Tangseng on the left. The three disciples sat on both sides of them. The other officials and guests sat at the other tables. The queen raised her glass of wine and gave a toast to all of the guests. She looked at Tangseng. Tangseng did not know what to do. Sun Wukong leaned towards him and whispered in his ear, "It's time for you to give a toast, Master!!" Then Tangseng gave a toast to the queen and all the guests.

The music stopped, and the guests began to eat and drink. Many different delicious foods were set out on the tables. Zhu pushed large quantities of food into his mouth followed by seven or eight cups of red wine. "Bring more wine!" he shouted. The servants brought more wine for him.

When the guests were finished eating and drinking, Tangseng stood up. He said, "Your majesty, thank you for this wonderful banquet. We had more than enough food and wine. Now, please sign our travel rescript, so that I can say goodbye to my disciples and send them on their way."

"Very well," said the queen.

The rescript was wrapped in cloth. Sha unwrapped it and handed it to Sun Wukong, who turned and gave it with two hands to the queen. The queen looked at the rescript. She saw the seals of the Tang Empire, and also seals from the Precious Image Kingdom, the Black Rooster Kingdom, and the Slow Cart Kingdom. She looked at Tangseng and asked, "Dear, why don't I see the names of your three disciples on this rescript?"

"My three troublemaking disciples are not from the Tang Empire," he replied. "My first disciple comes from Flower Fruit Mountain in the kingdom of Aolai. My second disciple comes from a village in Fuling Mountain. My third disciple comes from the River of Flowing Sand."

"Then why do they follow you?"

"All three broke the laws of Heaven. The Bodhisattva Guanyin saved them. Now all three are on the path of the Buddha. They travel with me and protect me on my journey to the west. When I left the Tang Empire many years ago, they were not with me. That is why their names are not on the rescript."

"May I add their names to the rescript?"

"My queen may do as she wishes."

The queen asked for ink and a brush. Using the brush she wrote the names of Sun Wukong, Zhu Bajie and Sha Wujing at the bottom of the rescript. She used her seal to stamp the rescript, then she signed her name under the stamp. She handed the rescript to Sun Wukong. He gave it to Sha. Sha wrapped it in cloth again and put it in his robe.

The queen gave a gold coin to Sun Wukong, saying, "Here is some money to help you journey to the west. When you return, I will give you a lot more money and gifts."

Sun Wukong replied, "Your Majesty, we who have left our families cannot accept these gifts. As we travel, we find places to beg for food. That is all we need."

The queen told one of her servants to give a large bolt of silk to Sun Wukong. She said, "Then please take this so that you can make clothing for yourselves."

Sun Wukong said, "Your Majesty, we who have left our families cannot wear silk clothing. We only wear cloth garments."

The queen then said, "Very well. Take three catties of rice, so you have something to eat."

Before Sun Wukong could say anything, Zhu shouted, "Thank you, Your Majesty!" and took the rice.

Tangseng stood up. He said to the queen, "Your Majesty, please ride with me in the phoenix chariot to the city's western gate. I want to say goodbye to my three disciples and give them a few final instructions. Then I will return, and we will spend the rest of our lives happy together as husband and wife."

They rode together to the western gate, followed by all the palace officials and hundreds of women and girls from the city. When they arrived at the western gate the three disciples said together, "Your Majesty need not go any further. We will leave now."

Then Tangseng stepped down from the chariot and said, "Goodbye, my queen. I must leave now."

The queen's face became pale with fear. She grabbed Tangseng's robe and cried, "My dear, where are you going? Tonight we will become husband and wife. Tomorrow you will sit on the throne of my kingdom. You have said yes. You have even eaten the wedding feast. Why do you change your mind now?"

Before Tangseng could say a word, Zhu rushed up to the chariot. He said to the queen, "How could a Buddhist monk marry a skeleton like you? let my master go on his journey!" This frightened the queen. She fell back into the chariot. Sha grabbed Tangseng and helped him mount his white horse. They turned to go, with Sha waving his staff to make the people move back.

Sun Wukong was just getting ready to use his magic to make the people immobile. But just then, a girl ran out from the crowd. She shouted, "Royal brother Tang, where are you going? I want to make love to you!" Sha tried to hit the girl with his staff, but he only hit the air. The girl called up a great wind. Then she grabbed Tangseng, and the two of them lifted into the air and disappeared.

Chapter 55

Sun Wukong heard the sound of the great wind. He turned around and shouted to Sha, "Where is Master?"

Sha replied, "A girl came out of the crowd. She grabbed Master. The two of them flew away in a great wind."

Sun Wukong used his cloud somersault to rise up to the sky. Shading his diamond eyes with his hand he looked in all four directions. Far to the northwest he saw a huge dark thundercloud. "Brothers," he shouted, "fly with me. We must save Master!" All three of them flew away to the northwest.

On the ground, all the women and girls of Western Liang saw this. They fell to the ground, crying and shouting, "We did not know that these men are holy sages who can fly to Heaven!"

One of the officials said to the queen, "Your Majesty, don't be frightened. This was no ordinary Chinese monk. He is a great sage. None of us could see this. Please sit down in your chariot, we will take you back to the palace."

We will leave the queen now and tell you about the three disciples. They flew rapidly to the northwest, following the dark thundercloud. Soon they came to a tall mountain. They dropped closer to the ground. Looking carefully, they saw a large green flat rock standing upright like a screen. They looked behind the rock and saw two stone doors. Zhu wanted to smash down the doors, but Sun Wukong stopped him, saying, "Don't be stupid, younger brother. We don't know if Master is behind this door. What if this cave belongs to someone else? We don't want to offend someone for no reason."

Sun Wukong said some magic words and shook himself. He changed into a small bee. He flew through a small crack in the stone doors. Looking around the cave he saw a comfortable chair surrounded by colorful flowers. A beautiful female demon sat on the chair. Nearby were several young girls dressed in silk robes. They were all talking about something.

Two more young girls approached the demon carrying two plates of hot steaming buns. "Madam," they said, "here are the buns you asked for. One plate has buns stuffed with human flesh. The other has buns stuffed with red bean paste."

"Little ones," said the demon, "bring out the Tang monk." Two of the girls went into the back of the cave. Soon they returned with Tangseng. His face was yellow, his lips were white, and his eyes were full of tears.

The beautiful demon said to Tangseng, "Relax, royal brother! Our home is not as large as the queen's palace, but you will find it to be quite comfortable. It is quiet and peaceful here. You will stay here for the rest of your life, chanting the name of the Buddha and studying your holy books. You will be my companion."

Tangseng was so frightened he could not speak. The demon smiled at him and continued, "I know that you did not eat much at the banquet. You must be hungry. Please, try some of our tasty buns!"

Tangseng thought to himself, "This demon is not like the queen. If I make her angry, she might kill me at any moment. I must keep her happy while I wait for my disciples to come and save me." So he said to the demon, "What is in the buns?"

The demon replied, "Some are filled with human meat. And some are filled with red bean paste. Which ones would you like to eat?"

"This poor monk has always been a vegetarian."

"Wonderful!" The demon called to her servants to bring some tea for Tangseng. Then she picked up a red bean paste bun, broke it into two pieces, and gave it to Tangseng. Tangseng picked up a meat bun and gave it to the demon but he did not break it open.

The demon laughed. "Dear, why did you not break open the meat bun?" she asked.

"This poor monk has always been a vegetarian. I dare not break open a meat bun."

Sun Wukong listened to this. He thought, "I don't know why they are talking so much about buns. But I am worried about Master. It's time to end this." Shaking his body, he returned to his true form. He shouted, "leave my master alone, you evil demon. Stop eating your buns and taste my rod instead!"

Quickly the demon blew out some fog to hide herself and Tangseng. Then she shouted for her servants to take Tangseng to the back of the cave. Turning to Sun Wukong she said, "Lawless monkey, what are you doing in my home? Don't run away from me. Taste this!" She smashed her trident down on Sun Wukong, who blocked it with his rod.

The demon and the monkey king fought, trident against rod, moving slowly out of the cave. Zhu and Sha waited outside the cave. When the two fighters came out of the cave, Zhu shouted to Sha, "Quick, move the horse and luggage away from here and guard them. I will help Old Monkey fight the demon." Then he shouted to Sun Wukong, "Stand back, elder brother, let me fight this bitch!"

The demon saw Zhu coming. Fire came out of her nose. She shook her body, and now she was fighting with three tridents instead of one. She shouted, "Sun Wukong, I recognize you but you don't recognize me. But I tell you, even your Buddha in Thunderclap Mountain is afraid of me."

The demon attacked the two disciples. The air was filled with the sound of tridents, rake and rod smashing against each other. The three of them fought as the sun went down in the west and the moon came up in the east. Neither side could win. But suddenly the demon leaped into the air and stabbed down on Sun Wukong's head. Sun Wukong did not see the weapon. He cried out in pain, grabbed his head, and ran away. Zhu followed him. The demon picked up her tridents and went back into her cave.

Sun Wukong held his head in both of his hands, crying, "Oh the pain, the pain!"

"This is strange," said Sha. "Your head is very hard. Other monsters and demons have hit you on the head and caused no pain at all. What happened this time?"

"I don't know," replied Sun Wukong. "Ever since I stole the golden elixir of Laozi, my head has been as strong as diamond. When I caused trouble in Heaven five hundred years ago, the Jade Emperor sent a whole army of warriors against me, but they could not hurt me. Then Laozi put me in his brazier for forty-nine days, and that could not hurt me. I don't know what weapon this demon used against me!"

"Let me see your head," said Sha. "Move your hands away." He looked closely but could not see any bruise.

"This demon knows me," said Sun Wukong. "and she knows what happened to us in the Country of Women. But I don't know who she is." He touched his head softly with his hand. "Well, it's late and my head hurts. I don't think Master is in any immediate danger. The demon does not want to kill him. I think she wants to marry him. Master's mind is strong, though. I don't think he will surrender to desire tonight. let's rest."

Back at the cave, the demon put away her weapons and smiled at her servants. "Little ones," she said, "shut the doors and watch them. We don't want that ugly monkey to come back." Pointing to two more servants, she said, "Go into the bedroom and light the candles. I want to spend the night with the royal brother Tang."

Tangseng was brought into the bedroom. The demon smiled at him and gently held his arm. She said, "The ancient ones say, 'Gold has its price but who knows the price of pleasure?' Let's play husband and wife. We will have fun!"

Tangseng said nothing. He did not want to say no to her, because he was afraid she might kill him. So he followed her into the bedroom. His body was shaking, his eyes were closed. The poem says,

> His eyes see nothing
> His ears hear nothing
> To her, his handsome face is like Heaven
> To him, her beautiful face is like dirt
> She takes off her clothes, her passion is strong
> He wraps his robe tighter, his will is stronger
> She only wants to seduce him
> He only wants to seek the Buddha
> She says, "I want you, my bed is ready."
> He says, "I am a monk, how can I go there?"
> She says, "I am as beautiful as Xishi[1]."
> He says, "I am as upright as King Yue[2]."

They talked and argued long into the night. Finally the demon could see that Tangseng had no interest in sleeping with her. So she had him tied up with ropes and dragged to the back of the cave. Then she put out the candles and went to sleep by herself.

The next morning, Sun Wukong was feeling much better. "My head does not hurt anymore. I just have a little itch."

Zhu laughed and said, "If you have an itch, you should ask the demon to smack it with her trident again."

---

[1] Xishi, the Lady of the West, was one of the Four Great Beauties of ancient China. It's said that when she looked at fish in the pond, the fish would be so overcome by her beauty that they would forget how to swim and would sink to the bottom of the pond.

[2] King Goujian ruled the Kingdom of Yue from 596 to 45 BC. He had no interest in kingly riches. He ate peasant food and slept at night on a bed of sticks.

Sun Wukong spat at him. "let's go, let's go, let's go!"

"All right. But last night, I think our Master was going wild, wild, wild!"

Sun Wukong said to Sha, "Little brother, stay here and guard the horses and luggage. I will go with Zhu and take care of this demon."

The two of them returned to the cave. "Wait here," said Sun Wukong. "I will go inside and see what's going on. If Master really gave up his yang last night, we can all leave without him. But if he remained strong, you and I must fight the demon and save him."

"Don't bother," said Zhu. "You know what the ancients say: 'You can give a cat a pillow made of fish meat, but the pillow will get a lot of scratches during the night.'"

"Stop babbling," replied Sun Wukong. He changed into a bee again and entered the cave. He saw that the demon was still sleeping. "Hmmm, she seems to be very tired," he thought. "I wonder what happened last night." He flew deeper into the cave and found Tangseng tied up like a hog. "Master!" he said.

"Wukong!" Tangseng cried. "Save me!"

"How did it go last night?" asked Sun Wukong.

"Don't worry, I did not do anything last night. The demon kept at me for half the night. But I did not take off my clothes, I did not touch her or the bed. Finally she got tired of trying to seduce me, so she had me tied up like this. Please save me so that I can continue on our journey."

The sound of their talking woke up the demon. She was angry but she also felt desire for Tangseng. She said to him, "So you really don't want to marry me? You would rather stay a monk and sleep on the ground by yourself every night?"

Sun Wukong flew out of the cave. He said to Zhu, "Don't worry, our Master did not sleep with the demon last night. He says that he did not take off his clothes, and he did not touch her. He only wants to stay on the path of the Buddha."

"All right then," replied Zhu. "He is still a monk. let's go and save him."

The monkey and the pig ran into the cave, holding their weapons. The demon met them and they began to fight again. Fire and smoke came from the demon's mouth, and she used her trident with great skill. Sun Wukong and

Zhu could not defeat her. Then she stabbed Zhu on the lip. "Oh, it hurts, it hurts!" he cried. He and Sun Wukong ran out of the cave.

They returned to the place where Sha was waiting with the horse and luggage. They sat on the ground. Zhu was crying in pain from the wound on his lip. Sun Wukong and Sha were discussing how to fight the demon. Then they saw an old woman coming up the mountain road. In her left hand she held a basket of vegetables. "Big brother," said Sha, "go talk with this woman. She lives in this area, maybe she knows something about the demon in the cave."

Sun Wukong walked towards the woman. As he got closer, he saw beautiful clouds all around her head. He dropped to his knees and said to the others, "Brothers, kowtow quickly! It's the Bodhisattva Guanyin!" All three kowtowed to her.

"Bodhisattva," said Sun Wukong, "please forgive us for not greeting you properly. Our master is in great danger and we have been unable to save him. Can you help us?"

Guanyin said, "Wukong, this demon is very, very dangerous. Her tridents are really her front claws. Your injuries came from the stinger in her tail. Yes, this monster is really a scorpion spirit. Once, a long time ago, she lived on Thunderclap Mountain. She heard a lecture by the Buddha himself. The Buddha saw her and he tried to push her away. She stabbed a finger on the Buddha's left hand. Even the Buddha found the pain to be terrible. He told some of his sages to capture her, but she ran away to this cave. She wants to become human, that is why she changed her form."

"Ah," said Sun Wukong. "Can the great Bodhisattva tell us how we can rescue our master from this scorpion spirit?"

"Go to the East Heaven Gate. Look for the Star Lord Mao[1]. He will know how to defeat this demon spirit." Then Guanyin changed to a golden beam of light and returned to the South Sea.

Sun Wukong told the other two disciples that he was going to the East Heaven Gate to find Star Lord Mao. He used his cloud somersault to get to the gate quickly. He was met by the four Grand Masters of Heaven. "Great Sage, where are you going?" asked one of the masters.

"I must find the Star Lord Mao," replied Sun Wukong.

---

[1] Mao is the Maned Head, the 18th of the 28 constellations in the Chinese zodiac. It has seven stars and corresponding to Pleiades in the Western zodiac.

"You will find him at the Stargazing Terrace."

Sun Wukong flew to the Stargazing Terrace. He saw a hundred soldiers crossing the terrace. Behind them walked the great Star Lord Mao. He wore a golden cap and a jade suit of armor. A sword of seven stars hung from a wide treasure belt around his waist. The soldiers saw Sun Wukong and stopped. Mao said, "Why has the Great Sage come here?"

"Sir, my master has been captured by a scorpion spirit. He is in great danger. I and my brother disciples have not been able to save him. Just now the Bodhisattva Guanyin said that you can help us to save our master."

"All right. Normally I would tell the Jade Emperor, but I can see that you are in a hurry. So I will not tell the Jade Emperor and I will not bring tea for you. let's go now!" Together they flew down from Heaven and arrived at the cave.

Sun Wukong said to Zhu and Sha, "Get up, get up! The Star God is here!"

Zhu said, "I cannot get up. My lip still hurts terribly!"

"Let me see it," said Mao. He looked at the lip, then blew on it with his sweet breath. Instantly the pain stopped and the lip returned to normal size.

"That's wonderful!" said Sun Wukong. "Can you blow on my head too?"

"What's wrong with your head? It looks all right to me."

"The scorpion spirit stabbed me yesterday. The pain has stopped, but it itches a lot and it feels numb." So the Star God blew sweet breath on Sun Wukong's head, and the itching and numbness disappeared.

"Now, let's take care of this scorpion spirit," said Mao. "You two, go to the cave and start a fight. Bring her outside. I will be waiting for her."

Sun Wukong and Zhu ran into the cave, weapons held high. They smashed the door to the second floor and shouted insults. The scorpion spirit was just getting ready to untie Tangseng and give him some food and drink. When she saw the two disciples coming, she jumped up and began fighting with them using her trident weapon. They fought for a few minutes. The scorpion spirit tried to stab them but they quickly ran out of the cave. The scorpion spirit followed them, stinger held high. "Quick, Star Lord, do it now!" shouted Sun Wukong.

The Star Lord changed into his true form, a giant rooster seven feet tall. He faced the scorpion spirit and crowed. The scorpion spirit changed into her true form, a scorpion about the size of a small dog. He crowed again, and the scorpion spirit fell down and died.

Without a word, the Star Lord flew into the sky and returned to the Heavens. The three disciples bowed to the sky and said, "Thank you. We are sorry for causing you this trouble. Another day we will come to your palace and thank you face to face."

The three disciples went back into the cave, ready to fight the scorpion spirit's helpers. But when they arrived, the helpers all fell to their knees. One of them said, "Fathers, we are not demons. We are girls and women from Western Liang, captured by the demon a long time ago. We have been slaves here for many years. You will find your master in a room in the back of the cave. He is crying."

Sun Wukong looked at them closely. He said, "I can see that you are not demons. All right, you can leave." The disciples ran to the back of the cave, where they found Tangseng.

"I am so glad to see you!" he said. "What happened to that woman?"

"That was no woman," said Sun Wukong. "That was a scorpion spirit. Guanyin appeared to us and told us that the Star Lord Mao was the only one who could help us. I went to the South Gate of Heaven and found the Star Lord. He came here and killed the scorpion spirit."

Tangseng thanked them again and again. Then they looked around the cave and found some rice and noodles. They had a small meal. When they finished eating, they helped the girls return to their homes. Then they lit a fire and burned everything in the cave.

After that, they set out again on their journey to the west.

Chapter 56

Spring had turned into summer. The travelers walked slowly westward along the Silk Road. They saw yellow birds flying above them, and they could smell fragrant flowers on the warm breezes.

One day in early summer they arrived at a large mountain. The path went upwards and became more difficult. They climbed the mountain. The air became cooler. They saw wild animals on both sides of the path. Far away they heard the sound of a tiger's roar.

After climbing for several hours, they reached the top of the mountain and began to travel down the western side. Tangseng's horse was very tired and began to walk slowly. Tangseng could not make the horse walk faster. Zhu shouted at it but the horse ignored him. Sun Wukong said, "Let me do it." He waved his golden hoop rod at the horse and shouted at it. Immediately the horse began to run. The Tang monk was frightened and held on tightly with both hands. The horse ran for twenty miles, taking Tangseng far ahead of his three disciples. Finally the horse came to level ground. It stopped running and began to walk again.

Tangseng had been very frightened while the horse was running. When the horse began walking again, he relaxed and looked up. Ahead on the road he saw a group of about thirty men standing in the road. They all held swords, spears and long rods. One of the men had a green face, long teeth, and looked like a powerful dragon. Another had red hair, big eyes, and looked like an angry tiger. Tangseng could see that they were bandits.

"Where are you going?" asked the green-faced bandit chief. "We don't want to hurt you, we just want your travel money. Give it to me right now!"

Tangseng got down from his horse. He pressed his palms together and replied, "Great Kings, this poor monk has been traveling for many years. Long ago I left the land of Tang. I am going to the Western Heaven to acquire holy scriptures. When I started my journey I had some money, but I spent it long ago. I ask you, Great Kings, to be kind and let me continue on my journey."

The bandit chief said, "We are guarding this road, and you must pay us. If you have no money, just give us your clothing and your horse. Then we will let you pass."

"This robe is old and threadbare. It is made of cloth begged from many different people. If you take it from me, it will be just like killing me. What will happen to you then? You might be a great king in this life, but in your next life you might return as an animal."

This made the bandit chief angry. He started to hit the monk with his rod. As the blows rained down on his head, Tangseng had an idea. He said, "Please stop hitting me. I have a young disciple who will arrive in a few minutes. He has a small bag of silver. I will tell him to give you the silver." The bandits stopped hitting Tangseng. They tied him up and hung him from a tree.

A short time later, the three disciples came near. Zhu looked and saw Tangseng hanging from a tree. "Look," he said, "our Master wanted to show us how strong he is, so he climbed a tree."

Using his diamond eyes, Sun Wukong saw the situation clearly. "You are a fool," he said to Zhu. "Stop talking. Wait here. I will go and see what's going on." He jumped up onto a small hill and looked again. Now he saw the bandits. He said to himself, "Ah, this is good. Business has come to my door!"

He shook his body and changed into a young monk about sixteen years old. He walked up to Tangseng and said, "Master, what's going on here? Who are these bad men?"

Tangseng cried, "Wukong, please save me! These are very bad men. They are bandits. They wanted money from me, but of course I had nothing to give them. So I told them that you were coming. I said that you would give them silver."

"Why did you tell them that?"

"I needed to make them stop hitting me!"

"Fine, fine. I like this. If you can keep doing this, Old Monkey will have lots of business!"

During this conversation the bandits quietly formed a circle around Sun Wukong. The green-faced bandit chief said, "Little monk, your master said that you had some money. Give it to us."

"No problem, I have quite a lot of gold and silver. But first you must let my master go." The bandit chief nodded his head, and a couple of the men released Tangseng. The monk ran to his white horse, jumped on the horse, and rode away as fast as he could. Sun Wukong started to follow him.

The bandit chief stopped him and said, "Where do you think you're going?"

Sun Wukong said, "All right, I will stay a little bit longer. But I think that the travel money should be divided in three parts."

The bandit chief laughed and said, "Ah, you are a clever little monk! You want some of the money for yourself, eh? All right then. Give us all your money and we will give you back a little bit. You can hide it in your robe and your master will never know."

"That's not quite what I meant," replied Sun Wukong. "What I meant was, bring out all the money that you have taken from other travelers. We will divide that money in three parts, two for me and one for you."

This made the bandits very angry. They all began to rain blows on Sun Wukong's head. Sun Wukong just stood without moving. The blows did not bother him at all. Finally he said, "Are you finished? Now I will show you something." He took a small needle from behind his ear and held it in his hand. "Change!" he whispered. Instantly the needle became his golden hoop rod, sixteen feet long and as thick as a rice bowl.

He put the rod on the ground and said, "If any of you can pick up this rod, you can keep it." The two bandit chiefs tried to pick it up, but it was like a fly trying to pick up a mountain. This was because the rod weighed thirteen thousand five hundred catties. Sun Wukong picked up the rod and said, "Now I'm afraid that your luck has just run out." He swung the rod twice, instantly killing both bandit chiefs. The rest of the bandits turned and ran for their lives.

Meanwhile, Tangseng was riding east as fast as he could towards the other two disciples. He reached Zhu and Sha and gasped, "Oh, disciples, go quickly to your elder brother. Tell him not to harm those poor bandits!"

Zhu ran toward Sun Wukong as fast as he could. He reached the monkey and said, "Elder brother, our master tells you not to kill any of the bandits."

"I have not killed anyone," replied Sun Wukong. He pointed to the two bandit chiefs lying dead on the ground and said, "These two are just sleeping."

"That's strange. Why are they sleeping in the middle of the road? Maybe they were awake all night drinking wine and singing songs." Zhu looked more closely. "And why are they sleeping with their mouths open?"

"That's because I hit them with my rod. They will never wake up."

"Ah, I understand," replied Zhu. He ran back to Tangseng and said, "Master, good news. The bandits have disbanded."

"That's good. Where did they go?"

"Two of them didn't go anywhere."

"Then why did you say they are disbanded?"

"They have been beaten to death. Isn't that disbanded enough for you?"

Tangseng was very angry when he heard this. "Zhu, use your rake to dig graves for these two. Then we will bury them. I will recite a prayer for the dead." Zhu started to use his rake to dig a hole. He dug about three feet down, then his rake struck some rocks. He dropped the rake and used his snout to quickly finish digging the graves. When he was finished, the holes were five feet deep. The disciples put the dead bandits in the holes, then covered them with dirt. Tangseng stood at the edge of the grave. He pressed his hands together and said,

> "Brothers, I bow to you, please listen to my words
> I come from the east, sent by the Tang Emperor
> I met you here on this road, face to face
> You wanted my clothing and my horse
> I begged you to let me pass but you did not listen
> You met my elder disciple and fell by his rod
> Now I pity your dead bodies
> If you meet Yama please remember
> My elder disciple's name is Sun
> My name is Chen
> My other disciples are Bajie and Wujing
> Tell Yama that Sun killed you, not us!"

Sun Wukong listened to this. When Tangseng was finished, he said, "Master, you are not being kind, are you? Yes, I killed these bandits. But I did it for you. This is your journey. I am just here to help you. If you had not decided to travel to the west, these men would not be dead. If you had not brought me as your disciple, these men would not be dead. This is your fault, not mine!" Then he turned to the graves and said angrily,

> "Listen to me, you stupid bandits
> You hit me on the head again and again
> You made me very angry
> Yes, killing you was a mistake
> But I am not afraid of you
> I am not afraid of Yama
> I am the Great Sage Equal to Heaven
> All ten Kings of the Underworld have served me

The Jade Emperor himself knows me
The guardian of Mount Tai fears me
All the gods of Heaven are my friends
You may go to hell and complain about me
I don't care!"

Tangseng listened to this. He was surprised that Sun Wukong was so angry. "Disciple, my words were meant to help you see the value of life, and make you a better person. Why are you taking this so hard?"

"Master," replied Sun Wukong, "your words were no joke." He started walking westward, then he turned and added, "Let's find a place to stay tonight." Tangseng and the other two disciples followed him. All four of them were unhappy and a little bit angry. There was tension in the air.

Soon they arrived at a small village. Looking around, they saw that it was a nice place. They heard dogs barking and they saw candles burning in the windows of small homes. An old man came out from one of the houses. Tangseng greeted him. "Hello, grandfather. We are traveling to the Western Heaven to seek the Buddha's holy scriptures. It's getting late, and we were hoping to find a place to stay for the night. Please do not be afraid of my disciples. They are ugly but they will not hurt you."

The old man looked at the disciples. He said, "They are extremely ugly. One of them looks like a yaksa, one is a horse-face, and one is a thunder god."

Sun Wukong was still angry. He shouted back, "Old man, the thunder god is my grandson, the yaksa is my great-grandson, and the horse-face is my great-great-grandson." When he heard this the old man became very frightened. His face turned pale and he fell on the ground. Tangseng helped him to stand up, saying, "Don't worry my friend, they are all quite rude and don't know how to speak politely. The one you called a thunder god is my eldest disciple, Sun Wukong. The one you called horse-face is my middle disciple Zhu Bajie. And the one you called a yaksa is my junior disciple, Sha Wujing. They are not demons. Don't be afraid."

"All right, come in," said the old man. They entered his house. The old man asked his wife to bring tea. She went to the kitchen to make the tea. A small boy followed her.

"Grandfather," said Tangseng, "what is your good surname and how old are you?"

"My surname is Yang. I have lived for seventy-four years. I have one son.

The little child you see here is my grandson."

"I would like to meet your son," said Tangseng.

"That young man is unworthy of meeting a holy monk like you. I wish he had a good job. But he only wants to kill people and take their money. His friends are bad men. He went out five days ago and has not returned."

Tangseng thought about this. He was wondering if Sun Wukong had killed their son on the road earlier that day. Before he could say anything, Sun Wukong said to the old man, "Sir, such a bad son can only bring troubles to you and your family. Why keep him? Let me go and find him. I can kill him for you!"

"Perhaps I would let you do that, but I have no other son. It's true that my son has become a bad person, but I need someone to dig my grave when I die."

Before Sun Wukong could reply, Sha said quickly, "Elder brother, you should mind your own business." Turning to the old man, he said, "Grandfather, you and your family have been very kind to us. Please show us where we can sleep tonight." The old man led them out to the barn. He put some clean straw down on the ground for the travelers to sleep on. Soon all four were asleep.

Now, Yang's son was indeed one of the bandits but he was not one of the bandit chiefs. Earlier that day, after Sun Wukong killed the bandit chiefs, Yang's son and the other bandits ran for their lives. That night after the travelers had gone to bed, the bandits knocked on the door of the Yang house. The old man opened the door. The bandits ran into the house, shouting, "We're hungry!" The wife of Yang's son woke up. She started to cook some rice for the bandits. Yang's son went out to the back of the house to get some firewood. He saw Tangseng's white horse. He returned to the house and asked his father, "What is that white horse in back of the house?"

The old man replied, "The horse belongs to some traveling monks. They are going to the Western Heaven . They asked if they could sleep here tonight."

Yang's son clapped his hands and said to his friends, "Good news, my friends! Our enemies are here! We can kill them tonight. We can take their horse and their money."

One of the other bandits said, "Let's wait. First, let's have some dinner and sharpen our knives. Later tonight we can kill them." So they all sat down to eat dinner and sharpen their knives.

While they were eating dinner, the old man quietly went out to the barn. He woke up the travelers and told them that the bandits were planning to kill them. "Run away!" he said. The travelers picked up their luggage, left the barn, and headed west on the road.

Around the time of the fifth watch, the bandits decided it was time to attack. They ran out of the house and into the barn. But of course the travelers were gone. The bandits started running west on the road, carrying knives and spears. Soon they caught up with the travelers.

Sun Wukong stopped and turned to face the bandits. "Disciple," said Tangseng, "you must not hurt these people. Just frighten them and make them go away."

Sun Wukong ignored him. The bandits formed a circle around Sun Wukong. They started to attack him with knives and spears. The Monkey King began to swing his golden hoop rod, faster and faster. When he hit the bandits, they fell like stars. A few escaped and a few were wounded, but most of them were killed. Their bodies lay dead on the ground.

Tangseng was very upset. He rode his horse away from the fight. Sun Wukong ran over to one of the wounded bandits and said, "Where is the son of Yang?" The bandit pointed to a man and said, "There, the one in yellow." Sun Wukong ran over to the one in yellow and cut off his head. Picking it up, he ran to Tangseng and said, "Master, here is the son of old man Yang. I have cut off his head."

Tangseng fell down on the ground and cried, "Take it away! Take it away!" Zhu kicked the head to the side of the road. Then he used his rake to dig a small hole and bury the head.

Sha went over to Tangseng and helped him to stand up. Tangseng began to recite the Tight Headband Spell. Immediately the headband on Sun Wukong's head became tighter. Sun Wukong cried out in pain. Tangseng said the Tight Headband Spell again and again and again. Ten times he said the spell. Ten times the headband became tighter. Sun Wukong was lying on the ground, his hands on his head, crying in pain, saying, "Master, please stop!"

Tangseng said to him, "I have nothing to say to you. I do not want you as my disciple anymore. Yang's son was no good, but he did not deserve to be killed by you. You have killed too many people and caused too much trouble. There is no kindness in you. Be gone, and don't come back!"

Sun Wukong held his head with both hands and cried, "Stop it!" Then he used his cloud somersault and disappeared.

Chapter 57

Sun Wukong had to leave, but where could he go? He thought about going home to Flower Fruit Mountain, but he was afraid that the other monkeys would despise him for not serving his master. He thought about going to the palace in Heaven, but he was afraid that the gods might not allow him to stay there. He thought about going to live with his friend the Dragon King of the Eastern Ocean, but he did not want to go there as a homeless monkey. Finally he decided to return to Tangseng and apologize.

He used his cloud somersault and came down in front of Tangseng's horse, saying, "Master, please forgive me. I will not hurt or kill others anymore. I beg you to let me travel with you to the Western Heaven."

But Tangseng was still angry at Sun Wukong. He just started reciting the Tight Headband Spell again and again, twenty times. Now the headband was so tight that it cut an inch into Sun Wukong's flesh. Then Tangseng said, "Why are you bothering me again? Just go away."

"Master, you need my help. Without me I don't think you will reach the Western Heaven."

Tangseng replied, "You are a murdering ape. I don't want you anymore. Maybe I will reach the Western Heaven, maybe I will not, but it's no concern of yours. Leave now. If you don't, I will continue saying the Tight Headband Spell and I won't stop until you are dead."

Sadly, Sun Wukong rose into the clouds again. He decided to go to Potalaka Mountain and visit the Bodhisattva Guanyin.

An hour later he arrived at the Great Southern Ocean. He flew on to Potalaka Mountain, then entered the purple bamboo forest where Guanyin lived. Guanyin's disciple Moksha greeted him, saying, "Why has the Great Sage come here?"

"I have something to tell the Bodhisattva."

Moksha wanted to ask him some questions, but just then a beautiful white bird came into view. It flew back and forth. This meant that Guanyin was ready to see him. Sun Wukong approached Guanyin. He started to cry. Guanyin said, "Wukong, tell me why you are crying. I will help you."

"You set me free from my prison and set me on the path of the Buddha. Since then, I have accompanied the Tang monk, protecting him from monsters, demons and wild animals. How could I know that he would be so ungrateful? Truly, he cannot tell black from white."

Guanyin smiled and said, "Wukong, tell me more about black and white."

Sun Wukong told her everything. He told her about the bandits. He told her how Tangseng had used the Tight Headband Spell. And he told her that there was no place in Heaven or on earth where he could go now.

Guanyin listened. Then she said, "The Tang monk is a holy monk, he would not kill even one person. But you have killed many. It's ok for you to kill a demon or a monster, but you must not kill a person. You could have easily frightened those people away without killing them. In my opinion, you have acted badly."

"I understand. But I should not be treated this way. I beg you, please show some kindness. Please release me from this magic headband. Let me return to Flower Fruit Mountain where I can live in peace."

"I'm sorry but I cannot do that. The Buddha himself gave me this headband to give to you. He also taught me the Tight Headband Spell. But I'm afraid there is no Loose Headband Spell."

"All right, then. I thank you. I will leave now."

"Where will you go?"

"I will go to see the Buddha himself, and ask him to remove my headband." He got up and prepared to leave.

"No, wait. I want to look into the future for you."

"Please do not. I don't want to see my future."

"Not your future. The Tang monk's future." She closed her eyes, and looked into the three worlds. She opened her eyes and said, "Wukong, soon your master will face death. He will need you. I will tell him to take you back so that both of you may reach the end of your journey and acquire wisdom." Sun Wukong did not dare say anything.

While Sun Wukong was visiting with Guanyin, Tangseng and the other two disciples continued on their journey. By late afternoon Tangseng was getting very hungry. He asked Zhu to find a village nearby where he could beg some rice. Zhu looked but did not see any nearby village. Tangseng said, "Well then, please get me some water from the river. I am extremely thirsty." Zhu left to get some water.

Tangseng and Sha waited for a long time, but Zhu did not return. Finally, Sha left to get some water. Tangseng was now alone, sitting by the side of the road. He heard a loud noise and looked up. Sun Wukong stood in front of him holding a bowl of water, saying, "Master, I have returned. Here is some water. Drink!"

But Tangseng was still angry. He said, "I don't want your water and I don't want you. It will be better for me to die of thirst than to take you back. Get out of here now!" Sun Wukong became angry. He hit Tangseng, knocking him to the ground. Then he grabbed the luggage and used his cloud somersault to fly away.

Zhu was getting ready to get water from the river, but he looked up and saw a little hut. He decided to go there to beg some food. He didn't want to frighten people with his appearance so he recited a spell and shook his body several times. He changed into a sickly old monk with yellow skin.

"Please, please," he said to the door of the house, "I am a poor monk. Please give me some rice!" Two women were inside the house. They were afraid of the sickly monk, so they quickly filled his begging bowl with rice and gave it to him.

As Zhu was returning with the rice, he met Sha on the road. They poured the rice from the begging bowl into a fold of Zhu's robe, then they filled the begging bowl with water from the river. Then they returned to the place where they'd left Tangseng. But when they arrived at that place, they saw Tangseng lying on the ground, face down. He looked like he was dead. The luggage was gone.

"That's it, that's it!" cried Zhu. "We are finished. No more talk about going to get scriptures in the Western Heaven. You stay here and keep an eye on Master's body. I will go to the next town and buy a coffin so we can bury him. After that, we can both go home and forget about this journey."

Sha turned Tangseng's body over and he bent down to look more carefully. He saw that Tangseng was breathing a little bit. "Master is still alive!" said Sha.

They waited until Tangseng took a few more breaths and opened his eyes. He said to his disciples, "It was that lawless monkey. Soon after you left, the monkey returned. I told him to go away. He hit me and left me for dead."

They returned to the little hut where Zhu had begged rice earlier that day. One of the two women opened the door and said, "What, more traveling monks? I saw an old sickly monk earlier today and gave him some rice. I have nothing more to give you. Please go away and don't bother me."

Zhu told the woman that he was the sickly monk that she had seen. Then Tangseng explained that they were traveling to the Western Heaven, and that his senior disciple had hit him on the head and then run away. He asked if they could rest in her house. She agreed, and gave them some hot tea to drink. Tangseng drank the tea. After a while he felt better. He said to his disciples, "One of you must go and find that lawless monkey. He has our luggage which contains our travel rescript. You must bring back our luggage so we can continue our journey."

"I will go," replied Zhu. "I have been to Flower Fruit Mountain before. I know the way."

"No," replied the Tang monk. "That monkey does not like you. And your words are often rude. He might become angry and attack you." Then turning to Sha Wujing he said, "Sha, you must go. Find the monkey. If he is willing to give you the luggage, just take it and return here. If he refuses, do not argue or fight with him. Just go to Potalaka Mountain, tell everything to Bodhisattva Guanyin, and ask her for help. We will wait here."

Sha Wujing traveled for three days to arrive at the Great Eastern Ocean. He smelled the salt water and felt the ocean winds. He flew across the ocean and soon arrived at Flower Fruit Mountain. Looking down, he saw Sun Wukong sitting on a high rock, surrounded by many other monkeys. Sha came down from the clouds and landed on the ground.

Immediately Sun Wukong shouted, "Seize him!" Dozens of monkeys surrounded Sha and grabbed his arms and legs so he could not move. They carried him to Sun Wukong, who said, "Who are you, to approach my cave without my permission?"

"I am your younger brother, Sha Wujing. Our master was angry at you and used the Tight Headband Spell on you. Your brother Zhu and I did not try to stop him. You asked him to stop using the spell but he refused. Then you hit him with your rod and flew here. If you have no anger towards us, return with me. Together we will continue on our journey to the west. But if you are still angry, just give me the luggage. You can stay here and enjoy your old age."

"Brother, you don't understand. I don't want to travel with you and the

Master. I have decided to go by myself to the Western Heaven. I will travel to Thunderclap Mountain, I will ask Buddha for the holy books, and I will deliver them to the Tang Emperor. My fame will last forever!"

"Elder brother, you are a little bit confused. The Buddha told the Bodhisattva Guanyin to find a monk in the eastern lands who would travel over a thousand mountains to reach the Western Heaven. It is the monk's fate to meet many troubles on the journey, that's why the three of us were released from our prisons and allowed to accompany him on the journey. The Buddha will never give the holy books to you alone."

"Ah, but I do have a Tang monk. And I have two other disciples. Monkeys, show him!" the little monkeys brought out a white horse. Riding the horse was a Tangseng. Standing next to him was a Zhu Bajie and a Sha Wujing.

Sha saw this and became furious. "Old Sand does not change his first name when he walks, he does not change his surname when he sits. There cannot be another like me!" Then he struck the second Sha with his staff, killing him instantly. The body of the dead Sha turned into a demon monkey spirit. Sun Wukong and the other monkeys surrounded Sha and started fighting with him. Sha flew away as fast as he could, saying to himself, "I need to see the Bodhisattva right away!"

A day and a night later he arrived at Potalaka Mountain. He came down slowly from the clouds. He was met by Moksha, who asked him, "Sha Wujing, why are you here? You should be with the Tang monk helping him to travel to the Western Heaven!"

"I must see the Bodhisattva!" replied Sha.

Moksha took him to see Guanyin. The Bodhisattva was sitting on a wooden platform in the purple bamboo forest. Underneath the platform sat Sun Wukong. He said to himself, "The Tang monk must be in trouble, that's why Sha is here."

Sha approached the platform. He planned to tell Guanyin his story. But before he could start, he looked under the platform and saw Sun Wukong sitting there. Instantly he tried to strike the monkey with his staff, shouting, "You lawless monkey! You tried to kill our Master! How dare you come here and try to fool the Bodhisattva?" Sun Wukong simply stepped aside, dodging the blow.

"Stop it!" said Guanyin. "Wujing, if you have a problem with this monkey, tell me. Don't hit him."

Sha put down his staff. He kowtowed to Guanyin and told her everything, starting with Sun Wukong killing the two bandit chiefs, and finishing with the story of the fight at Flower Fruit Mountain.

"Wujing, you are blaming the wrong person. Sun Wukong has been here with me for the last four days. I have not let him go anywhere."

"But I saw him at Flower Fruit Mountain! Do you think I am lying?"

"Please don't get upset. You and Wukong must go to Flower Fruit Mountain and take a look together. Lies will be destroyed but truth will remain." And so, Sun Wukong and Sha Wujing flew together to find the truth at Flower Fruit Mountain.

Chapter 58

Sun Wukong's cloud somersault was much faster than Sha's cloud flying. Soon he was far ahead of Sha. "Slow down," said Sha, "Don't try to arrive before me and change things before I see what's going on." So Sun Wukong slowed down to travel next to Sha.

After a day and a night of flying they arrived at Flower Fruit Mountain. Looking down, they saw a Sun Wukong sitting on a high rock. He looked just like the other Sun Wukong. He had a gold headband on his head, brown hair, diamond eyes, a hairy face with huge teeth. He wore a silk shirt, a kilt made of tiger skin, and deerskin boots. In his hand he held a golden hoop rod.

The real Sun Wukong shouted, "How dare you look like me, capture my little monkeys, and sit in my cave? Taste my rod!" The false Sun Wukong did not have time to reply. He raised his own rod. They began to fight. The poem says,

> Two iron rods
> Two fighting monkeys
> This fight was no small thing!
> Both wanted to travel to the west
> The true monkey follows the Buddha
> The false monkey follows no one
> They both have powerful magic
> Their fighting skills are equal
> They start fighting at the cave
> But soon rise into the air
> They fight a long time but neither can win

Sha watched the two fighting monkeys. He wanted to help Sun Wukong but he could not tell which was the truth and which was the false. Looking for something to do, he came down to the ground and killed the little monkey demons. Then he smashed all the stone furniture. Then he looked for the luggage but he could not find it, because the luggage was hidden behind a waterfall in Water Curtain Cave. Finally he flew up into the clouds again to continue watching the fight.

"Sha," shouted one of the monkeys, "go back to Master and tell him the situation. Let Old Monkey fight this demon. I will bring him to Potalaka Mountain and let Guanyin tell truth from false."

The other monkey shouted, "Sha, go back to Master and tell him the situation. Let Old Monkey fight this demon. I will bring him to Potalaka Mountain and let Guanyin tell truth from false."

Both monkeys sounded exactly the same and looked exactly the same. Sha did not know what to do, so he did what both monkeys told him to do. He returned to report to Tangseng.

The fight continued in the sky. The two monkeys used their cloud somersaults to fly to Potalaka Mountain, fighting all the way. They arrived at Potalaka Mountain. Moksha entered Guanyin's cave and told her, "Bodhisattva, two Sun Wukongs have just arrived. They are fighting."

Guanyin left her cave and went to see them, followed by Moksha and her other disciple Shancai. One of the monkeys said to her, "Bodhisattva, this demon resembles me but he is false. Our fight started on Flower Fruit Mountain and continues here. It is difficult for me to defeat this false one. Sha could not tell truth from false, so he could not help me. Please help your disciple. Tell truth from false, tell real from unreal!"

Then the other monkey said exactly the same thing.

Guanyin looked at them, then she said, "Both of you stop fighting. Stand apart, let me look at you." They stopped fighting and stood looking at her. She told Moksha to grab one of them and Shancai to grab the other. Then she recited the Tight Headband Spell. Both monkeys screamed and clutched their heads with their hands. They started rolling on the ground while still fighting each other.

Guanyin said to them, "Sun Wukong!" Both of them stopped fighting and looked at her. "Five hundred years ago you caused great trouble in Heaven. All the great ones in Heaven know you. Go there now, and let them tell which one of you is true and which is false."

The two Sun Wukongs both thanked her, then they flew up to the South Heaven Gate, fighting all the way. They flew through the gate and all the way to the palace of the Jade Emperor. The four masters of Heaven saw them coming and said to the emperor, "Two Sun Wukongs from the land below have arrived. They are fighting. They want to see Your Majesty." But before they were finished speaking, the two fighting monkeys flew into the palace and rolled around on the floor in front of the emperor's throne.

The emperor looked down at them and asked quietly, "Why are you here without permission, fighting in front of me? Are you both seeking death?"

One of them said, "Your Majesty! Your Majesty! I am sorry for disturbing you, but this demon has taken my form…" and then he told the entire story to the Jade Emperor. When he was finished, the other monkey said exactly the same words.

The emperor said to his servants, "Bring me the Demon-Reflecting Mirror!" They brought the magic mirror. He looked in the mirror at the two monkeys. Both monkeys looked back at him from the mirror, looking exactly the same. He said to them, "I cannot help you. Leave this place at once."

Rolling out of the palace, fighting all the way, they said to each other, "I will go and see Master!"

Back on earth, Sha Wujing had returned to the little hut where Tangseng and Zhu were staying. He told them, "I went to Flower Fruit Mountain. There I saw Sun Wukong. I also saw a Zhu and a Sha and a Master on a white horse. I killed the Sha and saw that it was a monkey demon spirit. Then I went to see Guanyin. When I arrived at her home, the true Sun Wukong was there. We went together back to Flower Fruit Mountain. The two monkey kings saw each other and started to fight. I could not tell the true from the false, so I returned here."

Just as he finished speaking, they heard a loud sound. They looked up in the sky. They saw the two monkey kings shouting and fighting with each other. Zhu said, "Let me see if I can tell them apart." He flew into the air towards them.

Both Sun Wukongs shouted at Zhu, "Brother, come and help me fight this demon!"

Down below in the little hut, the women saw the two monkeys fighting in the sky. One said, "Well, there certainly are a lot of people here! I must bring out more food." She started preparing rice and tea. The other woman said, "I wish they would stop fighting. I fear that they will cause great trouble in Heaven and on earth."

Sha said, "Don't worry, grandmother." Then he said to Tangseng, "Master, I will go up and tell these two to stop fighting. Zhu and I will bring them to you, and you can sort this out." Flying into the air, he said, "You two, stop fighting right now. Master wants to see both of you." They both stopped fighting and flew down to earth. They stood outside the house, waiting.

Tangseng told Zhu to grab one of the monkeys, and Sha to grab the other. He then recited the Tight Headband Spell. Both monkeys screamed and grabbed their heads with their hands. Tangseng stopped. "I cannot tell the two of you apart," he said.

The two monkeys said at the same time, "Brothers, take care of Master. I will go to see Yama, the King of the Underworld." The two of them flew off to see Yama.

After they left, Zhu asked Sha why he did not bring back the luggage from Flower Fruit Mountain. "I did not see it," replied Sha.

"You don't know that behind the waterfall is a secret cave called Water Curtain Cave. That's where the Monkey King lives. I think that he put our luggage there. This would be a good time for me to go and get the luggage."

"Be careful, brother," said Sha. "Over a thousand monkey demons are guarding the cave."

"Don't worry about me!" laughed Zhu, and he flew away to Flower Fruit Mountain.

The two fighting monkeys arrived at the underworld, at the Mountain of Darkness. The spirits of the underworld saw them coming. Terrified, they tried to hide. A few ran into the Hall of Darkness and said to the Ten Kings of the Underworld, "Great Kings, there are two Great Sages Equal to Heaven coming. They are fighting like two angry tigers." The ten kings gathered in the Hall of Darkness. They called all the soldiers of the underworld to come and capture the two monkeys. They waited in the dark. Soon they felt a strong cold wind, and the two fighting monkeys fell to the floor and rolled around, kicking and biting each other.

Yama, the greatest of the ten kings, said to them, "Why are the two of you coming and causing trouble here in my kingdom?"

One of the monkeys kicked away the other one. He stood up and said, "Your Majesty, I was traveling with the Tang monk towards the Western Heaven. We were attacked by a group of bandits. I killed a few of them. My Master was angry with me and sent me away. I went to see the Bodhisattva Guanyin to ask her for advice. While I was there, this demon," and he pointed to the other monkey, "took my form and went to my home at Flower Fruit Mountain. He wants to go by himself to the Western Heaven to see the Buddha and take the holy books for himself. I tried to stop him but I cannot win a fight against him because he is my equal. Nobody can tell us apart. I have asked the Jade Emperor and the Bodhisattva Guanyin and my Master, but none of them can help me."

The other monkey waited until he finished, then he said the exact same thing, word for word.

Yama called for one of his ministers to bring out the Long Life Book. This book has the names of all living beings in it – people, monkeys and animals. There was a special chapter in the book for Heaven born stone monkeys. That chapter had only one page, but it was crossed out. Yama said to the monkeys, "I cannot help you."

But before the two monkeys could leave, the Bodhisattva Dizang said, "Wait. Let me ask Investigative Hearing, maybe he can help us."

Investigative Hearing was a beast who lived under the desk of the Bodhisattva Dizang. He can instantly see truth or false among all creatures of the underworld, the earthly world, and the Heavenly worlds. The beast came out from under the desk. He looked carefully at the two monkeys. Then he said to the kings, "I know which one is the demon and which is the disciple of the Tang monk. But I cannot tell you."

"Why not?" asked Dizang.

"If I say which one is the demon, he will cause great trouble here. His powers are as great as Sun Wukong himself. He could destroy the Hall of Darkness and kill all of us. We are not strong enough to defeat him."

"What can we do?"

Investigative Hearing just said, "The Buddha's power has no limit."

Both monkeys jumped up and shouted, "Yes! I will go to Thunderclap Mountain and see the Buddha himself!" The great beings in the Hall of Darkness watched with relief as the two monkeys flew through the air, out of the Underworld, fighting all the way.

The two monkeys quickly arrived at Thunderclap Mountain in the Western Heaven. Thousands of monks and nuns were listening to a lecture by the Buddha. The lecture was about the real and the unreal, empty and non-empty, knowledge and non-knowledge. Then the Buddha said, "You all have one mind. But now look at two minds fighting against each other."

The monks and nuns looked up and saw the two fighting monkeys. The eight Golden Kings tried to stop them from entering, shouting, "Where do you two think you are going?"

One of the monkeys said, "A monster spirit has taken my appearance, I want to ask the great Buddha to tell the truth from the false." Then he told the entire story. When he was finished, the other monkey said the same thing.

They waited for the Buddha to speak. But while they waited, a pink cloud appeared, and Guanyin stepped out of the cloud. The Buddha smiled at her and said, "Guanyin, can you tell which is the true and which is the false?"

"I tried but I cannot. That is why I have come here, to beg you to do this, to help the Tang monk complete his journey."

The Buddha smiled again and spoke. "You have great knowledge and you can see very far, but you cannot know all things. There are five kinds of immortals and there are five kinds of creatures[1]. This fellow is not any of those."

Guanyin waited, and the Buddha spoke again. "However, there are four kinds of monkeys which do not belong to any of these ten kinds. The first is the Heaven-born stone monkey, it has great power and can change the path of the stars and planets. The second is the baboon, it understands the affairs of humans and has knowledge of yin and yang. The third is the gibbon, it can grab the sun and moon and destroy a thousand mountains. And the fourth is the six-eared macaque, it has knowledge of past and future and understands all things. This false Wukong must be a six-eared macaque because he has knowledge of events a thousand miles away[2]."

When the Buddha said this, the false Sun Wukong shook with fear. He jumped up and tried to fly away. The Buddha ordered the thousands of monks and nuns to encircle him. The true Sun Wukong ran to help, but the Buddha said to him, "Wukong, don't move. Let me capture him for you."

The false Sun Wukong changed into a bee and flew straight up into the air. The Buddha threw a golden begging bowl into the air. It caught the bee and brought it down to the ground. All the monks and nuns thought that the bee had escaped, but the Buddha said, "No, the monster spirit has not escaped. Look!" He lifted up the begging bowl. Under the bowl was a six-eared macaque.

Sun Wukong lifted his golden hoop rod and brought it down on the macaque, killing it instantly. The Buddha was not happy about this, but he simply

---

[1] The five kinds of immortals are the celestial, the earthbound, the divine, the human, and the ghostly. The five kinds of creatures are the short haired, the long haired, the scaly, the winged, and the crawling.
[2] This macaque's six ears represent the ears of a third party eavesdropping without permission on the Buddha's secret teaching.

looked at Sun Wukong and said, "Now it is time for you to return to your Master. You must help him on his journey."

Sun Wukong kowtowed to the Buddha and replied, "O great Buddha, I must tell you that my Master does not want me to return to him. He does not want my help. Please remove the headband from my head so that I can return to my old life on Flower Fruit Mountain."

"Stop this foolish talk and don't cause any more trouble," said the Buddha. "Guanyin will take you back to your Master. He will not turn you away. Later, when your journey is finished, you will sit on a lotus throne."

Guanyin pressed her palms together. The two of them rose up to the clouds and flew back to the little hut where Tangseng and Sha Wujing were waiting. She said to Tangseng, "Please don't be angry with Sun Wukong. He did not strike you. It was a false Sun Wukong, a six-eared macaque. The Buddha himself showed us the difference between the true and false Wukongs. Then the true Sun Wukong killed the false one. Your journey is not finished yet, and many dangers still wait for you on the path. You will need the protection of Sun Wukong on your journey. Please take him back."

Tangseng bowed to her and simply said, "I will do as you ask."

A short time later, Zhu returned from Flower Fruit Mountain with the luggage. He saw Guanyin and kowtowed to her. She told him the story of everything that had happened at Thunderclap Mountain. Then Tangseng and the three disciples all bowed to give thanks to Guanyin. She returned to her home in the South Sea. The travelers thanked the two women who had taken care of them. Then they left the little hut and continued on their journey to the west.

Chapter 59

The four travelers let go of their anger and continued on their journey to the west. The poem says,

> Anger weakens the Five Phases[1]
> But the demon's defeat brings light from Heaven
> Spirit returns, heart/mind is quiet
> Six senses are quiet, elixir is near

The travelers saw the end of summer's heat and the arrival of autumn. Green leaves turned yellow and red. Wild geese flew across the sky. The water in the streams became cold. There was morning frost on the grasses and trees, and they could see snow on distant mountaintops.

However, as the travelers approached a village, they felt the weather become warmer. Tangseng said, "Disciples, it is now autumn, why does it feel like summer?"

Zhu replied, "Master, I think we are approaching the Edge of Heaven. This is where the sun comes down to the Western Sea every evening. When the sun touches the water, huge clouds of steam come up from the sea. I think we are feeling the heat from that steam."

Sun Wukong laughed and said, "Zhu, you are an idiot. Master could travel for several lifetimes and still not reach the Edge of Heaven. There must be some other reason for this heat."

Soon they came to some buildings. The roofs were red, the doors were red, the brick walls were red, and the wooden benches were red. Tangseng pointed to one of the houses, saying, "Wukong, go to that house and try to learn why the weather is so hot."

Sun Wukong left the main road and walked towards the house. Just then an old man came out from the house. He wore a robe that was not quite yellow and not quite red. His hat was not quite blue and not quite black. His boots were not quite new and not quite old. His eyebrows were white and some of

---

[1] The five phases or natural forces are: fire (huǒ), water (shuǐ), wood (mù), metal or gold (jīn), and earth (tǔ). They form a cycle. A writing from the 6th century BC says, "Heaven has produced the five elements which supply humankind's requirements, and the people use them all. Not one of them can be dispensed with."

his teeth were gold. He became afraid when he saw Sun Wukong.

Sun Wukong bowed to the man and said, "Please don't be afraid, grandfather. I am a disciple of a monk from the Tang Empire. He was sent by the Tang Emperor to seek holy scriptures in the west. There are four of us. We have just arrived here. Right away we felt the heat. Can you please tell us why it is so hot here?"

The old man relaxed a bit, saying, "Please don't be offended, my friend. This old man cannot see very well. Where is your master? Please ask him to come here." Tangseng and the other two disciples walked towards the house, and the old man invited all four of them inside his house for tea.

"You have come to the Mountain of Flames," he said while pouring tea. "There is no springtime here and no autumn. All four seasons are hot. The mountain is about sixty miles west of here. The mountain's fire spreads for four hundred miles in both directions, blocking the road. You cannot get past it. And if you touch the mountain, you will burn or turn to liquid." When Tangseng heard this, he became very afraid.

Just then, a young man came to the door of the house. He was selling rice cakes. Sun Wukong pulled a hair from his head and turned it into a coin. He gave the coin to the young man to buy some rice cakes. But the cakes were so hot that Sun Wukong could not hold it in his hand. He threw it from one hand to the other, crying out in pain every time the cakes touched his hand.

"My friends," laughed the young man, "If you don't like heat, you should not be here!"

Sun Wukong replied, "Young man, if it is so hot here, how do you grow rice to make rice cakes?" The young man replied,

> "If it's rice you desire,
> You must from Immortal Iron Fan inquire."

"What does that mean?" asked Sun Wukong.

"Immortal Iron Fan has a magic plantain leaf fan. One wave of his fan puts out the fire. A second wave brings a cool breeze. A third wave brings the rain. When Immortal Iron Fan waves his fan, we can grow the five grains and have food to eat."

"Master," said Sun Wukong, "I will find this Immortal Iron Fan. I will ask him to give me the fan. First, we will use the fan to put out the fire on the mountain so we can travel to the west. Then I will give the fan to these people so they can grow the five grains in a normal way."

The old man said, "He will not give you the fan. You people don't have any gifts. Once every ten years, the Immortal Iron Fan meets with the families in this region. The families give him hogs, sheep, chickens, geese, wine and flowers. They beg him to control the fire so they can grow the five grains."

"Tell me where he lives."

"He lives on Jade Cloud Mountain, in a cave called Plantain Leaf Cave. It's about 1,450 miles from here. It will take you more than a month to get there. And there are many tigers and wolves."

"That won't be a problem," laughed the Monkey King. He jumped into the air and disappeared. A few seconds later he arrived at Jade Cloud Mountain. He looked down and saw a man cutting wood. He came down to the ground and walked up to the woodcutter, bowed and said, "Brother woodsman, please accept my bow. Would you please tell me where I can find Jade Cloud Mountain, Plantain Leaf Cave and the Immortal Iron Fan?"

The woodsman bowed and replied, "Greetings, sir. You have arrived at the correct mountain, and the cave that you seek is nearby. But I must tell you that there is nobody named Immortal Iron Fan. However there is Princess Iron Fan, also called Raksasi. She has a plantain leaf fan that can extinguish fires. She is the wife of the Bull Demon King."

Sun Wukong blinked in surprise. The Bull Demon King was his old friend and brother from five hundred years earlier. But Sun Wukong was almost burned to death by the king's son Red Boy when the boy tried to kill him with five carts full of magic fire. He also remembered Red Boy's uncle who was angry at Sun Wukong and refused to give him magic water at the Child Destruction Cave in the Country of Women. Now it looks like he will meet Red Boy's mother and perhaps his father.

The woodsman saw Sun Wukong lost in his thoughts. He said, "Elder, you are a monk. You have left the family. Do not worry about the past or the future. Go and see Raksasi. Think only of borrowing the fan, and do not hold onto any old grudges. I am sure you will get what you are seeking."

Sun Wukong bowed deeply and replied, "I thank brother woodsman for his wise words." He walked a short distance to the entrance to the Plantain Leaf Cave. He pounded on the door and shouted, "Open the door!"

The door opened slowly. A young girl walked out. She wore old rags and had a bunch of flowers in her hand. On her shoulder was a small rake. Sun Wukong said, "Little girl, please tell Raksasi that Sun Wukong from the land of Tang is here to see her. I wish to borrow her fan."

The girl went into the cave and reported this to Raksasi. When Raksasi heard that Sun Wukong had arrived, it was as if oil was poured on a fire. She jumped up and shouted, "That wretched ape is here? Maids, bring me my armor and my weapons!" She put on a robe with a belt made of two tiger tendons. In each hand she held a sword of blue steel. She looked more fierce than a yaksa. Running out of the cave, she shouted, "Where is Sun Wukong?"

Sun Wukong bowed and said to her, "Sister-in-law, old Monkey is here to greet you."

"How dare you call me sister-in-law?"

"Many years ago, your husband Bull Demon King was my old friend and brother. Why should I not call you sister-in-law?"

"Wretched ape, why did you capture my son?"

Sun Wukong pretended not to understand. "Who is your son?"

"He is Red Boy, the Great King Holy Child. You brought him down. I wanted revenge, and now here you are!"

Sun Wukong smiled and said, "Dear sister-in-law, I think you have not quite understood the situation. Your boy captured my master and wanted to cook and eat him. The Bodhisattva Guanyin captured the boy and rescued my master. He became a disciple of Guanyin and he is now quite happy. He is the same age as Heaven and Earth, he will live as long as the sun and moon. You should thank Old Monkey for helping your son!"

She spat at him. "You lying monkey. How can I ever see my son again?"

"That's not a problem. Just lend us your fan. We will put out the fire on the mountain so that my master can continue on his journey to the west. Then I will go to visit Guanyin and invite her and your son to come and see you."

"Stop flapping your tongue, you wretched monkey. Bend over and let me hit your head a few times with my blue steel sword. If you can endure the pain, I will lend you the fan."

Sun Wukong agreed to this. He bent over so that Raksasi could see his neck. Raksasi struck his neck with her blue steel sword ten or fifteen times. The sword just bounced off his neck. She turned and tried to run away, but Sun

Wukong said, "Sister-in-law, where are you going? Did you forget your promise? Have a taste of my rod!" He pulled his tiny golden hoop rod out of his ear and whispered "Change." It grew to a full-sized rod as thick as a rice bowl. He tried to strike Raksasi, but she blocked his blow with her swords. Soon they were fighting, completely forgetting about being friendly to each other.

Raksasi was a very skilled fighter and Sun Wukong could not easily defeat her. They fought for several hours, not even noticing that the sun had set. Raksasi started to become tired. She dropped one of the swords and waved her fan. A powerful gust of cold air blew towards the Monkey King. He was pushed far away like a leaf in the wind. Raksasi returned to her cave and closed the door.

Sun Wukong was blown by the wind all night. In the morning he finally was able to grab onto a mountaintop and stop moving. He rested for a few minutes. Then he stood up and looked around. He saw that he was on Little Sumeru Mountain. He thought, "I know this place. Several years ago, I fought the Demon Yellow Wind on this mountain. The Bodhisattva Lingji helped me then. Maybe I should find her and see if she can help us."

He walked down the mountain and approached a small temple. A temple worker saw him. The worker went inside and told the Bodhisattva, "That hairy faced ape is here again to see you."

Lingji greeted Sun Wukong, saying, "It's good to see you again, Wukong. Has your master reached the end of his journey yet?"

"No. In the years since you helped us defeat Demon Yellow Wind, we have climbed many mountains, walked many miles, and fought many monsters. Our path is now blocked by the Mountain of Flames. There is a fan that can put out the flames, but the owner of that fan will not give it to us. She is the wife of my old friend the Bull Demon King. But she is very angry with me because I helped to introduce her son to the Bodhisattva Guanyin. The boy is now Guanyin's disciple. She started a fight with me, then she waved her fan and blew me all the way here."

"I know her and I know that fan. It was created by Heaven and Earth many years ago, when the chaos was first divided. It can extinguish all fires. If a person is fanned by it, they will travel eighty-four thousand miles. You are very powerful so it only blew you fifty thousand miles."

"Wonderful fan!" exclaimed Sun Wukong. "How can my master overcome this?"

"You can relax. Many years ago, the Buddha himself gave me a Wind Arresting Elixir but I have never used it. I will give it to you. You can use it to take the fan, extinguish the fire, and help your master." She took out a small silk bag from her sleeve. Inside the bag was the Wind Arresting Elixir. She sewed the silk bag onto Sun Wukong's shirt. She said, "There's no time for us to drink tea. Go now!"

Using his cloud somersault, the Monkey King returned quickly to Jade Cloud Mountain. He pounded on the door with his rod, shouting, "Open the door! Old Monkey wants to borrow your fan!"

Raksasi was surprised that Sun Wukong had returned so quickly. She was a bit worried. But she put on her armor again, and walked out of the cave to meet him. She said, "So, you are seeking death again?"

"Dear sister-in-law, please lend me your fan. I am a real gentleman. I will always return what I borrow!"

"Have a taste of this old lady's swords!" she shouted, and attacked him with her two blue steel swords. Sun Wukong easily fought her off and began to beat her with his rod. She dropped one of the swords, grabbed her fan, and waved it at him. Nothing happened.

Sun Wukong smiled at her and said, "This time is not the same as last time. Wave that fan at me as much as you like. I am not going anywhere." Raksasi turned and ran back into the cave, locking the door behind her.

Sun Wukong pulled the silk bag off his shirt and popped the magic elixir into his mouth. Then he changed into a little cricket. He crawled under the door and into the cave. Raksasi was sitting in her chair, drinking a cup of hot tea. When she wasn't looking, he jumped into the teacup. She opened her mouth to sip her tea. Sun Wukong jumped into her mouth and went down into her stomach. Then he shouted, "Sister-in-law, lend me your fan!"

Raksasi was confused. She asked her maids, "Did you lock the door?" They told her that they did. "Where are you?" she cried.

"I'm just having a little bit of fun in my dear sister in law's stomach. How does this feel?"

He stomped his foot down, causing sharp pain in her lower abdomen. She fell to the floor, crying in pain. Then he jerked his head upward, causing sharp pain in her heart. She rolled around on the ground, the pain turning her face yellow. She cried out, "Please, brother-in-law, don't kill me!"

"Ah, so now I am your brother-in-law? Good. Give me the fan."

"I will. Just come out of my stomach."

"No. I want to see it first. And I will be kind to you and not make a hole in your stomach. Open your mouth and I will come out." She opened her mouth. A small cricket flew out of her mouth but she did not see it. She kept holding her mouth open, waiting for Sun Wukong to come out. Sun Wukong changed back into monkey form, picked up the fan, thanked her, and walked out of the cave.

He returned to Tangseng and the other disciples and told them the story of how he obtained the fan. Then the travelers thanked the old man and headed west. They walked about forty miles and got close to the Mountain of Flame. It was very, very hot. Sha and Zhu said that their feet were on fire. Even the white horse was uncomfortable. "Wukong, use the fan!" shouted Tangseng.

Sun Wukong waved the fan at the mountain. After one wave, the fire grew bigger than before. After the second wave, the fire grew a hundred times brighter than before. After the third wave, the fire leaped ten thousand feet into the air and started coming towards them. "Run away!" shouted Sun Wukong. "That princess has tricked me!" His hair and clothing started to burn.

Tangseng's horse galloped for twenty miles with Tangseng holding on tightly. The three disciples followed close behind. Tangseng began to cry, saying, "What shall we do? What shall we do?"

Sha said to Sun Wukong, "Elder brother, why did the fire burn you? I thought fire could not harm you."

"I was not prepared for the fire," he replied. "I had no time to make the fire repelling sign." Turning to Tangseng he said, "Master, perhaps we can head north and go around the mountain."

"I do not want to go north or south or east," said Tangseng. "The scriptures are in the west and that is where I want to go."

"Well, this is a problem," said Sha.

> "Where there are scriptures there is fire.
> Where there is no fire, there are no scriptures."

Just then, an old man arrived. On his shoulder was a demon with the head of a hawk and the face of a fish. "I am the local spirit of the Mountain of Flames," he said. "Raksasi has tricked you and given you a false fan."

"We know that," said Sun Wukong angrily. "What can we do now?"

The local spirit smiled and said,

> "If it's the real fan you desire,
> You must from the powerful King inquire."

Chapter 60

Sun Wukong said, "So, this fire was created by the Bull Demon King?"

The local spirit replied, "No. Please don't be angry at me for telling you this, but this fire was set by the Great Sage Equal to Heaven. That's you."

Sun Wukong's eyes grew big and he became angry. "How can you say that? Do you think I am someone who sets fires?"

"Please let go of your anger, Great Sage. You met me once before but you don't recognize me. Long ago, you caused great trouble in Heaven. Laozi put you in a brazier for forty-nine days. When he opened it, you jumped out and fought with everyone in Heaven. You did not notice that you knocked over the brazier. Two bricks from the brazier fell from Heaven to earth. Those bricks became the Mountain of Flames. At that time, I was a worker at the temple. My job was to take care of the brazier. Laozi blamed me for letting the bricks fall to earth, so he threw me out of Heaven and changed me into the mountain's local spirit."

"So, why must I go and see the Bull Demon King?"

"As you know, the Bull Demon King is the husband of Raksasi. Several years ago, he left her and now lives in Cloud Touching Cave on another mountain far from here. That cave was once the home of a fox demon, but after ten thousand years he died. The fox demon had a daughter named Princess Jade Face. This girl is also a fox demon. She inherited her father's cave and also his great fortune. Two years ago, she heard that the Bull Demon King had great magical powers. She became his girlfriend. He lives with her and has not visited Raksasi in two years."

He continued, "If you visit Bull Demon King and get the fan you can do three good deeds at once. You can help your master continue on his journey to the west. You can help the people in this region by eliminating the fire. And you will allow me to return to Heaven."

Sun Wukong nodded. "Where is this Cloud Touching Cave?"

"About three thousand miles south of here," replied the local spirit. Sun Wukong told Zhu and Sha to take care of Tangseng. He told the local spirit to stay there to guard them. Then he jumped into the air and flew away to the south.

Soon he arrived at the mountain that had the Cloud Touching Cave. It was a huge mountain. Its top touched the blue sky. He did not know where the cave was, so he dropped to the ground and began walking around. He heard a sound, looked up, and saw a young woman walking towards him. He hid behind a tree to watch her. What does she look like, you ask?

> She walks with slow careful steps
> Her face like Wang Qiang[1]
> Her face like a girl from Chu
> Like a beautiful flower
> Like a jade statue
> Her black hair is wound around her head
> Her green eyes shine like pools of water
> Red lips, white teeth
> Eyebrows as smooth as the River Jin
> She is more lovely than Zhuo Wenjun[2] and Xue Tao[3]

Sun Wukong came out from behind the tree and asked her, "Lady Bodhisattva, where are you going?"

She saw the ugly monkey and became frightened. "Where have you come from?" she asked. Sun Wukong tried to decide how to answer her. She waited for his reply, then said angrily, "Tell me who you are and why you dare question me?"

Sun Wukong finally found the words to say, "Madam, I have come from Jade Cloud Mountain. This is my first visit to your beautiful region. I am looking for Cloud Touching Cave. Can you tell me where I can find it?"

"Why do you seek this cave?"

"I was sent by Princess Iron Fan to find the Bull Demon King and bring him back to her."

Of course, the girl was Princess Jade Face. She became furious. She shouted, "That filthy slut! My lover, the Bull Demon King, has lived with me for two

---

[1] A brilliant and dazzlingly beautiful girl, a concubine of Emperor Yuan of Han, she volunteered to marry a chieftan of the nomadic Xiongyu tribes to help bring peace to the region. Over 700 songs and poems have been written about her.

[2] A poet in the 2nd century BC. As a young widow she eloped with a poet. Later he left her and took a concubine. She wrote him a letter about the inconstancy of male love, which became a famous poem, "White Haired Lament."

[3] A famous poet in the Tang Dynasty. Over 100 of her poems survive to the present day.

years. In that time, he has sent many gifts to her. He gave her jewels, diamonds and silk cloth. He gives her firewood to keep her warm, and rice to keep her fed. That woman has no shame! Why does she want you to bring him back to her?"

Sun Wukong realized who the girl was. He waved his golden hoop rod at her and bellowed, "You bitch! You used your father's wealth to buy the Bull Demon King. You are the one who should feel shame, not me!"

As he hoped, the girl turned and ran away, leading him back to the Cloud Touching Cave. She ran inside and locked the door. She ran into the back of the cave, where the Bull Demon King was sitting in the library reading a book. She jumped up and down, screaming at him, "You wretched demon! I took you in because I wanted protection and care. But now you have almost killed me! There is a hairy monkey outside the cave. He told me that your wife wants you to return to her. Then he waved his big rod at me and almost killed me."

Bull Demon King listened to this calmly. Then he said to her, "Pretty lady, there must be a mistake. My wife has studied the Way for many years. She is now an immortal. There are no men at her house. How could she send a man or a monkey to come here and make demands like that? It must be some kind of demon. I will go out and take a look."

He put on his armor, picked up an iron rod, and went outside the cave, saying, "Who is here causing trouble at my home?"

Sun Wukong bowed deeply and said, "Elder brother, don't you recognize me?"

"I think I know you. Aren't you Sun Wukong, the Great Sage Equal to Heaven?"

"Yes, I am. And I must say, my old friend, you are looking better than ever."

"Stop this talk! I have heard stories about you. I heard you caused trouble in Heaven and were trapped under Five Finger Mountain for five hundred years. And I heard that you have brought harm to my son Red Boy. I am really quite angry at you. Why are you here?"

Sun Wukong told the story of Red Boy's meeting with Guanyin and how he was now her disciple. Bull Demon King calmed down a little bit, but he said, "All right, but why did you try to hit my girlfriend?"

"I'm so sorry about that. I was trying to find you, and I asked her where your cave was. I did not know that she was my second sister-in-law. Please forgive me, old friend."

"All right, I forgive you. Now go away."

"I must ask a favor of you. I am helping the Tang monk journey to the Western Heaven. Our path is blocked by the Mountain of Flames. Your wife has a magic fan that can put out the fire so we can cross. We asked to borrow it, but she refused. I believe you have that magic fan. Please let us borrow it. As soon as we cross the mountain, I will return it to you."

"So, you are not here as my friend. You want something from me. All right, here's what we will do. We will fight. If you can last three rounds against me, you can borrow the fan." And before Sun Wukong could say anything, Bull Demon King brought his iron rod down on the monkey's head.

Sun Wukong stepped aside to avoid the rod. They began to fight. At first, they fought on the ground but they soon rose up into the air. They shouted insults at each other, forgetting their old friendship. They fought all day but neither one could win. Just before sunset, a voice called out from the mountaintop saying, "King Bull, my master invites you to dinner. Please come and enjoy a banquet at his home."

Bull Demon King stopped fighting and said, "Monkey, I must go now. We will continue this later." He dropped to the ground, went inside his cave and said to Princess Jade Face, "My dear, I must leave to go drink at a friend's house. Don't go outside, the ugly monkey is out there." He removed his armor and put on a green silk jacket. Then he was gone.

Sun Wukong saw Bull Demon King fly away. He followed him to another mountain, and he saw the old bull jump into a pool of water. Sun Wukong changed into a crab and jumped in after him. Diving down to the bottom of the pool, he saw a great banquet hall. Many guests were there. They were eating, talking, and listening to music played by fish and other aquatic creatures. Young boys played wooden flutes.

Bull Demon King sat in the seat of honor. Female dragon spirits sat on his right side and left side. Across from him sat an old dragon. Next to the old dragon were many sons, grandsons, daughters and granddaughters. They were all drinking wine and talking loudly.

Sun Wukong crab-walked into the middle of the room. The old dragon saw him and shouted, "Seize that crab!" Several of the dragon's sons rushed forward and grabbed him.

"Oh, don't kill me, don't kill me!" shouted Sun Wukong.

"Where do you come from, wild crab, and why are you here? Tell me quickly and we will not kill you."

"Great King, since birth I have lived in a small cave and looked for food in the lake. But I have never learned to walk properly. I am sorry if I did something to anger you, please forgive me!"

The dragon's sons asked the old dragon to let the crab leave, and the old dragon agreed. Sun Wukong crab-walked out of the banquet hall. He swam up and out of the pool of water and changed back into his original monkey form. He said to himself, "I don't think I should wait for Bull Demon King to leave, he might be there for several days. I will take his form and go to see Raksasi. I will try to get her to give me the fan. This plan is faster and safer." He changed into the form of the old bull and rode his cloud somersault back to Plantain Leaf Cave.

He knocked on the cave door, and servants let him in. He said to Raksasi, "Madam, it has been a long time!"

She looked at him and thought he was her husband. She replied, "I wish the Great King ten thousand blessings. It appears that he is so busy playing with his new girlfriend that he has forgotten this poor lady."

"I am sorry, my dear. I had many matters to attend to. But recently I heard that a monkey named Sun Wukong has come here to ask you for the fan. You must tell me if he comes back again. I will have him seized and chop him into small pieces."

"Oh husband, that monkey was here yesterday. He wanted to borrow the fan. I waved the fan at him and blew him away. But then he returned with some kind of magic that protected him from the fan's wind. He entered my stomach, causing me great pain. Then he took my fan and ran away."

"That is terrible! Why did you give him our greatest treasure?"

Raksasi laughed and said, "Please don't get angry. I gave him a fake fan."

"Ah, that's good. Where is the true fan?"

"Don't worry, I still have it. Now, my dear husband, please stay and have dinner with me." Servants brought food and wine. Sun Wukong dared not break his vegetarian diet, so he just ate a little fruit and drank a little wine.

Raksasi drank a lot of wine. She began feeling very friendly towards her husband. She moved closer to him and put her leg next to his. They both drank wine from the same cup. They gave fruit to each other. Sun Wukong had no choice but to laugh and pretend to be her husband. Raksasi became quite drunk. Sun Wukong saw his opportunity, so he asked her, "My dear, where did you put the real fan?"

Raksasi opened her mouth and spat out a tiny fan. Laughing, she handed it to him.

Sun Wukong stared at it. "How can this little thing extinguish eight hundred miles of flames?"

Raksasi swayed back and forth, barely able to sit up. She said, "Husband, you have spent the last two years playing with your little girlfriend. It has affected your mind and now you cannot remember anything at all. Remember, you touch the seventh red thread with your thumb. Then you say these magic words, *bi xu he xi Raksasi chui hu*[1]. The fan will grow to be twelve feet long, and it will easily put out the fires of the Mountain of Flame."

Sun Wukong took the tiny fan, popped it into his mouth, and changed back into his original monkey form. "Raksasi, take a good look at me. Am I your dear husband?" She fell to the ground, kicking and crying. He left the cave. He jumped into the air and immediately did what Raksasi told him. He touched the seventh red thread with his thumb and recited the magic words. Immediately the fan grew to be twelve feet long. "I wish I had learned the magic words to make it small again!" he thought.

Meanwhile back under the pool, Bull Demon King was finished eating and drinking with his friends. He got up to leave. "Where is that crab that was here earlier?" he asked. Nobody knew where the crab was. "Oh, now I understand. Before I came to this banquet, I was fighting with the Monkey King. He is very smart and has great skills. I think he took the form of a crab in order to find out what I was doing. I wonder if he has gone to see my wife to trick her into giving him the magic fan."

He leaped out of the pool and used a yellow cloud to fly to Plantain Leaf Cave. He entered the cave and found his wife crying and beating herself on the chest. "Where is Sun Wukong?" asked the Bull Demon King.

Raksasi hit him on the chest with her fists and shouted, "You idiot. How

---

[1] These words all are related to the act of expelling breath, which is part of Daoist practice of alchemy. It is said that only those who have perfected the Way (Dao) can utilize the power of these words.

could you allow that monkey to take your appearance and trick me?"

"Where is he?" repeated the king.

"He took our treasure, changed back to his original monkey form, and flew away. Oh, I am so angry I could die."

"Madam, take care of yourself and don't worry about that monkey. I will break every one of his bones." Then he shouted, "Bring me my armor and weapons!"

One of the maids said, "Sir, you don't live here anymore. Your armor and weapons are not here." Angrily, the Bull Demon King took off the silk jacket and threw it on the floor. He tightened up his belt around his undershirt, picked up his wife's two blue steel swords, and walked out of the cave to find Sun Wukong.

Chapter 61

The Bull Demon King saw Sun Wukong walking down the road, carrying the plantain leaf fan on his shoulders and singing a happy song. The King said to himself, "This monkey is very clever. He has taken the fan from my wife, and he also knows how to use it. If I just ask him for the fan, he will say no. He might even wave the fan at me. That would send me very far away. It would take me days to return." He thought some more. "I have heard that he is traveling with two other disciples, a pig-man and a flowing-sand spirit. I will change into the form of the pig-man and try to get my fan back."

Sun Wukong was feeling quite happy. He had tricked Raksasi into giving him the fan and the instructions for how to use it. So when he saw Zhu Bajie in the road, he did not even think that it might be a trick. He said to Zhu, "Brother, where are you going?"

Bull Demon King replied, "Master was worried because you did not return. He asked me to look for you."

"Here I am, and here is the fan! I saw Bull Demon King drinking and talking with his friends underwater. So I went to see Raksasi, pretending to be her husband. She was happy to see me. She drank a lot of wine, got drunk, and told me how to use it."

"That's wonderful. You look tired. Let me carry the fan for you."

Sun Wukong saw no problem with this, so he handed the fan to Bull Demon King. Immediately Bull Demon King changed into his true form and shouted, "Wretched ape, do you recognize me now?"

Sun Wukong shook his head slowly and said, "Oh, this is my fault. I have been hunting wild geese for years, and today a tiny goose has tricked me." Then he pulled his tiny golden hoop rod out of his ear, whispered "Change," and slammed the huge rod down hard on Bull Demon's head. Bull Demon moved aside to dodge the blow. Then he waved the fan at Sun Wukong. But Sun Wukong still had the Wind Arresting Elixir in his mouth so the fan did not move him at all.

Bull Demon King saw this and was frightened. He made the fan very small and popped it into his own mouth, then took his two blue steel swords and began to slash at Sun Wukong. The two kings fought like two dragons. Rocks, dirt and dust flew into the air, frightening ghosts and gods. As they fought, they hurled insults at each other. One used his rod, the other used his swords, but they had equal skill and neither could win. They fought for hours.

While the two kings were fighting, Tangseng was sitting by the side of the road. He was hot, hungry, thirsty and tired. "Where is that disciple?" he asked Zhu and Sha. "One of you should go and see where he is. Maybe he needs some help."

"I will go," said Zhu, "but I don't know how to get to Cloud Touching Cave."

"This humble deity knows the way," said the local mountain spirit. "I will go with the pig-man, if the sand spirit can stay and guard the holy monk." Sha, the sand spirit, agreed. So Zhu picked up his rake. He and the local spirit rose up into the clouds and fog and flew east to Cloud Touching Cave.

They arrived and saw Sun Wukong locked in battle with Bull Demon King. "Brother, I am here!" shouted Zhu.

"Is that really you?" shouted Sun Wukong. "You have tricked me once already today."

"What do you mean by that?"

"Earlier today I saw you coming towards me on the road. You wanted to carry the fan so I gave it to you. But then you changed into that wretched Bull Demon King. I have been fighting him ever since."

Zhu was very angry. He shouted at Bull Demon King, "How dare you take my form and cause trouble between me and my brother! Taste my rake!" He attacked Bull Demon King.

Bull Demon King was already tired from fighting all day against Sun Wukong. He turned to run away. But he saw the local mountain spirit and an army of ghost soldiers blocking his way.

The local spirit said, "Bull Demon King, you must stop now. Every god in Heaven will help the Tang monk finish his journey to the west. Everyone in the Three Regions knows about his journey. Quickly, use your fan to extinguish the flames on this mountain so that the monk may continue his travels. If you don't, everyone in Heaven will fight you and you will surely die."

Bull Demon King replied, "Local spirit, listen to me. This monkey has stolen my fan, insulted my girlfriend, tricked my wife, and taken my son away from me. I am so angry at him, I wish I could eat him, pass him through my stomach and out my rear end and feed him to my dogs! How can I give my treasure to him?"

The battle continued, with Bull Demon King fighting against Sun Wukong, Zhu, the local spirit and hundreds of ghost soldiers. They fought all evening and into the night. The moon rose, the stars came out, and still they fought. The next morning they were still fighting. They moved closer to the Cloud Touching Cave. Inside, Princess Jade Face heard the sound of the fighting. She looked out of the cave and saw her boyfriend fighting against an army of enemies. Quickly she called all her demon guards to join the fight. Over a hundred of them grabbed lances and rods and ran to help the Bull Demon King. They rushed at Zhu, who had to fall back in defeat. They rushed at Sun Wukong, who had to use his cloud somersault to escape. The local spirit and the ghost soldiers flew away in all four directions. Satisfied, the old bull and his demon guards returned to their cave and locked the door behind them.

Sun Wukong and Zhu were very tired. They sat down to talk. "How can we find a way to help Master cross this mountain?" asked Zhu.

The local spirit arrived and said, "Brother pig, there is no other way. Your master has said that he must travel west. Don't think about going north, south or east. You must walk on the correct road, no matter what!"

"Yes!" replied Sun Wukong. "We must fight to get the fan and extinguish the flames. Only then will we see the face of the Buddha."

Zhu jumped up and shouted, "Yes, yes, yes! Go, go, go! Who cares if the old bull says yes or no!"

The three of them were joined by the ghost soldiers. They rushed towards the cave door and smashed it. Bull Demon King and his demon guards rushed out of the cave, and the battle began again. The monkey used his rod, the pig used his rake, the old bull used his swords, and all the ghosts and demons used whatever weapons they had. The air was filled with fog, wind and rain. They fought in the sky from early morning until noon.

Exhausted, Bull Demon King turned and tried to return to his cave. But the local spirit blocked his way, shouting, "We are here, you cannot pass!" With nowhere else to go, the old bull threw down his weapons and armor, shook his body, changed into a white swan and flew into the air.

Sun Wukong shouted, "Zhu and local spirit, go back to the cave and kill all the demons. I will catch this old bull!" He flew high in the air, changed into a large vulture, and attacked the swan. Bull Demon King changed into an eagle and attacked the vulture. Sun Wukong changed into a huge black phoenix and attacked the eagle.

The old bull could not change into any other kind of bird, because the phoenix was the ruler of all birds and no bird would attack it. So he dropped to the ground and changed into a deer. Sun Wukong flew down, changed into a hungry tiger, and attacked the deer. Bull Demon King changed into a huge leopard and attacked the tiger. Sun Wukong changed from a tiger to a golden-eyed lion and attacked the leopard. Bull Demon King changed into a bear. The bear and the lion fought, rolling on the ground. Wukong changed into a huge gray elephant and tried to step on the bear.

Then Bull Demon King changed into his original form. He was a gigantic white bull. His head was like a mountain, his horns were like tall pagodas, his teeth were like long white swords. He was over a hundred feet tall. "Wretched ape, what will you do now?" he roared.

Sun Wukong changed into his own form, shouted "Grow!" and became as large as a mountain. His eyes were like the sun and moon, his teeth were like the doors of a palace. He lifted his mighty iron rod and brought it down on the old bull's huge head. They began to fight. The ground shook and mountains crumbled. The sound was so great that all the gods in Heaven heard it. The Golden Headed Guardian, the Six Gods of Darkness, the Six Gods of Light and the Eighteen Guardians of Monasteries all came. They surrounded Bull Demon King. The old bull attacked left, right, front and back, but each way was blocked by one or more of the gods of Heaven. With nowhere else to go, the old bull changed back to his normal size and ran away to join Raksasi in the Plantain Leaf Cave. He ran inside the cave and refused to come out.

Zhu ran up to the cave and smashed it with his rake. The doorway collapsed into a pile of rocks. Raksasi said to the old bull, "Dear husband, please, you cannot win. Just give them the fan."

He replied, "My dear, the fan is a small thing, but my anger is deep and wide. You wait here, I will fight them again."

He ran outside and began to slash at them with his blue steel swords. He could not win. He turned and flew to the north, where he was stopped by the Diamond Guardian of Vast Magical Powers who shouted at him, "Bull Demon, where are you going? I have been sent by Sakyamuni to capture you."

He turned and flew to the south, where he was stopped by the Diamond Guardian of Immeasurable Power, who shouted at him, "Bull Demon, the

Buddha himself told me to capture you."

His legs becoming weak, the old bull flew to the east. He was met by the Diamond Guardian of Great Strength, who shouted, "Where are you going, Bull Demon? I am here to arrest you."

Very afraid, the old bull turned and flew to the west. His way was blocked by the Diamond Guardian of Long Life, who shouted, "I am here by personal order of the Buddha of Thunderclap Mountain, I will not let you pass."

He looked all around and saw soldiers coming from all directions. He flew straight up. Devaraja Li and his son Prince Nata blocked his path. "Slow down!" they cried. "By the decree of the Jade Emperor we are here to arrest you."

He changed again into a huge white bull. But this time, Prince Nata changed into a man with three heads and six arms. He jumped onto the old bull's back. Nata brought his monster-killing sword down on the old bull's neck, cutting off its head. Nata prepared to jump off the old bull, but another head sprouted from the old bull's neck. Again Nata cut it off. Another head sprouted and Nata cut it off. This happened ten times.

Finally Nata grabbed his wheel of fire and placed it on one of the old bull's horns. The wheel began burning brightly with true immortal fire. The old bull tried to change its form, but Devaraja Li held the Demon Reflecting Mirror in front of the old bull, preventing it from changing form.

The old bull gave up. He said, "Please don't kill me. I will submit to the Buddha."

Nata replied, "If you want to save your own life, give us the fan quickly."

"I don't have it. My wife has it." Nata put a rope through the old bull's nose and led him back to the cave. All the gods of Heaven followed them. When they arrived at the cave, the Bull Demon King said, "Madam, please bring out the fan to save my life."

Raksasi heard his words. She took off all her jewelry and brightly colored clothing. She tied up her hair and put on a plain robe like a Buddhist nun. She walked out of the cave. She saw all the gods of Heaven standing in front of the cave. She fell to her knees, kowtowing to them. She said, "I beg the Bodhisattvas not to kill us. Here is the fan." Sun Wukong took the fan.

A few miles away, Tangseng and Sha still waited by the side of the road. They heard a sound and looked up. They saw dozens of gods and hundreds of warriors coming towards them. In front was Prince Nata, leading the old bull by his nose. Next to him was Devaraja Li, holding the magic mirror.

"What is going on?" Tangseng asked.

One of the guardians replied, "We are here to help you, by decree of the Buddha. You must continue on your journey. Do not give up, do not turn aside."

Sun Wukong turned to face the Mountain of Flame. He held the fan in his hand. He waved the fan once and all the fires went out, leaving just a little bit of golden light. He waved it a second time and everyone felt a cool breeze coming from the mountain. He waved it a third time. Clouds filled the sky and it began to rain. The poem says,

> The mountain of flames is eight hundred miles wide
> The fire burned all night, the elixir could not ripen
> But the plantain leaf fan brings clouds and cool rain
> The gods of Heaven have brought their power
> They lead the old bull to Buddha
> Water is joined to fire
> The world is calm.

The four travelers thanked the gods of Heaven, who all left to return to their various homes in Heaven. Devaraja Li and Prince Nata led the old bull to see Buddha at Thunderclap Mountain. Only the local spirit stayed. The local spirit and Sun Wukong both looked at Raksasi, who was still standing there.

"Raksasi," said Sun Wukong, "why are you still here?"

Raksasi got down on her knees and said, "I beg the Great Sage to please give me back my fan."

"What?" cried Zhu. "You don't know when to stop, do you?"

She ignored him and said to Sun Wukong, "Great Sage, you said that you would return the fan to me when you were finished using it. I will never hurt anyone again. I wish to follow the Buddha and the Way. Please give me back my fan, so I may start a new life."

The local spirit said, "Great Sage, this woman knows how to extinguish the flames forever. You should ask her to do it before you give her the fan. I will stay here and care for the people and creatures who live on this mountain."

Sun Wukong said to her, "The local people said that the flames are only extinguished for one year, then they return."

Raksasi said, "If you want the flames extinguished forever, you must wave the fan at the mountain forty-nine times."

Sun Wukong turned to face the mountain. He waved the fan forty-eight times. Then he waved it the forty ninth times. A great rain came. It extinguished all the fires on the mountain. But in the places where there was no fire, there was no rain.

The four travelers watched the rain for a while. Then they went into the cave and slept overnight. The next morning, they gave the fan back to Raksasi. Sun Wukong said to her, "I told you I would give the fan back to you, and now I have done that. Go now and don't cause any more trouble." She took the fan. She said a few magic words. The fan became very small and she popped it into her mouth. Then she left to study the Way of the Buddha.

The local spirit thanked the travelers. They began walking west towards the Mountain of Flames. The ground was cool and moist beneath their feet.

Chapter 62

Fire and water were in harmony, yin and yang were in balance. The minds of the four travelers were quiet. With no worries they crossed the cool mountain and continued on their westward journey.

Autumn was coming to an end; it was now the beginning of winter. In the mornings they saw frost on the ground. Ice appeared at the banks of streams and rivers. The days were bright. At night they could see thousands of stars in the sky.

After a few weeks of traveling, they came to a large city. Surrounding the city was a wide moat. A bridge crossed the moat and led to a pair of large city gates. The travelers saw that the streets were clean. There were flowers in the windows of the buildings. They could hear the voices of men singing in a tavern.

Tangseng said to his disciples, "This is a large city. It looks like the home of a powerful king."

The pig-man Zhu Bajie laughed and said, "It's just a city. How can you tell that it's the home of a king?"

"Just look at it," said Sun Wukong. "The wall that surrounds this city is probably a hundred miles long. It has at least ten gates. And look at the buildings, they are so tall that their tops are hidden by clouds. Master is right, this must be the home of a great king."

They crossed the bridge and entered the city. Looking around they saw that the people looked healthy and wore nice clothing. But when they walked a bit further, they saw a group of monks wearing old rags. The monks walked from door to door, begging for food.

Tangseng looked at the monks and said, "When the rabbit dies, the fox cries[1]. Wukong, go and ask those poor monks why they are begging for food and wearing old rags."

Sun Wukong walked up to them and asked, "Brother monks, you look poor and unhappy. Why are you suffering?"

---

[1] This is an old Chinese expression (tù sǐ hú bēi, literally, "rabbit dead fox sad"). It describes the sadness you feel when someone like yourself encounters misfortune because you worry that the same misfortune might come to you too.

One of the monks replied, "Father, I see that you are from another country. We are monks from Golden Light Monastery. It is not safe for us to stand in the street and talk about this matter. Please come with us to the monastery, I will explain everything."

 The travelers and the ragged monks walked together to the Golden Light Monastery. They entered. Tangseng looked around. It was a large monastery. At one time it had been beautiful, but now there were no monks in the building. There was dirt on the floors, the walls were covered with dust, and the main hall was silent. The only sound was a few birds flying across the hall.

They entered the main hall. In the back of the hall, several young monks were chained to pillars. Tangseng saw all this and he began to cry.

One of the monks said, "Father, please tell me, are you the travelers who come from the Tang Empire in the east?"

Sun Wukong was surprised to hear this. He said to the monk, "Brother, how do you know this? Do you have magic powers?"

"We have no magic powers. But we have suffered badly. Every day we call out to Heaven and earth asking for help. Last night each of us had the same dream. In our dreams we were told that a holy monk would arrive from the Tang Empire and save our lives. And now today you are here!"

"We may be able to help you," said Tangseng. "Please tell us your problems."

"Holy Father, this city is called the Sacrifice Kingdom. We are surrounded by four other kingdoms. In years past, all four of the neighboring kingdoms gave us tribute money[1]. We did not have to fight them."

Tangseng said, "If they paid you tribute, they respect and fear you. You must have an upright king, good ministers, and a strong army."

"Holy Father, our king is not upright, our ministers are not good, and our army is not strong. Our neighbors paid us tribute because of this Golden Light Monastery. In the daytime beautiful colored clouds appeared above the monastery. At night beams of light shone from the monastery and could be seen thousands of miles away. All four kingdoms saw this and gave us tribute."

"That sounds wonderful," said Tangseng.

"Yes, it was wonderful. But three years ago, at midnight on the first day of winter, there was a rainstorm of blood. It rained down on the entire city, and it covered the monastery. The monastery was covered with blood. After that, the colorful clouds did not appear in the daytime. The beams of light did not appear at night. The four kingdoms saw this and they stopped paying tribute. The king did not understand what happened. His ministers also did not understand, but they had to tell the king something. So they told the king that the monks of this temple had stolen treasures from the temple. The king believed their story. He had us arrested, beaten, and put in chains. Most of the monks are now dead, only a few of us are left alive. We beg you to save our lives and save our monastery!"

Tangseng was silent for a few minutes, thinking. Then he said, "I would like to meet with your king so that he can certify our travel rescript. However, I do not understand what has happened here. It is hard for me to speak with your king about this matter. So first, I would like to bathe and have some dinner. Then please give me a broom. I want to sweep out your pagoda. Then perhaps I can learn what caused the rain of blood. If I understand this matter, I will be

---

[1] Gòngpǐn, tribute, is a payment made by one nation to another as a sign of dependence.

able to talk with your king and try to help you."

The monks wanted to prepare a bath for Tangseng and fix dinner for the travelers, but they could not because they were chained to pillars in the back of the hall. Sun Wukong saw this. He waved his hand and used his lock-opening magic. Instantly the locks opened and the monks' chains fell to the floor.

The four travelers ate a vegetarian dinner prepared by the monks. Then Tangseng said to them, "You should all go to sleep. Let me sweep out the pagoda." He removed his cassock, put on a long undershirt, tied it with a sash, picked up a broom, and went to sweep out the pagoda.

Sun Wukong said, "Master, this rain of blood was caused by some kind of evil magic. Who knows what evil creatures are living in this pagoda? Please let me help you sweep the pagoda." Tangseng agreed. The monkey king picked up another broom. Together they went into the main hall. Tangseng burned some incense and prayed to the Buddha to reveal the source of the evil rain of blood. Then they began to sweep the pagoda.

The pagoda was very tall with thirteen floors. They started on the first floor, finished sweeping it, then went up to the second floor. They continued to sweep the pagoda, floor by floor. By the time they got to the tenth floor Tangseng was so tired that he could not stand up anymore. "Master," said Sun Wukong, "you are tired. Please let me finish the final three floors." Tangseng agreed, and he sat down to rest. Soon he fell asleep.

Sun Wukong was not tired. He swept the tenth and eleventh floor and walked upstairs to the twelfth floor. He heard two people talking. "That's strange!" he said. "It's now the hour of the third watch, why would anyone be up here at the top of the pagoda?" Quietly he put down his broom, flew out a window, and floated up to the top floor. There on the thirteenth floor, two monster spirits were sitting on the floor. In front of them on the floor was a pot of rice, two bowls, and a pot of wine. The monsters were playing a game of guess-fingers. Sun Wukong whipped out his golden hoop rod and shouted at them, "Aha! You are the ones who stole the monastery's treasures!"

The monsters jumped up and threw the pot of rice and the pot of wine at Sun Wukong. Sun Wukong easily moved aside to avoid the flying pots. He said to them, "I should kill you now but I won't. I need you alive so you can tell your story to the king!"

The monsters backed up until they were up against the wall. "Please don't kill us!" they cried. "We did not take the treasure. Someone else took it."

Sun Wukong grabbed each of them by the arm and dragged them down to the tenth floor. He woke up Tangseng and said to him, "Master, I have captured the thieves! I found them on the top floor of the pagoda. They were playing guess-fingers, eating rice and drinking wine. I wanted to kill them, but I decided to let them live so they could tell you where they put the monastery's treasure."

Before Tangseng could say anything one of the monsters started to speak. "Please don't kill us! I will tell you everything." Tangseng just waited quietly.

The monster continued, "I am called Bubble Busy, and my friend's name is Busy Bubble. We are both fish spirits. We were sent here by the All Saints Dragon King. He lives in Green Wave Lagoon. The Dragon King has a beautiful daughter. She is married to a powerful magician named Nine Heads. Two years ago, Nine Heads sent down a rain of blood onto this monastery. Then he stole the monastery's treasure, the sarira[1] of Buddha. Then the daughter went up to Heaven and stole a nine-lobed magic mushroom. Now the sarira and the magic mushroom are both at the bottom of the lagoon. They create beautiful mists and bright lights for the enjoyment of the Dragon King, his daughter, and the magician."

"I know this All Saints Dragon King," said Sun Wukong to Tangseng. "He was the one who invited Bull Demon King to an underwater banquet. I have already seen his green lagoon." Then turning to Bubble Busy he said, "And why are you here in the pagoda?"

"Recently we heard that a powerful monkey named Sun Wukong was coming here. The Dragon King sent us here to watch for him, so we could report back when he arrives."

Just then, Zhu Bajie arrived. Sun Wukong told him about the two fish spirits and the All Saints Dragon King. Zhu whipped out his rake and prepared to smash it down on the heads of the fish spirits. But Sun Wukong said, "Little brother, you have not thought this through. We want these two fish spirits alive, so they can tell their story to the king."

"All right," said Zhu. "But I would really like to use these two to make some fish soup for the monks."

---

[1] In Chinese Buddhist tradition, a sarira is a saint's relic, part of his or her body that remains after the saint is cremated. Usually it is shaped like an egg or pearl.

It was very late at night when Sun Wukong and Zhu led the two fish spirits down to the monastery. Several monks walked in front of them, holding their lanterns high. When they got to the main hall of the monastery, Sun Wukong said, "Tie up these two with iron chains. Guard them until tomorrow morning. We are going to sleep now." Then the travelers rested while the monks guarded the two fish spirits.

In the morning, Tangseng put on his best cassock and hat and went to the palace to meet the king. Sun Wukong wore his tiger skin and his silk shirt. "Should we bring the fish spirits to show the king?" he asked.

"No," replied Tangseng. "Let's just talk to the king first to let him know what happened. He can send someone to fetch them later if he wants to."

The two of them walked into the king's palace. When they reached the east gate, Tangseng said to one of the officials, "Please inform the king that this poor monk has been sent by the Tang Emperor to acquire the Buddha's scriptures in the Western Heaven. We would like to ask the king to certify our travel rescript." The official told this to the king, and the king agreed to see them.

Tangseng and Sun Wukong entered the throne room. The people in the throne room became afraid when they saw Sun Wukong. Tangseng bowed low to the throne, but Sun Wukong just stood with his arms crossed. He did not bow down. Tangseng said, "Your Majesty, we have been sent by the Tang Emperor to journey to the Western Heaven, to acquire the Buddha's scriptures. Our journey has taken us to your worthy kingdom, and we dare not pass without asking you to certify our travel rescript."

The king opened his hand. Tangseng approached the king and handed him the travel rescript. The king read it carefully. Then he said, "Your emperor was wise to select such an upright monk to make this journey to the west. Unfortunately, we do not have such monks in our kingdom. Our monks are only good for stealing and harming our people and their ruler."

Tangseng asked, "Your Majesty, how did your monks harm you and your people?"

"Our kingdom is the superior nation in this area. All four of our neighbors paid tribute to us every year because of the magic of the Golden Light Monastery. But three years ago, our monks stole treasure from the monastery. Now the four kingdoms do not pay tribute to us anymore."

"Your Majesty, when this poor monk arrived at your city last night, we met some monks who were begging in the streets. They invited us to stay at the Golden Light Monastery. During the night we found two fish spirit monsters hiding in the pagoda. I believe they stole the treasure."

"Where are these fish spirits now?"

"They are locked up in the Golden Light Monastery."

"I will send my guards to get them and bring them here."

"Very good. But may I suggest that my eldest disciple go with them?" The king agreed. He told his guards to bring a sedan chair for Sun Wukong. Eight strong guards picked up the sedan chair and carried Sun Wukong down the streets of the city. Riders on horseback rode ahead of them and behind them, calling out, "Get out of the way!"

They arrived at the Golden Light Monastery. Sun Wukong used his lock opening magic to release the two fish spirits. Zhu grabbed one of them, and the other disciple, Sha Wujing, grabbed the other one. They walked through the city and returned to the palace, with Sun Wukong again riding in the sedan chair.

Zhu and Sha brought the two fish spirits into the throne room. The king looked carefully at them. One of them was covered with black scales. He had a pointed mouth and sharp teeth. The other one had smooth skin, a big belly, and a large mouth. The king said to them, "You two look like fish! Who are you and where are you from? When did you come to our kingdom? What did you do with our treasures? Tell me everything."

The two fish spirits dropped to their knees. One of them said,

> "Your Majesty, three years ago
> On the first day of the seventh month
> The All Saints Dragon King arrived
> To live southeast of this kingdom
> He built a home underneath Green Wave Lagoon
> His daughter was beautiful
> She married Nine Heads, a powerful magician
> They learned of the pagoda's treasure
> They sent down a rainstorm of blood
> They stole your sarira treasure
> Then they went to Heaven
> and stole a nine-lobed magic mushroom
> Now your treasure lights up the Dragon King's home

Please don't punish us
We are not thieves
We are only servants of the Dragon King
We are telling you the truth!"

The king was pleased when he heard this story. He told his guards to put the two fish spirits in jail. Then he issued a decree that the chains should be removed from the monks of the city. He said to Tangseng and the disciples, "We thank you for your help. We wish to hold a banquet for you. At the banquet we will discuss how to arrest the Dragon King and bring back our treasures."

That night a great banquet was held in the king's palace. Tangseng sat at the head table in the place of honor. Sun Wukong sat on his left. Zhu and Sha sat on his right. Vegetables, rice, fruit and tea were placed on their table. The king sat at the table facing Tangseng. Lots of meat dishes were placed on the king's table. A hundred other tables were set up for the rest of the guests.

The king lifted his wine cup and toasted his honored guests. Tangseng dared not drink, but his three disciples all drank some wine. They all ate, but of course Zhu ate much more than the others.

When the banquet was nearly finished, the king said to Tangseng, "Honored guests, let's go to another room. We will discuss how to catch the Dragon King and get our treasures back."

"There is no need for that," replied Tangseng. "We will take care of this matter. My eldest disciple, the monkey king Sun Wukong, has some skill in this matter. He will catch the thief. My middle disciple, the pig-man Zhu Bajie, will assist him. My junior disciple, Sha Wujing, will stay here with me."

"Very good. What weapons can we give you?"

"We do not need any weapons," said Sun Wukong. "We have our own weapons and they are quite powerful. However please bring out the two fish spirits. We will bring them with us so they can give us valuable information." The guards brought out the two fish spirits. Sun Wukong grabbed one, Zhu grabbed the other, and together they rose into the sky and flew away.

Chapter 63

The king said, "Truly, these are great sages! This lonely one has eyes but could not see. We thought that your disciples were great warriors. But we did not realize that they were superior immortals who could ride the fog and fly above the clouds!"

Sha Wujing said to the king, "Your Majesty, my elder brother is the Great Sage Equal to Heaven. He caused great trouble in Heaven five hundred years ago. Even the Jade Emperor fears him. My other brother is the Marshal of Heavenly Reeds. Long ago he was the leader of eighty thousand soldiers. Compared to them I have very little power, but long ago I was the Curtain Raising Captain. We three are very good at catching monsters, fighting tigers and dragons, stirring up the oceans and rivers, that sort of thing. As for riding fog and flying above the clouds, well, that's really not a big deal at all."

After this, the king and his ministers began using the title "Great Buddha" for Tangseng and "Bodhisattva" for his disciples.

Meanwhile, Sun Wukong and Zhu Bajie dragged the two fish spirits through the sky. Soon they arrived at Green Wave Lagoon. Sun Wukong threw the two fish spirits in the water and said to them, "Go quickly and report to the All Saints Dragon King. Tell him that his father, the Great Sage Equal to Heaven, is here. Tell him to bring out the treasures of the Golden Light Monastery immediately. If he says even half a 'no' I will clear out this lagoon and kill every creature in it."

The two fish spirits swam quickly through the water, still dragging their chains. They swam into the palace of the Dragon King. They saw the king sitting on his throne, drinking with his son in law Prince Nine Heads. The fish spirits shouted, "Great King, disaster! Disaster! Last night we were in the pagoda of the Golden Light Monastery. We were captured by the Great Sage Equal to Heaven and the Tang monk. They bound us with iron chains and dragged us here to make a report to you. They say that you must give them the treasures of the monastery right away, or else they will kill every creature in this lagoon!"

The Dragon King was very afraid because he knew about the powers of Sun Wukong. But Nine Heads said, "Don't worry, father. Your foolish son in law has learned a few things about fighting. Let me go and fight with him for a few rounds. Soon he will be defeated and will kowtow to you."

Picking up his weapon, a large halberd, he swam up and out of the lagoon. From far away he looked like a man. But when Sun Wukong and Zhu looked closely, they could see that he had nine mouths. He had eighteen eyes all around his head so he could see in every direction at once. Using all nine mouths he shouted, "Where is this Great Sage? Come here now and give your life to me!"

Sun Wukong stood and looked at him. He held his Golden Hoop Rod in his right hand and tapped it against the palm of his left hand. "Here I am," he said.

Prince Nine Heads shouted at him, "Where do you come from? Why are you here in our kingdom? Why are you guarding the pagoda? And how dare you capture my two helpers and start a fight with me?"

"You monster! Don't you recognize your Grandfather Sun? Listen to this story. Long ago I lived on Flower Fruit Mountain in a cave behind a waterfall above the great ocean. I traveled many thousands of miles to find knowledge and acquire power. The Jade Emperor made me Great Sage Equal to Heaven. I caused big trouble in the halls of Heaven. All the gods of Heaven could not defeat me. They called on the Buddha himself. He made a bet with me and I lost. His hand and five fingers became a mountain with five peaks. He turned it upside down and trapped me for five hundred years. Bodhisattva Guanyin rescued me. She told me to help the monk Tangseng journey to the Western Heaven. We have been traveling for several years. Just yesterday we arrived in this kingdom. We heard that the pagoda has lost its light. My master wanted to learn the truth, so last night we swept the pagoda. We found your two monsters at the top of the pagoda. They told me that you were the thief. We told the king, and he sent us here to capture the thief and bring him to the king. Don't ask me any questions. Just return the treasures and you will live. If you fight us, I will drain this lagoon. I'll bring down this mountain and kill all of you!"

Nine Heads waited until Sun Wukong was finished. Then he said, "So, you are traveling west to find scriptures. Fine. That has nothing to do with us. Why do you care about this matter?"

"You wretched monster, it's because of you that my brothers, the monks of the temple, are suffering. And it's because of you that the temple is covered with blood. How could I not care?"

"All right, then we must fight. As the saying goes, 'the warrior avoids fighting unless it's necessary[1].' I will kill you quickly, and that will be the end of your monk's journey to the west."

Nine Heads raised his halberd and brought it down on Sun Wukong's head. The Monkey King easily blocked the halberd with his rod. They fought for thirty rounds, but neither could win. During the fight, Zhu watched from a short distance away, waiting for the right time to get involved. Finally he ran forward and tried to hit Nine Heads with his rake. But Nine Heads had eyes in the back of his head. He saw Zhu coming and blocked the rake with the handle of his halberd.

The fight continued for another six or seven rounds. Nine Heads became tired, he could not continue to fight against both Sun Wukong and Zhu Bajie. So he leaped into the sky and changed into his true form, a large, terrifying nine headed bird. His body was twelve feet long and covered with feathers. His feet were as sharp as knives. His nine heads formed a circle.

Zhu was frightened, but Sun Wukong said, "Let me go up there and fight him!" and jumped into the sky. Zhu followed him.

Sun Wukong tried to hit the bird with his rod. The bird darted to one side to avoid the blow. A new head popped out from the middle of its belly. The head grabbed Zhu. The bird flew down to the lagoon, pulling Zhu down under the water with him. When the bird reached the palace of the Dragon King it changed back to Nine Heads. He said to his father, "Take this monk and tie him up." A crowd of underwater creatures came, grabbed Zhu, and carried him inside the palace.

Sun Wukong was still in the clouds. He had seen the bird drag Zhu underwater. He did not want to fight the Dragon King and the bird underwater. So he changed into a crab and swam down to the Dragon King's palace. He crab-walked sideways into the palace and looked around. He did not see Zhu, but he saw the Dragon King and Nine Heads drinking and talking with their relatives. He crab-walked away from them. He found a few other crabs. He listened to them for a while, then he asked, "Have you seen the ugly pig that our king's son in law brought here? Is he alive or dead?"

"He's still alive," said one of the other crabs. "Can't you see him over there?" Sun Wukong looked and saw Zhu tied up to a pillar. He crab-walked towards

---

[1] In *The Art of War*, chapter 3, Sunzi says, "A hundred victories in a hundred battles is not the greatest good. Subduing the enemy's army without battle is the greatest good."

Zhu.

Zhu saw him and said, "Elder brother, what should we do?" Sun Wukong used his claw to cut the ropes holding Zhu to the pillar. Zhu said, "The monster took my rake. I think it's in the main hall."

Sun Wukong replied, "I will get your rake. Go and wait for me at the main gate." He crab-walked into the main hall. He saw Zhu's rake. He picked up the rake and used his magic power to hide the rake. Then he walked sideways to the main gate and gave the rake to Zhu.

"I am a better fighter underwater than you are," said Zhu. "You should go. I will fight my way back into the palace. Wait for me on the bank of the lagoon." Sun Wukong swam up to the surface of the lagoon. Zhu gripped his rake with both hands. Swinging the rake, he entered the palace. He smashed everything: windows, doors, tables, chairs, even wine cups. The Dragon King and his family all ran for their lives.

The nine headed monster made sure that his wife the princess was safe. Then he grabbed his halberd and ran towards Zhu, shouting, "You wretched pig! How dare you frighten my family!"

"How dare you capture me?" replied Zhu. They began to fight. But soon the Dragon King and his relatives all came out and joined the fight. Zhu could not fight them all. He turned and swam quickly out of the palace and towards the surface of the lagoon. He was followed by Nine Heads, the Dragon King, and all their relatives.

Zhu shot up out of the water. Sun Wukong was waiting on the bank of the lagoon. When the Dragon King came out of the water, Sun Wukong jumped up onto a cloud. He smashed his iron rod onto the Dragon King's head, killing him instantly. The dragon's dead body fell onto the water, and blood turned the water red. Nine Heads grabbed the dragon's body and carried him down to the underwater palace, followed by all the family members.

Sun Wukong and Zhu sat down on the bank of the lagoon to talk. Zhu said, "I'm glad that you beat that old dragon to death. Now they will be busy for a while, preparing for the funeral. They won't come out again tonight. It's getting late. What should we do now?"

Sun Wukong could see that Zhu was tired and did not want to fight anymore. He said, "Brother, don't worry about the time. This is our best chance to attack them. We can grab the treasures and bring them back to Master and the king!"

Just then, they heard a sound. They looked up and saw a large dark fog coming from the east. Sun Wukong used his diamond eyes to look carefully. He saw that it was Erlang and the Six Brothers of Plum Mountain. They were on a hunting trip. Each of them carried a bow and arrows, and each had a sharp knife in their hand.

Sun Wukong said, "I know these seven, they are my bond brothers. We should ask them to help us." Then he paused for a moment and added, "But Erland defeated me in battle a long time ago. I am a little bit embarrassed to ask him for help now. Zhu, please help me. Stand in front of them to block their path. When they come up to you, tell them that the Great Sage Equal to Heaven is here to greet them."

Zhu did as he was asked. Erlang asked his six brothers to invite Sun Wukong to see him. The six brothers all ran out of the camp and shouted, "Elder Brother Sun Wukong! Our elder brother requests that you come to see him."

Sun Wukong came out. He greeted each of the six brothers. Then together they walked into the camp. Erlang said, "Great Sage, you are acquiring merit by helping the Tang monk. Soon you will finish your journey and you will sit on a lotus throne."

"I have a long way to go," he replied. "The Tang monk rescued me and we are heading west. We are passing through this country and are trying to help some Buddhist monks. We are here to capture some demons and retrieve the treasure of their monastery. We saw you and your brothers passing nearby, and we humbly ask for your help. However, we don't know what your plans are or whether you will be pleased to help us."

"I have nothing else to do," smiled Erlang, "and I would be happy to help an old friend. Tell me more."

Sun Wukong told the whole story, how they arrived at Sacrifice Kingdom, saw the suffering of the Buddhist monks, found the two demons at the top of the pagoda, brought the demons to the king, went to the lagoon, fought Nine Heads, and killed the Dragon King. He finished by saying, "My brother Zhu and I were just talking about what to do next, when we saw you and your noble brothers coming."

Erlang replied, "Well, you have just killed the old dragon king. Now is the best time to attack!"

But his brothers disagreed. One of them said, "Don't be in a hurry, brother. The nine headed demon's family is here, so he will not run away. We have two guests now. And in our camp we have food and wine. Let's have a banquet tonight with our friends. There will be plenty of time tomorrow for a battle." Erlang agreed. Together they walked back to camp. They had a delicious vegetarian meal and talked for hours. Then they slept, with Heaven for their tent and the earth for their beds.

The next morning, Zhu got up. He had a couple of drinks, then he said, "It's getting light. I will go down and fight these monsters."

"Be careful," replied Erlang. "Just bring them up to the surface. My brothers and I will deal with them."

Zhu nodded his head, then grabbed his rake. He used his water-dividing magic to swim quickly down to the palace. With a loud shout he ran into the palace, swinging his rake. One of the dragon's sons was bending over the dragon's dead body. Zhu smashed his rake down on the son's head, making nine bloody holes in it.

"That pig has killed my son too!" cried the dragon king's widow. All of the dragon king's relatives ran out to fight with Zhu. Zhu turned and swam up to the surface of the lagoon and shot into the air. The relatives followed him. Sun Wukong and the seven brothers attacked them.

During the fight one of the dragon's grandsons was killed. Nine Heads saw that things were going badly. He turned into the huge nine-headed bird and began flying in circles over the battle. Erlang fired an arrow towards the bird, but did not hit it. The bird flew down and grew a new head to bite Erlang. But Erlang's dog jumped up and bit off the new head. The bird turned and flew away towards the Northern Ocean.

Zhu started to chase him, but Sun Wukong stopped him, saying, "Don't chase him. Never corner a defeated enemy[1]. I have a better idea. I will change my appearance so I look like Nine Heads. You chase me down into the palace. I will trick the princess into giving me the treasures."

Erlang said, "OK, we can wait if you want to. But it's not a good idea to let a monster like that live. It will just cause trouble for everyone in the future." And indeed, even today we see these bloody red monsters[2].

Sun Wukong changed his appearance to look like Nine Heads and dove into the water. Zhu followed him, shouting and yelling. They arrived at the palace gates. The queen said to Sun Wukong, "My dear son in law, why are you so frightened?"

Sun Wukong replied, "That pig has defeated me, and now he is trying to catch me down here. Quick, hide our treasures!"

The queen ran to the back of the hall, then came back with two boxes. One was made of gold, the other was white jade. She gave the golden box to Sun Wukong, saying, "This is the sarira, the Buddhist treasure." Then she gave the white jade box to him, saying, "And this is the nine-lobed magic mushroom. You must take these far away from here. I will fight with the pig for a few rounds. This will give you time to escape."

Sun Wukong shook his body, changing back to his true form. "Look at me

---

[1] In *The Art of War*, Sunzi says that a cornered enemy fighting on "death ground" is the most dangerous of all enemies because his only option is to fight to the death. He writes, "If death is certain, soldiers will fight to the end."

[2] It's not clear what animal the original author is referring to here, because the Nine Headed Beast (jiǔ tóu chóng tóu chóng) is variously described as a bird, a gigantic insect, or just a monster. Some say it is the mango bird, a kind of oriole found in India.

carefully, Queen," he said. "Am I really your son in law?" The queen tried to grab the boxes, but just then Zhu arrived. He hit her on the shoulder with his rake and she fell to the ground.

Zhu raised his rake to hit her again, but Sun Wukong held up his hand to stop him. He said, "Don't kill her! We should bring her back to the king's palace when we make our report."

Sun Wukong and Zhu swam up and out of the lagoon. Sun Wukong carried the two treasure boxes and Zhu dragged the queen by her hand. When they got to the bank of the lagoon, Sun Wukong said to Erlang, "Thank you my friend! We have the missing treasures and we have killed the thieves."

"We did nothing," replied Erlang. "It was because of the king's good fortune and your great power."

"Will you come with us to meet with the king?"

"No, we will leave now, brother monkey." And so Erlang and his six brothers returned to their hunting trip.

Sun Wukong and Zhu brought the queen back to the palace of the King of Sacrifice Kingdom. One of the monks saw them coming. He ran into the palace to tell the king and Tangseng that the monkey and pig had returned. Sun Wukong showed the two treasures to the king and told him the whole story of their visit to the lagoon. The king listened to the story. Then he asked, "Tell me, does the dragon queen know human speech?"

Sun Wukong replied, "She was the wife of the Dragon King for many years, and bore many sons and daughters. How could she not know human speech?"

"If she does, then she must now tell us everything about this matter. Who took the two treasures from the monastery?"

The queen replied, "I know nothing about stealing the Buddhist treasure. My dead husband did that, with help from Nine Heads. They were the ones who brought down the rain of blood on the monastery. As for the magic mushroom, that was the work of my daughter. She went up to Heaven and stole the mushroom."

"Tell us about the magic mushroom."

"Long ago it was planted by the Queen Mother of the West. It will live for a thousand years. Wave it with your hand and it will emit a thousand rays of colored light." She paused, then continued, "Now you have the magic mushroom and the Buddhist treasure. You have killed my husband and many of my relatives. I ask you to let me live."

Sun Wukong said to her, "An entire family is not responsible for the crimes of one or two family members. We will let you live. But you must remain at the monastery and become the guardian of the pagoda, for all the rest of your days."

She nodded. "An unhappy life is better than a good death. You may do with me as you wish."

"All right then," said Sun Wukong. He called for the monks to bring him an iron chain. Then he opened one of the links of the chain. He made a hole in her shoulder bone and passed the first link of the chain through the hole, then he closed the link again.

Then all of them went to the Golden Light Monastery and entered the pagoda. Sun Wukong used his magic to summon the local spirit of the city and the guardian spirits of the monastery. He told them that the queen would stay in the pagoda from this day onward. "Bring her food and water every three days," he said. "If she ever tries to escape, kill her immediately." They agreed.

Tangseng used the magic mushroom to sweep out all thirteen floors of the pagoda. Then he put the mushroom in a vase next to the sarira. The pagoda began to shine with colored light again. The light could be seen throughout the kingdom and also in all four neighboring kingdoms.

They all walked out of the pagoda. The king said to Tangseng, "I am glad that you and your three disciples came to our kingdom and got to the bottom of this matter."

Tangseng nodded. Sun Wukong said to the king, "Your Majesty, please think about changing the name of this monastery. Now it is called Golden Light. But gold can melt, and light is just glowing air. If you change the name to Defeated Dragon Monastery, it will last forever." The king agreed, and the name was changed.

That night, the king gave a great banquet for the four travelers. Artists came and painted portraits of the four travelers. Their names were carved in the Five Phoenix Tower. The king offered them gold and jewelry but of course they refused. So the king gave each of them two new sets of clothing, two sets of socks, two pairs of shoes, and two belts. He also gave them food and certified their travel rescript. Then the king gave them his own carriage to take them to the edge of the kingdom, so they could resume their journey.

Truly,

> Evil demons have been killed,
> The kingdom has been cleansed,
> The pagoda's light has returned,
> The world is bright again.

Chapter 64

When they reached the western edge of the kingdom, the four travelers got down from the king's carriage and resumed their journey. The king and his people walked with them for a few miles, then they said goodbye and turned back. But some of the monks from the monastery continued to follow them. Tangseng told them to return to the city but they continued to follow, saying that they wanted to stay with the four travelers all the way to the Western Heaven.

Finally, Sun Wukong took some hairs from his head, blew on them and said, "Change." Each hair became a large tiger. The tigers walked back and forth across the road, growling. The monks dared not follow. The four travelers continued walking, and after a few hours Sun Wukong retrieved his hairs.

A little while later their path was blocked again. In front of them was a huge field of brambles. It covered the road and extended as far as they could see to the left and right. The brambles were large and grew close together. It was impossible for a person or a horse to walk through them.

Zhu said, "These brambles are no problem for me. Using my rake, I can move them out of the way and clear a path for us."

"That won't work," replied Tangseng. "You are very strong but there are too many brambles. You would soon become tired. Wukong, please take a look and tell us how we can get past these brambles."

Sun Wukong jumped up into the air. He shaded his diamond eyes and looked in all directions. As far as he could see, brambles covered the ground. In between the brambles were many large trees covered with vines. All together they appeared to be a vast green cloud covering the earth.

He looked at the field of brambles for a long time. Then he came back down to earth. He said to Tangseng, "Master, this field is enormous. I cannot see the end of it. It must be a thousand miles long."

Tangseng was very unhappy. "What can we do?" he asked.

Sha said, "Don't worry, Master. Let's do what farmers do. We will just set fire to the brambles and clear a path that way."

Zhu laughed and said, "That won't work. If you want to burn the brambles you must do it in the tenth month when everything is dry. Right now, the brambles are green and growing, they won't burn."

Sun Wukong said, "Yes, and even if you could start a fire, it would be so big and so hot that it would probably kill all of us."

Zhu said, "Enough talking. I will take care of this matter." He made a magic sign with his fingers and said, "Grow!" Instantly he was three hundred feet tall. He stepped forward, swinging his huge rake back and forth along the ground. The brambles fell before the rake. He walked forward, clearing the path through the brambles. Tangseng walked behind him on his horse, followed by Sun Wukong and Sha.

They walked all day. When evening came, they arrived at a clearing. In the middle was a stone. The words "Bramble Ridge" were carved in large letters into the stone. Below it were these words:

Eight hundred miles of brambles
This is a road that few have traveled

Zhu read the words. He laughed and said, "Let Old Hog add a few more words!" Then he carved these words at the bottom of the stone:

But now Zhu Bajie has made a path
It leads us straight to the West

Tangseng was tired and wanted to rest for the night. But Zhu wanted to continue. So they kept walking, with Zhu clearing the path ahead of them. They walked all night and all the next day. The next evening the tired travelers arrived at another clearing. This clearing had a small shrine in the middle. As they looked at it, an old man walked out from the shrine. Next to him walked a small red-haired demon carrying a tray of cakes.

The old man fell to his knees and said to Tangseng, "Great Sage, this poor old man is the local spirit of Bramble Ridge. This is the only house for eight hundred miles. Please take some food and rest here tonight."

Zhu stepped forward to take the tray. But Sun Wukong shouted to him, "Stop!" Then he said to the old man, "Who are you? Why are you lying to us?"

Immediately the old man and the small demon disappeared. A powerful gust of cold wind came. It picked up Tangseng into the air and carried him away. The wind carried him for many miles. Finally it dropped him gently in front of a small fog-covered house. The old man and the small red-haired demon appeared again.

The old man said to Tangseng, "Please do not be afraid. We will not harm you. I am the Eighteenth Squire of Bramble Ridge[1]. It is a beautiful night; the moon and stars are looking down on us. I ask you to spend some time with me tonight, as a friend, to talk about poetry."

Tangseng looked around at the house and the clearing. It certainly was beautiful. Then he heard someone say, "Look, the Eighteenth Squire has brought the Tang monk here!" Three more old men arrived. One had hair as white as snow, the second one had a green face and hair, the third one had blue-black hair. They all bowed to Tangseng. One of them said to him, "Holy monk, we have heard that you are traveling to the west. We are happy that you are here with us tonight, and we ask that you give us some of your wisdom."

"Who are you?" asked Tangseng.

The one with white hair said,

> "I am Lord Lonely Upright.
> I have lived for a thousand years
> My branches touch the sky
> My shadow covers the ground
> My body is covered with snow
> I stand strong and tall
> Free from the dust of the world."

The one with green hair said,

> "I am Master of the Void.
> I have seen a thousand winters
> My body is tall and strong
> At night comes the sound of the rain
> My green leaves give shade to the earth
> Dragons and cranes live in my branches
> My roots know the secret of long life."

The one with the blue-black hair said,

> "I am Ancient Cloud Toucher.
> I have passed a thousand autumns

---

[1] As we will see, he is really the spirit of the pine tree. His name, Eighteenth Squire, consists of the characters for eight (八), ten (十) and squire (公) which together form the character for pine tree (松).

No anger here, just calm and relaxed
The seven wise men talk with me about the Way
My six friends sing and drink with me
I am one with Heaven
I travel with the gods."

Tangseng turned to the Eighteenth Squire and asked, "And what about you?"
Eighteenth Squire replied,

"I also have lived for a thousand years
I am tall, strong and green
My strength comes from rain and dew
I drink the wind and fog of the ravines
Immortals sit under my green branches
Playing chess and discussing the Way."

Tangseng smiled and said, "You have all lived a long time, you are strong and
handsome, and you have learned the Way. Wonderful!"

"And may we ask the age of the holy monk?" asked the four old men at the
same time.

Tangseng replied,

"Forty years ago I left my mother's womb
Even before my birth, trouble was my fate
I escaped and floated on the waves
I reached Golden Mountain and was saved
I studied the Way and read the holy books
I only wanted to worship the Buddha
Now His Majesty has sent me to the West
I am pleased to meet you ancient immortals!"

One of the old men said, "This holy monk is truly a superior monk. We are
fortunate to meet you here tonight. We beg you to teach us the Way. This has
been our desire for a thousand years."

And so, Tangseng sat with the four ancient ones and taught them the wisdom
of the Buddha. He spoke for a long time. The ancient ones listened.

But then Ancient Cloud Toucher said, "Holy monk, the Way began in China
and has been in China for thousands of years. But here you are, seeking
wisdom in the west, in India. What are you looking for? Has a stone lion
taken out your heart? You have forgotten the land of your birth. You seek the

wisdom of the Buddha but you ignore the wisdom that's right in front of you! You are as confused as the brambles here on Bramble Ridge. How can you teach and lead others? You must look carefully at your own life, and you must sit in stillness. Only then will you be able to raise water in a bottomless basket[1]."

Tangseng listened to this in silence, then he thanked Ancient Cloud Toucher and kowtowed to him. Master of the Void laughed and said, "Please get up, holy father. You don't have to believe everything our friend says. Let's not have any more serious discussions tonight. We should recite poetry, relax, and enjoy the night!"

And so, the five spent the rest of the night drinking tea, reciting poetry, and enjoying each others' company. One of them would say a line of poetry, something like "The empty mind is like the dustless moon," then another would add a second line, and another would add a third line. In this way, they created long poems of great beauty. Later, they each recited longer poems. After each one recited their poems, the others smiled and complimented him on the poem's beauty.

In this way they passed the night. Just as the morning sun began to glow in the eastern sky, Tangseng said to the four old men, "My friends, this has been wonderful. But now I must return to my disciples. I'm sure they are worried about me. And I must continue my journey to the west."

"Oh, please stay longer with us!" cried the old men. "Don't worry about your disciples. In a little while we will take you back to meet them again." Tangseng became a little bit worried about this, but he said nothing.

Just then, two young girls came into the clearing. They were wearing blue robes. Behind them was an immortal girl. She wore a pink skirt with pictures of purple plums, and a red blouse. Her eyes were like stars. She greeted the four old men. Then she saw Tangseng. She told the young girls to bring tea for everyone. Then she sat next to Tangseng, very close to him. She leaned towards him and whispered, "So, you are the guest who arrived yesterday evening! Will you give me one of your beautiful poems?"

Tangseng could not find words to reply to her. She continued, "What's the matter with you? If you don't want to have fun with me tonight, what are you

---

[1] This is an interesting defense of traditional Daoism. The "bottomless basket" in the last line is possibly a reference to Chapter 4 of the *Dao De Jing*, where Laozi says, "Dao is a bottomless cup that need not be filled. Profound and deep, it is the root of ten thousand things."

waiting for? Life is short, let's do it now!"

Still, Tangseng could not speak. Lord Lonely Upright said, "This holy monk has found the Way. He would not do anything improper. If the Apricot Fairy is willing, the two of them can be married right here and now."

Now Tangseng's face turned red. He jumped up and shouted, "You are all monsters, trying to lead me off the path of the Buddha. I am happy to recite poetry with you and drink tea, but I refuse to do this!"

The four old men listened to him but said nothing. But the little red-haired demon said coldly, "Apricot Fairy is my sister. What's wrong with her? You don't like her? You are making a mistake. You know, we might get angry. If we get angry, we will make sure you never leave this place, never marry, and never be a monk. Your life will be for nothing."

Tangseng realized that he was in serious trouble. Just then he heard Sun Wukong, Zhu and Sha calling his name. He shouted, "Disciples, here I am! Help me!"

As soon as he said this, the four old men, the beautiful woman and the little demon all disappeared. Tangseng told the disciples what happened. Sun Wukong looked around. At the edge of the clearing he saw a big juniper tree, an old cypress tree, an old pine tree, and an old bamboo tree. Behind the bamboo tree was a red maple tree. And nearby was an old apricot tree.

"I think I have found your demons," said Sun Wukong. "The Eighteenth Squire is the pine tree. Lord Lonely Upright is the cypress tree. The Master of the Void is the juniper tree. Ancient Cloud Toucher is the bamboo tree. The little red-haired demon is the maple tree. And the Apricot Fairy is the apricot tree. Your friends were the spirits of these trees, but during their thousand years they became confused. They are no longer kind; they have become dangerous."

Zhu heard this, and immediately rushed forward, holding his rake high above his head. He smashed the rake down, knocking all the trees to the ground. Tangseng tried to stop him, but Sun Wukong said, "Master, let go of your kind feelings towards these demons. If we don't do this now, they will only become more dangerous later." And so, Tangseng watched as Zhu smashed the trees into small sticks.

When he was finished, the disciples helped Tangseng up on his horse. They were close to the edge of the field of brambles. Zhu said the magic words and became big again. He finished clearing a path so that the travelers could escape the brambles. They found the road again, and resumed their journey to the west.

Chapter 65

I must tell you this:

> Always do good, avoid evil
> The gods know everything that you think
> Why try to be clever
> Why let yourself be a fool?
> Just let your mind become empty
> Do good while you are still alive
> Always seek the Dao, do not just drift
> Keep your eyes open, watch your thoughts
> Go through the three barriers[1]
> Fill up the dark sea
> You will ride the phoenix and the crane
> With joy you will rise to Heaven

You remember from our last story that the travelers escaped from the brambles and the tree-spirits who wanted to keep the Tang monk there. They continued walking westward along the Silk Road. Winter ended and spring arrived. The earth was covered with young grasses. Red flowers appeared on peach trees.

One day as they walked, they saw a huge mountain in the distance. Its peak was higher than the clouds. Tangseng said to Sun Wukong, "Look at that mountain. It touches Heaven!"

Sun Wukong replied, "No mountain can be so tall that it reaches Heaven." They followed the path as it led them up the side of the mountain. All around them they heard the cries of wolves, tigers and leopards. Tangseng began to feel afraid. But Sun Wukong shouted loudly and all the animals ran away.

They continued to climb until they reached a high pass, then they walked down the western side of the mountain. Soon they saw a large and beautiful

---

[1] In advanced Daoist practices, the student learns to go through three barriers or passes called guān on the spinal column: the Tailbone Gate just above the coccyx, the Narrow Ridge just below the shoulder blades, and the Jade Pillow at the base of the skull. One can open these passes by avoiding hunger for sex (Tailbone Gate), good food (Narrow Ridge), and desire (Jade Pillow).

building. Rays of colored light appeared above the building. They heard the music of bells.

"Disciples," said Tangseng, "go take a look. Tell me what kind of building this is."

Sun Wukong shaded his diamond eyes and looked carefully at the building. Then he said, "Master, this is a monastery. It is very beautiful. But I also feel that it has an air of silence. I have gone to the Western Heaven before and I have visited Thunderclap Mountain. This monastery looks a lot like Thunderclap, but something about it is not quite right. Please do not go inside yet. We must be careful. Some evil might be hiding inside."

Tangseng looked at him. "You say that this place reminds you of Thunderclap. Can this really be the place that we seek?"

Before the monkey king could reply, Sha Wujing said, "We do not need to worry about this. The road will take us right past the monastery's front gate. When we arrive at the monastery, we will know if it is Thunderclap or not."

Tangseng agreed. He urged his horse forward. Soon they arrived at the monastery's front gate. They looked up and saw large characters over the top of the front gate. The characters read, "Thunderclap Monastery."

Tangseng was so surprised that he fell off his horse. He landed on the ground. He jumped up and said angrily to Sun Wukong, "You wretched ape! You lied to me! This is indeed Thunderclap Monastery. We have reached the end of our journey."

Sun Wukong smiled and replied, "Master, there are four words above the front gate. You have only read three of them."

Tangseng looked again. There were four words, not three. He read them aloud, "Small Thunderclap Monastery." He thought for a minute, then said, "Well, even if it's only Small Thunderclap Monastery, there must be a Buddha living here. The scriptures say that there are three thousand Buddhas. They cannot all live in the same place! We all know that Bodhisattva Guanyin lives in the Southern Sea. I wonder which Buddha lives in this place. Let's go inside and see."

"I think that would be a mistake," said Sun Wukong.

"We will go inside," insisted Tangseng. "Even if there is no Buddha here, there must be a Buddha statue. I have vowed to pray at every Buddha statue that I see." He told Zhu to get his cassock and hat. After putting on the cassock and hat, they all walked forward into the monastery.

As soon as they entered the monastery, a loud voice called out, "Tang monk! You have come from the east to worship the Buddha. Why are you being so insolent now?" Immediately Tangseng kowtowed while Zhu and Sha knelt on the ground. Sun Wukong stood without moving, holding the horse. He felt that something was wrong here.

The three others moved forward slowly. They reached the inner gates. Inside was the Buddha Hall. Just outside the Buddha Hall was a large crowd of people. They saw five hundred teachers, three thousand guardians, eight Bodhisattvas, plus a lot of nuns, monks and ordinary people. Tangseng, Zhu and Sha kowtowed every step until they reached the Buddha Hall. Behind them, Sun Wukong walked slowly, not bowing.

The loud voice said, "Sun Wukong! Why don't you kowtow when you see the Buddha?"

Sun Wukong let go of the horse and whipped out his golden hoop rod. He shouted at the Buddha on the golden throne, "Evil monster, how dare you pretend to be the great Buddha! Stay right there!" Then he raised his rod and prepared to strike the Buddha. But before he could strike, two huge brass cymbals came down from the sky. They trapped Sun Wukong between them and joined together, making a mighty crashing sound. Sun Wukong was trapped inside. The crowd of people captured and tied up the other three travelers.

The travelers looked up and saw a Buddha on a golden throne. As they watched, the Buddha changed into his true form, and now the travelers could see that he was really a demon. The other people changed into their true forms and showed themselves to be little demons. The little demons picked up the two golden cymbals and put them on a platform. They expected Sun Wukong to be reduced to a puddle of blood in three days. They planned to steam and eat the three other travelers.

What happened here?

> The diamond-eyed monkey knew that the Buddha was false
> But the Tang monk used only his human eyes and was fooled
> He saw the appearance and not the truth
> The demon king was greater than the Dao

The travelers turned the wrong way
Now they might lose their lives!

Sun Wukong was trapped between the two cymbals. It was completely dark inside, and very hot. He tried pushing left and right but could not get out. He struck the cymbals with his golden hoop rod but they did not move. He used magic to grow to a thousand feet tall, but the cymbals grew with him. He became as small as a mustard seed, but the cymbals shrank with him. He pulled a hair from his head, whispered "Change" and became a five-pointed drill. He turned the drill a thousand times, but it had no effect on the cymbals.

Finally he recited the holy words, "Qián yuán hēnglì zhēn[1]." This was a call to the Six Gods of Light, the Six Gods of Darkness, and the Five Guardians. They all came quickly. They stood outside the cymbals and waited. Sun Wukong said to them, "I am trapped here because my master did not listen to me. I really don't care if they kill him, but I need to get out of here. It's so dark that I cannot see, and it's so hot that I cannot breathe!"

---

[1] These are the first five characters in the *I Ching*, the Book of Changes. The first, Qián, means sky or Heaven in Daoist cosmology. The next four mean beginning, prosperity, harmony and justice, and correspond to the four seasons of spring, summer, autumn and winter.

When they heard this, the Six Gods of Light ran away to protect Tangseng, the Six Gods of Darkness ran away to protect the two other disciples, four of the Guardians stayed and guarded the cymbals, and the fifth Guardian flew up to the South Heaven Gate. He flew right into the throne room of the Jade Emperor and threw himself at the Emperor's feet.

"Your Majesty," he said, "I am one of the Five Guardians. The Great Sage Equal to Heaven was traveling with the Tang monk to the Western Heaven. They came to a place called Small Thunderclap Mountain. The monk thought it was the true Thunderclap Mountain even though the Great Sage warned him that it was a trap. They entered anyway. Now the Great Sage is trapped between two large golden cymbals. He is going to die soon. That is why I have come here."

The Jade Emperor raised his hand and said, "Let the twenty-eight Constellations go and help the Great Sage." Right away the twenty-eight Constellations followed the Guardian back to the monastery.

They arrived about the time of the second watch. All the demons were sleeping. The Twenty-Eight Constellations walked quietly up to the golden cymbals. One of them said, "Great Sage we are here to help you escape, but we must be careful. If we hit the cymbals, they will make a great sound and wake up the demons. So we will try to make a small hole in one of the cymbals. As soon as you see even a little bit of light, you can escape." Then they began using their weapons to try and make a hole in the cymbals. But the two cymbals were like a dumpling whose edges were sealed together. For two hours they used every weapon they had, but they could not make a hole in the cymbals.

Finally one of the Constellations, the Golden Dragon said, "Let me try." He had a horn with a sharp tip. He made himself very small, so that his horn was the size of a tiny needle. Then he pushed as hard as he could. The tip of his horn slipped in between the two cymbals and pushed through to the inside. Sun Wukong could not see anything, but he could feel the horn's tip with his fingers. He used his golden hoop rod to make a tiny hole in the end of the horn. Then he made himself as small as a mustard seed. He crawled inside the hole at the end of the horn. "OK, pull out the horn!" he shouted.

Golden Dragon used all his strength and pulled his horn out, with Sun Wukong inside. Afterwards the dragon was so tired that he fell to the ground. Sun Wukong crawled out of Golden Dragon's horn and returned to his normal size.

Now Sun Wukong was angry. He smashed his golden hoop rod down on the cymbals, and they shattered into a thousand pieces. This made a huge noise that woke up the demon king and all the little demons. They rushed into the room and saw the broken cymbals on the floor. "Quick!" shouted the demon king, "Shut the doors!" But before they could shut the doors, Sun Wukong and the gods flew quickly out of the door and up to the ninth Heaven.

The demon king picked up his weapon, a mace with nine spikes like wolf's teeth. The demon had long hair, thick yellow eyebrows, a big nose, and long teeth. He looked like a man, but also like a beast. He shouted, "Wukong! A real man would not run away like this! Come down here and fight three rounds with me!"

Sun Wukong flew down to the ground. He replied, "What kind of monster are you? How can you be a false Buddha and create a false Thunderclap Mountain?"

"You don't know my name," the demon replied. "I am the Yellow-Browed Buddha, but the people around here call me King Yellow Brow. I have known about your journey for a long time. I used my magic to bring you and your master here. Now that you are here, let's have a test of strength. If you win, I will let you all go and you can continue on your journey to the west. But if you lose, I will kill all of you, and I will go myself to the real Thunderclap Mountain. I will get the scriptures and bring them back to China."

"You talk too much," replied Sun Wukong, and whipped out his golden hoop rod. They began to fight. The fight went much longer than three rounds. After fifty rounds they were still fighting. The little demons were shouting on one side of the fight, while the gods and soldiers of Heaven were shouting on the other side. Finally King Yellow Brow pulled an old white cloth from his belt and threw it into the air. It caught Sun Wukong and all the gods and soldiers of Heaven. He grabbed the cloth with everyone inside, and carried it back into the monastery. He told his little demons to tie up all the prisoners. Then the demons had a great feast, eating and drinking from morning till evening. When they were finished eating and drinking, they went off to sleep.

The prisoners were all feeling very weak, so they could not escape from their ropes. Sun Wukong heard the sound of crying. It was Tangseng, who said, "I wish I had listened to you. We could have avoided all of this. Now our work has come to nothing. How will we be saved from this terrible situation?"

Sun Wukong was happy to hear this! He made himself very small and easily escaped from the ropes that were tied around him. He then released Tangseng,

Zhu and Sha, then the twenty-eight Constellations and the other gods and soldiers of Heaven. He told Tangseng to get on the white horse and leave the monastery quickly. The twenty-eight Constellations used their magic to help the monk and his disciples travel away quickly.

Then Sun Wukong remembered that their luggage was still inside. "I must go back and get it," he said, "It has our travel rescript, Master's cassock and hat, and the golden begging bowl. These are great Buddhist treasures; we cannot leave them here." He went back inside to get the luggage. He picked up all the things and began carrying them outside. But the golden begging bowl fell out of his hands and dropped onto the floor with a loud crash. This woke up the demon king and his little demons. Sun Wukong dropped the rest of the luggage and used his cloud somersault to escape the monastery.

The demon king and his little demons ran out of the monastery. They followed Sun Wukong. Soon they arrived at the camp where the travelers, the twenty-eight Constellations, and the Five Guardians were resting.

"Brothers[1]!" shouted Golden Dragon, "The monsters are here!"

"Where do you think you're going?" shouted the demon king. Everyone in the camp except Tangseng and the horse rushed forward to join the battle. The three disciples fought the demon king, while the gods and soldiers of Heaven fought the thousands of little demons. The battle continued until the sun set in the west and the moon rose in the eastern sky.

Sun Wukong was fighting the demon king when he saw the demon king grab his white cloth. "This is bad," he thought. He shouted to the others to stop fighting and run away quickly, then he flew up to the ninth Heaven. But the others did not listen to him, they continued fighting. The demon king easily

---

[1] The Golden Dragon's brothers are the 27 other constellations of the Chinese zodiac: The Metal Dragon of the Gullet, the Earth Bat of the Woman, the Sun Hare of the Chamber, the Moon Fox of the Heart, the Fire Tiger of the Tail, the Water Leopard of the Winnower, the Wooden Unicorn of the Dipper, the Metal Bull of the Ox, the Earth Raccoon Dog of the Base, the Sun Rat of the Barrens, the Moon Swallow of the Roof, the Fire Pig of the House, the Water Beast of the Wall, the Wooden Wolf of the Strider, the Metal Dog of the Harvester, the Earth Boar of the Stomach, the Sun Cock of the Pleiades, the Moon Crow of the Net, the Fire Monkey of the Turtle, the Water Ape of Orion, the Wooden Hyena of the Well, the Metal Goat of the Ghosts, the Earth River Deer of the Willow, the Sun Horse of the Seven Stars, the Moon Deer of the Spread Net, the Fire Snake of the Wing, and the Water Worm of the Axle Tree.

captured all of them in his white cloth. He carried them back to the monastery and closed the door.

Sun Wukong flew down from the ninth Heaven and rested on the eastern slope of the mountain. "Oh Master!" he cried, "What did you do in your past lives to deserve these troubles? It's so hard to save you from suffering. What should we do?"

He did not know what to do. He thought about going to the Jade Emperor but he was afraid that the Emperor would be angry with him. Then he remembered that there was a great warrior called Demon Conquering Celestial Worthy who lived in Wudang Mountain. This warrior was also called the grand master. He decided to go and ask the grand master for help. He jumped into the air and used his cloud somersault to head south.

Chapter 66

Sun Wukong traveled to Wudang Mountain, the home of Demon Conquering Celestial Worthy. Sun Wukong had heard the story of the grand master's birth.

> His father was King Joy
> His mother was Queen Victory
> She dreamed that she had swallowed the sun
> Fifteen months later the child was born
> He grew up brave and strong
> He had no interest in his father's throne
> He only wanted to seek wisdom
> He left his parents' home
> He went to live in the mountains
> There he studied the mysteries of the Dao
> He learned how to fly to Heaven whenever he wanted.
> The Jade Emperor named him True Martial Lord
> Throughout the entire world
> From the beginning to the end of time
> He knows all truth
> He wins every fight
> He kills every demon

Sun Wukong arrived at Wudang Mountain and quickly passed through the first, second and third gates of Heaven. There he found a crowd of five hundred ministers. He asked to see the grand master. A few minutes later the grand master came out to greet him.

Sun Wukong said to him, "Sir, I need to ask you for help. I am Sun Wukong, the Great Sage Equal to Heaven. I am traveling with the Tang monk to seek the Buddha's scriptures in the Western Heaven. We arrived at a place called Little Thunderclap Mountain, where a demon tricked my master into thinking he was the true Buddha. The demon used a magic cloth to capture my master, myself, and my brother disciples. I called the Five Guardians for help. One of them went to see the Jade Emperor. The Emperor sent the twenty-eight Constellations to help us. But all the Constellations were captured and are now prisoners. I alone escaped. The others are all prisoners of the demon. I don't know what to do, so I am asking for your help."

The grand master nodded his head. He said, "In the old days I ruled the lands of the north. The Jade Emperor named me Zhenwu[1] and asked me to kill all the demons and fiends in the land. I rode barefoot on the turtle and the snake. I received help from the five thunder generals and several dragons, lions and other beasts. Together we ended the rule of the demons. Now I live peacefully here on this mountain."

He continued, "I am glad that you came to see me, but there is a small problem. On one hand I cannot help you without instructions from the Jade Emperor. If I did, he might become angry with me. But on the other hand, I cannot just refuse your request. So I will send General Turtle, General Snake and five magic dragons to help you. I am sure that they will capture this demon and rescue your master."

Sun Wukong bowed in thanks. Then he flew into the air, followed by the seven magic creatures. They all traveled quickly to Small Thunderclap Mountain. When they arrived, one of the little demons saw them and ran inside the monastery. He said to Yellow Brow, "That monkey has returned with some dragons, a turtle and a snake. I think they want to fight."

Yellow Brow put on his armor and picked up his wolf teeth mace. He walked outside and shouted, "Who are you, and how dare you come here to my immortal home?"

The magic creatures replied, "Wretched monster! We are General Turtle, General Snake, and five dragon gods. We were invited here by the Great Sage Equal to Heaven. Our master is the grand master, the Demon Conquering Celestial Worthy. Give us the Tang monk and the other prisoners and we will let you live. If you don't, we will chop you and your little demons into little pieces and burn all your buildings to ashes."

This made Yellow Brow very angry. He shouted, "Stay where you are and feel my power!" The battle began. The five dragons turned the clouds upside down and made heavy rain. The two generals brought clouds of dust and sand as they attacked with their weapons. Sun Wukong joined them using his rod.

They fought for about an hour. Then Sun Wukong saw the demon reach down for his white cloth. "Watch out, my friends!" he cried, and flew up above the

---

[1] Zhenwu, the Perfect Warrior, the protector of Wudang Mountain, has long unbound hair and is barefoot. He represents the North and is one of four Chinese astrological figures for the four directions. Originally he was called Xuanwu (玄武), the Dark Warrior, but during the Northern Song dynasty his name was changed to Zhenwu in order to avoid using the character 玄 from the Song Emperor's name.

ninth Heaven. The seven magic animals did not know what he meant by that. They stopped attacking with their weapons but they did not fly away. Yellow Brow threw the cloth into the air. It easily captured all seven magic animals. The demon tied up the cloth and carried the prisoners back into the monastery's cellar.

Sun Wukong saw this from the ninth Heaven. After the magic animals were captured, he returned to the side of the mountain. He said to himself, "This demon is very powerful!" He did not have any ideas for what to do next. He sat, not moving, with his eyes closed.

"Wake up, Great Sage!" came a voice from nearby. Sun Wukong opened his eyes, jumped up, and grabbed his rod. He saw the Day Sentinel.

"You wretched little god," he shouted, "I haven't seen you for several days. Why do you show up here now? You make me so angry, I think I'll hit your feet a few times just to make myself feel better."

The Day Sentinel replied, "Great Sage, please don't be angry. You know that I am here to give secret protection to the Tang monk."

"Well, you're not doing a very good job. Tell me, where does this monster keep my master, my brother disciples, the twenty-eight Constellations, and the other gods and magical creatures?"

"Your master and the other two disciples are tied up. They are hanging in a room by the side of the treasure hall. The rest are being kept in the cellar. You must go quickly to save them!"

Sun Wukong said, "Where can I go? I cannot go up to Heaven, I cannot go down to the seas, I am afraid to see the Bodhisattva, and I cannot go to see the Buddha himself. The seven magical animals cannot help me because they have been captured too. I dare not go back to the grand master and tell him that his magical animals have been captured. I have nowhere else to turn."

"Don't worry, Great Sage! You were just at Wudang Mountain. Nearby is Mount Xuyi. A great teacher lives there. He is called the Bodhisattva King Teacher. He has a disciple called Little Zhang Prince. There are also four powerful generals of Heaven there. I have heard that they are very good at fighting demons. You should go and ask them for help."

This made the monkey king feel a little bit better. He stood up and said, "All right, I will go. You stay here and take care of Master. Don't let any harm come to him." Then he used his cloud somersault to fly to Mount Xuyi.

Soon he arrived at Mount Xuyi. He saw a great monastery and a tall pagoda a thousand feet high. He entered the pagoda at the second floor. There he was met by Bodhisattva King Teacher and Little Zhang Prince. Sun Wukong bowed to them. Then he told Bodhisattva King Teacher about the capture of Tangseng and the others.

When Sun Wukong was finished telling the story, Bodhisattva King Teacher said, "The matters that you speak of are important to the success of our Buddhist religion, and I should go with you to help. But there is a small problem. Right now there is heavy rain in this area, and the nearby River Huai may flood. I recently had to fight the Great Sage Water Ape[1]. He is a troublemaking monkey! If the water touches him, he might cause trouble, and I am the only one who can defeat him. So I cannot leave. However, I will send my disciple Little Zhang and four great warriors. They should have no trouble capturing this demon."

Sun Wukong was a little bit worried about this, but he thanked Bodhisattva King Teacher. Together with Little Zhang and the four great warriors he returned to Little Thunderclap Monastery.

You can probably guess what happened next. A little demon reported to King Yellow Brow that Little Zhang, Sun Wukong and the four great warriors were standing outside the monastery. Yellow Brow came out and shouted at Sun Wukong, "Monkey! Who have you brought with you this time?"

Little Zhang stepped forward and replied, "You lawless monster! You have no flesh on your face and your eyes cannot see. That's why you don't recognize me! I am a disciple of Bodhisattva King Teacher, and I am coming to help the Great Sage Equal to Heaven. That is why I am here to arrest you."

Yellow Brow laughed and said, "You are just a little boy. Why do you dare to think you can fight against me?"

"I am the son of the king of Flowing Sand Kingdom. I left my home when I was a boy, and learned the secret of long life. I have traveled to the home of the Buddha himself. I have captured a water monster with my two hands. I have defeated tigers and dragons. And now I will defeat you too!"

---

[1] This ape is also known as Wuzhiqi, an aquatic demon with the appearance of a green macaque monkey. He lived in the Huai River. He was considered the god of water in ancient Chinese mythology. He was defeated by the emperor Yu the Great as part of the emperor's grand project to tame the Great Flood of Gunyu and is imprisoned under Turtle Mountain.

"Little prince, you are a fool to follow this monkey across a thousand mountains and ten thousand waters. You may be powerful enough to defeat a few tigers and dragons and water monsters, but you will lose your life if you try to fight me."

And so the battle began. Sun Wukong used his rod. Little Zhang used his weapon, a long white lance. The four warriors used their red swords. But Yellow Brow was very strong. He used his wolf-teeth mace and could not be defeated by the others.

They fought for a long time. Sun Wukong was watching Yellow Brow carefully. As soon as Yellow Brow reached for his white cloth, Sun Wukong shouted, "Watch out, all of you!" and he flew quickly up to the ninth Heaven. The others did not fly away quickly enough. They were all captured by the white cloth. Yellow Brow carried them back to the monastery and put them in the cellar with the other prisoners.

Sun Wukong sat down and cried. He sat for a long time, with no idea what to do next. After a while he looked up. A colorful cloud was approaching from the southeast. Behind the cloud, heavy rain fell on the distant mountains. A man was riding the cloud. He had big ears, a square face, broad shoulders, and a big belly. His eyes were bright and his voice was full of joy. Sun Wukong recognized at once that this was the laughing monk, Maitreya[1], the future Buddha.

Sun Wukong fell to his knees and kowtowed. He said, "Where are you going, Lord Buddha?"

Maitreya replied, "I am here because of the demon in Small Thunderclap Mountain."

"Thank you. May I ask, who is this demon? Where did he come from? And what is that white cloth treasure that he uses?"

"At one time he was a young man with yellow hair and yellow eyebrows. His job was to make music in my palace by striking two golden cymbals. Earlier this year I needed to go away for a while. I left him in the palace. He stole some of my treasures and came to earth, taking the form of the Buddha. His

---

[1] Mílè, known in English as Maitreya, is one of the thousands of forms taken by the Buddha. According to Buddhist legend, he will appear on earth in the future when the dharma (teachings) has been forgotten by most of the world. He will replace the current Buddha, Gautama, and will restore the dharma. Then the people of earth will lose their doubts, be freed from unhappiness, and lead joyous and holy lives.

white cloth was my 'bag of human seed[1].' His wolf-teeth mace was the stick used to strike the cymbals."

Sun Wukong said, "Ah, I am surprised that you let this boy escape and become a false Buddha!"

"Yes, I was careless. But it is your master's fate to suffer on this journey. He must pass through eighty-one trials, and you must fight a hundred monsters and demons. Now I will capture this monster for you."

"This monster has vast powers. You don't even have any weapons. How can you defeat him?"

Maitreya laughed. "That will not be a problem. At the bottom of this mountain there is a meadow. In the meadow I will set up a little hut and a field of melons. All the melons will be unripe. Go start a fight with the demon. Do not try to defeat him. Lead him to the melon field. When you get here, turn yourself into a ripe melon. The monster will be hungry and thirsty, so he will look for a ripe melon. He will find you and eat you. Then you will be in the monster's belly. At that point you can do whatever you like to him."

"That's a good idea. But why will the demon follow me to the melon field?"

"I will teach you a little bit of magic. Give me your hand." Sun Wukong held out his left hand. Maitreya licked his own finger then wrote the word "Forbid" on Sun Wukong's palm. He said, "Keep your left hand closed in a fist and only show it to the demon. When he sees it, he will follow you."

So Sun Wukong returned to the monastery. He shouted at Yellow Brow, "Evil monster, your master has returned. Come out now!"

A minute later Yellow Brow came out, saying, "It's you again. But you are alone. It looks like nobody wants to help you. This time you will lose your life." Then he saw that Sun Wukong was holding his rod with just one hand. "Why are you only using one hand?" he asked.

"You are a poor fighter, that's why you must always use that white cloth. I'll bet that if you fight me without the white cloth, I can defeat you with just one hand."

---

[1] A legendary tenth century wandering sage named Budai (or Hotei) was believed to be an incarnation of Maitreya. He carried a hemp bag full of gifts for local peasants, especially children. He is a fertility deity and is portayed as a disheveled, fat, laughing Buddha. A porcelain statue of Budai is often seen in Chinese restaurants.

"All right, go ahead and fight with one hand. I won't use my treasure." He ran forward to attack Sun Wukong. Sun Wukong opened his left fist and showed the magic word to Yellow Brow. Immediately Yellow Brow forgot about everything except using his mace to attack Sun Wukong. The monkey retreated towards the melon field, and Yellow Brow followed.

They reached the melon field. Sun Wukong changed into a large melon, ripe and sweet. Yellow Brow looked around but did not see the monkey anywhere. He walked up to the grass hut and said, "Who is the farmer here?"

"I am the farmer," said Maitreya, coming out of the hut. He had changed his appearance and looked like a simple farmer.

"Do you have any ripe melons? I am very thirsty."

"Yes of course. Please take one."

Yellow Brow looked around. He saw one ripe melon in the field. He picked it up and began to eat it. Sun Wukong jumped into his mouth and down to his belly. Then he started kicking Yellow Brow from the inside. The pain was terrible. Yellow Brow fell to the ground, crying. He shouted, "I am finished! I am finished! Who can help me?"

Maitreya walked over to him. He changed into his true form and said, "Wretched beast, do you recognize me now?"

Yellow Brow looked up and recognized his master immediately. He grabbed his belly with both hands while he kowtowed to Maitreya. "Master, please let me live! I will not do this again!"

Maitreya took the white bag from Yellow Brow's belt. Then he took the wolf's teeth mace. Sun Wukong was still inside Yellow Brow's belly, kicking as hard as he could. Maitreya shouted, "Sun Wukong, please stop kicking him!"

Sun Wukong did not listen. He was so angry, he continued to kick Yellow Brow from the inside.

"Let him go!" shouted Maitreya.

Finally Sun Wukong stopped. He said, "Open your mouth, you wretched beast, and let me come out." Yellow Brow opened his mouth. Sun Wukong jumped out. Then he grabbed his rod and got ready to bring it down on Yellow Brow's head. But before he could do that, Maitreya grabbed Yellow Brow, made him small, and dropped him into the white bag.

Maitreya looked around the melon field. Then he said to Yellow Brow in the bag, "What did you do with my golden cymbals?"

Yellow Brow cried, "That troublemaking monkey smashed them!"

"If they are smashed, then you must at least return the gold to me."

"The gold pieces are in a pile in the throne room of Little Thunderclap Monastery."

Maitreya and Sun Wukong walked together up the mountain to the monastery. When they got there, they saw that the gates were closed and locked. Maitreya waved his hand and the gates flew open. They walked inside. In the throne room was a pile of golden pieces. Maitreya blew on them and recited a spell. The gold changed into two small cymbals. He picked up the two cymbals. Then he put the cymbals and wolf-teeth mace in his robe. Then, holding the white bag with Yellow Brow inside, he flew up into the air and returned to his home in the highest Heaven.

Sun Wukong walked into the room and found Tangseng, Zhu and Sha. He untied them. Zhu was so hungry that he did not even thank Sun Wukong, he just ran into the kitchen and began putting rice in his mouth. After he finished eating two pots of rice, he brought some back for the others to eat.

Sun Wukong told them the story of his battles with Yellow Brow and the help he received from Maitreya. Then he went into the cellar and untied all the prisoners. The prisoners came out of the cellar. Tangseng, wearing his cassock and hat, was there to meet them and thank them for their help.

Then General Turtle, General Snake and the five magic dragons returned to Wudang Mountain. Little Zhang and the four warriors returned to their home. The twenty-eight Constellations returned to Heaven. The five Guardians, the Six Gods of Light and the Six Gods of Darkness also returned to their homes in Heaven.

Tangseng and the disciples fed the white horse. They stayed at the monastery and rested overnight. The next morning, they started a fire which burned the entire monastery to the ground.

Chapter 67

The four travelers continue walking west again. They walked for about a month. The weather grew warmer.

One day they saw a small mountain village. On the east side of the village was a small house under some trees. They walked up to the house. Tangseng knocked on the front door, saying, "Open the door! Open the door!"

An old man came out of the house. He was wearing a black cloth on his head and an old white robe. "Who's making all this noise?" he asked.

Tangseng folded his hands and bowed, saying, "Grandfather, we come from the land of the east. We are traveling to the Western Heaven to seek Buddhist scriptures. May we stay at your home tonight?"

"Sorry, you cannot get to the Western Heaven from here. This is the little Western Heaven. You seek the greater Western Heaven. But there is a problem. Just west of here is a large mountain, eight hundred miles wide. The entire mountain is covered by persimmon trees. There is only one road through the mountain. At this time of year, the persimmon trees drop their fruits. The fruits all end up in the mountain road. They completely fill it up so nobody can get through. And when the fruit rots, the whole area smells worse than any toilet. The people here call it 'Slimy Shit Mountain Pass.' Nobody can get through that mountain pass."

Sun Wukong laughed and said, "Old man, you are just trying to frighten us so that we go away. That's no problem. If your house is too small for us, we understand. We will just sleep under these nearby trees."

The old man looked carefully at Sun Wukong. "You are quite ugly. What are you?"

"Sir, you have eyes but you cannot see. I am the Great Sage Equal to Heaven. It's true that I am ugly but I do have some skills. I am quite skilled at catching and killing demons. I can frighten ghosts and gods. And I can even steal treasures from Heaven!"

When the old man heard this, he smiled and invited the four travelers to come into his house. He and his family served them a very good vegetarian meal. The travelers ate and drank until they were full. Later, when they were finished, Sun Wukong asked the old man, "Sir, when we first met you, you were not very friendly to us. But now you have given us a very good dinner, and we thank you for that. Can you tell us why you have given us such good food and drink?"

The old man replied, "Monkey, you said that you were good at catching and killing demons. We just happen to have a demon nearby."

"Oh good!" said Sun Wukong, clapping his hands. "Once again, business has come to my door! But I don't see any problems in this village, and your family appears to be healthy. Tell me why you want me to catch a demon for you."

"Our village was peaceful and happy for many years. But three years ago, a cold wind blew through the village and a monster spirit arrived. He ate all of our cows and pigs. He even ate some men and women and a few children. Since then, the monster spirit has returned several times to eat more animals and people. If you can capture and kill this monster, we will give you a great deal of money!"

"Old man, you are a fool. You say that this monster has been eating animals and people for three years. But there must be several hundred families in this village. If each family gave an ounce of silver, you would have enough money to pay a monster hunter to come here and kill this monster."

"We did just that. Two years ago, we paid a Buddhist monk to come here and catch the monster. The monk sang songs, burned incense and hit some bells. The monster heard this and came into our village. The monk and the monster fought. The monster easily won the fight. He killed the monk. We had to pay for the funeral. We also had to give some money to his disciples. What a mess!"

"Yes, that sounds bad. Did you try again?"

"Yes. A year ago, we paid a Daoist to come here and catch the monster. The Daoist waved his arms, calling on his gods to come. The gods did not come, but the monster came. The monster and the Daoist fought for a day. When it was over, we found the Daoist drowned in the river."

Sun Wukong laughed and said, "Well, you certainly have had some bad luck! Go now and call the village elders." The old man went out and soon returned with eight or nine village elders. They all stood in the courtyard outside the house. Sun Wukong asked them if they would allow him to catch and kill the monster. Of course, the elders agreed. They insisted on paying for this, but Sun Wukong said that he only wanted a little bit of rice and tea.

One of the elders said, "You are so small, monkey. The monster is huge. How can you fight him?"

"I will just treat him as my grandson. I will hit him and he will do as I say."

Just then, a great wind started to blow. All the elders ran into the house to hide. Tangseng, Zhu and Sha started to follow them, but Sun Wukong grabbed Zhu and Sha. He scolded them, saying, "Have you lost your minds? Stay out here with me! Let's see what kind of monster this is!"

Oh, what a wind!

> Tigers and wolves hid in their caves
> Ghosts and gods were frightened
> Mighty trees fell to the ground
> Rocks rolled down from mountaintops
> Villagers shut and locked their doors
> Children hid under their beds
> Black clouds covered the sky
> The whole earth became dark.

Sun Wukong stood unmoving as the wind howled around him. When the wind stopped, the world was quiet and dark. He looked up in the sky and saw two yellow lights. They looked like lanterns hung in the sky.

Sha said, "Those look like lanterns, but they are really the yellow eyes of the monster. If those are his eyes, how big is his mouth?"

Sun Wukong flew up into the air. He whipped out his golden hoop rod. He shouted at the monster, "Who are you? Where do you come from?" The monster did not reply. Sun Wukong began to hit the monster again and again with his rod. The monster did not say a word and he did not try to fight back. He only held up his weapon, a long lance, to block the monkey's blows.

Zhu also jumped into the fight, using his rake. Now the monster used a second lance to block the blows from the rake. Still, he said nothing.

"The monster does not know how to speak," said Sun Wukong. "Perhaps he has not learned human speech yet."

They fought all night. The monkey and the pig rained blows down on the monster, and the monster just blocked them with his two lances. As the morning sun rose in the east, the monster turned to run away. Sun Wukong and Zhu followed him. But soon they noticed a terrible smell. "What family is cleaning out their toilet?" asked Zhu. Of course, it was the rotting persimmons of Slimy Shit Pass.

The monster ran past the mountain pass. Then he turned into a huge red snake. The snake's body was so long that they could not see the far end. Its body was covered with hard red scales. Its eyes were like yellow stars, white fog came from its nose, its teeth were like long swords, and a long horn came from the center of its head.

Sun Wukong and Zhu attacked the snake. It turned and dived into a hole in the ground. Seven or eight feet of its tail stuck out from the hole. Zhu grabbed the tail and tried to pull the snake out of the ground. "Don't bother," said Sun Wukong. "You can't pull a snake out like that. The snake is quite large, and that hole is small. The snake cannot turn around. So there must be another opening somewhere else. That's where the snake will come out as it tries to escape."

Sun Wukong looked around and soon found the second hole. He shouted to Zhu to stab the snake's tail with his rake. Zhu brought his rake down on the snake's tail. And a few seconds later the snake came flying out of the second hole. Sun Wukong stood in front of it, waving his rod. The snake opened its huge mouth and swallowed the monkey.

"Oh no, my elder brother is dead!" cried Zhu.

"I am fine," said Sun Wukong from inside the snake. "Look, I will make a bridge for you." He pushed his rod against the top of the snake's belly. The snake picked up the middle of its body, resting its head and tail on the ground, so that it looked like a bridge.

"That's very nice," said Zhu. "What else can you do?"

"Now look, I will make a boat for you," said Sun Wukong. He turned his rod around, and started pushing his rod against the bottom of the snake's belly. The snake pushed its belly to the ground and picked up its head and tail. Now it looked like a riverboat.

"Also very nice," said Zhu, "but that boat needs a mast." So Sun Wukong made his rod grow until it was seventy feet long. He pushed it right through the top of the snake's belly and it stuck up in the air like the mast of a boat. The snake's body shook and it died. Sun Wukong climbed out through the hole in the snake's belly.

Back at the village, the old man was telling Tangseng that the two disciples were probably dead because they had not returned after a full day. "I am not worried," replied Tangseng. Just then they saw Sun Wukong and Zhu coming down the road. They were dragging the huge red snake behind them, shouting for the villagers to get out of the way.

"That is the monster spirit that has been eating our animals and people!" said the old man. "We are very glad that you have used your magic powers to kill this terrible monster. Now we will all be safe again."

The villagers insisted on thanking Tangseng and his disciples, so the four travelers had to stay in the village for several days, eating and drinking and resting. Finally, Tangseng said that they had to continue their journey to the west. They left the village and began walking westwards. All the people of the village followed them.

After a day's journey they came to the mountain road that was filled with rotting persimmon fruit. There were so many persimmons that it was impossible to walk through them. And the smell was terrible, like a toilet that had not been cleaned out for years.

Even Sun Wukong said, "This will be difficult."

Zhu said, "No, this will not be a problem at all." Turning to the old man he said, "Sir, please ask the villagers to prepare a large meal of rice, steamed buns, and bread. I will eat all of it. That will give me strength. And then I will open up a path through this pass."

The villagers prepared a huge feast for Zhu. The pig ate everything. Then he took off his black shirt and made a magic sign with his fingers. He changed into a huge hog a thousand feet high. He used his giant snout to dig out a narrow path through the rotting fruit. Tangseng, Sun Wukong and Sha followed him, being careful to avoid the huge piles of rotting fruit on both sides of the path.

Three hundred villagers followed them. They carried seven or eight piculs[1] of rice and dozens of plates of steamed buns for Zhu to eat.

After a full day, Zhu reached the end of the huge pile of rotting fruit. He wiped some persimmons off his snout. He was very hungry. He sat down and

---

[1] A picul was originally defined as the amount that a grown man can carry on a shoulder pole. It's equal to 100 catties, or about 143 pounds.

ate all the rice and buns. He did not care what kind of food was in front of him, he ate all of it.

When Zhu finished eating, he returned to his usual size. He put his black shirt back on and picked up the luggage. Tangseng mounted his white horse, then he turned and thanked the villagers for their kindness. The villagers thanked the travelers for killing the monster, and they all returned to their homes.

The travelers turned their faces to the west and continued their journey.

Chapter 68

The Buddhist monk Tangseng and his three disciples – the monkey king Sun Wukong, the pig-man Zhu Bajie, and the quiet man Sha Wujing – had been traveling towards the Western Heaven for several years. The cool and wet spring had turned to a hot and dry summer. One day as they walked, they saw a large city in front of them. A wide moat surrounded the high city walls.

Tangseng called out, "Disciples, look at that. What city is it?"

Sun Wukong said, "Master, it looks like you don't know how to read. The name of the city is written on that yellow banner. It says, 'Scarlet Purple Kingdom.'"

"I have never heard of this kingdom," said Tangseng. "We must stop here and get our travel rescript certified."

They crossed over the moat on a bridge and entered the city through the main gate. As they walked through the streets, they saw that the city was large and beautiful. Most buildings had a shop or restaurant on the first floor and homes on the upper floors. Boats came from far away, bringing goods to the people of the city. Great palaces rose towards the sky.

The streets were crowded with people shopping, talking, and doing business. But when the townspeople saw the four strangers, they stopped and stared. Tangseng said to his disciples, "Don't start any trouble. Keep your heads down and keep moving." Zhu and Sha lowered their heads, but Sun Wukong kept his head high, looking around for trouble.

After a while, most of the people stopped following them and returned to what they were doing before. But a group of young people continued to follow the travelers, laughing and throwing stones at Zhu. Tangseng became quite nervous, but they kept walking.

After a while they arrived at a building called the Hostel of Meeting[1]. "Let's stop here and rest," said Tangseng, "Later we can get our rescript certified so that we may continue our journey."

They entered the building. Two officials were sitting there. They looked up,

---

[1] Hostels of Meeting were established in the 13th century A.D. and were used as temporary lodging for visiting foreign envoys.

surprised. One of them said, "Who are you? What are you doing here?"

Folding his hands in front of his chest, Tangseng told them, "This poor monk is traveling from the Tang Empire to the Western Heaven to obtain Buddhist scriptures for our emperor. We just arrived at your worthy city and dared not leave without getting our travel rescript certified. We ask that you do this for us. We also ask that you let us stay here to rest and have a small meal."

The officials ordered some guest rooms to be prepared and food be brought to the travelers. Soon the travelers were given rice, green vegetables, tofu and mushrooms. But the officials told the travelers that they must cook the food themselves.

Tangseng asked the officials where he could find the king. One of them replied, "His Majesty is meeting with his ministers today. But if you want to meet him you must do it quickly. Tomorrow it might be too late. I don't know how long you will have to wait to see him."

Zhu removed the cassock and travel rescript from the luggage and handed them to Tangseng. Tangseng put on the cassock and put the travel rescript in his sleeve. He said to his disciples, "Stay here. Please don't cause any trouble." Then he walked down the street to the royal palace. He met the Maitreyan royal messenger. Tangseng told the messenger who he was and why he wanted to see the king. The royal messenger told the king, and the king agreed to see the Tang monk.

Tangseng entered the throne room and prostrated himself before the king. "Get up, get up," said the king, waving his hand. He asked Tangseng to show him the travel rescript. After reading it, he said, "Worthy monk, we have heard of your emperor. We have heard that at one time he was very ill. Tell us, how did he return to life after his illness?"

Tangseng said, "Your Majesty, our emperor is a great and wise ruler. North of Chang'an there lived a river dragon who was responsible for bringing rain to the kingdom. One day the dragon disobeyed the emperor's order to bring rain. Because of this, the emperor decreed that the dragon must die. He ordered his prime minister, a man named Wei, to kill the dragon. But before Wei could do this, the dragon appeared to the emperor in a dream and asked the emperor to let him live. The emperor agreed. The next day the emperor asked Wei to come and play chess with him. Wei came, but during the chess game Wei fell asleep. Wei killed the dragon in his dream."

"Ah," said the king, "that is terrible."

"After his death, the dragon was unhappy. He thought that the emperor had lied to him. So he went to the Kings of the Underworld to bring a lawsuit against the emperor. Shortly after that, the emperor became very ill. His soul left his body and traveled to the underworld. But just before the emperor died, Wei gave him a letter and told him to give it to a deceased courtier named Cui Jue. The emperor died, went to the underworld, met Cui Jue, and gave him the letter. After reading the letter Cui Jue agreed to help the emperor."

"Wonderful!" said the king. "How did he escape the underworld?"

"Cui Jue tricked the Kings of the Underworld. He changed the Book of Life to give the emperor twenty more years of life. The Kings of the Underworld read the Book of Life and saw that the emperor's life was not finished yet. So they allowed him to return to the land of the living. The emperor quickly recovered from his illness. But he never forgot his visit to the underworld. Later he sent me on this journey to the Western Heaven to obtain the Buddha's holy scriptures and bring them back to the Tang Empire."

"Thank you for that wonderful story, worthy monk. You come from a great nation. We have been ill for a long time, and we do not have any wise ministers like Wei who can save us." Just then, servants came with food and drink and they ate their dinner.

While Tangseng was meeting with the king, the three disciples were in the hostel. They were becoming quite hungry. Sha went into the kitchen to prepare the food. There was no oil or soy sauce, so he could not cook the vegetables. He asked Zhu to go out and buy these things. Zhu refused, saying that he was too ugly and would just cause trouble in the street. So Sun Wukong said that he would go with Zhu to buy the oil, salt and soy sauce.

Sun Wukong asked one of the officials where they could buy the food. The official said, "Go west on this street, then turn at the first corner. You will find the Zheng family grocery store. They have everything you need."

Sun Wukong and Zhu walked down the street towards the grocery store. They saw a large crowd of people nearby. Sun Wukong said to Zhu, "You wait here. Keep your head down." Then he walked towards the crowd. He saw that they were reading a large royal proclamation that was hung on a wall. The proclamation said,

> "Since we, the king of Scarlet Purple Kingdom, have ascended to the throne, the kingdom has been peaceful and happy. But three years ago, we became quite ill. None of our ministers could help us. So now we

invite scholars and doctors from anywhere in the world to come to the royal palace. If you can bring us back to health, we will give you half of our kingdom."

Sun Wukong said to himself, "Well, this looks like fun. I think we should stay in this city for a little while so Old Monkey can play doctor!" Then he picked up a handful of dirt, threw it in the air, and recited a spell. He became invisible. He blew out a huge breath. A powerful wind came and blew away all the people. Then he walked up to the proclamation and pulled it off the wall. He walked over to Zhu. He saw that Zhu had fallen asleep. He rolled up the proclamation and quietly put it inside Zhu's robe.

The crowd of people picked themselves off the ground, looked up, and saw that the proclamation was missing. Guards ran around looking for it. One of them saw Zhu standing nearby. The guard saw the proclamation sticking up out of Zhu's robe. The guard shouted, "You are a dead man! How dare you pull down the king's proclamation? You are either a great doctor or you are a thief. We will find out which one you are."

They tried to drag him away to the royal palace, but Zhu refused to move. It was like he was a tree with roots going deep into the ground. The guards pulled and pushed him but they could not move him.

A group of elderly eunuchs approached. One of them said to Zhu, "You are a strange looking man. Who are you and what are you doing here?"

Zhu replied, "I have come from the Tang Empire and am traveling to the Western Heaven. My master, a Buddhist monk, has gone to the royal palace to have our travel rescript certified. My elder brother and I were looking to buy some oil and other foods. I think he became invisible, grabbed the proclamation, and stuffed it in my robe."

The eunuch said, "Just a few minutes ago I saw a monk walking towards the royal palace. That must be your master. Your elder brother must have powerful magic. Where is he now?"

"His name is Father Sun. He is probably at the Hostel of Meeting."

"Come with us. We will go there and learn the truth of this matter." He told the guards to let Zhu go. Zhu walked back to the Hostel of Meeting, followed by the eunuchs, a dozen guards, and several hundred townspeople.

When they got to the hostel, Zhu saw Sun Wukong and shouted angrily at him. Sun Wukong just laughed. Then several of the eunuchs and palace guards stepped forward and bowed to Sun Wukong. They said, "Father Sun, we are glad that Heaven has sent you to us. We ask you to help our king recover from his illness. If you can do this, our king will give you half of his kingdom."

Sun Wukong stopped laughing. With a serious face he said, "I became invisible and took down the royal proclamation. I also arranged things so that my younger brother would bring you to me. Your king is ill and I can certainly help him. But you know the old saying,

> Be careful when you sell medicine
> Don't call just any doctor when you're sick

Tell your king to come here and ask me to help him. I can easily heal him."

Half of the eunuchs and guards stayed at the hostel, while the other half ran back to the royal palace. Without waiting to be announced they ran into the throne room. The king was still having dinner with Tangseng. One of them prostrated himself before the king and said, "Your Majesty, a holy monk from the Tang Empire has taken down your proclamation. We think he has powerful magic. The monk is now in the Hostel of Meeting. He asks that Your Majesty go there to seek his help."

The king was pleased to hear this. He said to Tangseng, "Worthy monk, how many disciples do you have?"

Tangseng replied, "I have three stupid disciples."

"Which of them is a doctor?"

"To tell you the truth, Your Majesty, they are all idiots. They can carry baggage, lead horses and travel over mountains and rivers. They also have some skill in killing monsters and demons. None of them know anything about medicine."

"Perhaps you are being too hard on them. We wish to see this Father Sun. But we are too weak to travel. He must come here." The king told the eunuchs and guards to return to the hostel and politely ask Father Sun to come to the palace.

The eunuchs and guards returned to the hostel. Kowtowing before Sun Wukong, they told him the king was too ill to travel, and would he please come to the palace. Sun Wukong agreed. Before he left the hostel, he told Zhu and Sha to stay at the hostel and take whatever medicines the people bring to them. They agreed.

Sun Wukong walked to the palace with the eunuchs and guards. They entered the throne room. The king said, "Who is the holy monk? Who is this great Father Sun?"

Sun Wukong stepped forward and shouted as loud as he could, "I am!" The king heard a loud voice and saw the monkey's ugly face. He fell back on his throne. The eunuchs helped him to leave the throne room. The ministers were angry at Sun Wukong and shouted at him. But Sun Wukong replied, "Don't talk that way to me, or your king will not get better in a thousand years."

"What do you mean?" asked one of the ministers. "A human life does not last that long."

"If I don't help him, he will die. Then he will be reborn as a sickly human and die again. And again, and again, for a thousand years. Listen:

> Medicine is a mysterious art
> You must use your eyes and ears
> Ask questions, feel the pulse[1]
> Examine the patient's vital energy
> Does he sleep well?
> Listen to his voice
> Is it clear or harsh?
> Are his words true or crazy?
> Ask how long has he been ill
> How does he eat, drink, go to the toilet?
> Feel the pulse
> Is it long or short, fast or slow?
> I must do all these things
> Or your king will never recover."

Hearing this, the ministers believed that Sun Wukong was a powerful doctor. They went to see the king and ask him if he would see Sun Wukong. "Just leave us alone," said the king. "We are too weak to see anyone."

The ministers went back to Sun Wukong and told him the king's words. "No problem," said Sun Wukong. "I do not need to touch the king. I will feel his

---

[1] Traditional Chinese Medicine practitioners diagnose illness by taking the patient's pulse at three locations on the wrist. Some pulse conditions are: floating, sunken, slow, rapid, surging, fine, vacuous, replete, long, short, slippery, rough, string-like, tight, soggy, moderate, faint, weak, dissipated, hollow, drumskin, firm, hidden, stirred, intermittent, bound, skipping, and racing.

pulse with hanging threads."

They returned to the king and told him this. The king said, "That is interesting. We have been ill for three years and nobody has ever tried that. We will allow it."

The ministers went back to Sun Wukong and told him that the king agreed to allow the use of hanging threads. Before he could say anything, Tangseng shouted, "You wretched ape! You will be the death of me! In all the years we have traveled together, I have never seen you cure a single person. You know nothing of drugs, and you have never read a medical book. How can you possibly use hanging threads to learn what his illness is?"

"Master, you don't realize that I can treat illness. I know I can cure the king. Look, here are my hanging threads!" He pulled three hairs from his tail and called out, "Change!" The hairs turned into three golden threads. Each was twenty-four feet long, to match the twenty-four periods of the year[1]. Then Sun Wukong turned and walked back into the room where the king was resting.

---

[1] The traditional Chinese calendar is divided into 24 equal periods. The first one, lìchūn, starts approximately on February 4th and marks the Chinese New Year. Each lìchūn represents 1/24th of the sky. Since there are 24 lìchūn and 12 astrological signs, two Chinese lìchūn equal one astrological sign.

Chapter 69

The king was tired and afraid of Sun Wukong, so he did not want the monkey to come near him. So Sun Wukong gave the three golden threads to the eunuchs. He said to them, "Tie these threads to the king's left wrist. Put the first at *cun*, the second at *guan*, and the third at *chi*[1]. Then pass the end of the threads out of the window to me." Then he left the room.

The eunuchs did as they were told. Sun Wukong held each of the three threads between the thumb and index finger of his right hand, one at a time, feeling the pulse at each point. Then he told the eunuchs to move the threads to the *cun*, *guan* and *chi* of the king's right wrist. After they moved the threads, he held each thread in his left hand and felt the pulse at each point.

When he was finished, he shook his body to return the hairs to his tail. Then he said in a loud voice, "Your Majesty, I have carefully felt your pulse. I have seen many things. You have pain in your heart, your muscles are tired, there is blood in your urine, there are female demons in your body, your belly is too full, and your body is cold. All together, this means that you are worried and afraid. This illness is called 'two birds separated.'"

The king was happy to hear that Sun Wukong had found out the cause for his illness. He told his ministers to tell the monkey to prepare medicine to cure his illness.

"What does 'two birds separated' mean?" asked the eunuchs.

"It's simple," said Sun Wukong. "When two birds are flying together in a storm, the wind may blow them in different directions. The male bird misses the female and the female misses the male. Now, I must go and prepare the king's medicine. Please deliver three catties of every medicine to the Hostel of Meeting right away."

"But there are 808 different kinds of medicine and 404 different illnesses. Which ones will you use?"

"Bring me all the medicines. You will see."

---

[1] In traditional Chinese medicine (TCM) one takes the pulse by placing three fingers next to each other on the underside of the wrist at three locations. The one closest to the base of the thumb is called cùn, the middle one is called guān, and and the furthest one is chǐ. In English these are sometimes called the inch, bar and cubit.

Tangseng got up to follow Sun Wukong back to the hostel. But the king stopped him and told him that he was to stay overnight in the palace. The king told Tangseng that the next day, after recovering from his illness, he would give gifts to the travelers and sign their travel rescripts. Tangseng knew what this meant. He said to Sun Wukong, "Disciple, he wants to keep me here as a hostage. If things don't go well, he will kill me!"

"Don't worry," replied Sun Wukong, "enjoy yourself in the palace. I am a very good doctor."

Sun Wukong returned to the hostel. He had a nice dinner with Zhu and Sha. He told them everything that happened. When they finished their dinner he said to Zhu, "All right, let's get started. Bring me a *tael* of rhubarb and make it into a powder. This will help the king's *qi* flow smoothly. It will also calm his belly." Zhu did not think this was the correct medicine for the king, but he fetched the rhubarb and made it into a powder.

Then Sun Wukong said, "Now get me a *tael* of croton[1] seeds. This will cure illnesses of the heart. Make this into a powder also. Then combine the two powders."

Zhu also did not believe this medicine would help the king, but he got it and prepared the powder. Then he asked, "You will need some more medicines, right?"

"No," replied Sun Wukong, "that's it. Now remove some of the black soot from the bottom of the cooking pots, make it into a powder, and bring it to me."

"I never heard of using soot in a medicine," muttered Zhu, but he did as he was told.

"Okay," said Sun Wukong, "now get me half a cup of our horse's piss."

Sha Wujing looked at him and said, "Brother, be careful. You know that horse piss smells very bad. You cannot use it in medicine. The king will smell it and throw up. And if he eats the rhubarb and croton seeds, he will be running to the toilet. Things will be coming out of him from both ends. That's no joke."

"You don't understand," replied Sun Wukong. "Our horse is not an ordinary horse, and his piss is not ordinary piss. Our horse used to be a dragon in the Western Ocean. His piss has magic powers. I just hope he will give us some.

---

[1] Croton is an herb used in traditional Chinese medicine.

Let's go get it."

The three of them went outside and asked the white horse to give them some piss. The horse became very angry and said in human language, "What? I remember when I was a flying dragon in the Western Ocean. I had to be very careful where I pissed. If I pissed in a river, the fish would drink it and turn into dragons. If I pissed on grass growing on the mountains, boys would eat the grass and have eternal life. I can't just let it flow into this world of dirt and dust."

"Be careful of what you say," said Sun Wukong. "We are in the city of a great king. We have to cure him or we won't be able to continue our journey. We just need a little bit of your piss."

And so, the horse squeezed out a few drops into a cup. The three disciples returned to the hostel. They mixed the horse piss with the rhubarb, the croton seeds, and the black soot. Then they formed the medicine into three large round balls. They put the three medicine balls into a wooden box. When they were finished, they all went to sleep.

The next morning, the king called for Tangseng to come and see him. Then the king sent a group of ministers to the hostel to get the medicine from Sun Wukong. The ministers prostrated themselves before Sun Wukong and said, "Father Sun, His Majesty has sent us to fetch the magic medicine." Sun Wukong nodded to Zhu, and Zhu handed the box of medicine to the ministers.

The ministers asked, "What is this medicine called?"

Sun Wukong replied, "It's called Black Gold Elixir."

"And how should the king take the medicine?"

"There are two different methods. The first method is to make a special kind of tea. You must use a fart from a fast-flying bird, piss from a fast-swimming fish, face powder from the Queen Mother of the West, black soot from Laozi's brazier, three threads from the Jade Emperor's hat, and five hairs from a tired dragon's beard. Boil these together and make a tea for the king to drink."

The ministers looked at each other. One of them said, "Great monk, we think it may be a little difficult for us to make this tea. What is the other method?"

"Have the king take the medicine with a cup of rootless water. Make it from rain that falls from the sky and does not touch the ground."

The ministers were happy to hear this. They took the box of medicine back to the king. They told him that the medicine was Black Gold Elixir, and should be taken with rootless water. The king called for his magicians and ordered them to bring rain.

Back at the hostel, Sun Wukong wanted to help the king get rootless water. He told Sha to stand on his left, and Zhu to stand on his right. Then he said a magic spell. Soon a dark cloud appeared in the east. It came closer and closer. A voice called out from the cloud, "Great Sage! It is me, Ao Guang, the Dragon King of the Eastern Ocean."

"Thank you for coming," replied Sun Wukong. "Could you help us a bit? The king needs some rootless water. Can you make some rain for him?"

"Great Sage, when you called me, you said nothing about making rain. I came alone. I did not bring any of my servants to make wind, cloud, thunder and lightning. How can I make it rain?"

"We don't need much rain, just enough for the king to take his medicine."

"All right. I think I can just spit out a bit for you." The old dragon moved his cloud until it was directly over the palace. Then he spat out some rain. The rain fell for about two hours on the palace but nowhere else. The king told everyone in the palace, young and old, high rank and low rank, to run outside and collect the rain before it hit the ground. When it was finished, they combined all the water that they had collected. It was about three cups. They gave it to the king.

The king took the first pill with a cup of rootless water. Then he took the second pill and a cup of water, then he took the third pill and a cup of water. Then he sat and waited. A few minutes later his stomach made a very loud sound. The king ran to the toilet and sat on the chamber pot. He stayed there a long time.

Afterwards he was so tired, he lay down on his royal bed and slept. Two of his servants went to look inside the chamber pot. They saw a very large amount of shit, and also a large hard ball of rice dumplings. "The root of the illness has come out!" they said.

After resting, the king was feeling much better. He walked back to the throne room. He saw the Tang monk and prostrated himself in front of him. Tangseng was surprised, and quickly prostrated in front of the king. The king reached out his hands and helped Tangseng to stand.

The king sent one of his ministers to the hostel to invite the three disciples to the palace. Then he ordered a great feast of thanksgiving to be held in the palace that evening. What a wonderful banquet! There were four tables of vegetarian food for Tangseng and the three disciples. There were ten times as many dishes as the travelers could eat. For everyone else there were vegetarian and meat dishes, also ten times as much as any of them could eat. There were

> A hundred rare dishes
> A thousand cups of fine wine
> Pork and mutton, goose and duck, chicken and fish
> Tasty noodles in hot soup
> Many kinds of fragrant fruits
> Sugar dragons wrapped around sweet lions
> Large cakes in the shape of phoenixes

and much, much more. The king held a cup of wine and toasted the Tang monk. Tangseng said, "I am a Buddhist monk. I cannot drink wine, Your Majesty. But my three disciples will drink for me."

The king gave a cup of wine to Sun Wukong. He drank the cup. The king gave him a second cup, and he drank that too. Then a third cup. Zhu was watching this. He really wanted some wine. When the king gave Sun Wukong a fourth cup, he could not wait anymore. He shouted, "Your Majesty, it was not just the monkey who helped you. We all made your medicine. We put horse…" Quickly, Sun Wukong pushed a cup of wine into Zhu's mouth. Zhu stopped talking and drank the wine.

Later, the king tried to give Sun Wukong some more wine. "Thank you, Your Majesty," said Sun Wukong, "but I cannot drink any more."

"We have been unhappy and sick for many years," said the king. "But your pills cured us."

"I saw that you were unhappy and sick, but I don't know why."

"The ancients say, 'A family should not talk about its dirt with strangers.'"

"You can speak freely with me, Your Majesty."

The king looked down into his wine cup for a minute. Then he said, "We used to have three queens, but now we only have two. The Golden Queen has been gone for three years."

"What happened to her?"

"Three years ago, we went to the Dragon Boat Festival with our three beautiful queens. We were watching the dragon boats, eating rice dumplings, and drinking wine. Suddenly a cold wind blew through the festival. An evil demon appeared in the air. He said, 'My name is Jupiter's Rival. I am lonely and need a wife. You must give me the Golden Queen right now. If you refuse, I will eat you, then I will eat all your officials and ministers. Then I will eat all the people in the city.' We had to protect our people, so we gave him the Golden Queen. He carried her away on the cold wind. The rice dumplings that we ate that day became as hard as rock and have been in our belly for three years. Also, we have been unable to sleep. That's why we have been ill for these three years. But you have given our life back to us!"

Sun Wukong smiled and said, "You were lucky to meet me! Would you like me to go and deal with this evil demon for you?"

The king fell to his knees and said, "We will give you our kingdom! We will take our three queens and go to live as common people."

Sun Wukong hurried to help the king get back to his feet. He said, "Tell me, Your Majesty, has this evil demon returned in the last three years?"

"Yes. From time to time he comes back. Every time, he demands that we give him two ladies to be the Golden Queen's servants. He has done this four times. We are afraid of him, so we have built an Avoiding Demons Shelter. When we hear the wind, we run and hide in the Avoiding Demons Shelter." The king showed them the shelter. It was an underground room twenty feet below the palace.

Just then, a strong wind began to blow from the south. One of the ministers had been listening to the conversation between the king and Sun Wukong. He cried out, "This monk knows the future! He speaks of the evil demon, and the evil demon comes!"

The king ran into the Avoiding Demons Shelter, along with Tangseng and the ministers and eunuchs. Sun Wukong stayed outside. Zhu and Sha tried to run into the Avoiding Demons Shelter, but Sun Wukong grabbed them and stopped them from running away. They looked up in the sky. What did they see?

> A great body nine feet tall
> Eyes like two golden lanterns
> Four steel fangs like long knives
> Red hair and eyebrows like flames
> A green face, a huge nose
> Bare feet and long hair
> Red muscled arms and green hands
> A leopard skin around his waist
> In his hand he held a long spear

The three disciples looked at the demon. Sun Wukong said to Sha, "Do you recognize him?"

Sha said, "No, I've never seen him before."

"Zhu, how about you?"

Zhu said, "No, I've never had a drink with this demon. He's no friend of mine."

Sun Wukong said, "He looks a little bit like the golden-eyed ghost of Eastern Mountain."

"No, ghosts only come out at night. It's ten in the morning, so it's no ghost. Maybe this is Jupiter's Rival."

"Zhu, you're not so stupid after all. You might be right. All right, you stay here and guard Master. I will ask this demon his name. Then I will rescue the Golden Queen and bring her back to the king."

Chapter 70

Sun Wukong jumped up into the air. He shouted at the demon, "Where do you come from, you lawless demon? Where do you think you're going?"

The demon replied, "I am a warrior for the great Jupiter's Rival. My master has ordered me to fetch two young women to serve Her Majesty the Golden Queen. Who are you and how dare you question me?"

"I am Sun Wukong, the Great Sage Equal to Heaven. I am traveling with the Tang Monk to the Western Heaven to obtain the Buddha's holy scriptures. We were passing through this kingdom. We know the evil things that your master has done here in this kingdom. I was looking for your master. Now here you are, ready to throw away your life."

The warrior threw his spear at Monkey, who blocked it easily with his rod. They began to fight in the sky. They fought for a little while, but Sun Wukong was stronger. He smashed his rod down on the warrior's lance and broke it in half. The warrior turned and flew away to the west as fast as he could.

The three disciples returned to the Demon Shelter to tell the king and Tangseng that it was safe to come out. They came out. The sky was clear, there was no wind, and the warrior was gone. The king thanked Sun Wukong and gave him another cup of wine. But just then, a minister came running up, shouting, "The western gate is on fire!"

When Sun Wukong heard this, he threw the cup of wine into the air. It fell to the ground. The king was surprised, and said to him, "Great monk, why did you throw the cup into the air? Did we do something to insult you?"

"Not at all," laughed Sun Wukong. A moment later another minister ran in to say, "There has been a sudden rainstorm at the western gate. The fire is out. The streets are flooded with water that smells like wine."

Sun Wukong said to the king, "Your Majesty, I was not insulted at all by your gift of wine. I knew that the warrior started that fire. So I used the cup of wine to put out the fire and save the people nearby."

The king was even happier than before. He invited Tangseng and the three disciples to come with him into the throne room. He planned to give the kingdom to them and become a common man. But before he could say anything, Sun Wukong said, "Your Majesty, that warrior said that his master was Jupiter's Rival. I defeated the warrior in a fight, so he will surely go back to his master and report what happened. Then his master will come here and want to fight me. That will be very bad for your city. I should meet him in his cave. Do you know where it is?"

"Yes. It is quite far, over a thousand miles. Please wait here. We will get you a fast horse and some dried food for your journey. You can leave tomorrow."

"Not necessary! I can get there in a few minutes."

"Holy monk, we hope you don't mind us saying this, but your handsome face looks much like an ape. How can you travel so fast?"

"Your Highness, I have studied the Way for many centuries. I have learned to use the cloud somersault to travel sixty thousand miles in a single jump. A thousand mountains are no problem for me, and a hundred rivers are nothing to me."

And without saying another word, Sun Wukong used his cloud somersault to fly away to the monster's mountain.

A few minutes later he saw a tall mountain covered with fog. He came down on the mountain's top. He looked around. It was a beautiful place. The mountain was covered with green pine trees. He heard the songs of birds and the sounds of wild animals. Mountain peaches hung from trees. Flowers were everywhere. He thought, "This is a place where evil immortals could live happily for the rest of their lives!"

Just then, a great fire leaped up from the base of the mountain. The flames reached up to the Heavens. A moment later the flames were followed by huge clouds of hot smoke. The smoke was not just black, but many different colors – blue, red, yellow, white and black. The smoke filled the air, killing and cooking wild animals. Birds who tried to escape the smoke lost their feathers.

Then a huge sandstorm came from the mountain. The sky was filled with sand and dust. Woodsmen gathering wood in the mountain became blinded and could not find their way home. Sun Wukong shook himself and turned into a fire-extinguishing hawk. He put out the fires on the mountain, then came back to the ground, returning to his usual form.

He saw a young demon walking down a mountain path. The demon was talking to himself. Sun Wukong wanted to hear what he was saying, so he turned into a small fly. He followed the young demon and heard him say, "Our king is terrible. First, he took the Golden Queen but he could not have her. Then he took several young women and killed them all. Now he is in trouble because of some monkey named Sun or something like that. Our king is declaring war on the human city. He will use fire, smoke and sandstorms. All the people of the human city will die. Our king will win, but this goes against Heaven."

Sun Wukong thought it was interesting that the young demon said, "he could not have her" and "this goes against Heaven" so he decided to talk with the demon. He changed his form so he looked like a Daoist boy. He walked up to the young demon and said, "What is your good name, sir, and where are you going?"

"My name is Gocome. I am going to the human city to deliver my king's declaration of war."

"Tell me, sir, has the Golden Queen slept with your king yet?"

"No. An immortal gave the Golden Queen a magic cloak to protect her. If our king tries to touch her, it hurts him terribly. So he cannot touch her."

"Is he in a bad mood then?"

"Oh yes, he is in a very bad mood! You should go and sing him some Daoist songs, that might make him feel better."

"Thank you," said Sun Wukong. Then he smashed his golden hoop rod down on Gocome's head, killing him instantly. He brought the body of the demon back to the palace. He showed it to the king, Tangseng, and the other two disciples.

Sun Wukong said to the king, "Tell me, Your Majesty, did the Golden Queen leave any of her things behind when she left with the demon king? I need to show her something when I go to rescue her. If I don't do that, she might not trust me."

"Yes," replied the king, "she left two gold bracelets. She had been planning to wear them to the Dragon Boat Festival, but she left them behind when the evil demon came and took her. We will give both of them to you."

Sun Wukong took the two bracelets, thanked the king, then used his cloud somersault to return quickly to the cave of Jupiter's Rival. He saw five hundred demon soldiers standing outside the cave. Quickly he changed his appearance to look like Gocome, the young demon.

He walked up to the cave. One of the soldiers said, "You're late, Gocome. Our king is waiting for your report."

Sun Wukong entered the cave. He looked up and saw a huge room with light coming in from eight windows. In the center was a large golden chair. The demon king was sitting in the chair.

"Gocome," said the demon king, "you're back, aren't you?"

Sun Wukong said nothing.

"Gocome," said the demon king, "you're back, aren't you?"

Still Sun Wukong said nothing.

The demon grabbed him and shouted, "Answer my question!"

"I didn't want to go, but you made me go. I saw many soldiers in the city. They saw me and grabbed me, shouting 'Seize the demon!' They dragged me to the palace to see their king. I gave him the declaration of war. The king was very angry. They whipped me thirty times and sent me out of the city."

"I don't care about their soldiers or their weapons. One fire will take care of all of them. Now, go see the Golden Queen. She has been crying. Tell her that the human king has a great army and will probably defeat us. That will make her feel better."

"Wonderful!" thought Sun Wukong. He went to see the Golden Queen. She was very beautiful, but her hair was long and messy and she wore no jewelry. She was sitting in her room. Several fox and deer servants were nearby.

"Hello," said Sun Wukong. "I am His Majesty's messenger. He sent me to deliver a declaration of war to the king of Scarlet Purple Kingdom. The human king gave me a private message to deliver to you. But I cannot tell you with these servants around."

The Golden Queen sent away the foxes and deer. "Tell me the private message," she said.

Sun Wukong rubbed his face and changed back to his normal form. "Don't be afraid of me. I am a monk, traveling with my master to the Western Heaven by order of the Tang Emperor. We came upon the Scarlet Purple Kingdom. We saw that the king was quite ill. I cured his illness. The king told me that you were carried off by an evil demon. I have some skill in killing demons, so he asked me to try to rescue you."

Of course, the Golden Queen did not believe him. So Sun Wukong showed her the two bracelets. He said, "If you don't believe me, look at these."

She began to cry. She said, "If you can return me to my husband, I will remember you until I am old and toothless."

"Tell me, how does the demon king create the fire, smoke and sandstorms?"

"He has three golden bells. When he shakes the first bell, flames a thousand feet high shoot out. When he shakes the second bell, a three-thousand-foot cloud of smoke shoots out. And when he shakes the third bell, a three-thousand-foot sandstorm begins. He keeps the bells on his belt all the time."

"For now, you must forget about your love for your husband. Let the demon king think that you love him. Bring him here and get the bells from him. I will steal them, defeat the monster, and return you to your true husband."

The Golden Queen went to see the demon king. She said to him, "Sir, for three years I have not allowed you to share my pillow. That is because you treat me as a stranger instead of your wife. When I was the queen of Scarlet Purple Kingdom, my husband trusted me to hold his treasures. But you will not let me. If you trust me, then let me hold your treasures. Then perhaps I will be willing to be your wife."

The demon king laughed and said, "Thank you for telling me that! All right, here are my treasures." Handing the three bells to her, he said, "Be very careful with these bells. Whatever you do, don't shake them!"

The queen told her servants to carefully put the treasures in her room. Then she told the demon king that she wanted to have a great feast with him, with lots of food and wine, so they could be together as husband and wife. The demon king was delighted. The two of them went off to another part of the cave, leaving Sun Wukong alone.

As soon as they were gone, Sun Wukong ran back to the queen's room and grabbed the three bells. But as he ran away with them, he accidentally shook them. Huge pillars of fire, smoke and sand came shooting out. Everything in the cave started to burn. Clouds of smoke and sand filled the cave.

The demon king came back and shouted, "Dirty slave, why did you steal my treasures? Arrest him!" Sun Wukong changed back to his monkey form, whipped out his golden hoop rod, and fought off the demon king and his soldiers. The demon king ordered the gates to the cave to be shut. Sun Wukong changed into a little fly and flew into a dark corner.

The demon king and his soldiers could not find Sun Wukong. One of his generals, a large bear, came up to him and said, "Your Majesty, the thief was Sun Wukong, the monkey king who defeated our warrior. I think he met

Gocome on the road, killed him, and took his form.”

“Yes, you must be right,” said the demon king. “Little ones, don’t open the gates. We will find that monkey!”

Chapter 71

The demon king and all the little demons searched for Sun Wukong for the rest of the day. They were looking for a monkey, of course, not a fly on the wall, so they did not find him. When night came, he flew to the Golden Queen's room and landed on her shoulder. She was crying, saying,

> In a past life I broke the incense sticks[1]
> Now I have been taken by an evil demon king
> When will I see my husband again?
> We are like two geese separated by a storm
> Today I had hope but now the monkey is dead
> Killed by his curiosity and the golden bells
> I long for my husband more than ever!

Sun Wukong said in her ear, "Don't be afraid, Your Majesty. It is me, the Monkey King. I'm still alive. I accidentally shook the bells. Fire, smoke and sand came out. Now the demon king has locked the doors and I cannot get out, and I don't have the bells. Please act like a wife, bring him here, and make him sleep. Then I can escape and rescue you later."

"How can I do that?" she asked, looking around but not seeing him.

"The ancients say, 'wine is best for ending a life,' and they also say, 'wine is best for solving problems.' Give him plenty of wine to drink. I will help. Show me one of your slave girls. I will change my appearance to look like her."

The queen called out, "Spring Beauty, please come here!" A beautiful young fox demon came into the room.

"Help me get ready for the demon king. Light the silk lanterns and burn some incense." The girl did as she was told. Then Sun Wukong landed on her head, pulled out a hair from his head, and changed it into a sleep insect. The sleep insect crawled into her nose. This caused Spring Beauty to fall asleep. As soon as she fell asleep, Sun Wukong changed his form so that he looked just like Spring Beauty. He dragged the real Spring Beauty into a dark corner of the room.

---

[1] A folk belief is that a person who offers the Buddha an incense stick with a "broken head" (duàn tóu xiāng) is fated to be separated from their loved ones in future lives.

The Golden Queen went to the demon king, smiled at him, and said, "Dear, you must be tired. Please come to bed." He followed her into her room. She said to the false Spring Beauty, "Bring wine for His Majesty, he is tired."

The false servant girl brought wine. The Golden Queen gave a cup to the demon king, then another, then another. The demon king started to become very sleepy and a bit drunk.

Sun Wukong needed to get his hands on the three golden bells. He pulled some hairs from his head, blew on them, and changed them into hundreds of fleas. The fleas crawled all over the demon king's clothing. This caused him to be extremely uncomfortable. "I am sorry, my dear," he muttered, with his eyes half closed, "but my clothing seems to be dirty."

"That is no problem, my dear," she said. "Let me take off your clothes." She removed his clothes, but he still had on his belt and the three bells. Sun Wukong made the fleas crawl onto the belt and the three bells. Now the bells were covered with the little insects.

"Your Majesty," said the false servant girl, "give me those bells. I will catch the fleas for you." The king was so sleepy and confused that he did as she asked. The false servant girl took the bells and hid them in her sleeve. Then she made three false bells using hairs from her head. The demon king did not see this.

"Be very careful with those," he mumbled, and then he fell asleep.

As soon as he fell asleep, Sun Wukong changed back to his usual form. The three bells were still in his sleeve. He became invisible. He walked to the front gate of the cave, used his lock opening magic to open the gates, and left the cave.

The next morning, Sun Wukong banged his rod on the gates and shouted for the demon king to come out and fight. "I'm your grandpa[1]. I've come from Scarlet Purple Kingdom to take back the Golden Queen." Then he smashed the front gate with his rod.

Some little demons heard this and ran back to the demon king, who had just gotten out of bed. "There's someone outside the cave, he says he is a foreign man," they said. "He just smashed the front gate."

---

[1] When Sun Wukong says he is a grandpa, he uses the word wàigōng which means maternal grandfather. But the two parts of the word are wài meaning "outside" or "foreign," and gōng which means "male" when used as a noun.

The demon king put on his armor and went outside. He saw Sun Wukong. He shouted, "How dare you come to my home causing trouble? Who are you?"

"Listen to my story," said Sun Wukong. Then he gave a long and detailed account of his entire life, starting with his birth as a little stone monkey on Flower Fruit Mountain. He spoke of causing trouble in Heaven and being trapped by the Buddha under a mountain for five hundred years. And he finished by saying that he was now helping the Tang Monk in his journey to the west.

"So, you're the lawless monkey who caused trouble in Heaven. Why are you here bothering me?"

"You shameless monster! The king of Scarlet Purple Kingdom asked me to help him, that's why I'm here. Now take a taste of my rod!"

The two of them began to fight. The monkey used his golden hoop rod, the demon king used a battle axe. They fought for fifty rounds. Then the demon said, "Monkey, stop this. I haven't had my breakfast yet. Wait here and I will be back soon."

"Of course. A good hunter does not chase a tired rabbit. Go have your breakfast, I'll wait here."

The demon king ran back into the cave. He said to the Golden Queen, "Quick! Where are the three golden bells?" She gave him the false bells that Sun Wukong had made.

The demon king ran outside again and shouted to Sun Wukong, "Stay where you are. Watch while I shake these bells."

Sun Wukong laughed and said, "Of course. But if you shake your bells, I will have to shake mine." He took the three bells out and showed them to the demon king.

The demon king saw them. He was shocked. "Where did you get those bells?" he asked.

"Where did you get yours?"

"My bells come from gold made in the Eight Trigrams Furnace. They were made by Lord Laozi himself."

"That's funny, my bells were made the same way. Mine are female, yours are male."

"You are a fool. These are treasures, not animals. They cannot be male or female." He shook his three bells, but nothing happened. He stared at the bells. He said, "Something is wrong. Perhaps the males are afraid of the females. They see the female bells, and that's why nothing comes out."

"Maybe. Let's see what my bells can do." Sun Wukong shook all three bells. Instantly, fire and smoke and sand came shooting out of the bells. The trees on the mountain started to burn. Smoke filled the Heavens; sand covered the earth. The demon king could not escape. He prepared to die.

Just then, Sun Wukong heard a woman's voice saying, "Sun Wukong, I am here." It was the Bodhisattva Guanyin. In her left hand she held a vase of water. In her right hand she held a willow branch. She shook the willow branch, and a few drops of water came out. The fire was extinguished, the smoke and sand disappeared.

Sun Wukong quickly put the bells in his robe, then kowtowed to the Bodhisattva. She said to him, "I am here to find this evil monster and take him."

"May I ask the Bodhisattva, who is this monster, and why are you taking the trouble to capture him?"

"He is a large golden-haired wolf that I used to ride. A servant boy was supposed to watch him, but the boy fell asleep and the wolf ran away. Then the wolf went to Scarlet Purple Kingdom to save the king."

Sun Wukong kowtowed again and said, "Bodhisattva, I must tell you, you have the story backwards. This demon did not save the king from trouble. He has brought trouble. For three years he has been doing terrible things to the king and queen of Scarlet Purple Kingdom."

"Wukong, you are the one who does not understand. One day, many years ago when the king of Scarlet Purple Kingdom was a young man, he went hunting. He saw a peacock and peahen. The peacock and peahen were really two children of the Buddha's mother in the west. The young king injured the peacock and killed the peahen. The Buddha's mother ordered that the king be separated from his wife for three years, so he could suffer separation just like the peacock and peahen. Also, she ordered that the king suffer the illness of 'two birds separated.'"

"What does that have to do with the demon?"

"I was riding my wolf nearby when the Buddha's mother said this. The wolf heard her words. When he escaped, he came here and took the king's wife to fulfill the Buddha's mother's wish. That was three years ago. Now the king's punishment is finished. You have cured his illness, and you have saved his wife. Do not kill the demon. I will take him back with me."

"If you take him back to the South Sea with you, you must not let him escape to the human world again."

Guanyin turned to the demon and said, "Evil beast! Change back to your own form!" The demon shook himself and became a yellow haired wolf. Guanyin mounted him. She was ready to ride away, but she looked down at his neck. The three golden bells were missing. "Wukong. Give me the three bells."

"I have not seen them."

"Thieving monkey! Give the bells to me at once, or I will have to recite the tight-headband spell."

"Don't say it! Don't say it! Here are the bells." He reached into his tiger skin robe, took out the bells, and handed them carefully to Guanyin. Guanyin attached the bells to the wolf's neck. Then, wrapped in golden cloth, the Bodhisattva flew away to the South Sea.

Sun Wukong went back into the cave. He killed all the little demons. In the back of the cave he found the Golden Queen. He told her everything that happened. He also told her why she had to be separated from her husband for the last three years. Then he gathered some soft grasses and made a straw dragon for her. He said to her, "Please sit on this and close your eyes."

They mounted the clouds and flew back to Scarlet Purple Kingdom. She entered the king's palace and walked into the throne room. The king was there. He jumped up and ran to her. He put his arms around her. Then he pulled his arms back, saying, "My hand! It hurts! It hurts!"

Zhu saw this and laughed, "Ha! No joy for the king!"

Sun Wukong said to Zhu and the rest of the people in the throne room, "The queen is wearing a poison cloak. Anyone who touches her feels terrible pain. That is why the demon king did not sleep with her for the three years that she was in his cave."

The ministers asked, "What can we do about this?"

Just then, they heard someone call out from above, "Great Sage, I have arrived!" They all looked up. Flying down from the sky was a man surrounded by beams of light and clouds of fog. Sun Wukong recognized him.

He said, "Hello, Zhang Boduan[1]. What are you doing here?"

Zhang replied, "Three years ago I was passing through this kingdom. I was at the Dragon Boat Festival when the demon king captured the Golden Queen. I was afraid that the queen would be harmed, so I made a special cloak and gave it to the demon king. He gave it to the queen as a wedding gift. As soon as she put on the cloak, poison thorns grew all over her body. This protected her from the demon king. Now I will remove the cloak and the poison thorns."

He pointed his finger at the queen. The cloak lifted off her body. Zhang raised his hands to say goodbye, then he rose up into the sky and disappeared.

Sun Wukong spoke to the king and queen, Tangseng, the other two disciples, and all the ministers in the palace. He told the entire story, from beginning to end. When he was finished, the king ordered a great banquet for them. Then he certified their travel rescript. Finally, he asked Tangseng to sit in the king's dragon carriage. The king, the three queens and the ministers pushed the monk's carriage with their own hands, while the three disciples rode in another carriage.

At the edge of the city, Tangseng and his three disciples got down from the carriages and began walking west again.

---

[1] Zhang Boduan (or Zhang Ziyang) was a 10th century civil servant who became a Daoist master and expert on Zen Buddhism. He wrote a famous book, "Folios on Awakening to Reality/ Perfection," a collection of 81 poems on Daoist inner alchemy.

Chapter 72

They traveled westwards for many months. They passed over many mountains and they crossed many rivers and streams. Autumn turned to winter, and winter turned to early spring. New leaves appeared on trees and the grass turned green again.

One day, the travelers came upon a group of houses under several large trees. The houses were surrounded by a stone wall. Tangseng got down from his horse and looked at the houses. "I am going to walk over there and beg some vegetarian food," he said.

Sun Wukong replied, "Master, please let me do the begging, not you. The ancients say, 'Once a teacher, always a father.' It is not right for you to go begging while your disciples stay here."

"Disciples, it is a beautiful day, there is no wind or rain. And the houses are very near. I will go. If I need help, I will call you." Zhu opened the luggage. He took the begging bowl out of the luggage and handed it to Tangseng along with his cassock and hat.

Tangseng approached the nearest house. In front of the house was a stone bridge. The bridge crossed a small stream and led to a courtyard. Large trees were all around. He could hear the songs of birds in the trees. He stood in front of the bridge. Looking in the window he saw four lovely young women inside the house, sitting and sewing.

Tangseng dared not enter a house with only young women it. So he stood outside for almost a half hour, waiting. He thought to himself, "If I cannot even beg a simple meal, what will my disciples think of me? Why would they be willing to travel with me to the Western Heaven?" He decided to cross the bridge and enter the courtyard.

When he entered the courtyard, he saw a small village inside the stone walls. He saw three more young women, just as beautiful as the other four. These three were playing a game. They kicked a ball that was full of air[1]. What were

---

[1] The game described here is cùjū, a game similar to soccer where players try to kick a ball through a net without using their hands. Kicking games date back to the Warring States period in the second or third century BC. Air-filled balls were introduced during the Tang dynasty in the seventh century AD. Cuju was very popular and was played by men and women across all classes of society.

they doing?

> They play with blue sleeves fluttering
> They run with yellow skirts flowing
> They kick the ball, passing it to each other
> Their necklaces sway as they run
> A turning kick is 'Flower Beyond the Wall'
> A backwards somersault is 'Crossing the Sea'
> Hitting the ball with their head is 'A Pearl On Buddha's Head'
> They kick the ball like the Yellow River flowing backwards
> The ball bounces like a goldfish on the river bank
> One has the ball, then others take it away
> They run, they shout
> Their clothes are wet with sweat
> Their hair is disheveled, their necklaces are askew
> Tired and happy, they shout to end their game.

Tangseng watched the game for a while. When it ended, he walked up to the house and called loudly, "Bodhisattvas, this humble monk begs that you give him a bit of food."

The four women stopped their sewing and looked up. One of them said, "Elder, please forgive us for not meeting you when you entered our poor village. Please come in, come in." She opened two large stone doors.

Tangseng entered the house. He saw that the house was strange. There was a stone table and some stone benches, but no other furniture. He noticed that the house was dark and cold. He realized that the house was really a cave. He began to worry. He thought, "This is an evil place."

"Honored elder, please sit down," said the woman. The house became even colder. Tangseng started to tremble. "Where are you from, sir?" she asked, "and why are you collecting money?"

"I am not collecting money," replied Tangseng, "I have been sent by the Tang Emperor to travel to Thunderclap Mountain in the Western Heaven. I have been commanded to fetch the Buddha's scriptures and bring them back to the land of Tang. We were passing by your noble home when we became hungry. I have come to beg a little bit of vegetarian food. Afterwards, we poor monks will be on our way again."

"Wonderful!" the women said, "We will give you vegetarian food as soon as we can!" Three of the women sat down and began talking with Tangseng, discussing Buddhism and Daoism. The fourth woman went into the kitchen to prepare some food. But the food that she prepared was not vegetarian. She cooked human flesh in a black sauce to make it look like gluten. She cut up human brains so it looked like tofu. Then she cooked it all in human fat.

When she was finished, she brought the food out of the kitchen. She put the dish on the stone table in front of Tangseng. "Please eat," she said. "I am sorry that we did not have time to prepare a better meal, but this will take care of your hunger."

Tangseng smelled the food. Right away he knew that it was human flesh. He said, "Bodhisattvas, I have been a vegetarian since my birth. I cannot eat this."

"But sir, this is vegetarian food."

"Dear ladies, I am under orders from the Tang Emperor to not harm any living creature. I thank you for this food. But if I eat it, I will be breaking my vows. Now, please let me go."

The women jumped up and blocked the door. One of them said, "Oh good, it looks like business has come to our door! You have as much chance of leaving here as of covering a fart with your hands."

Quickly they threw him to the ground and tied him up with rope. Then they hung him from the rafters. One of his hands was held up by a rope and was facing forwards. A second rope held his other hand to his waist. A third rope held up his legs. He hung from the rafters with his back facing up and his belly facing down. This is called "Immortal Pointing the Way."

Tangseng tried not to cry. He thought, "I thought I was begging a bit of vegetarian food from some good people. But now I have fallen into a fire. Oh disciples, where are you? Come quickly and save me!"

Then he saw that the women were starting to take off their clothes. Tangseng watched in fear. But the women only opened their blouses to expose their bellies. Silken ropes came out of each of their navels like flying silver. The ropes covered Tangseng and held tight. The ropes grew longer and longer. They covered the house, and then they grew to cover the entire village.

Meanwhile, the three disciples were waiting on the side of the road. Zhu and Sha were resting and keeping an eye on the luggage. Sun Wukong was jumping around in the trees searching for ripe fruits to eat. He looked up and saw a bright light coming from the place where Tangseng had gone. He

jumped down from the tree and shouted for the others to look. Then he whipped out his Golden Hoop Rod and ran towards the light.

When he arrived, he saw thousands of silken ropes lying in a great heap. He touched the ropes with his hand. They felt soft and sticky. He did not know what to do. He thought for a minute. Then he called the local spirit by making a magic sign with his hand and saying the word "Om."

A few seconds later the local spirit appeared. He was an old god, quite afraid of Sun Wukong. He got down on his knees.

"Get up, get up," said Sun Wukong. "I am not going to beat you. Tell me, what is this place?"

The local spirit replied, "Great sage, this is Spiderweb Mountain. Below it is Spiderweb Cave. Seven demon spirits live there."

"What kind of demon spirits are they?"

"They are all female demons. I don't know much about them. But three miles south of here is a hot spring. In the past it was used by the Seven Immortal Women of Heaven. But they left as soon as the seven demon spirits arrived. The demons bathe in the hot spring three times a day. They already bathed this morning. They will come again at noon today."

Sun Wukong told the local spirit that he could leave. Then he shook his body and changed into a tiny fly. He sat on a tree branch near the hot spring and waited.

He waited for about half the time it takes to drink a cup of tea. Then he heard the sound of loud breathing. It sounded like insects eating leaves, or waves on the beach. Seven young women arrived, laughing and talking. What did they look like?

> Like jade but more fragrant
> Like flowers that could speak
> Eyebrows like distant mountains
> Mouths surrounded by red lips
> Beautiful feathers in their hair
> Small feet below red skirts
> They looked like Chang'e[1] flying down to the world below
> Like immortals going down to earth

Sun Wukong laughed and said to himself, "I see why Master wanted to beg food from these beautiful women, but they could be trouble. If each of them wanted him, he would not live more than a couple of days. I must get closer and listen to their words."

He landed on the head of one of the young women. She was saying, "Sisters, let's bathe in the hot spring. Then we will go home and steam that fat monk for dinner." Laughing, they walked forward and pushed open two large wooden doors. Inside was a large pool of hot water. The pool was fifty feet wide, a hundred feet long, and four feet deep. Clouds of steam rose up from the pool. The water was so clear that you could see the bottom.

The young women took off their clothes and hung them on a nearby tree branch. Then they all jumped into the water. They played together in the hot water. Sun Wukong thought, "It would be so easy to kill them all now. But a real man does not fight women. It would hurt my reputation. However, I can

---

[1] Cháng'é is the Chinese goddess of the moon. Altars are set up to worship her during the Mid-Autumn Festival when the full moon appears in the eighth lunar month.

make things difficult for them."

He shook himself again and changed into a large eagle. He grabbed all seven sets of clothes in his claws. Then he flew away, carrying the clothes. He changed back to himself and returned to the place where Zhu and Sha were waiting.

"What are these?" asked Zhu, pointing to the clothes.

"These are the clothes of the seven evil demons," replied Sun Wukong.

"How did you take off their clothes?"

"I didn't have to take them off. This place is called Spiderweb Mountain, and the village is Spiderweb Cave. Seven evil demons live in the cave. They captured Master and hung him from the rafters inside the cave. Then they went off to bathe in a hot spring. I watched them take off their clothes and jump into the hot water. I changed into an eagle and grabbed their clothes. Now they are all trapped in the hot water. They are too embarrassed to come out. This is a good time for us to rescue Master."

Zhu replied, "Elder brother, you did not finish the job. You knew they were evil demons. You should have killed them then and there. If you don't, the demons will just wait until dark and then come out of the water when nobody can see them. They will put on some other clothes. Then they will kill and eat Master."

"I will not hit them. If you want to kill them, go and do it yourself."

Zhu picked up his rake. He ran straight towards the hot spring, holding his rake high in the air. He kicked open the gates and looked in. He saw the seven naked women sitting in the water. They were very angry, shouting at the eagle to bring back their clothes.

"You are a disgrace," said the women. "You are a monk and we are women. The ancients say, 'From age seven, boys and girls should not use the same mat together.' You must not bathe with us."

"I am sorry, ladies, but it is very hot today. I must jump in the water." Zhu stripped off his clothes and jumped into the water. The demons were very angry. They rushed at him, but he changed into a large fish spirit. Now he was too fast for them to catch him. If they grabbed east he jumped west, and if they grabbed west he jumped east. Often, he would swim between their legs. This continued for a while. Finally Zhu jumped out, changed back to his pig-man form, and put on his clothes.

The demons were very frightened. One of them said, "First you looked like a monk, then you looked like a large fish, now you look like a monk again. What are you?"

"Evil demons, you don't know who I am. I am a disciple of the Tang Monk, traveling to the Western Heaven to fetch holy scriptures. I am called Zhu Bajie. You have captured my master and you plan to eat him. Is my master just another bit of food for you? I'm going to smash you all with my rake."

The beautiful demons begged him to stop, but he began swinging his rake wildly. Even though they wore no clothes, the demons jumped out of the water and ran a short distance away. Then they turned towards Zhu. From seven navels came seven silken ropes. Zhu was covered by the silken ropes. He tried to move his feet but could not. He fell down, tried to get up, and fell down again. Finally he lay groaning on the ground. The demons tied him up and carried him back to the cave.

Each demon went into her own bedroom and found other clothes to put on. Then they all came out and called, "Where are you, children?"

Seven large insects arrived. They said, "What do you want us to do, mothers?" These seven insects had been captured long ago by the seven demons. The demons did not kill the insects. They let the insects live, but the insects became like sons to the demons, and the demons acted as their mothers.

The demons said to the insects, "Sons, we mistakenly captured a Tang monk. Now his disciples are angry and want to kill us. You must go out, find these disciples, and make them go away. When you are finished, meet us at your uncle's house. We are going there now."

The seven insects changed into the form of small demons and ran out of the cave towards the hot spring.

In the cave, the silken ropes that were covering Zhu suddenly disappeared. He stood up. He was in pain but unharmed. He saw Sun Wukong and told him what happened. Then Sha arrived. The three of them decided to go back to the cave to save their master. But before they arrived at the cave, they saw the seven small demons standing in front of them. The small demons said, "Not so fast, not so fast. We are here."

"These are just little kids," said Zhu, laughing, to his brothers. "They can't weigh more than eight or nine pounds each." Then he said to them, "Who are you?"

The small demons replied, "We are the sons of the seven immortal ladies. You have caused trouble here, now watch out!" The small demons attacked Zhu, who swung his rake wildly at them.

The small demons saw how powerful Zhu was. They changed back into insects. They flew into the air, shouting, "Change!" Each one became ten, each ten became a hundred, each hundred became a thousand, each thousand became ten thousand. The sky was filled with flying insects. They covered the disciples, biting and stinging them all over.

"I must tell you, Elder Brother," said Zhu, waving his hands at the biting insects, "it's not easy journeying to the west to fetch scriptures. Even the insects are giving us a hard time."

"Not a problem," replied Sun Wukong. He pulled out a few hairs, chewed them, and blew them out. He told the hairs to change into many different large birds. The birds flew quickly through the air. They grabbed the insects with their mouths or claws, or smacked them with their wings. In a few minutes, all the insects were dead. The ground was covered a foot deep in dead insects.

The three disciples ran over the bridge and into the cave. They found Tangseng still hanging from the rafters. Sun Wukong cut the ropes easily. He asked Tangseng, "Where are the evil demons?"

Tangseng replied, "All seven ran out the back door. They were calling for their sons."

The three disciples ran out the back door, weapons held high, but they did not see the seven evil demons. "They're gone," said Zhu, sadly. "Let's go back and smash everything in this cave, so they will not have a home to return to."

"That's too much work," said Sun Wukong. "Let's gather some firewood." They collected a large pile of branches, set them on fire, and watched the cave burn.

Chapter 73

After they burned Spiderweb Cave, the four travelers walked quickly down the road towards the west. A few hours later they arrived at a place with many tall towers. They saw lovely streams running between the buildings. Large trees filled with songbirds were nearby. Pairs of deer walked peacefully between the trees. It was as beautiful as the ancient Tiantai Cave of Liu and Ruan[1].

"Master," said Sun Wukong, "this is not the home of a rich man or a king. It looks like a Daoist temple or Buddhist monastery."

They reached the gates and saw a sign, "Yellow Flower Temple." Zhu said, "This is a Daoist place, so it must be all right for us to enter."

The four travelers went inside. On the sides of the inner gates they saw two more signs:

> Yellow buds, white snow, the home of an immortal
> Rare and wonderful flowers, the home of men with wings

"So," said Sun Wukong with a grin, "this is a place where a Daoist plays with alchemy[2]."

"Watch your words," replied Tangseng, "we don't know these people."

They went through the inner gate. A Daoist master sat on the floor making elixir pills. He wore a black Daoist robe tied with a yellow sash, a bright red and gold hat, and green shoes. His face was round like a melon. His eyes were as bright as stars.

"Greetings, sir!" said Tangseng.

The Daoist looked up, startled, and the elixir pills fell to the floor. He said, "Please, please, come in and sit down." The four travelers walked in and sat

---

[1] This refers to the legend of Liu Chen and Ruan Zhao who traveled to Tiantai Mountain to procure medicinal herbs. They encountered a couple of beautiful maidens in a valley of peach blossoms. They lived with the maidens for six months, then became homesick. But when they returned home, they discovered that hundreds of years had passed in their home village. Saddened, Liu and Ruan disappeared again, this time apparently forever.

[2] Chinese alchemy provides methods for extending life and purifying one's spirit, mind and body. Alchemists often mixed and drank elixirs containing toxic metals such as mercury, lead and arsenic in their quest for immortality.

down. The Daoist master sent two boys into the kitchen to fetch tea.

The seven demons from Spiderweb Cave were hiding in the back of the temple. They noticed the boys preparing tea. One of them said, "What visitors have arrived, boy?"

"Four Buddhist monks," replied one of the boys.

"Is one of them a pale fat monk?"

"Yes."

"And does one of them have a long snout and big ears?"

"Yes."

"Then bring them tea, and secretly tell your master to come here. We must speak with him."

The boy brought five cups of tea to his master and the four travelers. Then he winked at his master. The master said, "Excuse me for a minute," and went back into the kitchen. When he entered the kitchen, the seven demons fell to their knees. He said to them, "Why do you need to talk with me, sisters? I don't want any trouble here, I just want to live quietly. And right now you are keeping me from taking care of my visitors. How can you be so ill-mannered?"

One of the demons replied, "Dear brother, the boy just told us that four Buddhist monks just arrived here. One has a pale, fat face. Another has a long snout and big ears. Correct?" The Daoist nodded his head and said nothing. She continued, "We know this monk. He was sent by the Tang Emperor to fetch scriptures from the Western Heaven. He came to our cave this morning, begging food. We captured him."

"Why did you do that?"

"We have heard of this monk. He has studied the Way for ten lifetimes. Anyone who eats his flesh will live forever. That's why we captured him. Later, the monk with the long snout found us in the hot spring. He stole our clothes. Then he jumped into the water with us, the pig! He swam around in the water with us. Many times he swam right between our legs! He had no manners at all. Then he tried to kill us with his rake. We could not fight him, so we sent our seven sons to fight him. Then we came here for safety. We don't know if our sons are alive or dead. We beg you to take revenge on these evil monks!"

The Daoist became furious. "Don't worry, I will take care of these criminals. Come with me." He went into his room and climbed up to the rafters. He reached into the rafters and grabbed a small leather box. The box had a lock on it. The Daoist reached into his sleeve and pulled out a small key. He used the key to open the box. Then he brought out a cloth bag. What was in the bag?

> A thousand pounds of bird droppings
> Boiled for a long time until it was just a cupful
> Boiled again until it was just a spoonful
> Then fried, and cooked, and boiled again
> At last, it is the most powerful poison
> A man who eats just one grain will quickly see Yama
> Three grains will kill even a god or immortal

The Daoist took twelve grains out of the bag. He took twelve jujubes and made a small hole in each one. He pushed one grain of poison into each jujube. When he was finished, he put three poisoned jujubes into each of four different teacups. For himself, he put two jujubes without the poison into his cup.

He said, "I will ask them some questions. If I find out that they are from Tang, I will call for fresh tea. Bring these teacups. I will give them the poison tea. They will drink the tea and die. You will have your revenge."

He returned to the room where the four travelers were sitting. "Please forgive me, I had to take care of some matters in the kitchen. May I ask you, sir, where you are coming from?"

Tangseng replied, "I have been sent by the Tang Emperor to fetch scriptures from Thunderclap Monastery in the Western Heaven. We passed your temple and wanted to pay our respects."

"You are most welcome here," said the Daoist. Then turning to the boy he said, "Boy, bring some fresh tea for our guests right away!" The boy went into the kitchen. He took the tray of five teacups from the demon women and returned with the tea. The Daoist gave each of the travelers a cup with three jujubes. He took for himself the cup with just two jujubes.

Sun Wukong saw that the Daoist's cup had only two jujubes in it. "Sir," he said, "let's change cups."

The Daoist smiled and said, "Living here in the forest we do not have much food. I could only find twelve good jujubes. You are my honored guests, so I want you to have them. I will take these two old jujubes that are not as tasty."

Sun Wukong started to argue, but Tangseng jumped in and said, "Wukong, this man is being very kind. Drink your tea and don't argue with him." Sun Wukong stopped talking, but he did not drink his tea.

Zhu put his hand into the hot tea and grabbed his three jujubes. He ate them immediately. Tangseng and Sha were more polite, they drank their tea. In a few seconds, all three of them fainted and fell to the floor.

Sun Wukong jumped up and threw his teacup at the Daoist. "You brute!" he shouted, "look at what you've done. What have we ever done to you?"

The Daoist replied, "You asked for it, you beast. Didn't you beg for food at Spiderweb Cave? Didn't you bathe in the hot spring?"

"There were female demons in that hot spring! And since you know about it, you must be friends with them. You are probably an evil demon yourself. Stay where you are and taste my rod!" He whipped out his golden hoop rod and struck at the Daoist's face. The Daoist moved out of the way, whipped out a sword, and began to fight. The seven female demons heard the fighting. They ran out of the kitchen and opened their blouses. Magic silken ropes came from their navels and wrapped around Sun Wukong.

But this was not a problem for the monkey king. He said some magic words, did a cloud somersault, and flew up into the air. He had escaped but he was not happy. He thought, "This is terrible. I have never seen anything like this before. My master and my brothers are all poisoned. I don't know what to do. I think I will call that local spirit again."

So he came back down to the ground. He made a magic sign and spoke the word "Om." This made the old god come again.

The old god trembled with fear. He said, "Great sage, why are you here? I thought you went to rescue your master."

"I rescued him this morning," Sun Wukong replied. "Later we arrived at Yellow Flower Temple. The Daoist master there was very kind to us, but later he poisoned my master and my two brother disciples. He started talking about bathing at the hot spring, so I knew right away that he was a demon. We started to fight. Then the seven female demons came out of the kitchen and joined in the fight. They trapped me with their silken ropes, but I escaped. Now I need to know more about these demons. Tell me everything you know about them."

The trembling old god said, "The evil demons arrived here less than ten years ago. They are really spider spirits. And the silken ropes are really spiderwebs."

"That's all I need to know," Sun Wukong replied. He told the local god that he could leave. He pulled seventy hairs from his head, whispered "Change" and turned them into seventy little monkeys. Then he blew a magic breath on his golden hoop rod, whispered "Change" and turned it into seventy forks. He gave one fork to each little monkey. Then all the little monkeys attacked the demons. The demons tried to cover the little monkeys with silken ropes, but the little monkeys used their forks to wrap up all the silken ropes. Then the monkeys grabbed the seven demons, dragged them out of the cave, and tied them up with ordinary rope.

"Give me back my master and my brothers," shouted Sun Wukong to the spider demons.

"Elder Brother," screamed the spider demons to the Daoist master, "give the Tang monk back. Let us live!"

The Daoist master shouted from inside the cave, "No, I am going to eat the Tang monk. I cannot help you."

This made Sun Wukong angry. He pulled all seventy forks back into his golden hoop rod. Then he used the rod to kill all seven spider demons. When he finished killing the demons, he ran into the cave to fight with the Daoist.

It was a great battle. The monkey king and the Daoist were both fighting for the Tang monk. Sun Wukong was very strong, but the Daoist was very clever and fast. The rod and the sword smashed together again and again. They fought for fifty or sixty rounds. There was so much dust and dirt that the animals in the forest were frightened and ran away. The stars disappeared as the cloud of dust covered Heaven and earth.

After fighting for a long time, the Daoist became tired. He opened his belt and took off his black robe. "Ha!" said Sun Wukong. "If you cannot defeat me with your robe on, how can you defeat me with the robe off?"

But the Daoist had another weapon hidden under his robe. He raised both arms. On his chest were a thousand eyes. They glowed with a bright golden light, like fire. Thick yellow smoke came out of the eyes. Sun Wukong could not see anything. He tried to hit the Daoist with his rod, but he could not see his enemy. He got very hot. He jumped into the air, trying to smash the golden eyes. But he hit nothing. He fell to the ground. His head hurt.

"Well, this is bad," he thought. "I can't go left or right, I can't go forward or back, and I can't go up. I guess I will have to go down."

He said a magic spell, shook himself, and changed into a pangolin[1]. He dug into the ground with his sharp iron claws. He dug a tunnel six miles long. The golden light could only go about three miles. He dug a tunnel back up to the surface again. Then he lay on the ground, exhausted.

As he lay on the ground, he heard the sound of someone crying. He thought,

> One pair of crying eyes meets another
> One broken heart meets another

He said to her, "Lady, why are you crying?"

She said, "My husband was killed by the master of Yellow Flower Temple because of an argument over some business matter. The master used poisoned tea. Now I have come to burn some paper money at his grave."

"I am Sun Wukong, the senior disciple of the monk Tangseng. We are traveling to the Western Heaven and passed the Yellow Flower Temple. We stopped there to rest, but the Daoist master is the brother of seven evil spider demons. The Daoist master gave poison tea to my master and my two brothers. I did not drink the tea. The Daoist master and the seven spider demons attacked me. I fought them and killed the seven spider demons. Then I fought the Daoist master. He took off his shirt and used a thousand eyes to blind me. I escaped by turning into a pangolin and digging a tunnel underground."

"You don't know that Daoist master. He is Demon King Hundred Eyes. You must have great magical power to fight him and still live, because he is very powerful. I know a sage who can defeat the demon king, but I'm afraid that will not help your friends. The sage lives far from here, and the poison will kill your friends within three days."

"I can travel very fast. Tell me where this sage lives."

"All right. Three hundred miles due south of here is Purple Cloud Mountain. In that mountain is Thousand Flower Cave. And living in that cave is the sage Vairambha. She can defeat the demon."

After saying this, the crying woman disappeared. Sun Wukong looked up and

---

[1] The pangolin (chuān shān jiǎ), also called the scaly anteater, is a large nocturnal mammal that looks much like an armadillo. They nest in hollow trees or underground burrows and live on a diet of ants and termites.

saw her flying away. He flew after her and called, "Lady Bodhisattva, please tell me your name so I can thank you."

She replied, "Great sage, it's me." He looked more closely and saw that she was the Old Woman of Mount Li. She continued, "I was returning from the Dragon Flower Festival. I saw that your master was in trouble. Now hurry and find the sage. But don't tell her that I sent you. She can be rather difficult." Then she flew away.

Sun Wukong used his cloud somersault to travel quickly to Purple Cloud Mountain. He arrived and found Thousand Flower Cave. All around the cave were flowers of many colors. Above the cave he saw an auspicious cloud.

He was happy to see the beautiful flowers and the auspicious cloud above. But when he entered the cave, it was completely silent. He walked further and further into the cave. After walking for over a mile, he saw a Daoist nun. She was sitting on a couch. She wore a golden silk robe and an embroidered five-flowered hat. Her face was old but her eyes were bright, and her voice was like the song of a bird. He knew that this was Bodhisattva Vairambha, the Buddha of Thousand Flower Cave.

"Greetings, Bodhisattva Vairambha," he said.

"Greetings, Great Sage," she replied.

He was surprised to hear this. "How did you know my name?" he asked.

"When you caused trouble in Heaven, portraits of you were passed around. Everyone knows who you are."

"Truly, 'good deeds stay at home, but bad deeds are known far and wide.' You did not know that I am now a Buddhist. I need your help. My master is traveling to the Western Heaven to fetch the Buddha's scriptures. He was poisoned by the Daoist master of Yellow Flower Temple. I escaped but my master and two of my brothers are trapped in his cave. They will die soon if you cannot help them."

"How do you know of me? I have lived here three hundred years and nobody has heard of me."

"I am a demon of the earth; I can find you anywhere."

"All right. I shouldn't go, but I know that the Tang monk must succeed in his journey to the west. I will help you." Together, they started to fly towards Yellow Flower Temple.

As they flew together, Sun Wukong asked, "Lady Bodhisattva, please tell me what weapon you will use?"

"I have a small embroidery needle."

Sun Wukong laughed. "If I knew you were going to use an embroidery needle, I would not have come. I have lots of needles."

"Not like this one. Your needles are made of iron, steel or gold. My needle was made by my son, the Star Lord Mao. It was created in the fires of the sun. Watch this."

They were approaching Yellow Flower Temple. They could see a bright yellow light coming from it. Vairambha pulled the needle from her gown and threw it in the air. A few seconds later there was a loud noise. The golden light coming from the temple was extinguished. The needle returned to Vairambha's hand and she put it back in her gown.

"Wonderful!" said Sun Wukong.

They went into the cave. The Daoist master was standing there with his eyes closed, not moving. Sun Wukong whipped out his rod and prepared to smash the Daoist. But Vairambha said, "Don't hit him. Go find your master."

He went into the back of the cave. Tangseng, Zhu and Sha were lying on the floor, looking like they were going to die. Sun Wukong did not know what to do. "How can I help them?" he cried.

"Don't worry, Great Sage," said Vairambha. "Take these three pills and give one each to your master and your brothers." She handed him three red pills. He pushed one pill into each of their mouths. A few seconds later they all started vomiting up the poison tea. They immediately started feeling much better.

Sun Wukong told them about the poisoned tea, and that Bodhisattva Vairambha had saved them. Tangseng bowed to her in gratitude. Zhu became angry and ran towards the Daoist master with his rake held high.

"Stop, Marshal, said Vairambha. "Don't kill him. I have no servants in my cave. I am going to take this one back to my cave to be my servant."

Sun Wukong said, "Bodhisattva, thank you for your help. May we please see his true form?"

"That's easy," she replied. She stepped forward and pointed at the Daoist. He fell to the floor and changed into a giant centipede spirit, seven feet long. She picked him up with her little finger, and flew back to Thousand Flower Cave.

"That is one powerful lady," said Zhu, looking at the direction where Vairambha had flown.

Sun Wukong replied, "She told me that her son is the Star Lord Mao. He created her embroidery needle in the sun. Now, we know that the Star Lord is really a rooster. So his mother must be a hen. And we all know that hens are very good at dealing with centipedes. That's why it was so easy for her."

Tangseng kowtowed over and over again towards the direction where Vairambha had flown. Then he said, "Disciples, let's have some dinner." Sha went into the kitchen to fix some vegetarian food for dinner. Then they walked out of the cave. Sun Wukong started a fire in the kitchen. Soon everything in the cave was burning. They watched the fire for a little while. Then they turned and began walking west again.

Chapter 74

My dear child, please listen to these words:

> Study well the teachings of Buddha
> When desire leaves, wisdom arrives
> Be patient, let your heart be strong
> Be free of dust like the moon high in the sky
> Do your work without mistakes
> When it is done, you will be an enlightened immortal

Heavy rain washed away the last heat of summer. Cool autumn breezes moved through the trees, and crickets made music at night under the bright moon.

One day as they walked west, Tangseng looked up and saw a very tall mountain. He said, "That mountain is too tall, how can we get to the far side of it?"

Sun Wukong smiled and said, "Don't worry, Master. The ancients say, 'Even the highest mountain has a road, even the deepest water has a ferry boat.'"

Tangseng nodded his head and they continued walking. A few miles later they met an old man. He had long white hair and a long silver beard. He held a dragon's head staff in his hand. "Stop!" he called to the travelers. "There are terrible demons living in these mountains. They have already eaten all the people in this region. They will eat you too."

Tangseng was very frightened. His legs grew weak and he fell off his horse. Sun Wukong wanted to go and talk with the old man, but Tangseng said, "Disciple, your face is too ugly and the sound of your words is too harsh. I am afraid you will frighten the old man and he will refuse to talk to you."

"All right, I will change my appearance," the monkey king replied. He made a magic sign with his fingers. Now he looked like a young Daoist monk with a beautiful face and voice. "How's this?" he asked. Tangseng smiled and said that the ugly monkey was now very handsome.

Sun Wukong walked up to the old man and said, "Grandfather, this poor monk greets you!"

The old man patted him on the head and said, "Little monk, where did you come from?"

"We come from the empire of Tang in the east. We are traveling west to India. We want to find the Buddha's scriptures and bring them back to our people. Just now we heard you talking about the demons that live in this mountain. Would you please tell us more about them, so that we can defeat them?"

"You are a young man and you don't know anything. Let me tell you about these demons. If they send a letter to the Spirit Mountain, five hundred warriors will come to help them. These demons are friends with the dragons of the four oceans, the immortals of the eight caves, and all the gods of all the cities in this region."

"You seem to think very highly of these demons. Perhaps they are friends of yours, or maybe they are your relatives? No matter, I will defeat them. My surname is Sun and my given name is Wukong. My home is the Water Curtain Cave on Flower Fruit Mountain. Many years ago, I was also a monster spirit. One day I was drinking wine with some other demons. I fell asleep. Two men dragged me to the underworld to meet Yama and the Lords of Darkness. This made me angry. I used my golden hoop rod to beat the Lords of Darkness. They were very frightened, so they said that they would become my servants if I stopped beating them."

The old man laughed loudly. He said, "You have told me such an unbelievable story, you will never grow any taller yourself. How old are you?"

"Take a guess."

"Oh, maybe seven or eight years old."

"Multiply that by ten thousand and you will be closer to the truth, old man. Now I will show you my true appearance. Please don't be frightened." Sun Wukong wiped his face with his hand. Now he looked like a thunder god. He had long sharp teeth and a wide mouth. He wore a tiger skin robe and held a golden hoop rod in his hand. The old man was so frightened, he began to shake.

Sun Wukong asked, "Grandfather, how many demons are there on this mountain?" But the old man was too frightened to say any more. Sun Wukong turned and walked back to Tangseng and the others.

"Wukong," said Tangseng, "what did you find out?"

"Oh, it's nothing. The people here worry too much. There are just a few monsters. Let's continue our journey."

"Wait a minute," said Zhu. "We all know that elder brother is very good at telling stories and playing tricks. But if you want an honest person, look at me. I will find out the truth."

"All right. But do be careful, Wuneng," said Tangseng.

Zhu put his rake in his belt, smoothed out his black shirt, and walked up the road to speak with the old man. When the old man saw the ugly pig walking towards him, he cried, "What bad dream is this, that has such monsters in it? The first one was just ugly. But this one doesn't even look human!"

Zhu said, "Don't be afraid. I am the second disciple of the Tang monk. My elder brother frightened you, so I have come to ask you for some help. Please tell me, what mountain is this? What cave is in the mountain? How many demons are in the cave? And where is the road that can take us across the mountain?"

The old man pointed with his staff and said, "This mountain is Lion Mountain, it is eight hundred miles wide. It has a cave called Lion Cave. Three demons live in the cave."

"That's nothing," said Zhu. "Why should we care about three little demons?"

"You are a fool. These three demons are very powerful. They have many little demons under their command. There are five thousand on the south side, five thousand on the north side, ten thousand guarding the eastern road, ten thousand guarding the western road, five thousand on patrol, and ten thousand guarding the cave. Many more little demons tend the fires and gather wood. In all, there are about forty-eight thousand. All of them like to eat human flesh."

When Zhu heard these words, he ran back to Tangseng and the others. "Master, we must turn back! This mountain is full of demons! There are three large demons in a cave and nearly fifty thousand little demons nearby, and they all like to eat human flesh. If we continue, we will become food for them."

"Oh, stop this talk," said Sun Wukong. "The people here are easily frightened. I'm sure we can take care of a few demons."

"How can you defeat fifty thousand demons?" asked Zhu.

"It's easy. I will make my rod grow until it is four hundred feet long and eighty feet thick. When I roll it down the south side of the mountain, five thousand demons will die. When I roll it down the north side, another five thousand will die. And when I roll it east and west, there will be tens of thousands of dead demons."

Zhu nodded. "That's a good idea. I think you can do it in about four hours."

Tangseng also was feeling less frightened. He got back on his horse and they began walking up the mountain. The old man had disappeared. Sha said, "I think the old man was an evil spirit himself."

Sun Wukong said, "Let me take a look." He jumped up into the air and looked around. He saw bright colors in the sky. Looking closer, he saw the Bright Star of Venus. Sun Wukong grabbed him and said, "Long Lived Li[1], why did you pretend to be an old man and try to make a fool of me?"

"I'm sorry about that," said Li. "But these demons really are very powerful. You have great powers, but still, it will be very hard for you."

"Thank you. I hope you will go up to Heaven and ask the Jade Emperor to lend us some of his soldiers."

"Of course. Just say the word and you can have an army of a hundred thousand soldiers."

Sun Wukong returned to Tangseng and the others. "Wait here," he said, "I am going to take a look around. I'll find some demons. I will capture one, ask him questions, and learn what is going on here. Then I'll tell the demons to stay in their cave so we can pass though without trouble."

He changed into a fly and waited on a tree branch. For a long time he saw no one. Then a young demon came running along a mountain path. The young demon said to himself, "We must be careful. We must watch out for the one called Sun. He can even turn into a fly!" Sun Wukong waited until the young demon had run a little way ahead. Then he changed into a young demon, a little bit taller than the real young demon but dressed exactly the same.

He shouted, "Hey, wait for me!"

The young demon turned around and said, "Who are you? You are not one of us."

"I work in the kitchen."

----

[1] This is the immortal known as Bright Star of Venus. Sun Wukong is calling him by his personal name Chánggēng Lǐ, literally, "Long Lived Li."

"No, our king is very strict. The kitchen staff only works in the kitchen, and the mountain patrollers only work on the mountain. You should not be here."

Sun Wukong thought for a moment, then he said, "You don't know, but I did such a good job in the kitchen that I was given a new job patrolling."

"I don't believe you. Let me see your pass."

Of course Sun Wukong didn't have a pass because he did not know about it. He said, "Let me see your pass first."

The young demon took out his pass. It was a golden plate with the words "Junior Wind Cutter" on it. Sun Wukong looked at it, then he reached into the sleeve of his robe and pulled out a golden plate just like it, but with the words "Chief Wind Cutter" on it.

The young demon saw it and bowed quickly, saying, "Sir, I'm sorry. You just recently were given this job, that's why I did not recognize you."

Sun Wukong said, "That's all right, I'm not angry."

The two of them walked together for a mile or two until they arrived at a tall thin rock. Sun Wukong jumped up and sat on top of the rock. Then he said, "Come here." Young Wind Cutter stood near the rock. Sun Wukong said to him, "Our great king wants to kill and eat the Tang monk, but he is worried about Sun's magic powers. We have heard that Sun can change his appearance and look like one of us. That is why they made me Chief Wind Cutter, so I can find out if you really are a Wind Cutter. Tell me, what powers does our king have?"

Young Wind Cutter said, "Our king has great powers. He once ate a hundred thousand Heavenly warriors at once."

"That's crazy. No matter how big our king's mouth is, how could he eat a hundred thousand warriors?"

"Our king is called Blue Haired Lion. He can make himself as tall as the sky or as small as a vegetable seed. One day he was angry because the Queen Mother did not invite him to a banquet in Heaven. He started a war. The Jade Emperor sent a hundred thousand Heavenly soldiers to fight him. Our king gave himself a magical body with a mouth as big as a city gate. He was ready to eat all the soldiers, but they ran away and locked the gates of Heaven."

"That is correct. Now, tell me about the second king."

"Our second king is called Old Yellow Tusk Elephant. He is thirty feet tall, has a voice like a beautiful woman, and a nose like a dragon."

"That's right. And what about the third king?"

"Our third king is called Great Peng[1] of Ten Thousand Cloudy Miles. He is not from this world. He moves the wind and the seas. He carries a treasure called the Yin Yang Jar. Anyone put in that jar turns to liquid in a few minutes."

Sun Wukong thought, "I'm not scared of the bird, but I'd better watch out for that jar!" Turning to Young Wind Cutter he said, "That's right. Now tell me, which one wants to eat the Tang monk?"

"Don't you know, sir? They all do! Our first king and second king have lived here in Lion Mountain for many years. Our third king, the Great Peng, used to live a hundred miles away in a different country. Five hundred years ago he ate every person in the capital city, and turned the rest of the country's people into demons. Recently he heard about the coming of the Tang monk. He heard that anyone who eats the Tang monk's flesh will live forever and never grow old. But he is afraid of the monk's disciple Sun. So he came here. Now he and the Vairambha 's other two kings are working together to capture the Tang monk."

This made Sun Wukong very angry. "How dare they plan to eat my master?" he cried. He whipped out his rod and quickly killed the Young Wind Cutter demon. "Oh, I suppose he meant well," he thought, "but what is done is done. That's that."

He took the dead Young Wind Cutter's golden pass and tied it around his waist. Then he made a magic sign and changed his form to look exactly like the dead Young Wind Cutter. He ran towards Lion Cave. When he arrived, he saw forty groups of 250 soldiers each, for a total of ten thousand soldiers. He thought, "Long Lived Li was telling the truth after all!"

He walked up to the gate of the cave. Several soldiers stopped him and said, "You're back, Young Wind Cutter. Did you see the one they call Sun?"

---

[1] Péng is a huge bird of prey that transforms from a giant fish. The Daoist classic *Zhuangzi* begins with a famous story about this great bird: "In the northern darkness there is a fish and his name is Kun. The Kun is so huge I don't know how many thousand *li* he measures. He changes into a bird named Peng. The back of the Peng measures thousands of *li* across and, when he rises up and flies off, his wings are like clouds all over the sky. When the sea begins to move, this bird sets off for the southern darkness, which is the Lake of Heaven."

"Yes," Sun Wukong replied. "We all should be very afraid of Sun. He looks like a great god, several hundred feet tall. He was talking about how he was planning to use his magic rod to kill all the demons in this mountain. Now, I was thinking. Our king wants to capture this Tang monk. But the monk only has a few pounds of flesh. There is no way that our great king can give each of us some of the monk's flesh. So I think we should just run away and save our own lives."

"You're right!" they cried, and in a few minutes, all ten thousand soldiers had disappeared.

"Well, that was easy!" Sun Wukong said to himself. And he walked into the cave.

Chapter 75

What did Sun Wukong see when he walked into the cave?

Hills of skeletons
Mountains of corpses
Forests of bones
Piles of human heads and hair
Oceans of blood
The smell of cooking human flesh
Only the Monkey King would dare to enter!

He walked past the skeletons, corpses and bones. After passing through the second gate, he came to a part of the cave that was quiet, peaceful and beautiful. He walked two or three more miles and passed through the third gate. Here he saw a hundred and ten soldiers in armor. In the middle of the cave, three demons sat on chairs. What did they look like?

The demon in the middle had

A round head and a square face
A voice like thunder
Eyes that shine like lightning
He is the king of all animals
This is the senior demon, the Blue Haired Lion.

The demon on his left had

A white face like a bull
Golden eyes and two long yellow tusks
A long nose and silver hair
His head looks like a tail
A huge body but a voice like a young woman
This is the second demon, Old Yellow Tusk Elephant.

The demon on his right had

Golden wings and a huge head
Leopard eyes that shine like stars
He shakes the north when he flies south
Even dragons are frightened of him
He can fly thirty thousand miles through clouds
This is the third demon, Great Peng.

Sun Wukong was not afraid. He still looked like Young Wind Cutter. He walked up to the three demons and said, "Your Majesties, I went to find the disciple they call Sun. I found him. He is over a hundred feet tall. When I saw him, he was playing with his magical golden hoop rod. He said to himself that he was getting ready to attack Your Majesties."

"Quick!" shouted one of the generals, "Get everyone inside the cave, and shut the gates. Let the Tang monk and his disciples pass through our land."

One of the soldiers replied, "Sir, the little demons have all run away. They must be frightened."

The soldiers shut the gates to the cave. Sun Wukong said, "Be careful, Your Majesties. This Sun can change into a fly." Then he pulled a hair from his head, blew on it, whispered "Change!" and turned it into a golden fly.

The fly flew towards Blue Haired Lion's face. The lion shouted, "Brothers, he is inside our cave!" Sun Wukong laughed. But when he laughed his face turned back into its original monkey form for a few seconds.

The Great Peng saw this, ran forward and grabbed Sun Wukong. He shouted, "This isn't Young Wind Cutter, this is Sun himself! He must have killed the real Young Wind Cutter and taken his appearance to trick us." Great Peng knocked Sun Wukong to the ground, tied him up with ropes, and pulled off his clothes. Under the clothes he still looked like a monkey. He had a long tail and was covered with brown hair.

"We caught him!" shouted the Blue Haired Lion. "Quick, put him in the jar!" He told thirty-six little demons to fetch the jar. The jar was very small, only two feet four inches high. But it was very heavy because it was a treasure of ying and yang. Thirty-six people were needed to carry it, one for each of the stars in the Dipper[1]. The little demons brought the jar. They removed its lid. Immediately Sun Wukong was sucked inside by a magical fog that came from the jar. They put the lid back on the jar.

"Ha!" said the demons. "That monkey can forget about his journey to the west. The only way he will see Buddha is to go through the great Wheel of Rebirth." Then they all went into another room to relax and drink wine.

Sun Wukong made himself very small. He sat down inside the jar. It was cool

---

[1] In ancient Chinese astrology, the Big Dipper constellation has 36 stars representing Heavenly spirits and 72 stars representing demons. In the classic novel *The Water Margin* these 108 stars, called the Stars of Destiny, band together to fight for justice.

and quite comfortable. He laughed and said, "These demons were wrong. They said anyone in this jar would be dead in a few minutes. But it's so comfortable here, I could stay here for years."

But he did not know about the jar's magic. As long as the prisoner was quiet, the jar was cool and comfortable. But as soon as the prisoner spoke, the fires started. Inside the jar it quickly became burning hot. Sun Wukong made a magic sign with his hands to protect himself from the fire. Then forty snakes came to bite him. He grabbed them and broke them into eighty pieces. Then three fire dragons came and flew in circles above him.

He was worried about the fire dragons, so he made a magic sign and grew to be twelve feet tall. The jar grew also. Then he made himself as small as a vegetable seed. The jar became small. No matter what he did, he remained trapped in the jar. One of the fire dragons blew fire on his feet and they started to hurt badly.

He began to cry. But then he remembered something. He said to himself, "Many years ago, the Bodhisattva gave me three magic hairs. I wonder if I still have them." He ran his hands over his body. All his hairs were soft, but he found three rigid hairs on the back of his head.

He pulled the three rigid hairs out of his head, blew on them with magic breath and said, "Change!" The first hair became a drill, the second hair became a strip of bamboo, and the third hair became a silken cord. He put them together and made a magic drill. He drilled a small hole in the bottom of the jar. The yin and yang forces flowed out of the hole. The jar became cool. Sun Wukong changed into a tiny insect and escaped through the hole. He flew away and landed on the head of the Blue Haired Lion.

"Third brother," said the Blue Haired Lion, "has that monkey been turned to liquid yet?" Great Peng told some messengers to bring the jar.

"The jar is too light!" he shouted. Then he took off the lid and looked inside. "It's empty. The monkey has escaped. Find him!"

Sun Wukong ran out of the cave, shouting, "I made a hole in the jar and escaped. The yin and yang have also escaped. Now you can use your jar for a chamber pot!"

Shouting and dancing with glee, he flew on a cloud to Tangseng. When he came close, he looked down. Tangseng had his hands in front of his chest. He was saying,

Oh, you immortals in the clouds
Protect my disciple
His powers are great, his magic has no limits
The good monkey, Sun Wukong.

Sun Wukong came down to the ground. He gave Tangseng a full report of everything that had happened. When he finished, Tangseng said, "So, you did not fight the evil demons. Therefore, I dare not travel across this mountain."

"Master, there are three big demons and tens of thousands of little demons. How can I fight them all by myself?"

"Zhu and Sha also have some skills. Let them help you."

"All right." He turned to the other disciples. "Sha, you protect Master. Zhu, you come with me."

"Elder brother," said Zhu, "how can I help you? I can't do much of anything."

"You know the saying, 'even a fart can make the wind stronger.' I'm sure you can be helpful."

And so, Sun Wukong and Zhu flew back to the cave. The gates were shut. Sun Wukong shouted, "Open the gates, evil monsters! Come out and fight Old Monkey!"

Two of the demons were too afraid to come out, but Blue Haired Lion said to his brothers, "We already have a poor reputation in this region. If we don't fight Sun, our reputation will be even worse. I will go out there and fight him. If I can't last three rounds with him, I will return to the cave and we will let them pass through to the west."

Blue Haired Lion put on his golden armor and walked out of the cave. In a voice like thunder he said, "Who is knocking at my gates?"

"It's your grandfather Sun, the Great Sage Equal to Heaven," said Sun Wukong.

"I have never caused you any trouble. Why do you want to fight me now?"

"What? How can you say, 'no trouble'? Your foxes and dogs are trying to capture my master and eat him."

"All right, let's fight. But I will not use my soldiers, and you must not get help from anyone. Just you and me." Sun Wukong nodded his head and told Zhu to stay back.

Blue Haired Lion said, "Come here. Let me hit you on the head three times with my sword. If you are not killed, I will let you and your master pass through."

Sun Wukong stood without moving. Blue Haired Lion lifted his huge sword with both hands and brought it down onto the top of the monkey's head. There was a mighty sound, but his head was not hurt at all.

"You really do have a hard head!" said Blue Haired Lion.

"Your sword is not very sharp. Go ahead, hit me with it again."

Blue Haired Lion used all his strength to hit him again. This time, Sun Wukong's head was cut in two. He rolled on the ground and gave himself a second body. Blue Haired Lion was frightened by this. Zhu was watching from a short distance away. He laughed and said, "Go ahead, hit him again. You'll have four monkeys to fight!"

Blue Haired Lion tried to hit Sun Wukong a third time, but the monkey raised his golden hoop rod and blocked the blow. They began to fight. The monkey used his magic rod, the lion used his great sword. They fought on the ground and in the sky. The sky filled with clouds; the earth was covered with fog. Good and evil fought for twenty rounds but neither could win. Then Zhu ran in and joined the fight. The monster was frightened and ran away. Sun Wukong ran after him. The lion turned, opened his mouth wide, and swallowed the monkey in one bite.

Zhu saw this. He cried, "Oh brother, you are a fool. Why did you go towards the monster? Today you were a monk, but tomorrow you'll just be a pile of shit."

With his head down, Zhu walked slowly back to Tangseng and Sha. He said, "Sha, go and get the luggage. We should each take a few things and split up. You can go back to your river and continue eating people. I will go back to my village and see my wife. We can sell the white horse to buy a coffin for Master." Tangseng heard this and began to cry.

Meanwhile, Blue Haired Lion returned to his cave. "I caught one of them," he said to his brothers. "He's in my belly."

Great Peng said, "Elder brother, you should not eat the monkey. He is not good to eat."

"I am delicious," said Sun Wukong from inside Blue Haired Lion's belly. "And you will never be hungry again."

When the Blue Haired Lion heard a voice coming from his belly, he became frightened. He told some little demons to bring him some hot salt water. He drank it quickly, hoping that he would vomit Sun Wukong out of his belly. But Sun Wukong held on to the monster's belly and would not come out.

"I don't want to come out," he said. "I have been a monk for several years, and I'm always cold and hungry. But here it's very warm and there's lots of food to eat. I think I'll stay here all winter."

"Then I will stop eating and you will die from hunger."

"I don't think so. I have a nice cooking pan with me. I will make a fire and cook all the organs of your body. If there's too much smoke, I'll make a hole in your head and use it for a chimney. That will also give me some sunlight."

Blue Haired Lion called for some wine. He drank cup after cup of wine. As the wine came down into the monster's belly, Sun Wukong drank it. After a while he became drunk. He ran around, doing somersaults and kicking the monster from the inside. The pain was terrible. Finally the monster fell down on the floor, unconscious.

Chapter 76

The monster lay without moving for a few minutes, then he said to the monkey in his belly, "Oh Bodhisattva, Great Sage Equal to Heaven, be kind to me!"

"Oh, just call me Grandpa Sun," Sun Wukong replied.

"Grandpa Sun! Grandpa Sun! I should not have eaten you, I am sorry! Please let me live. I do not have any treasure to give you. But I will carry your master across the mountain on my sedan chair."

"That would be better than treasure. Open your mouth, I am coming out."

Just as the monster started to open his giant mouth, Great Peng said quietly, "When the monkey comes out of your mouth, bite him, chew him, and eat him. That will finish him." Sun Wukong heard all this, of course. So when Blue Haired Lion opened his mouth, Sun Wukong pushed his golden hoop rod out of the mouth. The monster bit down on the rod, breaking one of his teeth.

"So!" said Sun Wukong, "you are not a very nice monster. I let you live but you tried to kill me. Now I will just stay in your belly."

Great Peng heard this. He tried to make Sun Wukong angry. He said, "Monkey, I have heard how powerful you were outside the Southern Heaven Gate, and I have heard of the many demons you have killed. But now I think that you are very small and weak. You are hiding in my brother's belly. Come out and fight me now!"

"You know it would be easy for me to kill this monster from the inside. But that would hurt my reputation. So I will come out. But we should not fight in this cave, it's much too small. We must find a place where I can use my rod."

The other two demons carried Blue Haired Lion out of the cave. Thirty thousand little demons surrounded them. They all had weapons. They waited for Sun Wukong to come out of the monster's belly.

Sun Wukong pulled a hair from his head, said, "Change," and made it into a thin rope four hundred feet long. He tied one end around the monster's heart. He held the other end in his hand. Then he made himself very small. He did not want to risk going past the monster's sharp teeth, so he climbed up into the monster's nose. The monster sneezed, and Sun Wukong flew out of his nose.

The monkey immediately grew to thirty feet tall. He started to fight all three of the great monsters and the thousands of little demons. But there were too many enemies, so he used his cloud somersault to fly away to a nearby mountaintop. Then he pulled on the rope. It became tight around Blue Haired Lion's heart. The monster fell to the ground in pain.

Sun Wukong was angry. He shouted at them, "You are nothing but a gang of criminals. You promised to let me out of the monster's belly, then you tried to bite me. You promised to fight me one on one, then you brought thousands of soldiers to fight me. It's over between you and me. I will kill Blue Haired Lion and drag his body away to show it to my master."

"Please, don't do that!" they all cried.

"If I let him live, will you let us pass through your mountain?"

"Yes," said Great Peng. Sun Wukong thought he was telling the truth. So he released the rope from Blue Haired Lion's heart. Great Peng continued, "Please go back to your master, Great Sage. Tell him to prepare to leave. We will bring the sedan chair to him." All the little demons put down their weapons.

Sun Wukong returned to his master and the other two disciples. He saw Tangseng crying. Sha and Zhu were splitting up the luggage. "Oh no," thought Sun Wukong, "that idiot pig has told my master that I'm dead. That's why he's crying."

Zhu saw Sun Wukong. He said to the others, "With my own eyes I saw the monster eating him. This must be an evil ghost."

Sun Wukong slapped him in the face, hard. "Idiot! Do you still think I am an evil ghost?" Turning to Tangseng he said, "Master, don't worry. The monsters are coming with a sedan chair to carry you across the mountain."

Tangseng bowed and said, "Disciple, I have caused you great trouble. If I believed Zhu we would have been finished!" They sat down and waited by the side of the road for the monsters to arrive.

Back at the cave, the three demon brothers were making plans. Old Yellow Tusk Elephant said, "I thought Sun was a great warrior with nine heads and eight tails. But now I see that he is just a little monkey. We can capture him easily. Give me three thousand little demons."

Great Peng replied, "I will give you every little demon in my army." They gathered all the demon soldiers together. Then they sent a messenger to Sun Wukong, telling him that Old Yellow Tusk Elephant was ready to fight him.

Sun Wukong laughed when he heard this. He said to Zhu, "Well, it looks like their senior demon, Blue Haired Lion, doesn't dare fight me again. They are sending their second demon, Old Yellow Tusk Elephant. You should fight him, Zhu."

"All right, but give me that magic rope."

"Why? You can't jump inside the elephant's belly and tie it around his heart."

"I want you to tie it around my waist. Hold the end of the rope. If you see that I'm winning the fight, give me more rope. But if I'm losing, pull the rope and get me out of there."

Sun Wukong smiled and tied the rope around Zhu's waist. Zhu raised his rake and attacked the elephant. The elephant threw his spear at Zhu's face. Zhu blocked the spear. The two fought for seven or eight rounds. Zhu began to get tired. He shouted to Sun Wukong, "Elder brother, pull the rope, get me out of here!"

Sun Wukong laughed and dropped the rope onto the ground. Zhu turned and ran away from the monster. He didn't see the rope on the ground so he tripped on it and fell. The elephant caught up with Zhu, wrapped his trunk around him, held him high in the air and carried him back to the cave. All the little demons shouted and cheered.

Tangseng saw this. He was very angry at Sun Wukong for allowing his brother to be captured. Sun Wukong said, "Stop complaining, Master. I will go and rescue him." He turned into a little fly, flew into the cave, and landed on Zhu's ear.

The elephant demon threw Zhu on the ground and said to his brothers, "Look, I've caught one of them." Then he said to the little demons, "Tie him up and put him in a pool of water. Leave him there for a day. Then we can cut open his belly, salt him, and dry him in the sun. He will taste good with some red wine." The little demons dragged him away.

Sun Wukong said to himself, "Well, what should I do? Master wants me to save the pig. But he is always causing trouble. A few days ago I heard Sha say that Zhu has hidden some money. I wonder if that's true." So he changed his voice and said in the pig's ear, "Zhu Wuneng, Zhu Wuneng. I am a messenger from the Fifth King of the Underworld. He has sent me to drag you down to the underworld."

Zhu was frightened. He said, "Please go back and tell the Fifth King that I'm busy today, and please come back tomorrow."

"No. If the Fifth King decides that you will die on the third watch, you will not live to see the fourth watch. Come with me right now."

"Please, I want to live one more day. Wait until these evil monsters have captured my master and my brothers."

Sun Wukong smiled to himself. He said, "All right. I need to catch thirty other people today. I can wait until tomorrow, but you must give me some money."

"I am a poor monk, I don't have any money!"

"Too bad. Then you are coming with me right now."

"Wait, wait! I have been keeping little bits of silver that people have given to me over the years. In total it's about half an ounce. It's in my left ear. Take it!"

Sun Wukong looked in Zhu's left ear. Sure enough, deep inside his ear was a little silver ball. Sun Wukong reached into the ear, grabbed the silver ball, and held it in his hand. He laughed loudly. Zhu recognized that laugh. He said, "Damn you, coming here and stealing my money when I'm in such trouble."

"I've got you now, you coolie. You've been getting rich while I have suffered to protect our master."

"Rich? This is just enough for me to buy some cloth for a new robe. You stole it from me. Now give me back half of it."

"You won't get a penny of it." Sun Wukong grabbed Zhu's feet and dragged him out of the pool of water. "Now let's get going. And we are not going out through the back gate. We are leaving through the front gate."

Sun Wukong ran towards the front gate, swinging his rod and killing little demons left and right. Zhu saw his rake nearby. He grabbed the rake and also attacked the little demons. Old Yellow Tusk Elephant heard the fighting and ran towards Sun Wukong. The two of them began to fight.

> The elephant was sworn brother to the lion
> Together they planned to eat the Tang monk
> The monkey king had great powers
> He saved the foolish pig and killed the little demons

The elephant's spear moved like a snake in the forest
The monkey's rod moved like a dragon from the sea
They fought hard for the Tang monk

Zhu watched the fight. He shouted, "Elder brother, watch out for the trunk! Push your rod inside the trunk!" Sun Wukong heard this. He made his rod as thick as a chicken's egg and pushed it hard up inside the elephant's trunk. Then he grabbed the end of the trunk with his other hand. Zhu ran towards the elephant, his rake held high.

"Wait," shouted Sun Wukong, "don't kill the elephant. Master will be angry if you do. Use the other end of your rake." Zhu turned his rake around, and began hitting the elephant with the rake's handle. Sun Wukong dragged the elephant out of the cave and down the mountain path towards Tangseng.

Tangseng saw them coming. He said to Sha Wujing, "Wonderful! That is a very big evil spirit. Ask him if he will help us cross over the mountain."

Sha walked up to the elephant and asked him to take his master across the mountain. The elephant replied, "I will carry Lord Tang myself if you let me live."

Sun Wukong said to him, "We are good people. We will let you live. Go and fetch the sedan chair. But if you try to harm us again, we will certainly kill you." The monster kowtowed and left. Sun Wukong told Tangseng everything that had happened. Zhu was filled with shame. He walked away from the others. He took off his wet clothes and put them on some rocks to let them dry in the sun.

Back at the cave, Old Yellow Tusk Elephant told his two brothers what happened, and how the Tang monk had been kind to him. He said to them, "What should we do, my brothers? Should we help the monk?"

Great Peng said, "Of course we should get ready to carry them across the mountain. That is part of our plan to bring the tiger down from the mountain."

"What do you mean by that?" asked Old Yellow Tusk Elephant.

"Call ten thousand little demons to the cave. Choose one thousand from the ten thousand. Choose one hundred from the thousand. Then choose sixteen and thirty from the hundred. The thirty must be good cooks. Give them the best food. Tell them to go ten miles west of here, and prepare a great feast for the Tang monk. They should also prepare another meal twenty-five miles from here."

"And what about the sixteen?"

"Eight will carry the sedan chair. Eight will shout to clear the way. The three of us will walk next to the sedan chair. We will walk west until we reach my home city 150 miles away. I have a great army there."

The three great demons and the sixteen little demons went back to meet Tangseng and the three disciples. Eight little demons carried the sedan chair. "Please get into the sedan chair, my lord," said Old Yellow Tusk Elephant. Tangseng did not realize it was a trick. And even Sun Wukong did not look closely at the situation. He told Zhu and Sha to tie the luggage to the white horse and protect Tangseng. He walked in front of the group, clearing the way

with his rod. In this way they all began walking west.

They walked ten miles, then they all stopped and had a delicious vegetarian meal. After eating, they continued walking for another fifteen miles, where they had a second very good meal. After that they stopped for the night, resting comfortably.

In this way they traveled west for 150 miles. They arrived at a great walled city. Sun Wukong was in front and he saw the city first. What did he see?

There were large crowds of evil monsters and demons
Wolf spirits were at all four gates
Tigers were the generals
Deer were the messengers
Foxes walked the streets
Rabbits sold things in shops
Long snakes rested on the city walls
The city was filled with monsters
Once this was the capital of a Heavenly kingdom
Now it is a city of wolves and tigers!

Sun Wukong was looking at the city. He did not see that Great Peng had come up behind him, preparing to hit him on the head with his weapon. He heard the sound of wind and turned around quickly. He blocked the bird's blow with his rod. They began to fight. The lion began to fight with Zhu and the elephant fought with Sha. While all three disciples were busy, the sixteen little demons grabbed the white horse, the luggage and Tangseng. They carried them into the walled city.

"Your Majesty, what do we do now with the Tang monk?" asked one of the tiger generals.

"Do not frighten the monk," replied the elephant while he was fighting Sha. "It will make his flesh taste bad." So the little demons treated Tangseng very well. They gave him a seat of honor, offering him tea and food. Tangseng looked around, not seeing anyone that he knew. He became confused.

Chapter 77

The three disciples fought with the three demons all day and into the evening. Clouds gathered in the sky and it became dark. Zhu was tired. He tried to run away but Blue Haired Lion grabbed him. He threw Zhu to a group of little demons. They tied up the pig and took him to the throne room. Then the lion returned to the fight to help his brothers.

Sha saw that the fight was going badly. He also tried to run away. Old Yellow Tusk Elephant wrapped his trunk around him, gave him to the little demons, and told them to take also him to the throne room. Then he went to help Great Peng in his fight against Sun Wukong.

Now Sun Wukong was fighting against all three demon brothers. He saw that he could not win, so he flew away on his cloud somersault. Great Peng flew swiftly after him. Sun Wukong's cloud somersault lets him travel 36,000 miles in one somersault. But Peng could cover 30,000 miles with just one flap of his wings. So he quickly caught up to Sun Wukong, grabbing him in his claws. He carried the monkey back to the city, where the little demons tied him up with ropes and put him on the floor next to Zhu and Sha.

At the hour of the second watch, the little demons pushed Tangseng into the room where his three disciples lay on the floor, tied with rope. He fell crying to the floor next to Sun Wukong and said, "Oh disciple, you have always used your magic powers to defeat demons. But now even you have been defeated!"

Zhu and Sha also started to cry. But Sun Wukong just smiled and replied, "Relax, Master! You will not be harmed. We will escape soon. You think these ropes are heavy, but me they are like an autumn breeze blowing past my ears."

Just then, they heard the three monsters talking about how they would steam and eat the four travelers. "Listen," said Zhu, "those monsters are planning to steam and eat us. We are about to become neighbors of King Yama, and you're talking about autumn breezes!"

The little demons came. They picked up the four travelers. They put Zhu in the bottom layer of a large cooking pot. They put Sha in the second layer. Just before they picked up Sun Wukong to put him in the third layer, the monkey pulled a hair from his head, said, "Change," and turned it into a second monkey just like himself. His true body rose into the air where he could look down on the room. The little demons put the false monkey in the third layer, then put Tangseng on the top layer. Then they started a fire.

"I'd better do something quick," said Sun Wukong. "Master won't last long in that heat." He quickly made a magic sign in the air and said some magic words. At once Aoshun, the Dragon King of the North Sea, arrived and kowtowed to the monkey king.

"Please rise," said Sun Wukong. "I came here with Master Tang. He was captured by three terrible demons. They put him in that cooking pot. Please protect him and my brothers." Aoshun changed into a cool breeze. He blew himself towards the cooking pot and wrapped himself around it. The inside of the pot became quite cool.

Now it was too cool for Zhu. He said to the others, "You know, when we were first put into this pot it was nice and warm. Now it's cold. I have a little bit of arthritis and I liked the heat. This is too cold for me!"

Sun Wukong laughed when he heard this. Then he decided it was time to rescue Tangseng and his brothers. He remembered that he once played a game of guess-fingers with one of the Heavenly kings, and he had won a few sleep-causing insects. He reached into his tiger-skin kilt and found a few. He threw ten of them in the faces of the little demons. The insects crawled into the noses of the little demons, and all the demons fell asleep.

The monkey thanked the Dragon King. Then he lifted the cover off the pot. He untied Tangseng, Zhu and Sha and lifted them out of the pot. He said, "There are still many mountains ahead of us. Master will not be able to cross them on foot. And we need our travel rescript. So we must find our horse and luggage."

He went back to the throne room. He found the horse and untied it. Then he saw the luggage and picked it up. He brought the horse and luggage back to the others. Tangseng got on the horse. They all started walking towards the palace's front gate. But when they arrived at the front gate, they found that it was locked using magic, and Sun Wukong could not open the lock.

"This is not a problem," said Zhu. "Let's find a place where we can just lift Master up over a wall, and escape that way."

Sun Wukong laughed and said, "That's no good. When we return with the scriptures later, we don't want people to think that we are wall-climbing monks[1]!"

---

[1] In Chinese stories from this time period, wall climbing priests were usually thieves or

Zhu said, "This is not the time to worry about such things, brother. We have to run for our lives!"

Several more little demons heard the noise of the prisoners escaping. They ran to the three demon brothers to report. The demon brothers ran to the front gate, but saw that it was still locked. They ran to the back gate and saw it was also locked. Then they saw the four monks trying to climb a wall. The demons ran towards them, shouting. Tangseng fell off the wall and was captured. Zhu, Sha and the white horse were also captured. Only Sun Wukong escaped.

The demons tied Zhu and Sha to pillars in the main hall, but the elephant held on to Tangseng and started to open his mouth. Great Peng said to him, "Big brother, don't eat him now. The best way is to cook him and eat him slowly, with a good wine and music."

Old Yellow Tusk Elephant replied, "Quite right, brother. But we must be careful. Soon that wretched monkey will return and try to steal the monk."

"I have a large iron chest here in the palace. Hide the monk in the chest. Tell everyone that we have already eaten the monk. When the monkey comes here, he will hear people saying that the monk has been eaten and he will go away. Later we can eat the monk with no problems."

Sun Wukong flew to the Lion Cave and spent the rest of the day killing all the little demons that he found there. The next day he flew back to the city. He changed his appearance to look like a little demon. Walking through the streets of the city, he heard people saying that the Tang monk had been eaten by the demons brothers the previous night. He entered the palace and found Zhu and Sha tied up. "Where is Master?" he asked them.

Zhu replied, "The little demons are saying that Master was eaten last night. But I didn't see it with my own eyes. You should try to find out what really happened."

But Sha said, "Oh brother, last night the monster spirits ate our Master!"

Sun Wukong flew to a nearby mountain, where he sat down and cried for a while. Then he said to himself, "Why did the Buddha do this to us? If he really cared about us, he would have sent his scriptures to the East. But no, he didn't do that. He put the scriptures in India and made Master cross a hundred rivers and climb a thousand mountains, only to lose his life in this awful

----

adulterers.

place. I will go see Buddha myself. I will ask him to give me the scriptures to bring back to the Tang Empire. And if he won't do that, I will ask him to release me from the headband that's wrapped around my head."

He jumped up, using the cloud somersault. An hour later he was in India at Spirit Mountain, the home of the Buddha Tathāgata[1]. He walked up to the four guardians and said, "I must see the Buddha on some business."

The guardians replied, "You still have not thanked us for helping you with the Bull Demon. And this is not like the South Heavenly gate where you can just run in and out as you wish. This is the home of the Buddha himself. If you have business here, tell us first. We will tell the Buddha. You can enter when he calls for you."

Sun Wukong began to argue loudly with the four guardians. Tathāgata heard the arguing and called for Sun Wukong to enter. The four guardians stepped aside to let Sun Wukong enter.

"Wukong," said Tathāgata, "why are you unhappy?"

Sun Wukong told him the whole story – how they arrived at the city of demons, how the three demon brothers captured the four travelers, how he alone escaped, how the Dragon King helped to save the other three travelers, and how he heard that Tangseng had been eaten by the demon kings. He finished by saying, "Oh great Buddha, our journey has ended in defeat. I beg you, please remove this headband from my head so I may return to my home on Flower Fruit Mountain and live there for the rest of my days." Then he began to cry.

"Do not cry, Wukong. I know these three demons. Blue Haired Lion and Old Yellow Tusk Elephant have masters named Manjusri and Visvabhadra. They will take care of those two demons. But the third one, Great Peng, is actually related to me."

"Oh, really? On your father's side or your mother's side?"

"In the beginning there was chaos. Then chaos was separated and Heaven was born. After that, Earth was born, then Man was born. Heaven and Earth came together and the many creatures were born. One of those was the phoenix. Do you understand?"

---

[1] This is the Buddha Gautama. When referring to himself, the Buddha uses the Chinese word rúlaí, or Tathāgata in Sanskrit. The word means "one who has gone," that is, someone who is beyond all transitory phenomena.

"Yes."

"The phoenix gave birth to the peacock and the Great Peng. In those days the peacock was a very dangerous creature. One day it sucked me into its belly. To escape I had to cut a hole in its back and ride it back to Spirit Mountain. I kept it here and made it Buddha-mother, the Bodhisattva Sakyamuni. Since Great Peng and the Buddha-mother have the same parent, you could say that Great Peng is my uncle."

Sun Wukong laughed at this and said, "I beg you, please come and defeat this monster."

"All right." Tathāgata said to Manjusri and Visvabhadra, "how long have your beasts been missing?"

"Seven days," replied Manjusri.

"That is equal to several thousand years on earth," said Tathāgata. "We should go quickly."

They flew together to the demon city. "Tathāgata, look there," said Sun Wukong. "That place with black fog above it is the demon city."

The Buddha said, "Go there and begin fighting with the three monsters. You must not win. Retreat back here. I will deal with them."

Sun Wukong flew down to the demon city, approached the palace, and shouted, "You lawless beasts, come out and fight Old Monkey!" The three demon brothers ran out holding their weapons high. They all attacked Sun Wukong. The monkey fought them for a while, then he flew up into the clouds. The three demons followed him, shouting.

Sun Wukong ran behind Tathāgata and disappeared. Instead, the three demons saw three Buddhas – past, present and future, along with five hundred teachers and three thousand guardians. They surrounded the three demons.

The three demons attacked. Immediately Manjusri and Visvabhadra shouted, "Submit now, wretched beasts!" The lion and elephant both dropped their weapons and stopped fighting. Manjusri and Visvabhadra led them away.

But Great Peng refused to stop fighting. He looked down from the sky, saw Sun Wukong, and tried to grab him with his claws. Tathāgata shook his head. It changed into a piece of bloody meat. The monster tried to grab the meat. Tathāgata pointed his finger at the monster. Immediately the monster lost the ability to fly away. He was trapped in the sky above the Buddha.

"Tathāgata," shouted the monster, "why are you holding me?"

The Buddha replied, "You have killed many creatures and incurred a great debt. Follow me and change your ways."

"I cannot. Your place only allows a vegetarian diet, but I can only eat meat. If I follow you, I will die from hunger."

"There are many people who worship me. Some of them will give up their lives so that you may eat." When he heard this, the Great Peng had no choice but to surrender to the Buddha. Tathāgata put the great bird on the halo on his head, to serve as his guardian.

Sun Wukong reappeared. He kowtowed to Tathāgata and said, "Father Buddha, you have defeated the demons. But my master is dead."

Great Peng heard this. He said angrily, "Wretched monkey. I did not eat your master. He is hidden in an iron chest in my palace."

When he heard this, Sun Wukong bowed quickly to Tathāgata and flew back to the demon city. When he arrived, he saw that all the little demons had run away. He entered the palace, found the iron chest, opened it, and helped Tangseng get out. Then he freed his two brothers. He told them everything that happened. They found some rice in the palace and prepared a simple meal. After they finished the meal, they returned to the road and continued their journey to the west.

Chapter 78

They left the Lion Kingdom and traveled west again. The weather became cold. Ice appeared on the surface of ponds, leaves changed color to yellow and red, grasses lay flat on the ground, and snow clouds flew across the sky. In the daytime the travelers walked through the wind and snow, at night they slept on the cold ground.

One day they saw a great city with high walls surrounded by a moat. Tangseng got down from his white horse to join the three disciples as they walked through the city gates. Sun Wukong, the elder disciple, saw an old soldier sleeping on the ground next to the city wall. He walked over to the soldier. He shook the soldier's shoulder and said, "Wake up, son! We are monks from the east, traveling to the Western Heaven to fetch the Buddha's scriptures. We have just arrived in your city. Tell me, what is the name of this place?"

The soldier looked at Sun Wukong and thought he was a thunder god. He said, "My lord, this country used to be called Bhiksu, but the name has been changed. Now it is Boytown."

Sun Wukong walked to the others. He told them, "That soldier told me this country used to be called Bhiksu, but the name has been changed to Boytown."

Tangseng asked, "If it was Bhiksu, why is it now Boytown?"

Zhu Bajie, the pig-man who was Tangseng's second disciple, said, "Probably there once was a King Bhiksu. He died and his son became king, so they changed the name."

Sha Wujing, the large quiet man who was Tangseng's third disciple, said, "That can't be true. That old soldier was probably so frightened by Old Monkey that he could only speak nonsense."

They continued walking into the city. Looking around, they saw

> Wine shops and tea houses filled with loud customers
> Many beautiful shops and tea houses
> People selling gold, silver and silks, only wanting money
> Customers walking, talking and buying things
> A large and prosperous city!

But they saw something strange. In front of every house was a coop, like something that would hold geese. "Disciples," said Tangseng, "why do all these people put coops in front of their houses?"

Zhu smiled and replied, "Master, this must be a lucky day. Everyone is having a wedding!"

Sun Wukong said, "Nonsense, how can every family have a wedding? No. I will go and take a look." He did not want to frighten anyone, so he waved his hand, said some magic words, and turned into a bee. He flew up to a nearby coop and looked inside. He saw a little boy sitting inside. He flew to the next house and looked inside the coop. He saw another little boy. He looked at eight or nine houses. Each one had a little boy sitting inside the coop.

He returned to Tangseng and said, "Master, every coop has a little boy inside. The youngest is maybe four years old, the oldest is maybe six. I don't know why they are there."

They continued walking. Soon they came to a Hostel of Meeting. "Wonderful," said Tangseng. "Let's go inside. We can find out where we are. We can also rest the horse and sleep here tonight."

They entered the Hostel of Meeting. The manager met them and asked, "Sir, where are you from?"

Tangseng replied, "I am a poor monk, sent by the Tang Emperor to fetch the Buddha's scriptures from the Western Heaven. We have just arrived at your beautiful city. We ask that your king certify our travel rescript, and that you allow us to stay tonight at the Hostel of Meeting."

"Of course," replied the manager. "Please stay here and have dinner. You can sleep here tonight. Tomorrow morning you can meet with our king and have your travel rescript certified."

Tangseng thanked him. Some workers prepared beds for the travelers and cooked a vegetarian dinner for them. They all ate dinner. Afterwards it became dark, so the workers lit a lamp. Tangseng, his three disciples and the manager all sat together in the lamplight. Tangseng said to the manager, "Sir, please tell me, how do the people in this noble country raise their children?"

The manager replied, "People are the same everywhere, just as there are never two suns in the sky. The father's seed mixes with the mother's blood. Ten months later a child is born[1]. Children drink their mother's milk for three

---

[1] The manager is referring to lunar months. A lunar month is 29½ days, so ten lunar

years. They grow up. Everyone knows that."

"Yes," said Tangseng, "it is the same in my country. But when we arrived at your city, we saw a goose coop in front of every house, with a little boy in each coop. I do not understand this."

The manager leaned close to Tangseng and whispered into his ear, "Sir, please don't ask about that. Don't even think about it." Then the manager stood up and said, "Now, are you probably very tired. I think it's time for you to go to your beds for the night."

But Tangseng would not go to bed. He insisted on hearing an explanation. Finally the manager told all the workers to leave the room. After they left, he sat down and said to Tangseng, "The goose coops are there because our king is a bad ruler. Why do you insist on hearing about this?"

"I cannot rest until I understand this. How is he a bad ruler?"

"All right, I will tell you. This country used to be called Bhiksu Kingdom. Three years ago, an old Daoist came here with a fifteen-year-old girl. The girl was as beautiful as Bodhisattva Guanyin herself. The Daoist gave the girl to the king. The king fell in love with the girl. He forgot about everything. He forgot about his queens, his concubines, the affairs of the kingdom. All he wanted to do was play around in bed with the girl all the time. He stopped eating and drinking. Because of that, he has become very weak. He is close to death. The royal doctors have tried every medicine but nothing can help the king."

"And what about the Daoist?"

"Our king named him Royal Father-in-Law. The man told the king that he has a secret medicine that will let our king live for a thousand years. The Daoist traveled to ten continents and three magic countries to find the herbs needed to make this medicine. But now he needs to add one more thing. He must make a soup from the hearts of 1,111 little boys, and add that soup to the medicine. Those are the boys that you saw in the coops. The parents are too afraid to say anything. And that is why the city is now called Boytown."

The manager stood up again. He said, "When you go to the king's palace tomorrow, you must not say anything about this. Just get your travel rescript certified and continue your journey." He blew out the lamp and left the room.

---

months is 295 days. A more accurate answer would have been 9½ lunar months, since a normal pregnancy lasts 280 days.

After the manager left, Tangseng began to cry. "Foolish king! Your desire has almost killed you, and now you plan to kill all these young boys. How could you?"

Zhu walked over to him and said, "Master, what's the matter with you? It's like taking a stranger's coffin into your house and crying over it. You know the old saying,

> When the king wants the subject to die,
> The subject must die.
> When the father wants the son to die,
> The son must die.

Those boys are his own people. What are they to you? Come on, let's go to sleep."

Tangseng said, "Oh disciple, you have a hard heart! We are monks, we must help others. How can this king be so evil? I have never heard this nonsense that eating hearts will give long life. Of course it hurts me to hear of it!"

Sun Wukong said, "Master, let's not worry about this tonight. Tomorrow I will go with you to the palace. We will see this Royal Father-in-Law. If he is human and just thinks that medicine brings immortality, I will teach him the truth. If he is a monster, I will arrest him and show the king what he is, so the king can learn to control his desires and recover his strength. One way or another, I will not let him kill those children."

Tangseng said, "That is wonderful. But we must not say anything to the king. We don't want him to become angry at us."

"No problem. Tonight I will use my magic powers. I will move all the boys out of the city. The king will hear of this of course, but he will not think that we did it."

"How can you move the boys out of the city?"

"You know that I have some magical powers. Zhu and Sha, stay here with our master. If you feel a cold wind, you will know that it is the boys leaving the city."

Sun Wukong flew up into the air. He called the city god, the local spirits, the Six Gods of Darkness, the Six Gods of Light, and many more immortals. They all arrived quickly, asking, "Great Sage, why have you called us in the middle of the night?"

"Thank you for coming. I have just arrived at this city. The king is a bad man.

He is listening to an evil monster. Tomorrow, he plans to remove the hearts from over a thousand little boys to make a magic elixir that will let him live forever. My master has asked me to save the boys and capture the monster. That's why I have asked you all to come here. Please use your magic to lift up the boys. Carry them over the city wall to a safe place, far away in the forest. Keep them there for a day or two. Give them food to eat. Protect them, don't frighten them. When I have removed the evil from this city you can bring the boys back."

It was the time of the third watch when,

> A cold wind covered the stars in the sky
> The moon disappeared behind a magical fog
> The cold made peoples' clothing turn to iron
> Parents hid in their homes
> The coops and the young boys were carried away by the gods
> The night was terrible
> But joy was coming to everyone the next day.

Sun Wukong returned to the Hostel of Meeting. He told Tangseng that all the little boys were taken out of the city. Tangseng thanked him again and again. Then they all went to sleep.

The next morning, Tangseng put on his best clothing to meet with the king. The manager came up to him and whispered in his ear, telling him again to stay out of affairs that were none of his business. Tangseng nodded his head. Sun Wukong changed into a tiny insect. He flew to Tangseng and landed on the monk's gold-colored hat.

Tangseng walked to the king's palace. When he arrived, he told one of the palace eunuchs that he wanted to see the king. A few minutes later the king invited Tangseng to enter the throne room. Tangseng looked at the king. He saw that the man was extremely weak. He could hardly stand up and he had trouble speaking. When Tangseng handed the travel rescript to him, the king could not even read the words on it. With great difficulty the king signed the rescript and give it back to the Tang monk. Tangseng put the rescript in his robe.

Just then, a eunuch came in and said, "His Excellency the Royal Father-in-Law is here." Tangseng turned around. He saw an elderly Taoist walking with a swagger towards the throne.

What did he look like?

> On his head, a yellow silk cap
> On his body, a cloak of silk and feathers
> At his waist, a belt of blue cloth
> On his feet, cloud shoes made of straw
> In his hand, a staff with the head of a dragon
> His face was smooth like jade
> His eyes burned like fire
> His white beard blew around his face
> Clouds followed him as he walked
> Fragrant mists flowed around him
> The officials all shouted,
> "The Royal Father-in-Law has entered the court!"

The Royal Father-in-Law did not bow to the king. The king bowed to him and said, "We are fortunate that you have come to see us, Royal Father-in-Law."

The Daoist looked at Tangseng, then he said to the king, "Where is this monk from?"

"He has been sent by the Tang Emperor to fetch scriptures from the Western Heaven. He has come here to get his travel rescript certified."

The Daoist said, "The road west is covered in darkness. There is nothing good about it." Then he added, "We have heard that a monk who is a disciple of Buddha can live forever."

Tangseng said,

> "A monk knows that all things are empty
> He lives in the land of no birth
> He sees the true mysteries in silence
> He is not trapped by the Three Worlds[1]
> If you want knowledge you must know the mind
> Sit in silence
> Let the pure mind shine
> It illuminates all thoughts
> One with great wisdom looks like a fool
> He knows that one must do without doing
> The best plans require no thought
> Because everything must be left alone
> It is foolish to try to lengthen life through elixirs
> Let go of everything, let your mind be empty
> Live simply, let go of desires
> Then you will enjoy life without end, forever[2]."

When the Royal Father-in-Law heard this, he laughed. "What garbage!" he said. "You talk about understanding reality, but you really don't understand anything about where reality comes from. Listen to me,

> Sit, sit, sit, your ass will split
> Play with fire, you'll get burned
> One who seeks immortality has strong bones

---

[1] In Buddhism these are the three destinations for karmic rebirth: the world of desire, the world of form, and the world of formlessness. The human world is the world of desire and is populated by humans, animals, hungry ghosts, as well as some godlike creatures.

[2] These lines, spoken by a Buddhist monk in defense of Buddhism, are from a poem called "Rhymeprose on the Ground of the Mind" in the *Minghe Yuyin*, a 14th century collection of Daoist poems by various authors. Several of the lines echo lines from the *Dao De Jing*.

One who seeks the Way has a powerful spirit
I go to the mountains to visit my friends
I get a hundred herbs to help the world
I sing as people clap their hands
I dance and then I rest on clouds
I explain the Dao, I teach Laozi's words
I remove monsters with holy water
I take power from the sun and the moon
I make magic elixirs by mixing yin and yang
I ride the blue phoenix to the purple palace
I ride the white bird to the jade city
There I meet with the immortals of Heaven
How different from the deathly quiet of your Buddhism
The darkness of your peace
It can never lift you above this world
My mystery is the highest
My Dao is the greatest[1]!"

When he finished, the king and his ministers shouted, "That is wonderful! Dao is the greatest!" Tangseng looked at his shoes and said nothing. The king ordered a vegetarian banquet for the Tang monk. Tangseng ate his meal, then he thanked the king and turned to leave. As he was leaving, Sun Wukong flew into his ear and said, "Master, this Royal Father-in-Law is an evil spirit. The king is under his power. Please go back to the Hostel of Meeting. I will stay here and try to learn more."

Tangseng left the palace. Sun Wukong stayed and listened. A general came in and reported to the king, "Your Majesty, last night a cold wind blew through the city. It carried away all the little boys in the coops."

"This is terrible!" cried the king. "We have been sick for months. We need those boys. Royal Father-in-Law, how will we become well again?"

"No, this is wonderful news," said the Daoist. "We don't need those boys anymore. When I saw the Tang monk, I knew right away that he has been a monk for ten lifetimes. In each lifetime his *yang* has become greater[2]. If you can make soup from his heart and mix it with my elixir, you will live for ten

---

[1] These lines, spoken by a Daoist in defense of Daoism, are taken from the same poem as the previous one!

[2] Daoists believe that male energy, *yang*, accumulates in a man's body but is depleted during sex. Thus, a celibate monk can store up a great deal of *yang* over the course of ten lifetimes.

thousand years!"

The foolish king replied, "Why didn't you tell me sooner? I could have killed him when he was here, and taken his heart."

"It's not a problem. Right now he is probably at the Hostel of Meeting. Order the city gates to be closed. Send your soldiers to the Hostel of Meeting. Tell them to bring the Tang monk back to the palace. When he arrives, ask him politely for his heart. Tell him that you will build a shrine in his honor. If he refuses, just tie him up and cut out his heart anyway. Isn't that easy?"

The king agreed. He ordered the city gates to be closed, and he sent his soldiers to surround the Hostel of Meeting.

Sun Wukong flew quickly back to the Hostel of Meeting. He changed into his original form and reported to Tangseng everything he had just heard. Tangseng was frightened, but Sun Wukong said, "If you want to live, the old must become young, and the young must become old."

Sha asked, "What do you mean, elder brother?"

But Tangseng said, "It does not matter. If you can save my life, I will do anything you say."

Sun Wukong told Zhu to make some mud. Zhu dug up some dirt with his rake, but he could not leave the Hostel of Meeting to get water. So he lifted up his tunic and pissed on the dirt to make mud. He mixed it together, making a stinking ball of mud. He handed the ball to Sun Wukong. The monkey pressed the mud flat against his own face so that it took the shape of his face. Then he pulled it off his face and held it in his hands.

He told Tangseng to stand still and not move. Then he put the stinking mud on Tangseng's face and said some magic words. Now Tangseng looked just like the monkey. Tangseng and Sun Wukong gave each other their clothes. Tangseng put on the monkey's tiger skin kilt. Sun Wukong put on the monk's robes. Sun Wukong said some more magic words, and easily changed into the Tang monk.

Just as they finished, they saw a forest of spears and swords in front of the Hostel of Meeting. Three thousand soldiers had surrounded the building. An official entered the Hostel of Meeting. He said to the hostel manager, "Where is the gentleman from the Tang empire?"

"Over there, in the guest room," said the manager, very frightened.

The official entered the guest room and said, "Grandfather, His Majesty has asked you to come to the palace." The false monk walked out of the guest room, with Zhu and Sha on either side of him.

Chapter 79

The false Tangseng walked to the palace, surrounded by soldiers. When they arrived at the palace, the minister told the eunuch at the palace gate, "Please tell His Majesty that we have brought the Tang monk."

The eunuch told this to the king. The king ordered the monk to be brought into the throne room. Everyone in the room kneeled before the king except for the false Tangseng, who remained standing. He shouted, "King of Bhiksu, why did you bring me here?"

"We have been sick for a long time," replied the king. "The Royal Father-in-Law has prepared an elixir for us, but we need to add one more small thing. You have that thing. If you give it to us, we will build a temple to you. People will pray in the temple in all four seasons, and they will burn incense forever."

"I am a simple monk. I have nothing to give you."

"You have the thing that we need. We need your heart."

The false Tangseng smiled and said, "I have many hearts, Your Majesty. Which one do you want?"

The king was surprised. He said, "We want your black heart."

"All right. Give me a knife and I will open my chest. If there is a black heart in my chest, I will happily give it to you."

The king ordered one of his officials to give a knife to the false monk. The false Tangseng opened his robe, pressed his left hand against his chest, and made a deep cut with the knife. His chest opened and a pile of hearts fell out. The hearts fell onto the floor, dripping with blood. The false monk picked them up, one by one, and held them up for everyone to see. There was a red heart, a white heart, and a yellow heart. There was an evil heart, a frightened heart, a cautious heart, and a heart with no name. But there was no black heart.

The king was terrified. He shouted, "Put them away, put them away!"

Sun Wukong could not wait any longer. He changed back to his true form. He gathered the hearts and put them back in his chest. Then he said, "Your Majesty, you have eyes but you cannot see. We monks have good hearts. Only your father-in-law has a black and evil heart."

The Daoist saw that the monk had changed into Sun Wukong. He flew up into the clouds. Sun Wukong jumped into the air and shouted, "Where are you going? Taste my rod!"

The two of them began to fight in mid-air. Sun Wukong used his golden hoop rod to strike the Daoist's head. The Daoist blocked the blow with his dragon-head staff. The monkey's rod was like a tiger jumping off a mountain top, the Daoist's staff was like a dragon rising from the sea. Fog filled the sky. The king was frightened and ran away to hide.

The monkey and the Daoist fought for twenty rounds. The Daoist became tired. He changed into a cold beam of light and flew to the king's bedroom to find his daughter. She also changed into a cold beam of light. The two of them disappeared.

Sun Wukong returned to the palace. He said to the ministers, "Well, that's some Royal Father-in-Law you have." The ministers bowed to him and thanked him. Sun Wukong waved his hand and said, "Stop bowing and go find your king."

The ministers went into the king's bedroom. The king was not there. The girl was not there either. But then four or five eunuchs entered the throne room, helping the king to walk. The ministers told the king what happened. The king kowtowed to Sun Wukong and said, "Sir, when you came here this morning you were very handsome, why do you look different now?"

Sun Wukong replied, "Your Majesty, this morning you thought you were talking with my master, the holy monk Tangseng. He is the younger brother of the Tang Emperor. I am his senior disciple. My two brother disciples are here also. I came here to defeat the monster because I know that he wanted to kill my master and make a soup from his heart."

The king ordered his ministers to go to the Hostel of Meeting and fetch Tangseng and the other two disciples. But of course, Tangseng still had the mud mask on his face and looked like Sun Wukong. The ministers were confused, but Tangseng explained that he looked like Sun Wukong because he was wearing a mask. Tangseng walked with the ministers to the king's palace, with Zhu and Sha. When they arrived, Sun Wukong pulled the mud mask off his master's face and said a few magic words. Tangseng looked like Tangseng again.

Sun Wukong turned to the king and asked, "Your Majesty, do you know where these two monsters came from? We should catch both of them so they don't cause any more trouble."

The king replied, "When he came here three years ago, he said that he came from Pure Flower Village, about seventy miles south of here at a place called Willow Hill. He had no sons, only a daughter by his second wife. She was not married yet, so he gave her to us as a gift. We loved her and took her as our concubine. But after a while, we became very ill. The monster said that he had an elixir but it needed the hearts of 1,111 young boys. I was a fool to believe him."

"When were the boys to be killed?" asked Tangseng.

"They were going to take the hearts from the boys today. We did not know that you would come here and take the boys away. But the evil monster told us that you were a holy monk for ten lifetimes. He said that because your *yang* was very strong, your heart would make a stronger elixir than all of those boys' hearts. We were confused, we did not understand how evil this was. We are very grateful to you. Now, please use your vast magical power to stop this evil monster. We will give you everything that our nation has."

Sun Wukong said, "To tell you the truth, it was my master's idea to move the boys out of the city. That's why I did it. Please don't talk about giving us wealth. I only want to capture the evil monsters. Zhu, let's go."

Zhu put his hand on his belly and said, "I want to follow you, elder brother, but my belly is empty!" The king ordered a large vegetarian meal for the pig-man. Zhu ate all of it, then he rose up into the air and flew away with Sun Wukong.

The two disciples flew south for seventy miles until they arrived at Willow Hill. They looked down from the clouds. They did not see Pure Flower Village anywhere, they only saw a clear stream flowing between thousands of willow trees. Sun Wukong said some magic words to call the local spirit.

The local spirit arrived. He looked very worried. He kneeled and said, "Great Sage, the local spirit of Willow Hill kowtows to you."

Sun Wukong replied, "Don't worry, I won't beat you. Tell me, where is Pure Flower Village?"

"We have a Pure Flower Cave, but there is no Pure Flower Village. Why do you ask?"

"The king of Bhiksu has been tricked by an evil monster. But I saw the monster's true form. I defeated him in battle. The monster flew away by turning into a cold beam of light. The king says that the monster came from Pure Flower Village on Willow Hill. I see the hill but I don't see any village."

"Great sage, I would like to help you. But the evil monster has great powers. If I help you, he will come and punish me severely. So I cannot tell you where Pure Flower Village is. However, I can help you find Pure Flower Cave. Go to the south side of the stream. Find a willow tree with nine branches. Walk around the tree three times from left to right, then three more times from right to left. Lean against the tree with both hands and call out three times, 'Open the door.' You will see the cave."

Sun Wukong told the local spirit that he could go. He soon found the tree with nine branches. He said to Zhu, "Wait here. I will call the door to open. I will find the evil monster and chase him out of the cave. When you see him, help me to defeat him." Zhu agreed.

Sun Wukong walked around the tree three times from left to right, then three more times from right to left. He put both hands on the tree and called out, "Open the door!" three times. Instantly the tree disappeared. A pair of doors opened. Inside the doors he could see bright mists. He ran inside the cave.

It was beautiful inside the cave. White clouds of mist flowed out of the cave. Strange colorful flowers covered the ground. Bees and butterflies flew from flower to flower. The air was warm like springtime.

Sun Wukong ran through the cave. He saw a sign made of stone that read, "Pure Flower Immortal Palace." He ran around the stone sign. Behind the stone sign were the evil monster and the beautiful girl. They both said together, "We planned this for three years. It was going to be finished today. But that wretched ape ruined everything!"

Sun Wukong whipped out his golden hoop rod and shouted, "What are you talking about, you fools? Have a taste of my rod!" The evil monster picked up his dragon staff. They began to fight in the cave.

What a battle! Golden light came from the rod. Angry mist came from the staff. The monster shouted, "How dare you come into my cave!"

"I am here to defeat a monster!" replied Sun Wukong.

"My love for the king is no business of yours, why do you care about this?"

"A monk's business is compassion. We cannot let you kill these young boys."

They continued to fight. They stepped on the beautiful flowers. The bees and butterflies flew out of the cave. The cave's bright mists became dark. Only the monkey and the evil monster remained. Their battle raised huge winds that roared across the earth. Slowly their battle moved them towards the door of the cave where Zhu was waiting.

Zhu heard the sounds of battle. He really wanted to join the battle but he could not, so he used his rake to knock down the nine-branched willow. The tree fell to the ground and moaned. Zhu said, "Oh, this tree has become a spirit!"

Then the monster ran out of the cave. Zhu rushed forward, his rake held high, and he struck at the monster. The old monster saw that he could not win the fight. He shook himself, turned into a cold beam of light, and flew to the east. Sun Wukong and Zhu chased him.

But when they caught up with the monster, they saw that the Elderly Star of the South Pole had caught the cold beam of light. "Stop chasing the monster, Great Sage and Marshal. This old Daoist greets you!"

"Brother Elderly Star," replied Sun Wukong, "greetings! Where do you come from? And where is the evil monster?"

"He is here," smiled the Elderly Star. "Please don't hurt him."

"That evil monster is no relative of yours. Why do you speak up for him?"

"He is my messenger. I carelessly let him escape, and he became a monster here."

"Please change him back to his true form so we can see what he really is."

Elderly Star released the cold beam of light. He said, "Wretched beast! Show us your true form!" The monster turned into a white deer. The deer could not speak, it could only lie on the ground and cry.

> The deer had antlers like seven long knives
> When he was hungry he used to eat herbs
> When he was thirsty he used to drink from misty streams
> Over time, he taught himself to fly
> After many years he learned how to change his appearance
> Now he heard the words of his master
> He returned to his own form and lay down in the dirt.

Elderly Star helped the deer to stand up. He mounted the deer and prepared to fly away. But Sun Wukong stopped him. "Old brother," he said, "please don't leave yet. There are still two matters we must deal with."

"What two matters?"

"We must catch the beautiful girl. And we must return together to report to the Bhiksu king."

"All right, I will wait for you to capture the girl. Then we will go together to see the king."

The two disciples returned to the cave, shouting, "Catch the evil spirit!" The beautiful girl tried to run away, but there was no back door to the cave. She was trapped.

"Where are you going?" shouted Zhu. "Watch my rake, you stinking lying spirit." The girl had no weapon to fight with. She turned into a cold beam of light and tried to fly out of the cave. But Sun Wukong struck the beam of light with his rod, killing the girl. After she died, she turned into her true form, a white-faced fox spirit[1].

Zhu raised his rake, preparing to strike the fox again. But Sun Wukong said, "Don't hit her! We need to show the king what his girlfriend really was." Zhu grabbed the dead body of the fox spirit by the tail and dragged it out of the cave.

Outside the cave, Elderly Star was talking to the white deer. He said to the deer, "Evil beast, why did you run away from me and turn into an evil spirit?"

Zhu threw the fox spirit's body on the ground. He said to the deer, "Your daughter, I suppose." The deer nodded its head and cried.

Elderly Star said to the deer, "Evil beast, you are lucky to still be alive." He took off his belt and tied it around the deer's neck. He said, "Great Sage, let's go see the king."

"Not yet," replied Sun Wukong. He told the local spirit to get some dry firewood and start a fire. They piled up all the dry wood in the mouth of the cave. Then they lit the fire. Everything in the cave burned to ashes. Sun Wukong told the local spirit he could leave. Then they all flew back to the king's palace.

They walked up to the king's throne. Sun Wukong threw the body of the fox spirit on the floor in front of the king. "Here is your girlfriend," he said to the

---

[1] Beautiful fox spirits are believed to seduce both men and women, enticing them to exhaust themselves in endless lovemaking. The fox spirits feed off this energy, becoming stronger while the victims weaken and die. There are occasional exceptions, as told in our book *The Love Triangle*.

king. "Do you want to play around with her now?" The king began to shake. The king and all his ministers fell to their knees and kowtowed to Sun Wukong.

Sun Wukong smiled and said, "Why are you kowtowing to me?" He pointed to the white deer and said, "Here is the Royal Father-in-Law, maybe you should kowtow to him!"

The king was very embarrassed. He could only say, "I thank the Tang monk for saving the boys of my nation." Then he ordered a great vegetarian banquet for the four travelers and the Elderly Star.

While the banquet was being prepared, Tangseng asked the Elderly Star, "If the white deer is yours, how did it come here to harm people?"

The Elderly Star replied, "A while ago, the Great King of the East passed by my mountain home. I asked him to stay and play a game of chess with me. During the game, the wretched beast ran away. We could not find him. But I bent my fingers and learned that the beast had come to this place. I came here to find him. Just as I arrived, I met the Great Sage. If I had come a little bit later, I think my beast would be dead."

The banquet was ready. What a feast!

> The room was filled with many colors
> Incense smoke came from duck-shaped braziers
> The tables were heavy with vegetables
> Cakes shaped like dragons
> Candies shaped like lions
> Wine glasses shaped like birds
> Huge buns piled on golden trays
> Fragrant rice filling silver bowls
> Hot spicy noodles cooked in soup
> Many kinds of mushrooms
> Ten kinds of vegetables
> A hundred kinds of foods
> All were served to the visitors.

At the head table, the Elderly Star sat in the place of honor. The king sat next to him, and the Tang monk sat next to the king. The three disciples sat at the first side table. Three senior ministers sat at the other side table. Musicians and dancers performed. The king lifted his purple wine cup and toasted everyone. Everyone ate a lot, but of course Zhu ate more than all the rest of them together.

When the banquet ended, the Elderly Star stood up to leave. The king went up to him, kowtowed, and asked him for the secret of good health and long life. "I did not bring any elixir," said the Elderly Star. "Even if I had some elixir, you are too weak in body and spirit to use it. But I do have these three jujubes. I was going to give them to the Great King of the East. You can eat them instead of the Great King."

The king of Bhiksu ate the jujubes. Immediately he began to feel better. His illness was cured. And this may be the reason why his children and grandchildren had such long lives.

Zhu said to Elderly Star, "Hey, do you have any more of those jujubes?"

The Elderly Star replied, "Sorry, no. But next time I see you I will give you a few." He thanked the king. Then he jumped up onto the deer's back. They rose into the air and flew away. All the people in the palace bowed to the ground and burned incense.

Tangseng said to his disciples, "Gather the luggage. We must leave."

The king begged Tangseng to stay and teach him. Sun Wukong said to him, "Your Majesty, it is simple. You must control your desires. Do more good deeds. Let your strength make up for your weakness. This will get rid of your illness and give you long life."

The king ordered the royal carriage to carry the visitors out of the city. They began riding down the city streets towards the city gates. Suddenly there was the sound of a great wind. They looked up. One thousand one hundred and eleven goose coops dropped down from the sky and landed on the road. Inside each coop was a crying little boy. From the sky, the immortals shouted, "Great Sage, you told us to carry these boys out of the city. We heard that you defeated the evil monsters. So we have brought back every one of the little boys."

The king and his ministers all fell to their knees and kowtowed.

Sun Wukong called out, "I thank you for all your help. Please go back to your shrines now. I will ask these people to make offerings to you."

All the people of the city came and collected their children. They picked up the boys, called them "darling" and "dear." They laughed and danced. They told the children to take the hands of Tangseng, Sun Wukong, Zhu and Sha, and bring them to their homes. Nobody was frightened of the disciples' ugly faces. Each family wanted to give the visitors a feast. The travelers had to stay in the city for a month! Truly,

> Their good deeds were as big as a mountain
> They saved a hundred and a thousand lives

Chapter 80

Winter turned to spring; spring turned to summer. The weather was warm, and they saw many brightly colored flowers.

One day they saw that the road was blocked by a tall mountain. Tangseng said, "Disciples, we must be careful, there might be monster-spirits in this mountain."

Sun Wukong, the monkey king and the eldest disciple, said, "Master, you do not sound like a true traveler. You sound like someone who lives in a well and looks up at the sky. Remember, every mountain has a road that passes through it. I will take a look." Holding his golden-hooped rod in his hand, he jumped onto a high rock and looked all around.

He saw that the top of the mountain was covered in clouds and mist. He heard great waterfalls and small flowing streams. He smelled flowers, pine trees, willow trees and peach trees. Looking more carefully he saw a narrow path going upwards and around the mountain. He called Tangseng and the other two disciples, and together they walked up the path and around the mountain.

Soon they came to a huge, dark pine forest. Tangseng was worried. He said, "Wukong, do we have to pass through this dark forest? We must be careful!"

"What is there to be afraid of?" asked Sun Wukong.

Tangseng answered, "The ancients say, 'Beware of evil that appears to be good.' We have walked through many forests, but we have never seen one as large as this.

> See the trees from east to west,
> They reach to the end of the clouds
> See the trees from north to south,
> They touch the sky above
> You could stay in this forest for half a year
> And not know if the moon was in the sky
> You could travel in this forest for many miles
> And never see the stars
> There are trees ten thousand years old
> So many that not even a god could paint them
> Listen to the birds, they call, dance and sing
> See the great beasts wagging their tails

The tiger shows its teeth
Old foxes look like ladies
Gray wolves fill the air with their cries
If the king of Heaven came here
He might defeat demons but he could not defeat this forest!"

But Sun Wukong was not afraid. He led Tangseng and the other disciples through the forest. After they walked for half a day, Tangseng said he wanted to rest. He asked Sun Wukong to go and beg some vegetarian food.

Sun Wukong used his cloud somersault to jump up to the sky. Looking around, he saw auspicious clouds above Tangseng. He thought, "This is good. Five hundred years ago I caused great trouble in Heaven. I traveled to all four ends of the earth. I gave myself the name Great Sage Equal to Heaven. I removed my name from the Book of Life and Death. I was a demon king and I had 47,000 demons under me. Oh yes, I really was famous in those days! But now I am a disciple of the great Tang monk. Just look at these auspicious clouds above my master. I'm sure everything will turn out fine on this journey."

Just then, he saw some black clouds rising from the southern part of the forest. "Those black clouds mean that something evil is there," he thought. He looked carefully but could not see where the black clouds were coming from.

Meanwhile, Tangseng and the other two disciples were waiting on the ground. The pig-man Zhu Bajie and the big quiet man Sha Wujing walked around looking for flowers and fruit. Tangseng sat and meditated on the Buddha. Suddenly the monk heard someone cry, "Save me!"

"Who is that?" asked Tangseng. He stood up and walked towards the sound. He walked past thousand-year-old cypress trees and ancient pines. Soon he saw a young woman tied to a tree. The top half of her body was tied to the tree by vines, and her lower half was buried in the ground. Tangseng asked her, "Lady Bodhisattva, why are you tied up here? What crime have you committed? Tell me so that I can save you."

Now, of course this was a demon. Tangseng had eyes but he could not see, so he thought it was just a girl tied to a tree. She was crying, tears rolling down her lovely cheeks. She was so beautiful that birds seeing her would fall from the sky. Her eyes were as bright as stars.

"Master," she said, making up lies as she spoke, "I come from a small village seventy miles away. I was traveling through the forest with my parents when we were attacked by a group of robbers. My parents rode away on their horses, but I was too frightened to move. The robbers grabbed me and took me back to their camp. The bandit chief wanted me to be his girlfriend, the second in command wanted me to be his wife, the third and fourth in command just wanted me for my beauty. They all started fighting. None of them wanted the others to have me. So finally they tied me to this tree and left me here. I've been here for five days and I am near death. Please, sir, save my life. I won't forget you even when I die and journey to the nine springs of the underworld[1]." As she said this, her tears flowed like rain.

Tangseng listened to her story and also began to cry. He called to Zhu and said, "Disciple, untie this lady, we must save her life." Zhu took out his knife and started to cut the ropes.

Just then, Sun Wukong returned. He had seen the black clouds and knew that something evil was nearby. He saw Zhu cutting the ropes. Quickly grabbing one of the pig's ears, he threw him to the ground. "Younger brother," he said to Zhu, "don't untie her. She is an evil spirit."

"Wretched ape," shouted Tangseng, "why do you think this lovely girl is an evil spirit?"

Sun Wukong replied, "Master, in the old days I did the same thing when I wanted to eat some human flesh. You don't know what she is, but I do."

Zhu said, "Master, don't listen to him. He just wants us to leave her here. Then he will come back later and have some fun with her." This made Sun Wukong angry. He and Zhu began arguing loudly.

Finally Tangseng said, "Stop it, both of you. Sun Wukong is usually right about these things. Leave the evil spirit here. Let's get moving again." They began walking, leaving the beautiful girl tied to the tree.

The evil spirit was very angry. She thought, "I really wanted to carry off the Tang monk and have him for my husband. I have heard that he has been a monk for ten lifetimes and has great spiritual power. His *yang* is very strong. I want that power for myself! But that monkey is a problem."

She made the wind blow towards Tangseng. The wind carried her sweet voice to him. She told him, "Master, what kind of Buddhist monk are you? What's the use of you fetching holy scriptures if you won't even save the life of a poor girl like me?"

---

[1] Another name for the underworld is jiǔquán, the Nine Springs.

Tangseng heard this. He stopped his horse and said, "Wukong, go and get that girl. She is crying for help."

Sun Wukong said, "What did she say to you, Master?"

"She said, 'What's the use of me fetching holy scriptures if I refuse to save a life.' She is quite correct."

"Master, just think of all the demons we have met on our journey. Many of them have taken you into their caves. Many times they have wanted to eat you. And many times I have rescued you. We have killed tens of thousands of demons. Why can't you let this one demon die today?"

"Disciple, the ancients say, 'Don't fail to do a good deed just because it's small, don't do a bad deed just because it's small.' Go get her."

"Master, you have been a monk for your entire life. You know nothing about this world. This girl is young and beautiful. If people see us traveling with her, they will think we are doing evil things with her. We will all be arrested. You will lose your license to be a monk. Zhu and Sha will go to prison. Even I will suffer. All of us will be harmed." He thought for a minute, then he added, "And the girl will be destroyed."

"What do you mean?"

"She is already close to death. If we leave her there, she will die quickly and go to the underworld. But if we save her, she will not be able to keep up with us. She will fall behind. She will probably be attacked and eaten by a wolf or a tiger. Her body will be broken up into many small pieces."

"You are right. What should we do?"

Sun Wukong smiled. "She can ride with you on your horse."

Tangseng's face turned red. "Oh no. I could not possibly do that."

They stood and discussed this for a long time. Finally they decided that they would rescue the girl and leave her at the next temple or village that they came to. Zhu went back to where the girl was tied up. He cut the ropes, freeing the girl. Tangseng got down from his horse. They all began to walk westward.

In this way they walked for several miles. Just before evening they came to a tall building. It was a temple but in very bad condition. The buildings were falling down, the walls had collapsed, there were piles of broken bricks all around, and grass grew in the courtyard. Everything inside the building was covered in dust. The Buddha's golden statue had lost its color. They saw a statue of Guanyin that was broken, her willow vase fallen to the ground. They could not see any monks living here, it was only a home for foxes and tigers.

Tangseng walked slowly through the old temple. When he entered the broken bell tower, he saw a large brass bell that had long ago fallen to the ground. "Bell," he said,

> "Once you shouted from a high tower
> Calling from the painted beam where you hung
> Once you called the dawn
> And announced the evening
> Where are the monks who begged for your copper?
> Where are the craftsmen who created you?
> They are all in the underworld
> They have left you here, silent."

A man was standing nearby, burning incense. When he heard Tangseng he picked up a broken brick and threw it at the bell. The sound was so loud that the Tang monk fell down, jumped up, tripped over a tree root, and fell down again. "Bell," he said,

> "I was just talking about your life
> When suddenly you cried out
> On this lonely road to the west
> Over the years you have become a spirit."

The man walked over to Tangseng and helped him to stand up. "Please don't be afraid, sir. I take care of the incense here. I heard you talking. I was afraid you might be a demon, so I threw a brick at the bell to scare you away. This is not a spirit, it's just a bell. Please come inside."

The man led Tangseng through another pair of gates. There the monk saw a beautiful hall. The walls were made of blue bricks painted with pictures of white clouds. There were holy statues covered with gold. Blue light danced in the Buddha Hall. Looking out through the windows he saw a thousand bright bamboos and ten thousand beautiful pines. Auspicious clouds floating between the trees.

"Brother," said Tangseng, "why is the front of this monastery in such bad shape, while the back is so beautiful?"

"Sir, in this mountain there are many demons and bandits. They rob people in the daytime, then they come here to sleep at night. They sit on our statues.

They use our pillars for firewood. The monks here are not strong enough to fight them, so we have given the front of the monastery to them. We live here in the back."

Just then, a handsome and well-dressed lama came out to greet Tangseng. He was tall with eyes as bright as silver. Two bronze rings hung from his ears. He said, "Where have you come from, sir?"

Tangseng replied, "I have been sent by the great Tang Emperor to fetch the Buddha's scriptures from the Western Heaven in India. We were passing your noble monastery and were hoping to stay here tonight. We will leave early tomorrow morning."

"Sir, I am afraid you are speaking empty words. Between the Tang Empire and the Western Heaven are many mountains, many caves, many demons and many monsters. A monk like you could never travel all that way by yourself."

"Of course you are correct. I have three disciples who protect me. They are waiting outside."

Two of the lama's disciples went outside to look. They returned and said, "Sir, you are out of luck. Your disciples are gone. There are only three evil monsters out there. One looks like a thunder-god. One looks like a large pig. And one has a green face and large teeth. Oh, and there is a lovely girl with them."

"Ah yes. Those three ugly ones are my disciples. And the girl is someone I rescued in the forest."

The lama's disciples went back outside. One of them was shaking as he said brightly, "My lords, Lord Tang invites you to come inside."

Zhu asked Sun Wukong, "Why is that man shaking?"

Sun Wukong replied, "He is frightened because we are ugly."

"We were born this way. None of us chose to be ugly."

The disciples tied up the horse, then they all walked through the gates. The lama's disciples prepared sleeping rooms for the three disciples and gave all of them a hot vegetarian dinner.

Chapter 81

By the time they had all finished dinner, it was dark. The lamps were lit. The lama fell to his knees. Tangseng hurried to help him to stand. He asked him why he did that. The lama replied, "Please excuse me, father, but there is one matter I must ask you about. Of course you are welcome to spend the night here, and your disciples also. But it would not be right for the lady Bodhisattva to stay here. I don't know where she should stay tonight."

Tangseng replied, "You should not worry, Abbot. My disciples and I do not have evil thoughts. This morning we were walking through the forest. We found the girl tied to a tree. I rescued her."

"Very well. She can sleep on a bed of straw behind the Devaraja Hall." Tangseng agreed that this was a good idea. The lama's disciples showed the girl where she should sleep, and everyone went to bed.

In the morning they all wanted to leave. But Tangseng was not feeling good. Zhu put his hand on his master's forehead and said, "Master, you have a fever."

Tangseng said softly, "Disciple, I cannot even stand up. We will have to wait here for a bit." And so, the travelers did not leave that day. They stayed at the monastery. For three days the disciples took care of Tangseng. On the morning of the fourth day, Tangseng sat up and asked, "Wukong, have people been giving food to the lady Bodhisattva?"

"Of course," replied Sun Wukong. "Why are you worried about her?"

"No matter. Fetch me paper, brush and ink. I need to write a letter to the Tang Emperor in Chang'an."

"What do you wish to say to His Majesty?"

"I will say, 'Your subject hits his head three times on the ground and shouts three times, "Long live Your Majesty." I have been traveling for many years. There have been many troubles, many delays. Now I am so ill that I cannot even stand up. The gate to Buddha is as distant as the gate to Heaven. I fear I will not live to bring back the scriptures. I beg you to send another to take my place.'"

Sun Wukong laughed loudly. "Master, you should not worry about dying. I can protect you easily. I will find out which king of the Underworld is calling for you. I will go there, capture all ten kings of the Underworld, and beat them until they let you live."

Tangseng laughed a little bit and said, "Stop bragging, Wukong. Now I am thirsty. Get me some cold water to drink."

Sun Wukong took a begging bowl into the kitchen. There he saw a group of monks, all of them red-eyed and crying. "What's the matter?" he asked. "Have we been eating too much of your food? No worries, we will pay for everything."

"That's not it," said one of the monks. "There is an evil monster in the monastery. Every night for the last three nights, two monks have disappeared. In the morning we looked for them. We only found their hats, their shoes, and their bones. They had been eaten. We did not want to bother your master with this because we knew he was feeling sick."

Sun Wukong tried to hide his big smile. He was happy to hear that there was a monster in the monastery. "Don't say another word," he said. "I will kill this monster for you."

"If you can do that, it would be wonderful. But if you cannot kill the monster, things will be difficult for us."

"How so?"

"Sir, we have all been monks since we were children. Every morning we rise, wash our faces, and pray to Buddha. At night we burn incense and pray to Buddha. We try to understand the Buddha's teachings. When people come here to burn incense and worship Buddha, we strike the wooden fish and read from the holy books. When there are no people burning incense and worshiping Buddha, we put our hands together and meditate. We are simple monks. We cannot fight tigers or demons. So sir, if you make the monster angry, all of us will be a single meal for him. We will all fall onto the Wheel of Rebirth. This ancient monastery will be destroyed. And we will not see the face of the Buddha."

Sun Wukong listened to this and became angry. "You stupid little monks, don't you know who I am?"

"Really, we don't," they replied.

"Then I will tell you:

    I defeated tigers and dragons at Flower Fruit Mountain
    I traveled to Heaven and caused great trouble there

I was hungry and ate a few of Laozi's elixir pills
I was thirsty and drank a bit of the Emperor's own wine
When I look with my golden eyes, the sky turns pale
When I use my golden hoop rod, it strikes silently
I don't care about monsters big or little
They can try to run away
But they will be caught, cooked, and smashed
Don't worry, I will catch that evil spirit
Then you'll know who Old Monkey is!"

The monks listened to this. They all nodded their heads and said to each other, "Well, he talks big. Maybe he can do it."

Sun Wukong turned and left. He carried the bowl of water back to Tangseng. Tangseng drank the cold water and felt much better. "How long have we been here?" he asked.

"Three days. Tomorrow will be the fourth day."

"We should leave tomorrow."

"All right. But tonight I need to catch an evil spirit."

Tangseng was surprised to hear that there was an evil spirit in the monastery. "But how can you do this while I am still feeling sick? If you fail to catch the monster, it will try to kill me!"

"I have to tell you, Master. This evil spirit has been eating people. It's already eaten six of the monks." Tangseng agreed that Sun Wukong needed to catch and kill the evil spirit. So Sun Wukong told Zhu and Sha to stay with Tangseng and protect him.

That night, the stars were bright in the sky and the moon was still not up. Sun Wukong shook himself and changed his appearance. Now he looked like a young monk, eleven or twelve years old. He wore a yellow silk shirt and a white tunic. He held a wooden fish in one hand and struck it with the other while reciting the Buddha's sutras. He waited until the first watch. Nothing happened. During the second watch the moon rose. Suddenly there was a roaring wind. He waited. The wind died down. He looked up and saw a beautiful woman walking towards him. She put her arms around him and asked, "What is that sutra you are reciting?"

"It is the sutra I vowed to chant," he replied.

"Why are you reciting it when everyone else is asleep?"

"I made a vow. Why shouldn't I chant it?"

The woman kissed him on the lips. "Let's go out back and have some fun together."

Sun Wukong turned his head aside and said, "I think you are a little stupid."

"What kind of woman do you think I am?"

"To tell you the truth, I think you're a slut."

"You don't know a thing!" she shouted. "I am not a slut. Several years ago, I was married to a husband who was much too young. He did not know what to do in the bedroom. So I left him. Now tonight, the stars and moon are bright. We have traveled hundreds of miles to be together. Let's go to the garden and make love."

Now Sun Wukong understood how the six young lamas had died. He said, "Lady, I am a monk and also very young. I don't know anything about this."

"Come with me. I will teach you."

He decided to go with her to see what would happen. They walked to the garden, hand in hand. Then she tripped him and threw him to the ground. She shouted, "My dear!" and grabbed his crotch.

He said, "So, you really want to eat me!" He grabbed her hand and somersaulted her to the ground.

She laughed and said, "Dear, you really know how to make your girl fall!"

He thought to himself, "I must strike now. As the saying goes, 'Strike first and win, wait and lose.'" He jumped to his feet and changed back to his own form. Whipping out his golden hoop rod he struck at the demon's head.

She thought, "This young monk is a very good fighter!" Then she looked more closely and realized it was really Sun Wukong, the elder disciple of the Tang monk. She also changed into her own form. Now she had

> A golden nose, white fur,
> A home in a tunnel underground
> Three hundred years ago she was sent down from Heaven
> Daughter of the Heavenly king,
> Sister of Prince Nata,
> She had no fear
> She came and went like the mighty Yangtze River
> She moved up and down like Mount Tai

Seeing the beauty of her face
You would never know she was really a mouse-spirit

Now she held two silver swords, one in each hand. They rang out as she fought with the Monkey King. She did not look like a young girl anymore. She was a powerful warrior. Sun Wukong's rod flashed like lightning. The mouse-spirit's swords shone as bright as a star. They moved through the old monastery, smashing statues as they fought. But the mouse spirit was no match for Old Monkey. She turned and tried to fly away.

"Where do you think you're going?" shouted Sun Wukong.

The mouse spirit took off her left shoe, blew on it and said, "Change!" Immediately it changed into a copy of the mouse spirit, holding two swords and charging at Sun Wukong. Meanwhile she changed her real body into a clear breeze and disappeared. She headed straight towards Tangseng's room. She lifted the monk into a cloud and carried him away to her home in the Bottomless Cave.

When she arrived at the cave, she told her little demons to prepare a vegetarian wedding feast.

Meanwhile, Sun Wukong fought hard. After fighting for many rounds he used his rod to smash his enemy into the ground. His enemy turned into a shoe. Angry, he returned to see Tangseng. His master was not there, but Zhu and Sha were. Sun Wukong raised his rod and shouted, "You two idiots, I told you to guard Master. He's gone. I'll kill the pair of you!"

"If you kill us," said Sha, "who will take care of the luggage? Or the horse? Remember, 'To kill a tiger you need help from your brother.' I hope you will not kill us, so tomorrow we can work together to save our master."

Sun Wukong was still angry, but he put away his rod. The three of them tried to sleep but they could not. In the morning when the monks brought them some breakfast, they reported that the girl was missing. This was not a surprise to Sun Wukong of course. After breakfast they headed east, back to the place where they first saw the girl tied to a tree.

The angry Monkey King changed into the form that he used when he caused trouble in Heaven, with three heads, six arms, and three golden hoop rods. In his anger he smashed trees left and right. Soon the mountain god and the local deity came to see him.

Sun Wukong said to them, "Mountain god, local deity, you are worthless. I think you are working with the bandits in this mountain and the mouse demon. I think you helped her kidnap my master. Tell me where he is right now, or I will beat both of you."

"Great Sage," they cried, "we did not do anything. The evil spirit does not live in our mountain. But we have heard some things about her. We heard that she carried him to a place three hundred miles south of here. Void Trapping Mountain is there, and in that mountain is a cave called Bottomless Cave."

Sun Wukong turned away from the mountain spirit and local deity. He flew south, followed by Zhu and Sha. Soon they arrived at Void Trapping Mountain. The mountain was huge, with a peak touching the blue sky.

Zhu looked up at the mountaintop. He said, "Brother, this mountain is so high, there must be evil in it."

Sun Wukong replied, "Of course. Every high mountain has monsters, every high cliff has spirits. I will stay here with Sha. You go to the mountain and try to find the Bottomless Cave. When you find it, we will all go together to rescue Master."

The pig-man put down his rake, straightened his black shirt, and leaped down to the mountain to find the path.

Chapter 82

Zhu found the mountain path. He began to follow it up the mountain. After walking for almost two miles, he saw two female monsters pulling up water from a well. How did he know they were female monsters? Because both of them had long hair pulled up and held together by two very long bamboo sticks. This was a very unfashionable style.

"Hey, evil monsters!" he called to them.

This made the two monsters very angry. They began to beat him with their water-carrying poles. Zhu had no weapon, so after a few blows rained down on his head he had to run away. He ran back to Sun Wukong and said, "Go back, brother! These monsters are terrible! Two of them hit me again and again with their water-carrying poles, just because I spoke to them."

"What did you say?"

"I called them evil monsters."

"Well of course, then. Remember, soft words will get you anywhere you want to go, but use hard words and you won't go even a single step."

"I didn't know that."

"Younger brother, think about the willow and the sandalwood. The willow is soft, so craftsmen make statues out of it. They paint it, they cover it with gold and jewels and flowers, and the people give it many blessings. But sandalwood is hard. It's used to make oil. People hit it with hammers. It suffers because it is so hard."

"You should have told this to me earlier."

"Now go back there and try again. Use soft words. Bow to them. If they are younger than you, call them 'Miss.' If they are older, call them 'Lady.' But before you go you should change your appearance so they won't recognize you."

Zhu changed his appearance so he looked like a dark-skinned fat monk. He went back to the monsters and said, "Greetings ladies. May I ask why you are fetching water?"

One of the monsters said to the other one, "Well, this monk is much nicer than that ugly pig!" Then she said to Zhu, "You don't know this, monk. Our lady brought a Tang monk to our cave last night. Our water is not very clean, so she sent us to fetch clean water from this well. Tonight there will be a great feast, and our lady will marry the Tang monk!"

When Zhu heard this, he ran back to Sun Wukong and reported everything. The disciples followed the two monsters for five or six miles as they walked deep into the mountains. Then the monsters disappeared.

Sun Wukong said, "I think they went into a cave. Wait here while I take a look." Soon he saw an archway with these words on it, "Void Trapping Mountain Bottomless Cave." Nearby they saw a huge rock that was three miles wide. In the center of the rock was a round hole. This was the entrance to the cave. Sun Wukong put his head inside the hole and looked down. He said, "Brothers, the cave is very large and very deep. Maybe a hundred miles wide."

"Forget it," said Zhu. "We cannot save Master."

"Don't say that! Put down the luggage and tie up the horse. I want you and Sha to guard the entrance to the cave. I will go into the cave and look around."

He jumped through the hole. A cloud appeared under his feet, and he rode the cloud down to the bottom of the cave. It was bright and beautiful, filled with sunshine, soft breezes, flowers, and fruit trees. Nearby he saw a group of buildings. "This must be where the evil spirits live," he thought.

He shook himself and turned into a fly. He flew to one of the buildings and saw the mouse demon sitting comfortably in a pavilion. She was even more beautiful than Chang'e, the lady on the moon. She looked happy, thinking that soon she would share the marriage bed with the Tang monk. She said to her servants, "Prepare the feast, my little ones. Soon my darling monk and I will be husband and wife."

Sun Wukong thought, "I'd better find out what Master is thinking. If he really wants to marry this demon, I'm leaving him here." He flew over to Tangseng and landed on his head. "Master," he called in his little fly voice.

"Save me, disciple!" cried Tangseng.

"Master, it's too late. They are preparing the marriage feast. After the feast you two will be married. Soon you will have a son or daughter. Why are you unhappy?"

"Disciple, we have traveled together for several years. Have you ever seen me eat meat or have any evil ideas? This evil spirit wants me to mate with her. If I do that, I will lose my *yang*. I will fall off the great Wheel of Rebirth and I will be trapped forever behind the dark mountains."

"All right, I believe you. It was easy for you to enter this cave, but it will be difficult for you to leave. Here's my plan. The evil spirit will want to share a cup of wine with you[1]. You must drink a little bit. Then pour the wine into her cup quickly so it makes some bubbles. I will turn into a tiny insect and swim under the bubbles. When she drinks the wine, I will go into her belly. I'll rip her organs apart and kill her."

"That seems a bit cruel."

"Master, if you want to be kind to her, I cannot help you. Remember she has already killed many monks."

"Oh, all right. But you will have to stay close to me."

"Of course I will."

Just then, the evil spirit came to the door of the room and called, "Elder!" Tangseng did not reply. She said again, "Elder!" Tangseng did not reply. He was thinking that 'trouble starts when the tongue begins to move.' She said a third time, "Elder!"

He thought that if he did not reply at all, she might become angry and just kill him. So he replied, "Madam, here I am."

Hearing his reply, the evil spirit came into the room. She really was quite beautiful. Her eyebrows were like two willow leaves. Her cheeks were like peach blossoms. But the Tang monk had no feelings for her at all. She put her arm around him and said, "Elder, I have had a drink brought for you."

"Lady," said Tangseng, "I am a monk. I cannot take any impure food."

"I know. I have sent for some pure water from the mountains. It comes from the mating of *yin* and *yang* up in the mountains. I also have some fruit and vegetables for you. After that, we will have some fun together!"

She picked up a golden cup and filled it with wine. "My darling," she said, "please drink this cup of love."

---

[1] A Chinese wedding night tradition is jiāo bēi jiǔ, "have a glass of wine." The bride and groom drink cups of wine with their arms crossed. The word for wine, (jiǔ) sounds like (jiǔ) which means a long time, thus symbolizing that they will be together forever.

Tangseng prayed silently, "Gods of Heaven, please hear me. This poor monk thanks you for protecting me on my journey to the Western Heaven. Now I am trapped by a monster spirit who wants to marry me. If this wine is all right for me to drink, I will drink it and hope that I can still see Buddha. But if it is not all right for me to drink, may I fall again into the Wheel of Rebirth."

Sun Wukong was still a tiny fly. He sat near Tangseng's ear and told the monk that it was all right to drink the wine. Tangseng drank the wine. Then he poured another cup for the evil spirit. He poured it quickly, causing bubbles to appear in the cup. Sun Wukong jumped into the cup.

But the evil spirit did not drink the wine right away. She put the cup down and said some more words of love to Tangseng. When she picked up the cup again, the bubbles were gone. She looked down at the wine and saw a tiny insect. She lifted the insect out of the cup with her finger and tossed it away.

Sun Wukong's plans were ruined. Quickly he turned into a large hungry hawk. He flew up, knocking over the tables and sending all the fruit and vegetables crashing to the floor. The evil spirit was terrified. She grabbed Tangseng and said, "Dear, where did that bird come from?"

"I don't know," he replied.

"Heaven and earth must have sent that thing here because they don't like that I am holding you prisoner." Turning to the servants she said, "Get rid of all these broken dishes and food. Prepare another feast. It doesn't matter if it is vegetarian or not, just do it quickly. Then we will marry."

While they were waiting for the second feast, Sun Wukong flew out of the cave, changed back to his real form, and met up with Zhu and Sha. He said, "Our master and the demon just had a cup of wedding wine. Soon they will have a wedding feast. Then they will be married and she will have her way with him in the marriage bed. But don't worry, I will go back and rescue him."

Then he changed into a fly again and flew back into the cave. He landed on Tangseng's head. Tangseng saw him and said, "Monkey! You used your magic to smash all the dishes. But what good is that? The demon wants to mate with me more than ever! When will this end?"

"Don't worry, Master, I will rescue you. Behind this room is a garden. You must get her to take you into the garden to play with you. Sit with her under a peach tree. I will turn into a red peach. Give her the peach. She will swallow the peach and I will be in her belly. That will be the end of her!"

Tangseng was a little worried about this plan, but he nodded his head. He called out, "Lady! A few days ago, I became sick. Today I am feeling a little bit better, but I would like to relax a bit. Do you have a place where we can go and have a little fun?"

The demon was delighted to hear this. "So, my dear, you are feeling a little bit interested, eh? Let's go to the garden and have some fun there." They walked hand in hand into the garden. She whispered to him, "Here we are, my dear. Let's have some fun, it will make you feel much better!"

They walked through the garden, looking at the beautiful flowers and trees. Tangseng saw the peach tree. He stopped there and said, "Lady, look at that lovely peach tree. Tell me, why are some peaches green and some are red?"

"If the sky had no *yin* and *yang*, the sun and the moon would be unknown; if the earth has no *yin* and *yang*, plants and trees would not grow; if people have no *yin* and *yang*, there is no difference between men and women. Here, the peaches on the south side get the sun's heat and they ripen first. The peaches on the northern side get no sun and so they are not ripe[1]."

"Thank you, I did not know that." He picked a red peach and gave it to her. The evil spirit picked a green peach and gave it to him. He opened his mouth and started to eat the green peach. Delighted with this, the evil spirit opened her lovely mouth and started to eat the red peach. As soon as she did this, Monkey jumped into her mouth and rolled down to her belly.

"There's something wrong with this peach," she cried. "It rolled right into my mouth before I had time to bite it."

"It's because you love things that are beautiful," he replied.

From inside her belly, Sun Wukong said, "Master, you don't need to argue with her. I have succeeded."

"Who is talking?" asked the demon.

Tangseng said, "It's my disciple, Sun Wukong. He was in the red peach. Now he is in your belly."

"Oh, I am dead! Monkey, why did you do this?"

"I want to eat all of your organs, leaving just the bones behind."

The lovely demon grabbed Tangseng and said, "My dear, I thought we would be together forever. We were as close as fish and water. I never thought we would be apart. When will we see each other again?"

Sun Wukong heard this. He was afraid that his master would want him to be kind to the demon. So he started kicking and jumping around inside her body. The pain was so great that she stopped talking and fell to the ground. Her servants were waiting outside the garden. They rushed in when they heard the sounds. "Are you all right, Madam?" they asked.

"Don't ask any questions, just take the monk outside right away."

"No," said Sun Wukong from inside her belly. "You must take my master out yourself. Then I will spare your life."

"All right," she replied. "As long as the bright moon stays in the sky, I will find a different place to put my hook. I will take this man outside, then I will

---

[1] The original meaning of the word *yin* was "the shaded side of a hill" and *yang* was "the sunny side of a hill." Peasants would go to work when the sky was bright, and return home to rest when the sky was dark, living life in balance. So over time, *yin* and *yang* evolved as complements to each other and developed their modern meaning as the feminine and masculine aspects of *qi*, the fundamental energy of the universe.

find another one."

Riding on a cloud, she carried Tangseng up and out of the cave.

Chapter 83

The evil spirit carried Tangseng outside the cave and put him down on the ground. Sha walked up to him and asked, "Where is our elder brother?"

"He is in the demon's belly," replied Tangseng.

Zhu said, "It's really dirty in there. Elder brother, what are you doing in there? Come on out!"

From inside the demon's belly, Sun Wukong said, "Open your mouth, I'm coming out." She opened her mouth as commanded. Sun Wukong prepared to leave, but then he thought, "Maybe she will try to bite me." So he turned his golden hoop rod into a jujube stone and put it between her upper and lower teeth to keep her mouth open. Then he jumped out, took his own form, and grabbed his rod to strike her. She drew her two swords and the battle began.

> Two flying swords protected her face
> The golden hoop rod struck at her head
> One was a monkey born of Heaven
> The other was an earth girl changed into a spirit
> Both were angry
> When the rod was raised, cold fog appeared in the sky
> When the sword was used, the earth shook
> They fought for a long time
> The earth moved, the mountains shook, and the trees fell

Zhu and Sha watched the fight for a while. Then they ran towards the demon, striking at her with rake and staff. The demon flew over to Tangseng, put an arm around him, grabbed the luggage and the horse with her other arm, and flew away.

Sun Wukong was very angry, but Zhu started to laugh loudly. "What's so funny?" shouted the monkey.

Zhu replied, "The demon carried Master back to her cave. You have already been there twice. The third time you are sure to succeed!"

"All right, I will go. You two, guard the mouth of the cave." The Great Sage used his cloud somersault to enter the cave. He flew straight to the demon's home. The gates were closed but this was no problem for him. He smashed the gates with his rod. He entered the home and looked around. There was no one there. But then he smelled incense coming from another room.

He ran into the other room. There was no one there either. But there was an incense table. On the table was a golden tablet. In large letters it said, "Honored father, King Li." In smaller letters it read, "Honored elder brother, Prince Nata."

Sun Wukong grabbed the tablet and brought it back to show to Zhu and Sha. "Look," he said to them, "I found this in the demon's home. I think the demon is the daughter of King Li and the sister of Prince Nata. I think she longed to live in the human world, so she took human form. Now she has carried our Master away. I will take this tablet up to Heaven and complain to the Jade Emperor. He will force the demon to give our Master back to us."

"You'd better be careful," said Zhu. "If the emperor decides against you, you could lose your life!"

"This is what I will tell the emperor: 'An evil spirit has kidnapped my Master. This evil spirit is the daughter of King Li. The king has not properly controlled his daughter. He allowed her to run away and become an evil spirit. She has caused much trouble and has killed many people. She has now taken my Master to a place where he cannot be found. I beg Your Majesty to bring this demon under control and return my Master. I also ask that Your Majesty determine the correct penalty for this.'"

"That is excellent! Go quickly, before the demon harms our Master."

"I will return in the time it takes you to make a cup of tea."

Sun Wukong carried the tablet up to the South Gate of Heaven, then to the Hall of Light where the four teachers of Heaven greeted him. "I wish to submit a complaint against two people." The four teachers led him to the Hall of Mist, where Sun Wukong submitted his complaint to the Jade Emperor. One of the emperor's ministers, the Gold Star of Venus, took the written complaint and the tablet, and placed both of them on a table in front of the emperor. The emperor read the complaint and looked at the tablet. Then he sent Gold Star to summon King Li to the palace. Sun Wukong asked if he could go too, and the emperor agreed.

"What is this all about?" said King Li when they arrived at his palace.

Gold Star replied, "The Great Sage has made a complaint against you. He says that you allowed an evil spirit to kidnap his Master."

King Li read the complaint. He slammed his fist on the table and shouted, "Lies! All lies!"

"He says that your daughter kidnapped his Master."

"That cannot be true. I have only one daughter and she is just six years old. This monkey is lying. As you know, the penalty for a false complaint is three levels worse than the punishment for the crime itself. Tie up that monkey!" And three of his servants grabbed Sun Wukong and tied him up. The king continued, "Now wait here. I will get my sword and kill this troublemaking ape."

Before Gold Star could stop him, King Li grabbed his sword, walked over to Sun Wukong, and brought it down on the monkey's head. But just before it hit his head, another sword blocked it. Prince Nata held the sword. He said to the king, "Father, please let go of your anger."

Now, here is the story of Prince Nata. When he was born, the word *na* was written on his left hand and *ta* on his right hand, so he was named 'Nata.' Three days later, baby Nata jumped into the ocean, grabbed a dragon and killed it to make a belt for himself. The king saw this. He was so afraid of the boy that he decided to kill him.

Nata heard about his father's plan. Using a sword, Nata cut off his flesh and gave it to his mother. Then he gave his bones to his father. Having repaid his debts to his parents, he flew to the Western Heaven to ask the Buddha for help. The Buddha brought Nata back to life by giving him new bones made of lotus root and clothing from lotus leaves.

After coming back to life, Nata wanted to kill his father the king. The king asked the Buddha to save him. So the Buddha gave the king a great pagoda, with many statues of Buddha in it. Then the Buddha told Nata to look at these statues as if each of them was his father. This calmed Nata's anger.

But now, the king was afraid that once again Nata wanted to kill him. He said to Nata, "Son, why did you stop me from killing this ape?"

"Father, you have forgotten that you have another daughter. Three hundred years ago, an evil spirit became a monster. She stole incense and flowers from the Buddha's own temple. You caught her. You wanted to kill her, but the Buddha told you to let her live. Because you let her live, the girl bowed to you as her father, and she bowed to me as her elder brother. In her home she set up a table to burn incense for us. Do you remember now?"

"Son, I had forgotten this. What is her name?"

"She has three names. Originally in Heaven she was Golden-Nosed White-

Haired Mouse Spirit. Later she was called Half-Guanyin because she had stolen the Buddha's incense and flowers. And later, when she was sent down to the human world, she changed her name again to Lady Flowing-Earth."

King Li nodded and started to untie Sun Wukong. But Sun Wukong was angry and said to the king, "Don't you dare untie me. Bring me back to the Emperor just like this. I want the Emperor to see what you have done to me."

"Monkey," said Gold Star, "please don't cause trouble here. Remember the good things I did for you. Five hundred years ago when you caused trouble in Heaven, many people wanted to have you arrested. But I put in a good word for you, so instead of being arrested, you were given a job taking care of the Emperor's horses. Then you drank some of the Emperor's wine, but instead of being arrested for that, you were given the name 'Great Sage Equal to Heaven.' I was the one who helped you. Now I ask you to let the king untie you."

"Oh, all right. As the ancients say, 'Don't share a grave with an old man, you will have to listen to him complain forever.' Let the old king untie me."

Gold Star said, "One more thing. You have brought a complaint against King Li. The two of you may argue about this for a long time if you want to. But remember, one day in Heaven is a year in the human world. If you stay here much longer, your Master might already be married and have a baby monk in his arms!"

"You are right," said Monkey. "What should we do?"

"King Li and his soldiers can go with you to the human world and defeat the demon. I will tell the Jade Emperor that you have dropped your complaint." Sun Wukong agreed to this.

The Monkey King jumped up onto a cloud. King Li and Prince Nata met him there, along with their generals and commanders and thousands of soldiers. They all flew together down to the human world. They came down to the ground at Void Trapping Mountain.

Zhu and Sha were wide-eyed when they saw this great army coming from Heaven. Zhu said to the king, "Thank you for coming. We have caused you a lot of trouble."

King Li replied, "You don't know this, my pig friend, but the demon has been burning incense for us for many years. We accepted her offerings. And so it is partly our fault that she has captured your master. We are sorry it's taken us so long to come here. Now, where is the entrance to the cave?"

Sun Wukong led them for three or four miles until they reached the entrance to Bottomless Cave. When they reached the entrance, King Li said, "To capture the tiger, you must enter the tiger's cave. The Great Sage and my son will enter the cave with the soldiers. Zhu and Sha, you wait here with me, we will guard the entrance. She will not be able to escape."

Sun Wukong and Nata entered the cave. What did they see?

> Sun and moon in the sky inside the cave
> Rivers and hills just like the outside world
> Warm fog floats over beautiful pools of water
> Red houses, painted halls,
> Red cliffs, green farmland,
> Willows in spring, lotus trees in autumn
> This cave is like Heaven

They flew down to the demon's home. They went inside the home and looked around. They searched every room, they opened every door, they looked all around Bottomless Cave, they looked in the region outside the cave, but they could not find the demon or the Tang monk. They did not know that outside of the entrance to the Bottomless Cave there was another smaller cave. This cave had two tiny gates. Inside was a tiny house with flowers growing all around it. Here is where the demon had carried Tangseng. She was going to make him marry her.

Inside the small cave were also a few little demon servants. One of them poked his head outside the gates to look around. His head bumped into one of the soldiers from King Li's army. The soldier shouted, "Here they are!"

Sun Wukong ran into the small cave, holding his golden hoop rod. He saw the mouse demon, Tangseng, the horse, and their luggage. Prince Nata and several soldiers followed him into the cave. The demons had nowhere to hide. The mouse demon kowtowed to Prince Nata and begged for her life.

Prince Nata said to her, "We are here to arrest you on orders from the Jade Emperor. You have caused us a great deal of trouble." Then he shouted to his soldiers to tie up the mouse demon and all of the little demons too.

"Thank you!" said Sun Wukong to Prince Nata. He and Tangseng bowed to the prince.

Zhu was angry and wanted to chop up the mouse demon into little pieces. But

Prince Nata said, "Let go of your anger, my pig friend. The Jade Emperor wanted her arrested, so we must treat her well. We will bring her back to the emperor."

And so, the prince brought the mouse demon back to the emperor's palace. We don't know what happened to her. Sun Wukong guarded Tangseng, Sha gathered the luggage, and Zhu untied the horse. He held the horse so that Tangseng could mount it. Then the travelers headed back towards the main road that led to the west.

Truly,

> The silk net has been cut,
> The golden sea has been dried,
> The jade lock has been broken,
> All troubles have been left behind.

Chapter 84

As they traveled on the road towards India, the weather became warmer. Their faces were touched by warm breezes and early summer rains. The ground was covered with beautiful mountain flowers.

Suddenly an old woman walked out from between two tall willow trees. She held the hand of a young boy. She said, "Stop! Don't go any further, monk. Turn around and go back east. This road leads nowhere."

Tangseng was so surprised that he jumped down off his horse and bowed to her, saying, "Old Bodhisattva, the ancients say, 'The ocean is wide so fish can jump, the sky is empty so birds can fly.' How can there be no road to the west?"

The old woman looked at him and said, "About five or six miles from here is Dharma Destroying Kingdom. In a previous life the king became angry at Buddhism because some Buddhist monks treated him badly. In this life he has vowed to kill ten thousand Buddhist monks. So far, he has killed nine thousand, nine hundred and ninety-six monks. He is just waiting for four more. If you go to the city, you will be throwing away your lives."

"Thank you," replied Tangseng. "I am grateful for your words. Tell me, is there another road around the city?"

She laughed. "No, there is no other way, unless you can fly."

Zhu the pig-man said, "Mama, your words do not frighten us. We all can fly."

The Monkey King Sun Wukong was the only one who could see the truth of this woman. He saw that she was the Bodhisattva Guanyin who was protecting the four travelers on their journey. The boy was Guanyin's disciple Red Boy. Sun Wukong threw himself on the ground and said, "Bodhisattva, please pardon your disciple for not greeting you!"

Guanyin rose into the air on her colorful cloud. Tangseng and his three disciples kowtowed to her. After she left, the big quiet man Sha said, "It's a good thing she told us about the Dharma Destroying Kingdom. What should we do?"

"Don't be afraid," said Sun Wukong. "We have fought many demons and monsters. In this kingdom there are no demons, no monsters, just people. Why should we fear them?" He looked around and continued, "But it's getting late. We don't want the villagers to see us. They may be looking for four monks to kill. Let's get away from the road and find someplace where we can rest and talk."

They found a quiet place a short distance away from the road. They sat down on the ground. Sun Wukong said, "Zhu and Sha, you take care of Master. I will go into the city and look around."

He jumped into the air and flew above the city. Looking down, he saw a bright and prosperous city. It was early evening, the moon was rising in the east. People were finishing up their work and returning to their homes. Not wanting to be seen, Sun Wukong changed into a moth. He fluttered through the city, looking at the streets and shops. He saw a large inn with a sign, "Rest House for Travelers." Below that was a second sign with the name of the owner, Mr. Wang. Looking inside he saw eight or nine men, all travelers. They had finished eating their dinners and were getting ready to go to bed.

Sun Wukong thought he could steal the men's clothing, so that he and the other three travelers could look like everyone else in the city. But just as he thought this, Mr. Wang said, "Please be careful, gentlemen. There are thieves in this city. Keep an eye on your clothing and luggage."

Mr. Wang had a lantern in his hand. The men all gave their clothing and luggage to Mr. Wang. He carried all the luggage and the lantern into his own room. Then he closed the door.

Sun Wukong flew right into the lantern flame, extinguishing it. Then he turned into a rat. He grabbed the clothes and dragged them outside. Mrs. Wang saw this. She called to her husband, "Old man, this is terrible. A rat has changed into a spirit and taken the clothes of our guests!"

Sun Wukong changed back to his own form. He shouted, "Mr. Wang, don't listen to your wife. I am not a rat or a spirit. I am the Great Sage Equal to Heaven. I am protecting the Tang monk while he journeys to the Western Heaven. I must borrow these clothes to protect my master from your evil king. I will give them back to you later."

Sun Wukong returned to Tangseng and said to him, "Master, I have looked around this city and learned the local language. The king is a wicked man who kills monks. But he is also a true son of Heaven[1]. His city is happy and

---

[1] The concept of "Mandate of Heaven" (tiān jiàng dàrèn) originated in the Zhou Dynasty, where it was used to justify their deposing of the decadent and corrupt Shang Dynasty in 1046 BC. The Zhou claimed that Heaven gives its blessing to the

prosperous. I borrowed these clothes. We will wear them and go into the city. The hats will hide our bald heads. We will stay at the inn. Tomorrow morning, we will go out the gate and head west along the main road. If anyone tries to stop us, we will tell them that we have been sent by the Tang Emperor himself. Tang is known as a superior empire. This king will not dare to stop us."

The others agreed that this was a good plan. Tangseng took off his monk's robes and put on the borrowed clothing and hat. Sha also changed clothes. Zhu also tried, but his head was too big for his hat. Sun Wukong had to sew two hats together to make one very large hat. Finally, they all were wearing the borrowed clothing.

"All right," he said. "We must go now. But do not use the words 'master' or 'disciple' while we are here. We will call each other brothers. Master, you will be Tang the Eldest. I will be Sun the Second. Zhu, you are Pig the Third. And Sha, you are Sand the Fourth. When we arrive at the inn, I will do all the talking. I will say that we are horse merchants. I will say that the white horse is a sample, and we have many more horses waiting outside the city."

The four travelers entered the city. They approached the inn. They heard shouting. People were shouting, "My clothing is gone!" and "Where is my hat?" The travelers avoided that inn and went to another one further down the road.

This inn had a lantern at the door which meant that the inn was still open. They went inside. The innkeeper, a woman, asked them to come in. A man took the horse. They went upstairs and sat down at a table.

The innkeeper asked, "Where are you gentlemen from?"

Sun Wukong replied, "We are from the north. We have a hundred poor horses to sell."

She replied, "You have come to the right place. My name is Zhao. My husband died a few years ago, so this place is called 'Widow Zhao's Inn.' We have a big courtyard that will easily hold all of your horses. We have three different classes of service. Please tell me which class you want."

Sun Wukong replied, "Please explain the three different classes."

---

rulers who are most fit to rule. Later rulers such as the Tang Emperor Taizong embraced this and used the title "Son of Heaven" (tiānzǐ) to solidify their hold on power.

"If you choose first class you will receive a wonderful banquet with many kinds of fruit and dishes. Several young ladies will come to your table to sing and play with you if you want. The cost is five silver coins per head."

"That sounds very good. In my home town, five coins would not even pay for one young lady to come to the table. Tell me about second class."

"In our second class, you all eat from the same dishes of food. We will give you fruit and wine. There are no young ladies. The cost is two silver coins per head."

"That also sounds good. What about the third class?"

"I would not dare to tell you about it, because you are such fine gentlemen."

"There is no harm in telling us. Please!"

"All right. In our third class, nobody serves you. We give you a big pot of rice that you can share. We give you some straw which you can put on the floor to sleep on. In the morning you give us a few copper coins, it does not matter how many."

Zhu said, "Third class sounds fine to me. Bring out the big pot of rice, I'm hungry."

But Sun Wukong said, "No. We have a few silver coins. Innkeeper, give us the first class."

The innkeeper was delighted. She called to her workers, "Make some good tea. Tell the kitchen to get ready. Kill some chickens and geese." She paused, then she added, "Also, kill a pig and a sheep. And get some good wine."

Tangseng was not happy about all this meat being prepared. Sun Wukong stamped his foot and said, "Mrs. Zhao, please come here." He waited until she arrived. He told her, "Please don't kill any living creatures. We are all eating vegetarian food today."

"What, are you all vegetarians?"

"We are on the *gengshen* diet[1]. Today is *gengshen*, so we must eat vegetarian. Tomorrow will be *xinyou* and we can eat meat again. So please, prepare vegetarian dishes for us tonight. We will pay you the same."

---

[1] The traditional Chinese calendar uses a sixty day cycle. The 57th day of the cycle is Gēngshēn, the Metal Monkey. The 58th day is Xīnyǒu, the Metal Rooster. There is also a sixty year cycle, with Gēngshēn and Xīnyǒu being the 57th and 58th years.

This made the innkeeper very happy, because vegetarian food was much less expensive than meat dishes. Sun Wukong continued, "We will also have a little wine, but Elder Brother Tang will not have any. And please don't send any girls to us. Today is a *gengshen* so we want to avoid having fun with the girls. But we will certainly want the girls tomorrow."

The innkeeper went away to help prepare the vegetarian food, and to tell the girls not to come upstairs. The four travelers finished their meal. Hotel workers removed the dishes.

Tangseng said to Sun Wukong, "Where will we sleep? It's too dangerous upstairs. If anyone comes in and sees our bald heads, we will be trapped."

"You're right," he replied. He stamped his foot to call the innkeeper again. When she arrived, he told her, "Madam, I'm afraid there is no place for us to sleep. Two of my brothers are a little bit sick, they cannot sleep in the upstairs room because of the breeze. And my elder brother and I cannot sleep if there is any light in the room."

The innkeeper went away and told her daughter, "We have a problem. Four wealthy horse merchants arrived tonight. They wanted first class service and I was hoping to earn some money from them. But they don't want to sleep in the inn because of the breezes and the light that comes in. I may have to tell them to leave. If I do that, we will lose all the money they were going to pay us."

The daughter replied, "Mother, don't worry. When father was alive, he made a big wooden trunk. It's four feet wide, seven feet long, and three feet high. It's big enough for several people to sleep in. And when the trunk is closed there's no breeze and no light. It's perfect for our guests."

This made the innkeeper very happy. She told Sun Wukong about the trunk and he agreed to use it. Some workers brought out the trunk and opened the lid. The four travelers got inside. They told the innkeeper to tie up the white horse next to the trunk. Then they told her to close the trunk, lock it, and put paper over any gaps that might let in some light.

"You are very strange," she said, but she did as they asked. Then everyone went to bed.

During the night, the travelers were all very uncomfortable. The trunk was too hot, there was no breeze, and everyone was too close together. They all tried to sleep.

Sun Wukong wanted to make a little bit of trouble. He pinched Zhu on the leg to wake him up. He said in a loud voice, "Brother, we sold those horses last week for three thousand silver coins. We have another four thousand in our bags, and tomorrow we will sell the rest of the horses for three thousand more. That's not bad, eh?"

Outside the trunk, several hotel workers were listening. They were in cahoots with the local bandits. When they heard this, some of them ran to tell the bandits that there were guests in the inn with lots of money. Twenty bandits came to the inn. Widow Zhao and her daughter saw them coming. They were frightened so they locked themselves in their room.

The bandits looked around. They did not see any travelers but they saw the big, locked trunk. The leader said, "This trunk is probably full of money, silk and jewels. Let's take it outside the city. We can open it up and take everything." Several strong bandits picked up the trunk and started to carry it away. Some other bandits took the white horse.

Inside the trunk, the travelers all woke up. They knew that the trunk was moving but they didn't know what was going on. Sun Wukong said, "Bandits are carrying us. Keep quiet. Maybe they will carry us all the way to the Western Heaven, so we won't have to walk."

But the bandits headed east. They killed some guards at the city gate and escaped the city. People saw this and reported it to the commander of the army. A large number of soldiers rushed out of the city to try to catch the bandits. The bandits saw them coming. They dropped the trunk, let go of the white horse, and ran away into the forest.

The soldiers carried the trunk back into the city. The commander looked at the white horse. What did he see?

> Silver threads grow in his mane
> Jade strands grow in his tail
> His bones can bring a thousand gold coins
> He can run for three thousand miles
> He climbs mountains to meet the green clouds
> He neighs at the moon as white as snow
> He is truly a dragon from the ocean
> A jade kirin[1] in the human world

---

[1] The kirin (qílín) is a benevolent horned beast in Chinese mythology. Males kirins are

The commander rode the white horse back to the king's palace. The soldiers carried the trunk into the palace. They put the trunk down so the king could look at it in the morning.

During the night, Sun Wukong used his magic to drill a small hole in the bottom of the trunk. He changed into a small cricket. He crawled out and changed back to his true form. Now it was time for some interesting magic!

He pulled all the hairs from his right arm, blew on them and whispered, "Change!" Each hair turned into a little monkey. He pulled all the hairs from his left arm, blew on them and whispered, "Change!" Each hair turned into a sleep insect. Then he grabbed his golden hoop rod, pinched it, and whispered, "Change!" The rod shattered and became a thousand small razors.

He gave a sleep insect and a razor to each little monkey. He told them to go and find everyone in the palace and government offices. He told them to give a sleep insect to each person they met, wait for them to fall asleep, then shave their heads with the razor.

A few hours later the work was done. Sun Wukong shook himself to bring all the hairs back to his arms. He brought the razors together again to make his golden hoop rod. He made the rod small and put it in his ear. Then he changed back into a small cricket and crawled back into the trunk.

In the morning there was chaos in the palace. When the palace ladies woke up, they went to wash their hair and found that they were bald. The men found that they were also bald. The queen woke up, looked beside her in the royal bed, and saw a monk sleeping there. She cried out. The monk sat up, and she saw that it was the king, completely bald. He looked at her and said, "Why are you bald, my queen?" "You are the same, Your Majesty," she replied.

The king looked at her and cried. He said to her, "This must be because of all the monks we have killed."

<hr>

qí, females are lín. They are peaceful, bearded, with a dragon-like appearance and a jewel-like brilliance. In Buddhist tradition, kirins walk on clouds to avoid harming even a single blade of grass.

Chapter 85

Later that morning, the king met with all his ministers. The ministers said, "Your Majesty, we don't know why, but all of your servants lost their hair last night." The ministers and the king agreed that they would not dare to kill any more monks.

Then the commander of the army approached the king and said, "Your Majesty, last night we captured a large wooden trunk and a white horse from some bandits. We beg Your Majesty to decide what to do."

"Bring it here," replied the king. Several soldiers picked up the heavy trunk and carried it into the throne room.

Inside the trunk, Tangseng was very worried. "What will we say to the king?" he asked.

"Stop worrying," replied Sun Wukong. "I have everything under control. When the trunk is opened, the king will bow to us. I just hope that Zhu can keep his mouth shut."

Before Tangseng could say anything, the soldiers put the trunk down in the throne room. They opened the lid. Zhu jumped out, frightening everyone in the room. Sun Wukong climbed out next, helping Tangseng. Sha climbed out last, carrying the luggage.

The four travelers stood in the throne room, waiting. The king stood up from his throne and walked down several steps until he stood in front of the travelers. He bowed and asked, "What brings you gentlemen here?"

Tangseng answered, "I have been sent by the Tang Emperor to go to Thunderclap Monastery in India, to worship the living Buddha and bring back sacred books to the Tang empire."

"And why were you in the trunk?"

"I knew that Your Majesty had vowed to kill ten thousand Buddhist monks. That is why we dressed as villagers instead of monks. Last night we slept in the trunk because we were afraid of bandits. Our trunk was stolen by the bandits, with us still inside it. Your army commander rescued us. Now that I see your noble face, the clouds have disappeared and the sun has come out. I hope you will allow me to continue on my journey. My gratitude will be as deep as the ocean."

"Honored master, it was wrong of us not to welcome you to our kingdom. A long time ago, some monks said terrible things about me. In anger, I vowed to kill ten thousand of them. We never thought that we would all become monks! I beg you, honored master, please take us as your disciples."

Zhu laughed loudly. "If you are going to be our disciples, what gifts do you have for us?"

The king replied, "Master, if you accept us as your disciples, everything in our kingdom is yours."

Sun Wukong said, "We are monks, we are not interested in your wealth. Please sign our travel rescript and let us leave your city safely. Your kingdom will last forever and you will have a long and happy life."

The king agreed to this at once. Then he asked the travelers to change the name of his country. Sun Wukong said, "The name 'Dharma Kingdom' is good, it's the 'Destroying' word that is the problem. If you change the name of your kingdom to 'Dharma Honoring Kingdom' you will have

Clear waters and calm seas for a thousand years
Rain and wind in the proper season
Peace throughout your kingdom

The king thanked the four travelers and gave them the royal carriage to take them to the western edge of Dharma Honoring Kingdom.

When they reached the western edge of the kingdom, they got out of the carriage and continued their journey. Sun Wukong explained to the others how he had used his magic the night before to shave the heads of everyone. Everyone laughed.

Just then, they saw another large mountain blocking their path. Tangseng said, "Disciples, look at that tall mountain. It looks a little bit evil. I am beginning to feel frightened."

Sun Wukong replied, "Master, have you forgotten the Heart Sutra that was given to you by the Chan Master? Remember these words from the sutra,

Do not go far seeking Buddha on Spirit Mountain
Spirit Mountain lives in your heart
In each person there is a Spirit Mountain shrine
At this shrine you will be transformed

When the mind is pure it shines like a lantern. When the mind is at peace the world becomes clear. But if you make a mistake, you will not succeed even in ten thousand years. Be strong and Thunderclap Mountain will be right in front of you. Let yourself become frightened and Thunderclap Mountain will remain far away. So forget your fears and just come with me."

Tangseng felt much better when he heard these words. They continued walking and reached the mountain. Looking up, they saw many colors, with white clouds near the peak. The mountain was covered with thousands of pine trees and a few bamboo trees. From far away they heard the sounds of gray wolves, tigers, wild apes, and birds singing in the trees. Then they heard the sound of wind.

"I hear a wind," said Tangseng, frightened.

"Of course. There are winds in all four seasons. Why are you frightened by this one?"

"It is blowing very hard." Suddenly a thick fog arose from the ground. The sun disappeared, the birds stopped singing, and they could not see anything. "And why is there fog when the wind is still blowing?"

"I'll take a look. Please get down off your horse, Master." Tangseng got down. Sun Wukong leaped into the air. He shaded his eyes to look in all four directions. Looking down, he saw a monster spirit sitting by a cliff. He had a big strong body, long fangs, a big nose like a jade hook, golden eyes, and a silver beard. Thirty or forty little demons were sitting near him, all in a straight line and all blowing fog from their mouths.

Sun Wukong laughed and said to himself, "Well, Master was right, it was an evil wind after all. I could kill this monster right now, but that would ruin my reputation. I'll give this business to Zhu."

He returned to Tangseng and said, "Master, my eyes are usually good, but this time I was wrong. There is no monster. The fog is gone now. I think it came from a nearby village where the villagers are making steamed rice."

Zhu heard this. he was hungry of course. He whispered to Sun Wukong, "Did you eat their food?"

The monkey replied, "I just tasted a little bit. It had too much salt for me."

"I don't care how much salt the food has, I would eat it anyway." Zhu walked up to Tangseng bowed and said, "Master, elder brother has just told me that there are people in a nearby village who feed monks. Let me go and beg some food."

Tangseng agreed. As Zhu was leaving, Sun Wukong said to him, "Brother, they only feed good-looking monks. You are quite ugly." So Zhu said some magic words and shook himself. He changed into a short skinny monk holding a wooden fish and beating it with a stick. He did not know any scriptures to recite, so he just said, "Oh great one" again and again.

Zhu walked down the road. Soon he walked right into a group of little demons. The demons grabbed him. Zhu said, "Don't pull me! You can let me eat at each of your houses, one at a time."

One of the little demons replied, "So you want to eat, eh monk? You don't know this, but we like to eat monks. We catch monks, take them to our homes, steam them until they're cooked, and eat them."

Zhu was afraid and angry. He changed back to his true form and began swinging his rake at the little demons. The demons ran away and rushed back to the senior demon. "Disaster, Your Majesty! We caught a little monk. We were going to keep him and eat him later. But then he transformed into a large pig-man. He hit us with a rake."

"Let me go and have a look," said the senior demon. He went for a closer look and saw Zhu, holding the magical nine-toothed rake in his hands. The senior demon shouted, "Where are you from? What's your name? Tell me know and I'll let you live."

"What, you don't recognize me?" replied Zhu.

> I was once Marshal of the Heavenly Reeds
> I was the commander of eighty thousand soldiers on the river of Heaven
> One day in the Heavenly palace I insulted the beautiful Chang'e
> Then I ate the Queen Mother's magic mushrooms
> The Jade Emperor hit me with a hammer two thousand times
> And sent me down to the human world
> I became an evil monster like you
> I married a farm girl in Gao Village
> Then I met my elder brother the Monkey King
> He defeated me with his golden hoop rod
> I had to bow and take a Buddhist vow
> Now I am a coolie for the Tang monk
> My surname is Zhu
> My Buddhist name is Zhu Bajie!"

The monster shouted, "So, you are the Tang monk's disciple. I've heard his flesh is tasty. Now taste my mace!"

The monster and the pig began to fight.

> The pig's rake was like a howling wind
> The mace's blows came as thick and fast as rain
> Zhu's rake was like a dragon from the ocean
> The monster's mace was like a snake from a pond
> Their shouts shook mountains and rivers
> They terrified all the creatures in the underworld

As they fought, Sun Wukong laughed and said to Sha, "That pig really is a fool. I told him that there was food, so he went to find out. He probably ran into the demons by now. Well, I'd better go and see how he's doing."

Sun Wukong saw Zhu fighting with the monster. He shouted, "Relax, pig. Old Monkey is here!" Zhu and Sun Wukong fought the monster together. Soon the monster and his little demons ran away in defeat.

The two disciples returned to Tangseng. Zhu was tired from fighting. He was covered with sweat and snot was running from his nose. "What happened to you?" asked Tangseng. "I thought you went to get some rice from the village."

"Elder brother tricked me," said Zhu. "He told me there was a village full of people who would give us food. But there was a crowd of evil demons. They gave me a difficult fight. Monkey helped me and we defeated them."

"Is there really a monster there?" asked Tangseng.

Sun Wukong replied, "There are a few little devils, but they won't give us any trouble. Let's get going. Zhu, you walk in front and clear the path. If the senior demon shows up again, you fight him. I know you can defeat him."

Zhu said, "Brother, you know,

> A prince at a banquet
> Will either be drunk or fed
> A soldier in a battle
> Will either be wounded or dead"

"That sounds bad. Why do you say those things?" asked Sun Wukong.

"By saying this now, I will make myself stronger later." The four travelers continued walking westward on the road to India.

Meanwhile, the senior demon and the little demons returned to their mountain cave. The senior demon was in a very bad mood. One of the junior demons asked, "Why are you so sad today, Your Majesty?"

He replied, "Little ones, usually when I go out on patrol, I can find a few people or animals to bring back for you to eat. But today I met a very dangerous monk, the pig-man Zhu Bajie. He has come here with his master, a Tang monk. I want to eat the monk's flesh but I cannot defeat his disciple."

One of the little demons said, "Your Majesty, I used to live in the Lion Cave. I worked for the demon of Lion Ridge. My boss also wanted to eat the Tang monk. But the monk's senior disciple, a monkey named Sun, killed my boss and many of the other demons. I escaped through the cave's back door and came here. That is how I know about Sun's powers. He made trouble in Heaven five hundred years ago, and all the gods of Heaven are afraid of him. You should forget about eating the Tang monk. It's too dangerous."

This story frightened the senior demon. But then another little demon stepped up. He said, "Don't be afraid, Your Majesty. I have a plan for capturing the Tang monk. It's called 'Dividing the Petals of the Plum Flower.'"

The senior demon asked, "What do you mean, 'Dividing the Petals of the Plum Flower'?"

"Call all of your little demons. From all of them, choose the best hundred. From that hundred choose the best ten. From that ten choose the best three. They must be able to change their appearance. Tell the three to change their appearance so they all look just like Your Majesty, with your armor and weapons. Send one to fight Zhu Bajie, one to fight Sha Wujing, and one to fight Sun Wukong. While they are all busy fighting, you can grab the Tang monk. It's easy."

The senior demon clapped his hands and said, "That is a wonderful plan! If it works, I will make you commander of all the little demons." The little demon kowtowed, then went off to call the little demons. Soon, the best three little demons were selected. They all changed their appearance to look like the senior demon. Then they went to wait for the monk and his disciples to arrive.

Tangseng was riding on his horse, surrounded by his three disciples. They heard a loud crashing sound. A demon jumped out and ran straight towards Tangseng. Sun Wukong shouted, "The demon is here. Get him, Zhu!"

Zhu whipped out his rake and began battling with the demon. A minute later, a second demon jumped out and ran towards Tangseng. Sun Wukong said, "I guess Zhu let the demon escape. I will fight him." He began to fight the second demon.

Soon afterwards, there was a great wind and a third demon ran towards Tangseng. "What is going on here?" asked Sha Wujing. But he whipped out his staff and began to fight the third demon.

Now all three disciples were fighting. The senior demon flew down from the sky. He grabbed Tangseng and carried him off to his cave. He entered the cave, carrying Tangseng on his shoulder. "Commander!" he shouted. The little demon who'd given him the plan stepped forward. The senior demon said, "Your plan was a complete success. You are now commander of all my demons. Tell the others to get water, firewood and a large pot. We will steam the Tang monk. Then you and I will eat his flesh and live forever."

The commander replied, "Your Majesty, we must not eat the monk yet. That monkey Sun is really, really dangerous. If he finds out that we've killed and eaten his master, he won't even bother to fight with us. He will just bring down the entire mountain on our heads and kill us instantly."

"What do you suggest?"

"I think we should bring the Tang monk out to the back garden, tie him up, and keep him there for a couple of days. That will clean out his insides. We will wait for the three disciples to go away. Then we can steam the monk and enjoy him in a relaxed way. Okay?"

"Yes," laughed the senior demon, "that's a very good plan."

They took Tangseng to the back garden and tied him to a tree. He began to cry, saying, "Disciples, where are you? I have been captured by an evil demon. When will I see you again?"

As he cried, he heard a voice nearby saying, "Elder, you are also here!"

"Who's that?" asked Tangseng.

"I am a woodcutter who lives on this mountain. I was captured three days ago and tied up. I think they plan to eat me."

"Woodcutter, I am sorry to hear that. But if you die, it will only be you. If I die it will be much worse."

"Why do you say that? You are a man who has left the family. You have no parents, no wife, no children."

"I have been sent by the Tang emperor to fetch holy scriptures from the Western Heaven. If I die here, I will fail my emperor and his ministers. Countless souls in the underworld will never be able to escape the Wheel of Rebirth. All of my work will be as dust in the wind."

"That is sad indeed. But my death will be even worse. I live alone with my mother. She is eighty-two years old, and I am the only one to care for her. If I die, who will bury her?"

"My friend, serving one's emperor and serving one's parents are both the same. You are moved by your mother's kindness; I am moved by my emperor's kindness."

Chapter 86

While Tangseng and the woodcutter were locked up in the demon's cave, Sun Wukong defeated one of the three false demons. He ran back to the place where his master was waiting for him. But he did not see Tangseng, he only saw the white horse and the luggage. He began searching for Tangseng.

Soon he was joined by Zhu and Sha. There was a lot of confusion, because each of the three disciples thought that they had been fighting the same demon. Each one thought that the others had let the demon escape. Finally Sun Wukong jumped up and shouted angrily, "He's fooled me! He's fooled me!"

"What do you mean?" asked Sha.

"He used the old 'Dividing the Petals of the Plum Flower' trick. He got all three of us to fight other demons, then he jumped down and carried off our master." He started to cry, saying, "What will we do now?"

Zhu said, "Elder brother, don't cry. He must be close. Let's go look for him." They began searching the mountain. After a while they found a large stone gate to a cave at the base of a large cliff. There was a stone tablet above the gate. These words were carved into the stone in large letters, "Hidden Mist Mountain, Broken Peak, Joined Rings Cave."

"This is where the demon lives," said Sun Wukong. "Zhu, go get him." Zhu raised his rake, ran forward, and smashed the stone gate.

The young commander heard the sound. He ran towards the gate and saw the pig-man. He turned and ran back to the senior demon, saying, "Don't worry, Your Majesty. It's just Zhu Bajie. He's no problem. Just watch out for the monkey."

Zhu heard this. He turned and called to Sun Wukong, "They're not frightened of me, elder brother, but they are definitely frightened of you. You'd better come here quick." Immediately, Sun Wukong ran up to the gate and began shouting for the demons to release his master. Sha followed him.

The demon king heard this. He said to the commander, "You brought this disaster down on us with your 'Dividing the Petals of the Plum Flower' nonsense. How will this end for us?"

"Don't worry, Your Majesty," replied the commander. "I know this monkey.

He is a powerful warrior, but he is also quite vain. Let's say some flattering things to him, and trick him into thinking that we've already eaten his master."

"How will we do that?"

"I will make a fake human head. We will show the head to Sun and tell him that it's the head of his dead master."

The commander used his axe to cut a piece of willow root. He shaped it so it looked somewhat like a human head. He bit his lip and let some blood drip onto the head. Then he told one of the junior demons to put the head on a tray and bring it to Sun Wukong, saying, "Oh Great Sage, please let go of your anger and allow us to speak to you."

The junior demon was afraid, but he walked slowly towards the disciples, carrying the head on a tray. Zhu was about to smash the junior demon with his rake. But Sun Wukong liked to be called 'Great Sage' so he held up his hand and said, "Wait a minute, brother. Let's hear what they have to say."

The junior demon said, "Oh Great Sage, I'm afraid that some of the demons in this cave have done a very bad thing. They have eaten all of your master except his head. I have the head right here."

Sun Wukong replied, "Well, if you've eaten him, that's that. Show me the head." The junior demon threw the head. It landed at Sun Wukong's feet.

"Something's not right," said Sun Wukong to Zhu. "When you throw a real human head and it hits the ground, it's quiet. But when this hit the ground it made a loud sound, like hitting two pieces of wood together." He then hit the head with his rod. The head split open, and they could see that it was just a piece of willow root.

The junior demon ran back into the cave and reported this to the senior demon. "Well then," said the senior demon, "we just need to show him a real head. Get one from the kitchen."

The junior demon went to the kitchen, found a pile of human heads, and picked one up. He used a knife to remove most of the flesh from the head. Then he brought it out to Sun Wukong and Zhu, saying, "Great Sage, the first head that I showed you was false. But this really is the head of your master." And he threw the second head on the ground towards Sun Wukong.

Sun Wukong began to cry. He believed that the head was really his master. The three disciples picked up the head. They found a peaceful place not far from the cave. Zhu dug a hole with his rake. They put the head in the hole, covered it with dirt, and placed a few willow branches and stones on top.

Sun Wukong wiped his eyes and said, "Sha, you guard the tomb and keep an eye on the horse and luggage. Zhu, you and I will go and capture that monster and break his body into a thousand little pieces." The pig-man picked up his rake, the Monkey King raised his golden hoop rod, and the two of them ran straight towards the cave. They ran into the cave and began hitting all the little demons.

"What should we do?" said the commander to the senior demon.

He replied, "The ancients say, 'put your hand in a basket of fish, and your hand will stink.' We have started this, now we have to finish it. Stand your ground!" Then he picked up his weapon, an iron mace. He ran outside the cave, followed by the commander and hundreds of little demons. He shouted at Sun Wukong and Zhu, "Don't you know who I am? I am the Great King of the Southern Mountains. I've been here for hundreds of years. I've eaten your master. What will you do about it?"

Sun Wukong replied, "How dare you call yourself Great King of the Southern Mountains? Even Laozi, Tathagata Buddha and Kongzi don't dare call themselves Great King. You are nothing."

The Great Sage and the Great King stood and hurled insults at each other for a while. Finally the monster jumped forward and tried to hit Sun Wukong with his iron mace. The monkey king easily blocked the blow, and the fight began. While they fought, Zhu battled the commander. Sun Wukong saw hundreds of little demons coming. He quickly used his body-dividing magic to make hundreds of little monkeys. Each little monkey began to fight a little demon.

What a battle!

> The monk from the east was traveling west
> The great demon of the southern mountains blocked his way
> Foolishly the monster had captured the Tang monk
> Then he met the Monkey King and the famous Zhu Bajie
> Dust clouds rose, the sky darkened
> Shouts from the demons rose above the battle
> The Great Sage and the pig showed their strength
> The monster and his commander showed their hunger
> The Great Sage and the pig wanted revenge
> The monster and his commander wanted the monk's flesh

The four of them fought for a long time
But neither side could win

Finally the Great King of the Southern Mountain saw that he could not win the fight. He flew back into his cave. The commander could not fly away. He was struck down by the monkey king's rod. His body changed into his true form, a gray wolf. Sun Wukong and Zhu looked at the body of the wolf. Then they flew after the Great King.

The Great King told his little demons to block the cave entrance with rocks and dirt. Zhu tried to smash the rocks with his rake, but the rocks did not move. "Don't bother with that," said Sun Wukong. "They have blocked the front gate, but there must be a back entrance to the cave. I'll go and look for it."

"Don't get yourself killed," said Zhu. "We have already cried for Master, I don't want to have to cry for you too."

Sun Wukong walked around the mountain for a while. He heard the sound of flowing water. Looking down, he saw a small stream coming out of a small gate in the ground. He said to himself, "I can turn into a water snake and get in the cave that way. But Master would not like it if I became a long and thin creature. How about a crab? No, Master would not like that either, too many legs." Finally he decided to turn into a water rat. He ran through the gate and followed the flowing water up into the cave.

Soon he found himself in the back of the cave. Looking up, he saw some little devils preparing human flesh for eating. He felt sick when he saw this. "I'd better find out what's going on here," he said to himself. Then he turned into a small bee. He flew through the cave to the room where the senior demon was sitting.

A junior demon ran up to him and said, "Your Majesty, I was just on patrol outside the cave. I saw the Tang monk's three disciples. They were all standing around a grave, crying loudly. I think they must have thought that the head we gave them was really their master."

Sun Wukong was happy to hear this. He looked around the room. On one side of the room was a very small door. He flew under the door. He found himself in a large garden. He heard the sound of crying. He saw Tangseng and another man. Both of them were tied to trees.

He turned back into his true form and greeted his master. "Is that you, Wukong?" asked Tangseng. "Get me out of here quickly!"

"Don't worry, Master. Wait for a little bit. I have to kill the evil demon first."

He changed back into a small bee and returned to the room where the senior demon was. The demons were talking about how to cook the Tang monk. Should they steam him, fry him, or boil him? One said that they should salt him and take their time eating him. This made Sun Wukong very angry. He said to himself, "What did my master ever do to you?"

He flew up to the ceiling where nobody could see him, and changed into his true form. Then he pulled some hairs from his arm, whispered, "Change!" and turned them into sleep insects. The sleep insects crawled into the noses of the demons, putting them to sleep. The Great King was much larger and he did not fall asleep. So Sun Wukong sent several more sleep insects into his nose. Finally the Great King yawned twice and fell asleep.

When they were all asleep, Sun Wukong broke down the door to the garden. He was about to untie Tangseng, but then he said, "Wait, Master, I need to kill the evil demon first." He ran back into the other room and raised his staff. Then he said, "Oh, wait. Maybe I should rescue Master first." He ran back to the garden. He ran back and forth several times, not sure which thing to do first. Finally he untied Tangseng.

As Tangseng got up to walk away, the other man cried out, "Please save me too, my lord!"

"Who's that?" asked Sun Wukong.

Tangseng said, "He is a woodcutter, also captured by the demons. His mother is very old and he is worried about her. Untie him too."

Sun Wukong led both of them out of the cave. They walked to the grave where Zhu and Sha were standing. Zhu thought that Tangseng was a ghost, but Sun Wukong told him all about the fake head and how he had rescued Tangseng.

Sun Wukong and Zhu went back into the cave. They found the demon who called himself Great King. They tied up the demon and carried him, still sleeping, outside the cave. Then they piled up a lot of dry firewood at the back entrance of the cave. They set it on fire. Zhu flapped his ears to make the fire grow faster. It burned everything in the cave, killing all the little demons.

They returned to Tangseng. They saw that the Great King was waking up. Quickly Zhu smashed him with his rake. The dead Great King turned into a leopard. Sun Wukong said, "Leopards can kill tigers and humans. By killing him we have saved many lives."

The monk and the three disciples got ready to leave. But the woodcutter said, "Gentlemen, my home is not far from here. Would you please come to my home, meet my mother, and let us prepare a meal for you?"

They followed the woodcutter. Soon they saw a small cottage. It was surrounded by a bamboo fence. A stone path led from the gate to the front door. Flowers and trees were all around. An old woman was standing in front of the door, looking all around and calling out, "My son, where are you?"

"I am here, Mother!" he shouted. He ran up to her and knelt before her, crying.

The old woman hugged him. She said, "My boy, you have been gone for several days. I thought the mountain lord had captured you. What happened?"

"Mother, the mountain lord did capture me. I was tied up for several days. They were going to eat me. But these gentlemen saved me. They are holy monks from the Tang Empire, traveling to the Western Heaven to fetch the Buddha's scriptures. They killed the mountain lord and all of his little demons. If it were not for them, your son would be dead."

Mother and son both kowtowed to the Tang monk and his disciples. Then they hurried into the cottage to prepare a vegetarian meal.

After they had eaten the meal, Tangseng thanked the woodcutter's mother. Then he asked the woodcutter to show them how to return to the main road to the west. The five of them walked for several miles, over hills and across rivers, until they found the main road again.

"Disciples," said Tangseng,

> "I have traveled far on this journey
> Meeting disaster at every river and mountain
> Escaping death from monsters and demons
> My mind is only on the Buddha scriptures
> My thoughts are only on Heaven above
> When will this journey end?
> When will I return home?"

The woodcutter heard him and replied, "Don't worry, sir. Three hundred miles from here is India. You are very close to the Western Heaven."

This made Tangseng happy. He thanked the woodcutter. The monk and disciples turned their faces to the west and continued their journey.

Chapter 87

My dear child, listen to these words!

> The great Dao is hidden and deep
> It becomes large, it becomes small
> Its story frightens gods and ghosts
> It surrounds Heaven and earth
> It divides darkness and light
> It brings happiness to the world
> In front of Vulture Mountain[1]
> Pearls and jewels appear
> They glow with five colors
> They illuminate Heaven and earth
> Those who know it will live as long as mountains and seas

After Tangseng and the woodcutter were rescued, the four travelers continued walking westward. After a few days they came to a large walled city.

"Wukong," said Tangseng, "have we arrived in India?"

"No," he replied. "The Buddha lives in Thunderclap Monastery in India. It's located on a great mountain called Vulture Mountain, but there is no city there. But I do think we are close to the Indian border."

They entered the city. Tangseng got down from his horse. They walked through the streets. They saw that the people all looked hungry and poor. They wore black clothing. Soon they came to a group of officials standing in the road. The officials did not move when the travelers approached, so Zhu shouted, "Get out of the way!"

This frightened the officials. One of them bowed and said, "Who are you and where are you from?"

Tangseng, wishing to avoid trouble, replied, "I am a monk sent by the Tang Emperor to worship the Buddha at Thunderclap Mountain, and bring back

---

[1] Vulture Mountain, also known as Holy Eagle Mountain, was the Buddha's favorite retreat in the ancient city of Rajagriha (now called Rajgir) in northeastern India. He gave many famous sermons there, including the Heart Sutra which appears in this book.

holy books to the Tang Empire. Our journey has brought us to this treasure place. We hope we have not insulted you by entering your city."

The official said, "This is Fengxian, on the eastern border of India. We have had no rain here for several years. The prefect has sent us to put up this sign." He held up a large sign. The travelers looked at it. It said,

> Shangguan, the Prefect of Fengxian, is seeking an enlightened Dharma master to help us. We have had no rain for many years. The rivers are dry, and there is no water in the wells. The rich have very little to eat, and the poor are dying. A picul of rice costs a hundred pieces of silver. Girls are sold for three pints of rice; boys are given away to anyone who will take them. The rich are selling their things to buy food, but the poor are becoming bandits and thieves. I am looking for a wise man to pray for rain and help the people of this city. You will receive a thousand pieces of silver if you can bring rain. This I promise!

Tangseng said to his disciples, "If any of you know how to bring rain, do it and save these people. If you don't, then we must be on our way."

Sun Wukong asked, "What's so hard about bringing rain? I can turn rivers upside down. I can move stars and mountains. I can kick the sky and push the moon. Bringing rain is easy."

Two of the officials heard this. They ran to tell the prefect, "Your Excellency, we were carrying your sign to the marketplace. We met four monks. They said that they have come from the Tang Empire in the east and are headed towards Thunderclap Mountain to worship the Buddha. They say that they can bring rain!"

The prefect jumped up from his chair. Not waiting for a sedan chair, he hurried to the marketplace. He walked up to Tangseng and his three ugly disciples. Showing no fear, he kowtowed and said, "I am Shangguan, the prefect of this city. I beg you to pray for rain to save these people."

Tangseng bowed and said, "Sir, we cannot talk here in the street. Please take us to a monastery."

The prefect led them back to his home. He ordered that tea and vegetarian food be brought to the guests. When the food arrived they all ate, but Zhu ate like a hungry tiger. The servants brought bowl after bowl of soup, and plate after plate of rice. Finally he was full and he stopped eating.

When the meal was over, Tangseng asked the prefect why there was no rain. The prefect replied, "It has not rained here for three years. The grass does not grow, the five grains have all died. Two thirds of the people are now dead. For the rest, their lives are like a candle flame in the wind. We are fortunate that you have come to visit us. If you can bring an inch of rain, you will receive a thousand silver coins."

Sun Wukong laughed and said, "If you offer us silver, you will not get even a drop of rain. But if you practice compassion and honor the Buddha, Old Monkey will give you plenty of rain."

"Of course," replied the prefect, bowing to him. "I will never turn my back on these things."

Sun Wukong stood up and said some magic words. Soon a dark cloud appeared in the east and moved until it was in front of the house. This was Aoguang, the ancient dragon of the Eastern Ocean. Aoguang took on human form and walked up to the monkey. Bowing low, he asked, "Great Sage, why have you sent for this poor dragon?"

"Please rise, my friend," said Sun Wukong. "Thank you for coming here. This place has had no rain for three years. Would you please send some rain?"

Aoguang replied, "I can certainly make rain, but I would never dare to do so without Heaven's command. Also, I must have my Heavenly warriors here to help me. Now I will go back to the Eastern Ocean to get my warriors. You must go to the palace of Heaven. Ask the Jade Emperor to command the rain, and ask the officials to release the dragons. Then I will bring the rain that the Emperor commands."

Aoguang returned to the ocean. Sun Wukong told Zhu and Sha to guard Tangseng. Then he vanished.

"Where did the monkey go?" asked the frightened prefect.

"He has gone up to Heaven on a cloud," replied Zhu, smiling. The prefect then commanded all the people of the city to worship the dragons. He also told them to place willow sprigs in jars of clean water and place them in front of their gates.

Sun Wukong arrived at the Western Gate of Heaven. He was met by Heavenly King Protector. He said to the king, "My master and I have arrived at the city of Fengxian on the border of India. It has not rained there for three years. I asked Aoguang the Dragon King to bring rain, but he tells me that he cannot do it without a command from the Jade Emperor."

The Heavenly King Protector opened the gate. Sun Wukong went through the gate and flew to the Hall of Brightness where he was met by the four Heavenly teachers. He told the same story to the four teachers. One of the teachers said, "But it's not supposed to rain there!"

"Maybe it is, maybe it isn't. But please let me ask the Jade Emperor for myself."

The four teachers brought Sun Wukong to the Hall of Divine Mists. They said to the Jade Emperor, "Your Majesty, Sun Wukong has arrived at the city of Fengxian on the border of India. He wants it to rain there."

The Jade Emperor told Sun Wukong, "Three years ago, on the twenty-fifth day of the twelfth month, we were traveling through the three worlds. We came to the city of Fengxian. We saw the prefect, Shangguan. We saw him knock over the Heavenly offerings and feed them to the dogs. Then he said evil words about us. Because of that, we set up three things in the Hall of Fragrance." Turning to the four teachers, he said, "Take Sun Wukong to see these three things." Then to Sun Wukong he said, "When the prefect has done what we asked, we will give the command. Until then, mind your own business."

The four teachers led the monkey to the Hall of Fragrance. He saw three things. On the left was a mountain of rice a hundred feet high. Beside the mountain was a chicken about the size of a fist, occasionally eating a bit of rice. In the middle was a mountain of noodles two hundred feet high. Beside this mountain was a small golden-haired dog, occasionally licking a noodle with its tongue. And on the right was a large golden padlock about fifteen inches high. It hung from an iron rod. Just below the padlock was a small candle. The candle flame just touched the bottom of the padlock.

Sun Wukong did not understand what he was seeing. "What is this?" he asked the teachers.

"The Jade Emperor set this up after he saw what the prefect did. When the chicken has eaten all the rice, when the dog has eaten all the noodles, and when the lamp has melted the lock, then it will rain in Fengxian."

Sun Wukong's face turned pale. He said nothing. He turned to leave the hall. "Don't feel bad, Great Sage," said one of the teachers. "If the prefect has a single thought of kindness and goodness, the rice mountain and noodle mountain will collapse and the lock will be broken. Perhaps you will be able to persuade the prefect to turn to the path of kindness and goodness."

Sun Wukong flew quickly back to the prefect's house. He entered the main office. Many people crowded around him asking him questions. He ignored them. He shouted at the prefect, "Do you know why there is no rain here? It's because three years ago, on the twenty fifth day of the twelfth month, you did something that angered Heaven and earth. That's why there is no rain, and that's why your people are suffering. Why did you knock over the Heavenly offerings and feed them to the dogs?"

The prefect said, "It is true. On that day I was making offerings to Heaven. My wife and I were arguing. In my anger I knocked over the table of offerings. The food fell on the floor. I called the dogs to eat it. I did not know that Heaven would know about this. Please, what can I do now?"

"The Jade Emperor has set up three things in the Hall of Fragrance in Heaven. There is a mountain of rice with a small chicken eating a little bit from time to time. There is a mountain of noodles with a small dog taking a bit from time to time. And there is a lock with a candle burning underneath it. It will rain here when the chicken finishes eating the rice, the dog finishes eating all the noodles, and the candle burns through the lock."

Zhu said, "That's no problem, brother. Take me with you. I can eat all the rice and the noodles, and I can break the lock."

"Don't be an idiot," replied Sun Wukong. "This was set up by the Emperor. You won't get near that place."

"Then what can we do?" asked Tangseng.

Sun Wukong said to the prefect, "Your Excellency, I was told that if your heart turns to goodness, the problem will be solved. If you don't, then your life cannot be saved."

The prefect kneeled on the ground and said, "I will do as you say, great teacher." Then he ordered all the Buddhist and Daoist monks to prepare their ceremonies. He led his people in burning incense and worshipping. He asked Tangseng to recite sutras. And he asked every family to burn incense and pray to Buddha.

After a couple of days of this, Sun Wukong felt it was time to return to Heaven. He told Zhu and Sha to look after Tangseng. Then he flew straight to the Western Gate of Heaven. He said to the Heavenly King Protector, "The prefect has returned to the right path." Several messengers arrived a moment later, bringing letters written by the Buddhist and Daoist monks. The king allowed the messengers to carry the letters to the Hall of Brightness to give to the Jade Emperor.

Sun Wukong started to follow the messengers, but the Heavenly King Protector stopped him, saying, "Great Sage, you do not need to see the Jade Emperor again. You should go to the Office of the Seasons in the Ninth Heaven. There you can borrow some thunder gods."

The monkey king agreed with this. He went to the Office of the Seasons in the Ninth Heaven. He said to one of the officials there, "I wish to see the Heavenly Honored One."

The Heavenly Honored One came into the room and greeted Sun Wukong. Then the monkey said, "I have a favor to ask you. I am assisting the Tang monk in his journey to the west. We have come to the city of Fengxian. It has not rained there for three years. I have promised to make it rain. But I need help from some of your thunder gods."

The Heavenly Honored One replied, "I have heard that the prefect has angered the Emperor, and that three things have been set up. Nobody has told me that rain is due to fall there."

"Those three things are the mountain of rice, the mountain of noodles, and the golden lock. They are still set up, and rain cannot fall in Fengxian until those things fall. But the four Heavenly teachers told me that Heaven will help the prefect if he begins to do good in the world. Good things are starting to happen in Fengxian. I believe the Emperor will allow rain to fall soon. That is why I am asking for your thunder gods to help bring the rain."

"All right, Great Sage, you can have four thunder gods and Mother Lightning."

Sun Wukong flew back to Fengxian with the thunder gods and Mother Lightning. When they came near the city, the thunder gods began to use their magic. Truly, there was

Lightning like snakes of purple gold
Thunder like a million sleeping insects awakening
Bright light like flying flames
Thunder that smashes mountain caves
Arrows that light up the Heavens
Noise that shakes the earth
Red gold that wakens seeds under the ground
It shakes rivers and mountains for three thousand miles

The people of the city all fell to their knees, held burning incense, held willow sprigs in their hands, and said, "We submit to the Buddha!"

While the storm was beginning in Fengxian, the messengers came into the Hall of Mist and submitted the letters to the Jade Emperor. The Emperor looked at the letters, then said to his officials, "Go and see what has happened to the three things." The officials went to the Hall of Fragrance and saw that the rice mountain and noodle mountain had both collapsed and the lock was broken.

Just then, the local god and the city god came in. They bowed to the Emperor and said, "Our prefect and every person in the city is now worshipping the Buddha and Heaven. Please show compassion and send rain to save the people."

The Jade Emperor was pleased. He said, "Let the gods of wind, cloud and rain go to the city of Fengxian. Let the clouds cover the sky, let the thunder roar, and let three feet and forty-two drops of rain fall."

The rain began to fall. There were thick clouds, black mist, crashing thunder and flashing of lightning. The land was dark for a thousand miles. The rain fell, filling the rivers and seas. It pounded on roofs and windows. It flooded the streets. Dry grasses turned green and withered trees began to grow new leaves. The five grains began to grow again in the farms. Farmers went to work in the fields. Truly, when the wind and rain come, the people are happy. When the rivers and seas are quiet, the world is at peace.

Exactly three feet and forty-two drops of rain fell. The weather gods were getting ready to leave, but Sun Wukong stopped them. He said, "Gods, please stay for a minute. Please show yourselves to the prefect so that he will see you and make offerings to Heaven."

And so,

> The dragon king appeared
> The thunder gods were revealed
> The cloud boys were seen
> The lords of the wind came down
> The dragon king appeared
> With a silver beard and an ashen face
> The thunder gods were revealed
> With powerful bodies and crooked mouths
> The cloud boys were seen
> With gold crowns over jade faces
> The lords of the wind came down
> With large eyes and bushy eyebrows
> The people looked up
> They burned incense and kowtowed
> The people looked up and saw the gods and Heavenly generals
> Cleansing their hearts as they all turned to goodness

The gods and Heavenly generals stayed for two hours while the people kowtowed and prayed. Finally Sun Wukong said, "Thank you for your help. You may now return. But please send wind every five days and rain every ten days." The gods agreed, and they returned to Heaven.

The travelers wanted to leave that day. But the prefect asked them to stay while a temple was built in their honor. So they stayed. The temple was built very quickly. After half a month it was finished. Tangseng named it the Temple of Salvation by Rain. From that day forward, monks came from far and near to pray and burn incense at the temple. The prefect also built temples for the thunder gods and dragon gods to thank them.

Finally, the travelers could stay no longer. The prefect and his officials had tears in their eyes as they watched them leave.

Chapter 88

As Tangseng and his disciples continued their journey to the west, summer gave way to autumn. Leaves turned red. The nights were cool, the stars were bright in the sky, and the moon shone white in the windows.

One day they saw the walls of a great city. "Wukong," said Tangseng, "there is another city. I wonder what it is?"

"We have never seen this city before," he responded, "so how could I know? Let's find out."

Just then, an old man came out from behind some trees. He was holding a wooden staff and wore straw sandals. Tangseng got down from his horse and greeted the man. The man returned the greeting and asked, "Where are you from, sir?"

"I am a poor monk set by the Tang Emperor to worship the Buddha and fetch holy scriptures. Can you tell us what city we see in the distance?"

"Master, you are in India. This is the Jade Flower Kingdom. The lord of our city is a prince, a relative of the King of India. He is a good man. He respects both Buddhist and Daoist priests, and cares about the people. If you see him, he will treat you with respect." And then the man walked back into the forest.

The travelers walked a little bit further and entered the city through the main gate. There were many people in the streets. There were stores, wine shops and tea houses. It looked like a prosperous city.

Tangseng thought to himself, "I have never been to India, but this is really no different from the land of Tang." He saw people buying and selling, and he heard that one could buy a picul of rice for just four tenths of an ounce of silver, and a catty of oil for just a penny. Truly this was a prosperous city!

They walked through the city until they arrived at the prince's palace. "Wait here," said Tangseng to the disciples. "I will ask the prince to sign our travel rescript. If he offers me a meal, I will send for you to share it. While you wait, you can go to that hostel over there and get some grain for the horse."

Soon Tangseng was invited inside the palace to see the prince. He handed his travel rescript to the prince. The prince looked at it. He saw many signatures from many countries. He signed it and returned it to Tangseng. "Great teacher," he said, "you have passed through many countries. How long have you been traveling?"

"I have already seen fourteen winters and summers on my journey," replied Tangseng. "I have met thousands of monsters, and I cannot tell you how much suffering."

The prince ordered a meal to be prepared for his visitor. Tangseng asked that his three disciples be invited to share in the meal. But when the prince's ministers went outside, they could not see anyone. So they walked across the street to the hostel. "Who are the disciples of the Tang monk?" they asked. "His Royal Highness has invited them to a meal."

Zhu heard the word "meal" and jumped up, saying, "We are! We are!"

This terrified the hostel's workers. They shouted, "A pig demon! A pig demon!"

Monkey grabbed Zhu and told him to be quiet. The hostel's workers saw him and shouted, "A monkey spirit! A monkey spirit!"

Sha raised his hands and tried to tell them not to be frightened. But the hostel's workers saw him and shouted, "A kitchen god! A kitchen god!"

Finally the three disciples just walked out of the hostel. They followed the ministers back to the palace. The prince was also frightened when he saw them, but Tangseng said, "Don't be frightened, Your Royal Highness. They are ugly and they do not know how to act in polite company, but they have good hearts."

The palace servants brought out the food and everyone ate. Later, the prince returned to his own rooms. His three sons saw that his face was pale. "What has frightened you, Father?" they asked.

"A monk has arrived from the Great Tang in the East. I invited him to eat with us. He said he had three disciples, so I invited them to eat with us also. They are all very ugly, they look like demons. That's why I look so pale."

Now, these three young men were all skilled fighters. They jumped up and said to their father, "These must be evil spirits from the mountains. We will fetch our weapons and see what they are." The eldest picked up a rod, the second picked up a nine-toothed rake, and the youngest picked up a staff. They ran through the palace shouting, "Where are the monsters?"

"They are having a vegetarian meal in the pavilion," replied the kitchen master.

The three young men ran into the pavilion and shouted, "Are you men or monsters? Tell us now and we will let you live."

Tangseng saw them and was so frightened that he dropped his bowl. He said, "I am a poor monk, not a monster."

The princes said, "Yes, you look like a man. But the three ugly ones are definitely monsters."

Sun Wukong said, "We are all human. Our faces may be ugly but our hearts are good. Now, where are you from and why are you speaking such foolish words?"

The kitchen master said quietly, "These are the sons of His Royal Highness."

"Well, Your Highnesses," said Zhu, "why are you carrying those weapons? Do you want a fight?" The second prince tried to hit Zhu with his rake, but Zhu just laughed. He pulled out his own rake from his belt and swung it around over his head. Ten thousand beams of golden light came from the rake. The prince was so frightened that he dropped his own rake.

The oldest of the young princes was holding a rod. Sun Wukong took his own rod out of his ear and whispered, "Change!" It grew to be as thick as a rice bowl and twelve feet long. He slammed it into the ground, pushing it three feet into the dirt. "Here," he said, "take my rod. Go ahead." The young prince grabbed the monkey's rod but he could not move it at all.

The youngest prince attacked Sha with his staff. Sha easily dodged the blow, then whipped out his own staff. Bright colored lights came from the staff. Everyone stopped what they were doing to look at the lights. Then the three young princes dropped their weapons, kowtowed, and said, "Great teachers, we are sorry that we did not recognize you. Please show us how you use these weapons."

The three disciples put on a show for the young princes. Sun Wukong jumped up on to a golden cloud and swung his golden hoop rod rapidly until it was moving too quickly to be seen. Zhu swung his rake up and down, left and right, forward and backward, filling the air with a howling wind. And Sha showed them 'Red Phoenix Facing the Sun' and 'Hungry Tiger Seizing Its Prey,' his staff glowing with a golden light. Then they came back down to the ground, bowed to Tangseng, and sat down again.

The young princes ran back to the palace. They said to their father, "Did you see the three dancers in the sky? Those were not gods or immortals. They were the three ugly disciples of the Tang monk. Their skills are wonderful. We want them to be our teachers, so we can learn their skills and protect our country. What do you think?" The old prince agreed that this would be a good idea.

The old prince and his three sons hurried to the pavilion. The four travelers were getting ready to leave. The old prince said to Tangseng, "Tang master, I want to ask you a favor. When I first saw you and your disciples, I thought you were just men. But now I see that you are immortals and Buddhas. My wretched sons wish to become your disciples and learn some of your fighting skills. I beg you to agree. If you do, I will give you all the riches of this city."

Sun Wukong laughed and said, "Your Royal Highness, you don't understand. We are happy to take your sons as disciples. But we do not want any of your riches." The old prince was very happy. He ordered a great banquet in the main hall of the palace. There was singing, dancing, music, and wonderful vegetarian food.

The next day, the three young princes came to see Sun Wukong, Zhu and Sha. The princes asked, "May we have a look at your weapons?" Zhu threw his rake on the ground. Sha leaned his staff against a nearby wall. Two of the young princes tried to pick up the weapons, but they could not move them at all. It was like a butterfly trying to move a stone pillar.

Zhu smiled and said, "My rake is not heavy. It's 5,048 pounds including the handle[1]."

---

[1] This number probably is inspired by a famous collection of Buddhist teachings, the *Digest of the Catalog of Buddhist Teachings Compiled During the Kaiyuan Reign of the Great Tang*, completed in 730 A.D. during the Tang Dynasty. It consists of 5,048 volumes.

Sha added, "My staff is also 5,048 pounds."

"And what about your weapon, Great Sage?" they asked Sun Wukong.

He answered,

> "This rod was made at the beginning of time
> It was made by Great Yu himself[1]
> He used it to find the depth of rivers and seas
> Later it floated to the gate of the Eastern Ocean
> It rested there and glowed with a colored light
> I found the rod and made it my own
> I can make it grow to fill the universe
> I can make it as small as a tiny pin
> It is the only one in Heaven and Earth
> It weights 13,500 pounds
> It can bring life or death
> It can defeat dragons and tigers
> It can kill monsters and demons
> It helped me when I made trouble in Heaven
> Heaven and earth, gods and demons all fear it
> It comes from the birth of time
> This is no ordinary iron rod!"

The young princes all begged to learn how to use the three weapons. But Sun Wukong said, "We can teach you, but you are not strong enough to use these weapons. The ancients say, 'A badly drawn tiger just looks like a dog.' You need to be strong to use these weapons."

This made the three young princes very happy. They washed their hands, brought in an incense table, lit the incense sticks, and bowed to Heaven. Then they asked the teachers to teach them.

Sun Wukong, Zhu and Sha all bowed to Tangseng and asked his permission to teach the young princes. Tangseng agreed. Then Sun Wukong led the three young princes into a quiet room behind the pavilion. He told them to lie down and close their eyes. Then he said some magic words and blew a magic breath

---

[1] Yu the Great, sometimes called "Great Yu Who Controlled the Waters," was a legendary king in ancient China. He labored for thirteen years to build China's first system of flood control. Emperor Shun was so impressed that he passed over his own son to name Yu as emperor at age 53. Yu reigned for 45 years.

into their hearts. This gave them new muscles and bones. When he was finished, the young princes could pick up any of the three heavy weapons with no trouble at all.

The next day, the three disciples began to teach the young princes. The young princes were now able to pick up the weapons, but they had difficulty using them. Also, the weapons were magic. They changed form as the princes were trying to use them. At the end of the day, the princes said, "Thank you for showing us how to use these weapons. But it is very difficult for us to use them. We would like to make three new weapons. They would look like your weapons but would be made of ordinary steel. Would that be all right with you?"

"Sure," said Zhu. "We need to use our weapons anyway, to protect the Dharma and defeat monsters." So the princes called for ironsmiths. The ironsmiths brought ten thousand pounds of iron. Working in the courtyard, they melted the iron and began to make steel. When the steel was ready, they asked the three disciples to bring out their weapons so they could be copied. The three disciples left their weapons in the courtyard for the ironsmiths to look at.

But trouble was nearby. An evil spirit lived on Leopard Head Mountain in Tiger Mouth Cave about twenty-five miles away. He saw the light from the ironsmiths' fires and came to see what was happening in the courtyard. He saw the three magic weapons lying in the courtyard. "Wonderful weapons!" he exclaimed. "This is my lucky day. I will take them." He created a powerful wind, picked up the weapons, and carried them back to his cave.

Truly,

> You cannot leave the Dao
> The Dao that can be left is not the true Dao[1]
> When the Heavenly weapons are stolen
> The work of the disciples is in vain

---

[1] This is taken almost word for word from the beginning of the Doctrine of the Mean, written by Zisi, grandson of Confucius: "The path may not be left for an instant. If it could be left, it would not be the path."

Chapter 89

The next morning the ironsmiths came to the courtyard to begin their work. But the magic weapons were gone. The ironsmiths looked everywhere but could not find them. They went to the princes, kowtowed, and said, "Young masters, we don't know what happened to the weapons."

The princes ran to tell the three disciples. They all returned to the courtyard and saw that the weapons were gone. Zhu was angry. He said to the ironsmiths, "You stole our weapons! Give them back right now or I will kill you all."

But the ironsmiths cried and kowtowed, saying, "Your Lordship, we all went to sleep last night, we were so tired. This morning we came to work and saw that the weapons were gone. We are not gods, we are just men. We could not move these heavy weapons."

Sun Wukong said, "This is our fault. We should not have left the weapons here last night. I think a monster came and stole them."

The disciples stood in the courtyard and argued for a while. Then the old prince arrived. He said to them, "Nobody here stole your weapons. Your weapons are magic. Even a hundred people could not move them. Besides, the people in this city are good, they would not steal anything from you."

Sun Wukong said, "Your Royal Highness, tell me, are there any evil monsters living nearby?"

"Well, yes. North of the city is Leopard Head Mountain. In that mountain is Tiger Mouth Cave. I have heard that a monster lives in that cave."

Sun Wukong was pleased to hear this! He told Zhu and Sha to stay and take care of Tangseng and the city. Then he jumped into the air and used his cloud somersault to fly quickly to Leopard Head Mountain. He looked around. He heard voices and saw two wolf-headed monsters walking and talking to each other. He turned into a butterfly and followed them.

He heard one of them say, "Our master is so lucky! Last month he met a beautiful woman and she is now living with him in the cave. And last night he found three magic weapons. Tomorrow there will be a Rake Festival, that will be fun!"

The other monster replied, "You and I are also lucky. Our master gave us twenty taels of silver to buy pigs and sheep for the festival. Let's get a bottle of wine. When we buy the pigs and sheep, we can keep two or three *taels* for ourselves. We can use that money to buy warm jackets for the winter."

Sun Wukong heard their words. He fluttered ahead of them on the path. Then he turned back into his original form. When the monsters came close, he said a few magic words. The monsters stopped moving. They could not move and they could not speak. Sun Wukong walked over to them. He took the twenty *taels* of silver from one of them. He saw that they both were carrying passes. Their names were "Shifty Freaky" and "Freaky Shifty." He took the passes.

Sun Wukong returned to the palace. He told everyone what he had seen. "Zhu, you turn yourself into Shifty Freaky. I will turn into Freaky Shifty. Sha, you will be a trader selling pigs and sheep. We will go to Tiger Mouth Cave, grab our weapons, and kill the monsters. Then we can continue our journey."

"But how can I turn into Shifty Freaky?" asked Zhu. "I've never met him." So Sun Wukong blew a magic breath on the pig, and now the pig looked just like Shifty Freaky. He changed himself to look like Freaky Shifty. Sha dressed himself so he looked like a trader. Then the three of them walked towards the cave, driving pigs and sheep ahead of them.

As they walked along the path, they met another demon. His name was Greenface. He had red hair like fire, a red nose, sharp teeth, big ears, and a green face. He wore a yellow tunic and straw sandals. He was carrying a small box. When he saw the three disciples he called out, "Freaky Shifty, good to see you! Did you get some pigs and sheep?"

"Of course," replied Sun Wukong. "Can't you see them?"

"Who's that?" said the demon, pointing to Sha.

"He's a trader. We owe him some silver, so we are going home to get it for him. What's in the box?"

"These are invitations to the Rake Festival. It's tomorrow morning. Our chief will be there, and about forty other guests. Look for yourself." The demon picked up one of the invitations and showed it to Sun Wukong. It read,

Oh great one, Ninefold Spiritual Sage, I hope you can join us tomorrow
for the Rake Festival. I hope you will not refuse. With gratitude, your
grandson Yellow Lion kowtows a hundred times.

Sun Wukong gave the invitation back to Greenface. The demon walked away
down the mountain path. When he was gone, Sun Wukong told the others
what the invitation said. Then they continued walking until they reached the
cave. Just outside the cave a crowd of little demons played under the trees.
When the little demons saw the pigs and sheep, they caught them and tied
them up. The demon king heard the noise and came outside.

"So, you're back," he said. "How many pigs and sheep did you buy?"

Sun Wukong replied, "Eight pigs and seven sheep. The pigs cost us sixteen
taels of silver, the sheep nine taels. You gave us twenty taels, so we owe this
trader five taels."

The demon king told one of the little demons, "Go and get five taels for this
trader."

"My lord," said Sun Wukong, "I told the dealer that he could stay for the
banquet. He's hungry and thirsty."

"Damn you, Freaky Shifty, I sent you to buy some pigs and sheep, not to
invite people to our banquet." Handing the five taels to the trader, he said,
"Here's your silver. Come with me to the back of the cave and get something
to eat and drink. But don't touch anything, and don't tell anyone what you see
here."

They walked into the back of the cave. There on a table was Zhu's nine-
toothed rake, glowing with many colors. Next to it was Monkey's golden
hoop rod, and at the end of the table was Sha's staff. As soon as Zhu saw the
rake, he could not stop himself. He grabbed it and changed back to his own
form. He ran towards the demon king, swinging the rake in the air. Sun
Wukong and Sha also grabbed their weapons and changed back to their own
forms.

The demon king ran and grabbed his own weapon, a four-light shovel[1] with a
long handle and a sharp end. "Who are you to steal my treasures?" he

---

[1] The four lights may refer to the four openings in Daoist sacred mountains, which
allow light from the sun, moon, stars and constellations to shine through.

shouted.

Sun Wukong shouted at him, "I'll get you, you hairy beast! You don't know me. I'm a disciple of the Tang monk. When we came here, the prince told his three sons to ask us for fighting lessons. They were making their own weapons to look like ours. We left our weapons in the courtyard overnight. You stole them! And now you say that we are stealing your treasures. Stay there and taste my rod!"

What a fight!

> The rod was like the wind
> The rake came down like rain
> The staff filled the sky with fog
> The demon's four-light shovel gave off white clouds
> The three disciples showed their power
> The evil spirit should not have stolen their treasures

They fought until the sun was low in the west. After a while, the demon became tired and could not fight any more. He ran out of the cave and flew like the wind to the southeast.

Zhu started to fly after him, but Sun Wukong said, "Let him go. Let's leave him nothing to come back to." They killed all the little demons in the cave. When the little demons died, they turned into tigers, wolves, tigers, leopards, deer and goats. Sha found some dry wood and lit it. Zhu flapped his ears to help the fire grow. It burned everything in the cave. Then they carried some of the dead animals back to the city.

They met the old prince and told him everything. The prince was happy to hear that they'd won the fight, but he was afraid that the demon king would return to the city later and cause trouble.

"Don't worry, Your Highness," said Sun Wukong. "This morning we learned that there will be a banquet tomorrow. One of the guests will be a demon named Ninefold Spiritual Sage. I think this is the demon king's grandfather. The demon king's name is Yellow Lion. I think the demon king has gone to see his grandfather. And I think they will return tomorrow to get their revenge." The old prince thanked him. They all had dinner and went to bed.

Now, Yellow Lion did indeed go to see his grandfather. He flew all night and arrived at his grandfather's cave around the time of the last watch when the sun was rising in the east. He went inside. When he saw his grandfather, he prostrated himself on the ground and cried.

"Worthy grandson, why are you crying?" asked Ninefold Spiritual Sage. "I was just getting ready to come to your banquet."

"There will be no banquet today," cried the demon king. "I wanted to have a banquet to show you the three fine weapons I found. I sent two of my servants to buy some sheep and pigs for the banquet. They returned with the animals, and they brought a third man with them, a trader. The trader was hungry so I gave him something to eat. When he saw the weapons, all three of them changed into terrible demons and began to fight me. One had a hairy face and looked like a thunder god. One had a long snout and big ears. And the third was a big man with a scary face. They said that they are disciples of the Tang monk who is traveling to the west. They are all very good fighters. I could not win. So I came here to see you. If you love your grandson, please help me get revenge on these three."

The grandfather was silent for a minute, then he said, "Grandson, you were wrong to mess with these three. The one with the big ears is Zhu Bajie. The big man is Sha Wujing. They're not too bad. But the one with the hairy face is Sun Wukong. Five hundred years ago he caused trouble in Heaven, and a hundred thousand soldiers could not stop him. Why did you anger him? Well, never mind. I'll help you."

Yellow Lion kowtowed his thanks. Ninefold Spiritual Sage called six more of his grandsons, all of them lion demons. The eight of them traveled with the wind, arriving quickly at Leopard Head Mountain. But when they got to the cave, all they saw was smoke and fire. In front of the cave, Shifty Freaky and Freaky Shifty were sitting on the ground, crying.

"Are you really Shifty Freaky and Freaky Shifty?" shouted Yellow Lion.

"It's really us," they replied, still crying. "Yesterday we met a monk with a face like a thunder god. He said some magic words and after that we could not move. He stole our silver and our passes. This morning we could finally move. We came here and saw that everything in the cave was burned."

Yellow Lion stamped his foot on the ground and shouted, "Evil beasts! How could you do this? You burned my cave and killed everyone, even my girlfriend. I'm so angry I could die!" Then he threw himself against the side of the mountain, banging his head against the rocky wall. He only stopped when two of his brothers grabbed him. Then they all left the cave and flew towards the city.

The people in the city looked up and saw a cloud of angry demons flying towards them. They all ran inside and locked their doors. The old prince saw the flying demons and asked, "What should we do?"

"Don't worry about that," replied Sun Wukong. "It's just that evil spirit from Tiger Mouth Cave, and that guy who calls himself Ninefold Spiritual Sage, and maybe a few other demons. No problem. Tell everyone to stay in their homes. We will take care of it." Then he flew into the sky, with Zhu and Sha, to battle the demons.

Chapter 90[1]

The three disciples saw the cloud of demons coming towards them. In front was the demon king called Yellow Lion. His six brothers were behind him. In the middle was the nine headed lion called Ninefold Spiritual Sage. The demon Greenface held a canopy of flowers above the nine-headed lion. On each side, Shifty Freaky and Freaky Shifty carried red flags.

When they got closer, Zhu shouted at the lions, "Monsters! Thieves! Treasure stealers!"

Yellow Lion shouted back, "Why did you burn my cave and kill my family? My hatred is as great as the ocean. Stay there and taste my four-light shovel!"

Now the battle began. Yellow Lion and two of his brothers fought Zhu. The other four lions attacked Sha and Sun Wukong. What a fight!

> Seven lions with seven powerful weapons
> Shouting as they surround the three monks
> The Great Sage's rod is powerful
> Sha's staff has no equal in the world
> Zhu's rake emits a bright colorful light
> They battle against the seven lions
> In the city the prince's soldiers beat drums and gongs
> They fight in the sky until Heaven and earth turn dark

The battle lasted for half a day. As night came, Zhu grew tired. He tried to fly away but he was caught by two of the lion demons. They carried him to Ninefold Spiritual Sage and said, "Grandfather, we caught one of them!"

Meanwhile, Sun Wukong and Sha battled the other five lion demons. They

---

[1] Each chapter in this novel has a title as well as a number. To keep things simple we have not shown the chapter titles in these books. But the title of this chapter is a fun one. It's 师狮授受同归一盗道缠禅静九灵 (shī shī shòu shòu tóng guī yī dào dào chán chán jìng jiǔ líng). As you can see, it's a series of word pairs that have the same sound. For example, 师狮 is shī shī and means "teachers and lions." 授受 is shòu shòu and means "give and receive," and so on. The whole title is somewhat cryptic but could be translated as "Teachers and lions, giving and receiving, return to the One. Thieves and Dao, entangled in meditation, pacify the Ninefold Spirit."

caught two lion demons but the others escaped.

Ninefold Spiritual Sage saw this. He said, "Tie up the pig but don't kill him. When they give us our lions back, we will give them the pig. If not, then we will kill him."

Sun Wukong and Sha brought their two lion prisoners back to the city. Soldiers tied them up. Tangseng asked if Zhu was still alive. "Yes," replied Sun Wukong, "but don't worry. We will trade the two lions for Zhu tomorrow. They won't hurt him."

At dawn the next day, Ninefold Spiritual Sage told Yellow Lion his plan. "You must capture the monkey and the other monk. I will try to capture their master, the old prince, and his three sons. We will all meet in my cave afterwards."

So Yellow Lion and his four brothers went back to fight Sun Wukong and Sha. The battle filled the sky. It knocked down trees, frightened tigers and wolves, and worried gods and demons. While they fought in the sky, Ninefold Spiritual Sage flew to the city. He shook his nine lion heads, frightening the soldiers on guard. Then he used five of his mouths to grab Tangseng, the old prince, and the three young princes. He carried them to the place where Zhu was being held prisoner. He opened another one of his mouths and grabbed Zhu.

Now six of his mouths were holding prisoners. With his other three mouths, he shouted to his grandsons, "I have my prisoners, I am leaving now!" The other lions fought even harder against Sun Wukong and Sha. But Sun Wukong pulled all the hairs from his arm, chewed them, and spat them out. The hairs turned into a thousand little monkeys. All the little monkeys attacked the lions. This was too much for the lions. The little monkeys killed Yellow Lion and captured the other four lions. Freaky Shifty, Shifty Freaky and Greenface escaped.

Sun Wukong carried the lions back to the city. The soldiers opened up the city gates. They tied up the four lions and put them with the other two lion prisoners. Sun Wukong said to the soldiers, "Skin the Yellow Lion. Make sure the other six lions can't escape. And bring us some dinner."

The next morning, Sun Wukong and Sha flew to Bamboo Mountain where Ninefold Spiritual Sage lived. They stopped and looked around. Suddenly they saw Greenface. "Where are you going?" shouted Sun Wukong. Greenface turned to run away, but he fell down a ravine. The two monks went down into the ravine to look for him. They could not find him, but they found a cave entrance with a pair of stone gates. Above the gates was a sign saying, "Bamboo Mountain. Nine Bend Cave."

Inside the cave, Greenface reported to Ninefold Spiritual Sage, "My lord, there are two ugly monks outside. But I haven't seen any of your grandsons."

Ninefold Spiritual Sage bowed his head and cried, saying, "This is terrible. My grandsons are probably dead. How will I get my revenge?"

Zhu was tied up nearby. He heard this. He laughed and said, "Don't be sad, old man. My elder brother has won. He has captured all the demons. Now he will rescue us."

Without saying another word, Ninefold Spiritual Sage threw open the stone gates and stepped outside the cave. He opened his mouths and quickly grabbed Sun Wukong and Sha. He brought them into the cave. He said to Sun Wukong, "All right. You have captured my seven grandsons. But I have all four monks and four princes. We can trade. But first, you need to be beaten. Little ones, get started!"

Three of the little demons started beating Sun Wukong with willow rods. But this did not bother him at all. The demons kept beating him all day and into the evening. Finally the old demon said to them, "That's enough for now. Go get something to eat and drink. I'm going to bed."

The three little demons continued to beat Sun Wukong through the night, but after a while they got tired and fell asleep. As soon as they fell asleep, Sun Wukong used his magic to become small. He escaped from the ropes that were holding him. He took his golden hoop rod out of his ear, grew it to twenty feet long, and smashed it down on the heads of the three little demons, killing them instantly.

Ninefold Spiritual Sage heard the noise. He ran into the main hall carrying a lamp. Sun Wukong had to leave quickly. He freed Sha, then he flew out of the cave. Ninefold Spiritual Sage captured Sha and tied him up again.

Sun Wukong flew quickly back to the city. As he was traveling, he was met in mid-air by the Golden Headed Guardian, the Six Gods of Darkness and the Six Gods of Light. They were guarding a local spirit. They said, "Great Sage, we have captured this demon and brought him here for you."

Sun Wukong said, "Why are you here? You should be back at the city, protecting my master."

"Great Sage," they replied, "after you left Nine Bend Cave, the nine-headed lion captured your younger brother Sha again. This lion is very powerful. So we captured this local spirit, he is in charge of Bamboo Mountain where the lion's cave is located. We hope that he knows something about this lion. You may question him if you like."

Sun Wukong looked down at the local spirit. The local spirit trembled and said, "The demon came to Bamboo Mountain the year before last. Nine Bend Cave used to be the home of six lions. When the nine-headed demon came, the lions took him to be their grandfather. If you want to defeat him, you must go to Wonderful Cliff Palace in the east. Find the lion's master and tell him what has happened. Nobody else can help you."

"I know that place," said Sun Wukong. "It is the home of the Celestial Worthy. There is an animal there, a nine headed lion, that lives underneath his throne. I will go there. You all stay here. Protect the city and my master."

Sun Wukong used his cloud somersault to fly up to Heaven. He reached the Eastern Gate of Heaven. King Virupaksa[1] saw him and asked where he was going. He replied, "I am going to Wonderful Cliff Palace in the Eastern Heaven."

"But why?" asked Virupaksa.

"We were traveling to the west. We came to the Jade Flower Kingdom and met the prince of the city. His three sons wanted us to teach them how to use weapons. But our weapons were stolen by a gang of lion monsters. They are holding my master and my brothers prisoner. Now I must ask the Celestial Worthy to subdue the leader of the lion monsters."

"This is your fault. You wanted to be a teacher, and that caused the trouble with the lions."

---

[1] Virupaksa, known in Chinese as Guǎngmù Tiānwáng. is one of the Four Heavenly Kings in Buddhism. He has red skin, wears armor, and often is shown holding a red lasso which he uses to snare people into the Buddhist faith. He can see great distances and knows the karma of sentient beings.

"That's true."

Virupaksa and his soldiers moved aside to let Sun Wukong pass. The monkey king continued on until he reached the Wonderful Cliff Palace. It was a huge building covered with a golden roof. Flowers grew everywhere. Sun Wukong came to the palace gate. A boy saw him. He went to the Celestial Worthy and reported, "My lord, the Great Sage Equal to Heaven who caused trouble in Heaven is here."

The Celestial Worthy came down from his throne to greet Sun Wukong, saying, "Great Sage, I haven't seen you for many years. I heard that you had given up Daoism and you are now a Buddhist. Have you and your master reached the Western Heaven yet?"

"We are getting close. We have come to Jade Flower Kingdom. The prince has three sons. They asked us to teach them how to use our magic weapons. One night, someone stole our weapons. I found out that they were taken by a demon named Yellow Lion. I tried to get the weapons back, but Yellow Lion was joined by six other lion demons, plus a very powerful demon named Ninefold Spiritual Sage. He is a lion with nine heads. Perhaps you know something about him?"

The Celestial Worthy turned his head and told one of his officers to fetch his lionkeeper slave. The officers found the slave asleep on the floor. They dragged him to the throne room. The Celestial Worthy asked him, "Where is my nine headed lion?"

The slave kowtowed and said, "My lord, please don't kill me. I stole a jug of wine and drank it. I must have fallen asleep. The lion escaped."

"You fool. That wine was given to me by the great Laozi. If you drink it, you fall asleep for three days. How many days has the lion been gone?"

Sun Wukong answered, "The Ninefold Spiritual Sage has lived in his cave for two or three years, I think."

"That's right. A day in Heaven is equal to a year in the human world." Then he said to the lionkeeper, "Get up. I will let you live. Come to the human world with the Great Sage and me. We will get the lion."

The three of them returned to Bamboo Mountain. There they met the Six Gods of Darkness and Six Gods of Light. All the gods bowed to the Celestial

Worthy. "Nothing has happened here," they said. "The Ninefold Spiritual Sage was so angry that he went to sleep. He has not harmed the monk or anyone else."

The Celestial Worthy said, "He is a good lion, he would not harm anyone. Great Sage, go to the gates of his cave, call him, and bring him out so we can capture him."

Sun Wukong went to the cave gates and shouted for a while. But the lion demon was asleep and did not hear him. Finally Sun Wukong used his rod to smash the stone gates. This woke up the lion demon. He ran towards Sun Wukong, shouting, "I'm coming for you!" Sun Wukong turned and ran away. The lion demon chased him, shouting, "Where do you think you're going?"

Sun Wukong ran away a little bit, turned, and said, "What, don't you see your master here?"

Just then, the Celestial Worthy said, "I'm here, my little sage." The lion demon looked and saw his master. He stopped running and lay down with all four feet on the ground, kowtowing.

The lionkeeper ran over to him and punched him, saying, "Why did you run away? You caused me a lot of trouble!" He kept punching the lion until his fist was tired. Then he put a rope around the lion's neck, led him onto a colored cloud, and flew back to Wonderful Cliff Palace.

Sun Wukong thanked the Celestial Worthy and the other gods and local spirits. Then he went into the cave and freed the old prince, Tangseng, Zhu, Sha, and the three young princes. They all walked out of the cave. Zhu gathered some dry wood, started a fire, and burned everything in the cave. Sun Wukong told Zhu and Sha to carry the four princes back to the city. Then he and Tangseng walked back to the city. It was dark by the time they arrived at the city. A vegetarian feast was prepared for everyone. Then they all went to bed.

The next day after breakfast, Sun Wukong asked that the six lion prisoners be killed and their meat cut up. The meat of one lion was given to the palace workers. The meat of another lion was given to the palace officers. The meat of the other four lions was cut into very small pieces and given to all the soldiers and citizens of the city. This was to let everyone taste the lion meat and conquer their fear.

The ironsmiths finished their work. They had made a golden hoop rod that weighed a thousand pounds, a nine-toothed rake weighing eight hundred pounds, and a staff weighing eight hundred pounds. The three young princes came out.

Their father said to them, "These weapons almost caused all of us to lose our lives. We are alive thanks to the power of our great teachers. Now the evil demons are gone. We will have no trouble from them anymore."

The travelers stayed in the city for a few more days. The three disciples taught the three young princes how to use their new weapons. The young princes had great strength thanks to some magic from Sun Wukong's breath. They learned quickly, and soon they could use the heavy weapons with great skill.

We have a poem for this:

> They had good luck finding three teachers
> They did not know their studies would bring lion spirits
> Evil is destroyed, the nation is at peace
> The travelers are as one against the bandits
> The nine headed lion's power is gone
> The Way has returned
> The dharma will live forever
> Jade Flower Kingdom will be at peace

The old prince thanked the travelers again and again. He tried to give them gold and silver. But Zhu said, "We cannot take gold or silver. But those lions really tore up our clothes. If you could give us a change of clothing, we would be grateful." The prince gave the command, and new clothing was made quickly. The travelers put on the clothing, gathered their luggage, and set off again.

As they walked down the streets of the city, everyone came out of their houses to say goodbye. Music played, flags fluttered overhead, colored lanterns were hung, and incense was burned.

The travelers reached the western gate of the city. Free from worry, free from thought, they walked towards the land of the Buddha.

Chapter 91

My dear child, how should you practice the Way?

> Cut off the horse's thoughts and the ape's mind[1]
> Bind them tight, they will glow with the five colors
> Let them escape, you will walk the three paths of suffering[2]
> Seek the easy life, Heaven's elixir will leak and your jade will wither.
> Sweep away anger, joy and worry, you will understand the wonderful mystery

After leaving the city, the travelers resumed their journey to the west. They walked for five or six days, then they saw another city.

"This is strange," said Sun Wukong, looking at the city. "I see a flagpole but no flag. Let's go inside and learn more."

Just outside the city gate they came to a busy marketplace with tea houses, wine shops and stores selling rice and oil. The people stared at the Chinese monk and his three disciples，the monkey king Sun Wukong, the pig-man Zhu Bajie, and the tall dark man Sha Wujing. The four travelers ignored them. They continued walking until they came to a monastery with a sign saying, "Mercy Cloud Temple."

"Let's go inside," said Tangseng. "We can rest the horse and beg some food."

They entered the monastery. It was full of people worshipping Buddha and climbing the pagoda. A golden bell was ringing and monks were chanting Buddhist sutras. A monk walked up to Tangseng and asked, "Welcome travelers! Where did you come from?"

Tangseng replied, "This poor monk has traveled from the land of Tang in China. My disciples and I are seeking holy scriptures from the Buddha at Spirit Mountain."

The monk kowtowed to Tangseng. Tangseng, surprised, helped the monk back to his feet and asked why he kowtowed. The monk said, "Great teacher,

---

[1] The poem's first line says that the wandering mind must be brought under control. It refers to the Chinese expression xīn yuán yì mǎ, literally "the mind of an ape, the desire of a horse," that is, a wandering and restless mind.

[2] The three paths of virtue (sān tú) in Buddhism are the paths of fire, swords and blood. But without mental discipline one ends up instead on the three paths of suffering and karmic retribution: the paths of hell, hungry ghosts, and beasts.

in this region the monks chant sutras and pray to Buddha, hoping that in their next life they will be born in China. You are from China, so you must be a great soul."

Tangseng smiled and said, "No, I am just a poor monk who travels and begs for food. You have a quiet and comfortable life here. You are the one who is blessed!" Then he asked, "Tell me, what is the name of this treasure region, and how far away is Spirit Mountain?"

"This is Gold Level Prefecture, on the eastern border of India. We are about two thousand miles from our capital city, but we do not know how far it is to Spirit Mountain."

Tangseng thanked him for telling him this. Then the monk asked Tangseng to stay for a few days to enjoy the Lantern Festival. He said, "Lanterns and lights will be set up, and there will be music all night long." The travelers agreed to stay. Their hosts gave them a vegetarian dinner, then in the evening they all went outside to see the lanterns burning on Golden Lamp Bridge.

The next day they rested and had breakfast and lunch. In the afternoon they went for a walk around the city. And in the evening, they went out again to look at the lanterns burning on Golden Lamp Bridge.

On the third day, Tangseng said, "This poor monk once vowed to sweep out a pagoda every time I came to one. Would you please let me to sweep out your pagoda?" The monk agreed. He opened the pagoda door. Tangseng and Sha went in. Tangseng used a broom to sweep out the first floor. They walked up to the second floor and Tangseng swept it out. They continued like this until they reached the top. They rested for a short time on the top floor, looking out at the city below. Then they walked down to the ground level. By this time it was evening again.

"Great teacher," said the monk, "you have seen our lanterns the last two nights. Tonight is the main festival night. Let's go into the city and watch the lanterns there!"

Tangseng agreed. He and the three disciples walked into the city. What did they see?

    Thousands of lanterns hanging in the marketplace
    In the sky, the moon is like a round silver dish
    The moonlight shines on the lanterns, making them even brighter
    Snowflake lanterns, plum blossom lanterns
    Like bits of ice in spring

Embroidered screen lanterns, painted screen lanterns
Made of every color
Blue lion lanterns, white elephant lanterns
Hanging high on the city walls
Goat lanterns, rabbit lanterns
Bringing the houses to life
Eagle lanterns, phoenix lanterns
Hanging in two long rows
Tiger lanterns, horse lanterns
Carried together down the street
Lanterns on thousands of houses
Making clouds and smoke for miles
Behind curtains beautiful shy girls watch the fun
On the bridge drunken tourists laugh and play
The music and songs continue all night

People were everywhere. Some were dressed as ghosts, others as elephants. Many were dancing and singing.

Tangseng and the others came to the bridge. They saw three huge lanterns with bases the size of large barrels. Surrounding the lanterns were towers made of colored glass. Tangseng asked, "What kind of oil do you burn in these lanterns?"

One of the monks replied, "Great teacher, in our district there are many families. Each year we select 240 families to be 'oil families.' They must make a special oil. Each barrel holds 500 catties of oil, so together 1,500 catties of oil are needed to fill the three barrels. It costs 48,000 taels of silver every year to fill all three barrels."

Sun Wukong asked, "But how can you burn so much oil in just one night?"

"Each lantern has forty-nine wicks. Each wick is as thick as a chicken egg. We light the lanterns, and sometime during the night the Lord Buddhas appear. The oil disappears and the lights go out."

Zhu smiled and said, "Ah, I suppose the Buddhas take all the oil."

"That's right. It has been this way since ancient times." Just then, they heard a howling wind in the sky. All the people ran from the bridge. The monks also ran, shouting, "Great teacher, we need to leave now. The wind has arrived. The Lord Buddhas are coming!"

Tangseng did not move. He said, "This poor monk chants the name of

Buddha and worships Buddha. If there are Buddhas coming here now, I will pray to them."

The monks all ran away. Tangseng looked up and saw three Buddhas flying down from the sky. He ran to the top of the bridge and kowtowed to them. Sun Wukong ran up to him and shouted, "Master, these are not Buddhas, they are evil!" But it was too late. The lamps all went dark and the Tang monk was swept away by the wind.

The three disciples looked everywhere and shouted for Tangseng. The monks asked, "What happened?"

Sun Wukong laughed and replied, "You all have eyes but you cannot see. For years you have been tricked by these three monsters. You thought they were true Buddhas coming to enjoy the oil from the lamps, but they are monsters. Because I was too slow in coming up onto the bridge, they were able to grab my master and take him away. Now I will find him!"

The monkey king quickly jumped up and smelled the air. Smelling a foul odor coming from the northeast, he used his cloud somersault to fly quickly towards the smell. Soon he arrived at a huge mountain, ten thousand feet high. He heard tigers and leopards, he saw deer, and he heard a river flowing swiftly down the mountainside. He looked around but did not see any monsters. But then he saw four men with goats. Looking more closely, he saw that they were the Four Sentinels of Time: Year, Month, Day and Hour.

Quickly he whipped out his Golden Hoop Rod and shouted, "Where do you four think you are going?"

The Four Sentinels quickly replied, "Great Sage, please forgive us. Your master has become a little bit lazy recently. He spent a long time eating and resting in the Mercy Cloud Temple. This weakened his spirit and allowed the monsters to capture him. We were afraid that you would not know where to find him, so we came here to help you."

"If you wanted to help me, what's with the goats?"

"We brought these three goats to remind you of the old saying, 'With three *yang* begins prosperity[1].' This should help your master."

---

[1] This saying refers to the 11th hexagram in the book called yì jīng, known in English as the *I Ching* or *Book of Changes*. This hexagram is called *tai*. It has three broken lines on top representing the feminine *yin* and three solid lines underneath representing the masculine *yang*. This hexagram is associated with the first month of

Sun Wukong put away his rod and asked, "Is this where the monsters live?"

"Yes. The three monsters are named Great King Cold Avoider, Great King Heat Avoider, and Great King Dust Avoider. They have lived here at Green Dragon Mountain for a thousand years. They learned how to make themselves look like Buddhas and trick the people of this region into giving them the special oil. This year they saw your master and knew that eating his flesh would give them immortality. So they plan to kill and eat him soon."

Sun Wukong told the Four Sentinels that they could go. Then he looked around and found the monsters' cave. Its entrance was a stone building with a pair of stone doors. The doors were open. Sun Wukong stuck his head inside

---

the year and the renewal of spring. Of course 羊, *yáng,* is also the Chinese word for goat!

and shouted, "Give me my master at once, you monsters."

Several bull-headed demons came out and shouted at him, "Who are you to yell at us?"

"I am the senior disciple of the Tang monk. We were looking at lanterns when your demon kings carried him off. Now give him back to me. If you don't, I will turn your cave upside down and kill you all."

The bull demons ran inside and told the three demon kings what had just happened. One of the demon kings said, "We've just caught this monk, we haven't even had time to ask him his name and where he is from. Little ones, bring him here so we can question him."

The bull demons grabbed Tangseng and dragged him in front of the demon kings. One of the demon kings said, "Where are you from, and why did you run towards us instead of running away like everyone else?"

Tangseng replied, "Your Majesties, I have been sent by the great Tang Emperor to worship the Lord Buddha and fetch holy scriptures from Thunderclap Monastery. My birth name is Chen Xuanzang. I was given the name Sanzang because there are three rooms full of holy scriptures that I must bring back. But now people simply call me Tangseng. Last night on the bridge I saw Your Majesties coming down from the clouds, and I kowtowed to you because I thought you were real Buddhas."

"Who is traveling to the west with you?"

"I have three disciples. The eldest is called Sun Wukong, he is also called Great Sage Equal to Heaven."

The demon kings were surprised by this. "Is this the Great Sage who made so much trouble in Heaven five hundred years ago?"

"Yes, yes. My second disciple is Zhu Bajie, formerly the Marshal of Heavenly Reeds. And my third disciple is Sha Wujing, the Curtain Raising Captain."

The demon kings told their little demons to lock up Tangseng with heavy iron chains. Then they gathered a large army of bull demons and went outside to do battle. Sun Wukong stood behind a large rock and looked at them. Each demon king was very large, with two horns and four pointed ears. Behind them were hundreds of bull demons, tall and short, fat and thin, old and young. They all were holding weapons. Above them were three large banners reading Great King Cold Avoider, Great King Heat Avoider, and Great King

Dust Avoider.

Sun Wukong stepped forward and shouted, "You lawless thieves! Don't you recognize Old Monkey?"

One of them replied, "So you are the one who caused trouble in Heaven, eh? We know your name but not your face. Now we see that you are just a little monkey."

"You oil stealing thieves! Stop talking and return my master now!"

The monsters came at him with their weapons: an ax, a sword and a cane. The monkey king fought to save his master's life, the three monsters fought for a taste of the monk's flesh and immortality. They fought all day, over a hundred and fifty rounds. Finally the monsters surrounded Sun Wukong. He used his cloud somersault to escape back to Mercy Cloud Temple.

"Brothers!" he said to Zhu and Sha. "After our master was taken, I followed the bad smell of the wind. I met the Four Sentinels of Time. Then I found a cave, and inside the cave were three monster kings and a large number of bull demons. The three monsters have been stealing oil from the city for years, pretending to be Buddhas. I fought all of them for an entire day but I could not win the battle, so I used my cloud somersault to come back here."

The monks from the temple arrived and offered dinner to the three disciples. "I don't need to eat anything," said Sun Wukong. "I once went five hundred years without any food or drink." The monks thought he was joking. They brought food, and the three disciples ate dinner. Sun Wukong said, "Let's get some sleep, we can fight the monsters tomorrow."

But Sha said, "What are you saying, elder brother? If the monsters cooked and ate our master tonight, what would we do then? Better to go back now and save him."

Zhu and Sun Wukong both agreed. So they told the monks to guard their horse and luggage. Sun Wukong said, "We will capture these false Buddhas and bring them back here. Then the people will not have to produce all that oil. Wouldn't that be nice?"

Chapter 92

Sun Wukong, Zhu and Sha flew back to the cave at Green Dragon Mountain to find the three monsters. Zhu lifted his rake and was getting ready to smash the stone gates. But Sun Wukong said, "Wait, brother. Let's find out first whether Master is alive or not."

"But the gates are locked," replied Zhu. "How can we get in?"

"With magic, of course!" The monkey said a few magic words and changed into a little firefly. He flew inside the cave. Looking around, he saw many large bull demons asleep all over the floor. The sound of their snoring filled the air. Flying deeper into the cave, he heard the sound of crying. There he found Tangseng tied to a pillar. He was saying,

> "Since leaving Chang'an over ten years ago
> I have crossed thousands of mountains and rivers
> Happy to find a lantern festival
> I climbed the Golden Lantern bridge
> I could not tell true from false
> So once again I must suffer
> I hope my disciples come soon
> I hope their great powers will save me!"

Looking up, he saw the firefly. He said, "What is this? It's only the first month but already there are fireflies!"

The firefly said, "Master, I am here! You could not tell true from false. You did not listen to me, and you let these monsters take you away. I am here now with Zhu and Sha. All the monsters are asleep. Let's get out of here."

Sun Wukong changed back to his original form. He used magic to open the lock, freeing Tangseng. They started to walk out of the cave. But just then, one of the monster kings said to a bull demon, "Little ones, why is nobody on patrol tonight?" Of course, all the monsters were exhausted from fighting all day. When the monster king said this, a few of them got up and walked to the back of the cave to look at the Tang monk. They ran right into master and disciple.

One of the bull demons said, "My good monk, you have escaped from the chains, but where are you going now?"

Sun Wukong whipped out his golden hoop rod and killed two little bull demons. The rest ran back and banged on the door to the monster kings' bedroom, shouting, "It's bad! It's bad! The hairy ape has killed two of us!"

Sun Wukong called his two brothers, and the three of them fought against the monsters. But they had to leave Tangseng in order to fight. The monster kings captured Tangseng again and chained him up again. One of them said, "So, your little friends came into our cave to get you, eh? Well now we are awake and we won't let you escape!"

The monster kings turned to fight against the three disciples. The battle lasted for a long time but neither side could win. Finally, Great King Cold Avoider called for the bull demons to come and help him. They all rushed up to Zhu and fought him. Zhu fell to the ground, surrounded by bull demons. They dragged Zhu inside the cave and tied him up. Then they all ran towards Sha, surrounding and hitting him. Sha also fell to the ground and was tied up by the bull demons. Sun Wukong knew he could not win by himself against so many demons, so he flew away.

He returned to Mercy Cloud Temple. The monks there asked him if he had rescued Tangseng. "No," he replied, "there are quite a few monsters there and they are very powerful. I think my master is safe, because he is receiving help from the Six Gods of Light, the Six Gods of Darkness, and the Guardians of the Five Quarters. But still, I will need some help. I must go up to Heaven. You all stay here and keep an eye on the horse and luggage."

Quickly he flew up to the western gate of Heaven. There he ran into Gold Star Venus and some other immortals. Gold Star greeted him and asked him where he was going.

Sun Wukong replied, "I have traveled with my master to the eastern regions of India. We were staying at Mercy Cloud Temple and were enjoying the lantern festival. We went to Golden Lantern Bridge where three huge lanterns were burning a special oil. The people of that city thought that the oil was their gift to the Buddha every year, but three monster spirits have been taking the form of Buddhas every year and stealing the oil for themselves. My master did not understand this. He bowed to the false Buddhas. The false Buddhas captured him and brought him back to their cave on Green Dragon Mountain. I tried fighting these monsters, but they are too powerful for me. Now I have come to ask the Jade Emperor to help me understand who they are, and make them submit."

Gold Star smiled and said, "I know these monsters. They are rhinoceros spirits. Their forms can be seen in Heaven, and they have studied the Way for many years so they now have vast magical powers. They can fly in the clouds and walk on the fog. They have magic in their horns. If you want to capture them, you must get help from the Four Wood Bird Stars."

"How can I find these Four Wood Bird Stars?"

"They are in the sky, just outside of the Bull Fighting Palace. If you want to know more, go ask the Jade Emperor."

Sun Wukong thanked him, then he went inside the gate and flew to the Hall of Perfect Light. There he explained his situation to the Four Celestial Masters. They allowed him into the Hall of Divine Mists to see the Jade Emperor.

The Emperor listened while Sun Wukong told him the story. He was about to order some Heavenly warriors to take care of the problem, but Sun Wukong said, "Just now, Gold Star of Venus told me that these monsters are rhinoceros spirits. He said that only the Four Wood Bird Stars can subdue them." The Jade Emperor agreed, and sent someone to give instructions to the four stars. They were Horn Wood Dragon, Dipper the Wood Unicorn, Strider Wood Wolf, and Well Wood Hound[1].

When Sun Wukong saw them, he laughed and said, "Oh, it's you four! If I'd known that I should see the four woods of the twenty-eight constellations, I would have come to see you directly, without needing to ask the Emperor!"

"How can you say that?" they replied. "We cannot do anything unless the Emperor decrees. Now, what do you want from us?"

"There are some rhinoceros spirits living in a cave on Green Dragon Mountain."

Dipper the Wood Unicorn said, "You don't need all of us for this. Just ask Well Wood Hound, he is very powerful. He can climb mountains to eat tigers, and he can go under the ocean to catch rhinos."

"No!" said Sun Wukong. "You don't understand, these rhinos have mastered the Way through centuries of study. They are extremely powerful. I need all four of you."

And so Sun Wukong and the four Wood Stars went down to the cave on Green Dragon Mountain. The bull demons had put wooden planks across the cave entrance, since the stone gates were broken. Sun Wukong shouted for the

---

[1] These four constellations are collectively known as Sì Mù Qín Xīng, the Four Wood Birds.

monster kings to come out. A short time later, all three monster kings came out in full armor. They were accompanied by a large herd of bull demons, all holding knives and spears, waving banners and beating war drums. The monster kings told the bull demons to spread out and encircle Sun Wukong. But suddenly, all four Wood Stars ran forward with their weapons and shouted, "Evil beasts, don't move!"

"Oh, no!" shouted the monster kings. "This is bad! Little ones, run for your lives!" All the bull demons changed back to their original forms. They were mountain buffalo, water buffalo and yellow buffalo. All were madly running all around the mountain. The three monster kings also returned to their true forms. They dropped their weapons, their hands became front legs, and their bodies turned into large rhinoceros bodies. With legs pounding the ground like thunder they ran towards the northeast, chased by Sun Wukong and two of the Wood Stars, Well and Horn. The other two Wood Stars, Dipper and Strider, ran to the cave and freed Tangseng, Zhu and Sha.

Tangseng bowed to Dipper and Strider and thanked them. He said, "But where is my disciple Wukong?" The Wood Stars explained that he was chasing the monster kings. Tangseng touched his forehead to the ground, then prostrated himself.

"Enough of this," said Zhu. "There's no need for you to keep bowing. These stars are just following the Emperor's commands. Now, let's destroy this cave. Then we can return to the temple and wait for Elder Brother."

Dipper and Strider agreed, and they left to help Sun Wukong and the other two stars. Zhu and Sha removed all the gold and jewels from the cave, then they started a fire that burned everything in the cave to ashes.

> Disaster comes at the height of success[1]
> One should meet evil with joy
> For love of lanterns the Dharma was disturbed
> The monk's heart was weakened by the lovely glow
> Always guard the great way of alchemy[2]
> Lose it and you will lose your way

---

[1] The idea that victory holds the seeds of defeat, and vice versa, is common in Chinese thought. The yin-yang symbol illustrates this. And the *Dao De Jing* says, "Emptiness and existence transform into each other, difficult and easy come from each other, long and short compared to each other, high and low flow from each other, before and after follow each other."

[2] Daoist inner alchemy teaches how to purify one's spirit, mind and body. This brings health, wisdom and long life.

Keep a tight grip, don't let it go
A moment's laziness will bring disaster

Dipper and Strider caught up with Sun Wukong and explained how they had rescued Tangseng, Zhu and Sha. "Thanks!" said Sun Wukong. "The three monster kings have jumped into the ocean. Well and Horn jumped in after them, but they told me to stay here and guard the shore. Now that you're here, though, I will go into the ocean to help them."

Sun Wukong grabbed his rod. He made a magic sign with his fingers to divide the waters. Then he flew down to the bottom of the ocean. He found the three monster kings battling with Well and Horn. When the monster kings saw that Sun Wukong had joined the battle, they turned and ran for their lives, with Sun Wukong, Well and Horn close behind.

As they all rushed through the ocean, they passed a couple of yakshas who were out on patrol. The yakshas swam quickly back to their boss, Aoshun the Dragon King of the Western Ocean. They told Aoshun that three rhinos were being chased by Sun Wukong and two constellations. Aoshun immediately knew that he needed to help Sun Wukong. He ordered his soldiers to rush out of the palace and help. They formed up in front of the three monster kings, blocking them. The monster kings were trapped. Each one went off in a different direction.

One of the monster kings, Dust Avoider, was quickly surrounded by the dragon king and his soldiers. Sun Wukong shouted, "Don't kill him, we want him alive!" The soldiers tied him up and put an iron hook through his nose.

Heat Avoider was also captured. But Cold Avoider was not so lucky. By the time Sun Wukong reached him, the soldiers had already captured and killed him. They dragged the dead rhino back to the palace. Sun Wukong told the soldiers to cut off the horns and skin, but to give the meat to the dragon king.

Then they returned to the Gold Level Prefecture. Horn led Dust Avoider by a rope through his nose. Well led Heat Avoider the same way. They were joined by the other two Wood Stars, Strider and Dipper.

When they came close to Gold Level Prefecture, Sun Wukong shouted from the clouds, "All people of this region, hear me! We are monks sent by the great Tang to seek scriptures in the Western Heaven. We have learned the truth about the creatures who pretended to be Buddhas and took your special oil. They are actually rhino spirits. These spirits stole your lantern oil and abducted my master. The gods of Heaven have helped us to subdue these rhino spirits. From now on, there is no need for you to make this special and expensive oil."

After this, Sun Wukong and the Wood Stars came down to the ground and brought the two living and one dead rhino spirits to the home of the prefect. They were joined by Zhu and Sha, and by Tangseng, who was carried on a sedan chair by some of the local monks. Sun Wukong told everyone the story about his visit to Heaven, the decree by the Jade Emperor, the help provided by the Four Wood Stars, and the great final battle under the ocean.

As Sun Wukong told the story, Zhu became more and more angry. Finally he grabbed a large knife[1] and cut off the heads of Heat Avoider and Dust Avoider.

Sun Wukong said, "Let the four Wood Stars cut off the horns of these two rhinos and give them to the Jade Emperor with our thanks. As for the horns of the third rhino, we will give one horn to the people of Gold Level Prefecture to remind you in future years of what happened here. And we will take one with us, to give to the Buddha when we arrive on Spirit Mountain."

The four travelers thought that they were finished at Gold Level Prefecture. But the prefect would not let them leave yet. First, he held a great vegetarian feast. Then he issued a decree that there would be no Lantern Festival the following year, and that no family would need to give any more special oil for future festivals. He also decreed that the meat from the dead rhinos be distributed to all the people. And he decreed that a temple be built so that the people would always remember the victory of the four Wood Stars over the rhino monsters.

Each of the 240 oil lamp families was very grateful and wanted to give the travelers a feast at their homes, one every night for 240 days. So every night they ate at a different home, and every night Zhu took a couple of jewels from his sleeve and gave them to the family. After a month of this, Tangseng had enough. He told Sun Wukong to give the rest of the jewels to the temple, and he told his disciples that they would be leaving the next morning before dawn. He said, "I'm afraid that if we stay too long here enjoying ourselves, the

---

[1] This is a special knife, jièdāo, literally "knife to guard against evil," also called a precept knife. It was worn by monks but only used to cut clothing, slice food, and trim hair and fingernails, never used for killing. According to legend, when Buddha Shakyamuni lived in the world the monks needed to mend their clothing but they had no cutting tools, so some monks resorted to tearing cloth with their hands and teeth. Seeing this, Buddha allowed the monks to use a special knife for this purpose.

Buddha might become angry and we will run into more troubles."

The next morning Tangseng was awake by the fifth watch. He told Zhu to get the horse ready. Zhu was unhappy about this, saying, "Why are we leaving? All 240 families want to give us meals, but we have only eaten at thirty of them so far."

Tangseng snapped, "You fat coolie, stop crying. If you keep complaining I will ask Wukong to knock out your teeth with his golden hooped rod!"

Zhu blinked in surprise when he heard these angry words. Then he picked up the luggage. Sha also finished his work. And so, before the sun rose in the sky, the four travelers left Gold Level Prefecture. They were

Letting the phoenix escape from the jade cage
Opening the locks to let the dragon go free

Chapter 93

Tangseng and his three disciples left Gold Level Prefecture and walked for about half a month. One day they came to another tall mountain. Tangseng said that they must be careful, but Sun Wukong just laughed and said, "We are so close to the land of the Buddha. There cannot be any monsters or demons here!"

"That's true," said Tangseng, "but remember what the monks told us at Gold Level Prefecture. They said that the capital of India is still two thousand miles away. I wonder how far we have traveled?"

"Master, have you forgotten again the Heart Sutra taught to you by the Chan master?"

"Of course not. The Heart Sutra is like my cassock or my alms bowl, it is always with me. I could say it backwards."

"You know how to say it, but do you know what it means?"

"You stupid ape head, of course I know what it means. Do you?"

"Yes, I do."

The two of them were silent for a long time. Zhu thought this was all very funny. He said, "We three disciples all started off as monster spirits. We are not dharma monks, we have never heard the sutras explained by Buddhist monks. I think Old Monkey is just telling us a tall tale."

But Tangseng said to Zhu, "Wukong understands the language that has no words. That is true wisdom."

By this time, they had passed by the tall mountain. They came to a monastery. It was not too big, not too small. The roof was green and it was surrounded by a red brick wall. On the gates was a large sign saying, "Gold Spreading Monastery."

Tangseng said, "That's interesting. There is an old story about Jetavana Park in the city of Sravasti. A man named Sudatta wanted to buy it from Prince Jeta so that the Buddha could use it for giving lectures. But the prince said that the park was not for sale. When Sudatta asked him again, the prince said, 'The only way you can buy this park is if you cover the whole thing with gold.' So Sudatta covered the entire park with gold bricks. The prince sold him the park, and Sudatta invited the Buddha to come and teach there."

They entered the monastery. A monk met them and said, "Master, where do you come from?"

"This poor monk is Chen Xuanzang, sent by the great Tang emperor to worship Buddha in the Western Heaven and bring back scriptures. We were just passing your treasure monastery, and were hoping we could stay here for one night."

The monk agreed, and invited them to come inside for tea and a vegetarian meal. They all sat down. Tangseng began to say a prayer, but Zhu immediately started pushing food into his mouth. Sha said quietly to him, "Second elder brother, remember that there are many gentlemen in the world, but they all have bellies just like us." Zhu thought about this and stopped eating.

Tangseng asked the monk whether this was indeed the famous Jetavana Park. "Yes," the monk replied, "this used to be Jetavana. But after Sudatta covered it with gold and bought it, the name was changed to Gold Spreading Monastery. Even now, after a heavy rain, we sometimes will find small bits of gold on the ground."

"And why are there so many travelers here? When we came through the gates, we saw many horses and carts."

"Our mountain is called Hundred Legs Mountain. It used to be quite safe. But recently there have been some centipede spirits on the mountain. They have attacked people on the roads. Nobody has been killed, but people are afraid to travel at night. So when evening falls, the merchants stay here overnight. They leave when the cock crows in the morning."

"We will do the same," said Tangseng.

Later, Tangseng and Sun Wukong went for a walk in the moonlight. An old monk holding a bamboo staff came up to Tangseng and asked, "Is this the master who came from China?"

"I dare not accept that honor," Tangseng replied.

"What is the master's age?"

"I have passed forty-five years in vain. And you?"

"I have foolishly spent sixty years more than the master."

Sun Wukong said, "So, you are a hundred and five. How old do you think I am?"

"My eyes do not see well in the moonlight, it's hard for me to tell your age."

They walked in comfortable silence for a while. They went out through the rear gate and came to a terrace. Suddenly Tangseng heard the sound of someone crying. "Who is that?" he asked.

The elderly monk replied, "On this day a year ago, this poor monk was meditating on the relationship between ourselves and the moon. I heard a sound. Looking around, I saw a lovely young girl. I asked her who she was. She told me, 'I am the daughter of the King of India. I was blown here by a strong wind.' Immediately I thought she must be a monster of some kind, so I had her locked in an empty room. I had the door covered with bricks to make it like a prison, with just a small hole through which one could pass a rice bowl. The girl was afraid that the other monks would try to have sex with her. So during the day she pretends to be crazy, lying in her own shit and piss and saying nonsense words. But at night she cries and calls out quietly for her parents. I don't know what to do with her. But now that the great master has come here, I hope you can shed some light on this matter."

Tangseng and Sun Wukong returned to their room and went to sleep. In the morning, all four travelers prepared to leave when the cock crowed. As they were leaving, the old monk said to them, "Don't forget that matter about the weeping girl!"

"Of course not," said Sun Wukong. "When I get to the city, I will find out the truth." They left the monastery along with a large group of merchants. They climbed up the mountain pass, and in late morning they saw the walls of the city. Coming down the other side of the mountain, the merchants all went to their own hotels and inns. Tangseng and the disciples came to the Hostel of Meeting. Tangseng greeted the manager there, and asked if he could stay at the Hostel of Meeting while he got his travel rescript certified.

The manager agreed, and offered the travelers a room and a vegetarian meal. Tangseng could see that the manager was very afraid of the three disciples, so he said, "Please don't be afraid. These are my disciples. They may look ugly but they all have good hearts. As the saying goes, 'An ugly face, a kind person.' Tell me sir, what is the age of your treasure country?"

"This is the Great Kingdom of India. It is five hundred years old. Our king is a man who loves mountains and streams, flowers and plants. His name is Emperor Yizong and he has ruled for twenty-eight years."

"Do you think this poor monk can see your great king today, to get our travel rescript certified?"

"Yes, this is a very good day. Our princess, the king's daughter, recently had her twentieth birthday. Today she will throw down an embroidered ball to find out who Heaven has chosen to be her husband. I believe the king's court is still open. You should go now."

Tangseng invited Sun Wukong to come with him to see the king. He said, "The people here are very much the same as the people of Great Tang. And I have heard the story of my mother, who met her husband by throwing down an embroidered ball. It hit him on the head, and they were married that same day."

"We should go and see this," said Sun Wukong.

"No, we are not wearing the proper clothing."

"But master, have you forgotten the words of the old monk at Gold Spreading Monastery? We need to tell truth from lies. If we go, we can get a good look at this princess."

Tangseng agreed to go. But he did not know that they were like a fisherman who tries to catch a fish but ends up catching big trouble! He did not know that a year earlier the king had gone with the queen and princess into the palace garden to enjoy the moonlight. When nobody was looking, a monster removed the princess and sent her far away. Then the monster took the form of the princess. The monster knew that the Tang monk would be coming a year later, so she asked her father to arrange the throwing of the embroidered ball for this very night. She wanted to mate with the Tang monk, absorb his *yang* energy, and become immortal[1].

Well, you can guess what happened next. Just after noon, Tangseng and Sun Wukong approached the tower. The false princess saw them and quickly threw the embroidered ball at Tangseng. It hit him on the head, knocking off his hat. Tangseng tried to grab the ball but it rolled inside one of the sleeves of his robe.

"It hit a monk! It hit a monk!" shouted the people on the tower. Everyone ran towards Tangseng. Sun Wukong roared and stretched his body until he was thirty feet tall. The people ran away. Sun Wukong returned to his normal size.

---

[1] Daoists believe that a man's male energy (yang) is transferred to his partner during sex in exchange for the woman's female energy (yin).

"What do I do now?" cried Tangseng.

"Relax, Master. Go inside and meet with the king. I will return to the Hostel of Meeting. If the princess does not want to marry you, then just get the travel rescript certified and we will leave. But if she does want you, then tell the king that you must give some instructions to your disciples. Then we will come to the court, and I will be able to tell truth from lies."

Tangseng agreed to this. Then he walked to the tower, surrounded by the palace maidens. The princess came down from the tower. She led him to the imperial chariot, and they rode together to the palace. The king was not happy when he heard that the princess's ball had hit a monk. But he invited them both to come into the Hall of Golden Chimes. He asked Tangseng, "Where did you come from, and how did it happen that you were hit by our daughter's ball?"

Tangseng prostrated on the floor. He said, "This poor monk was sent by the great Tang Emperor to worship Buddha and seek holy scriptures. I came here simply to have our travel rescript certified. My path took me under the tower. I never expected to be hit by your daughter's ball! This poor monk has left the family and follows a strange religion. I could not possibly become your daughter's husband. I beg you, please pardon me for being so stupid and send me off quickly to Spirit Mountain."

The king replied, "The ancients say, 'A thread can bring together lovers across a thousand miles.' This is a very auspicious year, month, day and hour for finding a husband or wife. We are not pleased that she hit a monk with her ball, but we do not know how the princess herself feels."

"Father King," she said, kowtowing to him, "you know the old saying,

> If you marry a chicken, you follow a chicken
> If you marry a dog, you follow a dog

I made a vow to Heaven and earth that I would marry the man that is struck by my ball. Do I dare to break that vow? I will take him as the royal son in law."

Now the king smiled. He told the court astronomer to select the best day for the wedding. But just as he was preparing to announce the wedding to everyone in the kingdom, Tangseng just said, "Release me, oh king!"

The king growled, "What, you don't want to become the royal son in law? You would rather persist in seeking your scriptures? Well, if you don't want to marry our daughter, you will lose your head!"

Tangseng was shaking. He replied, "I thank Your Majesty for his kindness. But please, I need to give instructions to my three disciples. They are waiting for me at the Hostel of Meeting." The king sent some of his officials to fetch the disciples.

Meanwhile, Sun Wukong had returned to the Hostel of Meeting. He was laughing and telling Zhu and Sha about what happened with the embroidered ball. Zhu stamped his feet and shouted, "I knew that I should have gone there instead of you! If you hadn't stopped me, I would have gone to the tower and the ball would have landed on my head. The princess would have had to marry me. We would play all day and all night, what fun!"

Sha rubbed Zhu's face and said, "What a mouth you have! It's like, 'With three coins you buy an old horse, then tell everyone how you can ride it.' Who would want a disaster like you for a husband or a son in law?"

The two of them argued for a while, until a minister arrived and said, "His Majesty wants the three of you to come to the palace right away. The old monk was lucky and was struck by the princess's embroidered ball, and will become the new royal son in law."

Sun Wukong said, "All right, let's go."

Chapter 94

Sun Wukong, Zhu and Sha followed the minister into the palace. They walked into the throne room. They did not bow to the king. The king asked them, "What are your names? Where do you live? Why did you become monks? What scriptures do you seek?"

Sun Wukong stepped towards the throne. Several guardians moved in between him and the king. Tangseng was standing to one side of the king. He said to Sun Wukong, "Disciple, His Majesty is asking you some questions. Please reply properly to him."

Sun Wukong became angry. He shouted at the king, "Your Majesty, you want us to treat you with respect, but you do not respect others. If you want our master as your son in law, why do you make him stand? Why is he not allowed to sit down?"

The king became frightened. Hiding his fear, he asked his attendants to bring out a comfortable cushion for the Tang monk to sit on. Once this was done, Sun Wukong answered the king, saying,

> "This old monkey's home is Water Curtain Cave
> on Flower Fruit Mountain in the kingdom of Aolai
> My father was Heaven, my mother was earth
> I was born when a rock broke apart
> A Daoist master taught me the Way
> I defeated dragons in the ocean
> I captured wild animals in the mountains
> I removed our names from the Book of Life and Death
> I went to Heaven and lived there happy every day
> But then I caused trouble in Heaven
> The Lord Buddha placed me under a mountain
> For five hundred years I ate no food, drank no tea
> Then my master came and set me free
> I am now a student of the Buddha
> My name is Sun Wukong!"

The king nodded his head, then turned to Zhu and waited for him to speak. Zhu said,

> "In my previous lives old Pig was a slave to pleasure
> My life was in chaos, my mind was confused

One day I met an Immortal who changed my life
I became his student and studied the Way
The Jade Emperor made me Marshal of Heavenly Reeds
Leading his troops on Heaven's river
But I became drunk at a festival and tried to play with Chang'e
The Emperor sent me down to earth
Through a mistake, I was born to a pig instead of a woman
I became a pig demon and did much evil
Thanks to Guanyin I became a Buddhist
Now I protect the Tang monk
My name is Zhu Bajie!"

Then Zhu laughed loudly and flapped his big ears at the king. Tangseng said, "Bajie, control yourself!" Zhu put his hands together and stood quietly. The king looked at Sha, who said,

"Old Sand was once an ordinary man
Fear of death made me seek the Way
I walked the clouds and wandered the shores of Heaven
I met some immortals
I raised the baby boy to mate with the lovely girl[1]
I flew above the sky into the dark void of Heaven
I was named the Curtain Raising Captain
But at a festival I dropped and broke a treasure cup
I was sent down earth to live as a monster
I ate travelers who entered my home in Flowing Sand River
Bodhisattva Guanyin saved me and told me to wait for the Tang monk
I became his disciple and started a new life
My name is Sha Wujing!"

Listening to these three stories, the king was happy to hear that his daughter was to marry a living Buddha, but he was terrified that the man's disciples were such powerful monsters. While he was thinking about this, the royal astronomer entered and told the king that the most auspicious day for the wedding was the twelfth day of the month, four days in the future. The king

---

[1] In Daoist alchemy, "baby boy" refers to lead and "lovely girl" to mercury, and the combination was said to yield the golden elixir of immortality. But since both chemicals are extremely toxic, those who drank these often died. So Daoists eventually shifted from this so-called external alchemy to internal alchemy, where lead and mercury are treated as symbols or metaphors which must be extracted and purified through study with a Daoist master.

commanded that a building be prepared for the Tang monk and his three disciples. Then he discussed wedding preparations. Finally he left the throne room, and the four travelers walked into the garden to have some dinner.

Tangseng shouted at Sun Wukong, "You wretched ape! I told you all I wanted was to get our travel rescript certified. And I told you not to go near that tower. Why did you take me there?"

Sun Wukong replied, "Master, you were telling me about your mother who met her husband in that same way. I thought you were longing for the past. Also, I was thinking about the words of the abbot from Gold Spreading Monastery. I wanted to get a good look at the princess. Just now I thought the king looked a little bit evil. But I don't know about the daughter yet."

"What will you do if you see her?"

"My diamond eyes can tell truth from lies, and good from evil. So let's just wait until the wedding day, I will be able to get a good look at her then."

"Oh stop talking, you evil ape. Our journey is almost finished, but still you try to stab me with your poisonous tongue. The next time you cause trouble, I will recite the Tight Headband Spell."

"Please don't do that! If we find out that she is a real princess, I promise to cause chaos, and get you out of there."

Zhu said, "Master, it's late. Let's discuss things tomorrow. It's time to go to sleep." Tangseng agreed, and they stopped arguing and went to sleep.

The next morning, the king sat on his throne and ordered his ministers to take the three disciples back to the hostel to enjoy a vegetarian breakfast. Then he ordered musicians to play at the hostel for the disciples, and also in the imperial garden for the Tang monk. But Zhu flapped big his ears and said, "Your Majesty, we have never been apart from our master. We want to be with him today. Otherwise, you will not be able to have the wedding."

The king was frightened by Zhu's words and his appearance, so he agreed. He ordered two tables to be set up in the garden for the king and Tangseng, three tables nearby for the three disciples, plus more tables for the queen, the princess, and her servants. They all enjoyed a walk through the garden, followed by a delicious vegetarian feast. Tangseng smiled and appeared to enjoy himself, but he did not let anyone see how worried he was.

Tangseng noticed four large screens hanging on the walls. Each screen had a poem written by a famous scholar. There was one poem for spring, one for summer, one for autumn, and one for winter. The first line of the first poem was "The great wheel of nature has made its turn." Tangseng studied the poems carefully.

The king saw Tangseng looking at the screens. He said, "I see the royal son in law enjoys poetry. Perhaps you could give us a reply to each poem, using the same rhymes?"

Tangseng's mind was full of these beautiful poems. Without thinking, he said, "The sun melts the ice as the great wheel turns."

The king was delighted to hear this. "Please, tell us more!" and ordered that brush and ink be given to Tangseng. Tangseng took the brush. Without hesitating he wrote replies to each of the four poems, using the same rhymes as the originals.

The king read Tangseng's poems and said, "This is really quite good!" He ordered the court's musicians to set the poems to music. In this way, the king and the monk spent the entire day.

They spent the next three days enjoying themselves, and finally the auspicious twelfth day of the month arrived. The king's officials told him that the wedding banquet was ready. Five hundred tables were set up for the guests. Another official came in and said, "Your Majesty, the queen and princess wish to meet with you."

The king went to the ladies' quarters and greeted the queen and princess. The princess kowtowed to him and said, "Your Majesty, my father, please forgive me for asking you this favor. I have been told that the Tang monk has three very ugly disciples. Because of my poor health, I am afraid that seeing them would terrify me and lead to disaster. Please keep them away from the wedding."

The king said, "Of course, dear daughter. We will certify their rescript this morning, and command the disciples to leave the city at once." The king returned to the throne room and commanded Tangseng and the three disciples to come and see him.

Tangseng was just saying to Sun Wukong, "It is now the twelfth day. What do we do now?"

Sun Wukong replied, "I really need to see the princess. But I expect that today the king will order the three of us to leave the city. Don't worry. I will come right back in secret, and I'll protect you." And a few minutes later, an official arrived to bring the three disciples to see the king.

When they arrived at the throne room, the king said, "Give us your travel rescript. We will sign it. We will also give you some money to help you get to Spirit Mountain. Our son in law will remain here. Don't worry about him."

Sha handed the travel rescript to the king. The king signed it and handed it back. Then he gave the pilgrims ten bars of yellow gold and twenty bars of white gold as wedding gifts. Sun Wukong thanked the king. The three of them turned to leave. Tangseng ran over to Sun Wukong and grabbed him, saying, "Are you leaving me here?"

Sun Wukong winked at him and said, "Relax, master, and enjoy your wedding and your new wife. We will see you after we have acquired the scriptures." Tangseng held onto the monkey for a minute, then let him go.

The three disciples walked back to the Hostel of Meeting. Sun Wukong said, "You two stay here, don't talk to anyone. I am going back to protect Master." Then he pulled a hair from his arm, blew on it and whispered, "Change!" It changed into a form of himself which stayed with Zhu and Sha. His true self jumped into the air and changed into a little yellow bee. He flew back towards the palace. He saw Tangseng sitting by himself in the garden, looking quite sad. He landed on Tangseng's hat and whispered, "Don't worry, Master, I am here."

This made Tangseng feel much better. A little while later, an official came and told him that the wedding banquet was ready, and the princess was waiting for him. The king came up to him, and he led Tangseng inside the palace.

Chapter 95

Tangseng followed the king into the inner palace, with Sun Wukong hiding on his hat. They heard flutes and drums. They saw two rows of beautiful young women wearing colorful clothing, so the place looked like a garden of flowers. The women were beautiful, but Sun Wukong saw that his master was unmoved by their beauty. "Marvelous monk!" he thought, "Walking through such beauty, his heart is not moved and his mind is not confused."

Soon the princess and the queen walked towards them, surrounded by the concubines. They all shouted, "Long live Your Majesty! Long live Your Majesty!" Sun Wukong looked carefully at the princess. He saw a little bit of demon cloud floating above her head. He whispered to Tangseng, "Master, that princess is fake."

Tangseng whispered back, "If she is not the true princess, how can we make her show her true form?"

"I will show her my magic body[1]."

"No! That would frighten the king. Better to wait until the king and queen have left the room."

But the old monkey could not stop himself. He roared and changed back to his original form. Running forward, he grabbed the princess and shouted, "You damned beast! It's bad enough that you are here, enjoying life in the palace instead of the true princess. But why do you want to trick my master and steal his true *yang*?"

There was chaos in the palace. The king was frozen with fear. The queen and concubines fell to the ground in every direction. Palace workers ran around crazy with fear. Only the fake princess was unafraid. She freed herself from Sun Wukong's hands. She ripped off all her clothes and jewels. She ran to a nearby shrine and grabbed a short heavy club. Turning, she smashed the club at Sun Wukong. He quickly blocked it with his rod. Shouting at each other, the two of them rose up into the sky and fought in the clouds and fog.

What a battle!

The golden hoop rod is famous

---

[1] Sun Wukong refers to his true form as his magic body. Here, he must change back to his true form to fight the demon.

The club is unknown to all
The monk has come seeking true scriptures
The demon has come for love of strange flowers
She has heard of the Tang monk, she longs for his powerful *yang*
A year earlier she took the true princess's form
Now the Great Sage knows the truth
The club does its work, hitting the head
The rod does its work, hitting the face
Loudly the two of them fight in the sky
As fog and cloud hide the sun

Down on the ground, Tangseng reached out and took the frightened king's hands. He said, "Your Majesty, please don't be afraid! That woman is actually a demon who has taken on the form of your daughter. When my disciple captures her, you will understand." The king calmed down a bit. Together, they watched the battle in the sky.

In the sky, the monkey and the monster fought for half a day. Then Sun Wukong threw his rod into the air and shouted, "Change!" One rod became ten; ten became a hundred; a hundred became many thousands. Like a cloud of snakes, the rods attacked the monster. She changed into a clear breeze and flew up towards Heaven. Sun Wukong collected the rods back into one and followed her.

They both came to the western gate of Heaven. He shouted, "Block that monster, don't let her escape!" The four Grand Marshals blocked her path, each holding his weapon. The monster turned around and began fighting Sun Wukong again.

As they fought, Sun Wukong looked at the monster's weapon. He asked, "Cursed beast, what sort of weapon is that? Tell me now or I will smash your head!"

"So," she replied, "you don't know about my weapon?

This is a piece of mutton fat jade
Cut and polished for thousands of years
It was mine when the chaos was first parted
It was mine when the world began
It stayed with me in the Hall of the Moon[1]

---

[1] The Hall of the Moon, sometimes called the Cold Palace, is the home of Chang'e, the Goddess of the Moon. The beautiful Chang'e stole the elixir of immortality from her

For love of flowers I came down to earth
I went to India, taking the form of a young girl
My only wish is to wed the Tang monk
How could you destroy this beautiful wedding?
Chasing me across the sky like a beast
My weapon is older than your iron rod
It once was used to make drugs in the Hall of the Moon
One blow from it and your life is ended!"

"Ha!" said Sun Wukong. "If you lived in the Hall of the Moon, you must know of Old Monkey. Why do you fight me? You will surely lose!"

"Oh yes, I know you. You're the one who took care of the Jade Emperor's horses and caused such trouble in Heaven. I should run away from you. But you are trying to prevent my wedding, that is as bad as killing one's parents. I must fight you!"

Sun Wukong hated to be reminded about his job tending the Emperor's horses. So he raised his rod to hit her. She blocked the blow, and they started to battle again at the gate of Heaven. They fought for a while. The monster realized that she could not win the fight. So she shook her body and changed into a shaft of golden light. The light flew down to earth and entered a mountain cave. Sun Wukong followed the light to see where it went. Then he turned around and returned to the kingdom.

"Master, I'm back!" he cried.

Tangseng replied, "Be careful, Wukong, don't frighten His Majesty. Tell me, what happened with the princess?"

"And if that princess is a monster, where is our real princess?" asked the king.

Sun Wukong said, "The false princess is definitely a monster. I fought with her for half a day, then I chased her to the gate of Heaven. The guards at the gate blocked her way, so she turned and fought with me again. Then she changed into a beam of golden light and flew to a mountain south of here. I could not find her so I was afraid she might try to harm you, so I came back right away."

The king said, "We beg you, please rescue our real princess and return her to

---

husband who had hidden it under their bed. She drank it and floated up to the moon. Later, the Jade Emperor gave her the Hall of the Moon as a gift. Longing to return to the human world, she asked the Jade Rabbit to help her make medicine by pounding drugs with a mortar and pestle.

us!"

"Your Majesty, please return to the main hall with my master. Please summon my two brothers to come and guard you and my master. Then I will leave and subdue the monster."

The king agreed, and also arranged for a vegetarian meal for the monk and disciples. Sun Wukong explained the situation to Zhu and Sha. Then he used his cloud somersault to fly south to the mountain.

He searched the mountain but could not find the monster. This was because the monster had crawled into a small cave and blocked the entrance with rocks. After searching for a while, Sun Wukong summoned the local spirit and mountain god.

They arrived and kowtowed, saying, "Please don't hit us! We didn't know anything about this matter."

"I won't hit you yet. Tell me, what is the name of this mountain, and what monsters live here?"

"Great sage, this is called Mount Hairbrush. There have never been any monsters living here. There are just three rabbit lairs."

"Let's go look at them." The three of them went to search for the three rabbit lairs. At the first lair they only saw a few rabbits. But the second lair was blocked by two large stones. Sun Wukong used his rod to push away the stones. As soon as he did that, the monster spirit rushed out, attacking him and the two deities. They all rose up on to the air.

Sun Wukong was stronger and was almost ready to kill the monster spirit. But suddenly a voice came down from the Ninefold Heaven, saying, "Great Sage, don't raise your hand!"

The monkey looked up and saw it was the Star Lord of the Moon. He was traveling on a pink cloud. Chang'e and all the other goddesses of the moon followed him. Sun Wukong put away his rod, bowed, and said, "Old man, where are you going? I'm sorry for not stepping out of your way."

The Star Lord replied, "That monster who you were fighting is the jade rabbit who lives in my Hall of the Moon. Her job is to make my Mysterious Frost Elixir. A year ago, she opened the jade locks and escaped from the palace. I thought she might be in danger, so I came here to rescue her. Please don't kill her."

"Of course, of course," replied Sun Wukong. "I cannot refuse you. So, she's just a little rabbit! But do you know, your rabbit took the form of the princess of India. She wanted to mate with my master and steal his *yang*. This is a very serious crime."

"There are things that you also do not know. The daughter of the king is no ordinary girl. Eighteen years ago, she was Lady White of the Palace of the Moon. One day she slapped the little jade hare on the face. Then, longing to live in the world below, her soul entered the belly of the Queen of India and she was born a princess. But the little rabbit never forgot that slap. That is why she ran away, and that is why she sent Lady White out of the palace. However, you are right, she should not have tried to mate with your master. Please give her back to me."

Sun Wukong laughed and said, "Now I understand. But if you take away the little rabbit, I'm afraid the king may not believe my story. Would you please come back with me to the palace and tell the king the same story that you told me?"

"Of course," said the Star Lord. Then turning to the monster he said, "Evil beast, it's time for you to return to what is right!"

The monster rolled onto the ground. In a few seconds she had turned into a little rabbit. She had sharp teeth, a split lip, red eyes, soft ears, and a cream-colored little nose. Her body was covered with fur-like jade. Sun Wukong laughed, and they all flew back to the king's palace.

They arrived at the palace around sunset, when the moon was rising. The king, Tangseng, Zhu and Sha were all in the court. They looked up and saw a bright colorful cloud approaching from the south. They heard the Great Sage calling out, "Your Majesty of India, please come out and look. Here is the Star Lord of the Moon. With him is Chang'e, the lunar goddesses, and this little jade rabbit who once was the false princess. Now you see her true form."

They all looked up. Zhu was overcome by desire. He leaped into the air and reached for one of the goddesses of the moon. He cried, "Sister, you and I are old friends. Let's go have some fun!" Sun Wukong grabbed him and slapped him on the face, then pushed him down to the ground.

Ignoring this, the king asked, "Now that the false princess has been captured by your powerful magic, where can we find the true princess?"

Sun Wukong replied, "Your daughter is really the immortal Lady White of the Palace of the Moon. She wanted to live in this world, so she entered the belly of the Queen and was born as your daughter. Right now she is living in

Gold Spreading Monastery where she is pretending to be insane. Let's all get some sleep. In the morning I will return your daughter to you."

The next morning, the king held court as usual. He asked Tangseng to go and look for his daughter.

Tangseng replied, "Your Majesty, we recently passed near the Gold Spreading Monastery and stayed there to rest. One night we heard the sound of a girl crying. An elderly monk told us that a year earlier, a strange wind had carried the girl to the monastery and dropped her in the Jetavana Garden. She told the monk that she was the daughter of the king of India. The monk was afraid that the other monks might cause trouble for her, so he shut her in a room for her own protection. Every night she cried for her parents. The old monk told us that he had visited the capital to learn more about this matter, but he saw that the princess was still living in the palace and appeared to be ok. Because of this, he dared not say anything to the king. But when we arrived at the monastery, he asked us to use our powers to find out the truth of the matter. Now we all know the truth. The rabbit has been taken back by the Star Lord, and your daughter is still at the monastery."

The king cried with joy. He asked, "How far is this Gold Spreading Monastery?"

"No more than sixty miles," said Tangseng.

Immediately the king ordered carriages for himself, the Queen, Tangseng, and the disciples. They set out for the monastery. But Sun Wukong jumped out of the carriage and flew ahead, arriving quickly at the monastery. He said to the monks, "Where is that elderly monk? Tell him to come out quickly. And all of you, prepare to receive the king and queen of India!"

The elderly monk came out. Sun Wukong told him the whole story about the lantern festival, the false princess, the battles in the sky, and the arrival of the Star Lord of the Moon. The elderly monk kowtowed again and again. Sun Wukong said, "Stop bowing! Get ready to meet the king and queen!"

A short time later, the carriages carrying the king and queen arrived. They were met by the monks of the monastery, and standing with the monks was Sun Wukong. "How did you get here so quickly?" asked the king.

Sun Wukong replied, "It was easy for Old Monkey. Why did you get here so slowly?"

The group entered the monastery. The elderly monk led them to the room where the princess was pretending to be mad. The monk went to his knees and said, "Your Highness, inside this room is the lady princess."

The king ordered the door to be opened. The king and queen looked inside and recognized their daughter, even though she was extremely dirty. "Our poor child!" they cried, and all three of them embraced and cried for a long time.

Later, the princess bathed and put on clean clothes, and they all climbed up on the imperial chariot. As they were getting ready to depart, Sun Wukong approached the chariot. He said to the king, "Your Majesty, there is one small matter I wish to discuss with you."

"Of course, we will do anything you ask of us."

"There is a mountain here called Hundred Legs Mountain. It has many centipedes that have become evil spirits. They are harming people in the night. I ask you to select a thousand roosters and scatter them throughout the mountain. They will eat all the centipedes. Also, you should change the name of the mountain. And you should provide some money for the repair of this old monastery."

The king did everything that Sun Wukong asked. A thousand roosters were sent to eat the centipedes. The name of the mountain was changed to Precious Flower Mountain. Money and materials were provided for the repair of the monastery, which was renamed Gold Spreading Monastery of Precious Flower Mountain. The elderly monk was named a monk-official and given a stipend of 36 bushels of grain. And there were many banquets held to celebrate the return of the princess.

The travelers stayed for five or six days, but they wanted to continue on their journey. The king provided them with the royal chariot to take them to the western gate of the city. They got out of the chariot and began walking westward again. Truly,

> Washing away the words of thanks, they return to the true nature
> Leaving the sea of gold, they awaken to the true void

My dear child, Tangseng has now been traveling to the west for over fourteen years. His journey is almost finished, but we don't know how it will end.

Chapter 96

My dear child, the world is not as it appears! Think deeply about this:

> In the beginning, form had no form
> And emptiness was not really empty
> Sound and not-sound, talking and not-talking are all the same
> Why speak of dreams from within a dream?
>
> The useful, when used, is useless
> The powerless gives power to power
> When fruit ripens it turns red on its own
> Don't ask the seed how it grows

After they saved the princess, the four travelers continued their journey to the west. It was now early summer. The weather was sunny, plums were ripening after the rain, the whole world seemed bright. Every day the four travelers ate breakfast at dawn, walked all day, and found a place to sleep at sunset.

They had no trouble for two weeks. Then they came to another city. Tangseng asked his senior disciple Sun Wukong, "What sort of place is this?"

Sun Wukong replied, "I don't know, I have passed this way before, but I was always high up in the clouds. I did not see anything."

They continued walking. Tangseng saw two old men sitting by the side of the road. They were talking about this and that. "Disciples," said the monk, "wait here and don't cause any trouble. I am going to talk with these two men." Then he went up to the men, put his hands together, and said, "Gentlemen, this poor monk greets you!"

The men looked up at him. One of them said, "What do you have to say to us, sir?"

"I have come from far away to worship the Lord Buddha. Can you tell me what this place is called, and where I might beg a bit of food?"

"You have come to the city of Bronze Tower. If you want food there is no need to beg. Go down this street. You will see a gate tower that looks like a sitting tiger. That is the home of Squire Kou. You'll see a sign saying, 'Ten Thousand Monks Welcome.' There you can get all the food you want."

Tangseng thanked them. He returned to the three disciples and told them what the old man had said. Sha Wujing, the junior disciple, said, "We are now in the land of Buddha, that's why they are happy to give food to monks. Let's go and eat."

They walked down the street, pushing through crowds of people. "Don't cause trouble, don't cause trouble!" said Tangseng to his troublemaking disciples. After a short walk they arrived at the home of Squire Kou. They saw the sign saying, 'Ten Thousand Monks Welcome.'

The second disciple, the pig-man Zhu Bajie, started to walk right into the building. But Sun Wukong told him to wait and see if someone would come out to meet them. They waited outside the building. A little while later a servant came out. When he saw the four travelers he quickly ran back inside. "Master!" he said, "four strange looking monks are standing outside."

Squire Kou had been walking around the courtyard, reciting the name of the Buddha. When he heard this, he went outside to welcome his guests. He was not frightened at all. "Come in, come in!" he said.

The four travelers followed Squire Kou into the house. Kou showed them the various rooms of the house, including the Buddha Hall. Tangseng put on his cassock to worship the Buddha and entered the hall. What did he see?

Clouds of incense and bright candles
Bundles of silk and flowers
A golden bell hangs from a red frame
A drum rests on a wooden stand
A thousand Buddha statues are covered in gold
There are bronze vases, carved boxes and glass bowls
Lamps burn brightly, bells ring long and slow
This is a treasure house more beautiful than a temple

Squire Kou washed his hands, kowtowed and worshipped. Then he led the travelers to the library. They saw too many scriptures to count. Several tables were covered with paper, ink and brushes.

Squire Kou asked Tangseng who he was. "I have been sent by the emperor of Tang," the monk replied, "to find the Lord Buddha in your country and ask for scriptures. I have heard that in your home you honor monks, so we beg for a bit of food. Then we will be on our way."

The squire smiled and said, "My name is Kou Hong. I have foolishly lived for sixty-four years. When I was forty years old, I vowed to feed ten thousand monks. Having nothing else to do, I have counted them all, and so far, I have fed 9,996 monks. Today Heaven has sent you four to me. I hope you will stay

627

with me for a month and help me celebrate this. Then I will send you on horses and sedan chairs to Spirit Mountain. It is only eight hundred *li*[1] from here." Tangseng agreed to this at once.

Several servants went into the kitchen to prepare a meal of rice, noodles and vegetables. The squire's wife saw the servants working. She asked why they were preparing a meal. One of them replied, "Four monks have arrived. One is handsome but the other three are quite ugly. They told our master that they were sent by the great Tang emperor to worship Buddha at Spirit Mountain. Our master thinks they have come from Heaven. He asked us to prepare a vegetarian meal."

"You know nothing," smiled the wife. "When you see someone who is ugly, strange or unusual, they must have come down from Heaven. Now go and tell your master that I am coming to see the visitors."

The servants ran to tell Squire Kou and the four visitors. A few minutes later the wife came into the room. She looked carefully at Tangseng, then she looked at the three disciples. She believed that they had indeed come down from Heaven, but she was a bit nervous when she kowtowed to them.

Tangseng bowed back to her and said, "Lady, I do not deserve this honor."

Just then, another servant came in and said, "The two young masters have arrived." Two young men entered the room, saw the visitors, and bowed low to them.

Kou said, "These are my two sons. They are named Kou Liang and Kou Dong. They have just come back from school and have not had lunch yet. They heard that you were here, and came to bow to you."

"What fine sons!" said Tangseng. "Truly, the success of your sons and grandsons depends on how they study at school."

"Where have these lords come from?" one of the sons asked his father.

"From far away," he replied. "The Tang Emperor himself has sent them."

"We have read that there are four continents in the world. We are in the western continent, and you come from the southern continent[2]. How long

---

[1] One lĭ is about 1/3 of a mile. Most people know the famous proverb from the Dao De Jing, "A journey of a thousand miles begins with a single step" but it actually refers to a thousand *li*, not miles.

[2] In ancient Buddhist teachings, there are four island-continents which surround Mount Meru. They are Purvavideha in the East where Sun Wukong was born,

have you been traveling?"

"A very long time," replied Tangseng. "Over the last fourteen winters and summers we have met many demons and monsters, and suffered a great deal. I owe much to my three disciples."

Just then, the banquet was ready. Squire Kou and the four travelers sat down to eat, while Kou's wife and the young men went back into the house. There was vegetable soup, rice, steamed bread, and many kinds of fruit. Servants ran around serving the food while four or five cooks worked in the kitchen. Many bowls of food disappeared into Zhu's mouth like clouds blown away by the wind. Everyone ate until they were full.

When they were finished, Tangseng thanked Squire Kou. The travelers prepared to leave. But Kou said, "Teacher, why don't you stay here for a few days and relax? As the ancients say, 'It is easy to start a journey but hard to end one.' Please stay until I have celebrated the completion of my vow to feed ten thousand monks."

They stayed for about a week. At the end of the week, twenty-four local Buddhist monks came and performed a ceremony.

> There were banners hung in the halls
> Rows and rows of candles and burning incense
> Music from drums, gongs and flutes
> The sound of monks reciting the sutras
> Everyone bowed low to the Buddha statues
> Lamps were lit
> The Water Ceremony was performed
> The Garland Sutra[1] was recited
> Everywhere monks are the same!

After the ceremony, Tangseng thanked his host and prepared to leave. Kou looked at him and said, "Teacher, you really want to leave. I think we must have treated you badly while we were busy preparing for the ceremony."

Aparagodaniya in the West where Sun Wukong first traveled and met his first teacher, Jambudvipa in the South where the Tang Empire is located, and Uttarakuru in the North past the Himalayas. Each continent has human inhabitants with different characteristics, except for the Chamara region of Jambudvipa which is inhabited by demons.

[1] This is the Avatamsaka Sutra, written in the 3rd or 4th century. It describes the universe as seen by an enlightened being who sees all phenomena as empty and interpenetrating.

Tangseng replied, "Sir, we have put you to a great deal of trouble, we cannot ever repay you. But when I left my home, my Emperor asked me how long I would be traveling. Foolishly I told him three years. It has already been fourteen years. I don't know if we will ever get the scriptures, and I don't know how long it will take to return to Tang. How can I fail to obey my Emperor's command? Please let us go. Next time we are here, I will be able to stay much longer."

Zhu heard this and became angry. He said, "Master, you don't care about us at all. This old man is very rich, and he wants us to stay. What harm is there in staying here for a year or more? Why leave all this good food just so we can go out and beg from strangers?"

Tangseng shouted at him, "All you care about is food, you coolie! You care nothing about learning how to become a better person. Truly, you are a beast who only cares about filling his belly. If you want to stay here that's fine, I will go the rest of the way alone."

Hearing this and seeing his master's anger, Sun Wukong hit Zhu on the head and said, "You idiot, you've made Master angry now."

Kou heard this. Smiling, he said to Tangseng, "Don't be so angry, teacher. You have only been here for two weeks. Please relax for the rest of the day. Tomorrow we will help you leave."

Kou's wife said that she had a little bit of money and would be happy to use it to pay for the monks to stay for another two weeks. The two sons also offered to feed the monks for another two weeks.

"Please," said Tangseng, "I dare not stay any longer. If I do not leave now, my Emperor will surely kill me for disobeying his orders."

Again, Zhu asked his master to stay longer. Again, Tangseng shouted at him. Sun Wukong laughed at something that Zhu said, causing Tangseng to threaten to recite the tight headband spell.

Squire Kou listened to all the arguing for a while, then he spoke. "Please don't argue, teachers. You can leave tomorrow." He invited a hundred of his friends and neighbors to come the next day to say goodbye to the monks. And he told his servants to prepare another great banquet. He had twenty large colored flags made. He hired a group of musicians, and brought in several Buddhist and Daoist monks to say prayers.

The servants worked all night to prepare the banquet and make the colored flags. The monks and musicians traveled all night to get to Kou's house by morning. Early the next morning, Tangseng and his disciples got up and prepared to leave. Zhu was unhappy but he packed up the luggage. Sha saddled the horse. Sun Wukong picked up his master's staff and gave it to him, then he hung their travel rescript around his own neck. They were all ready to leave.

Squire Kou came and invited them to a large sitting room where the banquet was set out. This banquet was even larger than the one they had eaten the day before.

"Brothers," said Zhu, "relax and eat as much as you can. There won't be any more food like this after we leave here."

"Don't fill your belly too full," replied Sun Wukong. "We have to walk after we leave here."

It was almost noon by the time Tangseng raised his chopsticks and said a sutra to begin the meal. They all ate, but Zhu quickly ate six bowls of rice. Then he stuffed a lot of food into his sleeves, no matter if the food was good or bad.

As they were leaving the house, the Buddhist and Daoist monks arrived. Squire Kou said to them, "Gentlemen, you are too late. Our teacher is in a hurry to leave so I cannot feed you." Then the four travelers, surrounded by a crowd of Kou's friends and relatives, began walking west. The air was filled with the music of drums, gongs and flutes. Colorful flags fluttered in the wind.

They all walked together for three or four miles. They came to a pavilion where food and drink were set out. They all raised cups and toasted each other.

Squire Kou tried not to cry and he said, "Teacher, please visit us when you return from Spirit Mountain."

Tangseng replied, "If I reach Spirit Mountain and see the Lord Buddha, the first thing I will do is praise you. And we will certainly visit you when we return." They continued walking to the west, and eventually Kou and his friends turned back, leaving the four travelers to continue on their own.

They walked another forty or fifty *li*. By now it was getting dark. "It's late," said Tangseng. "Where will we stay tonight?"

Zhu was still unhappy. He said, "You are the one who wanted to leave good food and a warm bed, to go walking again. It's very late now. What if it starts to rain?"

"Evil beast," said Tangseng. "If Heaven lets us visit the Lord Buddha, fetch the true scriptures and bring them back to the Tang Emperor, I will let you eat in the royal kitchens for years and years. Then you will become so fat that you will burst. That will teach you to be a hungry demon." Zhu smiled to himself but did not say another word.

Sun Wukong saw some buildings by the side of the road. He said, "Let's rest over there!"

Tangseng walked over to one of the buildings. He saw a sign, old and covered with dust. It said, "Bright Light Travel Palace." He said to the others, "The Bodhisattva Bright Light was a disciple of the Buddha of Flames and Five Lights. He was punished for killing the Demon King of Poison Fire. There must be a shrine here."

They all went in together. The place was in ruins. The walls had fallen down, and vegetation covered everything. They would have left, but outside it had started to rain. So they stayed the night, just sitting or standing in the dark.

Chapter 97

While the four travelers were resting in the Bright Light Travel Palace, a group of bandits was sitting and talking in Bronze Tower City. These bandits came from good families, but they all had spent their money on drinking and gambling. Now they needed money. So they decided to get together and steal from the richest families in Bronze Tower City.

One of the bandits said, "There is no need to think too much about this. We all know that the richest man in the city is Squire Kou. Tonight it is raining, so nobody will be out in the streets. Let's steal his money. Then we can go gambling and have fun with the girls!"

The other bandits agreed. So they went out in the rain towards Mr. Kou's house. They carried knives, swords, staffs, ropes and torches. They threw open the gates to Squire Kou's house. All the people in the house ran away. The bandits ran through the house, holding torches and looking for treasure. They grabbed all the gold, silver, jewels and fine clothes that they could hold.

Squire Kou could not stand to see this. He ran back into the house and cried, "Please, Great Kings, take as much treasure as you want. Just leave me a few clothes to be buried in!" But the bandits kicked him to the ground. His three souls drifted back to the underworld and his seven spirits slowly left the human world[1].

When the bandits left, the rest of the family came back into the house. They saw Squire Kou lying dead on the floor. They all started crying and said, "Oh Heavens, our master has been killed!"

Mrs. Kou felt that Tangseng and his three disciples were responsible for this disaster. She said to her sons, "Your father fed ten thousand monks. Who would have thought that the last four would come back to his home and kill him?"

"Mother," said the brothers, "how do you know that they did this?"

---

[1] In Chinese tradition each person has two kinds of souls. The spiritual part of a person is hún. It is *yang*, comes from the Heavens, and returns there upon death. The animal or physical part of a person is pò. It is *yin*, comes from the underworld, and rejoins it after death. There are three kinds of hun and seven kinds of po. But in this story, for some reason, Squire Kou's three hún and seven pò seem to head in the wrong directions.

"I was hiding under the bed. I saw the Tang monk holding the torches, Zhu Bajie was holding a knife, Sha Wujing took the gold and silver, and that evil monkey killed your father."

"If you saw this, mother, then you must be correct. They were here for two weeks and knew the house very well. They must have desired our treasure and came back in the dark and rain to take it. How evil! In the morning we will report this to the prefect."

Now the prefect of Bronze Tower City was a good man. As a boy he had studied by the light of the snow[1] and taken the examinations to become a government official. His mind was filled with kindness. His name will be remembered for a thousand years.

The next day, Kou Liang and Kou Dong went to see the prefect. They said, "Your Honor, we have come to tell you of some bandits and murderers."

The prefect replied, "I heard that your family just completed your vow of feeding ten thousand monks. How could this have happened?"

"Your Honor, our father fed monks for twenty-four years. The last four monks were with us for two weeks. They learned everything about our house and our treasures. They left yesterday morning, and last night they returned with weapons. They stole our treasures and killed our father. We beg you to help us avenge our father's death!" The prefect agreed, and sent a hundred and fifty men west to capture the Tang monk and his disciples.

After killing Squire Kou, the bandits traveled west. They passed by Bright Light Travel Palace where Tangseng and his disciples were staying. The bandits stopped on the side of the road a few miles west of Bright Light Travel Palace and divided up the treasures. While they were doing this, Tangseng and his disciples came upon them on the road.

"Look," said one of the bandits, "aren't these the monks that left Kou's house yesterday?"

"Oh good!" said the other bandits. "These monks spent a long time at Kou's house. I bet they have a lot of his gold and silver. Let's take their treasure and

---

[1] This is a reference to the legend of Sun Kang, a poor young man who wanted to study at night. He could not afford lamp oil and there were no fireflies in winter, so he went outdoors in the freezing cold and read books by moonlight reflected off the snow-covered ground. Thus the saying rú náng yíng, rú yìng xuě, "like a bag of fireflies, like the snow's reflection," describes anyone who studies hard despite poverty.

their white horse." They stood in the middle of the road, waving their weapons and shouting, "Stay where you are, monks. Give us your gold and silver and your horse. If you say even half a 'no' we will kill you without mercy."

Sun Wukong smiled and said to the others, "Don't be frightened. I'll go and ask them a few questions." He walked up to the bandits, put his hands together in front of his chest, and asked, "What are you gentlemen doing?"

"Don't you care if you live or die?" they shouted at him. "Hand over your treasures right now!"

"Oh Great Kings, I am only a poor monk from the countryside. I do not know what to say, please don't be angry. You can have all of our money, that's no problem. But let the other three go. The man on the horse is my master. All he can do is recite sutras, he's forgotten all about wealth and sex. The black-faced one is a simple man who just takes care of the horse. And the one with the big ears is a coolie, he just carries stuff. Please let them go. I will get you the money."

"Well, you seem like a monk who speaks the truth. All right. Tell the other three to leave everything here. They can go." Sun Wukong turned and gave them a look. Tangseng, Zhu and Sha walked west on the road a little way. Sun Wukong bent down to pick up one of the bundles of luggage. He grabbed a bit of dust from the road, said some magic words, and threw the dust into the air. He shouted, "Stop," and all the bandits found that they could not move at all.

Sun Wukong waved his hand at Tangseng. The monk turned his horse around and returned to Sun Wukong. He said, "Wukong, why have you called us back?"

"Please get off your horse and sit down, Master. Listen to what these bandits have to say. Brother Zhu, tie up the bandits so we can hear their story."

"Sorry, I don't have any rope," said Zhu. Sun Wukong pulled some hairs from his head, blew on them with magic breath, and turned them into thirty lengths of rope. The disciples tied up all thirty of the bandits. Then Sun Wukong said some words to end the magic.

"Little thieves," said Sun Wukong, "how many years have you been robbing people? How many have you killed? Tell us everything."

"Please, your lordships," said the robbers. "We are all from good families. We threw away our families' wealth on gambling, drinking, and women. We needed money. We knew that Squire Kou was the wealthiest man in the city, so last night we entered his house and took his gold, silver, jewelry and clothing. Then we escaped to this place so we could divide up the treasure. We saw your heavy luggage and thought that you also had some treasure. But we did not know you had such divine powers! Please spare our lives. You can take all the treasure."

"Wukong," said Tangseng, "how did Squire Kou bring this disaster upon himself?"

Sun Wukong replied, "Master, it was because Kou wanted to show off his wealth with the flags, the drummers, the monks, the feasts, and all the rest[1]."

Tangseng replied, "We owe the Kou family a huge debt of gratitude for their kindness. We should return this treasure to them." So the three disciples packed up all the treasure. Sun Wukong wanted to kill all the bandits but he was afraid that Tangseng would be angry with him. So he released the bandits. They ran away into the forest.

The four travelers turned back to Bronze Tower City to return the treasure. But the poem says,

> Kindness is rarely rewarded
> Often goodness is exchanged for hatred
> Save someone from drowning and you may fail
> Think twice before you act, you won't suffer

They were walking eastwards on the road when they were met with a large group of soldiers carrying spears and swords. The leader said, "You are a fine bunch of monks. First you rob a house, then you show off your stolen treasure." They dragged Tangseng from his horse and tied him up. Then they tied up the three disciples to long bamboo poles and carried them back to the city, two soldiers carrying each pole.

Tangseng was shaking, crying, and speechless. Zhu was unhappy and complaining. Sha was talking but secretly feeling a bit nervous. Sun Wukong laughed to himself, getting ready to use his powers.

The soldiers took them to the prefect's court. The prefect thanked the soldiers and told them to return the treasure to the Kou family. Then he said to

---

[1] Chapter 9 of the *Dao De Jing* says: "Filling up isn't as good as knowing when to stop / A sharp point can't be maintained for long / When gold and jade fill a room no one can protect it / Wealth leads to arrogance and invites mistakes / Achieve success then let it go / This is the Dao of Heaven."

Tangseng, "You say that you are poor monks traveling to the Western Heaven to worship the Buddha. But I think you are bandits."

Tangseng said, "Your Honor, we are not bandits. We can show you our travel rescript so you can see where we have traveled. We encountered the bandits on the road and took the treasure from them so we could return it to the Kou family. I beg you to study this matter more closely."

"If you really met those robbers, why didn't you capture them?"

Tangseng had no answer for this. The prefect told the soldiers to put a head-clamp on Tangseng. But Sun Wukong said, "Please, Your Majesty, don't squeeze that monk's head. I was the one who lit the torches, carried the sword, stole the treasure, and killed Squire Kou." The soldiers put the head-clamp on Sun Wukong's head and made it tight. It did not hurt him at all, no matter how tight they made the clamp.

Just then, someone came in to report that the Lord Guardian Chen had arrived. The prefect went to meet his boss. As he was leaving, he told the soldiers to put the four travelers in prison and beat them for a while. The soldiers dragged the four travelers into the prison, then they started beating them.

"What can we do?" cried Tangseng.

"These soldiers just want some money," replied Sun Wukong.

"But we have no money!"

"Clothes will do. Give them the cassock."

Tangseng was very unhappy about the thought of losing his beautiful cassock, but he just said softly, "Do what you must, Wukong."

"Gentlemen," called Sun Wukong to the soldiers, "you don't need to beat us anymore. In that bundle over there is a beautiful cassock that is worth a fortune. Take it, it's yours." The soldiers looked in the bundle. In the bottom, covered by oiled paper, was something glowing brightly. They took it out and looked at it. The cassock was covered with shining pearls, with embroidered dragons and flying phoenixes around the edges. They looked at the cassock with wide eyes.

"What's going on?" said the head soldier, coming over to look.

"Sir, the prefect told us to put these four in prison and beat them for a while. They gave us this cassock. We don't know what to do with it. It would not be right for just one of us to have it. But if we rip it into pieces, it will be ruined. What should we do?"

The head soldier looked at the cassock. Then he saw the travel rescript and looked at it carefully. He said to the soldiers, "You fools, these monks are not bandits. Do not touch their luggage. I will tell the prefect about this tomorrow."

The soldiers left the prison, and the four travelers lay down to get some rest. Around the fourth watch, Sun Wukong thought, "Master needed to have this hardship, that's why I said nothing to the prefect. But his suffering is almost finished. I'd better get us out of here." So he shook himself and turned into a tiny fly. He flew out of the prison and through the night, towards the gates of the Kou house.

Across the street was the home of a husband and wife. They were both tofu-makers. The husband said to her, "Wife, I went to school with old man Kou. In those days he owned a little bit of farmland but he was too kind to the farmers and sometimes forgot to collect their rent. When he was twenty years old, he married the daughter of a man named Zhang. Her name was Zhang Wang, and she certainly brought prosperity to her husband. Everything he did was successful and he made a lot of money. When he turned forty, he began to feed the monks. And now he's dead at only age sixty-four. How sad!"

Sun Wukong listened to this. Then he flew across the street to the Kou house. A coffin was in the main room. Around the coffin were incense, candles and fruit. Mrs. Kou and her two sons were there, crying. Sun Wukong landed on the head of the coffin and coughed. The people were terrified. The mother banged the head of the coffin with her fist and said, "Have you come back to life, old man?"

Sun Wukong used Squire Kou's voice and said, "King Yama brought me back to talk to you. Zhang, you have been telling lies!"

Mrs. Kou, whose childhood surname was Zhang, fell to her knees and cried, "What lies have I been telling?"

"Didn't you say, 'I saw the Tang monk holding the torches, Zhu Bajie was holding a knife, Sha Wujing took the gold and silver, and that evil monkey killed your father'? Your lies have caused those good men a great deal of trouble. They met the bandits on the road and took back your treasure to return it to you. But you made up some lies. Now these good men are in prison. The local god and the city god were so angry that they went to King

Yama. King Yama sent me here to say this to you. Get these men freed from jail as soon as possible. If you don't do as I say, nobody in this house, not even the dogs and chickens, will be spared from my anger!"

The sons kowtowed and begged, saying, "Please go back, Father, and don't harm us. We will get those monks freed from jail. We only want peace for the living and the dead."

"Burn paper money," said Sun Wukong. "I am leaving now." But Sun Wukong did not go back to the jail yet. He flew to the house of the prefect. It was now early morning. He saw that the prefect was out of bed and praying to a picture of his uncle. Sun Wukong landed on the picture and coughed. The prefect jumped and said, "Uncle, I pray to you every day. Why do you speak to me today?"

"Nephew, you have always been a good and honest man. But how could you be so stupid yesterday? You took four holy monks and threw them in prison without listening to their story. The local god and the city god are quite angry with you. They reported this to King Yama, and he told me to talk to you. You must find out the truth and release these monks. If you don't, you will join me soon in the underworld. Now burn some paper money, I am leaving."

Leaving the kowtowing prefect, Sun Wukong had one more stop to make. He went to the city courtroom. It was now morning, and the court officials were gathered there. He changed into a huge man. Standing in the middle of the courtroom, he said, "Listen to me, you officials. I am Wandering Spirit, sent by the Jade Emperor. He says that four holy monks have been thrown in jail and beaten for no reason. Release them at once. If you don't, I will kill you all and destroy your entire city." The officials all fell to their knees and kowtowed.

Sun Wukong left the courthouse, changed back into a fly, and flew back to the jail. He changed back into his original form and went to sleep.

Later that morning, the prefect began his work in the courtroom. Immediately the two Kou sons rushed in and begged the prefect to release the four monks, saying, "Your Honor, last night our father's spirit appeared to us and told us that the four monks did not take the treasure or kill our father. He said that if the four monks are not released from prison, everyone in our house will be killed!"

The prefect thought to himself, "It is not unusual for a new ghost to appear to the living. But my uncle has been dead for over five years. He appeared to me this morning. It looks like I did make a mistake yesterday."

Then a group of officials rushed in and said, "Your Honor, the Jade Emperor sent the Wandering Spirit to tell us to release those four monks from prison immediately. If you don't, he will destroy our city!"

Of course, the prefect ordered the four monks to be released from prison and brought to the courtroom. The prefect said he was sorry about the mistake. Sun Wukong became angry. He said, "Give us back our white horse and all our luggage right now. Now tell us, what is the punishment for throwing innocent people into prison?"

The prefect was terrified. He had the horse and luggage returned to the monks. And he said that it was Mrs. Kou who was responsible for this mistake. Tangseng said to Sun Wukong, "Let's go to the Kou house and find out the truth."

So Tangseng, the three disciples, the prefect, and all the court officials walked to the Kou house. There they saw Mrs. Kou, kneeling and weeping at her husband's coffin.

"Stop yelling, you lying old woman," shouted Sun Wukong. "You tried to get an innocent man killed. Wait until I call your husband back from the underworld. We'll see what he has to say!" And with that, he jumped into the sky and went straight to the underworld. Seeing this, the prefect and the court officials fell to their knees.

The Ten Kings of the Underworld came out to meet Sun Wukong. The monkey said, "Where is the ghost of Kou Hong who used to feed monks in Bronze Tower City?"

"Kou Hong is a good man," said the Ten Kings. "We did not have to drag him here, he came on his own. He is now with Bodhisattva King Ksitigarbha[1]." Sun Wukong went to the palace of King Ksitigarbha and asked to see Kou.

King Ksitigarbha said, "Kou Hong's life has been completed, that's why he came here. I have given him a job here in my palace, writing down good deeds in my book. But since you have come here for him, I will give him twelve more years of life. He can leave with you."

Kou came out to see Sun Wukong. The monkey blew a magic breath that changed Kou to vapor. Then Sun Wukong put the vapor in his sleeve and

---

[1] Ksitigarbha is the Bodhisattva of all beings in the underworld. He has taken a vow to not achieve Buddhahood until all hells are emptied.

used his cloud somersault to return to the Kou house in the human world. He pushed the vapor into the coffin. A moment later, Squire Kou sat up in the coffin. He climbed out, kowtowed to Tangseng and the three disciples. Then he said, "Thank you, thank you! I was wrongly killed and sent to the underworld, but you brought me back to life!" Then he looked around the room and saw the crowd of people. "Why are these lords in my house?" he asked.

The prefect answered, "Your sons said that these holy monks killed you. Later, we learned that the monks had met the real bandits on the road, taken your treasures from them, and were bringing the treasure back to your house. Last night a spirit appeared to me, and the Wandering Spirit came to the county offices. They all said that I should release the monks, so that's what I have done."

Squire Kou said, "Sir, on the night of my death thirty bandits came to my house with torches and weapons. I tried to talk with them but they kicked me to death. These four monks did nothing wrong." Then turning to his wife, he said, "Why did you lie about who killed me?"

The wife had no answer for this. However, the prefect was a kind man. He decided not to punish Squire Kou's family. Everyone kowtowed to the prefect. Then Squire Kou held another banquet to thank the prefect and the monks, but the prefect left the house before the banquet began.

The next day, Squire Kou again put up the sign saying, "Ten Thousand Monks Welcome." He again asked Tangseng to stay for a while, but of course Tangseng refused. After the banquet was over, the monk and disciples set out again on the road. Truly,

> Many people do evil in the wide world
> Although Heaven is high, it protects good people
> The four travelers walk towards the Buddha
> Certain that they will reach the gate of Spirit Mountain

Chapter 98

The travelers were now getting quite near to Spirit Mountain. This was indeed the land of the Buddha. Everyone that they met was kind and offered to feed the traveling monks. They saw other travelers reciting Buddhist sutras.

They walked for six or seven days. Then they saw a group of buildings a hundred feet high. There were beautiful palaces and gardens. Lovely flowers grew everywhere, and colorful birds flew through the sky. Tangseng pointed and said, "Wukong, this is a fine place!"

Sun Wukong laughed and said, "Master, we have seen many places with false Buddhas, and you have kowtowed to those places. Now we have reached the home of the true Buddha but you won't even get off your horse. Why is that?" As soon as he said this, Tangseng jumped down from his horse and walked towards the main gate.

A young Daoist stood in front of the gate. He wore a silk robe and held a small statue of a jade elk in his hand. His face was quite handsome. He said, "Are you the monk from the East who seeks holy scriptures?"

Tangseng looked at the young man but did not recognize him. But Sun Wukong did. He said, "Master, this is the Great Immortal of the Golden Head. He lives here at the base of Spirit Mountain." Then Tangseng bowed to the young man.

"So, you are finally here!" said the young man. "The Bodhisattva Guanyin told me more than ten years ago that you would be coming within two or three years. I have waited for you for many years."

Tangseng put his hands together and said, "I am very grateful for your kindness, Great Immortal, very grateful!"

The four travelers entered the Daoist temple, carrying the baggage and leading the horse. They had a vegetarian meal. Then some Daoist boys heated scented water for the travelers to bathe in. When night came, they slept in the temple.

The next morning, Tangseng put on his fine silk cassock and his hat. Holding his monk's staff in his hand, he climbed the steps of the main hall. The Great Immortal smiled and said, "Yesterday you were dirty and in rags. Today you are dressed like a true son of Buddha! Now let me show you the way."

Sun Wukong said, "There is no need. Old Monkey knows the way."

"No, you have always traveled through the clouds. The Tang monk cannot do that yet. He must walk on the road." The Great Immortal led Tangseng out the back gate. They stepped outside. He pointed to Spirit Mountain and said, "Holy monk, do you see those lights in the sky? That is Spirit Mountain, the land of the Holy Buddha." Tangseng saw it and bowed low.

Sun Wukong said, "Master, we still have a long way to walk. If you continue to stop and hit your head on the ground, we will never get there."

The Great Immortal waved goodbye to them. Sun Wukong led them slowly up Spirit Mountain. They walked for a couple of miles. They came to a great river three miles wide.

"Wukong," said Tangseng with a worried voice, "we have come the wrong way. This river is too wide and the waves are too large. How will we cross it?"

Sun Wukong pointed and said, "Look, there's a bridge." They looked and saw a sign, "Cloud Touching Bridge." Next to the sign was a single tree trunk that went all the way across the river. The trunk was very narrow and slippery. There were no handrails.

"Wukong," said Tangseng, "no one can cross that bridge."

"It's easy!" Sun Wukong replied. He jumped up onto the tree trunk and ran across the river. Then he called out, "Come over, come over!" But Tangseng, Zhu and Sha refused to climb up onto the tree trunk. Sun Wukong ran back and grabbed Zhu, saying, "Come with me, you idiot." But Zhu lay down on the ground and refused to move. The two of them started to fight and pull at each other.

After a while, Tangseng called out, "Look, a ferry boat is coming." Sun Wukong looked with his diamond eyes. He saw that the ferryman was The Royal Buddha of Brightness[1]. "Come over here!" he called. The ferryman brought the boat to the shore. Looking into the boat, Tangseng saw that the boat had no bottom. He could see nothing in the boat but the river water.

---

[1] This Buddha is probably Amitābha, whose name means "the Buddha of immeasurable light and life." It is said that Amitābha achieved buddhahood and created a pure land called Sukhāvatī (Sanskrit for "possessing happiness") in the far west beyond the bounds of our own world. Amitābha enables all who call upon him to be reborn into this pure land and ultimately become bodhisattvas and buddhas.

"How can this boat carry anyone?" cried Tangseng.

"Ah," said the boatman,

> "My boat has been famous since the chaos first parted
> I have used it with no changes at all
> It is steady in wind and steady in waves
> It is peaceful with no beginning or end
> Untouched by dust it can return to the One
> It moves calmly through all kinds of trouble
> A bottomless boat cannot cross the ocean
> But it can ferry anyone across this river!"

Tangseng was afraid to climb into the bottomless boat, but Sun Wukong grabbed him and pushed him into the boat. The monk fell into the water. The boatman reached down, grabbed him, and put him back in the boat. Zhu and Sha followed, leading the horse and carrying the luggage.

The Buddha pushed the boat away from the shore. They saw a dead body floating by. Tangseng was frightened. But Sun Wukong said, "Don't be frightened, Master. That is you."

Zhu and Sha started clapping their hands and sang, "It's you, it's you" over and over. Soon the boatman joined in the song. They continued singing until the boat reached the far shore. Then Tangseng jumped lightly out of the boat. Truly,

> Throwing aside their flesh and bone
> The spirit finds friendship and love
> Their work finished, they become Buddhas this day
> Six six kinds of dust are washed away[1]

When they looked back, the bottomless boat was gone. Tangseng thanked the three disciples for helping him to reach this place. "We have helped each other," replied Sun Wukong. "You showed us how to achieve the right fruit, and we protected you and helped you to leave behind your human body."

They continued walking up Spirit Mountain. After a while they arrived at Thunderclap Monastery. Its roofs were high enough to reach the Heavens, its

---

[1] In Buddhism there are six *gunas* or dusts, these are impure qualities that come from the sense organs: sight, sound, smell, taste, touch, and thoughts. There are also six roots, corresponding to the sense organs themselves: eyes, ears, nose, tongue, body and mind. The Diamond Sutra describes the world of the six dusts as "a dream, a mirage, a bubble, a shadow."

roots went deep into the mountain. In the east and west were palaces full of flowers, in the north and south were many pavilions and tall buildings. In the center, colored light and purple flames streamed from the main hall.

They walked to the main gate of the monastery. People smiled and waved at them from both sides of the path. Four guardians met them at the gate, asking, "Has the sage monk arrived?"

Tangseng bowed low and replied, "Your disciple Xuanzang has arrived."

"Please wait here," they said. They sent a report to the four guardians of the middle gate, and they sent a report to the four guardians of the inner gate. Those guardians reported to Tathagata Buddha that the Tang monk had arrived.

The Lord Buddha was pleased. He called together eight Bodhisattvas, five hundred teachers, three thousand protectors, eleven stars and eighteen temple guardians, and told them to form two rows. Then Tangseng was called to enter the inner hall. He entered the inner hall, accompanied by the three disciples. Zhu Bajie carried the baggage while Sha Wujing led the horse.

They prostrated themselves on the floor and kowtowed to the Buddha and the others to their left and right. Then Tangseng handed his travel rescript to the Buddha. The Buddha read it and returned it to Tangseng.

 Tangseng said, "Your disciple has made the long journey to your treasure monastery at the command of the great Tang Emperor, to beg you to give scriptures to save all living beings."

The Buddha opened his holy mouth and spoke these words, "Your land is large and has many people. But there is too much greed, killing, lying and anger. People do not honor my teachings. They do terrible things to each other. They have brought upon themselves the suffering of hell. Many will be reborn as beasts, to pay their debts by being made into food for people. Confucius gave them wisdom teachings, many kings and emperors have made good laws, but still the people are fools and criminals."

He continued, "I have three baskets of scriptures that can save these people. One basket speaks of Heaven, one basket speaks of earth, and one basket speaks of ghosts in the underworld. Altogether there are thirty-five volumes in 15,144 scrolls. These scriptures are the path to immortality. I would like to give them all to you. But unfortunately, the people of your region are too stupid to understand these teachings."

Then he called out, "Ananda and Kasyapa[1], take these four to the room under the treasure tower. Give them a vegetarian meal. Then select a few scrolls from each of the thirty-five volumes so that these travelers can bring them back to the East with our blessings."

Ananda and Kasyapa led the four travelers to the room under the treasure tower. Immortal foods and drinks were given to them. As Zhu and Sha ate the immortal food, their bodies were given new flesh and bones.

Then Ananda and Kasyapa led them to the treasure pavilion. When the doors were opened, a thousand colors of light shone from the room where scriptures rested on shelves. Each scripture had a red label where the name of the

---

[1] Ananda is the Buddha's primary attendant and one of the ten principal disciples of Gautama Buddha. Kasyapa (also called Mahākāśyapa) was a disciple of Gautama Buddha and assumed leadership of the community of disciples after his teacher's death in 483 BC.

scripture was carefully written.

Ananda and Kasyapa said to Tangseng, "Great monk, what small gifts do you have for us? Show us, then we will be happy to give you the scriptures that you want."

Tangseng replied, "I'm sorry, we have come a great distance and faced many difficulties. We don't have any gifts for you."

Then Sun Wukong said to Tangseng, "Master, this is not right. Let's go tell Tathagata about this. He should come here and give us the scriptures himself."

"Shut up," said Ananda. "Where do you think you are? Don't act like this. Come here and get the scriptures." Sun Wukong was very angry, but Zhu and Sha stopped him from saying or doing anything more. Ananda and Kasyapa started handing the scrolls to the disciples. Some were put on the horse's back, then the rest were packed into bundles, to be carried by Zhu and Sha. Then everyone returned to the Buddha's throne, kowtowed to him again, and headed back down the mountain.

While the scrolls were being given to Tangseng and the disciples, the ancient Buddha called Dipamkara[1] was watching and listening. Dipamkara knew that the scrolls given by Ananda and Kasyapa had no words written on them. He smiled and said to himself, "Those stupid monks did not know what they were getting." Then he called to one of the arhats, "Go quickly to the Tang monk. Tell him what happened. Then take the wordless scrolls from him and tell him to come back to get the true scriptures." The arhat flew away so fast that waves flowed backwards in the rivers and seas, and trees were broken in the forests.

The arhat flew to Tangseng and the disciples. He reached down his hand and grabbed the scrolls. Then he ripped them into little pieces, dropped them on the ground, and flew away. Tangseng fell to his knees and picked up some pieces, crying and saying, "Disciples, even in this holy land, there are demons who want to cheat us."

But Sha looked at some of the pieces. They were as white as snow. "Master," he said, "there is nothing written on these scrolls." Tangseng, Sun Wukong

---

[1] Dipamkara is one of the Buddhas of the past. He is said to have lived on Earth one hundred thousand *kalpas* ago, where each *kalpa* is 4.32 billion years. It is said that Dipamkara was a previous Buddha who attained Enlightenment many millenia before Gautama Buddha, the historical Buddha.

and Zhu picked up more pieces and saw that there was no writing on them.

Tangseng said, "What are we to do now? If I return to Tang with empty hands, the Emperor will kill me."

Sun Wukong said, "Master, I think Ananda and Kasyapa gave us these scrolls because we did not have any gifts for them. This is extortion. Let's go back and tell Tathagata." Tangseng agreed, and the four of them hurried back up the mountain to Thunderclap Monastery.

They entered the main hall. Sun Wukong shouted at Tathagata Buddha, "Sir, we have traveled for thousands of miles and fought many demons and monsters to come here. You instructed Ananda and Kasyapa to give us scriptures, but the scrolls that they gave us had no words. What good are those? I beg you, punish those two and give us good scrolls."

Tathagata Buddha smiled and said, "I know that those scrolls had no words on them. They were true wordless scriptures, but you people from the East are so stupid that you cannot use them. So we will have to give you scrolls that have words on them. Ananda and Kasyapa, fetch a few scrolls that have words on them."

Once more, Ananda and Kasyapa led the four travelers to the scripture room. "What do you have for us this time?" they asked. Tangseng handed over his begging bowl of purple gold, the one given to him by the Tang Emperor. Ananda accepted the bowl without saying a word. Kasyapa picked up 5,048 scrolls and handed them all to Tangseng.

"Disciples," said the monk, "look carefully at each scroll!" They looked at each scroll and saw that each one had words written on it. The travelers packed up the scrolls. Then they returned to the main Buddha Hall. Tathagata asked Ananda and Kasyapa how many scrolls were given to the Tang monk. Ananda told him the names and numbers of each scroll.

The Buddha nodded and said, "These scriptures have power beyond your understanding. They are the root of the Three Religions. When you bring them back to your region, let nobody touch them unless they have bathed and fasted first. Then they will find the key to immortality and timeless wisdom."

Tangseng prostrated himself three times and thanked the Buddha. Then he and his three disciples left Thunderclap Monastery.

After they left, Bodhisattva Guanyin walked up to the Buddha. She put her hands together and said to him, "Lord, it has been fourteen years since the

Tang monk started his journey. That is 5,040 days[1]. If you let him return to the East in eight days, that will be a perfect number[2]."

Tathagata agreed. He said to the Eight Guardians, "Use your magic powers to carry the Tang monk quickly back to the East. As soon as he has given the scriptures to his emperor, bring him back here. Do all this within eight days." The Eight Guardians flew to catch up with Tangseng and the disciples. They picked up all four of them, plus the horse and baggage and scriptures, and carried them off through the clouds.

---

[1] In ancient times, the Chinese year was made up of six 60-day periods totaling 360 days, as Guanyin says here. But later this was refined to make the year more accurate. By the first century BC, the length of a year according to the Tàichū calendar was 365 plus 385/1539 days, or 365.2502 days. This is very close to the modern figure of 365.2422 days, differing by only about 20 minutes per year.

[2] The journey of the historical Tang monk actually took seventeen years. But in this story the journey is said to last only fourteen years, or 5,040 days. Adding 8 to this gives 5,048.

Chapter 99

While the Eight Guardians were carrying Tangseng and the disciples back to the East, several of the Heavenly beings were talking with the Bodhisattva Guanyin. She said to them, "Tell me about the Tang Monk's journey."

They replied, "Your disciples have watched him carefully. He has suffered greatly through his many trials. There have been eighty trials so far. They are[1]:

1. As Golden Cicada, he was sent out of the Buddha's home.
2. He was almost killed as a newborn baby. [9]
3. He was thrown in the river as a one-month-old baby. [9]
4. He searched for his parents and vengeance for his father's death. [9]
5. He fell into a pit and was captured by three demon kings. [13]
6. His two companions were cooked and eaten by the demons. [13]
7. He was attacked by a tiger and saved by Liu Boqin. [13]
8. He was attacked by bandits on the road near Mountain of Two Frontiers. [14]
9. He lost his horse to a dragon at Eagle Grief Stream. [15]
10. He was nearly burned to death by a fire set by monks at Guanyin Hall. [16]
11. His cassock was stolen by a black bear demon. [16]
12. He defeated Zhu Bajie and made him a disciple. [19]
13. He was kidnapped by a demon at Yellow Wind Ridge. [20]
14. His disciple Sun Wukong was blinded, but healed by an old man. [21]
15. He crossed Flowing Sands River guarded by a sand demon. [22]
16. He defeated Sha Wujing and made him a disciple. [22]
17. His Zen mind is tested by a mother and her three beautiful daughters. [23]
18. He refused to eat magic ginseng fruit because they looked like babies. [24]
19. He was nearly boiled in oil by Great Immortal Zhenyuan. [26]
20. He sent away Sun Wukong for killing monsters. [27]
21. He was captured in the forest by the Yellow Robed Monster. [28]
22. He was forced to send a letter to the king of Precious Image Kingdom. [29]

---

[1] For each of these eighty trials, the chapter(s) where the event happened is also shown.

23. He was changed into a tiger by a tiger demon. [30]
24. He was captured by Great Kings Silver Horn and Golden Horn. [33]
25. He was hung from the rafters in a cave. [33]
26. In a dream he met the drowned king of Black Rooster Kingdom. [37]
27. He met a demon who looked exactly like him. [39]
28. He found the demon Red Boy tied to a tree in the forest. [40]
29. He was carried off by the wind sent by Red Boy. [40]
30. He saw Sun Wukong nearly killed by Red Boy's magic fire. [41]
31. He was nearly eaten by Red Boy and the Bull Demon King. [42]
32. He was dragged underwater and nearly eaten by a crocodile demon. [43]
33. He saw Buddhists suffer at Slow Cart Kingdom. [44]
34. He entered a meditation contest against a Daoist demon. [46]
35. He entered a guessing game against a Daoist demon. [46]
36. He met a demon king who eats two children every year. [47]
37. He fell through the ice into the River of Heaven. [48]
38. He saw Guanyin change a demon into a goldfish. [49]
39. He was captured by a buffalo demon. [50]
40. He saw Prince Nata fail to defeat the buffalo demon. [51]
41. He asked Laozi to defeat the buffalo demon. [52]
42. He became pregnant in the Kingdom of Women. [53]
43. He is almost married to the Queen of the Kingdom of Women. [54]
44. He suffered at the cave of a beautiful scorpion demon. [55]
45. He sent away Sun Wukong for killing too many bandits. [56]
46. He was beaten up by a six eared macaque who looked like Sun Wukong. [57]
47. His path was blocked by the Mountain of Flames. [59]
48. He sought the palm-leaf fan. [60]
49. He saw his disciples battle the Bull Demon King. [61]
50. He swept the pagoda at Sacrifice Kingdom. [62]
51. He recovered treasure to save the monks. [63]
52. He was lost in the woods and chanted poetry with three tree spirits. [64]
53. He met a false Buddha at Little Thunderclap Monastery. [65]
54. He saw celestial warriors imprisoned by King Yellow Brow. [66]
55. His way was blocked by a giant snake at Slimy Shit Mountain Pass. [67]
56. He let Sun Wukong try to cure the sick king of Scarlet-Purple Kingdom. [68]
57. He sees Sun Wukong heal the king of Scarlet-Purple Kingdom. [69]
58. He sees Sun Wukong fight a monster to save a queen. [71]
59. He is tied up and almost eaten by seven beautiful spider demons. [72]
60. He saw Sun Wukong wounded by Demon King Hundred Eyes. [73]

61. His path was blocked by Great Peng and his brothers. [74]
62. He was captured by demons serving Great Peng. [76]
63. He was put in a steamer by Great Peng and his brothers. [77]
64. He needed to ask the Buddha for help subduing demons. [77]
65. He saved the children in cages at Bhiksu Kingdom. [78]
66. His heart is almost eaten by a Daoist at Bhiksu Kingdom. [79]
67. He found a female demon tied to a tree in a forest. [80]
68. He fell sick in a monastery. [81]
69. He was imprisoned by a demon in Bottomless Cave. [83]
70. He had to hide in a wooden box in Dharma-Destroying Kingdom. [84]
71. He was captured by demons serving the Great King of South Mountain. [85]
72. He brought rain at Phoenix-Immortal Prefecture. [87]
73. He lost weapons at Phoenix-Immortal Prefecture. [88]
74. He was captured by the Nine Headed Lion. [89]
75. He saw Sun Wukong fight the Celestial Worthy's guards. [90]
76. He was captured by three false Buddhas at the Lantern Festival. [91]
77. He saw Sun Wukong fight three rhino demons. [92]
78. He was hit by an embroidered ball thrown by a demon princess in India. [93]
79. He was jailed because of bandits killing Squire Kou. [97]
80. He gave up his mortal body at Spirit Mountain. [98]

Altogether, the Tang monk has journeyed one hundred and eight thousand miles and suffered eighty trials."

Guanyin said, "In the school of Buddhism, nine times nine is the path to perfection. The Tang monk needs one more trial to reach the sacred number 81. Go now. Find the Eight Guardians and tell them that one more trial is needed."

One of the Heavenly beings immediately flew above the clouds to meet up with the Eight Guardians. He whispered in their ears. The Eight Guardians dropped Tangseng, his three disciples, the horse and the luggage on to the ground.

Tangseng picked himself up off the ground and looked around. "Where are we, Wukong?"

Sun Wukong said, "Master, we are on the west bank of the River of Heaven."

"Yes, I remember. The Chen Family Village is on the east bank. They wanted to build a boat to take us across the river, but a great turtle came and carried us across. What do we do now?"

"This is no problem," said Sha. "Master now has an immortal body; he can just fly across the river with us."

Sun Wukong laughed and said, "No, my brother. That won't work." This wasn't true. But the monkey knew that Tangseng had only endured eighty trials, and needed one more to reach the sacred number of nine times nine.

As they were talking, they heard a voice calling, "Tang Monk, Tang Monk! Come here!" They looked and saw a great turtle. This was the same turtle that had carried them across the river several years earlier. The turtle said, "Master, I have waited for you for many years."

Tangseng replied, "Old turtle, you helped us once, and today we meet again. Will you help us again?"

The turtle walked slowly up onto the river bank. The four travelers climbed on its back, with Sha leading the horse and Zhu carrying the baggage. Then the turtle walked into the water and started swimming swiftly across the river. They traveled east for nearly a day. When they saw the eastern riverbank approaching, the turtle said to Tangseng, "Great master, you remember that the last time we met, I begged you to speak to Tathagata Buddha, to ask him how I can lose my original form and be reborn in human form."

Tangseng's entire heart and mind was set on worshipping the Buddha, and he had completely forgotten about his promise to the turtle. He could not lie, but he did not want to say the truth, so he just stood on the turtle's back and said nothing. After a few moments the turtle understood that Tangseng had forgotten his promise. Without a word he shook his body. All the travelers and the horse fell off the turtle's back and into the cold water.

If this had happened before Tangseng's visit to Spirit Mountain, his mortal body would have sunk to the bottom of the river. But now, his immortal body did not sink. Sun Wukong grabbed him and swam to the eastern river bank, along with Zhu, Sha and the horse. Everything was soaked with water, including the bundles of sacred scrolls.

No sooner had they climbed out of the river than the sky turned dark. Thunder crashed, lightning crossed the sky like golden snakes, the wind blew, and heavy rain started to fall. Demons surrounded them trying to grab the sacred scrolls. Tangseng, Zhu and Sha held the scrolls tightly, while Sun Wukong swung his golden hoop rod to keep the demons away. He fought the demons all night until the sun came up in the morning.

"What was that all about?" Tangseng asked Sun Wukong.

The monkey king replied, "Master, you don't understand. When the Buddha gave us these sacred scrolls, we were robbing Heaven and earth of their power. That is why the demons and gods attacked us last night. They wanted to take the scriptures away from us so we could not give them to the people. They were stopped by your dharma body which could not be harmed, and of course by my golden hoop rod. Now it is morning. This is the time when *yang* is stronger than *yin*, so they cannot attack us."

The others thanked Sun Wukong for fighting off the demons. They all set out the scrolls on some flat rocks in the sun to dry. Truly,

> The pure yang body faces the light
> Invisible demons cannot continue to fight
> When water is strong, the true scriptures will win
> Unafraid of thunder, lightning, rain or wind
> The travelers will now awaken to the truth
> They will reach the land of the immortals
> These rocks will remain forever
> Never again will demons come to this place

Two fishermen saw the travelers. When they returned to Chen Family Village, they found old man Chen. They told Chen that the teachers who traveled to the west had returned. Chen went to see them and said, "My lords, now that you have the holy scriptures, your work is done. Please come to my house and rest for a while."

Tangseng agreed. They picked up the scrolls off the flat rocks and packed them away. But several rolls of the Buddhacharita Kavya Sutra were still wet and they could not pull the scrolls away from the rocks. That is why even today, the Buddhacharita Kavya Sutra is not complete, and you can see the writing on those rocks if you go there[1].

Tangseng was unhappy about the damage to the sutra, but Sun Wukong said, "Heaven and earth are incomplete. The scriptures were complete, but now they are torn, so they will also be incomplete. This is divine mystery."

Back at the village, one person told ten, ten told a hundred, a hundred told a thousand, until everyone in the village came out to welcome the travelers.

---

[1] Buddhacharita, the "Acts of the Buddha," is an epic poem on the life of Gautama Buddha written in Sanskrit by Asvaghosa of Saketa in the early second century AD. The poem was originally 28 cantos, but the final 14 cantos have been lost.

Musicians played and incense was burned. The villagers brought out tea and vegetarian food, but Tangseng had lost all desire for mortal food. Sun Wukong and Sha ate very little. Even Zhu only ate a bowl of rice.

"Idiot, aren't you eating any more food?" asked Sun Wukong.

"I don't know why," replied Zhu. "My stomach is weak."

The villagers asked Tangseng to tell them the story of his visit to the Buddha at Spirit Mountain. So Tangseng told them the whole story. Then he took out one of the scrolls and read one of the sutras. Many families came and asked the travelers to come to their homes to eat. They visited many homes but only ate a few bites at each home. Zhu shook his head and said, "This is just my bad luck. When I was hungry, nobody had any food for me. Now I don't want any food and every family wants me to eat with them." He tried to eat and finished off twenty or thirty steamed buns.

Night came. Tangseng sat quietly guarding the scrolls. He saw Sun Wukong and said to him, "Wukong, you know the saying, 'The wise one does not show his face; the one who shows his face is not wise.' I think we should go."

"You are right, Master," said Sun Wukong. "Let's leave tonight." Quietly they all packed up their luggage. The main gate was locked, but Sun Wukong used his magic and easily opened the locks. They started walking east. The Eight Guardians looked down, saw them, picked them all up and carried them towards the east.

Chapter 100

After several days of traveling through the clouds, the Eight Guardians and the four travelers saw in the distance the city of Chang'an.

Many years earlier, about three years after Tangseng began his journey, the Tang emperor Taizong commanded that a tower be built. This tower was for the people of Chang'an so they could watch for the return of the Tang monk. Once every year Taizong visited the tower. This very day when Taizong visited the tower and climbed to the top, he looked to the west. He saw colored clouds and smelled a fragrant wind.

The Eight Guardians stopped a few miles away from the city. They said to Tangseng, "Holy monk, we must leave you here. We do not want the people of Chang'an to see us. You must go alone, without us and without your three disciples. We will wait here in the clouds and watch you."

Sun Wukong said to them, "My master could not possibly carry all the holy scriptures and lead the horse all the way to the city. May we please take him to the city?"

"No. Bodhisattva Guanyin has already told Tathagata Buddha that this journey must be completed in just eight days. We have already spent four days traveling east. If we go with you to the city, the pig will delay us while he asks for blessings and eats too much food. We cannot stay here any longer."

Zhu said to them, "Oh, no. Our master has become a Buddha, and I want to be one too. You wait here. We will take our master to the city. Then we will quickly return to you." And without waiting for an answer, the three disciples brought their cloud down to the ground. They picked up the scriptures and baggage. Leading the horse, they walked with Tangseng towards the city.

They arrived at the city gates. Emperor Taizong met the travelers at the gate. He said, "Imperial younger brother, you are back." Tangseng fell to his knees and kowtowed. Taizong continued, "Who are these three?"

"They are my disciples. They have traveled with me to the home of the Buddha."

Taizong was pleased when he heard this. He invited Tangseng to follow him back to the palace. Sha led the horse. Sun Wukong followed just behind him, twirling his golden hoop rod and smiling. Zhu carried the luggage on his shoulder. Together they walked towards the palace.

They walked towards the monastery where Tangseng had lived many years before. In the monastery the monks saw that the branches of several large pine trees were leaning towards the east. "How strange!" they said. "There is no wind, but the trees look like the wind is blowing them towards the east."

One of them, a monk who used to be a disciple of Sanzang, said, "Our master has returned!" When the other monks did not understand him, he continued, "When our master left many years ago, he said that these trees would lean towards the east when he returned from the Western Heaven. Let's go see him." The monks all hurried out of the monastery. They saw the emperor and Tangseng walking towards the palace. They dared not approach the royal carriage, so they waited a bit and then followed behind them.

Emperor Taizong invited Tangseng to enter the throne hall and sit down. "Tell us," he said, "how many scriptures are there? And how did you fetch them?"

"When your subject reached Spirit Mountain and saw the Lord Buddha, the Buddha told two of his attendants to give us the scriptures. But the two attendants told us that they wanted gifts first. We had nothing to give them. They gave us some scriptures. But later we were in a great storm. The storm blew the scriptures all over the place. My disciples gathered them again but saw that there were no words on the scrolls. So we returned to Thunderclap Mountain and asked Buddha to give us different scrolls. Again he told his two attendants to give us scrolls, and again they demanded gifts. This time I understood that the Buddha wanted us to give them something. So I gave them the purple gold begging bowl that you gave me many years ago. This time, they gave us thirty-five scriptures, with several scrolls from each scripture. Altogether there are 5,048 scrolls[1]."

"Wonderful!" said Taizong. Then he looked at the three disciples standing nearby. "Who are your noble disciples and where are they from?"

Tangseng replied, "My senior disciple's name is Sun Wukong. He is from the Water Curtain Cave on Flower Fruit Mountain in the country of Aolai. He caused great trouble in Heaven five hundred years ago and was locked in a prison by the Lord Buddha. The Bodhisattva Guanyin helped him to become a

---

[1] In the year 730 A.D., the Kaiyuan Era Catalog (kāiyuán shìjiào lù) listed all the Chinese Buddhist scriptures known at that time. It named 1,076 works contained in 5,048 volumes or scrolls. Based on this, the entire body of Buddhist scriptures was customarily said to consist of 5,048 volumes.

Buddhist and my disciple. He has protected me on the journey. My second disciple is Zhu Wuneng. He was a monster in Gao Village until he was subdued by Sun Wukong and found Buddhism. He has carried our baggage all along the way and been very useful in crossing rivers. My third disciple is Sha Wujing. He used to be a monster in the Flowing Sands River. He also found Buddhism and has helped me greatly."

"And what of the horse?"

"The horse that you gave me many years ago was killed and eaten by a river monster, the son of the Dragon King of the Western Ocean. The river monster also became a Buddhist and changed into a horse that looked just like the one that he ate. This is the horse you see now. He has helped us greatly in our journey."

"How far was your journey?"

"I remember Bodhisattva Guanyin saying that it was 36,000 miles, but I have no idea if that is correct. We have traveled for fourteen winters and summers, crossed thousands of rivers and mountains, and fought many monsters and demons. I have met many kings. Disciples, show our travel rescript to His Majesty."

Taizong looked at the travel rescript. It had seals from Precious Image Kingdom, Black Rooster Kingdom, Slow Cart Kingdom, the Kingdom of Women, the Sacrifice Kingdom, the Scarlet-Purple Kingdom, the Lion Camel Kingdom, the Bhiksu Kingdom, and the Dharma-Destroying Kingdom. There were also the seals of the Phoenix-Immortal Prefecture, the Jade-Flower County, and the Gold Level Prefecture. After reading through it, Taizong put it away.

Just then, an attendant informed the Emperor that the banquet was ready. The Emperor asked Tangseng, "Are your noble disciples familiar with the etiquette of the royal court?"

"Your Majesty, my humble disciples all began as monsters. They have never been taught the etiquette of the Chinese court."

Taizong laughed and said, "Not a problem, not a problem! Let's go eat!" The travelers and all the officials of the court stood on left and right while Emperor Taizong sat in the middle. There was singing, dancing and music. The banquet lasted the rest of the day. Truly,

> This banquet was greater than that of the ancient kings

The true scriptures have brought great blessings
This story will be told forever
The light of Buddha shines throughout the capital

After the banquet ended, Taizong went to his living quarters. The officials all went to their homes. Tangseng and the disciples went back to Tangseng's monastery where they were welcomed by the other monks. The monks told Tangseng about the pine trees leaning to the east.

This time, Zhu did not call for food and wine and did not cause any trouble. Sun Wukong and Sha also behaved well. Their journey finished, they had no reason to cause trouble. When night came, they all went to bed.

The next morning, Taizong said to his officials, "We did not sleep at all last night. We kept thinking about the wonderful things our younger brother told us. We have a few words to say. We hope they will show our gratitude."

Then he began to speak, while the officials quickly wrote down all of his words. He spoke for a long time[1].

He spoke about the invisible powers of yin and yang, Heaven and earth, and the ten thousand things of this world.

He said how difficult it is to understand the way of Buddhism which speaks of the void. The void is full of mysteries, deep, far and silent. It controls the entire world. It has no birth, no death, and lasts forever.

He spoke of the great Buddha and his teachings. He spoke of how the people worshipped Buddha's image without understanding the deeper truth behind the image. He spoke of the Buddha's scriptures, and the Great and Small Vehicles[2].

He spoke of the monk Xuanzang, brighter than the dew of Heaven and the greatest jewels. This monk rose above the six senses and placed his mind completely on the truths of the Buddha's teachings. He longed for the pure

---

[1] Taizong's proclamation is far too long and esoteric to include all of it this book. It's based on an actual document called the *Preface to the Holy Religion* (shèng jiào xù) composed by the actual Emperor Taizong in 648 AD in gratitude for Xuanzang's translation of one of the sutras.

[2] The more conservative form of Buddhism is xiǎo chéng, called Theravada or the "Small Vehicle." It is a discipline for personal salvation by one who accumulates enough meritorious karma. The other main branch is dà chéng, called Mahayana or the "Great Vehicle." It teaches that salvation is possible to all sentient beings because they possess the Buddha nature in them and hence all have the potential to become enlightened.

land and set out for the Western Heaven. He faced snowdrifts in the morning and sand storms in the evening, he crossed ten thousand mountains and streams, he pushed aside smoke, frost, rain and snow. He traveled for fourteen years all the way to Spirit Mountain in the land of India. Going deep into the mysteries of the Buddha's teachings, he learned the most difficult lessons.

Finally, he spoke of the holy scriptures themselves. He said that when the people of China can read the scriptures in their own language, they will spread the truths of Buddhism across the country to all people. Like water putting out the fire in a burning house, Buddhism will save all people. Like a golden beam of light on dark waters, it will lead travelers to safety on the far shore. He said, may these scriptures last as long as the sun and the moon, and spread their light across the universe!

The Emperor's officials wrote all this down carefully. Then Tangseng was invited into the throne room. He kowtowed to the Emperor. Then he was given the Emperor's document. He read it, kowtowed again, then said, "Your Majesty's writing is wonderful. But what is this document called?"

The Emperor replied, "We only thought of this last night. We would call it 'Preface to the Holy Religion.' Is this all right?" Tangseng kowtowed and thanked the Emperor again and again. The Emperor said, "Our words are very poor compared to the scriptures you have brought from the west. It is like spilling ink on golden tablets, or dropping stones into a forest of pearls. It is beneath your notice, and you should not thank us. Tell us, younger brother, would you please recite some of these holy scriptures for us?"

"Of course, my lord," replied Tangseng. "But we cannot do it here in your treasure palace. We must go to a monastery."

Tangseng asked his officials which monastery was the most pure. They replied that the Wild Goose Pagoda Monastery would be the most pure. Tangseng and his disciples walked with the Emperor and his officials to the monastery. As they walked, Tangseng said to Taizong, "My lord, it would be best to make copies of these scriptures before we start carrying them around your empire." Taizong agreed, and several officials immediately began to make copies of the scrolls.

They arrived at Wild Goose Pagoda Monastery. Tangseng picked up one of the scrolls. He was just starting to recite when a gust of wind came. Everyone looked up and saw the Eight Guardians. The Guardians called out, "You who are reciting scriptures! Put them down and come with us!" Tangseng carefully put the scroll down. Then he, his three disciples and the dragon horse all rose up into the air and were carried rapidly towards the west.

We will say no more about Emperor Taizong, except to say that he commanded a Grand Mass of Land and Water to be held at Wild Goose Pagoda Monastery. The monks of the monastery were told to recite the scriptures so that souls trapped in the underworld would be freed, and so that goodness would spread throughout the Tang empire.

Meanwhile, the Eight Guardians brought the travelers back to Spirit Mountain. The Guardians said to Tathagata Buddha, "We have obeyed your golden command. We have brought the holy monks back to the land of Tang where they delivered the scriptures. Now our work is done."

Tathagata Buddha nodded. Then he told the travelers to step forward. He said to Tangseng, "Holy monk, in your previous life you were my disciple, Golden Cicada. You did not listen to my laws and you had no respect for my teachings. You were sent to the land of the east for ten lifetimes. Since then, you have never forgotten my teachings. I now give you the job of Buddha of Sandalwood Merit[1].

"Sun Wukong, you caused great trouble in Heaven, and I had to use great power to imprison you under Five Finger Mountain. However, you have embraced Buddhism and you have worked hard to subdue evil and protect the Tang monk. For this reason, I now give you the job of Victorious Fighting Buddha.

"Zhu Bajie, you were once a god of the Heavenly river, but you got drunk at a festival and insulted the divine maiden. For this reason, you were sent to the region below to live as a beast. You have accepted our religion and protected the Tang monk. But you still cause trouble, and you still have desire for food, drink, money and sex. For carrying the Tang monk's baggage, I give you the job of Janitor of the Altars."

"What?" cried Zhu. "They all became Buddhas and I am to be a janitor?"

The Buddha smiled and replied, "You are still quite hungry. Throughout the four great continents, wherever there are Buddhist services you will clean the altars. That will give you lots of food. How bad could that be?"

Then the Buddha continued, "Sha Wujing, you were once the great Curtain Raising Captain. But you broke a valuable cup during a festival and were sent

---

[1] Sandalwood (zhāntán) is a fragrant wood often used for carving statues of the Buddhas. It is said to have anti-demonic properties.

to the region below. There, you lived as a monster who ate humans. However, you have embraced our religion and you have protected the Tang monk. I now give you the job of the Golden Body Arhat."

Buddha turned to the white horse and said, "You were once the son of the Dragon King of the Western Ocean. You went against your father's command. For this crime you were to be killed. But you submitted to the law, then you carried the Tang monk during his journey to the west. For this, I now name you one of the dragons in the Eight Legions[1]." One of the protectors led the horse to the Dragon Transforming Pool and pushed him into the water. Golden scales grew over his body and a silver beard appeared on his face. The horse, now a golden dragon, flew out of the pool and circled in the sky high above the monastery.

Sun Wukong said to Tangseng, "Master, now that I am a Buddha like you, it isn't right that I should still be wearing the headband. You wouldn't want to punish a Buddha by reciting the tight headband spell, would you? Please take this off my head."

Tangseng replied, "Now that you are a Buddha, the headband is gone. See for yourself." Sun Wukong put his hand on his head and found that the headband was gone.

The five travelers moved to their proper places. All the deities who had come to hear the Buddha's words left to return to their proper places.

Look around. What do you see?

> Colored mists and clouds surround Spirit Mountain
> Golden dragons lie quietly, jade tigers are all quiet
> Black rabbits come and go as they want
> Turtles and snakes circle as they wish
> Red and green phoenixes play in the forest
> Black apes and white deer enjoy themselves
> Flowers bloom, fruit grows in all four seasons
> Tall pines, ancient cypress, blue-green juniper, thin bamboo
> Plums of every color, peaches ripe and unripe
> A thousand kinds of flowers

---

[1] The Eight Legions of Heavenly Dragons, also called the Eight Classes of Supernatural Beings, is a group of Buddhist deities whose function is to protect the Dharma.

All of them put their hands together and said,

> I submit to the Buddha
> I submit to the past, present and future Buddhas
> I submit to the Buddha of Pure Joy
> I submit to the Buddha Maitreya
> I submit to the Buddha Amitabha
> I submit to the Buddha of the Dragon Kings
> I submit to the Buddha of Water and Sky
> I submit to the Buddha of the Jeweled Banners
> I submit to the Buddha of Compassion and Power
> I submit to the Buddha of Golden Light
> I submit to the Buddha of the Sun and Moon
> I submit to the Buddha of Great Wisdom
> I submit to the Buddha of Sandalwood Merit
> I submit to the Buddha of Victorious Fighting
>
> I submit to the Bodhisattva Guanyin
> I submit to the Bodhisattva of the Great Ocean
> I submit to the Bodhisattva of the Western Heaven
> I submit to the Bodhisattva of the Three Thousand Guardians
> I submit to the Bodhisattva of the Five Hundred Teachers
> I submit to the Bodhisattva the Janitor of the Altars
> I submit to the Bodhisattva of the Heavenly Dragon of Eight Legions
>
> I submit to all the Buddhas in the ten directions and the three worlds
> I submit to all the Bodhisattvas, the Mahasattvas, and the Great Perfect
> Wisdom
>
> I will go to the pure land of the Buddha
> I will repay the four kindnesses
> I will save those who suffer
> In the three paths of life
>
> For all those who see and hear
> Your mind will find true wisdom
> May you be reborn in the land of joy
> And live with us in Heaven

Here ends the Journey to the West.

About the Author

Jeff Pepper (author) is President and CEO of Imagin8 Press, and has written dozens of books about Chinese language and culture. Over his thirty-five-year career he has founded and led several successful computer software firms, including one that became a publicly traded company. He's authored two software related books and was awarded three U.S. patents.